Contents

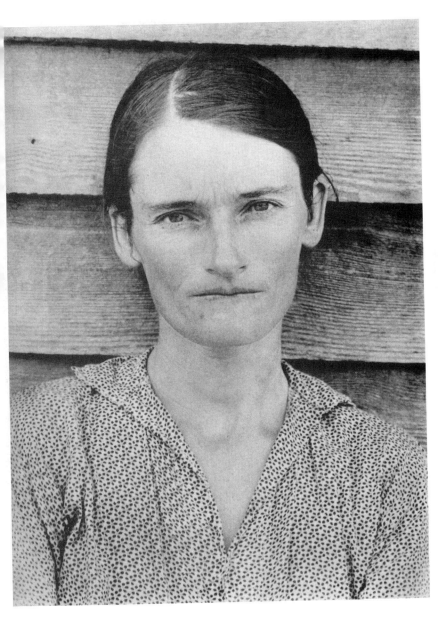

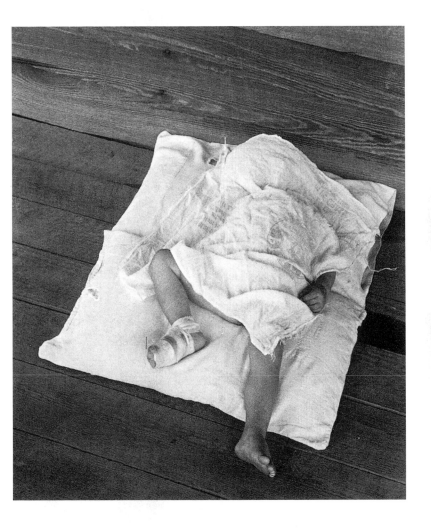

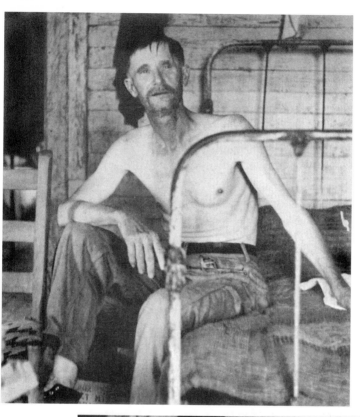

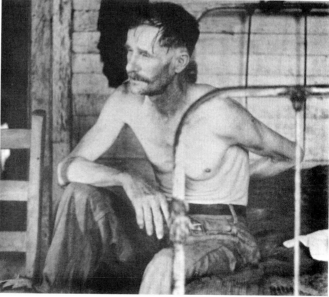

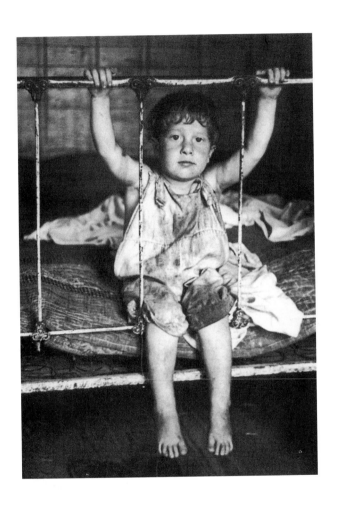

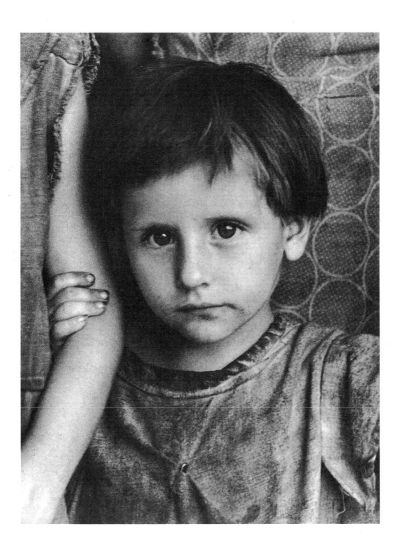

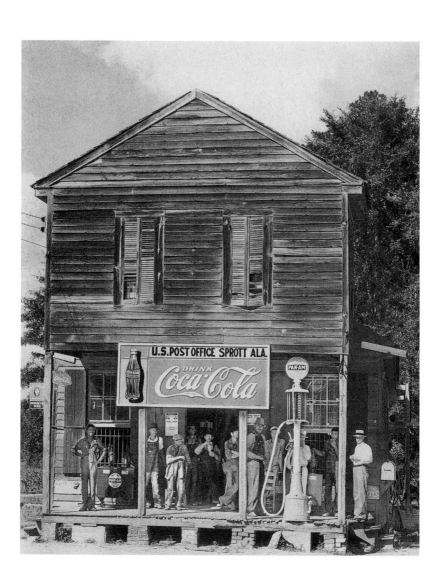

THREE TENANT FAMILIES

LET US NOW PRAISE
FAMOUS MEN

JAMES AGEE   WALKER EVANS

To those of whom the record is made.
In gratefulness and in love.
                                    J. A.
                                    W. E.

JAMES AGEE IN 1936

by Walker Evans

AT THE TIME, Agee was a youthful-looking twenty-seven. I think he felt he was elaborately masked, but what you saw right away—alas for conspiracy—was a faint rubbing of Harvard and Exeter, a hint of family gentility, and a trace of romantic idealism. He could be taken for a likable American young man, an above-average product of the Great Democracy from any part of the country. He didn't look much like a poet, an intellectual, an artist, or a Christian, each of which he was. Nor was there outward sign of his paralyzing, self-lacerating anger. His voice was pronouncedly quiet and low-pitched, though not of "cultivated" tone. It gave the impression of diffidence, but never of weakness. His accent was more or less unplaceable and it was somewhat variable. For instance, in Alabama it veered towards country-southern, and I may say he got away with this to the farm families and to himself.

His clothes were deliberately cheap, not only because he was poor but because he wanted to be able to forget them. He would work a suit into fitting him perfectly by the simple method of not taking it off much. In due time the cloth would mold itself to his frame. Cleaning and pressing would have undone this beautiful process. I exaggerate, but it did seem sometimes that wind, rain, work, and mockery were his tailors. On another score, he felt that wearing good, expensive clothes involved him in some sort of claim to superiority of the social kind. Here he occasionally confused his purpose, and fell over into a knowingly comical inverted dandyism. He got more delight out of factory-seconds sneakers and a sleazy cap than a straight dandy does from waxed calf Peal shoes and a brushed Lock & Co. bowler.

Physically Agee was quite powerful, in the deceptive way of

3

uninsistent large men. In movement he was rather graceless. His hands were large, long, bony, light, and uncared for. His gestures were one of the memorable things about him. He seemed to model, fight, and stroke his phrases as he talked. The talk, in the end, was his great distinguishing feature. He talked his prose, Agee prose. It was hardly a twentieth century style; it had Elizabethan colors. Yet it had extraordinarily knowledgeable contemporary content. It rolled just as it reads; but he made it sound natural—something just there in the air like any other part of the world. How he did this no one knows. You would have blinked, gaped, and very likely run from this same talk delivered without his mysterious ability. It wasn't a matter of show, and it wasn't necessarily bottle-inspired. Sheer energy of imagination was what lay behind it. This he matched with physical energy. Many a man or woman has fallen exhausted to sleep at four in the morning bang in the middle of a remarkable Agee performance, and later learned that the man had continued it somewhere else until six. Like many born writers who are floating in the illusory amplitude of their youth, Agee did a great deal of writing in the air. Often you had the impulse to gag him and tie a pen to his hand. That wasn't necessary; he was an exception among talking writers. He wrote—devotedly and incessantly.

Night was his time. In Alabama he worked I don't know how late. Some parts of *Let Us Now Praise Famous Men* read as though they were written on the spot at night. Later, in a small house in Frenchtown, New Jersey, the work, I think, was largely night-written. Literally the result shows this; some of the sections read best at night, far in the night. The first passage of *A Country Letter* (p. 57), is particularly night-permeated.

Agee worked in what looked like a rush and a rage. In Alabama he was possessed with the business, jamming it all into the days and the nights. He must not have slept. He was driven to see all he could of the families' day, starting, of course, at dawn. In one way, conditions there were ideal. He could live inside the subject, with no distractions. Back-country poor life wasn't really far from him, actually. He had some of it in his blood, through relatives in Tennessee. Anyway, he was in flight from New York magazine editorial offices, from Greenwich Village social-intellectual evenings, and especially from the whole world of high-minded, well-bred, money-hued culture, whether authoritarian or libertarian. In Alabama he sweated and scratched with submerged glee. The families understood what he was down there to do. He'd explained it, in such a way that they were interested in *his* work. He wasn't playing. That is why in the end he left out certain completed passages that were entertaining, in an acid way. One of these was a long, gradually hilarious aside on the subject of hens. It was a virtuoso piece heightened with allegory and bemused with the pathetic fallacy.

He won almost everybody in those families—perhaps too much—even though some of the individuals were hardbitten, sore, and shrewd. Probably it was his diffidence that took him into them. That non-assurance was, I think, a hostage to his very Anglican childhood training. His Christianity—if an outsider may try to speak of it—was a punctured and residual remnant, but it was still a naked, root emotion. It was an ex-Church, or non-Church matter, and it was hardly in evidence. All you saw of it was an ingrained courtesy, an uncourtly courtesy that emanated from him towards everyone, perhaps excepting the smugly rich, the pretentiously genteel, and the police. After a while, in a round-about way, you discovered that, to him, human beings were at least possibly immortal and literally sacred souls.

The days with the families came abruptly to an end. Their real content and meaning has all been shown. The writing they induced is, among other things, the reflection of one resolute, private rebellion. Agee's rebellion was unquenchable, self-damaging, deeply principled, infinitely costly, and ultimately priceless.

New York, 1960

PREFACE

(Serious readers are advised to proceed to the book-proper after finishing the first section of the Preface. A later return will do no harm.)

DURING July and August 1936 Walker Evans and I were traveling in the middle south of this nation, and were engaged in what, even from the first, has seemed to me rather a curious piece of work. It was our business to prepare, for a New York magazine,* an article on cotton tenantry in the United States, in the form of a photographic and verbal record of the daily living and environment of an average white family of tenant farmers. We had first to find and to live with such a family; and that was the object of our traveling.

We found no one family through which the whole of tenantry in that country could be justly represented, but decided that through three we had come to know, our job might with qualified adequacy be done. With the most nearly representative of the three we lived a little less than four weeks, seeing them and the others intimately and constantly. At the end of August, long before we were willing to, we returned to the north and got our work ready.

For reasons which will not be a part of this volume the article was not published. At the end of a year it was, however, released to us; and in the spring of 1938 an agreement was reached with a New York publisher for an expansion of the same material in book form. At the end of another year and a half, for reasons which, again, will receive later attention, the completed manuscript was rejected, or withdrawn. In the spring of 1940 it was accepted by those who now publish it, on condition that certain words be deleted which are illegal in Massachusetts.

The authors found it possible to make this concession and, since it rather enhanced a deception, to permit prominence to the immediate, instead of the generic, title.

———

*Evans was on loan from the Federal Government.

This volume is designed in two intentions: as the beginning of a larger piece of work; and to stand of itself, independent of any such further work as may be done.

The title of this volume is *Let Us Now Praise Famous Men.*

The title of the work as a whole, this volume included, is *Three Tenant Families.*

The nominal subject is North American cotton tenantry as examined in the daily living of three representative white tenant families.

Actually, the effort is to recognize the stature of a portion of unimagined existence, and to contrive techniques proper to its recording, communication, analysis, and defense. More essentially, this is an independent inquiry into certain normal predicaments of human divinity.

The immediate instruments are two: the motionless camera, and the printed word. The governing instrument—which is also one of the centers of the subject—is individual, anti-authoritative human consciousness.

Ultimately, it is intended that this record and analysis be exhaustive, with no detail, however trivial it may seem, left untouched, no relevancy avoided, which lies within the power of remembrance to maintain, of the intelligence to perceive, and of the spirit to persist in.

Of this ultimate intention the present volume is merely portent and fragment, experiment, dissonant prologue. Since it is intended, among other things, as a swindle, an insult, and a corrective, the reader will be wise to bear the nominal subject, and his expectation of its proper treatment, steadily in mind. For that is the subject with which the authors are dealing, throughout. If complications arise, that is because they are trying to deal with it not as journalists, sociologists, politicians, entertainers, humanitarians, priests, or artists, but seriously.

The photographs are not illustrative. They, and the text, are coequal, mutually independent, and fully collaborative. By their fewness, and by the impotence of the reader's eye, this will be misunderstood by most of that minority which does not wholly ignore it. In the interests, however, of the history and future of photography, that risk seems irrelevant, and this flat statement necessary.

The text was written with reading aloud in mind. That cannot be recommended; but it is suggested that the reader attend with his ear to what he takes off the page: for variations of tone, pace, shape, and dynamics are here particularly unavailable to the eye alone, and with their loss, a good deal of meaning escapes.

It was intended also that the text be read continuously, as music is listened to or a film watched, with brief pauses only where they are self-evident.

Of any attempt on the part of the publishers, or others, to disguise or in any other way to ingratiate this volume, the authors must express their regret, their intense disapproval, and, as observers awaiting new contributions to their subject, their complaisance.

This is a *book* only by necessity. More seriously, it is an effort in human actuality, in which the reader is no less centrally involved than the authors and those of whom they tell. Those who wish actively to participate in the subject, in whatever degree of understanding, friendship, or hostility, are invited to address the authors in care of the publishers. In material that is used, privately or publicly, names will be withheld on request.

CONTENTS

Poor naked wretches, wheresoe'er you are,
That bide the pelting of this pitiless storm,
How shall your houseless heads and unfed sides,
Your loop'd and window'd raggedness, defend you
From seasons such as these? O! I have ta'en
Too little care of this! Take physick, pomp;
Expose thyself to feel what wretches feel,
That thou may'st shake the superflux to them,
And show the heavens more just.

Workers of the world, unite and fight. You have nothing to lose but your chains, and a world to win.*

*These words are quoted here to mislead those who will be misled by them. They mean, not what the reader may care to think they mean, but what they say. They are not dealt with directly in this volume; but it is essential that they be used here, for in the pattern of the work as a whole, they are, in the sonata form, the second theme; the poetry facing them is the first. In view of the average reader's tendency to label, and of topical dangers to which any man, whether honest, or intelligent, or subtle, is at present liable, it may be well to make the explicit statement that neither these words nor the authors are the property of any political party, faith, or faction.

1. The Great Ball on Which We Live.

The world is our home. It is also the home of many, many other children, some of whom live in far-away lands. They are our world brothers and sisters. . . .

2. Food, Shelter, and Clothing.

What must any part of the world have in order to be a good home for man? What does every person need in order to live in comfort? Let us imagine that we are far out in the fields. The air is bitter cold and the wind is blowing. Snow is falling, and by and by it will turn into sleet and rain. We are almost naked. We have had nothing to eat and are suffering from hunger as well as cold. Suddenly the Queen of the Fairies floats down and offers us three wishes.

What shall we choose?

'I shall wish for food, because I am hungry,' says Peter.

'I shall choose clothes to keep out the cold,' says John.

'And I shall ask for a house to shelter me from the wind, the snow, and the rain,' says little Nell with a shiver.

Now everyone needs food, clothing, and shelter. The lives of most men on the earth are spent in getting these things. In our travels we shall wish to learn what our world brothers and sisters eat, and where their food comes from. We shall wish to see the houses they dwell in and how they are built. We shall wish also to know what clothing they use to protect themselves from the heat and the cold.*

*These are the opening sentences of *Around the World With the Children,* by F. B. Carpenter (published by The American Book Company), a third-grade geography textbook belonging to Louis Gudger, aged ten, daughter of a cotton tenant.

PERSONS AND PLACES

Fred Garvrin Ricketts	. . . . a two-mule tenant farmer, aged fifty-four.
Sadie (Woods) Ricketts	. . . . his wife, aged forty-nine.
Margaret	. . . . aged twenty.
Paralee	. . . . aged nineteen.
John Garvrin	. . . . aged twelve.
Richard	. . . . aged eleven.
Flora Merry Lee	. . . . aged ten.
Katy	. . . . aged nine.
Clair Bell	. . . . aged four.
Thomas Gallatin Woods (Bud)	. . . . a one-mule tenant farmer, aged fifty-nine.
Ivy Woods	. . . . his second wife; middle twenties.
Miss-Molly	. . . . her mother; early fifties.
Gallatin	. . . . Woods' son by first marriage; a half-cropper; middle thirties.
Emma	. . . . a daughter of the first marriage; aged eighteen; married.
Pearl	. . . . Ivy's daughter by common law-marriage to a man prior to Woods; aged eight.
Thomas	. . . . son of Woods and second wife; aged three.
Ellen	. . . . child of second marriage; aged twenty months.
George Gudger	. . . . a one-mule half-cropper, aged thirty-one.
Annie Mae (Woods) Gudger	. . . . his wife, aged twenty-seven.
Maggie Louise	. . . . aged ten.
George Junior	. . . . aged eight.
Burt Westly	. . . . aged four.
Valley Few (Squinchy)	. . . . aged twenty months.

Chester Boles	. . . . Gudger's landlord.
T. Hudson Margraves Michael Margraves	} . . . . landlords to Woods and Ricketts.
Harmon	. . . . a landowner and New Deal executive.
Estelle	. . . . a middle-class young woman.
James Agee	. . . . a spy, traveling as a journalist.
Walker Evans	. . . . a counter-spy, traveling as a photographer.
William Blake Louis-Ferdinand Celine Ring Lardner Jesus Christ Sigmund Freud Lonnie Johnson Irvine Upham Others	} . . . . unpaid agitators.
Birmingham	. . . . a large Southern industrial city.
Cherokee City	. . . . a county seat; population *c.* 7000.
Centerboro	. . . . county seat for these tenants; *c.* 1500.
Cookstown	. . . . their landlords' town, and theirs; *c.* 300.
Madrid	. . . . a crossroads; two stores, four houses.
Hobe's Hill	. . . . a low plateau of clay, where the tenants live.

It is two miles to the highway; three to Madrid; seven to Cookstown; seventeen to Centerboro; twenty-seven to Cherokee City; eighty to Birmingham. Transportation, for these families, is by mule or by mule wagon or on foot. This is not far from the geographic center of the North American Cotton Belt.

Sadie Ricketts is a half-sister of Woods; Annie Mae Gudger is his daughter.

Since none of the characters or incidents of this volume are fictitious, the names of most persons, and nearly all names of places, are altered.

The ages given, and tenses throughout, save where it is otherwise obvious or deliberately ambiguous, are as of the summer of 1936.

BOOK TWO

DESIGN OF BOOK TWO

(To Walker Evans.

AGAINST time and the damages of the brain
Sharpen and calibrate. Not yet in full,
Yet in some arbitrated part
Order the façade of the listless summer.

Spies, moving delicately among the enemy,
The younger sons, the fools,
Set somewhat aside the dialects and the stained skins of
   feigned madness,
Ambiguously signal, baffle, the eluded sentinel.

Edgar, weeping for pity, to the shelf of that sick bluff,
Bring your blind father, and describe a little;
Behold him, part wakened, fallen among field flowers shallow
But undisclosed, withdraw.

Not yet that naked hour when armed,
Disguise flung flat, squarely we challenge the fiend.
Still, comrade, the running of beasts and the ruining heaven
Still captive the old wild king.

' I SPOKE of this piece of work we were doing as "curious." I had better amplify this.

It seems to me curious, not to say obscene and thoroughly terrifying, that it could occur to an association of human beings drawn together through need and chance and for profit into a company, an organ of journalism, to pry intimately into the lives of an undefended and appallingly damaged group of human beings, an ignorant and helpless rural family, for the purpose of parading the nakedness, disadvantage and humiliation of these lives before another group of human beings, in the name of science, of "honest journalism" (whatever that paradox may mean), of humanity, of social fearlessness, for money, and for a reputation for crusading and for unbias which, when skillfully enough qualified, is exchangeable at any bank for money (and in politics, for votes, job patronage, abelincolnism, etc.*); and that these people could be capable of meditating this prospect without the slightest doubt of their qualification to do an "honest" piece of work, and with a conscience better than clear, and in the virtual certitude of almost unanimous public approval. It seems curious, further, that the assignment of this work should have fallen to persons having so extremely different a form of respect for the subject, and responsibility toward it, that from the first and inevitably they counted their employers, and that Government likewise to which one of them was bonded, among their most dangerous enemies, acted as spies, guardians, and cheats,† and trusted no judgment, however authoritative it claimed to be, save their own: which in many aspects of the task before them was untrained and uninformed. It seems further curious that realizing the extreme corruptness and difficulty of the circumstances,

*Money.
†Une chose permise ne peut pas être pure.
  L'illégal me va.
            Essai de Critique Indirecte.

23

and the unlikelihood of achieving in any untainted form what they wished to achieve, they accepted the work in the first place. And it seems curious still further that, with all their suspicion of and contempt for every person and thing to do with the situation, save only for the tenants and for themselves, and their own intentions, and with all their realization of the seriousness and mystery of the subject, and of the human responsibility they undertook, they so little questioned or doubted their own qualifications for this work.

All of this, I repeat, seems to me curious, obscene, terrifying, and unfathomably mysterious.

So does the whole course, in all its detail, of the effort of these persons to find, and to defend, what they sought: and the nature of their relationship with those with whom during the searching stages they came into contact; and the subtlety, importance, and almost intangibility of the insights or revelations or oblique suggestions which under different circumstances could never have materialized; so does the method of research which was partly evolved by them, partly forced upon them; so does the strange quality of their relationship with those whose lives they so tenderly and sternly respected, and so rashly undertook to investigate and to record.

So does the whole subsequent course and fate of the work: the causes for its non-publication, the details of its later acceptance elsewhere, and of its design; the problems which confronted the maker of the photographs; and those which confront me as I try to write of it: the question, Who are you who will read these words and study these photographs, and through what cause, by what chance, and for what purpose, and by what right do you qualify to, and what will you do about it; and the question, Why we make this book, and set it at large, and by what right, and for what purpose, and to what good end, or none: the whole memory of the South in its six-thousand-mile parade and flowering outlay of the façades of cities, and of the eyes in the streets of towns, and of hotels, and of the trembling heat, and of the wide wild opening of the tragic land, wearing the trapped frail flowers of its garden of faces; the fleet flush and flower and fainting of the human crop it raises; the virulent, insolent, deceitful, pitying, infinitesimal and frenzied running and searching, on this colossal peasant

map, of two angry, futile and bottomless, botched and over-
complicated youthful intelligences in the service of an anger
and of a love and of an undiscernible truth, and in the frightening vanity of their would-be purity; the sustaining, even now,
and forward moving, lifted on the lifting of this day as ships on
a wave, above whom, in a few hours, night once more will
stand up in his stars, and they decline through lamplight and
be dreaming statues, of those, each, whose lives we knew and
whom we love and intend well toward, and of whose living we
know little in some while now, save that quite steadily, in not
much possible change for better or much worse, mute, innocent, helpless and incorporate among that small-moted and
inestimable swarm and pollen stream and fleet of single, ir-
reparable, unrepeatable existences, they are led, gently, quite
steadily, quite without mercy, each a little farther toward the
washing and the wailing, the sunday suit and the prettiest
dress, the pine box, and the closed clay room whose fraily decorated roof, until rain has taken it flat into oblivion, wears the
shape of a ritual scar and of an inverted boat: curious, obscene,
terrifying, beyond all search of dream unanswerable, those
problems which stand thickly forth like light from all matter,
triviality, chance, intention, and record in the body, of being,
of truth, of conscience, of hope, of hatred, of beauty, of indignation, of guilt, of betrayal, of innocence, of forgiveness, of
vengeance, of guardianship, of an indenominable fate, predicament, destination, and God.

Therefore it is in some fear that I approach those matters at
all, and in much confusion. And if there are questions in my
mind how to undertake this communication, and there are
many, I must let the least of them be, whether I am boring
you, or whether I am taking too long getting started, and too
clumsily. If I bore you, that is that. If I am clumsy, that may indicate partly the difficulty of my subject, and the seriousness
with which I am trying to take what hold I can of it; more certainly, it will indicate my youth, my lack of mastery of my socalled art or craft, my lack perhaps of talent. Those matters,
too, must reveal themselves as they may. However they turn
out, they cannot be otherwise than true to their conditions,
and I would not wish to conceal these conditions even if I

could, for I am interested to speak as carefully and as near truly as I am able. No doubt I shall worry myself that I am taking too long getting started, and shall seriously distress myself over my inability to create an organic, mutually sustaining and dependent, and as it were musical, form: but I must remind myself that I started with the first word I wrote, and that the centers of my subject are shifty; and, again, that I am no better an "artist" than I am capable of being, under these circumstances, perhaps under any other; and that this again will find its measurement in the facts as they are, and will contribute its own measure, whatever it may be, to the pattern of the effort and truth as a whole.

I might say, in short, but emphatically not in self-excuse, of which I wish entirely to disarm and disencumber myself, but for the sake of clear definition, and indication of limits, that I am only human. Those works which I most deeply respect have about them a firm quality of the superhuman, in part because they refuse to define and limit and crutch, or admit themselves as human. But to a person of my uncertainty, undertaking a task of this sort, that plane and manner are not within reach, and could only falsify what by this manner of effort may at least less hopelessly approach clarity, and truth.'

'For in the immediate world, everything is to be discerned, for him who can discern it, and centrally and simply, without either dissection into science, or digestion into art, but with the whole of consciousness, seeking to perceive it as it stands: so that the aspect of a street in sunlight can roar in the heart of itself as a symphony, perhaps as no symphony can: and all of consciousness is shifted from the imagined, the revisive, to the effort to perceive simply the cruel radiance of what is.

This is why the camera seems to me, next to unassisted and weaponless consciousness, the central instrument of our time; and is why in turn I feel such rage at its misuse: which has spread so nearly universal a corruption of sight that I know of less than a dozen alive whose eyes I can trust even so much as my own.'

'If I had explained myself clearly you would realize by now that through this non-"artistic" view, this effort to suspend or destroy imagination, there opens before consciousness, and within it, a universe luminous, spacious, incalculably rich and wonderful in each detail, as relaxed and natural to the human swimmer, and as full of glory, as his breathing: and that it is possible to capture and communicate this universe not so well by any means of art as through such open terms as I am trying it under.

In a novel, a house or person has his meaning, his existence, entirely through the writer. Here, a house or a person has only the most limited of his meaning through me: his true meaning is much huger. It is that he *exists*, in actual being, as you do and as I do, and as no character of the imagination can possibly exist. His great weight, mystery, and dignity are in this fact. As for me, I can tell you of him only what I saw, only so accurately as in my terms I know how: and this in turn has its chief stature not in any ability of mine but in the fact that I too exist, not as a work of fiction, but as a human being. Because of his immeasurable weight in actual existence, and because of mine, every word I tell of him has inevitably a kind of immediacy, a kind of meaning, not at all necessarily "superior" to that of imagination, but of a kind so different that a work of the imagination (however intensely it may draw on "life") can at best only faintly imitate the least of it.'

'The communication is not by any means so simple. It seems to me now that to contrive techniques appropriate to it in the first place, and capable of planting it cleanly in others, in the second, would be a matter of years, and I shall probably try none of it or little, and that very tortured and diluted, at present. I realize that, with even so much involvement in explanations as this, I am liable seriously, and perhaps irretrievably, to obscure what would at best be hard enough to give its appropriate clarity and intensity; and what seems to me most important of all: namely, that these I will write of are human beings, living in this world, innocent of such twistings as these which are taking place over their heads; and that they were dwelt among, investigated, spied on, revered, and loved, by other quite monstrously alien human beings, in the employment of still others still more alien; and that they are now being looked into by still others, who have picked up their living as casually as if it were a book, and who were actuated toward this reading by various possible reflexes of sympathy, curiosity, idleness, et cetera, and almost certainly in a lack of consciousness, and conscience, remotely appropriate to the enormity of what they are doing.

If I could do it, I'd do no writing at all here. It would be photographs; the rest would be fragments of cloth, bits of cotton, lumps of earth, records of speech, pieces of wood and iron, phials of odors, plates of food and of excrement. Booksellers would consider it quite a novelty; critics would murmur, yes, but is it art; and I could trust a majority of you to use it as you would a parlor game.

A piece of the body torn out by the roots might be more to the point.

As it is, though, I'll do what little I can in writing. Only it will be very little. I'm not capable of it; and if I were, you would not go near it at all. For if you did, you would hardly bear to live.

As a matter of fact, nothing I might write could make any difference whatever. It would only be a "book" at the best. If it were a safely dangerous one it would be "scientific" or "political" or "revolutionary." If it were really dangerous it would be "literature" or "religion" or "mysticism" or "art," and under one such name or another might in time achieve the emasculation of acceptance. If it were dangerous enough to be of any remote use to the human race it would be merely "frivolous" or "pathological," and that would be the end of that. Wiser and more capable men than I shall ever be have put their findings before you, findings so rich and so full of anger, serenity, murder, healing, truth, and love that it seems incredible the world were not destroyed and fulfilled in the instant, but you are too much for them: the weak in courage are strong in cunning; and one by one, you have absorbed and have captured and dishonored, and have distilled of your deliverers the most ruinous of all your poisons; people hear Beethoven in concert halls, or over a bridge game, or to relax; Cézannes are hung on walls, reproduced, in natural wood frames; van Gogh is the man who cut off his ear and whose yellows became recently popular in window decoration; Swift loved individuals but hated the human race; Kafka is a fad; Blake is in the Modern Library; Freud is a Modern Library Giant; Dovschenko's *Frontier* is disliked by those who demand that it fit the Eisenstein esthetic; *nobody* reads *Joyce* any more; Céline is a madman who has incurred the hearty dislike of Alfred Kazin, reviewer for the *New York Herald Tribune* book section, and is, moreover, a fascist; I hope I need not mention Jesus Christ, of whom you have managed to make a dirty gentile.

However that may be, this is a book about "sharecroppers," and is written for all those who have a soft place in their hearts for the laughter and tears inherent in poverty viewed at a distance, and especially for those who can afford the retail price; in the hope that the reader will be edified, and may feel kindly disposed toward any well-thought-out liberal efforts to rectify the unpleasant situation down South, and will somewhat better and more guiltily appreciate the next good meal he eats; and in the hope, too, that he will recommend this little book to really sympathetic friends, in order that our publishers may at least cover their investment and that (just the merest perhaps) some kindly thought may be turned our way, and a little of your money fall to poor little us.'

'Above all else: in God's name don't think of it as Art.

Every fury on earth has been absorbed in time, as art, or as religion, or as authority in one form or another. The deadliest blow the enemy of the human soul can strike is to do fury honor. Swift, Blake, Beethoven, Christ, Joyce, Kafka, name me a one who has not been thus castrated. Official acceptance is the one unmistakable symptom that salvation is beaten again, and is the one surest sign of fatal misunderstanding, and is the kiss of Judas.

Really it should be possible to hope that this be recognized as so, and as a mortal and inevitably recurrent danger. It is scientific fact. It is disease. It is avoidable. Let a start be made. And then exercise your perception of it on work that has more to tell you than mine has. See how respectable Beethoven is; and by what right any wall in museum, gallery or home presumes to wear a Cézanne; and by what idiocy Blake or work even of such intention as mine is ever published and sold. I will tell you a test. It is unfair. It is untrue. It stacks all the cards. It is out of line with what the composer intended. All so much the better.

Get a radio or a phonograph capable of the most extreme loudness possible, and sit down to listen to a performance of Beethoven's Seventh Symphony or of Schubert's C-Major Symphony. But I don't mean just sit down and listen. I mean this: Turn it on as loud as you can get it. Then get down onto the floor and jam your ear as close into the loudspeaker as you can get it and stay there, breathing as lightly as possible, and not moving, and neither eating nor smoking nor drinking. Concentrate everything you can into your hearing and into your body. You won't hear it nicely. If it hurts you, be glad of it. As near as you will ever get, you are inside the magic; not only inside it, you are it; your body is no longer your shape and substance, it is the shape and substance of the music.

Is what you hear pretty? or beautiful? or legal? or acceptable in polite or any other society? It is beyond any calculation savage and dangerous and murderous to all equilibrium in human life as human life is; and nothing can equal the rape it does on all that death; nothing except anything, anything in existence or dream, perceived anywhere remotely toward its true dimension.'

'Beethoven said a thing as rash and noble as the best of his work. By my memory, he said: "He who understands my music can never know unhappiness again." I believe it. And I would be a liar and a coward and one of your safe world if I should fear to say the same words of my best perception, and of my best intention.

Performance, in which the whole fate and terror rests, is another matter.'

The house had now descended

All over Alabama the lamps are out

THE HOUSE and all that was in it had now descended deep beneath the gradual spiral it had sunk through; it lay formal under the order of entire silence. In the square pine room at the back the bodies of the man of thirty and of his wife and of their children lay on shallow mattresses on their iron beds and on the rigid floor, and they were sleeping, and the dog lay asleep in the hallway. Most human beings, most animals and birds who live in the sheltering ring of human influence, and a great portion of all the branched tribes of living in earth and air and water upon a half of the world, were stunned with sleep. That region of the earth on which we were at this time transient was some hours fallen beneath the fascination of the stone, steady shadow of the planet, and lay now listing toward the last depth; and now by a blockade of the sun were clearly disclosed those discharges of light which teach us what little we can learn of the stars and of the true nature of our surroundings. There was no longer any sound of the settling or ticking of any part of the structure of the house; the bone pine hung on its nails like an abandoned Christ. There was no longer any sound of the sinking and settling, like gently foundering, fatal boats, of the bodies and brains of this human family through the late stages of fatigue unharnessed or the early phases of sleep; nor was there any longer the sense of any of these sounds, nor was there, even, the sound or the sense of breathing. Bone and bone, blood and blood, life and life disjointed and abandoned they lay graven in so final depth, that dreams attend them seemed not plausible. Fish halted on the middle and serene of blind sea water sleeping lidless lensed; their breathing, their sleeping subsistence, the effortless nursing of ignorant plants; entirely silenced, sleepers, delicate planets, insects, cherished in amber, mured in night, autumn of action, sorrow's short winter, waterhole where gather the weak wild beasts; night; night: sleep; sleep.

In their prodigious realm, their field, bashfully at first, less timorous, later, rashly, all calmly boldly now, like the tingling and standing up of plants, leaves, planted crops out of the earth into the yearly approach of the sun, the noises and natures of the dark had with the ceremonial gestures of music and of erosion lifted forth the thousand several forms of their entrancement, and had so reasonantly taken over the world that this domestic, this human silence obtained, prevailed, only locally, shallowly, and with the childlike and frugal dignity of a coal-oil lamp stood out on a wide night meadow and of a star sustained, unraveling in one rivery sigh its irremediable vitality, on the alien size of space.

Where beneath the ghosts of millennial rain the clay land lay down in creek and the trees ran thick there disposed upon the sky the cloud and black shadow of nature, hostile encampment whose fires were drenched, drawn close, held sleeping, near, helots; and it was feasible that within a few hours now, at the signaling of the primary changes of the air, the wave which summer and darkness had already so heavily overcrested that it leaned above us, snaring its snake-tongued branches, birnam wood, casually would lounge in and suddenly and forever subdue us; at most, some obscure act of guerrilla warfare, some prowler, detached from his regiment, picked off in a back country orchard, some straggling camp whore taken, had; for the sky:

The sky was withdrawn from us with all her strength. Against some scarcely conceivable imprisoning wall this woman held herself away from us and watched us: wide, high, light with her stars as milk above our heavy dark; and like the bristling and glass breakage on the mouth of stone spring water: broached on grand heaven their metal fires.

And now as by the slipping of a button, the snapping and failures on air of a spider's cable, there broke loose from the room, shaken, a long sigh closed in silence. On some ledge over-leaning that gulf which is more profound than the remembrance of imagination they had lain in sleep and at length the sand, that by degrees had crumpled and rifted, had broken from beneath them and they sank. There was now no further extreme, and they were sunken not singularly but companionate among the whole enchanted swarm of the living, into a region prior to the youngest quaverings of creation.

(*We lay on the front porch:*

July 1936

Late Sunday Morning

THEY CAME into the Coffee Shoppe while we were finishing breakfast, and Harmon introduced the other, whose name I forget, but which had a French sound. He was middle-sized and dark, beginning to grizzle, with the knotty, walnut kind of body and a deeply cut, not unkindly monkey's face. He wore dark trousers, a starched freshly laundered white collarless shirt, and a soft yellow straw hat with a band of flowered cloth. His shoes were old, freshly blacked, not polished; his suspenders were nearly new, blue, with gold lines at the edge. He was courteous, casual, and even friendly, without much showing the element of strain: Harmon let him do the talking and watched us from behind the reflecting lenses of his glasses. People in the street slowed as they passed and lingered their eyes upon us. Walker said it would be all right to make pictures, wouldn't it, and he said, Sure, of course, take all the snaps you're a mind to; that is, if you can keep the niggers from running off when they see a camera. When they saw the amount of equipment stowed in the back of our car, they showed that they felt they had been taken advantage of, but said nothing of it.

Harmon drove out with Walker, I with the other, up a loose wide clay road to the northwest of town in the high glittering dusty sunday late morning heat of sunlight. The man I drove with made steady conversation, in part out of nervous courtesy, in part as if to forestall any questions I might ask him. I was glad enough of it; nearly all his tenants were negroes and no use to me, and I needed a rest from asking questions and decided merely to establish myself as even more easygoing, casual, and friendly than he was. It turned out that I had not been mistaken in the French sound of his name; ancestors of his had escaped an insurrection of negroes in Haiti. He himself, however, was entirely localized, a middling well-to-do landowner with a little more of the look of the direct farmer about him than the average. He was driving a several-years-old tan sedan, much the sort of car a factory worker in a northern city drives, and was pointing out to me how mean the cotton was on this man's land, who thought he could skimp by on a low grade of fertilizer, and how good it was along this pocket and high lift, that somehow caught whatever rain ran across this part of the country, though that was no advantage to cotton in a wet year or even an average; it was good in a drowt year like this one, though; his own cotton, except for a stretch of it along the bottom, he couldn't say yet it was going to do either very good or very bad; here we are at it, though.

A quarter of a mile back in a flat field of short cotton a grove of oaks spumed up and a house stood in their shade. Beyond, as we approached, the land sank quietly away toward woods which ran tendrils along it, and was speckled near and far with nearly identical two-room shacks, perhaps a dozen, some in the part shade of chinaberry bushes, others bare to the brightness, all with the color in the sunlight and frail look of the tissue of hornets' nests. This nearest four-room house we were approaching was the foreman's. We drew up in the oak shade as the doors of this house filled. They were negroes. Walker and Harmon drew up behind us. A big iron ring hung by a chain from the low branch of an oak. A heavy strip of iron leaned at the base of the tree. Negroes appeared at the doors of the two nearest tenant houses. From the third house away, two of them were approaching. One was in clean overalls; the other wore black pants, a white shirt, and a black vest unbuttoned.

Here at the foreman's home we had caused an interruption that filled me with regret: relatives were here from a distance, middle-aged and sober people in their sunday clothes, and three or four visiting children, and I realized that they had been quietly enjoying themselves, the men out at the far side of the house, the women getting dinner, as now, by our arrival, they no longer could. The foreman was very courteous, the other men were non-committal, the eyes of the women were quietly and openly hostile; the landlord and the foreman were talking. The foreman's male guests hovered quietly and respectfully in silence on the outskirts of the talk until they were sure what they might properly do, then withdrew to the far side of the house, watching carefully to catch the landowner's eyes, should they be glanced after, so that they might nod, smile, and touch their foreheads, as in fact they did, before they disappeared. The two men from the third house came up; soon three more came, a man of forty and a narrow-skulled pair of sapling boys. They all approached softly and strangely until they stood within the shade of the grove, then stayed their ground as if floated, their eyes shifting upon us sidelong and to the ground and to the distance, speaking together very little, in quieted voices: it was as if they had been under some sort of magnetic obligation to approach just this closely and to show themselves. The landlord began to ask of them through the foreman, How's So-and-So doing, all laid by? Did he do that extra sweeping I told you?—and the foreman would answer, Yes sir, yes sir, he do what you say to do, he doin all right; and So-and-So shifted on his feet and smiled uneasily while, uneasily, one of his companions laughed and the others held their faces in the blank safety of deafness. And you, you ben doin much coltn lately, you horny old bastard?—and the crinkled, old, almost gray-mustached negro who came up tucked his head to one side looking cute, and showed what was left of his teeth, and whined, tittering, Now Mist So-and-So, you know I'm settled down, married-man, you wouldn't— and the brutal negro of forty split his face in a villainous grin and said, He too *ole*, Mist So-and-So, he don't got no sap lef in him; and everyone laughed, and the landowner said, These yer two yere, colts yourn ain't they?—and the old man said they were, and the landowner said, Musta found *them* in the woods, strappin young niggers as that; and the old man said, No sir, he got the both of them lawful married, Mist So-and-So; and the landowner said that eldest on em looks to be ready for a piece himself, and the negroes laughed, and the two boys twisted their beautiful bald gourdlike skulls in a unison of shyness and their faces were illumined with maidenly smiles of shame, delight and fear; and meanwhile the landowner had loosened the top two buttons of his trousers, and he now reached his hand in to the middle of the forearm, and, squatting with bent knees apart, clawed, scratched and rearranged his genitals.

But now three others stood in the outskirts who had been sent for by a running child; they were young men, only twenty to thirty, yet very old and sedate; and their skin was of that

sootiest black which no light can make shine and with which
the teeth are blue and the eyeballs gold. They wore pressed
trousers, washed shoes, brilliantly starched white shirts, bright
ties, and carried newly whited straw hats in their hands, and
at their hearts were pinned the purple and gilded ribbons of a
religious and burial society. They had been summoned to sing
for Walker and for me, to show us what nigger music is like
(though we had done all we felt we were able to spare them
and ourselves this summons), and they stood patiently in a stiff
frieze in the oak shade, their hats and their shirts shedding
light, and were waiting to be noticed and released, for they
had been on their way to church when the child caught them;
and now that they were looked at and the order given they
stepped forward a few paces, not smiling, and stopped in rigid
line, and, after a constricted exchange of glances among themselves, the eldest tapping the clean dirt with his shoe, they
sang. It was as I had expected, not in the mellow and euphonious Fisk Quartette style, but in the style I have heard on
records by Mitchell's Christian Singers, jagged, tortured, stony,
accented as if by hammers and cold-chisels, full of a nearly paralyzing vitality and iteration of rhythm, the harmonies constantly splitting the nerves; so that of western music the nearest
approach to its austerity is in the first two centuries of poly-
phony. But here it was entirely instinctual; it tore itself like a
dance of sped plants out of three young men who stood sunk
to their throats in land, and whose eyes were neither shut nor
looking at anything; the screeching young tenor, the baritone,
stridulant in the height of his register, his throat tight as a fist,
and the bass, rolling the iron wheels of his machinery, his hand
clenching and loosening as he tightened and relaxed against
the spraining of his ellipses: and they were abruptly silent;
totally wooden; while the landowner smiled coldly. There was
nothing to say. I looked them in the eyes with full and open
respect and said, that was fine. Have you got time to sing us
another? Their heads and their glances collected toward a
common center, and restored, and they sang us another, a
slow one this time; I had a feeling, through their silence before
entering it, that it was their favorite and their particular pride;
the tenor lifted out his voice alone in a long, plorative line that
hung like fire on heaven, or whistle's echo, sinking, sunken,

along descents of a modality I had not heard before, and sank along the arms and breast of the bass as might a body sunken from a cross; and the baritone lifted a long black line of comment; and they ran in a long and slow motion and convolution of rolling as at the bottom of a stormy sea, voice meeting voice as ships in dream, retreated, met once more, much woven, digressions and returns of time, quite tuneless, the bass, over and over, approaching, drooping, the same declivity, the baritone taking over, a sort of metacenter, murmuring along monotones between major and minor, nor in any determinable key, the tenor winding upward like a horn, a wire, the flight of a bird, almost into full declamation, then failing it, silencing; at length enlarging, the others lifting, now, alone, lone, and largely, questioning, alone and not sustained, in the middle of space, stopped; and now resumed, sunken upon the bosom of the bass, the head declined; both muted, droned; the baritone makes his comment, unresolved, that is a question, all on one note: and they are quiet, and do not look at us, nor at anything.

The landlord objected that that was too much howling and too much religion on end and how about something with some life to it, they knew what he meant, and then they could go.

They knew what he meant, but it was very hard for them to give it just now. They stiffened in their bodies and hesitated, several seconds, and looked at each other with eyes ruffled with worry; then the bass nodded, as abruptly as a blow, and with blank faces they struck into a fast, sassy, pelvic tune whose words were loaded almost beyond translation with comic sexual metaphor; a refrain song that ran like a rapid wheel, with couplets to be invented, progressing the story; they sang it through four of the probably three dozen turns they knew, then bit it off sharp and sharply, and for the first time, relaxed out of line, as if they knew they had earned the right, with it, to leave.

Meanwhile, and during all this singing, I had been sick in the knowledge that they felt they were here at our demand, mine and Walker's, and that I could communicate nothing otherwise; and now, in a perversion of self-torture, I played my part through. I gave their leader fifty cents, trying at the same time, through my eyes, to communicate much more, and said I was sorry we had held them up and that I hoped they would not be late; and he thanked me for them in a dead voice, not looking me in the eye, and they went away, putting their white hats on their heads they walked into the sunlight.

At the Forks

O N A ROAD between the flying shadows of loose woods toward the middle of an afternoon, far enough thrust forward between towns that we had lost intuition of our balance between them, we came to a fork where the sunlight opened a little more widely, but not on cultivated land, and stopped a minute to decide.

Marion would lie some miles over beyond the road on our left; some other county seat, Centerville most likely, out beyond the road on our right; but on which road the woods might give way to any extension of farm country there was no deducing: for we were somewhere toward the middle of one of the wider of the gaps on the road map, and had seen nothing but woods, and infrequent woods farms, for a good while now.

Just a little behind us on our left and close on the road was a house, the first we had passed in several miles, and we decided to ask directions of the people on the porch, whom, in the car mirror, I could see still watching us. We backed slowly, stopping the car a little short of the house, and I got slowly out and walked back toward them, watching them quietly and carefully, and preparing my demeanors and my words for the two hundredth time.

There were three on the porch, watching me, and they must not have spoken twice in an hour while they watched beyond the rarely traveled road the changes of daylight along the recessions of the woods, and while, in the short field that sank behind their house, their two crops died silently in the sun: a young man, a young woman, and an older man; and the two younger, their chins drawn inward and their heads tall against the grained wall of the house, watched me steadily and sternly as if from beneath the brows of helmets, in the candor of young warriors or of children.

They were of a kind not safely to be described in an account claiming to be unimaginative or trustworthy, for they had too much and too outlandish beauty not to be legendary. Since, however, they existed quite irrelevant to myth, it will be necessary to tell a little of them.

43

The young man's eyes had the opal lightings of dark oil and, though he was watching me in a way that relaxed me to cold weakness of ignobility, they fed too strongly inward to draw to a focus: whereas those of the young woman had each the splendor of a monstrance, and were brass. Her body also was brass or bitter gold, strong to stridency beneath the unbleached clayed cotton dress, and her arms and bare legs were sharp with metal down. The blenched hair drew her face tight to her skull as a tied mask; her features were baltic. The young man's face was deeply shaded with soft short beard, and luminous with death. He had the scornfully ornate nostrils and lips of an aegean exquisite. The fine wood body was ill strung, and sick even as he sat there to look at, and the bone hands roped with vein; they rose, then sank, and lay palms upward in his groins. There was in their eyes so quiet and ultimate a quality of hatred, and contempt, and anger, toward every creature in existence beyond themselves, and toward the damages they sustained, as shone scarcely short of a state of beatitude; nor did this at any time modify itself.

These two sat as if formally, or as if sculptured, one in wood and one in metal, or as if enthroned, about three feet apart in straight chairs tilted to the wall, and constantly watched me, all the while communicating thoroughly with each other by no outward sign of word or glance or turning, but by emanation.

The other man might have been fifty by appearance, yet, through a particular kind of delicateness upon his hands, and hair, and skin—they were almost infantine—I was sure he was still young, hardly out of his twenties, though again the face was seamed and short as a fetus. This man, small-built and heavy jointed, and wandering in his motions like a little child, had the thorny beard of a cartoon bolshevik, but suggested rather a hopelessly deranged and weeping prophet, a D. H. Lawrence whom male nurses have just managed to subdue into a straitjacket. A broken felt hat struck through with grass hair was banged on flat above his furious and leaky eyes, and from beneath its rascally brim as if from ambush he pored at me walleyed while, clenching himself back against the wall, he sank along it trembling and slowly to a squat, and watched up at me.

—

None of them relieved me for an instant of their eyes; at the intersection of those three tones of force I was transfixed as between spearheads as I talked. As I asked my questions, and told my purposes, and what I was looking for, it seemed to me they relaxed a little toward me, and at length a good deal more, almost as if into trust and liking; yet even at its best this remained so suspended, so conditional, that in any save the most hopeful and rationalized sense it was non-existent. The qualities of their eyes did not in the least alter, nor anything visible or audible about them, and their speaking was as if I was almost certainly a spy sent to betray them through trust, whom they would show they had neither trust nor fear of.

They were clients of Rehabilitation. They had been given a young sick steer to do their plowing with; the land was woods-clearing, but had been used as long as the house (whose wood was ragged and light as pith); no seed or fertilizer had been given them until the end of May. Nothing they had planted was up better than a few inches, and that was now withering faster than it grew. They now owed the Government on the seed and fertilizer, the land, the tools, the house, and probably before long on the steer as well, who was now so weak he could hardly stand. They had from the start given notice of the weakness and youth of the steer, of the nearly total sterility of the soil, and of the later and later withholding of the seed and fertilizer; and this had had a great deal to do with why the seed was given them so late, and they had been let know it in so many words.

The older man came up suddenly behind me, jamming my elbow with his concave chest and saying fiercely *Awnk, awnk,* while he glared at me with enraged and terrified eyes. Caught so abruptly off balance, my reflexes went silly and I turned toward him questioning 'politely' with my face, as if he wanted to say something, and could, which I had not quite heard. He did want urgently to say something, but all that came out was this blasting of *Awnk, awnk,* and a thick roil of saliva that hung like semen in his beard. I nodded, smiling at him, and he grinned gratefully with an expression of extreme wickedness and tugged hard at my sleeve, nodding violently in time to his voice and rooting out over and over this loud vociferation of a frog. The woman spoke to him sharply though not unkindly (the young man's eyes remained serene), as if he were a dog masturbating on a caller, and he withdrew against a post of the porch and sank along it to the floor with his knees up sharp and wide apart and the fingers of his left hand jammed as deep as they would go down his gnashed mouth, while he stayed his bright eyes on me. She got up abruptly without speaking and went indoors and came back out with a piece of stony corn-bread and gave it to him, and took her place again in her chair. He took the bread in both hands and struck his face into it like the blow of a hatchet, grappling with his jaws and slowly cradling his head like a piece of heavy machinery, while grinding, passionate noises ran in his throat, and we continued to talk, the young woman doing most of the talking, corrobo-rative and protective of the young man, yet always respectful toward him.

The young man had the asthma so badly the fits of it nearly killed him. He could never tell when he was going to be any good for work, and he was no good for it even at the best, it was his wife did the work; and him—the third—they did not even nod nor shift their eyes toward him; he was just a mouth. These things were said in the voice not of complaint but of statement, quietly stiff with hatred for the world and for living: nor was there any touch of pride, shame, resentment, or any discord among them.

Some niggers a couple of miles down a back road let them have some corn and some peas. Without those niggers there was no saying what they'd be doing by now. Only the niggers hadn't had a bit too much for themselves in the first place and were running very short now; it had been what was left over from the year before, and not much new corn, nor much peas, was coming through the drought. It was——

The older man came honking up at my elbow, holding out a rolled farm magazine. In my effort to give him whatever form of attention could most gratify him I was stupid again; the idea there was something he wanted me to read; and looked at him half-questioning this, and not yet taking what he offered me. The woman, in a voice that somehow, though contempuous (it implied, You are more stupid than he is), yielded me for the first time her friendship and that of her husband, so that hap-piness burst open inside me like a flooding of sweet water, said, he wants to give it to you. I took it and thanked him very much, looking and smiling into his earnest eyes, and he stayed at my side like a child, watching me affectionately while I talked to them.

They had told me there was farm country down the road on the right a piece: the whole hoarded silence and quiet of a lonesome and archaic American valley it was to become, full of heavy sunflowers and mediocre cotton, where the women wore sunbonnets without shyness before us and all whom we spoke to were gracious and melancholy, and where we did not find what we sought. Now after a little while I thanked them here on the porch and told them good-bye. I had not the heart at all to say, Better luck to you, but then if I remember rightly I did say it, and, saying it or not, and unable to communicate to them at all what my feelings were, I walked back the little distance to the car with my shoulders and the back of my neck more scalded-feeling than if the sun were on them. As we started, I looked back and held up my hand. The older man was on the dirt on his hands and knees coughing like a gorilla and looking at the dirt between his hands. Neither of the other two raised a hand. The young man lowered his head slowly and seriously, and raised it. The young woman smiled, sternly beneath her virulent eyes, for the first time. As we swung into the right fork of the road, I looked back again. The young man, looking across once more into the woods, had reached his hand beneath the bib of his overalls and was clawing at his lower belly. The woman, her eyes watching us past her shoulder, was walking to the door. Just as I glanced back, and whether through seeing that I saw her I cannot be sure, she turned her head to the front, and disappeared into the house.

Near a Church

I T WAS a good enough church from the moment the curve
opened and we saw it that I slowed a little and we kept our
eyes on it. But as we came even with it the light so held it that
it shocked us with its goodness straight through the body, so
that at the same instant we said *Jesus.* I put on the brakes and
backed the car slowly, watching the light on the building, until
we were at the same apex, and we sat still for a couple of minutes at least before getting out, studying in arrest what had hit
us so hard as we slowed past its perpendicular.

It lost nothing at all in stasis, but even more powerfully
strove in through the eyes its paralyzing classicism: stood from
scoured clay, a light lift above us, no trees near, and few weeds;
every grain, each nailhead, distinct; the subtle almost strangling strong asymmetries of that which has been hand wrought
toward symmetry (as if it were an earnest description, better
than the intended object): so intensely sprung against so
scarcely eccentric a balance that my hands of themselves spread
out their bones, trying to regiment on air between their
strengths its tensions and their mutual structures as they stood
subject to the only scarcely eccentric, almost annihilating stress,
of the serene, wild, rigorous light: empty, shut, bolted, of all
that was now withdrawn from·it upon the fields the utter statement, God's mask and wooden skull and home stood empty in
the meditation of the sun: and this light upon it was strengthening still further its imposal and embrace, and in about a
quarter of an hour would have trained itself ready, and there
would be a triple convergence in the keen historic spasm of the
shutter.

I helped get the camera ready and we stood away and I
watched what would be trapped, possessed, fertilized, in the
leisures and shyness which are a phase of all love for any object:
searching out and registering in myself all its lines, planes,
stresses of relationship, along diagonals withdrawn and approached, and vertical to the slightly off-centered door, and
broadside, and at several distances, and near, examining merely
the ways of the wood, and the nails, the three new boards of

differing lengths that were let in above the left of the door, the staring small white porcelain knob, the solesmoothed stairlifts, the wrung stance of thick steeple, the hewn wood stoblike spike at sky, the old hasp and new padlock, the randomshuttered windowglass whose panes were like the surfaces of springs, the fat gold fly who sang and botched against a bright pane within, and within, the rigid benches, box organ, bright stops, hung charts, wrecked hymnals, the platform, pine lectern doilied, pressed-glass pitcher, suspended lamp, four funeral chairs, the little stove with long swan throat aluminum in the hard sober shade, a button in sun, a flur of lint, a torn card of Jesus among children:

While we were wondering whether to force a window, a young negro couple came past up the road. Without appearing to look either longer or less long, or with more or less interest, than a white man might care for, and without altering their pace, they made thorough observation of us, of the car, and of the tripod and camera. We spoke and nodded, smiling as if casually; they spoke and nodded, gravely, as they passed, and glanced back once, not secretly, nor long, nor in amusement. They made us, in spite of our knowledge of our own meanings, ashamed and insecure in our wish to break into and possess their church, and after a minute or two I decided to go after them and speak to them, and ask them if they knew where we might find a minister or some other person who might let us in, if it would be all right. They were fifty yards or so up the road, walking leisurely, and following them, I watched aspects of them which are less easily seen (as surrounding objects are masked by looking into a light) when one's own eyes and face and the eyes and face of another are mutually visible and appraising. They were young, soberly buoyant of body, and strong, the man not quite thin, the girl not quite plump, and I remembered their mild and sober faces, hers softly wide and sensitive to love and to pleasure, and his resourceful and intelligent without intellect and without guile, and their extreme dignity, which was as effortless, unvalued, and undefended in them as the assumption of superiority which suffuses a rich and social adolescent boy; and I was taking pleasure also in the competence and rhythm of their walking in the sun, which was incapable of being less than muted dancing, and in the

beauty in the sunlight of their clothes, which were strange
upon them in the middle of the week. He was in dark trousers,
black dress shoes, a new-laundered white shirt with lights of
bluing in it, and a light yellow, soft straw hat with a broad
band of dark flowered cloth and a daisy in the band; she glossy-
legged without stockings, in freshly whited pumps, a flowered
pink cotton dress, and a great sun of straw set far back on her
head. Their swung hands touched gently with their walking,
stride by stride, but did not engage. I was walking more rapidly than they but quietly; before I had gone ten steps they
turned their heads (toward each other) and looked at me
briefly and impersonally, like horses in a field, and faced front
again; and this, I am almost certain, not through having heard
sound of me, but through a subtler sense. By the time I raised
my hand, they had looked away, and did not see me, though
nothing in their looking had been quick with abruptness or
surreption. I walked somewhat faster now, but I was overtaking them a little slowly for my patience; the light would be
right by now or very soon; I had no doubt Walker would do
what he wanted whether we had 'permission' or not, but I
wanted to be on hand, and broke into a trot. At the sound of
the twist of my shoe in the gravel, the young woman's whole
body was jerked down tight as a fist into a crouch from which
immediately, the rear foot skidding in the loose stone so that
she nearly fell, like a kicked cow scrambling out of a creek, eyes
crazy, chin stretched tight, she sprang forward into the first
motions of a running not human but that of a suddenly terrified wild animal. In this same instant the young man froze, the
emblems of sense in his wild face wide open toward me, his
right hand stiff toward the girl who, after a few strides, her
consciousness overtaking her reflex, shambled to a stop and
stood, not straight but sick, as if hung from a hook in the spine
of the will not to fall for weakness, while he hurried to her and
put his hand on her flowered shoulder and, inclining his head
forward and sidewise as if listening, spoke with her, and they
lifted, and watched me while, shaking my head, and raising my
hand palm outward, I came up to them (not trotting) and
stopped a yard short of where they, closely, not touching now,
stood, and said, still shaking my head (*No; no; oh, Jesus, no, no,
no!*) and looking into their eyes; at the man, who was not

knowing what to do, and at the girl, whose eyes were lined with tears, and who was trying so hard to subdue the shaking in her breath, and whose heart I could feel, though not hear, blasting as if it were my whole body, and I trying in some fool way to keep it somehow relatively light, because I could not bear that they should receive from me any added reflection of the shattering of their grace and dignity, and of the nakedness and depth and meaning of their fear, and of my horror and pity and self-hatred; and so, smiling, and so distressed that I wanted only that they should be restored, and should know I was their friend, and that I might melt from existence: 'I'm *very sorry!* I'm *very* sorry if I scared you! I didn't mean to scare you at all. I wouldn't have done any such thing for anything.'

They just kept looking at me. There was no more for them to say than for me. The least I could have done was to throw myself flat on my face and embrace and kiss their feet. That impulse took hold of me so powerfully, from my whole body, not by thought, that I caught myself from doing it exactly and as scarcely as you snatch yourself from jumping from a sheer height: here, with the realization that it would have frightened them still worse (to say nothing of me) and would have been still less explicable; so that I stood and looked into their eyes and loved them, and wished to God I was dead. After a little the man got back his voice, his eyes grew a little easier, and he said without conviction that that was all right and that I hadn't scared her. She shook her head slowly, her eyes on me; she did not yet trust her voice. Their faces were secret, soft, utterly without trust of me, and utterly without understanding; and they had to stand here now and hear what I was saying, because in that country no negro safely walks away from a white man, or even appears not to listen while he is talking, and because I could not walk away abruptly, and relieve them of me, without still worse a crime against nature than the one I had committed, and the second I was committing by staying, and holding them. And so, and in this horrid grinning of faked casualness, I gave them a better reason why I had followed them than to frighten them, asked what I had followed them to ask; they said the thing it is usually safest for negroes to say, that they did not know; I thanked them very much, and was seized once more and beyond resistance with the wish to clarify and set right, so that again, with my eyes and smile wretched and out of key with all I was able to say, I said I was awfully sorry if I had bothered them; but they only retreated still more profoundly behind their faces, their eyes watching mine as if awaiting any sudden move they must ward, and the young man said again that that was all right, and I nodded, and turned away from them, and walked down the road without looking back.

Aᴌᴌ ᴏᴠᴇʀ Alabama, the lamps are out. Every leaf drenches the touch; the spider's net is heavy. The roads lie there, with nothing to use them. The fields lie there, with nothing at work in them, neither man nor beast. The plow handles are wet, and the rails and the frogplates and the weeds between the ties: and not even the hurryings and hoarse sorrows of a distant train, on other roads, is heard. The little towns, the county seats, house by house white-painted and elaborately sawn among their heavy and dark-lighted leaves, in the spaced protections of their mineral light they stand so prim, so voided, so undefended upon starlight, that it is inconceivable to despise or to scorn a white man, an owner of land; even in Birmingham, mile on mile, save for the sudden frightful streaming, almost instantly diminished and silent, of a closed black car, and save stone lonesome sinister heelbeats, that show never a face and enter, soon, a frame door flush with the pavement, and ascend the immediate lightless staircase, mile on mile, stone, stone, smooth charted streams of stone, the streets under their lifted lamps lie void before eternity. New Orleans is stirring, rattling, and sliding faintly in its fragrance and in the enormous richness of its lust; taxis are still parked along Dauphine Street and the breastlike, floral air is itchy with the stilettos and embroiderings above black blood drumthroes of an eloquent cracked indiscoverable cornet, which exists only in the imagination and somewhere in the past, in the broken heart of Louis Armstrong; yet even in that small portion which is the infested genitals of that city, never free, neither of desire nor of waking pain, there are the qualities of the tender desolations of profoundest night. Beneath, the gulf lies dreaming, and beneath, dreaming, that woman, that id, the lower American continent, lies spread before heaven in her wealth. The parks of her cities are iron, loam, silent, the sweet fountains shut, and the pure façades, embroiled, limelike in street light are sharp, are still:

PART ONE

A COUNTRY LETTER

A COUNTRY LETTER

IT IS late in a summer night, in a room of a house set deep and solitary in the country; all in this house save myself are sleeping; I sit at a table, facing a partition wall; and I am looking at a lighted coal-oil lamp which stands on the table close to the wall, and just beyond the sleeping of my relaxed left hand; with my right hand I am from time to time writing, with a soft pencil, into a school-child's composition book; but just now, I am entirely focused on the lamp, and light.

It is of glass, light metal colored gold, and cloth of heavy thread.

The glass was poured into a mold, I guess, that made the base and bowl, which are in one piece; the glass is thick and clean, with icy lights in it. The base is a simply fluted, hollow skirt; stands on the table; is solidified in a narrowing, a round inch of pure thick glass, then hollows again, a globe about half flattened, the globe-glass thick, too; and this holds oil, whose silver line I see, a little less than half down the globe, its level a very little—for the base is not quite true—tilted against the axis of the base.

This 'oil' is not at all oleaginous, but thin, brittle, rusty feeling, and sharp; taken and rubbed between forefinger and thumb, it so cleanses their grain that it sharpens their mutual touch to a new coin edge, or the russet nipple of a breast erected in cold; and the odor is clean, cheerful and humble, less alive by far than that of gasoline, even a shade watery: and a subtle sweating of this oil is on the upward surface of the globe, as if it stood through the glass, and as if the glass were a pitcher of cool water in a hot room. I do not understand nor try to deduce this, but I like it; I run my thumb upon it and smell of my thumb, and smooth away its streaked print on the glass; and I wipe my thumb and forefinger dry against my pants, and keep on looking.

In this globe, and in this oil that is clear and light as water, and reminding me of creatures and things once alive which I have seen suspended in jars in a frightening smell of alcohol—serpents, tapeworms, toads, embryons, all drained one tan pallor of absolute death; and also of the serene, scarved flowers in untroubled wombs (and pale-tanned too, flaccid, and in the stench of exhibited death, those children of fury, patience and love which stand in the dishonors of accepted fame, and of the murdering of museum staring); in this globe like a thought, a dream, the future, slumbers the stout-weft strap of wick, and up this wick is drawn the oil, toward heat; through a tight, flat tube of tin, and through a little slotted smile of golden tin, and there ends fledged with flame, in the flue; the flame, a clean, fanged fan:

I :

THE LIGHT in this room is of a lamp. Its flame in the glass is of the dry, silent and famished delicateness of the latest lateness of the night, and of such ultimate, such holiness of silence and peace that all on earth and within extremest remembrance seems suspended upon it in perfection as upon reflective water: and I feel that if I can by utter quietness succeed in not disturbing this silence, in not so much as touching this plain of water, I can tell you anything within realm of God, whatsoever it may be, that I wish to tell you, and that what so ever it may be, you will not be able to help but understand it.

It is the middle and pure height and whole of summer and a summer night, the held breath, of a planet's year; high shored sleeps the crested tide: what day of the month I do not know, which day of the week I am not sure, far less what hour of the night. The dollar watch I bought a few days ago, as also from time to time I buy a ten cent automatic pencil, and use it little before I lose all track of it, ran out at seventeen minutes past ten the day before yesterday morning, and time by machine measure was over for me at that hour, and is a monument. I know of the lateness and full height by the quietly starved brightness of my senses, which some while ago made the transition past any need for sleep without taking much notice of it, as, in the late darkness, the long accustomed liner loses the last black headland, and quietly commends her forehead upon the long open home of the sea: and by a quality in the night itself not truly apparent to any one of the senses, yet, by some indirection, to every sense in one, of a most complete and universally shared withdrawal to source, like that brief paralysis which enchants a city while wreaths are laid to a cenotaph, and, muted, a bugle's inscription shines, in the tightening just before the relaxation of this swarmed, still, silence, till, hats-on, gears grow and smooth, the lifted foot arrested in the stopshot completes its step, once more the white mane of the drayhorse flurrs in the sunny air: now vibrates all that vast stone hive: into resumption, reassumption, of casual living.

And it is in these terms I would tell you, at all leisure, and in all detail, whatever there is to tell: of where I am; of what I perceive.

Lamplight here, and lone, late: the odor is of pine that has stood shut on itself through the heat of a hot day: the odor of an attic at white noon: and all of the walls save that surface within immediate touch of the lamp, where like water slept in lantern light the grain is so sharply discerned in its retirement beyond the sleep of the standing shape of pines, and the pastings and pinnings of sad ornaments, are a most dim scarce-color of grayed silver breathed in yellow red which is the hue and haze in the room; and above me, black: where, beyond bones of rafters underlighted, a stomach sucked against the spine in fear, the roof draws up its peak: and this is a frightening dark, which has again to do with an attic: for it is the darkness that stands just up the stairs, sucking itself out of sight of the light, from an attic door left ajar, noticed on your way to bed, and remembered after you are there: so that I muse what not quite creatures and what not quite forms are suspended like bats above and behind my bent head; and how far down in their clustered weight they are stealing while my eyes are on this writing; and how skillfully swiftly they suck themselves back upward into the dark when I turn my head: and above all, why they should be so coy, who, with one slather of cold membranes drooping, could slap out light and have me: and who own me since all time's beginning. Yet this mere fact of thinking holds them at distance, as crucifixes demons, so lightly and well that I am almost persuaded of being merely fanciful; in which exercise I would be theirs most profoundly beyond rescue, not knowing, and not fearing, I am theirs.
Above that shell and carapace, more frail against heaven than fragilest membrane of glass, nothing, straight to the terrific stars: whereof all heaven is chalky; and of whom the nearest is so wild a reach my substance wilts to think on: and we, this Arctic flower snow-rooted, last matchflame guarded on a windy plain, are seated among these stars alone: none to turn to, none to make us known; a little country settlement so deep, so lost in shelve and shade of dew, no one so much as laughs at us. Small wonder how pitiably we love our home,

cling in her skirts at night, rejoice in her wide star-seducing smile, when every star strikes us sick with the fright: do we really exist at all?

> This world is not my home, I'm, only passing through,
> My treasures and my hopes, are, all, beyond the sky,
> I've many, friends, and kindreds, that's gone, along before,
> And I can't, feel, at home, in this world, any, more.

And thus, too, these families, not otherwise than with every family in the earth, how each, apart, how inconceivably lonely, sorrowful, and remote! Not one other on earth, nor in any dream, that can care so much what comes to them, so that even as they sit at the lamp and eat their supper, the joke they are laughing at could not be so funny to anyone else; and the littlest child who stands on the bench solemnly, with food glittering all over his cheeks in the lamplight, this littlest child I speak of is not there, he is of another family, and it is a different woman who wipes the food from his cheeks and takes his weight upon her thighs and against her body and who feeds him, and lets his weight slacken against her in his heavying sleep; and the man who puts another soaked cloth to the skin cancer on his shoulder; it is his wife who is looking on, and his child who lies sunken along the floor with his soft mouth broad open and his nakedness up like a rolling dog, asleep: and the people next up the road cannot care in the same way, not for any of it: for they are absorbed upon themselves: and the negroes down beyond the spring have drawn their shutters tight, the lamplight pulses like wounded honey through the seams into the soft night, and there is laughter: but nobody else cares. All over the whole round earth and in the settlements, the towns, and the great iron stones of cities, people are drawn inward within their little shells of rooms, and are to be seen in their wondrous and pitiful actions through the surfaces of their lighted windows by thousands, by millions, little golden aquariums, in chairs, reading, setting tables, sewing, playing cards, not talking, talking, laughing inaudibly, mixing drinks, at radio dials, eating, in shirt-sleeves, carefully dressed, courting, teasing, loving, seducing, undressing, leaving the room empty in its empty light, alone and writing a letter urgently, in couples married, in separate chairs, in family parties, in gay parties, preparing for bed, preparing for sleep: and none can care, beyond that room; and none can be cared for, by any beyond that room: and it is small wonder they are drawn together so cowardly close, and small wonder in what dry agony of despair a mother may fasten her talons and her vampire mouth upon the soul of her struggling son and drain him empty, light as a locust shell: and wonder only that an age that has borne its children and must lose and has lost them, and lost life, can bear further living; but so it is:

A man and a woman are drawn together upon a bed and there is a child and there are children:

First they are mouths, then they become auxiliary instruments of labor: later they are drawn away, and become the fathers and mothers of children, who shall become the fathers and mothers of children:

Their father and their mother before them were, in their time, the children each of different parents, who in their time were each children of parents:

This has been happening for a long while: its beginning was before stars:

It will continue for a long while: no one knows where it will end:

While they are still drawn together within one shelter around the center of their parents, these children and their parents together compose a family:

This family must take care of itself; it has no mother or father: there is no other shelter, nor resource, nor any love, interest, sustaining strength or comfort, so near, nor can anything happy or sorrowful that comes to anyone in this family possibly mean to those outside it what it means to those within it: but it is, as I have told, inconceivably lonely, drawn upon itself as tramps are drawn round a fire in the cruelest weather; and thus and in such loneliness it exists among other families, each of which is no less lonely, nor any less without help or comfort, and is likewise drawn in upon itself:

Such a family lasts, for a while: the children are held to a magnetic center:

Then in time the magnetism weakens, both of itself in its tiredness of aging and sorrow, and against the strength of the growth of each child, and against the strength of pulls from outside, and one by one the children are drawn away:

Of those that are drawn away, each is drawn elsewhere toward another: once more a man and a woman, in a loneliness they are not liable at the time to notice, are tightened together upon a bed: and another family has begun:

Moreover, these flexions are taking place every where, like a simultaneous motion of all the waves of the water of the world: and these are the classic patterns, and this is the weaving, of human living: of whose fabric each individual is a part: and of all parts of this fabric let this be borne in mind:

Each is intimately connected with the bottom and the extremest reach of time:

Each is composed of substances identical with the substance of all that surrounds him, both the common objects of his disregard, and the hot centers of stars:

All that each person is, and experiences, and shall never experience, in body and in mind, all these things are differing expressions of himself and of one root, and are identical: and not one of these things nor one of these persons is ever quite to be duplicated, nor replaced, nor has it ever quite had precedent: but each is a new and incommunicably tender life, wounded in every breath, and almost as hardly killed as easily wounded: sustaining, for a while, without defense, the enormous assaults of the universe:

So that how it can be that a stone, a plant, a star, can take on the burden of being; and how it is that a child can take on the burden of breathing; and how through so long a continuation and cumulation of the burden of each moment one on another, does any creature bear to exist, and not break utterly to fragments of nothing: these are matters too dreadful and fortitudes too gigantic to meditate long and not forever to worship:

Just a half-inch beyond the surface of this wall I face is another surface, one of the four walls which square and collaborate against the air another room, and there lie sleeping, on

two iron beds and on pallets on the floor, a man and his wife
and her sister, and four children, a girl, and three harmed boys.
Their lamp is out, their light is done this long while, and not in
a long while has any one of them made a sound. Not even
straining, can I hear their breathing: rather, I have a not quite
sensuous knowledge of a sort of suspiration, less breathing
than that indiscernible drawing-in of heaven by which plants
live, and thus I know they rest and the profundity of their
tiredness, as if I were in each one of these seven bodies whose
sleeping I can almost touch through this wall, and which in the
darkness I so clearly see, with the whole touch and weight of
my body: George's red body, already a little squat with the
burden of thirty years, knotted like oakwood, in its clean white
cotton summer union suit that it sleeps in; and his wife's beside him, Annie Mae's, slender, and sharpened through with
bone, that ten years past must have had such beauty, and now
is veined at the breast, and the skin of the breast translucent,
delicately shriveled, and blue, and she and her sister Emma are
in plain cotton shifts; and the body of Emma, her sister,
strong, thick and wide, tall, the breasts set wide and high, shallow and round, not yet those of a full woman, the legs long
thick and strong; and Louise's green lovely body, the dim
breasts faintly blown between wide shoulders, the thighs long,
clean and light in their line from hip to knee, the head back
steep and silent to the floor, the chin highest, and the white
shift up to her divided thighs; and the tough little body of
Junior, hardskinned and gritty, the feet crusted with sores; and
the milky and strengthless littler body of Burt whose veins are
so bright in his temples; and the shriveled and hopeless, most
pitiful body of Squinchy, which will not grow:

But it is not only their bodies but their postures that I know,
and their weight on the bed or on the floor, so that I lie down
inside each one as if exhausted in a bed, and I become not my
own shape and weight and self, but that of each of them, the
whole of it, sunken in sleep like stones; so that I know almost
the dreams they will not remember, and the soul and body of
each of these seven, and of all of them together in this room
in sleep, as if they were music I were hearing, each voice in
relation to all the others, and all audible, singly, and as one

organism, and a music that cannot be communicated: and thus they lie in this silence, and rest.

Burt half-woke, whimpering before he was awake, an inarticulated soprano speaking through not quite weeping in complaint to his mother as before a sure jury of some fright of dream: the bed creaked and I heard her bare feet slow, the shuffling soles, and her voice, not whispering but stifled and gentle, Go to sleep now, git awn back to sleep, they aint nothin agoin to pester ye, git awn back to sleep, in that cadence of strength and sheltering comfort which anneals all fence of language and surpasses music; and George's grouched, sleepy voice, and hers to him, no words audible; and the shuffling; and a twisting in beds, and grumbling of weak springs; and the whimpering sinking, and expired; and the sound of breathing, strong, not sleeping, now, slowed, shifted across into sleep, now, steadier; and now, long, long, drawn off as lightest lithest edge of bow, thinner, thinner, a thread, a filament; nothing: and once more that silence wherein more deep than starlight this home is foundered.

I am fond of Emma, and very sorry for her, and I shall probably never see her again after a few hours from now. I want to tell you what I can about her.

She is a big girl, almost as big as her sister is wiry, though she is not at all fat: her build is rather that of a young queen of a child's magic story who throughout has been coarsened by peasant and earth living and work, and that of her eyes and her demeanor, too, kind, not fully formed, resolute, bewildered, and sad. Her soft abundant slightly curling brown hair is cut in a square bob which on her large fine head is particularly childish, and indeed Emma is rather a big child, sexual beyond propriety to its years, than a young woman; and this can be seen in a kind of dimness of definition in her features, her skin, and the shape of her body, which will be lost in a few more years. She wears a ten cent store necklace and a sunday cotton print dress because she is visiting, and is from town, but she took off her slippers as soon as she came, and worked with Annie Mae. According to her father she is the spitn image of her mother when her mother was young; Annie Mae favors her father and his people, who were all small and lightly built.

Emma is very fond of her father and very sorry for him, as her sister is, and neither of them can stand his second wife. I have an idea that his marrying her had a lot to do with Emma's own marriage, which her father so strongly advised her against. He married the second time when Emma was thirteen, and for a long while they lived almost insanely, as I will tell you of later, far back in a swamp: and when Emma was sixteen she married a man her father's age, a carpenter in Cherokee City. She has been married to him two years; they have no children. Emma loves good times, and towns, and people her own age, and he is jealous and mean to her and suspicious of her. He has given her no pretty dresses nor the money to buy cloth to make them. Every minute he is in the house he keeps his eye right on her as if she was up to something, and when he goes out, which is as seldom as he can, he locks her in: so that twice already she has left him and come home to stay, and then after a while he has come down begging, and crying, and swearing he'll treat her good, and give her anything she asks for, and that he'll take to drink or kill himself if she leaves him, and she has gone back: for it isn't any fun at home, hating that woman the way she does, and she can't have fun with anyone else because she is married and nobody will have fun with her that way: and now (and I think it may be not only through the depression but through staying in the house because of jealousy and through fear of living in a town with her, and so near a home she can return to), her husband can no longer get a living in Cherokee City; he has heard of a farm on a plantation over in the red hills in Mississippi and has already gone, and taken it, and he has sent word to Emma that she is to come in a truck in which a man he knows, who has business to drive out that way, is moving their furniture; and this truck is leaving tomorrow. She doesn't want to go at all, and during the past two days she has been withdrawing into rooms with her sister and crying a good deal, almost tearlessly and almost without voice, as if she knew no more how to cry than how to take care for her life; and Annie Mae is strong against her going, all that distance, to a man who leaves her behind and then just sends for her, saying, Come on along, now; and George too is as committal over it as he feels will appear any right or business of his to be, he a man, and married, to the wife of another man, who is no kin to him, but only the sister of his wife, and to whom he is himself unconcealably attracted: but she is going all the same, without at all understanding why. Annie Mae is sure she won't stay out there long, not all alone in the country away from her kinfolks with that man; that is what she keeps saying, to Emma, and to George, and even to me; but actually she is surer than not that she may never see her younger sister again, and she grieves for her, and for the loss of her to her own loneliness, for she loves her, both for herself and her dependence and for that softness of youth which already is drawn so deep into the trap, and in which Annie Mae can perceive herself as she was ten years past; and she gives no appearance of noticing the clumsy and shamefaced would-be-subtle demeanors of flirtation which George is stupid enough to believe she does not understand for what they are: for George would only be shocked should she give him open permission, and Emma could not be too well trusted either. So this sad comedy has been going on without comment from anyone, which will come to nothing: and another sort has been going on with us, of a kind fully as helpless. Each of us is attractive to Emma, both in sexual immediacy and as symbols or embodiments of a life she wants and knows she will never have; and each of us is fond of her, and attracted toward her. We are not only strangers to her, but we are strange, unexplainable, beyond what I can begin yet fully to realize. We have acted toward her with the greatest possible care and shyness and quiet, yet we have been open or 'clear' as well, so that she knows we understand her and like her and care for her almost intimately. She is puzzled by this and yet not at all troubled, but excited; but there is nothing to do about it on either side. There is tenderness and sweetness and mutual pleasure in such a 'flirtation' which one would not for the world restrain or cancel, yet there is also an essential cruelty, about which nothing can be done, and strong possibility of cruelty through misunderstanding, and inhibition, and impossibility, which can be restrained, and which one would rather die than cause any of: but it is a cruel and ridiculous and restricted situation, and everyone to some extent realizes it. Everyone realizes it, I think, to such a degree even as this: supposing even that nothing can be helped about the marriage, supposing she is going away and on with it, which she shouldn't, then if only Emma could spend her last few days alive having a gigantic good time in bed, with George, a kind of man she is best used to, and with Walker and with me, whom she is curious about and attracted to, and who are at the same moment tangible and friendly and not at all to be feared, and on the other hand have for her the mystery of glamour almost of mythological creatures. This has a good many times in the past couple of days come very clearly through between all of us except the children, and without fear, in sudden and subtle but unmistakable expressions of the eyes, or ways of smiling: yet not one of us would be capable of trusting ourselves to it unless beyond any doubt each knew all the others to be thus capable: and even then how crazily the conditioned and inferior parts of each of our beings would rush in, and take revenge. But this is just a minute specialization of a general brutal pity: almost any person, no matter how damaged and poisoned and blinded, is infinitely more capable of intelligence and of joy than he can let himself be or than he usually knows; and even if he had no reason to fear his own poisons, he has those that are in others to fear, to assume and take care for, if he would not hurt both himself and that other person and the pure act itself beyond cure.

But here I am going to shift ahead of where I am writing, to a thing which is to happen, or which happened, the next morning (you mustn't be puzzled by this, I'm writing in a continuum), and say what came of it.

The next morning was full of the disorganized, half listless, yet very busy motions of ordinary life broken by an event: Emma's going away. I was going to take her and Annie Mae to her brother Gallatin's house near Cookstown, where she was to meet the man with his truck, and I was waiting around on the front porch in the cool-hot increasing morning sunlight, working out my notes, while the morning housework was done up in special speed. (George was gone an hour or more ago, immediately after the breakfast they had all sat through, not talking much. There had been a sort of lingering in eating and in silences, and a little when the food was done, broken by talk to keep the silences from becoming too frightening; I had let the breakfast start late by telling him I would take him in the car; then abruptly he got up saying, 'Well, Jimmy, if you——' Whether he would kiss Emma goodbye, as a sort of relative, was on everybody's mind. He came clumsily near it: she half got from her chair, and their bodies were suddenly and sharply drawn toward each other a few inches: but he was much too shy, and did not even touch her with the hand he reached out to shake hers. Annie Mae drawled, smiling, What's wrong with ye George; she ain't agoin' to bite ye; and everyone laughed, and Emma stood up and they embraced, laughing, and he kissed her on her suddenly turned cheek, a little the way a father and an adolescent son kiss, and told her goodbye and wished her good luck, and I took him to work in the car, and came back. And now here I was, as I have said, on the porch.) Here I was on the porch, diddling around in a notebook and hearing the sounds of work and the changing patterns of voices inside, and the unaccustomed noise of shoe-leather on the floor, because someone was dressed up for travel; and a hen thudded among dried watermelon seeds on the oak floor, looking, as they usually do, like a nearsighted professor; and down hill beyond the open field a little wind laid itself in a wall against the glistening leaves of the high forest and lay through with a long sweet granular noise of rustling water; and the hen dropped from the ledge of the porch to the turded dirt with a sodden bounce, and an involuntary cluck as her heaviness hit the ground on her sprung legs; and the long lithe little wind released the trees and was gone on, wandering the fringed earth in its affairs like a saturday schoolchild in the sun, and the leaves hung troubling in the aftermath; and I heard footsteps in the hall and Emma appeared, all dressed to go, looking somehow as if she had come to report a decision that had been made in a conference, for which I, without knowing it, seemed to have been waiting. She spoke in that same way, too, not wasting any roundabout time or waiting for an appropriate rhythm, yet not in haste, looking me steadily and sweetly in the eyes, and said, I want you and Mr. Walker to know how much we all like you, because you make us feel easy with you; we don't have to act any different from what it comes natural to act, and we don't have to worry what you're thinking about us, it's just like you was our own people and

had always lived here with us, you all are so kind, and nice, and
quiet, and easygoing, and we wisht you wasn't never going to
go away but stay on here with us, and I just want to tell you
how much we all keer about you; Annie Mae says the same,
and you please tell Mr. Walker, too, if I don't see him afore I
go. (I knew she could never say it over again, and I swore I
certainly would tell him.)

What's the use trying to say what I felt. It took her a long
time to say what she wanted so much to say, and it was hard
for her, but there she stood looking straight into my eyes, and
I straight into hers, longer than you'd think it would be possible to stand it. I would have done anything in the world for
her (that is always characteristic, I guess, of the seizure of the
strongest love you can feel: pity, and the wish to die for a person, because there isn't anything you can do for them that is at
all measurable to your love), and all I could do, the very most,
for this girl who was so soon going on out of my existence
into so hopeless a one of hers, the very most I could do was
not to show all I cared for her and for what she was saying,
and not to even try to do, or to indicate the good I wished I
might do her and was so utterly helpless to do. I had such tenderness and such gratitude toward her that while she spoke I
very strongly, as something steadier than an 'impulse,' wanted
in answer to take her large body in my arms and smooth the
damp hair back from her forehead and to kiss and comfort and
shelter her like a child, and I can swear that I now as then
almost believe that in that moment she would have so well
understood this, and so purely and quietly met it, that now as
then I only wish to God I had done it; but instead the most I
did was to stand facing her, and to keep looking into her eyes
(doing her the honor at least of knowing that she did not want
relief from this), and, managing to keep the tears from running down my face, to smile to her and say that there was
nothing in my whole life that I had cared so much to be told,
and had been so grateful for (and I believe this is so); and that
I wanted her to know how much I liked them, too, and her
herself, and that I certainly felt that they were my own people,
and wanted them to be, more than any other kind of people in
the world, and that if they felt that of me, and that I belonged
with them, and we all felt right and easy with each other and

fond of each other, then there wasn't anything in the world I
could be happier over, or be more glad to know (and this is so,
too); and that I knew I could say all of the same of Walker (and
this, too, I know I was true in saying). I had stood up, almost
without realizing I was doing it, the moment she appeared and
began to speak, as though facing some formal, or royal, or ritual action, and we stayed thus standing, not leaning against or
touching anything, about three feet apart, facing each other. I
went on to say that whatever might happen to her or that she
might do in all her life I wished her the best luck anyone could
think of, and not ever to forget it, that nobody has a right to
be unhappy, or to live in a way that makes them unhappy, for
the sake of being afraid, or what people will think of them, or
for the sake of anyone else, if there is any way they can possibly do better, that won't hurt other people too much. She
slowly and lightly blushed while I spoke and her eyes became
damp and bright, and said that she sure did wish me the same.
Then we had nothing to say, unless we should invent something, and nothing to do, and quite suddenly and at the same
instant we smiled, and she said well, she reckoned she'd better
git on in and help Annie Mae, and I nodded, and she went,
and a half-hour later I was driving her, and Annie Mae, and her
father, and Louise, and Junior, and Burt, and the baby, to her
brother's house near Cookstown. The children were silent
and intent with the excitement of riding in the car, stacked on
top of each other around their mother on the back seat and
looking out of the windows like dogs, except Louise, whose
terrible gray eyes met mine whenever I glanced for them in the
car mirror. Emma rode between me and her father, her round
sleeveless arms cramped a little in front of her. My own sleeves
were rolled high, so that in the crowding our flesh touched.
Each of us at the first few of these contacts drew quietly away,
then later she relaxed her arms, and her body and thighs as
well, and so did I, and for perhaps fifteen minutes we lay
quietly and closely side to side, and intimately communicated
also in our thoughts. Our bodies were very hot, and the car
was packed with hot and sweating bodies, and with a fine salt
and rank odor like that of crushed grass: and thus in a short
while, though I knew speed was not in the mood of anyone
and was going as slowly as I felt I could with propriety, we

covered the short seven mileage of clay, then slag, to Cookstown, and slowed through the town (eyes, eyes on us, of men, from beneath hatbrims), and down the meandering now sandy road to where her brother lived. I had seen him once before, a man in his thirties with a bitter, intelligent, skull-formed face; and his sour wife, and their gold skinned children: and now here also was another man, forty or so, leathery-strong, blackshaven, black-hatted, booted, his thin mouth tightened round a stalk of grass showing gold stained teeth, his cold, mean eyes a nearly white blue; and he was sardonically waiting, and his truck, loaded with chairs and bed-iron, stood in the sun where the treeshade had slid beyond it. He was studying Emma coldly and almost without furtiveness, and she was avoiding his eyes. It was impossible to go quite immediately. We all sat around a short while and had lemonade from a pressed-glass pitcher, from which he had already taken at least two propitiatory glasses. It had been made in some hope of helping the leavetaking pass off as a sort of party, from two lemons and spring water, without ice, and it was tepid, heavily sweetened (as if to compensate the lack of lemons), and scarcely tart; there was half a glass for each of us, out of five tumblers, and we all gave most of it to the children. The children of the two families stayed very quiet, shy of each other; the others, save the black-hatted man, tried to talk, without managing much; they tried especially hard when Emma got up, as suddenly as if she had to vomit, and went into the next room and shut the door, and Annie Mae followed her. Gallatin said it was mighty hard on a girl so young as that leaving her kinfolks so far behind. The man in the hat twisted his mouth on the grass and, without opening his teeth, said Yeah-ah, as if he had his own opinions about that. We were trying not to try to hear the voices in the next room, and that same helpless, frozen, creaky weeping I had heard before; and after a little it quieted; and after a little more they came out, Emma flourily powdered straight to the eyes, and the eyes as if she had cried sand instead of tears; and the man said—it was the first kind gesture I had seen in him and one of the few I suspect in his life, and I am sure it was kind by no intention of his: 'Well, we can't hang around here all day. Reckon you'd better come on along, if you're coming.'

With that, Emma and her father kiss, shyly and awkwardly, children doing it before parents; so do she and her brother; she and Annie Mae embrace; she and I shake hands and say goodbye: all this in the sort of broken speed in which a family takes leave beside the black wall of a steaming train when the last crates have been loaded and it seems certain that at any instant the windows, and the leaned unpitying faces, will begin to slide past on iron. Emma's paper suitcase is lifted into the truck beside the bedsprings which will sustain the years on years of her cold, hopeless nights; she is helped in upon the hard seat beside the driver above the hot and floorless engine, her slippered feet propped askew at the ledges of that pit into the road; the engine snaps and coughs and catches and levels on a hot white moistureless and thin metal roar, and with a dreadful rending noise that brings up the mild heads of cattle a quarter of a mile away the truck rips itself loose from the flesh of the planed dirt of the yard and wrings into the road and chucks ahead, we waving, she waving, the black hat straight ahead, she turned away, not bearing it, our hands drooped, and we stand disconsolate and emptied in the sun; and all through these coming many hours while we slow move within the anchored rondures of our living, the hot, screaming, rattling, twenty-mile-an-hour traveling elongates steadily crawling, a lost, earnest, and frowning ant, westward on red roads and on white in the febrile sun above no support, suspended, sustained from falling by force alone of its outward growth, like that long and lithe incongruous slender runner a vine spends swiftly out on the vast blank wall of the earth, like snake's head and slim stream feeling its way, to fix, and anchor, so far, so wide of the strong and stationed stalk: and that is Emma.

But as yet this has not happened, and now she sleeps, here in this next room, among six others dear in their lives to me, and if I were but to section and lift away a part of this so thin shell and protection of wall, there they would be as in a surgery, or a medical drawing, the brain beneath the lifted, so light helmet of the skull, the deep-chambered, powerful and so vulnerable, so delicately ruined, emboweled, most vital organs, behind the placid lovedelighting skin; and a few hours past, they were going to bed, and not long before, they were eating supper, and because of their sadness, and because of the excitement of her being here, supper had in its speaking and its whole manner a tone out of the ordinary, a quality of an occasion, almost of a party, almost of gaiety, with a pale chocolate pudding, made out of cocoa and starch, for dessert, and a sort of made-conversation and joking half forced by fear of sadness, and half genuinely stimulated by her presence and by a shyness and liking for us: and in the middle of the table stood the flower of the lighted lamp, more kind, more friendly in the still not departed withering daylight and more lovely, than may be set in words beneath its fact: and when the supper was finished, it disintegrated without suture or transition into work, sleep, rest: Annie Mae, Emma, Louise, the three women, rising to the work they had scarcely ceased during the meal (for they had served us, eating betweentimes), clearing, scraping, crumbing the damp oilcloth with damp cloth in the light, dishwashing, meanwhile talking (Louise not talking, listening to them, the older women, absorbing, absorbing deeply, grain by grain, ton by ton, that which she shall not escape): the women lifting themselves from their chairs into this work; the children meanwhile sinking and laid out five fathom five mile deep along the exhausted floor: and we, following manners, transferred with George, a few feet beyond the kitchen door, in the open porch hall, leaned back in chairs against the wall, or leaned between our knees and our planted feet, he, with his work shoes off, his feet taking, thirstily drinking like the sunken heads of horses at the trough, the cool and beauty quiet of the grained and gritted boards of the floor; and he talking a little, but too tired for talk, and rolling a damp cigarette and smoking its short sweetness through to the scorching of the stony thumb, with a child's body lifted sleeping between his knees:

and when the women are through, they may or may not come out too, with their dresses wet in front with the dishwashing and their hard hands softened and seamed as if withered with water, and sit a little while with the man or the men: and if they do, it is not for long, for everyone is much too tired, and has been awake and at work since daylight whitened a little behind the trees on the hill, and it is now very close to dark, with daylight scarcely more than a sort of tincture on the air, and this diminishing, and the loudening frogs, and the locusts, the crickets, and the birds of night, tentative, tuning, in that great realm of hazy and drowned dew, who shall so royally embroider the giant night's fragrant cloud of earth-shade: and so, too, the talking is sporadic, and sinks into long unembarrassed silences; the sentences, the comments, the monosyllables, drawn up from deepest within them without thought and with faint creaking of weight as if they were wells, and spilled out in a cool flat drawl, and quietly answered; and a silence; and again, some words: and it is not really talking, or meaning, but another and profounder kind of communication, a rhythm to be completed by answer and made whole by silence, a lyric song, as horses who nudge one another in pasture, or like drowsy birds who are heavying a dark branch with their tiredness before sleep: and it is their leisure after work; but it does not last; and in fifteen minutes, or a half-hour at most, it is done, and they draw themselves into motion for bed:

one by one, in a granite-enameled, still new basin which is for that single purpose, they wash their feet in cold water—for this is a very cleanly and decent family—and begin to move into the bedroom: first the children, then the women, last George: the pallets are laid; the lamp is in the bedroom; George sits in the porch dark, smoking another cigarette. Junior, morose and whimpering and half blind with sleep, undresses himself, sliding the straps from his shoulders and the overalls from his nakedness and sinking in his shirt asleep already, along the thin cotton pallet. Burt scarcely half awakens as his sister strips him, a child of dough, and is laid like a corpse beside his cruel brother. Squinchy is drugged beyond doom-crack: his heavy tow head falls back across her bent arm loose as that of a dead bird, the mouth wide open, the eyelids oily gleaming, as his mother slips from his dwarf body the hip length, one-button dress; and the women, their plain shifts lifted from the closet nails, undress themselves, turned part away from each other, and careful not to look: the mother, whose body already at twenty-seven is so wrung and drained and old, a scrawny, infinitely tired, delicate animal, the poor emblems of delight no longer practicable to any but most weary and grunting use: her big young sister, childless still, and dim, soft as a bloomed moon, and still in health, who emanates some disordering or witless violation: and the still inviolate, lyric body of a child, very much of the earth, yet drawn into that short and seraphic phase of what seems unearthliness which it will so soon lose: each aware of herself and of the others, and each hiding what shames or grieves her: and the two elder talking (and the child, the photographic plate, receiving: These are women, I am a woman, I am not a child any more, I am undressing with women, and this is how women are, and how they talk), talking ahead, the two women, in flat, secure, drawled, reedy voices, neither shy nor deliberately communicative, but utterly communicative, the talk loosening out of them serenely and quietly steady and in no restraint of uncertainty of one another like the alternate and plaited music of two slow-dribbling taps; and they are in bed and George throws his cigarette, hurdling its spark into the night yard, and comes in, and they turn their faces away while he undresses; and he takes the clean thin union suit from its nail by the scrolled iron head of the bed; and he slides between the coarse sheets and lets down his weight; and for a little while more, because they are stimulated, they keep talking, while the children sleep, and while Louise lies looking and listening, with the light still on, and there is almost volubility in the talk, and almost gaiety again, and inaudible joking, and little runs of laughter like startled sparrows; and gradually this becomes more quiet, and there is a silence full of muted thought; and George, says; Well; and fluffs out the lamp, and its light from the cracks in my wall, and there is silence; and George speaks, low, and is answered by both women; and a silence; and Emma murmurs something; and after a few seconds Annie Mae murmurs a reply; and there is a silence, and a slow and constrained twisting on springs and extension of a body, and silence; and a long silence in the darkness of the peopled room that is chambered in the darkness of the continent before the unwatching stars; and Louise says, Good night Immer, and Emma says, Good night Louise; and Louise says, Good night mamma; and Annie Mae says, Good night Louise; and Louise says, Good night daddy; and George says, Good night Louise; good night George; night, Immer; night, Annie Mae; night, George; night, Immer; night, Annie Mae; night, Louise; night; good night, good night:

Bᴿɪɴɢ: Bring up:
Thou wound thy mien before the jurying stars:

And wild earth lifted streams in peace so noble, the wide
        dreaming forehead
and water mapped of earth, serene, serene;

O infant skull, back-fallen from an arm upon tall starlight,
        that ran in the bright barnyard:
Old world, thou richly peopled, thou sober-steering ark, quiet
        stone, thou granule,
        that finds no ararat:

O thou girl's breast:

II:

THERE are on this hill three such families I would tell you of: the Gudgers, who are sleeping in the next room; and the Woods, whose daughters are Emma and Annie Mae; and besides these, the Ricketts, who live on a little way beyond the Woods; and we reach them thus:

Leave this room and go very quietly down the open hall that divides the house, past the bedroom door, and the dog that sleeps outside it, and move on out into the open, the back yard, going up hill: between the tool shed and the hen house (the garden is on your left), and turn left at the long low shed that passes for a barn. Don't take the path to the left then: that only leads to the spring; but cut straight up the slope; and down the length of the cotton that is planted at the crest of it, and through a space of pine, hickory, dead logs and blackberry brambles (damp spider webs will bind on your face in the dark; but the path is easily enough followed); and out beyond this, across a great entanglement of clay ravines, which finally solidify into a cornfield. Follow this cornfield straight down a row, go through a barn, and turn left. There is a whole cluster of houses here; they are all negroes'; the shutters are drawn tight. You may or may not waken some dogs: if you do, you will hardly help but be frightened, for in a couple of minutes the whole country will be bellowing in the darkness, and it is over your movements at large at so late and still an hour of the night, and the sound, with the knowledge of wakened people, their heads lifted a little on the darkness from the crackling hard straw pillows of their iron beds, overcasts your very existence, in your own mind, with a complexion of guilt, stealth, and danger:

But they will quiet.

They will quiet, the lonely heads are relaxed into sleep; after a little the whippoorwills resume, their tireless whipping of the pastoral night, and the strong frogs; and you are on the road, and again up hill, that was met at those clustered houses; pines on your left, one wall of bristling cloud, and the lifted hill; the slow field raised, in the soft stare of the cotton, several acres, on the right; and on the left the woods yield off, a hundred yards; more cotton; and set back there, at the brim of the hill, the plain small house you see is Woods' house, that looks shrunken against its centers under the starlight, the tin roof scarcely taking sheen, the floated cotton staring:

The house a quarter-mile beyond, just on the right of the road, standing with shade trees, that is the Ricketts'. The bare dirt is more damp in the tempering shade; and damp, tender with rottenness, the ragged wood of the porch, that is so heavily littered with lard buckets, scraps of iron, bent wire, torn rope, old odors, those no longer useful things which on a farm are never thrown away. The trees: draft on their stalks their clouds of heavy season; the barn: shines on the perfect air; in the bare yard a twelve-foot flowering bush: in shroud of blown bloom slumbers, and within: naked, naked side by side those brothers and sisters, those most beautiful children; and the crazy, clownish, foxy father; and the mother; and the two old daughters; crammed on their stinking beds, are resting the night:

Fred, Sadie, Margaret, Paralee, Garvrin, Richard, Flora Merry Lee, Katy, Clair Bell; and the dogs, and the cats, and the hens, and the mules, and the hogs, and the cow, and the bull calf:

Woods, and his young wife, and her mother, and the young wife's daughter, and her son by Woods, and their baby daughter, and that heavy-browed beast which enlarges in her belly; Bud, and Ivy, and Miss-Molly, and Pearl, and Thomas, and Ellen, and the nameless plant of unknown sex; and the cat, and the dog, and the mule, and the hog, and the cow, and the hens, and the huddled chickens:

And George, and his wife, and her sister, and their children, and their animals; and the hung wasps, lancing mosquitoes, numbed flies, and browsing rats:

All, spreaded in high quietude on the hill:

Sadie the half-sister of Bud, and drowned in their remembrance: that long and spiral shaft they've climbed, from shacks on shale, rigid as corn on a cob, out of the mining country, the

long wandering, her pride of beauty, his long strength in marriage, into this: this present time, and this near future:

George his lost birthright, bad land owned, and that boy-
hood among cedars and clean creeks where no fever laid its
touch, and where in the luminous and great hollow night the
limestone shone like sheep: and the strong, gay girls:

Fred, what of him: I can not guess. And Annie Mae, that
hat; which still, so broken, the death odor of feathers and silk
in menthol, is crumpled in a drawer; and those weeks when
she was happy, and to her husband and to her heart it was
pleasing to be alive:

She is dreaming now, with fear, of a shotgun: George has
directed it upon her; and there is no trigger:

Ivy, and her mother: what are the dreams of dogs?

Margaret, of a husband, and strong land, and ladies nodding
in the walks.

And all these children:

These children, still in the tenderness of their lives, who will
draw their future remembrance, and their future sorrow, from
this place: and the strangers, animals: for work, for death, for
food: and the scant crops: doing their duty the best they can,
like temperless and feeble-minded children: rest now, between
the wrenchings of the sun:

O, we become old; it has been a long, long climb; there
will not be much more of this; then we will rest: sorrow nor
sweating nor aching back, sickness, nor pity, hope gone,
heaven's deafness; nothing shall take or touch us more: not
thunder nor the rustling worms nor scalding kettle nor weeping child shall rouse us where we rest: these things shall be the
business of others: these things shall be the business of our
children, and their children; we will rest:

In what way were we trapped? where, our mistake? what,
where, how, when, what way, might all these things have been
different, if only we had done otherwise? if only we might have
known. Where lost that bright health of love that knew so
surely it would stay; how, how did it sink away, beyond help,
beyond hope, beyond desire, beyond remembrance; and where
the weight and the wealth of that strong year when there was

more to eat than we could hold, new clothes, a grafanola, and money in the bank? How, how did all this sink so swift away, like that grand august cloud who gathers—the day quiets dark and chills, and the leaves lather—and scarcely steams the land? How are these things?

In the years when we lived down by the river we had all the fish we wanted, and yellow milk, enough to sell, and we bought two mules:

When we moved in here I wanted to make the house pretty, I folded a lot of pattern-paper and cut it into a pretty lace pattern and hung it on the mantelpiece: but now I just don't care any longer, I don't care how anything looks:

My mother made me the prettiest kind of a dress, all fresh for school; I wore it the first day, and everyone laughed and poked fun at me; it wasn't like other dresses, neither the cloth, nor the way it was cut, and I never . . .

I made her such a pretty dress and she wore it once, and she never wore it away from home again:

Oh, thank God not one of you knows how everyone snickers at your father.

I reckon we're just about the *meanest* people in this whole country.

George Gudger? Where'd you dig *him* up? I haven't been back out that road in twenty-five year.

Fred Ricketts? Why, that dirty son-of-a-bitch, he *brags* that he hasn't bought his family a bar of soap in five year.

Ricketts? They're a bad lot. They've got Miller blood mixed up in them. The children are a bad problem in school.

Why, Ivy Pritchert was one of the worst whores in this whole part of the country: only one that was worse was her own mother. They're about the lowest trash you can find.

Why, she had her a man back in the woods for years before *he* married her; has two children by him.

Gudger? He's a fair farmer. Fair cotton farmer, but he hain't got a mite a sense.

None of these people has any sense, nor any initiative. If they did, they wouldn't be farming on shares.

Give them money and all they'll do with it is throw it away.

Why, times when I envy them. No risk, we take all the risk; all the clothes they need to cover them; food coming up right out of their land.

So you're staying out at Gudgers', are you? And how do you like the food they give you? Yeah, aheh-heh-heh-heh, how do you like that fine home cookin'; how do you like that good wholesome country food?

Tell you the honest truth, they owe us a big debt. Now you just tell me, if you can, what would all those folks be doing if it wasn't for us?

How did we get caught? Why is it things always seem to go against us? Why is it there can't ever be any pleasure in living? I'm so tired it don't seem like I ever could get rest enough. I'm as tired when I get up in the morning as I am when I lay down at night. Sometimes it seems like there wouldn't never be no end to it, nor even a let-up. One year it'll look like things was going to be pretty good; but you get a little bit of money saved, something always happens.

I tell you I won't be sorry when I die. I wouldn't be sorry this minute if it wasn't for Louise and Squinchy-here. Rest vmd git along all right:

(But I am young; and I am young, and strong, and in good health; and I am young, and pretty to look at; and I am too young to worry; and so am I, for my mother is kind to me; and we run in the bright air like animals, and our bare feet like plants in the wholesome earth: the natural world is around us like a lake and a wide smile and we are growing: one by one we are becoming stronger, and one by one in the terrible empti- ness and the leisure we shall burn and tremble and shake with lust, and one by one we shall loosen ourselves from this place, and shall be married, and it will be different from what we see, for we will be happy and love each other, and keep the house clean, and a good garden, and buy a cultivator, and use a high grade of fertilizer, and we will know how to do things right; it will be very different:) (? :)

((?)   )   :)

How were we caught?

What, what is it has happened? What is it has been happening that we are living the way we are?

The children are not the way it seemed they might be:

She is no longer beautiful:

He no longer cares for me, he just takes me when he wants me:

There's so much work it seems like you never see the end of it:

I'm so hot when I get through cooking a meal it's more than I can do to sit down to it and eat it:

How was it we were caught?

And seeing the multitudes, he went up into a mountain; and when he was set, his disciples came unto him:

And he opened his mouth and taught them, saying:

Blessed are the poor in spirit: for theirs is the kingdom of heaven.

Blessed are they that mourn: for they shall be comforted.

Blessed are the meek: for they shall inherit the earth.

Blessed are they which do hunger and thirst after righteousness: for they shall be filled.

Blessed are the merciful: for they shall obtain mercy.

Blessed are the pure in heart: for they shall see God.

Blessed are the peacemakers: for they shall be called the children of God.

Blessed are they which are persecuted for righteousness' sake: for theirs is the kingdom of heaven.

Blessed are ye when men shall revile you, and persecute

you, and shall say all manner of evil against you falsely, for my sake.

Rejoice, and be exceeding glad: for great is your reward in heaven: for so persecuted they the prophets which were before you.

III:

NEVERTHELESS:

Oh, nevertheless:

Spired Europe is out, up the middle of her morning, has brought her embossed cities, her front of country snailed with steel;

the Atlantic globe is burnished, ship-crawled, pathed and paved of air, brightens to blind;

shoulder clean shoulder from their hangar, Brazil and Labrador; flash flame;

from stone shore, bluff-browed tree, birds are drawn sparkling and each plant: erects upon his root, lifts up his head, accepts once more the summer:

and so must these: while the glistening land drives east: they shall be drawn up like plants with the burden of being upon them, their legs heavy, their eyes quiet and sick, the weight of the day watching them quietly from the ceiling, in the sharpening room; they will lift; lift—there is no use, no help for it—their legs from the bed and their feet to the floor and the height of their bodies above their feet and the load above them, and let it settle upon the spine, and the width of the somewhat stooped shoulders, the weight that is not put by; and are drawn loose from their homes a million upon the land, beneath the quietly lifted light, to work:

And here:

Watch from the crackling mattress how the stars, through the roof, though strong, are yet so tired.

The night has dried.

Nothing is yet visible in the room, but one begins again to be aware: of the walls, and their odor and lightness, facing each other; and of the postures of the furniture. The bureau, squared on a corner, and its blind mirror receiving, reflecting, the blindness of the bed. The iron of the bed. The sewing-machine, the tin trunk, and the wicker chair. The beauties on the walls.

Outside, from near, there is a new sound. It happens every night, and it is most sorrowful. It is the voice of a blond, fat, and craven rooster, a creature half-frightened of his own wives; and in this poor voice of his, lugubrious, almost surreptitious, he is making a statement he so misbelieves that it is rather a question that expects no answer save the utter scorn and denial of silence; and it gets none: but serves only to remind one of the noises of the night, which perhaps have not at any time ceased.

They have perhaps at no time ceased, but that will never be surely known, they are, after a while, so easily lost: and one hears them once again with a quiet sort of surprise, that only slowly becomes the realization, or near certainty, that they have been there all the while:

They are still there, they still convey to one no merely intimate vicinity, but the whole blind earth dispread: they chainlike stream like water violins, a straight and upward rain extracted from the world: yet they are in this hour so profoundly retired upon themselves, they are scarcely the echo of an echo, music's remembrance in a dying dream, lashed through with weltering whippoorwill, the mourner and genius of great summer night: and even that weeping bird now twice has faltered, and on blurred bark-hued flight has taken his song more deeply among the groves. And the land:

The land, pale fields, black cloudy woodlands, and the late lamps in the central streets of the rare and inexpiable cities: New Orleans; Birmingham; whose façades stand naked in the metal light of their fear:

the land, in its largeness: stretches: is stretched:

it is stretched like that hollow and quietness of water that is formed at the root of a making wave, and it waits: not a leaf, not a grass blade, trembles even: but is stretched: stretched: stretched: and waits (the blood stream stridence meanwhile coursing): waits (the whippoorwill has established in a much nearer tree; one almost knows the feathers that work at his larynx; but he is uncertain):

not suddenly, nor with fright, but certainly with no line of crossing, no beginning, there has been a change in the air, a crisis passed in sleep; for now, that in the same instant it seems was so enchanted still, there is a nearly noiseless trembling of every leaf of the vegetation of all this part of the world, so delicate a turning in fright of sleep as that needle which records a minute disturbance on the far side of the thick planet, and so nearly noiseless, yet so unanimous, it is the indistinguishable and whispered sigh of all the generations of the dead, the crumbling of a world-long wave so distant, that one yard more removed, could not be audible:

yet that shuddering: that of a body hopeless standing, though the air is mild: does not break, but rather intensifies the waiting (this is happening not only here but in a stripe, a few miles wide, straight up through Canada, and down the Andes): the air darkens to black violet, and the stars refresh:

and casually, and with rending triumph, the signal is delivered on the dusk: the sure wild glittering yell of a rooster; light on a lifted sword.

He is some long distance away, it seems infinite miles, the utmost ledge of the universe, to the east. He has a little while ago awakened, full awake immediately, and intensely aware, as one wakes and is aware, in the total darkness, of someone alien in the room, and his round eye has sharpened on the dark a fierce button, the head cocked, and whole being listening; what is it: what is it; tightening with excitement and premonition, a sort of joyful fear, the hackles roughed with it:

And with the brusqueness of an epileptic seizure a power much stronger than himself has taken him whole; it must be the voice of another rooster, who received it from another, and so to the brim of the continent, where the first, their bright backs warm and splendid in the light, are stabbing at corn; he is taken whole; he clenches the whole strength of his body and his fiery soul deep into one fist, and strives it at the sky, all his strength shuddering:

and it is heard: and distant though it is, it cleaves in its full fortissimo: so valiant a noise as rescuing bugle, or tenor broke his throat for: and no answer:

and then the answer: deep, steep back behind beneath my prostrated head:

(the violet grays; the gray walks through the walls)

silence: the whippoorwill; pleading; deploring:

the first again, much fiercer:

and, almost interrupting him, a third, beyond the woods:

('*whip*-pa*will!*   *whipp*-a*willl!*')

The second again; at last, our blond, his androgynous voice chortling with fake confidence: a fourth: the first (the country is taking shape): another: now the third (it is emerging like a print in a tank; I see distinctly the walls of the room, and on the earth the medallioned cities): three new ones now: another: now another: strain on their horn toes and shout.

By now it is full glass light, clean, whitening gray, without shadow, and the air is cold, with an odor of pork and damp earth, and the spiring of the roosters has become a commonplace. The whippoorwill has stayed it out long beyond the last ditch, whispering almost visible from among the distinct gray leaves of a near tree; now he is sunk and gone, and the air is brisk with small and skillful birds, who whistle, and beat metals with light hammers; and a dog comes casually though somewhat stiffly round the corner of the house, and smoke sprowls up from chimneys: and the light still whitens:

But much earlier, while it was not yet light, at about the crowing of the second cock, Annie Mae woke, on her back, and watched up at the ceiling; and at this time Margaret Ricketts is already a half-hour up, and the stove crackling, and she is cooking by lamp before the windows are even pale, for her father suffers from stirrup corns, and has four miles through the woods to walk to work. And Fred, and his wife, and Paralee, lie in their beds collecting their strength, and the children still sleep:

Annie Mae watches up at the ceiling, and she is as sick with sleep as if she had lain the night beneath a just-supportable weight: and watching up into the dark, beside her husband, the ceiling becomes visible, and watching into her eyes, the weight of the day. She has not lacked in utter tiredness, like a load in her whole body, a day since she was a young girl, nor will she ever lack it again; and is of that tribe who by glandular arrangement seem to exhaust rather than renew themselves with sleep, and to whom the act of getting up is almost unendurably painful. But when the ceiling has become visible there is no longer any help for it, and she wrenches herself up, and wriggles a dress on over her head, and shuffles barefooted across the porch to the basin, and ladles out two dippers of water from the bucket, and cups it in her hands, and drenches her face in it, with a shuddering shock that straightens her; and dries on the split flour sack that hangs from a nail; and is capable of being alive, to work:

Her first work being, to build the fire, and to cook biscuits and eggs and meat and coffee:

With the noise at the stove, George wakes. Without having to look for it, he reaches on the floor by the bed and finds the book of cigarette papers and the tobacco, and the sweatproof matchbox he has made of a truncated Prince Albert tin. In a skillful and beautiful collusion of his stiff, thick fingers he rolls a cigarette, and he props his head, and smokes it, staring through the ornate iron at the wall, while the birds whet and sweeten:

(Ivy is meantime up: she was wakened in the serene quietness of a woods animal, neither tired nor rested, but blank and fresh like water; her fine big feet soothe and seethe the floor, and Bud comes to, lifting his sardonic-gentle, innocent, dimly criminal, birdlike, little-boy's head a little from the pillow, the sheet drawn to his chin: the cleaning light is cool: the children sleep; Pearl, pale, adenoidal, already erotic; and Thomas like a dance, frog-legged, his fists in his eyes; and Ellen, like a baby, fish-mouthed between her enormous cheeks:)

The cleaning light is cool; the older Ricketts are hurrying through breakfast. There is a rapid smattering of feet and Clair Bell sprints in affrighted: that her father has left for work before kissing her good-bye. They take her on their laps assuring her that he would never do no such a thang, and help her drink her coffee:

I used as a child in the innocence of faith to bring myself out of bed through the cold lucid water of the Cumberland morning and to serve at the altar at earliest lonely Mass, whose words were thrilling brooks of music and whose motions, a grave dance: and there between spread hands the body and the blood of Christ was created among words and lifted before God in a threshing of triplicate bells, and from the rear of the empty church stole forward a serene widow and a savage epileptic, softly blind, and knelt, and on the palms of their hands and at their mouths they took their strength and, blind, retired: and the morning was clangorous with the whole of a roused school when we were done, and out, and that was the peace of a day: and it is in no beauty less that the gestures of a day here begin; and in just such silence and solitude: the iron lids are lifted: the kindling is laid in the grate: and the lids replaced: and a squirting match applied beneath: and the flour is sifted through shaken window-screen, and mixed with lard and water, soda, and a little salt: the coffee is set on the stove, its grounds afloat on the cold water: more wood laid in: the biscuits poured, and stuck into the oven: all these things with set motions, progressions, routines and retracings, of bare feet and of sticklike arms, stick hands, contractions of the sharp body: and the meat sliced and sliding, spitting, in the black skillet; and the eggs broken, and their shells consigned; and the chairs lifted from the porch to the table, and the sorghum set on, and the butter, sugar, salt, pepper, a spoon straightened, the lamp set at the center; the eggs turned; the seething coffee set aside; the meat reheated; the biscuits looked at; the straight black hair, saturated with sweat and smoke of pork, tightened more neatly to the head between four black pins; the biscuits tan, the eggs ready, the coffee ready, the meat ready, the breakfast ready:

and they come in, by order of age, masked with the chill of the water that holds them together, and silent with sleep; and the animals raise themselves out of the floor and establish themselves beneath the table, lifting open heads:

and breakfast is too serious a meal for speaking; and it is difficult and revolting to eat heavily before one is awake; but it is necessary, for on this food must be climbed the ardent and steep hill of the morning, steadily hotter, up to noon, and for Fred and George then a cold lunch only, and resumption, and hours more of work: so that your two halves are held together and erect by this food as by a huge tight buckle as big as the belly, giving no ease but chunk, stone, fund, of strength: endurance in it, or leverage on the day, like a stiff stone: this slowly thaws and is absorbed more evenly throughout the body, and the strength becomes easy leather:

it is much the same at the Woods', a little different; Ivy drawls and chaffers like water, her loose hair lays around on her head; and Pearl's face at the edge of the table is a solemn pouch with swampy eyes; and Woods, his body is elderly, not strong, he must draw it together like strings into a knot; and his eyes look out at the morning, from his intelligent unequipped brain, with a sort of sour part-smiling, hopeless speculation, while he talks a little:

and at the Ricketts', more vivacious, for there are many people; the father talks continuously, and though he has now gone, walking as if barefoot on a field of burrs, there are accidents to food and to children, and enough confusion over who is at what task, to keep them going;

and the breakfasts ended, the houses are broken open like pods in the increase of the sun, and they are scattered on the wind of a day's work.

(*How was it we were caught?*)

IV:

F OUR MILES back into the northeast, on a relaxation to flatness in the middle of the low, roiling, and tree-mantled
hills, there is a long rectangle cut clean of timber, and beyond
it, standing pine.

The rectangle is stacked along the middle with fresh lumber
that stands in a yellow nimbus. The road splits round it between tall drenched weeds and meets itself at the far end
where, still close within the cold, dark, early shade, are the
soot-black scaffolded structures of sawmill machinery and of
power; the tall black candle of stack torched-off with clear
curling heat beneath the stained flag of rust-lighted smoke;
and a negro waiting, glancing frequently at his watch with a
little left in him, after years of habituation, of a child's excitement in responsibility and in power: and the space is meanwhile struggling full of more and more men, not really many,
yet in this woodland and keen morning quietness they seem a
crowd, drawn in on rattling wagons and by truck and afoot
through the chill hickory smell and fronded shade of the
morning forest; and the sun is strong.

It is strong already, and steadfastly strengthening like the
held note of a horn. It is lifted square in the middle of the far
end among the tops of the black pines and burns a whorl of
cobwebs through them, and the pines are sheeted and shred-
ded, carded wool, in a keen mist its brightness refracts among
and burns and brightens, so that they are lifted slowly and
splendidly in long planes and slashed uncoiling streamers, and
there is a sheen on the whole of the clear air of such intensity
that it all but hurts the eyes.

Over to the left the brass padlock hangs loosened on the
new pine shed of tools and slung harness, and in a barked enclosure behind it are the mules, and along the fence the wagons are ranged in a line, their tongues in the air like a salute of
elephants. They are long, low skeleton wagons of tough
beams, no sides, for hauling logs; some of them auto-wheeled
and rubber-tired; and their oak wood is now blanching with

warmth, and their details of metal already warm to the touch.
The mules loiter in a hooved muck of tattered water in a tract
of brownlighted shadow slivered with sun, a sapling grove
licked leafless within their reach, the trunks rubbed slick: very
naked-looking and somehow shy without harness, as if they
had not quite the right to nature, they stand, they drift, they
wait, they glide among the vertical wax saplings in the camou-
flaging light, and lift back their cynical heads like flowers as the
men who master their days lift open the gate and advance
toward them: some stand docile, and accept the halter with a
kind of sneering meekness; others quietly lift their hoofs in the
chopped earth and drift, as a matter of decent form rather than
rebellion; two or three draw themselves back as deep among
the narrow trees as the squared sharp wire will allow them, and
abide a close approach, then slither away, and these are kicked
in the belly and slashed along the jaws and across the eyes:
there is among these negroes a scarred yet pure white mule,
whose presence among them in this magic light is that of an
enslaved unicorn: and these are led out and stood along the
shafts and harnessed in teams in geometries of leather, rope
and bird-jingling metal as sweet in their stresses as the rigging
of sloops; and the men now wait quietly and in a casually tense
listlessness, talking a little, rolling damp cigarettes, and ad-
justing the iron violence of their breakfasts inside them; and
a negro, harnessing his mules, lifts forth wet-throated, joyfully,
three times into the emblazoned morning the long black
sorrow-foundered and incompleted phrase of anarchaic mode
in whose glorying he begins each day; and the men still wait;
and the trapped mules, twitching the metal flies, conniving
their long heads: and though the air is still cool, there is now
the cutting odor of grass and weeds, and a cool sweat starts out
and faintly stings in patterns upon the forehead, the wrists, the
beam of the shoulders, and the spine; and down in the short-
ening and uncooling shade at the black altar of machinery, the
negro stands with one hand hung in a triangular wire and with
time like a lake in the palm of the other, into whose surface he
gazes, and on the second, he pulls down on the wire; and in a
stiff standing-out of steam, the air is one rich reeking shriek
through which the sunlight is vibrated: and the mules tighten;
and the negro slides the watch, which is tethered to him by a

still new black shoestring, back into the small pocket at the center of his chest; and the whistle is cut off like a murder, leaving the aquarium clearing weak with silence from all sides of which are reflexed in diminishment the noise like a weltering, withering flat of the contour waves from a center: they are spread on the hills like the explosive sudden flowering of a steel rose and it is retracted to the root: and there is a tightening of strength against harness under slashing of sharp leather and they move, the long clattering wagons, in a drawn line round the stacked pine lumber and down the far side of the clearing and on, past the machinery and uphill to the right along a wide broken trough of stumps rank weeds iron shade and iron and splendid light, and are deployed along the ragged and stump-spiked woodlands into the resumption of yesterday's work: chopping, sawing, snaking, hauling, the shearing surflike shriek of the saw: and it is now thirty-two minutes past six, and among these men are George Gudger and——

COLON

CURTAIN SPEECH

COLON

B UT there must be an end to this: a sharp end and clean
silence: a steep and most serious withdrawal: a new and
more succinct beginning:

Herein I must screen off all mysteries of our comminglings
—all these, all such, must be deferred—and must here set in
such regard as I can the sorry and brutal infuriate yet beautiful
structures of the living which is upon each of you daily: and
this in the cleanest terms I can learn to specify: must mediate,
must attempt to record, your warm weird human lives each in
relation to its world:

Nor may this be lightly undertaken: not lightly, not easily by
any means: nor by any hope 'successfully':

For one who sets himself to look at all earnestly, at all in purpose toward truth, into the living eyes of a human life: what is
it he there beholds that so freezes and abashes his ambitious
heart? What is it, profound behind the outward windows of
each one of you, beneath touch even of your own suspecting,
drawn tightly back at bay against the backward wall and blackness of its prison cave, so that the eyes alone shine of their own
angry glory, but the eyes of a trapped wild animal, or of a furious angel nailed to the ground by his wings, or however else
one may faintly designate the human 'soul,' that which is angry, that which is wild, that which is untamable, that which is
healthful and holy, that which is competent of all advantaging
within hope of human dream, that which most marvelous and
most precious to our knowledge and most extremely advanced
upon futurity of all flowerings within the scope of creation is of
all these the least destructible, the least corruptible, the most
defenseless, the most easily and multitudinously wounded,
frustrate, prisoned, and nailed into a cheating of itself: so situ-
ated in the universe that those three hours upon the cross are
but a noble and too trivial an emblem how in each individual
among most of the two billion now alive and in each successive

instant of the existence of each existence not only human
being but in him the tallest and most sanguine hope of god-
head is in a billionate choiring and drone of pain of generations upon generations unceasingly crucified and is bringing
forth crucifixions into their necessities and is each in the
most casual of his life so measurelessly discredited, harmed,
insulted, poisoned, cheated, as not all the wrath, compassion,
intelligence, power of rectification in all the reach of the future
shall in the least expiate or make one ounce more light: how,
looking thus into your eyes and seeing thus, how each of
you is a creature which has never in all time existed before
and which shall never in all time exist again and which is not
quite like any other and which has the grand stature and
natural warmth of every other and whose existence is all measured upon a still mad and incurable time; how am I to speak
of you as 'tenant' 'farmers,' as 'representatives' of your 'class,'
as social integers in a criminal economy, or as individuals,
fathers, wives, sons, daughters, and as my friends and as I
'know' you? Granted—more, insisted upon—that it is in all
these particularities that each of you is that which he is; that
particularities, and matters ordinary and obvious, are exactly
themselves beyond designation of words, are the members of
your sum total most obligatory to human searching of perception: nevertheless to name these things and fail to yield
their stature, meaning, power of hurt, seems impious, seems
criminal, seems impudent, seems traitorous in the deepest: and
to do less badly seems impossible: yet in withholdings of speci-
fication I could but betray you still worse.

Let me say, then, how I would wish this account might be
constructed.

I might suggest, its structure should be globular: or should
be eighteen or twenty intersected spheres, the interlockings of
bubbles on the face of a stream; one of these globes is each of
you.

The heart, nerve, center of each of these, is an individual
human life.

We should first meditate and establish its ancient, then more
recent, its spreaded and more local, history and situation: how
it is a child of the substance and bowels of the stars and of all
space: how it is created forth of an aberration special to one

speck and germ and pollen fleck this planet, this young planet, on that broadblown field: how on the youth of this planet it is youngest, scarcely yet breathed-upon yet born, into its future growth: how it is blossomed forth upon that branch most sportive, most precarious, most propitious, potential and most frightful in known creation, of human existence, of human consciousness, of human possibility to build itself ruin or wonder: how it is the bearer of whatever the future shall be: how in itself, no matter which individual mote it is, it is in its beginning capable, in its terms, of health, which is perfection, which is holiness, which is simple and salted, blooded functioning of each animal in his own best: and is capable likewise of all harm to itself and to others: how all that is to make all this difference is circumstance, physical and mental: how there is nothing within consciousness and the receiving of our senses which is not incorporate of this bulk and strength to shape of circumstance, and nothing so minute but that it impounds more power, more importance, more meaning of impingement upon this human life, than most exact or violent words might ever tell:

At this center we set this seed, this flower, whose genealogy we have suggested and whose context in eternal history, his royalty, his miraculousness, his great potentiality: we try at least to suggest also his incomparable tenderness to experience, his malleability, the almost inimaginable nakedness and defenselessness of this wondrous fivewindowed nerve and core: the size, the pity, the abomination of the crimes he is to sustain, against the incredible sweetness, strength, and beauty of what he might be and is cheated of:

Never relaxing the simultaneity of his ancestral and brotherly stars, we bring his sources into a more near convergence in local place of time: how he is brought forth of a chain and weaving, a texture of sorrowful and demented flesh, which in all previous centuries has scarcely in few meaningless hundreds wrought up a head from the blind bottom of the human sea and breathed one cup of brightness and plain air, and in these disadvantagings were drawn up and woven upon the crookedness of one continent and were drawn upon seas and upon a newer to no better faring, and here a few generations have dwelt in the woodlands and dead clays in bestial freedom or in servitude, shaken with fevers, grieved and made sick with foods, wrung-out in work to lassitude in the strong sun and to lack of hope or caring, in ignorance of all cause, all being, all conduct, hope of help or cure, saturated in harm and habit, unteachable beliefs, the germens they carry at their groins strained, cracked, split, tainted, vitiate to begin with, a wallet of cheated coinage:

Here we have two, each crucified, further crucify one another upon the shallow pleasure of an iron bed and instigate in a woman's belly a crucifixion of cell and whiplashed sperm: whose creature is our center, our nerve we spoke of; in this instant already his globe is rounded upon him and is his prison, which might have been his kingdom: it is begun in a redblack cherishing of a blind and beating of hurt unvanquishable blood and is informed entirely of the ferment of this blood, of whom likewise hard work is done, indecent diet is taken, there is fright and sorrow in dream, and not much or no love at all, a weaponless mind is meditating as it may; this creature, the motive even of his creation, is sprung, is sprained, is slaved and ordered by a crimesoaked world: for he is made for work, for a misuser, not his own even illusive master nor even mere slave of his parents or a healthful state, but of misuse without which he shall not live at all: and it is in obedience to these pressures that the marriage was made and that he was conceived, and that he is nursed and emboweled among the discouragements of this beating of beaten blood; and it is toward this bondage that the germ unfurls and flowers, climbs from that soft and floated sea through darkness and petting blood the steep ladder through all shifts of nature and, low helmet huge and cowering mild, hands covering lightless eyes, knees, feet drawn tight as if he were receiving the blow of a bayonet in his solar plexus, he floats steadily upward in balance upon his deafness and at length, like the bursting beating of the lungs of a deep diver, is broken forth on gladness of the air

to find himself:

how should he know it, how should these poor parents who so earnestly wish him well, ever suspect it better than a little, how in their ignorance and skinned sadness shall they ever learn, how all the help they would do him is but harm

to find himself:

weakened, internally hurt already beyond all use of estimate, yet still amenable of all goodness were it there:

and defenseless and unknowing, without choice, without knowledge for choice if he had it, without power of choice if he had knowledge

to find himself

Ahh, so set about so pressed upon, so searched to the very soul already by poisons, monsters, all shapes of ruin, smiling jaws of traps, that that true-mythic natural man of racial dream, that self-venturous hero, that strong young man were much more fortunate who at the end of so steep and arduous a journey and flight from the floor of creation revisited, his lungs ready to burst his heart breaking, his body naked, his primal weapons lost that he might swim at all, bursts bleeding into freedom of his breathing element to find, surrounding him, not just in circle on a floor in closured den as Daniel, but in such complex of such circle as blows round him one bubble and sutureless globe, his grinning grincing machinearmed scorcheyed lovetaloned raving foes:

For this man is aware; he may have skill; it is by skill; by consciousness by innocence by intelligence by love, by magic we shall win and only thus; this skill he may have and by this skill may speak; may talk or flute such mild commodious language that these beasts dissolve their brows, yearn sweetly in quaverings and sobs of ardor toward and upon him, roll down before, and undefend their gold inhuman bellies at his feet in all heaven's astonishment:

and if he lack; or if he fail; his death is soon, is done, as a shock of lightning:

whereas this other: *his* death, *his* destroying, it is quiet, subtle, continuous, very slow, in quite great part deluded, in some part the doing of most tenderly intended love, his foes being of this silent, insinuous, and masked kind, and he void of all skill against:

This creature, this center, soul, nerve, see he is now born, and I have said, how he is globed round, with what shall make and harm him: what are the constituents of this globe? What are the several strengths of their forces upon him?

It was beyond all use of hoping to say, while yet he was in his mother's blood scarce conscious, when this globe was at its simplest and least: how then should we say more now, when with a few hours' wrenching he is wrung out of this haven through such cataclysmic change to take forever, no retreat, his uprooted, root-cut and human place in so immane and outrageous, wild, irresponsible, dangerous-idiot a world: how still shall we better than blankly suggest, or lay down, a few possible laws?

Our five or twenty known human senses: there is no reason to assume but they are few, are crudely woven, that swarms of immediacy slide through these nets at best, assisted though they be by dream, by reason, and by those strictures of diamond glass and light whereby we punch steep holes in the bowels of the gliding heavens, taste out the salt smell of the earth, step measurements upon the grand estate of being: nevertheless: nevertheless and at their weakest, weakest and most weaponless of these instruments, their taking is titanic beyond exhaustion of count or valuation, and is all but infinitely populous beyond the knowledge of each moment or a lifetime: and that which we receive yet do not recognize, nor hold in the moment's focus, is nevertheless and continuously and strengthfully planted upon our brains, upon our blood: it holds: it holds: each cuts its little mark: each blown leaf of a woodland a quarter-mile distant while I am absorbed in some close exactitude: each of these registers, cuts his mark: not one of these is negligible: and they measure, not only by multitudes within each granular instant, but by iteration, which is again beyond our counting not alone but as well the remotest realization of our flesh and even brain: and with each iteration the little cut is cut a little distincter, a little deeper, a little more of a scar and a shaping of a substance which might have taken other shape and which in each reregistration loses a little more and a little more the power to meet this possibility: and more and more inexorably and fixedly is drawn and shaped into that steepest-sunken of all graves wherein human hope is buried alive, the power and blindness, stiffness and helplessness of habituation, of acceptance, of resignation so totally deep it has sailed beyond memory of resignation or thought of other possibility: a benumbing, freezing, a paralysis, a turning to stone, merciful in the middle of all that storm of torture, relatively resistant of much further keenness of harm, but always in measure of that petrifaction obtuséd ten times over against hope, possibility, cure:

Moreover, these globular damagements are of many kinds and degrees and colors and of an infinite talent for deceit: being of as many kinds as that particular set of senses and that particular intelligence at their heart can perceive and can receive and can react to and reflect upon: all that is 'physical,' all that is of the 'mind,' all that is of the 'emotions,' all that is of the 'economic' and the 'mental' and the 'glandular' and the 'medical' predicament, all that is of 'belief,' and is of 'habit,' and is of 'morality,' and is of 'fear,' 'pride,' need of 'love,' 'warmth,' 'approbation,' all that is attached in the 'meanings' of 'ideas,' 'words,' 'actions,' 'things,' 'symbols': all these apart, all these in orchestral complex wherein they interlock, interform one another, and conspire in their companionship still sharper fiercer stricter subtler more bonebiting traps and equations of destruction than is in the power of any one or five of them independent of one another:

Here, again, in the midst of all these, is this human creature, born, awaiting their touch:

We specialize him a little more: yes, he is of the depth of the working class; of southern alabamian tenant farmers; certain individuals are his parents, not like other individuals; they are living in a certain house, it is not quite like other houses; they are farming certain shapes and strengths of land, in a certain exact vicinity, for a certain landholder: all such things as these qualify this midge, this center, a good deal:

Born otherwise, he would break his shell upon other forms of madness: he might, for instance, have sprung up in the sheltering and soft shame and guilt of money, which in this earth at present is had at the expense of other spirits and of human good, and which brings on its own diseases, so ghastly that one cannot in wisdom and honesty either envy or hate the image, say, of the landowner whom I suggest beside this child: Or otherwise again, in the guilty sheltering even of a little ease, the mind, the spirit, the heart, which in him shall all so swiftly be killed or obtunded, this might have grown its fight, and

would discover, and have to bear, something of the true pro-
portions of the savageness of the world, and something of the
true weight of responsibility which each human being must
learn to undertake for all others, and something of the true
magnitude of the terror and the doubt in which in each human
being this responsibility must be searched out and undertaken;
and might easily have deceived himself, and become an instrument of poison, or, less deceived, have sustained those further
agonies of perception so great that one may very doubtfully
feel any glad or guiltless embrace of the joys and lacerations of
this consciousness short of the whole uncompromised and seldom piercing and intention of 'genius' itself: see, in this 'consciousness,' what a swarm and slime of monsters he would
encounter, whose skill, pain, disease, deceitfulness is multiplied
in proportion to the reach and edge of this same 'consciousness' which is our one hope, this monster world's one sure,
most shriveling enemy: of this particular world of hope and of
smile-masked horror he is nearly free, for in his world few such
beasts exist, and the instruments whereby he might see them if
they did, or of his own born doing; the lenses of these are
smashed in his infancy, the adjustment screws are blocked; his
is more nearly purely a tactile, a fragrant, a visible, physical
world, wherein through his deep isolation these plainfeatured
physiques drive and impose their stresses all the more keenly
upon him; and should he by faint and most irregular chance
make his little, terrific, faithful struggle to escape, into a sphere
how much less tortured shall this escape be made: for this human sphere is all one such interlocked and marvelously variegated and prehensile a disease and madness, what man in ten
million shall dare to presume he is cleansed of it or more so
than another, shall dare better than most hesitantly to venture,
that one form of this ruin is more than a millionth preferable
to another?

Here then he is, or here is she: here is this tender and helpless human life: subjected to its immediacy and to all the en-
largéd dread of its future: out of a line, weight, and burthen of
sorrow and poison of fatigue whereof its blood is stained and
beneath which it lifts up its little trembling body into standing,
wearing upon its shoulders the weight of all the spreaded

generations of its dead: surrounded already, with further pressures, impingements: the sorrow, weariness, and nescience of
its parents in their closures above and round it: the ghastly influence of their lovelessness, their lack of knowledge hope or
chance, how to love, what is joy, why they are locked together
here: his repeated witness of the primal act, that battling and
brutality upon a bed which from his pallet on the floor of the
same room he lifts his head and hears and sees and fears and is
torn open by: their hopeless innocence how to 'raise' him, an
ignorance no less enormous than in the parents of the rest of
the world, yet not less relevant nor less horrifying on that account: the food which is drawn out of his mother distilled of
the garbage she must eat; and the garbage to which he gradu-
ates: the further structures of psychological violence, strangling, crippling, which take shape and stress between him and
his brothers and his sisters and between all of these and their
parents; for of all these all are utterly innocent, totally helpless:
the slow, silent, sweet, quiet yet so profoundly piercing enlargement of the physical sensual emotional world whereof, as
we have said, not the least detail whose imposure and whose
power to trench and habituate is not intense beyond calculation: all such that in the years of his very steepest defenselessness, who shall always be defenseless, and in the years of his
extremest malleability, by the time he is five or six years old, he
stands at the center of his enormous little globe a cripple of
whose curability one must at least have most serious doubt:
and now new worlds open upon him in the manifold swift un-
foldings of a great flower, and in each opening he is the more
firmly shut upon, his first wounds the more salted, the little slit
graves of angelic possibility the more savagely danced on and
defiled beyond memory of their existence: all accepted, all
taken in, all new burdens taken on, the early laboring, sub-
servience, acclimation to insult and slendering of forms of
freedom, the hideous jokes of education and their sharp finish
into early worse, the learning of one's situation relative to the
world and the acceptance of it, the swellings and tremblings
of adolescence, the bursting free from home into wandering,
the fatal shining and sweet wraths of joy in love and the locked
marriage and the work, the constant lack of money, need,
leanness, backbroken work, knowledge of being cheated,

helplessness to protest or order this otherwise, clothes worn, landlords imposed on one, towns traded in——

This is all one colon:

Here at a center is a creature: it would be our business to show how through every instant of every day of every year of his existence alive he is from all sides streamed inward upon, bombarded, pierced, destroyed by that enormous sleeting of all objects forms and ghosts how great how small no matter, which surround and whom his senses take: in as great and perfect and exact particularity as we can name them:

This would be our business, to show them each thus transfixed as between the stars' trillions of javelins and of each the transfixions: but it is beyond my human power to do. The most I can do—the most I can hope to do—is to make a number of physical entities as plain and vivid as possible, and to make a few guesses, a few conjectures; and to leave to you much of the burden of realizing in each of them what I have wanted to make clear of them as a whole: how each is itself; and how each is a shapener.

We undertake not much yet some, to say: to say, what is his house: for whom does he work: under what arrangements and in what results: what is this work: who is he and where from, that he is now here; what is it his life has been and has done to him: what of his wife and of their children, each, for of all these each is a life, a full universe: what are their clothes: what food is theirs to eat: what is it which is in their senses and their minds: what is the living and manner of their day, of a season, of a year: what, inward and outward, is their manner of living; of their spending and usage of these few years' openness out of the black vast and senseless death; what is their manner of life:

All this, all such, you can see, it so intensely surrounds and takes meaning from a certain center which we shall be unable to keep steadily before your eyes, that should be written, should be listed, calculated, analyzed, conjectured upon, as if all in one sentence and spread suspension and flight or fugue of music: and that I shall not be able so to sustain it, so to sustain its intensity toward this center human life, so to yield it out that it all strikes inward upon this center at once and in all its intersections and in the meanings of its interrelations and interenhancements: it is this which so paralyzes me: yet one can write only one word at a time, and if these seem lists and inventories merely, things dead unto themselves, devoid of mutual magnetisms, and if they sink, lose impetus, meter, intension, then bear in mind at least my wish, and perceive in them and restore them what strength you can of yourself: for I must say to you, this is not a work of art or of entertainment, nor will I assume the obligations of the artist or entertainer, but is a human effort which must require human co-operation.

That steep withdrawal and silence and meditation of whose need I spoke; we are now drawn back at the peak of in quite silence: whence let me hope the whole of that landscape we shall essay to travel in is visible and may be known as there all at once: let this be borne in mind, in order that, when we descend among its windings and blockades, into examination of slender particulars, this its wholeness and simultaneous living map may not be neglected, however lost the breadth of the country may be in the winding walk of each sentence.

PART TWO

SOME FINDINGS AND COMMENTS

MONEY

You are farmers; I am a farmer myself.
—Franklin Delano Roosevelt

Woods and Ricketts work for Michael and T. Hudson Margraves, two brothers, in partnership, who live in Cookstown. Gudger worked for the Margraves for three years; he now (1936) works for Chester Boles, who lives two miles south of Cookstown.

On their business arrangements, and working histories, and on their money, I wrote a chapter too long for inclusion in this volume without sacrifice of too much else. I will put in its place here as extreme a précis as I can manage.

Gudger has no home, no land, no mule; none of the more important farming implements. He must get all these of his landlord. Boles, for his share of the corn and cotton, also advances him rations money during four months of the year, March through June, and his fertilizer.

Gudger pays him back with his labor and with the labor of his family.

At the end of the season he pays him back further: with half his corn; with half his cotton; with half his cottonseed. Out of his own half of these crops he also pays him back the rations money, plus interest, and his share of the fertilizer, plus interest, and such other debts, plus interest, as he may have incurred.

What is left, once doctors' bills and other debts have been deducted, is his year's earnings.

Gudger is a straight half-cropper, or sharecropper.

Woods and Ricketts own no home and no land, but Woods owns one mule and Ricketts owns two, and they own their farming implements. Since they do not have to rent these tools and animals, they work under a slightly different arrangement. They give over to the landlord only a third of their cotton and a fourth of their corn. Out of their own parts of the crop, however, they owe him the price of two thirds of their cotton fertilizer and three fourths of their corn fertilizer, plus interest; and, plus interest, the same debts on rations money.

Woods and Ricketts are tenants: they work on third and fourth.

A very few tenants pay cash rent: but these two types of arrangement, with local variants (company stores; food instead of rations money; slightly different divisions of the crops) are basic to cotton tenantry all over the South.

From March through June, while the cotton is being cultivated, they live on the rations money.

From July through to late August, while the cotton is making, they live however they can.

From late August through October or into November, during the picking and ginning season, they live on the money from their share of the cottonseed.

From then on until March, they live on whatever they have earned in the year; or however they can.

During six to seven months of each year, then—that is, during exactly such time as their labor with the cotton is of absolute necessity to the landlord—they can be sure of whatever living is possible in rations advances and in cottonseed money.

During five to six months of the year, of which three are the hardest months of any year, with the worst of weather, the least adequacy of shelter, the worst and least of food, the worst of health, quite normal and inevitable, they can count on nothing except that they may hope least of all for any help from their landlords.

Gudger—a family of six—lives on ten dollars a month rations money during four months of the year. He has lived on eight, and on six. Woods—a family of six—until this year was unable to get better than eight a month during the same period; this year he managed to get it up to ten. Ricketts—a family of nine—lives on ten dollars a month during this spring and early summer period.

This debt is paid back in the fall at eight per cent interest.

Eight per cent is charged also on the fertilizer and on all other debts which tenants incur in this vicinity.

At the normal price, a half-sharing tenant gets about six dollars á bale from his share of the cottonseed. A one-mule, half-sharing tenant makes on the average three bales. This half-cropper, then, Gudger, can count on eighteen dollars, more or less, to live on during the picking and ginning: though he gets nothing until his first bale is ginned.

Working on third and fourth, a tenant gets the money from two thirds of the cottonseed of each bale: nine dollars to the bale. Woods with one mule, makes three bales, and gets twenty-seven dollars. Ricketts, with two mules, makes and gets twice that, to live on during the late summer and fall.

What is earned at the end of a given year is never to be depended on and, even late in a season, is never predictable. It can be enough to tide through the dead months of the winter, sometimes even better: it can be enough, spread very thin, to take through two months, and a sickness, or six weeks, or a month: it can be little enough to be completely meaningless: it can be nothing: it can be enough less than nothing to insure a tenant only of an equally hopeless lack of money at the end of his next year's work: and whatever one year may bring in the way of good luck, there is never any reason to hope that that luck will be repeated in the next year or the year after that.

The best that Woods has ever cleared was $1300 during a war year. During the teens and twenties he fairly often cleared as much as $300; he fairly often cleared $50 and less; two or three times he ended the year in debt. During the depression years he has more often cleared $50 and less; last year he cleared $150, but serious illness during the winter ate it up rapidly.

The best that Gudger has ever cleared is $125. That was in the plow-under year. He felt exceedingly hopeful and bought a mule: but when his landlord warned him of how he was coming out the next year, he sold it. Most years he has not made more than $25 to $30; and about one year in three he has ended in debt. Year before last he wound up $80 in debt; last year, $12; of Boles, his new landlord, the first thing he had to do was borrow $15 to get through the winter until rations advances should begin.

Years ago the Ricketts were, relatively speaking, almost prosperous. Besides their cotton farming they had ten cows and sold the milk, and they lived near a good stream and had all the fish they wanted. Ricketts went $400 into debt on a fine young pair of mules. One of the mules died before it had made its first crop; the other died the year after; against his fear, amounting to full horror, of sinking to the half-crop level where nothing is owned, Ricketts went into debt for other, inferior mules; his cows went one by one into debts and desperate exchanges and by sickness; he got congestive chills; his wife got pellagra; a number of his children died; he got appendicitis and lay for days on end under the ice cap; his wife's pellagra got into her brain; for ten consecutive years now, though they have lived on so little rations money, and have turned nearly all their cottonseed money toward their debts, they have not cleared or had any hope of clearing a cent at the end of the year.

It is not often, then, at the end of the season, that a tenant clears enough money to tide him through the winter, or even an appreciable part of it. More generally he can count on it that, during most of the four months between settlement time in the fall and the beginning of work and resumption of rations advances in the early spring, he will have no money and can expect none, nor any help, from his landlord: and of having no money during the six midsummer weeks of laying by, he can be still more sure. Four to six months of each year, in other words, he is much more likely than not to have nothing whatever, and during these months he must take care for himself: he is no responsibility of the landlord's. All he can hope to do is find work. This is hard, because there are a good many chronically unemployed in the towns, and they are more convenient to most openings for work and can at all times be counted on if they are needed; also there is no increase, during these two dead farming seasons, of other kinds of work to do. And so, with no more jobs open than at any other time of year, and with plenty of men already convenient to take them, the

whole tenant population, hundreds and thousands in any lo-
cality, are desperately in need of work.

A landlord saves up certain odd jobs for these times of year:
they go, at less than he would have to pay others, to those of
his tenants who happen to live nearest or to those he thinks
best of; and even at best they don't amount to much.

When there is wooded land on the farm, a landlord ordinarily permits a tenant to cut and sell firewood for what he can
get. About the best a tenant gets of this is a dollar a load, but
more often (for the market is glutted, so many are trying to
sell wood) he can get no better than half that and less, and
often enough, at the end of a hard day's peddling, miles from
home, he will let it go for a quarter or fifteen cents rather than
haul it all the way home again: so it doesn't amount to much.
Then, too, by no means everyone has wood to cut and sell: in
the whole southern half of the county we were working mainly
in, there was so little wood that the negroes, during the hard
winter of 1935–36, were burning parts of their fences, outbuildings, furniture and houses, and were dying off in great
and not seriously counted numbers, of pneumonia and other
afflictions of the lungs.

WPA work is available to very few tenants: they are, technically, employed, and thus have no right to it: and if by chance
they manage to get it, landlords are more likely than not to
intervene. They feel it spoils a tenant to be paid wages, even
for a little while. A tenant who so much as tries to get such
work is under disapproval.

There is not enough direct relief even for the widows and
the old of the county.

Gudger and Ricketts, during this year, were exceedingly
lucky. After they, and Woods, had been turned away from government work, they found work in a sawmill. They were given
the work on condition that they stay with it until the mill was
moved, and subject strictly to their landlords' permission: and
their employer wouldn't so much as hint how long the work
might last. Their landlords quite grudgingly gave them permission, on condition that they pay for whatever help was
needed in their absence during the picking season. Gudger

hired a hand, at eight dollars a month and board. Ricketts did not need to: his family is large enough. They got a dollar and a quarter a day five days a week, and seventy-five cents on Saturday, seven dollars a week, ten hours' work a day. Woods did not even try for this work: he was too old and too sick.

SHELTER

I will go unto the altar of God

SHELTER: An Outline

A home in its fields
The spring: the garden: the outbuildings

. . .

The Gudger House

  The house is left alone

  In front of the house: its general structure
  In front of the house: the façade

.

  The room beneath the house

.

  The hallway
  Structure of four rooms

  Odors
  Bareness and space

. .

   I. The Front Bedroom

    General
    Placement of furniture

    The furniture

    The altar
    The tabernacle

  II. The Rear Bedroom

    General

    The fireplace
    The mantel
    The closet
    The beds

 III. The Kitchen

    General

    The table: the lamp

  IV. The Storeroom

    Two essentials

    In the room

SHELTER

A home in its fields

GEORGE GUDGER has of Chester Boles a little over twenty acres of open farm land, a few more acres of woods and of hillside ravines, a house, a barn, a smokehouse, a henroost, a garden, and a spring, all suspended and emplaced in solitude out at the end of a mile of dwindled branch road, and not within sight nor within a half-mile's walk of any other inhabited house. A little of his land is on the flat crest of the hill; the rest is broken into large patches among ravines and woods along the falling shapes of the hill and into little patches along the road that leads him out. The house and outbuildings, the garden and the spring, stand about midway in the main pieces of this land, and about halfway down the hill.

The top three acres are a long flat rectangle of keenly red clay and are planted in cotton. Between the edge of the hill and his barnyard there is nothing planted, only wild weeds and briars on a scrubbed-looking set of rounded and trenched surfaces, and a narrow path slid winding among them, but from this edge, standing at the edge of the cotton, you see the house and barnyard, resembling a large museum model or an establishment for large dolls, set at the middle of the slope, back-to-you, facing due west, and the two large fields in front of it and on its left which make up most of the rest of the farm, the whole bound in by a bluff horizon of trees. Now and then a faint windy noise of speed or a noise of grinding, sweeping a western crescent beyond the trees and through one thin sector of trees, for two seconds, the uncertain glimpse of a gliding bulk: and these are the thinly spaced sedans and trucks which use a minor artery between two county seats profoundly distant to a walking man.

One of these fields begins very deep behind the house on its left, and along its left flank the cotton plants nearly touch the wall; it is nearly all in cotton. Back beyond it and beneath it, in a clearing in the tall woods, is a smaller patch of corn. The field that falls away two hundred yards in front of the house is all in adolescent corn, softly flashing, ending at tall forest whose leaves run like quicksilver wheat in the lesions of heated air. Out at the right of the house is the rough stretch of mid-hill, partly bare, fluted with rain, not planted, sprung with tall weeds and smoky grasses and with berry briars, young pines and little runs and islands of young trees, seeming open, yet merged before long in a solid coastline of well-grown woods. Out along the road that, beginning just below the house, leads out to the right and north, there are further small floors and slivers of farm land, all but one less than an acre, and lying much within the moistures of trees during several hours of the day, in cotton, in corn, in sorghum cane, in peanuts, in watermelons, and in sweet potatoes. Some of this land of Gudger's is sandy clay, dull-orange to a dead sort of yellow; some is dark sand; a little is loam. He has in all about eleven acres in cotton, nine in corn, a quarter in sorghum cane, about half an acre divided among the melons, peanuts, and potatoes, and there are field peas planted in the corn rows.

These fields are workrooms, or fragrant but mainly sterile workfloors without walls and with a roof of uncontrollable chance, fear, rumination, and propitiative prayer, and are as the spread and broken petals of a flower whose bisexual center is the house.

Or the farm is also as a water spider whose feet print but do not break the gliding water membrane: it is thus delicately and briefly that, in its fields and structures, it sustains its entity upon the blind breadth and steady heave of nature.

Or it is the wrung breast of one human family's need and of an owner's taking, yielding blood and serum in its thin blue milk, and the house, the concentration of living and taking, is the cracked nipple: and of such breasts, the planet is thickly and desperately paved as the enfabled front of a goddess of east india.

The fields are organic of the whole, and of their own nature, and of the work that is poured into them: the spring, the garden, the outbuildings, are organic to the house itself.

The spring

The garden

The outbuildings

The spring is out to the rear of the house and above it, about a hundred and fifty yards away to the right, not a short distance to walk for every drop of water that is needed. The path lifts from the end of the back hall between the henroost and the smokehouse to just below the barn, swings left here, parts from the hill path, and runs narrowly, but slick as a scalp, among thick weeds under sunlight and toward trees whose green-brown gloom and coolness is sudden and whose silence, different from that of the open light, seems to be conscious and to await the repetition of a signal. Not five feet deeper, a delicate yet powerful odor of wetness in constant shade, a broad windless standing-forth of a new coolness as from a re-frigerator door, and a diminutive wrinkling noise of water: and ten feet deep within the roof of leaves, low, on the upward right, the spring, the dirt all round dark and strong-rooted and fra-grant, tamped smooth as soap with bare feet, and a mottled piece of plank to kneel to water on. The water stands forward from between rounded strata of submerged dark stone as from between lips or rollers, in a look not of motion yet of quiet compulsion, into a basin a foot deep floored with dead oak-leaves and shored up with slimy wood. On a submerged shelf small crocks of butter, cream, and milk stand sunken to their eyes, tied over with pieces of saturated floursack. A sapling next the spring has been chopped short to make a stob, and on it hangs a coffee can rusted black and split at the edges. The spring is not cowled so deeply under the hill that the water is brilliant and nervy, seeming to break in the mouth like crystals, as spring water can: it is about the temper of faucet water, and tastes slack and faintly sad, and as if just short of stale. It is not quite tepid, however, and it does not seem to taste of sweat and sickness, as the water does which the Woods family has to use.

Ten feet below, in a little alcove cleared at the edge of the woods, the water lets out through a rusted pipe and rambles loose. There is a brute oak bench here for washtubs,* and burnt stones are squared round the bright ashes of wood fires, and, next these stones, is one of those very heavy and handsome black iron kettles in which people one remove more primitive still make their own soap.

So, at the end of a slim liana of dry path running out of the heart of the house, a small wet flower suspended: the spring.

The garden plot is close on the right rear of the house. It is about the shape and about two thirds the size of a tennis court, and is caught within palings against the hunger and damage of animals. These palings are thin slats of split pine about three and a half feet tall and an inch and a half wide, wired together vertically, about their width apart from each other. The erratic grain and cleavage of this pine have given each of them a different welter and rippling streaming of surface and pattern structure; the weather has made this all as it were a muted silver and silk, exquisitely sensitive to light; and these slats closely approximate yet seldom perfect their perpendiculars; so that when the sun is on them, and with the segments of garden between each of them, there is here such a virtuosity as might be watched by speechless days on end merely for the variety and distinction of their beauty, without thought or any relevant room for thinking, and without possibility of absorbing all that is there to be seen. Outside, the frowsy weeds stand halfway up these walls: inside, the planting is concentrated to the utmost possible, in green and pink-veined wax and velvet butter beans, and in rank tomatoes, hung low, burst against the ground, in hairy buds of okra, all these sprung heavy with weeds and smothered in textured shades of their leaves, blown like nearly exploding balloons in the full spread of the summer, each in its shape and nature, so that the whole of this space is one blowsy bristling pool and splendor of worm- and insect-embroidered plants and the savage odors of their special lusts that sting the face in gathering, nuzzling the paling as the bars of a zoo: waist-deep to wade in, so twined and spired and reached among each other that the paths between rows are discernible

---

*There was also a split, mended washboard whose ribblings were homesawn out of a thick section of pine plank.

only like steps confounded in snow: a paling gate, nearest the kitchen, is bound shut against their bursting with a piece of wire.

Behind the house the dirt is blond and bare, except a little fledging of grass-leaves at the roots of structures, and walked-out rags of grass thickening along the sides. It lifts up gently, perhaps five feet in twenty yards: across the top line of this twenty yards is the barn, set a few feet to the right of center of the rear of the house. Half between the barn and house, symmetrical to the axis of the house, the henroost and the smoke-house face each other across a bare space of perhaps twelve feet of dirt.

These, like the house, are all made of unpainted pine. In some of this wood, the grain is broad and distinct: in some of it the grain has almost disappeared, and the wood has a texture and look like that of weathered bone.

The henroost is about seven feet square and five high, roofed with rotted shingles. It is built rather at random of planks varying in width between a foot and four inches, nailed on horizontally with narrow spaces between their edges. On the uphill side a short pole leans against the roof with chips and sticks nailed along it for steps and a box nailed at the top with straw in it; but most of the eggs are found by the children in places which are of the hens' own selection and return. Inside the roost, three or four sections of saplings, so arranged that the hens will not dirty each other; these poles rubbed smooth by their feet; the strong slits of light between the boards; the odor of closured and heated wood; and the nearly unbearably fetid odor of the feathers and excretions of the hens.

The smokehouse is about eight feet square and about seven tall to the peak of the roof. It is built of vertical boards of uniform width. The door is flush to the wall without a frame and is held shut by a wood button. On the uphill side, at center of the wall and flat to it, hangs a nearly new washtub, the concentrics on its bottom circle like a target. Its galvanized material is brilliant and dryly eating in the sun; the wood of the wall itself is not must less brilliant. The natural usage of a smoke-house is to smoke and store meat, but meat is not smoked here: this is a storage house. Mainly, there are a couple of dozen tin cans here, of many differing sizes and former uses, now holding sorghum; four hoes; a set of sweeps; a broken plow-frame; pieces of an ice-cream freezer; a can of rusty nails; a number of mule shoes; the strap of a white slipper; a pair of greenly eaten, crumpled workshoes, the uppers broken away, the soles worn broadly through, still carrying the odor of feet; a blue coil of soft iron wire; a few yards of rusted barbed wire; a rotted mulecollar; pieces of wire at random:* all those same broken creatures of the Ricketts' porch, of uselessness and of almost endless saving.

It should hardly be called a 'barn,' it is too thin an excuse for one: a long low shed divided into three chambers, a wired-in yard, a hog wallow and the hog's dirty little house. One room is made of thick and thin logs, partly stopped with clay, and this is the stall for the mule when he is there: the rest is pine boards. The next partition is for the cow. In one corner of the small wired yard which squares off this part of the barn, in somewhat trampled and dunged earth, is the hogpen, made of logs; beyond that, a room used, in turn, as a corncrib and as a storage house for cotton prior to ginning. There is no hayloft. The whole structure is about twenty feet long and not more than seven high and seven or eight deep. The floor, except of the corncrib, is earth.

Here I must say, a little anyhow: what I can hardly hope to bear out in the record: that a house of simple people which stands empty and silent in the vast Southern country morning sunlight, and everything which on this morning in eternal space it by chance contains, all thus left open and defenseless to a reverent and cold-laboring spy, shines quietly forth such grandeur, such sorrowful holiness of its exactitudes in exis-

---

*Invention here: I did not make inventory; there was more than I could re-member. I remember for certain only the sorghum cans, the sweeps, the hoes, the work shoes, the nails; with a vaguer remembrance of random pieces of har-ness and of broken machinery: there may also have been, for instance, a ruined headlight and a boy's soggy worn-out cap. Many of the sorghum cans, by the way, were almost the only bright and new-looking things on the farm. Gudger may have bought them. If so, they are notable, for tenants seldom buy any-thing new.

tence, as no human consciousness shall ever rightly perceive, far less impart to another: that there can be more beauty and more deep wonder in the standings and spacings of mute furnishings on a bare floor between the squaring bourns of walls than in any music ever made: that this square home, as it stands in unshadowed earth between the winding years of heaven, is, not to me but of itself, one among the serene and final, uncapturable beauties of existence: that this beauty is made between hurt but invincible nature and the plainest cruelties and needs of human existence in this uncured time, and is inextricable among these, and as impossible without them as a saint born in paradise.

But I say these things only because I am reluctant to entirely lie. I can have nothing more to do with them now. I am hoping here only to tell a little, only so well as I may, about an ordinary* house, in which I lived a little while, and which is the home, for the time being, of the Gudger family, and is the sort of home a tenant family lives in, furnished and decorated as they furnish and decorate. Since it is so entirely static a subject, it may be slow going. That is as it may be.

*The whole problem, if I were trying fully to embody the house, would be to tell of it exactly in its ordinary terms.

The Gudger House

The house is left alone

S LOWLY they diminished along the hill path, she, and her
daughter, and her three sons, in leisured enfilade beneath
the light. The mother first, her daughter next behind, her
eldest son, her straggler, whimpering; their bare feet pressed
out of the hot earth gentle explosions of gold. She carried her
youngest child, his knees locked simian across her, his light
hands at her neck, and his erected head, hooded with night,
next hers, swiveled mildly upon the world's globe, a periscope.
The dog, a convoy, plaited his wanderings round them through
the briars. She wore the flowerlike beauty of the sunbonnet in
which she is ashamed to appear before us. At length, well up
the hill, their talking shrank and became inaudible, and at that
point will give safe warning on the hill of their return. Their
slanted bodies slowly straightened, one by one, along the
brim, and turned into the east, a slow frieze, and sank beneath
the brim in order of their height, masts foundered in a horizon; the dog, each of the walking children, at length; at last,
the guileless cobra gloatings of the baby, the mother's tall,
flared head.

They are gone.

No one is at home, in all this house, in all this land. It is a
long while before their return. I shall move as they would trust
me not to, and as I could not, were they here. I shall touch
nothing but as I would touch the most delicate wounds, the
most dedicated objects.

The silence of the brightness of this middle morning is increased upon me moment by moment and upon this house,
and upon this house the whole of heaven is drawn into one
lens; and this house itself, in each of its objects, it, too, is one
lens.

I am being made witness to matters no human being may
see.

There is a cold beating at my solar plexus. I move in exceeding slowness and silence that I shall not dishonor nor

awaken this house: and in every instant of silence, it becomes more entirely perfected upon itself under the sun. I take warmed water from the bucket, without sound, and it brings the sweat out sharply and I wipe it away, remembering in shame his labor, George, at this instant, hard, in the strenuous heat, and upon the tanned surface of this continent, this awful field where cotton is made, infinitesimal, the antlike glistening of the sweated labors of nine million. I remember how in hot early puberty, realizing myself left alone the whole of a cavernous and gloomed afternoon in my grandfather's large unsentineled home, I would be taken at the pit of the stomach with a most bitter, criminal gliding and cold serpent restiveness, and would wander from vacant room to vacant room examining into every secrecy from fungoid underearth to rare-hot roof and from the roof would gaze in anguish and contempt upon the fronded suffocations of the midsummer city; trying to read; trying to play the piano; ravening upon volumes of soft-painted nudes; staring hungrily and hatefully into mirrors; rifling drawers, closets, boxes, for the mere touch at the lips and odor of fabrics, pelts, jewels, switches of hair; smoking cigars, sucking at hidden liquors; reading the piteous enthusiasms of ribboned letters stored in attic trunks: at length I took off all my clothes, lay along the cold counterpanes of every bed, planted my obscenities in the cold hearts of every mirror in foreknowledge, what unseen words and acts lurked ambushed in those deep white seas before the innocent fixtures of a lady's hair: I permitted nothing to escape the fingering of my senses nor the insulting of the cold reptilian fury of the terror of lone desire which was upon me:

It is not entirely otherwise now, in this inhuman solitude, the nakedness of this body which sleeps here before me, this tabernacle upon whose desecration I so reverentially proceed: yet it differs somewhat: for there is here no open sexual desire, no restiveness, nor despair: but the quietly triumphant vigilance of the extended senses before an intricate task of surgery, a deep stealthfulness, not for shame of the people, but in fear and in honor of the house itself, a knowledge of being at work. And by this same knowledge, along with the coldness, the adoration, the pity, the keen guilt at the heart, complete casualness. I am merely myself, a certain young man, standing in my sweated clothes in the rear of a dividing porch of a certain house, foundered as stone in sea in deepest Alabamian rurality, beneath the white scorch of a calm white morning; the leaves, sluicing most gently in their millions what open breadth of earth I see, beneath upward coilings of transparent air, and here, their home; and they have gone; and it is now my chance to perceive this, their home, as it is, in whose hollow heart resounds the loud zinc flickering heartbeat of the cheap alarm two hours advanced upon false time; a human shelter, a strangely lined nest, a creature of killed pine, stitched together with nails into about as rude a garment against the hostilities of heaven as a human family may wear.

We stand first facing it, squarely in front of it, in the huge and peaceful light of this August morning:

And it stands before us, facing us, squarely in front of us, silent and undefended in the sun.

In front of the house: its general structure

Two blocks, of two rooms each, one room behind another. Between these blocks a hallway, floored and roofed, wide open both at front and rear: so that these blocks are two rectangular yoked boats, or floated tanks, or coffins, each, by an inner wall, divided into two squared chambers. The roof, pitched rather steeply from front and rear, its cards met and nailed at a sharp angle. The floor faces the earth closely. On the left of the hall, two rooms, each an exact square. On the right a square front room and, built later, behind it, using the outward weatherboards for its own front wall, a leanto kitchen half that size.

At the exact center of each of the outward walls of each room, a window. Those of the kitchen are small, taller than wide, and are glassed. Those of the other rooms are exactly square and are stopped with wooden shutters.

From each room a door gives on the hallway. The doors of the two front rooms are exactly opposite: the doors of the rear rooms are exactly opposite. The two rooms on either side of the hallway are also connected inwardly by doors through their partition walls.

Out at the left of the house, starting from just above the side window of the front room, a little roof is reached out and rested on thin poles above bare ground: shelter for wagon or for car.

At the right of the house, just beneath the side window of the front room, a commodious toolbox, built against the wall. It is nailed shut.

The hallway yields onto a front porch about five feet long by ten wide, reaching just a little short of the windows at either side, set at dead center of the front of the house. A little tongue of shingles, the same size, is stuck out slightly slanted above it, and is sustained on four slender posts from which most of the bark has been stripped.

Three steps lead down at center; they are of oak: the bottom one is cracked and weak, for all its thickness. Stones have been stacked beneath it, but they have slid awry, and it goes to the ground sharply underfoot. Just below and beyond it is a wide flat piece of shale the color of a bruise. It is broken several ways across and is sunken into the dirt.

The forty-foot square of land in front of the house, the 'front yard,' is bare of any trees or bushes; there is nothing at all near the house of its own height, or bestowing of any shade. This piece of land is hunched a little on itself in a rondure. Through the dry haze of weeds and flowering fennels its dead red yellowness glows quietly, a look of fire in sunlight, and it is visible how intricately it is trenched and seamed with sleavings of rain; as if, the skull lifted off, the brain were exposed, of some aged not intellectual being who had lived a long time patiently and with difficulty.

Where we stand, square toward the front, the house is almost perfectly symmetrical. Its two front walls, square, balanced, each of a size, cloven by hallway; the lifted roof; at center of each wall, a square window, the shutters closed; the porch and its roof and the four little posts like candles:

Each window is framed round with a square of boards.

Ten or twelve feet out in this yard, and precisely in line with these front windows, as if they were projections of them, and of about the same size, two hollow squares of wood are laid upon the earth and are sunk level with it: and these are in fact two projections and are related with these windows, and indeed are windows, of a sort: for they are intended to let through their frames from the blank wall and darkness of the earth a particular and gracious, pleasing light; they are flower-beds. The one at the left is sprung through with the same indiscriminate fennels of the yard; the one on the right, the same. But here among this rambling of bastardy stands up, on its weak stem, one fainting pale magenta petunia, which stares at its tired foot; and this in the acreage of these three farms is the one domestic flower.

Now raising the eyes, slowly, in face of this strength of sun, to look the house in its blind face:

In front of the house: The façade

The porch: stands in its short square shade:

The hall: it is in shadow also, save where one wall, fifteen feet back, is slantingly slashed with light:

At the far end of this well of hall, the open earth, lifted a little, bald hard dirt; the faced frontages of the smokehouse and the henhouse, and a segment of the barn: and all of this framed image a little unnaturally brilliant and vital, as all strongly lighted things appear through corridors of darkness:

And this hall between, as the open valve of a sea creature, steadfastly flushing the free width of ocean through its infinitesimal existence: and on its either side, the square boxes, the square front walls, raised vertical to the earth, and facing us as two squared prows of barge or wooden wings, shadow beneath their lower edge and at their eaves; and the roof:

And these walls:

Nailed together of boards on beams, the boards facing the weather, into broad cards of wood inlet with windows stopped with shutters: walls, horizontals, of somewhat narrow weatherboarding; the windows bounded by boards of that same width in a square: the shutters, of wide vertical boards laid edge to edge, not overlapped: each of these boards was once of the living flesh of a pine tree; it was cut next the earth, and was taken between the shrieking of saws into strict ribbons; and now, which was vertical, is horizontal to the earth, and another is clamped against the length of its outward edge and its downward clamps another, and these boards, nailed tightly together upon pine beams, make of their horizontalities a wall: and the sun makes close horizontal parallels along the edges of these weatherboards, of sharp light and shade, the parallels strengthened here in slight straight-line lapse from level, in the subtle knife-edged curve of warping loose in another place: another irregular 'pattern' is made in the endings and piecings-out of boards:

And the roof:

It is of short hand-hewn boards so thick and broad, they are shingles only of a most antique sort: crosswise upon rigid beams, laths have been nailed, not far apart, and upon these laths, in successive rows of dozens and of hundreds, and here again, though regularly, with a certain shuffling of erratism against pure symmetry, these broad thick shingles are laid down overlapping from the peak to the overhung edge like the plumage of a bird who must meet weather: and not unlike some square and formalized plumage, as of a holy effigy, they seem, and made in profligate plates of a valuable metal; for they have never been stained, nor otherwise touched or colored save only by all habits of the sky: nor has any other wood of this house been otherwise ever touched: so that, wherever the weathers of the year have handled it, the wood of the whole of this house shines with the noble gentleness of cherished silver, much as where (yet differently), along the floors, in the pathings of the millions of soft wavelike movements of naked feet, it can be still more melodiously charmed upon its knots, and is as wood long fondled in a tender sea:

Upon these structures, light:

It stands just sufficiently short of vertical that every leaf of shingle, at its edges, and every edge of horizontal plank (blocked, at each center, with squared verticals) is a most black and cutting ink: and every surface struck by light is thus: such an intensity and splendor of silver in the silver light, it seems to burn, and burns and blinds into the eyes almost as snow; yet in none of that burnishment or blazing whereby detail is lost: each texture in the wood, like those of bone, is distinct in the eye as a razor: each nail-head is distinct: each seam and split; and each slight warping; each random knot and knothole: and in each board, as lovely a music as a contour map and unique as a thumbprint, its grain, which was its living strength, and these wild creeks cut stiff across by saws; and moving nearer, the close-laid arcs and shadows even of those tearing wheels: and this, more poor and plain than bone, more naked and noble than sternest Doric, more rich and more variant than watered silk, is the fabric and the stature of a house.

It is put together out of the cheapest available pine lumber, and the least of this is used which shall stretch a skin of one thickness alone against the earth and air; and this is all done according to one of the three or four simplest, stingiest, and thus most classical plans contrivable, which are all traditional to that country: and the work is done by half-skilled, half-paid men under no need to do well, who therefore take such vengeance on the world as they may in a cynical and part willful apathy; and this is what comes of it: Most naïve, most massive symmetry and simpleness. Enough lines, enough off-true, that this symmetry is strongly yet most subtly sprained against its centers, into something more powerful than either full symmetry or deliberate breaking and balancing of 'monotonies' can hope to be. A look of being most earnestly hand-made, as a child's drawing, a thing created out of need, love, patience, and strained skill in the innocence of a race. Nowhere one ounce or inch spent with ornament, not one trace of relief or of disguise: a matchless monotony, and in it a matchless variety and this again throughout restrained, held rigid: and of all this, nothing which is not intrinsic between the materials of structure, the earth, and the open heaven. The major lines of structure, each horizontal of each board, and edge of shingle, the strictness yet subtle dishevelment of the shingles, the nail-heads, which are driven according to geometric need, yet are not in perfect order, the grain, differing in each foot of each board and in each board from any other, the many knots in this cheap lumber: all these fluencies and irregularities, all these shadows of pattern upon each piece of wood, all these in rectilinear ribbons caught into one squared, angled, and curled music, compounding a chord of four chambers upon a soul and center of clean air: and upon all these masses and edges and chances and flowerings of grain, the changes of colorings of all weathers, and the slow complexions and marchings of pure light.

Or by another saying:

'In all this house:

'In all of this house not any one inch of lumber being wasted on embellishment, or on trim, or on any form of relief, or even on any doubling of walls: it is, rather, as if a hard thin hide of wood has been stretched to its utmost to cover exactly once, or a little less than once, in all six planes the skeletal beams which, with the inside surface of the weatherboarding, are the inside walls; and no touch, as I have said, of any wash or paint, nor, on the floors, any kind of covering, nor, to three of the rooms, any kind of ceiling, but in all places left bare the plain essences of structure; in result all these almost perfect symmetries have their full strength, and every inch of the structure, and every aspect and placement of the building materials, comes inevitably and purely through into full esthetic existence, the one further conditioner, and discriminator between the functions and proprieties of indoors and out, being the lights and operations of the sky.'

Or by a few further notes:

'On symmetry: the house is rudimentary as a child's drawing, and of a bareness, cleanness, and sobriety which only Doric architecture, so far as I know, can hope to approach: this exact symmetry is sprung slightly and subtly, here and there, one corner of the house a little off vertical, a course of weatherboarding failing the horizontal between parallels, a window frame not quite square, by lack of skill and by weight and weakness of timber and time; and these slight failures, their tensions sprung against centers and opposals of such rigid and earnest exactitude, set up intensities of relationship far more powerful than full symmetry, or studied dissymmetry, or use of relief or ornament, can ever be: indeed, the power is of another world and order than theirs, and there is, as I mentioned, a particular quality of a thing hand-made, which by comparison I can best suggest thus: by the grandeur that comes of the effort of one man to hold together upon one instrument, as if he were breaking a wild monster to bridle and riding, one of the larger fugues of Bach, on an organ, as against the slick collaborations and effortless climaxes of the same piece in the manipulations of an orchestra.'

Or again by materials: and by surfaces and substances: the build and shape of walls, roof, window frames, verticals of shutters, opposals and cleavings of mass as I have said, and the surfaces and substances: 'The front porch of oak two-by-twelves so hard they still carry a strong piercing fell of splinters; the four supporting posts which have the delicate bias and fluences of young trees and whose surface is close to that of rubbed ivory; in the musculatures of their stripped knots they have the flayed and expert strength of anatomical studies: and the rest of the house entirely of pine, the cheapest of local building material and of this material one of the cheapest grades: in the surfaces of these boards are three qualities of beauty and they are simultaneous, mutually transparent: one is the streaming killed strength of the grain, infinite, talented, and unrepeatable from inch to inch, the florid genius of nature which is incapable of error: one is the close-set transverse arcs, dozens to the foot, which are the shadows of the savage breathings and eatings of the circular saws; little of this lumber has been planed: one is the tone and quality the weather has given it, which is related one way to bone, another to satin, another to unpolished but smooth silver: all these are visible at once, though one or another may be strongly enhanced by degree and direction of light and by degree of humidity: moreover, since the lumber is so cheap, knots are frequent, and here and there among the knots the iron-hard bitter red center is lost, and there is, instead, a knothole; the grain near these knots goes into convulsions or ecstasies such as Beethoven's deafness compelled; and with these knots the planes of the house are badged at random, and again moreover, these wild fugues and floods of grain, which are of the free perfect innocence of nature, are sawn and stripped across into rigid ribbons and by rigid lines and boundaries, in the captive perfect innocence of science, so that these are closely collaborated and interinvolved in every surface: and at points strategic to structure: and regimented by need, and attempting their own symmetries, yet not in perfect line (such is the tortured yet again perfect innocence of men, caught between the pulls of nature and science), the patternings and constellations of the heads of the driven nails: and all these things, set in the twisted and cradling planet, take the benefit of every light and weather which the sky in their part of the world can bestow, this within its terms being subtly unrepeatable and probably infinite, and are qualified as few different structures can be, to make full use of these gifts. By most brief suggestion: in full symmetry of the sun, the surfaces are dazzling silver, the shadows strong as knives and

India ink, yet the grain and all detail clear: in slanted light, all slantings and sharpenings of shadow: in smothered light, the aspect of bone, a relic: at night, the balanced masses, patient in the base world: from rain, out of these hues of argent bone the colors of agate, the whole wall, one fabric and mad zebra of quartered minerals and watered silks: and in the sheltered yet open hallway, a granite gray and seeming of nearly granitic hardness, the grain dim, the sawmarks very strong; in the strength of these marks and peculiar sobriety of the color, a look as if there has been a slow and exact substitution of calcium throughout all the substance: within the rooms, the wood holds much nearer its original colors of yellows, reds, and peasant golds drawn deep toward gray, yet glowing quietly through it as the clay world glows through summer.'

But enough.

The room beneath the house

The rear edges of the house rest in part on stacked stones, in part on the dirt; in part they overhang this dirt a little. Beneath the house this dirt sinks gently, so that the flanks and forward edges are lifted to level in part on taller stacks of stone, in part on thick rounded sections of logs. The porch floor, and the forward parts of the house, are about two and a half feet off the ground.

This cold plaque of earth beneath, which wears the shape of the house and is made different from other earth, as that part of a wall against which a picture has been hung for years: which might have been field, pasture, forest, mere indiscriminate land: by chance:

At a bright time in sun, and in a suddenness alien to those rhythms the land had known these hundred millions of years, lumber of other land was brought rattling in yellow wagonloads and caught up between hammers upon air before unregarding heaven a hollow altar, temple, or poor shrine, a human shelter, which for the space of a number of seasons shall hold this shape of earth denatured: yet in whose history this house shall have passed soft and casually as a snowflake fallen on black spring ground, which thaws in touching.

There in the chilly and small dust which is beneath porches, the subtle funnels of doodlebugs whose teasing, of a broom-straw, is one of the patient absorptions of kneeling childhood, and there, in that dust and the damper dust and the dirt, dead twigs of living, swept from the urgent tree, signs, and relics: bent nails, withered and knobbed with rust; a bone button, its two eyes torn to one; the pierced back of an alarm clock, greasy to the touch; a torn fragment of pictured print; an emptied and flattened twenty-gauge shotgun shell, its metal green, lettering still visible; the white tin eyelet of a summer shoe; and thinly scattered, the desiccated and the still soft excrement of hens, who stroll and dab and stand, shimmying, stabbing at their lice, and stroll out again into the sun as vacantly as they departed it. And other things as well: a long and slender infinitesimally rustling creek and system of ants in their traffic: the underside of the house, so sparsely lifted even at the front, and meeting the quietly swollen earth so close there is scarcely light at all at the rear: and here the earth is cold, continually damp, and in the odors of mold and of a well, and there are cold insects, sutured and plated, rapid on many feet that run in a rill and nimbus along their narrow bodies; and strong spiders here, and dead ones, pale as mushrooms, suspended in the ruins of their lives, or strong, avid, distinct among their clean constructions, still, slowly palpitant in their thick bodies, watching you with a poison sharpness of eye you cannot be sure you see, sudden to movement and swift, and some who jump: and the clean pine underside of the house, blond like the floor of a turtle, that sun has never and weather has scarcely touched, so that it looks still new, as if yet it had sustained no sorrow above, but only a hope that was still in process of approach, as once this whole house was, all fresh and bridal, four hollowed rooms brimmed with a light of honey:

(*O therefore in the cleanly quiet, calm hope, sweet odor, awaiting, of each new dwelling squared by men on air, be sorrowful, as of the sprung trap, the slim wrist gnawn, the little disastrous fox:*
   It stands up in the sun and the bride smiles: quite soon the shelves are papered: the new forks taste in the food:
   Ruin, ruin is in our hopes: nor hope, help, any healing:)

it is hung and strung with their frail structures, and closes with the cool damp dirt in almost darkness: and is of this noiseless and variegated underworld the flat scarce-lifted stone, the roof and firmament: and above:

This underside, and firmament, and shelter and graveyard of sharp alien and short lives, and drifting lot of orts of usage, and retirement of hens, and relief of dogs, and meditation space of children, and gradation of constant shade, and yielder upward of harsh winter damp, slid through likewise from time to time with snakes, and sterilizer of earth which contiguous, just beyond its region of rule, sick as it is, streams and inaudibly shrieks with green violence: this likewise on its upward surface is the floor and basis of still other living, a wide inch-thick plat of wood, swept with straws and not seldom scrubbed, soaped and spreaded with warmth of water, that drains in its seams, and kneeling, hard breathing, with hard straws scoured and pure: the walls stand up from its edges and face one another; and its surface sustains the distributed points and weights of the furnishings of living, and the motions and directions of desire, need, work, and listlessness: a floor, a sustainer of human living; whereto children and dogs droop in their tiredness and rest, and sleep, and on a pallet a baby lies, spread over with a floursack against infringement of flies, and sleeps and here a moving camera might know, on its bareness, the standing of the four iron feet of a bed, the wood of a chair, the scrolled treadle of a sewing machine, the standing up at right angles of plain wood out of plain wood, the great and handsome grains and scars of this vertical and prostrate wood, the huge and noble motions of brooms and of knees and of feet, and how with clay, and animals, and the leaning face of a woman, these are among the earliest and profoundest absorptions of a very young child.

The hallway

Structure of four rooms

The hallway is long courses of weatherboard facing one another in walls six feet apart, featureless excepting two pair of opposite doors, not ceiled, but beneath the empty and high angling of the roof: perhaps because of the blankness of these walls, and their facing closeness relative to their parallel length, there is here an extremely strong sense of the nakedness and narrowness of their presence, and of the broad openness, exposing the free land, at either end. The floor is laid along beams rather wide apart. In all the rear end it yields to the ground under much weight: the last few feet lie solid to the ground, and this is a strong muck in wet weather.

The one static fixture in the hallway is at the rear, just beyond the kitchen door. It is a wooden shelf, waist-high, and on this shelf, a bucket, a dipper, a basin, and usually a bar of soap, and hanging from a nail just above, a towel. The basin is granite-ware, small for a man's hands, with rustmarks in the bottom. The bucket is a regular galvanized two-gallon bucket, a little dented, and smelling and touching a little of a fishy-metallic kind of shine and grease beyond any power of cleaning. It is half full of slowly heating water which was not very cold to begin with: much lower than this, the water tastes a little ticklish and nasty for drinking, though it is still all right for washing. The soap is sometimes strong tan 'kitchen' soap, sometimes a cheap white gelatinous lavender face soap. It stands on the shelf in a china saucer. The dipper again is granite-ware, and again blistered with rust at the bottom. Sometimes it bobs in the bucket; sometimes it lies next the bucket on the shelf. The towel is half a floursack, with the blue and red and black printing still faint on it. Taken clean and dry, it is the pleasantest cloth I know for a towel. Beyond that, it is particularly clammy, clinging, and dirty-feeling.

A few notes of discrimination may be helpful:

The towels in such a farmhouse are always floursacks. 'Kitchen' towels are of another world and class of farmer, and 'face' and 'turkish' towels of still another.

By no means all poor farmers use any sort of 'toilet' soap. Some seldom use soap at all. When they use other than kitchen soap, it is of one of about three kinds, all of them of the sort available in five-and-tens and small-town general stores. One is 'lava' or 'oatmeal' soap, whose rough texture is pleasing and convincing of cleanliness to a person who works with his hands. The white soaps smell sharply of lye: again, the odor is cleansing. Or if the soap is more fancy, it is a pink or lemon or purple color, strongly and cheaply scented and giving a big lather. No cheap yet somewhat pleasantly scented soap such as lux is used.

Rather more often than not, the basin and the dipper are plain unenameled tin. I expect, but am not sure, that this is a few cents cheaper. In any case the odor, taste, and shiny, greasy texture soon become strong. The use of enamel ware is a small yet sharp distinction and symptom in 'good taste,' and in 'class,' and in a sort of semi-esthetic awareness, choice and will. The use of gray as against white is still another discriminative. That they bought small sizes, which are a very few cents cheaper, speaks for itself. So does the fact that they have afforded still another basin, not quite big enough for its use, to wash their feet in.

At times, there is also a mirror here, and a comb; but more often these are on the bedroom mantel.

The hall and front porch are a kind of room, and are a good deal used. Mrs. Gudger and her children sit in the porch in empty times of the morning and afternoon: back in the rear of the hall is the evening place to sit, before supper or for a little while just after it. There are few enough chairs that they have to be moved around the house to where they are needed, but ordinarily there is a rockingchair on the porch and a straight chair in the rear of the hall next the bedroom door. This rockingchair is of an inexpensive 'rustic' make: sections of hickory sapling with the bark still on. On the hard and not quite even porch floor the rocking is stony and cobbled, with a little of the sound of an auto crossing a loose wooden bridge. Three of the straight chairs are strong, plain, not yet decrepit hickory-bottoms, which cost a dollar and a half new; there is also a kitchen-type chair with a pierced design in the dark scalloped wood at the head, and the bottom broken through.

When we first knew the Gudgers they had their eating-table in the middle of the hall, for only in the hall is there likely to be any sort of breeze, and the kitchen, where nearly all farm families eat, was so hot that they could at times hardly stand to eat in it. This was only an experiment though, and it was not successful. The hall is too narrow for any comfort in it for a whole family clenched round a table. If it were even two feet wider, it would be much more use to them, but this would not have occurred to those who built it, nor, if it had, would anything have been done about it.

——

Four rooms make a larger tenant house than is ordinary: many are three; many are two; more are one than four: and three of these rooms are quite spacious, twelve feet square. For various reasons, though, all of which could easily enough have been avoided in the building of the house, only two of these rooms, the kitchen and the rear bedroom, are really habitable. There is no ceiling to either of the front rooms, and the shingles were laid so unskillfully, and are now so multitudinously leaky, that it would be a matter not of repairing but of complete re-laying to make a solid roof. Between the beams at the eaves, along the whole front of the house, and the top of the wall on which the beams rest, there are open gaps. In the front room on the right, several courses of weatherboarding have been omitted between the level of the eaves and the peak of the roof: a hole big enough for a cow to get through. The walls, and shutters, and floors, are not by any means solid: indeed, and beyond and aside from any amount of laborious calking, they let in light in many dozens of places. There are screens for no windows but one, in the rear bedroom. Because in half the year the fever mosquitoes are thick and there are strong rainstorms, and in the other half it is cold and wet for weeks on end with violent slanted winds and sometimes snow, the right front room is not used to live in at all and the left front room is used only dubiously and irregularly, though the sewing machine is there and it is fully furnished both as a bedroom and as a parlor. The children use it sometimes, and it is given to guests (as it was to us), but storm, mosquitoes and habit force them back into the other room where the whole family sleeps together.

But now I want to take these four rooms one by one, and give at least a certain rough idea of what is in each of them and of what each is 'like,' though I think I should begin this with a few more general remarks.

Odors

Bareness and space

The Gudgers' house, being young, only eight years old, smells a little dryer and cleaner, and more distinctly of its wood, than an average white tenant house, and it has also a certain odor I have never found in other such houses: aside from these sharp yet slight subtleties, it has the odor or odors which are classical in every thoroughly poor white southern country house, and by which such a house could be identified blindfold in any part of the world, among no matter what other odors. It is compacted of many odors and made into one, which is very thin and light on the air, and more subtle than it can seem in analysis, yet very sharply and constantly noticeable. These are its ingredients. The odor of pine lumber, wide thin cards of it, heated in the sun, in no way doubled or insulated, in closed and darkened air. The odor of woodsmoke, the fuel being again mainly pine, but in part also, hickory, oak, and cedar. The odors of cooking. Among these, most strongly, the odors of fried salt pork and of fried and boiled pork lard, and second, the odor of cooked corn. The odors of sweat in many stages of age and freshness, this sweat being a distillation of pork, lard, corn, woodsmoke, pine, and ammonia. The odors of sleep, of bedding and of breathing, for the ventilation is poor. The odors of all the dirt that in the course of time can accumulate in a quilt and mattress. Odors of staleness from clothes hung or stored away, not washed. I should further describe the odor of corn: in sweat, or on the teeth, and breath, when it is eaten as much as they eat it, it is of a particular sweet stuffy fetor, to which the nearest parallel is the odor of the yellow excrement of a baby. All these odors as I have said are so combined into one that they are all and always present in balance, not at all heavy, yet so searching that all fabrics of bedding and clothes are saturated with them, and so clinging that they stand softly out of the fibers of newly laundered clothes. Some of their components are extremely 'pleasant,' some are 'unpleasant'; their sum total has great nostalgic power. When they are in an old house, darkened, and moist, and sucked into all the wood, and stacked down on top of years of a moldering and old basis of themselves, as at the Ricketts', they are hard to get used to or even hard to bear. At the Woods', they are blowsy and somewhat moist and dirty. At the Gudgers', as I have mentioned, they are younger, lighter, and cleaner-smelling. There too, there is another and special odor, very dry and edged: it is somewhere between the odor of very old newsprint and of a victorian bedroom in which, after long illness, and many medicines, someone has died and the room has been fumigated, yet the odor of dark brown medicines, dry-bodied sickness, and staring death, still is strong in the stained wallpaper and in the mattress.

Bareness and space (and spacing) are so difficult and seem to me of such greatness that I shall not even try to write seriously or fully of them. But a little, applying mainly to the two bedrooms.

The floors are made of wide planks, between some of which the daylighted earth is visible, and are naked of any kind of paint or cloth or linoleum covering whatever, and paths have been smoothed on them by bare feet, in a subtly uneven surface on which the polished knots are particularly beautiful. A perfectly bare floor of broad boards makes a room seem larger than it can if the floor is covered, and the furniture too, stands on it in a different and much cleaner sort of relationship. The walls as I have said are skeleton; so is the ceiling in one of these rooms; the rooms are twelve feet square and are meagerly furnished, and they are so great and final a whole of bareness and complete simplicity that even the objects on a crowded shelf seem set far apart from each other, and each to have a particularly sharp entity of its own. Moreover, all really simple and naïve people* incline strongly toward exact symmetries, and have some sort of instinctive dislike that any one thing shall touch any other save what it rests on, so that chairs, beds, bureaus, trunks, vases, trinkets, general odds and ends, are set very plainly and squarely discrete from one another and from walls, at exact centers or as near them as possible, and this kind of spacing gives each object a full strength it would not otherwise have, and gives their several relationships, as they stand on shelves or facing, in a room, the purest power such a relationship can have. This is still more sharply true with such people as the Gudgers, who still have a little yet earnest wish that everything shall be as pleasant and proper to live with as possible, than with others such as the Woods and Ricketts, who are disheveled and wearied out of any such hope or care.

*And many of the most complex, and not many between.

I. The Front Bedroom

General: placement of furniture

ITS west wall is the front of the house; its north wall, the hall-way; its east wall, the partition; its south wall, the side of the house. At the center of the partition wall is a fireplace. At the center of the side wall and of the front wall is an exactly square window, about three feet each way. At the center of the north wall a door leads into the rear bedroom. The doors are very wide vertical planks, not paneled, but crosslaid with planks in a Z. They are held shut by block wood buttons and are kept shut most of the time. The square shutters, hung on sagged and rusted, loud hinges, are less broad verticals. Always at night and nearly always during the day they are drawn shut and secured, one by a leather strap over a nail, the other by a piece of rag over a nail. When they are shut, the room is dark and has a special heat and odor of daylight darkness; but also there is a strong starlight of sunshine with slits and blades and rods of light through the roof and two outward walls and, looking through the floor, the quiet sunless daylighted grain of the earth can be seen, strange to see as at the bottom of a lake; and in this oddly lighted darkness, certain flecks of the room are brilliantly picked out, and every part of it is visible. When one of the shutters is opened, the light is new and un-easy in the room, as if the objects were blinking, or had been surprised in secret acts, or, even, as an archaeologist who first lets daylight into an unviolated Egyptian tomb: and the feeling and odor of its particular darkness never leaves it: and here, on the bare floor, between the squarings of the wide bare walls, the furniture stands: the furniture, its clothing, and each little ornament on wall and shelf, and the contents of each box and drawer, and the cleanliness of the central floor, such that it might be licked with the tongue and made scarcely cleaner, and the lint curled back against itself under the bed and be-hind the sewing machine and thick beneath the bureau, and the pine walls, which outside are weathered so pure, still holding their reds and yellows among their grays, clear in their grain, and lined in strong parallels on the far sides of the strongly nailed pine two-by-fours, through the sides of which, here and there, nails have split their points among splinters of fresh-looking wood.

The bed, between the hall door and the front wall, in the angle of the two walls, the head toward the wall, about six inches out from each wall, the foot at the window.

On the other side of the hall door, at center between this door and the angle of the partition wall, a 'settee.'

Directly before the fireplace, but not touching it, a small table. Above the fireplace, a mantel.

Again out from the walls, symmetrically across the right angle made by the partition wall and the side wall, its tall mirror erect above it, a bureau.

Exactly beneath the window of the side wall, again a little out from the wall, a trunk:

Exactly across the angle of the side and front walls, and still again, not touching these walls, a sewing machine.

Exactly at center behind and beneath the sewing machine, on the floor, a square-based and square-bowled lamp of clear heavy glass, dusty, and without its chimney, the base broken and the broken piece fitted but not mended into place:

Exactly beneath the center of the table, on a shelf just above the floor, their toes pointed parallel into the center of the fireplace, a large and still nearly new pair of men's black sunday oxfords, the heels clayed and the shining black upward heels narrowly streaked with clay of the color of angry gold.

On the bureau shelf, the mantel, the table and one wall, objects; small, simple and varied: which, the only adorned or decorated creatures of this room, bestow upon its nakedness the quality of an altar.

The furniture

The dark castiron treadle of the sewing machine spells out squarely, in the middle of its curlings, the word CONQUEST. This is repeated in gold on the split wooden hood, but most of the gold has been rubbed off.

The 'settee': rather fancily bent out of thin canes; loud and broken; too uncomfortable to make much use of. The seat is badly broken through. A thin homemade cushion, stuffed with raw cotton; the slip is the frailest and cheapest kind of cotton cloth, dirty white, splotched with wide pink roses.

It is a small, elderly, once gay, now sober, and very pretty trunk, the lid shallowly domed, somewhat tall and narrow, and thus bearing itself in a kind of severe innocence as certain frame houses and archaic automobiles do. It is surfaced with tin which was once colored bright red and bright blue, and this tin, now almost entirely gone brown, is stamped in a thick complex of daisies and studded with small roundheaded once golden nails; and the body of the trunk is bound with wood and with two recently nailed ribbons of bluish iron. The leather handles are gray-green and half-rotted, the hinges are loose, the lock is wrenched. Opening this light trunk, a fragrance springs from it as if of stale cinnamon and fever powders and its inward casket is unexpectedly bright as if it were a box of tamed sunlight, in its lining of torn white paper streaked with brown, fresh yellow wood grained through the torn places, the bright white lining printed with large and bright mauve centerless daisies. In this trunk: an old slightly soiled cotton slip; a little boy's stiff cheap gray cap; a baby's dress; a gray-white knit shoe for a baby; a pair of ten-cent hard thin mercerized bold-patterned electric-blue socks, worn through at the heels, with a strip of green checked gingham tied through the top of one, for a garter, and a strip of pink gingham through the other. In one corner of the floor of the trunk, staring blue with black centers, waxed to the ends of a wire wishbone whose juncture is a light lead weight, the eyes of a small doll.

The bed-frame is not tall or at all ornate, as many iron frames are. Its former surface of hard white paint is worn almost entirely away to the bare, blue-brown iron. It is a three-quarter bed, which means a double bed so far as tenant usage is concerned. Because it is the guest and parlor bed, and little used, it is covered with a thin, brittle, magenta spread of chemical silk.

The bureau was at some time a definitely middle-class* piece of furniture. It is quite wide and very heavy, veneered in

---

*More accurately, it would have been a lower-middle-class imitation of a middle-class piece, mimicking weight, bulk, gloom, ornament, and expense.

gloomy red rich-grained woods, with intricately pierced metal plaques at the handles of the three drawers, and the mirror is at least three feet tall and is framed in machine-carved wood. The veneer has now split and leafed loose in many places from the yellow soft-wood base; the handles of the three drawers are nearly all deranged and two are gone; the drawers do not pull in and out at all easily. The mirror is so far corrupted that it is rashed with gray, iridescent in parts, and in all its reflections a deeply sad thin zinc-to-platinum, giving to its framings an almost incalculably ancient, sweet, frail, and piteous beauty, such as may be seen in tintypes of family groups among studio furnishings or heard in nearly exhausted jazz records made by very young, insane, devout men who were soon to destroy themselves, in New Orleans, in the early nineteen twenties. The surface of this bureau is covered with an aged, pebble-grained face towel, too good a fabric to be used in this house for the purposes it was made for. Upon this towel rest these objects: An old black comb, smelling of fungus and dead rubber, nearly all the teeth gone. A white clamshell with brown dust in the bottom and a small white button on it. A small pincushion made of pink imitation silk with the bodiced torso of a henna-wigged china doll sprouting from it, her face and one hand broken off. A cream-colored brown-shaded china rabbit three or four inches tall, with bluish lights in the china, one ear laid awry: he is broken through the back and the pieces have been fitted together to hang, not glued, in delicate balance. A small seated china bull bitch and her litter of three smaller china pups, seated round her in an equilateral triangle, their eyes intersected on her: they were given to Louise last Christmas and are with one exception her most cherished piece of property. A heavy moist brown Bible, its leaves almost weak as snow, whose cold, obscene, and inexplicable fragrance I found in my first night in this house.

I shall not fully list the contents of the bureau drawers. They contain, among other things, schoolbooks; and in one drawer there are a number of pieces of wrapping paper, each folded separately and very carefully to make no more new creases than is necessary. Some of this paper is dark blue with large gold bells and stars and small gold houses on it. Some is red and green holly on a white ground. Some is plain red or white or green or blue tissue. One is plain brown wrapping paper but has glued to it several seals of santaclaus and of scotch terriers and of bells in holly garlands. These papers are now torn in a number of places, rather somber and faded, and are intricately seamed and ridged over all their surfaces with years of wrapping and unfolding. They smell stale and old. There are also red, frayed gold and silver strings here, wound some on spools, some on matches or nails.

And, centered one upon another and at center of their squarespread partition wall, all squarely opposite the square window, the table and the fireplace and the mantel which, with the wall, create a shrine and altar:

The altar

The three other walls are straight and angled beams and the inward surfaces of unplaned pine weatherboards. This partition wall is made of horizontals of narrow and cleanly planed wood, laid tightly edge to edge; the wood is pine of another quality, slenderly grained in narrow yellow and rich iron-red golds, very smooth and as if polished, softly glowing and shining, almost mirroring bulks: and is the one wall of the room at all conducive to ornament, and is the one ornamented wall. At its center the mantel and square fireplace frame, painted, one coat, an old and thin blue-white: in front of the fireplace, not much more than covering the full width of its frame, the small table: and through, beneath it, the gray, swept yet ashy bricks of the fireplace and short hearth, and the silent shoes: and on the table, and on the mantel, and spread above and wide of it on the walls, the things of which I will now tell.

On the table: it is blue auto paint: a white cloth, hanging a little over the edges. On the cloth, at center, a small fluted green glass bowl in which sits a white china swan, profiled upon the north.

On the mantel against the glowing wall, each about six inches from the ends of the shelf, two small twin vases, very simply blown, of pebble-grained iridescent glass. Exactly at center between them, a fluted saucer, with a coarse lace edge, of pressed milky glass, which Louise's mother gave her to call her own and for which she cares more dearly than for anything else she possesses. Pinned all along the edge of this mantel, a broad fringe of white tissue pattern-paper which Mrs. Gudger folded many times on itself and scissored into pierced geometrics of lace, and of which she speaks as her last effort to make this house pretty.

On the wall, pasted or pinned or tacked or printed, set well discrete from one another, in not quite perfected symmetric relations:

A small octagonal frame surfaced in ivory and black ribbons of thin wicker or of straw, the glass broken out: set in this frame not filling it, a fading box-camera snapshot: low, gray, deadlooking land stretched back in a deep horizon; twenty yards back, one corner of a tenant house, central at the foreground, two women: Annie Mae's sister Emma as a girl of twelve, in slippers and stockings and a Sunday dress, standing a little shyly with puzzling eyes, self-conscious of her appearance and of her softly clouded sex; and their mother, wide and high, in a Sunday dress still wet from housework, her large hands hung loose and biased in against her thighs, her bearing strong, weary, and noble, her face fainted away almost beyond distinguishing, as if in her death and by some secret touching the image itself of the fine head her husband had cared for so well had softly withered, which even while they stood there had begun its blossoming inheritance in the young daughter at her side.

A calendar, advertising ——'s shoes, depicting a pretty brunette with ornate red lips, in a wide-brimmed red hat, cuddling red flowers. The title is Cherie, and written twice, in pencil, in a schoolchild's hand: Louise, Louise.

A calendar, advertising easy-payment furniture: a tinted photograph of an immaculate, new-overalled boy of twelve, wearing a wide new straw hat, the brim torn by the artist, fishing. The title is Fishin'.

Slung awry by its chain from a thin nail, an open oval locket, glassed. In one face of this locket, a colored picture of Jesus, his right hand blessing, his red heart exposed in a burst spiky gold halo. In the other face, a picture by the same artist of the

Blessed Virgin, in blue, her heart similarly exposed and haloed, and pierced with seven small swords.*

Torn from a child's cheap storybook, costume pictures in bright furry colors illustrating, exactly as they would and should be illustrated, these titles:

> The Harper was Happier than a King
> as He Sat by his Own Fireside.

> She Took the Little Prince in Her Arms and Kissed Him.
> ('She' is a goosegirl.)

Torn from a tin can, a strip of bright scarlet paper with a large white fish on it and the words:

> SALOMAR
> EXTRA QUALITY MACKEREL

At the right of the mantel, in whitewash, all its whorlings sharp, the print of a child's hand.

The Tabernacle

In the table drawer, in this order:

A delicate insect odor of pine, closed sweated cloth, and mildew.

One swooning-long festal baby's dress of the most frail muslin, embroidered with three bands of small white cotton-thread flowers. Two narrow courses of cheap yet small-threaded lace are let in near the edge of the skirt. This garment is hand-sewn in painfully small and labored stitchings. It is folded, but not pressed, and is not quite clean.

One plain baby's dress of white cotton; a torn rag: home-sewn, less studiously; folded.

Another, as plain, save for pink featherstitching at the cuffs. Torn, not folded.

Another, thinlined gray-blue faded checks on a white ground. The silhouettes of two faded yellow rabbits, cut out at

---

*If the Gudgers realized that this is Roman Catholic, they would be surprised and shocked and would almost certainly remove it. It is interesting and mysterious to me that they should have found it anywhere in their country, which is as solidly anti-catholic as the Province of Quebec is roman.

home, are stitched on the front, the features are x'd in in pink thread.

A nearly flat blue cloth cat doll, home-made, a blue tail, nearly torn off, the features in black thread.

A broad and stiff-brimmed soft-crowned hat, the brim broken in several places, the fabrics stained and moldered. The crown is gold, of thin plush or the cheapest velvet. The ribbon is wide plaid woodsilk weltering lights of orange and of pearl. It is striped white at the edges and the stripes are edged in gold thread. The brim is bordered an inch wide with gold brocade. The underbrim is creamcolored mercerized cotton, marked in one place by an indelible pencil. Through a tear the pasteboard brim is visible: it was cut out of a shoe-box. The stitching throughout is patient, devoted, and diminutive. The hat is one broken, half-moist, moldered chunk.

A blue foursided tall box of Dr. Peters Rose Talcum Powder, empty save for some small hard object which rattles. The odor of the powder, a little like that of perfume-machines in theater toilets.

One smallchecked pink and white baby's dress.

One baby's dress, a rag. Blue featherstitching in mercerized thread.

One child's brown cotton glove, for the right hand. The index finger ends in a hole.

A scissored hexagon of newsprint:

> *GHAM NEWS*
> hursday afternoon, March 5, 1936
> Price: 3 cents
> > in G
> > (else
>
> Thousa
> are on d
> througho
> cording its
>
> for the Birm

(over two photographs:)
> Glass and night sticks fly in strike

(caption:)

> between police and strike sympathizers now
> York. A cameraman was right o
> venty-second St.

(the photographs, both flashlighted night scenes:)

1. A man in civilian clothes including gloves, back to, is doing someting unidentifiable to what may be an elevator door.

2. A street. Two policemen. One is balanced in recoil from an action just accomplished. The face signifies uh-huh. The other, glasses, a masterful head, his nightstick just rebounding from the palm-clenched skull of a hatless top-coated civilian whose head is level with his hips. Flashlighted pavement, spotted with grease or blood. On the black background hands, a shirtfront, watch, poised ready to run, beneath a faint oval of hatface bisected by dark hatband.

(To the left:)

> NEW STRIKE MOVE
> EARED AS PEACE
> NFAB SPLITS UP
>
> —
>
> fer to Arbitrate is
> Down by Real
> e Group
>
> ——
>
> s Owners
> f Parley
> Labor
> reat
>
> ANY EXPANDS ARMAMEN
>
> HASES
> MPLETION
>
> Program planned
> Keep Pace with
> Greater Army

(caption above small photograph:)
> Veteran Chinese War
> Lord Prepares For
> Communist Conflict

(below:)
> Marshal Yen Hsi-Suan
> An impending threat of 10,000 Chinese Communists against Tai-Yuan, Shensi Province, China, led Marshal Yen Hsi-Suan, veteran war lord, to declare an emergency and mobilize an army to halt their approach. Twenty-six American missionaries may be in danger. (Associated Press Photo.)

> SHAW CONFESSES
> HE'S A 'WASHOUT'
> British satirist admits he's
> a failure, since world
> won't mind him

(Above photograph:)
> TINY TOT FACES

(below:)
> Altho 4 months old Kenneth House, Jr.
> physicians with X-rays are watching progres
> which he swallowed six days ago, to date
> operation will be necessary to remove it.
> its mother, Mrs. Betty House, at Denver, C

> National Whirligig

> ———

> continued from page 1

> T   O   U

Held against the light, the contents of both sides of the paper are visible at once.

> The two parts of a broken button.
> A small black hook, lying in its eye.
> Another small black hook.

In the corners of the pale inward wood, fine gray dust and a sharpgrained unidentifiable brown dust.

In a split in the bottom of the drawer, a small bright needle, pointed north, as the swan above it is.

II. The Rear Bedroom

General

I<small>T IS</small> half as bright and opened-seeming (and seems more so) as the room we left was and remains dark: all but the window of the side wall, whose shutter is laid back flat, and which is nailed over with a square of fresh gray screening: yet after a minute it seems somewhat somber too; or thus: the floor from the window in a wide fan and all the opposite wall is clearly lighted, none of it in direct sun: but the rear wall and the corner to the right are much less lighted.

There are two beds here, both three-quarter size, set parallel, their heads near the rear wall, their sides near the two side walls. One is directly opposite this partition door, its foot frame comes just short of the kitchen door: the other is directly opposite the door of a very shallow closet built out from the partition. The fireplace, in the partition wall, faces the closed rear shutter down the bare aisle of transverse planks between them: and the two of them together almost fill their side of the room. These beds are both sheeted in tightly drawn white sheets, and at the central head of each, a hard thin white-cased pillow is slightly tilted from the mattress case. On each of these surfaces is a thin constellation of perhaps a dozen black flies. Once in a while several at once will move a sharp inch or two in straight lines, or one will suddenly spiral off and butt the windowscreen: but for minutes on end they all stand still together. Both these beds are iron. This one we face, which is George's bed, and his wife's, the iron is dark and smooth and the pattern is plain, a few round verticals, and taller verticals at the head: the other is of more slender, white rods, bent into balanced curves.

Above the head of this nearer bed, suspended on two forked sticks nailed to the wall, is a light-gauged shotgun.

On a nail just beside the window hangs the white summer union suit George sleeps in.

There is a trunk beneath the side window, very similar to the trunk in the front room.

The fireplace

All the frame and mantel of the fireplace and the rather dark, blank wall, to a squared-off height of perhaps five and a half feet, and some of the wall beyond the frame, are whitewashed, long enough ago that the wash is scarred with matches and the grain is strong through it, yet a very cold and fine white, the edges of the work carefully labored and inexpert. Up by the right of the fireplace, and not balanced on the other side, is a wide vertical board, creating between its structural dominance and the centrality of the fireplace a not wide yet sharp dilemma of symmetries. The whitewash, with bold and fine instinct, is applied to follow the symmetry of the wood, so that the fireplace is sprung a few inches off center within its large white framing; yet, since it still has so strong a central focus in its wall, a powerful vibration is set up between the two centers.

The mantel

On the mantel above this fireplace:
A small round cardboard box:
> (on its front:)
>> Cashmere Bouquet Face Powder
>> Light Rachel

> (on its back:)
>> The Aristocrat of Face Powders.
>> Same quality as 50¢ size.

Inside the box, a small puff. The bottom of the box and the bottom face of the puff carry a light dust of fragrant softly tinted powder.

A jar of menthol salve, smallest size, two thirds gone.

A small spool of number 50 white cotton thread, about half gone and half unwound.

A cracked roseflowered china shaving mug, broken along the edge. A much worn, inchwide varnish brush stands in it. Also in the mug are eleven rusty nails, one blue composition button, one pearl headed pin (imitation), three dirty kitchen matches, a lump of toilet soap.

A pink crescent celluloid comb: twenty-seven teeth, of which three are missing; sixteen imitation diamonds.

A nailfile.

A small bright mirror in a wire stand.

Hung from a nail at the side of the fireplace: a poker bent out of an auto part.

Hung from another nail, by one corner: a square pincushion. Stuck into it, several common pins, two large safety-pins, three or four pins with heads of white or colored glass; a small brooch of green glass in gilded tin; a needle trailing eighteen inches of coarse white thread.

Above the mantel, right of center, a calendar: a picture in redbrown shadows, and in red and yellow lights from a comfortable fireplace. A young darkhaired mother in a big chair by the fire: a little girl in a long white nightgown kneels between her knees with her palms together: the mother's look is blended of doting and teaching. The title is Just a Prayer at Twilight.

The closet

On nails on the inside of the door of the shallow closet:

A short homesewn shift of coarse white cotton, square beneath the arms and across the chest and back: a knot in the right shoulderstrap.

A baby's dress, homemade. The top is gray denim; the collar is trimmed in pink; the skirt, in a thinner material, is small yellow-and-white checks.

A long homemade shift of coarse white cotton, same rectilinear design as above. A tincture of perspiration and of sex.

On the closet floor, to the left, a heap of overalls, dresses, shirts, bedding, etc., ready for laundering.

On a shelf above, three or four patchwork quilts of various degrees of elaborateness and inventiveness of pattern, and in various degrees of raggedness, age, discoloration, dirt absorption, and sense-of-vermin, stuffed with cotton and giving off a strong odor.

On nails along the wall, overalls, dresses, children's clothing; the overalls holding the shape of the knee and thigh; an odor of sweated cloth.

On the floor to the right, folded one on the other, two homemade pallets for children: flat rectangular sacks of thin white cloth thinly padded with cotton.

On the floor at center, two by two, toes to the wall, a pair of woman's black slippers, run-over at the low heels. A pair of workshoes, very old, molded to the shape of the feet. A pair of girl's slippers, whited over scrubbed clay and streaked again with clay. A pair of little-boy's high black shoes, broken at the toes and worn through the soles, the toes curled up sharply; looped straps at the heels: thick clay scrubbed off. A pair of little-girl's slightly narrower and softer high tan button shoes, similarly worn and curled, similarly scrubbed. A pair of little-boy's high black button shoes, similarly worn, curled, and scrubbed. One infant's brown sandal. These shoes, particularly those of the children, are somewhat gnawn, and there are rat turds on the floor.

The beds

The children's bed in the rear room has a worn-out and rusted mesh spring; the springs of the other two beds are wire net, likewise rusty and exhausted. Aside from this and from details formerly mentioned, the beds may be described as one. There are two mattresses on each, both very thin, padded, I would judge, one with raw cotton and one with cornshucks. They smell old, stale, and moist, and are morbid with bedbugs, with fleas, and, I believe, with lice. They are homemade. The sheaths are not ticking, but rather weak unbleached cotton. Though the padding is sewn through, to secure it, it has become uncomfortably lumpy in some places, nothing but cloth in others. The sheeting is of a coarse and beautiful unbleached but nearly white cotton, home-sewn down the length of each center with a seam either ridged or drawn apart. It is cloth of a sort that takes and holds body heat rapidly, and which is humid with whatever moisture may be in the air, and the fabric is sharp against the skin. The pillows are storebought, the cheapest obtainable: thin, hard, crackling under any motion of the head; and seem, like the mattresses, to carry vermin. The pillowcases are homemade, of the sheeting; one is a washed, soft, fifty-pound floursack. The striped ticking shows strongly through the cloth. The beds are insecure enough in their joints that motions of the body must be gentle, balanced, and to some extent thought out beforehand. The mattresses and springs are loud, each in a different way, to any motion.

The springs sag so deeply that two or more, sleeping here, fall together at the middle almost as in a hammock. The sheets are drawn tight in making the bed, in part out of housework ritual, in part, I believe, in the wish to make the chronically sagged beds look level. Sometimes this succeeds. At other times the bed, neatly made though it is, looks like an unlucky cake.

Very often, Burt cannot get to sleep except in his mother's arms. During nearly all the year, the whole family sleeps in this one room. The youngest of them never sleeps elsewhere. Even when they are in the next room, the partition is very thin. Even if there were no children, such parents are limited enough that they are deeply embarrassed and disturbed by noises coming of any sexual context and betraying it. Even if there were no noises, the bed frames are insecure, the springs sag weakly, the mattresses are thin and lumpy, the sheets are not very pleasant.

On these beds, however, and among their children, they get whatever sexual good they ever have of each other, as noiselessly and with as little movement as possible; and on these beds, after spending two thirds of their life in hard wearying work and in conscious living in every way hurtful and distortive of the 'mind,' 'emotions,' and 'nerves,' they spend a third of their lives getting the refreshment and rest of sleep.

III. THE KITCHEN

General

THERE is a tin roof on the kitchen. It leaks only when the rain is very heavy and then only along the juncture with the roof of the main house. The difficulty is more with heat. The room is small: very little more than big enough to crowd in the stove and table and chairs: and this slanted leanto roof is quite low above it, with no ceiling, and half the tin itself visible. The outdoor sunlight alone is in the high nineties during many hours of one day after another for weeks on end; the thin metal roof collects and sends on this heat almost as powerfully as a burning-glass; wood fires are particularly hot and violent and there is scarcely a yard between the stove and one end of the table: between the natural heat, the cumulated and transacted heat striven downward from the roof, and the heat of the stove, the kitchen is such a place at the noon meal time that, merely entering it, sweat is started in a sheet from the whole surface of the body, and the solar plexus and the throat are clutched into tight kicking knots which relax sufficiently to admit food only after two or three minutes.

This is a leanto room. The forward wall is the former outside of the house. The hall door is at center of its wall; there is another door just beyond the head of the table, about four feet from the far end of the room, leading into the front room; at center of the rear wall is a window; there is another at center of the side wall. These windows are glassed, thin rippled and dimpled panes, and are in two parts, but lacking weights, are held open with stovewood. The stove stands in the corner between them, the 'cupboard' stands against the front wall beyond the door to the storeroom, the table along the front wall between that door and the hall, the meal bin and foot basin in the corner made between the rear and hall walls; the woodbox stands along the near side of the stove; under the stove is the dishpan; the coffee-pot and a kettle stand on it, set back; pots are hung on nails along the walls of the stove-corner; lids are stuck between the walls and a two-by-four; one of the skillets stands out nearly level; its handle is stuck through a rift between two boards of the wall and through this rift a small piece of the outdoors is visible. The broom stands in the corner at the foot of the table and above, on nails, hang the round crockery head of the churn, and the dasher. It is pleasantly bright here, with no sunshine, but an almost cool-looking, strong, calm light, of the sort that takes up residence in any piece of glass without glittering in it.

The room is a little small for comfort, and here, as is unnecessary in the other rooms, everything that can be is blocked back hard against the wall. There are no chairs on the wall side of the table, but a long and quite narrow bench, close against the wall, and the table is brought up close against it so that the children have to climb to their places with a fair amount of difficulty: and in spite of this economizing, the table juts out beyond the hall door, the chairs along that side a little more, and when everyone is seated the room is pretty nearly blocked. The chair at the foot is crowded in close, too, for there is just enough room between the hall door and the storeroom door. The stove has to be set well out from the walls of its corner, a couple of feet from each at least, and this leaves just room and no better between the stove and the corner of the table. In spite of all the open air, the kitchen smells powerfully of the cooking, for the walls are saturated with it.

The 'cupboard,' a carry-all for kitchen implements, china, eating-tools, and the less perishable of the chronic cooking supplies, is never known in the rural south as a cupboard, but always as a safe.* The ordinary safe is a tall, dark, flimsy wood cabinet with several shelves, with double doors faced in rusted tin pierced in ventilative patterns of geometry and of radiant flowers, and smelling stuffily yet rather sweetly of hens, butter, and fried pork and of the cheap metals of its forks. I speak of this because the Gudgers' safe veers so wide of the ordinary as to seem comic or even surrealist in this setting, as a frigidaire might. It is of bright yellow shellacked pine and the doors are white enameled metal in narrow frames, and the door-latches

---

*I don't know how this got started, but it seems to me of some interest that farm families, whose most urgent treasures are the food they eat, use for its storage-box the name used among middle-class people for the guardian of money, ledgers, and 'valuable papers.'

are not buttons shaped like jazz-bows, as in the ordinary nine-teenth-century-type safe, but are bright nickel, of the sort used on refrigerators; and it is more capacious than the old-fashioned safe. There is a metal-lined bin for flour, and there are enameled and labeled cans for SUGAR, COFFEE, SALT, TEA, which look to have come with the house. It is a really good piece of furniture; and has a sort of middle-class lovenest look to it which connects it to advertisements in women's maga-zines and to the recipe voices of radio women, so that it is here peculiarly insulting and pathetic; and already it has picked up tenant-kitchen redolences for which it was never intended.

The stove is of baroque rusting iron, with an oven. It is small, and low enough that it must be leaned above at a rather deep angle. A large black iron kettle stands at the back of it; on nails behind it, in its corner, a few dark pots and flat baking pans are hung, and a heavy black skillet; the skillet is stuck by its handle through a rift in the wall and extends its round hand flat toward the center of the room.

The mealbin is a fifty-pound lard can half full. It is topped off by a sifter, homemade of windowscreen which is broken, and three trapped flies, covered with meal, brain themselves against the lower side.

The broom is of the cheap thirty-to-forty-cent kind and is nearly new, but do not be misled: the old one, still held in limbo because nothing is thrown away, was well used before it was discarded: it has about the sweeping power of a club foot.

The dasher is made deliciously mild and fragrant by milk and butter, and glows as ivory might against the raw wall.

The chairs sit in exact regiment of uneven heights with the charming sobriety of children pretending to be officers or judges.

The table: the lamp

The table is set for dinner.

The yellow and green checked oilcloth is worn thin and through at the corners and along the edges of the table and along the ridged edges of boards in the table surface, and in one or two places, where elbows have rested a great deal, it is rubbed through in a wide hole. In its intact surfaces it shines prettily and bluntly reflects the window and parts of the objects that are on it, for it has been carefully polished with a wet rag, and it shows also the tracings of this rag. Where it has rubbed through, the wood is sour and greasy, and there are bread crumbs in the seams and under the edges of the cloth, which smell of mold, and these odors are so mingled with that of the oilcloth that they are in total the classic odor of a tenant eating-table.

There are two stainless steel knives and forks with neat black handles which would have cost a dime apiece, and against what little we could do about it these are set at our places: but by actual usage they belong to the two parents.

Aside from these the forks and knives and spoons are of that very cheap, light, and dull metal which seems to be almost universal among working-class families, and in the more charitable and idealistic kinds of institutions, and which impart to every ounce of food they touch their peculiar taste and stench, which is a little like that of a can which has contained strong fish. The tines of nearly all the forks are bent, then rippled back into approximate order; the knives are saw-edged.

Almost no two of the plates, or cups, or glasses, or saucers, are of the same size or pattern. All of the glasses except one are different sizes and shapes of jelly glass. One of the cups is thin, blue, Woolworth's imitation of willow plate: the handle is gone, two others are thick and white, of the sort used in lunch-wagons, but of lower quality, flinty, and a little like sandstone at their brims; one of these is chipped; the fourth is a taller cup of the same sort, with a thready split running its full height. Two of the plates are full dinner size, of the same thick lunch-wagon china, another is translucent white of a size between saucer and dinnerplate; another, deep cream-colored, netted with brown cracklings, is pressed with a garland of yellow corn and green leaves. The children eat mainly out of saucers and bowls. The food will be served in part out of pans, and in part out of two wide shallow soup plates and a small thick white platter. At the middle of the table is a mason jar of sorghum, a box of black pepper, and a tall shaker of salt whose top is green, all surrounding the unlighted lamp which stands in the bare daylight in the beauty of a young nude girl.

IV. The Storeroom

Two essentials

TWO ESSENTIALS, I cannot hope to embody even mildly but must say only, what they are, and what they should be if they could be written: one is of the house as a whole; one may be realized in terms of any single room. The first is true of any house of more than one room. The second is the privilege only of houses such as this one I am talking of.

The first is this: In any house, standing in any one room of it, or standing disembodied in remembrance of it, it is possible, by sufficient quiet and passive concentration, to realize for a little while at a time the simultaneity in existence of all of its rooms in their exact structures and mutual relationships in space and in all they contain; and to realize this not merely with the counting mind, nor with the imagination of the eye, which is no realization at all, but with the whole of the body and being, and in translations of the senses so that in part at least they become extrahuman, become a part of the nature and being of these rooms and their contents and of this house: or in a kind of building-dream, a disembodied consciousness stands in an open platform of floor, no walls nor roof: and in a fluttering of hammers and with wide quiet motions from all sides of this consciousness, at the edges of the platform there are swept up the wide cards of the wooden walls like the sped closing of the petals of flowers, and their edges join in a stitching of nails, and beginning vertical and matched against one another along the ridgepole like the closed wings of a butterfly, the great wings of the roof are spread open and sweep downward either side in darkening, to come to rest at length along the upward edges of this squared wooden pit: and where these walls are risen and clasped, their square surfaces face one another two and two and make an inward square, a chamber, and all the four rooms of this house where the Gudgers live are here at once each in its space and each in balance of each other in a chord: and it is the full bodily recognition of this chord that I speak of particularly, which can so arrest the heart: and of how all these furnishings and objects, within these rooms, are squared and enchanted as in amber.

The second, this too is true of any place, yet it is most powerful where all the materials of structure are bare before one, as they are here. It is, having examined scientifically or as if by blueprint how such a house is made from the ground up, in every strictly sized part of its wood, and in every tightening nail, and with nearly every inch of this open to the eye as it is within one of these rooms, to let all these things, each in its place, and all in their relationships and in their full substances, *be*, *at once*, driven upon your consciousness, one center: and there is here such an annihilating counterpoint as might be if you could within an instant hear and be every part, from end to end, of the most vastly spun of fugues: and this first essence of one of the things a bare house is, the plain shell, in which the fates of successive families shall live as they may, can best be realized in this dark room in front of the kitchen, for it is scarcely used, and is never opened to the open daylight, and is nearly empty, and there reside there mainly the mere walls, and floor, and roof, facing one another and one center as pine mirrors.

But of this room I can only make these suggestions, and can tell very little about it, of another kind.

In the room

The way in is by the kitchen door. The hall door and the shutters are nailed shut. Because it is so constantly closed, the heat and darkness and wood odor are different here from elsewhere in the house; and because it is so little used the silence is so powerfully impacted and compounded upon itself that it is almost a solid block, stretching the walls apart. What light there is comes in by the gap above the hall, and by the eaves, and through the many imperfections of the walls and roof, splintering on the floor. There is an odor of sackcloth and a dry odor of storage and of a vault or tomb. Along the north wall there are long shelves with jars on them. From a nail by the kitchen door hang four or five cobs of red and yellow popcorn, years old. Toward the middle of the floor are several sacks, some full, some empty. Up in the high roof a wasp cruises, stricken now and then by sunlight; at such instants he is an electric spark. There are dim smoky cobwebs on beams in corners. Excepting a path along the shelves and to the sacks, it is a floor of gentlest, rat-trailed dust, so full the grain of wood is hardly visible. Nothing else is in the room. One of the sacks is heavy, its head nodded above its belly, it is two-thirds full of cornmeal. Another is part full of dried peas. Another is light, full of unshelled peas. Several lie empty. They will hold peas and meal for the winter. Out at their left are scraps of shattered leaves and twigs. They are peanut leaves, a good feed for stock. There is also a floursack nearly full of dried peaches. Along the shelves, using very little of their space, stand perhaps three dozen mason jars of which about twenty are empty, and fifteen or twenty jelly glasses, of which six or eight are being used: apple and wild berry jellies and jams, and canned peaches, tomatoes, string beans: One or two have already begun to fester. There is almost none of last winter left here now, but at this time of summer, the shelves are beginning to be banked against next winter. By cold weather, every jar here will be used, and every other that Mrs. Gudger can get.

In the Front Bedroom: The Signal

I LIE where I lay this dawn.)
If I were not here; and I am alien; a bodyless eye; this would never have existence in human perception.

It has none. I do not make myself welcome here. My whole flesh; my whole being; is withdrawn upon nothingness. Not even so much am I here as, last night, in the dialogue of those two creatures of darkness. What is taking place here, and it happens daily in this silence, is intimately transacted between this home and eternal space; and consciousness has no residence in nor pertinence to it save only that, privileged by stealth to behold, we fear this legend: withdraw; bow down; nor dare the pride to seek to decipher it:

At this certain time of late morning, then, in the full breadth of summer, here in this dark and shuttered room, through a knothole near the sharp crest of the roof, a signal or designation is made each day in silence and unheeded. A long bright rod of light takes to its end, on the left side of the mantel, one of the small vases of milky and opalescent glass; in such a way, through its throat, and touching nothing else, that from within its self this tholed phial glows its whole shape on the obscurity, a sober grail, or divinity local to this home; and no one watches it, the archaic form, and alabastrine pearl, and captured paring of the phosphor moon, in what inhuman piety and silent fear it shows: and after a half minute it is faded and is changed, and is only a vase with light on it, companion of a never-lighted twin, and they stand in wide balance on the narrow shelf; and now the light has entirely left it, and oblates its roundness on the keen thumbprint of pine wall beside it, and this, slowly, slides, in the torsion of the engined firmament, while the round rind of the planet runs in its modulations like a sea, and along faint Oregon like jackstrewn matches, the roosters startling flame from one another, the darkness is lifted, a steel shade from a storefront.

Here also, his noise a long drawn nerve behind him, the violin wasp returns to his house in the angle of the roof, is silent a half minute, and streams out again beneath eaves upon broad light.

But he: he is not unwelcome here: he is a builder; a tenant. He does not notice; he is no reader of signs.

The return

But now on that hill whose mass is hung as a wave behind us I hear her voice and the voices of her children, and in knowledge of those hidden places I have opened, those griefs, beauties, those garments whom I took out, held to my lips, took odor of, and folded and restored so orderly, so reverently as cerements, or priest the blessèd cloths, I receive a strong shock at my heart, and I move silently, and quickly.

When at length I hear the innocence of their motions in the rear of the hall, the noise of the rude water and the dipper, I am seated on the front porch with a pencil and an open notebook, and I get up and go toward them.

In some bewilderment, they yet love me, and I, how dearly, them; and trust me, despite hurt and mystery, deep beyond making of such a word as trust.

It is not going to be easy to look into their eyes.

O N THE Woods' and Ricketts' houses I must be much more brief. Do not, through the relative brevity, presume that they are more sparsely furnished, or that they seem to me of less significance, than the Gudgers' house.

THE WOODS' HOUSE

The Woods' house is set quite far back from the road as I have described. It faces south: first a short yard of tough thick grass and weeds, next its garden plot, whose palings are half down, and beyond this a long deep field of very moderately good cotton. Out at the right of the house there are a log corn-crib, a small and rotted barn, and a large convulsed apple tree whose yield is small and sour. It is a three-room house: two rooms built end to end and a kitchen leaned-to the far room from the barn. The single, west room, had an opening for a front door and the marks of steps which no longer exist. In front of the door into the far room, there is a porch. It is of soft pine, broken through in one place, and ragged at all the outward ends of the boards. During the afternoon a quilt is hung across nails between two of the posts to guard off the sun. There are two windows in the west room, glassed, and with thin white curtains, and three in the east room, glassed, with no curtains, and one glassed window about eighteen inches square in the kitchen, whose main light and ventilation comes through two opposite doors, one into the yard, the other into the front room. The west room is a bedroom, about ten by twelve feet, empty of floor furniture except for a small tin trunk, a broken hickory-bottom chair, and a three-quarter bed of florid iron spread with a mainly white quilt of uncommonly talented pattern.* On the wall beyond this bed hangs a blunt officer's sword in a rusted scabbard; it was used by an ancestor of Mrs. Woods. Next the door there is a mirror in an

*The work of Mrs. Woods' mother. She also excellently embroidered a pair of pillowcases, in pinkish-brown thread, following out only the simplest lines and dots a child would draw. One was the head of a man, and a balancing flower; the other, with a flower, the head of a woman.

early to middle nineteenth century frame of pressed and rusty tin: stars, and an eagle grasping crossed thunder javelins. Along the back wall from nails hang overalls, shirts, and a dirty dress, and a clean dress on a wire hanger.

The east room, about ten feet square, is the combined bedroom and sitting-room. The iron bed is so weak in its joints that Woods has nailed it into the wall. It is unmade and is flung over with a wrecked quilt nearly dead-gray with dirt, the dark, crudded cotton leaking from its wounds. Though none of the outside of the house has ever been touched, the walls of this room and of the kitchen have been whitewashed and between the resinous streakings of the grain, the wash still thinly shows. There is an iron ice-cream chair here with a homemade seat of fresh bright pine: and on one table, next the lamp, a pot of paper flowers stemmed with still bright tin; and above this, on the wall, 'Just a Prayer at Twilight,' and on the rear wall, a photograph with caption, cut from some inexplicable magazine, of Barbara Drake, aged three, and of John B. Drake III, aged perhaps six, of Chicago, who has already perfected the poisonous expression which in due time will serve him so well in his social-financial-sexual career. The caption is 'The Little Drakes,' and they sit beside water.

The kitchen, eight feet square, contains chiefly a small and heroic wood stove which has already served the lifetime of one family and is well into another. It falls a little further beyond adequate repairing, however, each time they move, and Woods is sure that the rigors of one more moving will end its usefulness for good. In the opposite side of the kitchen is a small bare table from which they eat; and on the walls, what you may see is one of the photographs.

The Woods' spring

Out behind, ten feet or so of scarred red yard, then the dirt is sharply bent and goes steeply down sixty feet to a near-level: and a little out beyond the lower edge of this bank, a small warm spring, guarded in wooden walls. The bank is steep enough that much of it must be climbed on the hands and knees: but that is necessary only when the device for getting water breaks down. This device, which stands close at the edge of the yard, is called a lazyboy. It consists in a windlass, a rope, a bucket, and a heavy rock. The bucket, which is battered nearly shapeless, is let fall rapidly, for the fun of it; the stone ballast insures that it will strike the water right and fill itself. The rope is sectioned together of pieces of sheeting, small rope, a clothesline, and is frayed in several places to parts of a single strand and is knotted and reknotted where it has broken almost in every foot: the windlass is so insecurely mounted that on the uphill winding it is necessary to guard it against collapse with one hand while you wind with the other: and even so, a third to half the water is sloshed out by the time the bucket comes within reach. Sometimes it will go without much trouble as long as two or three days on end; then, as if it had taken it into its head to be contrary, the rope slips its pulley at the far end, or the crank slips loose under the guarding hand, or the rope breaks in mid-climb, and the whole bucket goes banging to hell and has to be gone down after, as many as one trip in any two.

This water, as I have said, is warm and has an ugly, feathery, sickening taste; they believe it is full of fever. And they strongly attribute this sickness of the water to the fact that the spring is also used by a family of negroes who live beneath them in the hollow. For this reason Pearl will hide in watch at the top of her bank and, when the negro children appear (they always come as a pair; they're afraid to come alone), or even the father and mother, pelts down rocks at them which she has collected, and chunks of wood. And in retaliation, the children have a few times had the courage to slip the rope from its pulley, or once, even, to stand there and empty the bucket three times in a row before, coming to their senses, they stopped laughing and ran as hard as they could go into the woods below. But mainly they know better than to fight back, and try simply to come for their water at times of day when they will be least expected.

The Ricketts' House

T HE Gudgers' and Woods' houses are solidly of the tenant type and were that when they were new and first built. The Ricketts, living in sight of Woods a few hundred yards further up the road, occupy an entirely different sort of place: that is, a house which was originally the property of the man who lived in it, a small-farmer, not a tenant, and designed and constructed in the order of his class. Whereas, for instance, their houses are of the simplest kind of expanded crate construction imaginable, and are low in proportion to their ground space, and are made of knotty lumber which has never been painted or even whitewashed, this Ricketts home is built as an ordinary lower-middle-class frame house is, and simulates both solidity to the earth and the height and bulk of a second floor which it lacks, and the exterior wood is still rubbed with the last dust and scalings of a dull yellow paint with chocolate trim. Moreover, and again as they are not, it is overhung by two strong large shade trees, and there is a flowering bush in the rubbed, bare, and large though shapeless yard; the barn, though it is now shattered into the look of makeshift and weathered white silver, is barn-size, with actual stalls and a hayloft; and beyond the far side of the house there is a wide pit of rocks and rotted planks surrounding a narrower shaft, . . . at the bottom of this shaft, the scummed and sullen glitter of a former well, and behind the house another pit and other rotted planks and a sudden violent spume of weeds where there was once a privy: in fact, a very different and at first glance more prosperous type of establishment; but this man, whoever he may have been, evidently lost his house and land, however much he may have cared for and tried to keep it, and probably by foreclosure, and in all probability to the Margraves brothers, who now own it, and who drew most of their twenty-six hundred acres from beneath the feet of just such families and by just such careful observation of the letter of the law: and this regardless of the fact that it was from just such a family of small-farmers that they themselves came: so now the house and land

are let to tenants; and for four years the tenants have been
Fred Ricketts and his family.

The long side lies along the road. First the side porch and
kitchen; next the bedroom, connected with the kitchen by a
windowless hall bedroom just wide and long enough to hold a
three-quarter bed and still allow passage: this bedroom is the
front of the house, which is at right angles to the road. All
across the front of it is a wide porch, the roof so deep and
overhanging that little light can get in by the window on this
side: beyond this porch another large square room built in a
unit to itself; and between this and the main house, the porch
is extended fifteen feet or so back along the side of the house,
where in the last five feet its rotted boards are broken beneath
a broken roof, and above a shallow and evil-smelling pit which
was once a basement; and beyond this, an open stretch of high
weeds, and the garden palings, and forward and swept wide on
the left, a large field of cotton which joins the Woods' land;
and living here, a man and his wife and seven of the fifteen
children they have brought into existence.

The front porch is the social and resting place and is kept
nearly clear of junk. The floor gives very noticeably, with sounds
of warning, under the legs or rockers of any chair an adult
weight sits in, and is caved in in a number of places; yet in general it is still safe, and the unsteady hickory-bottom and the
kitchen rocker, its broken seat stopped with a cushion, which
are not needed at the kitchen table, are always there, along
with Clair Bell's infant-size chair.

The side porch along the kitchen is utilitarian: it is littered
and in one corner stacked high with lard tins, muleshoes, broken pieces of machinery and tools, all such things as cannot
properly be called junk because they are here in the idea that a
use will be found for them; and the washstand and cistern are
also here. The wash basin is an old and dented hub-cap of the
wide disk kind, and there is no soap because it is foolish to
waste money that can be eaten with on soap when any fool
knows there is nothing cleaner than water. The drinking and
cooking water is caught off the roof and routed through
crumpled gutterpipes into storage beneath the porch. How
sound the walls of this cistern are seems to me of possible importance, 'esthetically' at least, because the wide hole in the

hall porch above the former basement, about fifteen feet away, is used for nocturnal convenience. Because this cistern water must be used as sparingly as possible even for drinking and cooking if they are to avoid using the fever-water the Woods have to use, and even so is usually exhausted during the hot part of the summer, the laundry is always done at the Woods' spring, a third of a mile and a steep hill away: and because of this, and because, too, degrees of dirt and the bearable or proper are in a sense so highly relative and social in conception, the laundry is almost never done, and beyond their faces and hands the people, and their clothing and bedding, and their pans and dishes, and their house, are generally by standards other than their own insanely or completely dirty, or almost beyond possibility of being dirtier, short of a deliberated or cult-like acquisition of dirtiness.

Here again as at the Gudgers' there are four rooms; but here again that does not mean what it appears to. The room built independent of the house, though it is quite large, and is the best lighted part of the house, is not used to live in. Several of the windowpanes are broken out and though some of these are stopped with rags and with squares of cardboard, that is not enough: for the whole rear wall of the fireplace is burst through, letting in a large hole of daylight, and the stone chimney has fallen in on itself; and so this room is of no use for living, and there is no furniture in it, but only the odor of apples and the nearly fainting munificent odor of warm muskmelons, in their time, or during picking season the terrible ether odor of hot stored cotton. At the center of the stone chimney, between two windows, and in line above the stove-in tunnel of bright gasping country, hang a hat and a sign. The hat is round, and is homemade of brilliant cornshucks. The sign is made on the smooth side of a rectangular of corrugated cardboard, in blue crayon, part in print and part in a lopside running hand, and reads:

PLEAS!
be
QUITE

and is the relic of a religious effort I will speak of later.

So the living is done in three rooms, the kitchen very

spacious, perhaps fifteen feet long by twelve wide, so that in its meager and widely spaced furnishing and empty floor it seems larger than it is; and the front bedroom twelve feet square, filled up thick, mainly with two beds; and the third connecting room so small, dark, and stifled that it seems hardly honest to count it as a 'room.'

But all these three rooms are dark, for that matter. It is partly because of the set of the windows, but it is still more that the once whitewashed walls are so dirty. They have in the course of years absorbed smoke and grease and dirt into a rich dark patine so labored into the wood that sweeping and scrubbing affect it as scarcely as if it were iron; so that even in the kitchen, where two windows are not shaded with porch or trees, but are free to the sky's whole blaze, the brightness though powerful is restricted, fragile and chemical like that of a flash bulb, and is blunted or drowned in the iron blackness of every wall.

These faced surfaces also compel upon the room a steel-hard fragrance of their own and in this air amorphous and hairy as Spanish moss, as slab as old wet garments and corrupted meats, hang the odors of the bedding, and of the cooking, and of the people in the sweating and sleeping between whose hands their living is cradled: but this becomes bearable and generalized, indeed nearly unnoticeable, so that the odor of the eating-table, in the kitchen, is a thing in itself: for here the oilcloth is rotted away into scarcely more than a black net, and the cloth and the wood have stored up smoke and rancid grease and pork and corn and meat to a degree which extends a six-foot globe of almost uncombatable nausea thick and filming as sprayed oil.

In the front room, parallel, heads opposite the fireplace, and filling all their part of the room except the path to the door between them, are two beds not of iron but of wood. One of these beds is of simply designed and not very heavy wood; the other is of dark, heavy and ornate victorian wood, high and florid at the head against the dark plank wall, and scarred and chopped with many years of use, and these are spread with nearly black gashed quilts, considerably further gone than are ordinarily found on dump heaps, and at the heads are pillows, some bare and some in slips, in either case the ticking or slip-

cloths torn and reduced to a festered gray and the urine yellow
that is the stain of hair.

The Ricketts' fireplace

The fireplace opposite these beds is broad and high, and
handsome in its Greek panelings.

The Ricketts are much more actively fond of pretty things
than the other families are, and have lived here longer than
they have, and in obedience of these equations the fireplace
wall is crusted deep with attractive pieces of paper into the intricate splendor of a wedding cake or the fan of a white pea-
cock: calendars of snowbound and staghunting scenes pressed
into bas-relief out of white pulp and glittering with a sand of
red and blue and green and gold tinsel, and delicately tinted;
other calendars and farm magazine covers or advertisements of
dog-love; the blesséd fireside coziness of the poor; indian vir-
gins watching their breasts in pools or paddling up moonlit
aisles of foliage; fullblown blondes in luminous frocks leaning
back in swings, or taking coca-cola through straws, or beneath
evening palmleaves, accepting cigarettes from young men in
white monkey-coats, happy young housewives at resplendent
stoves in sunloved kitchens, husbands in tuxedos showing
guests an oil furnace, old ladies leaning back in rocking chairs,
their hands relaxed in their needlework, their faces bemused in
lamplight, happy or mischievous or dog-attended or praying
little boys and girls, great rosy blue-eyed babies sucking their
thumbs to the bone in clouds of pink or blue, closeups of
young women bravely and purely facing the gravest problems
of life in the shelter of lysol, portraits of cakes, roasts of beef,
steaming turkeys, and decorated hams, little cards by duplicate
and a series depicting incidents in the life of Jesus with appropriate verses beneath, rich landscapes with rapid tractors in the
foreground, kittens snarled in yarn, or wearing glasses, or
squinting above pink or blue bows, white bulldogs in tophats
wearing monocles, girls in riding-habits making love to the
long heads of horses, color photographs of summer salads,
goateed and ruddy colonels smiling over cups of coffee or receiving Four Roses whiskey from vicariously delighted negroes,
slenderly drawn little girls, boys, adolescent girls, adolescent
boys, and young matrons in new play frocks, rompers, two-part

playsuits, school frocks, school suits, first-party dresses, first
long suits, sports sweaters, house frocks, afternoon frocks, and
beach slacks, dickensians at Christmas dinner, eighteenth-
century gentlemen in a tavern, medievalists at Christmas dinner, country doctors watching beside sick children, three-
quarter views of locomotives at full speed, young couples
admiring newly acquired brown and brocade davenports: all
such as these overlaid in complexes and textured with the
names and numberings of days months years and phases of the
moon and with words and phrases and names such as ——'s
Shoes; —— Furniture, Hay, Grain and Feed, Yellow Stores,
Gen'l Merchandise, Kelvinator, Compliments of, Wist ye not
that I am about my Father's Business, Mazola, Railroad Age,
Maxwell House, They Satisfy, Mexico Mexico, The Pause that
Refreshes, Birmingham, The Progressive Farmer, After Six,
Congoleum, Farm and Fireside, Love's Gift Divine, You Can't
Afford *NOT*, Soft, Lovely Hands, You Owe It to Her, You
Owe It to Him, You Owe It to Them, Country Gentleman,
Daughters of Jerusalem, weep not for me but for your chil-
dren, and your children's children, Energize, Save, At Last,
Don't Be a Stick-in-the-Mud, et cetera.*

The connecting room is entirely furnished and filled by an
iron three-quarter bed and, on the facing wall, by clothes very
thickly hung from nail-heads. The two eldest daughters sleep
here; four of the younger children sleep in the simpler of the
two other beds. Mr. and Mrs. Ricketts and Clair Bell sleep in
the large bed. The children sleep either in short shirts or entirely naked.

The kitchen contains the table I have spoken of, surrounded
by chairs and a bench; another chair stands out in the middle
of the room; near the corner opposite the table is a large, very
old, nearly unmanageable, and almost inconceivably foul
stove, stacked with unwashed pans; and next this a broken
table whose unpainted wood surface is coal black and on
which the biscuit dough is made. These are the entire contents
of the kitchen.

*These are in part by memory, in part composited out of other memory, in
part improvised, but do not exceed what was there in abundance, variety, or
kind. They are much better recorded in photographs for which there is no
room in this volume.

NOTES

These notes, which might well be the proper device for any amount of expansion, redefinition and linkage, must be just as brief as I can make them. It will probably be necessary to make unsupported statements, and to raise problems rather than to try to answer them. Of the unsupported statements, please know that I have considered their backgrounds as scrupulously as I am able; and of the problems, that I want to 'answer' or at least to consider them as fully as possible in the course of time.

'Beauty'

It is my belief that such houses as these approximate, or at times by chance achieve, an extraordinary 'beauty.' In part because this is ordinarily neglected or even misrepresented in favor of their shortcomings as shelters; and in part because their esthetic success seems to me even more important than their functional failure; and finally out of the uncontrollable effort to be faithful to my personal predilections, I have neglected function in favor of esthetics. I will try after a little to rectify this (not by denial); but at present, a few more remarks on the 'beauty' itself, and on the moral problems involved in evaluating it.

The houses are built in the 'stinginess,' carelessness, and traditions of an unpersonal agency; they are of the order of 'company' houses. They are furnished, decorated and used in the starved needs, traditions and naiveties of profoundly simple individuals. Thus there are conveyed here two kinds of classicism, essentially different yet related and beautifully euphonious. These classicisms are created of economic need, of local availability, and of local-primitive tradition: and in their purity they are the exclusive property and privilege of the people at the bottom of that world. To those who own and create it this 'beauty' is, however, irrelevant and undiscernible. It is best discernible to those who by economic advantages of training have only a shameful and thief's right to it: and it might be said that they have any 'rights' whatever only in proportion as they recognize the ugliness and disgrace implicit in their privilege of perception. The usual solution, non-perception, or apologetic perception, or contempt for those who perceive and value it, seems to me at least unwise. In fact it seems to me necessary to insist that the beauty of a house, inextricably shaped as it is in an economic and human abomination, is at least as important a part of the fact as the abomination itself: but that one is quali-fied to insist on this only in proportion as one faces the brunt of his own 'sin' in so doing and the brunt of the meanings, against human beings, of the abomination itself.

But consider this merely as a question raised: for I am in pain and uncertainty as to the answers, and can write no more of it here.*

Another question comes up, of course: are things 'beautiful' which are not intended as such, but which are created in con-vergences of chance, need, innocence or ignorance, and for entirely irrelevant purposes? I can only answer flatly here: first, that intended beauty is far more a matter of chance and need than the power of intention, and that 'chance' beauty of 'irrele-vances' is deeply formed by instincts and needs popularly held to be the property of 'art' alone: second, that matters of 'chance' and 'nonintention' can be and are 'beautiful' and are a whole universe to themselves. Or: the Beethoven piano con-certo #4 *IS* importantly, among other things, a 'blind' work of 'nature,' of the world and of the human race; and the partition wall of the Gudgers' front bedroom *IS* importantly, among other things, a great tragic poem.

Relations and averages

Briefly again, I want to relate these houses to 'the tenant average' (or averages), so far as I know it, and to other relevant southern houses.

By location or setting in the land, the Gudgers' house is far false to the average: the land is much too uneven, the house is too remote, the cultivated land of one farm is closely walled in by thick woods. By all this appearance it better suggests a fron-tier house in 1800 in newly cleared country, or a 'moun-taineer's' home, than a tenant's.

---

*The 'sin,' in my present opinion, is in feeling in the least apologetic for perceiving the beauty of the houses.

The Woods' and Ricketts' setting is better. A lonely two miles of low hill road, among a dozen used and three or four abandoned houses, it meets very well one important 'average': that of the inhabitants of the little back roads in the rarely traveled, deeply populated and huge country which lies between the inconceivably narrow horizons of the highways. Yet I must emphatically mention that by still another and perhaps more common 'average,' tenants live in nearly flat and much less timbered country, enough houses in sight of one another to give a sense of a world: so that there is, in a two-mile horizon, or the fledging of a lonely road, the 'feeling' of seeing a large yet little part of an enormously populated yet as enormously attenuated one-trade and monotone city: i.e. a city of nine million, stretched thin against a cottonfield which in turn is drawn over earth three hundred miles one way and sixteen hundred the other.

Again, in certain respects of outward frame and appearance, none of these houses meets an average.

The 'averages' might briefly be described thus:

The one-room shack is of vertical planks, a door at center front and center rear, square shuttered glassless windows, a chimney of clay and sticks; the house is, save for the roof, an almost perfect cube.

The two-room is more often than not a three-room, the third being a leanto. This house is most often made of vertical planks, yet quite often of horizontals, clapboards, or even weatherboards or matched edges. Fairly often a small glass window in the kitchen leanto; the others are square and shuttered. The two doors are at center front and rear, and there is usually a small roofed front porch. The rooms, all end-to-end so that the façade is two rooms wide.

All tenant houses have pretty strongly in common these characteristics: wood unpainted and weathered or once whitewashed and weathered; raised off the ground so that earth and daylight are clear under the whole of them; one of two or three of the simplest conceivable designs; hard bare dirt yard; either no shade or that of a bush; no trees near, the low house is much the tallest thing in sight; no flowers or very few; other very similar or even identical houses visible, several at once,

yet in each a look of deep remoteness and solitude; the outbuildings small and low beyond proportion to a 'farm'; the
house very clearly an enlarged crate or box, scarcely modified
to human use; in the whole establishment the look of the
utmost possible extreme of flimsiness and nudity.

Such a house can be mistaken for nothing else in its country
except, occasionally, the home of the weakest and poorest sort
of small-owner. In turn, what you think of as his 'type' of
house can easily turn out to be inhabited by a tenant.

By first appearance Ricketts' place is that of a sloppy but by
no means hopeless small-farmer. Seen more clearly, it could
still as easily as not be the home of an owner at the bottom of
the owning class.

Neither the Woods' nor the Gudgers' house would at all
likely belong to a small-owner, no matter how small.

On the other hand, and though they fulfill any number of
the 'average' tenant characteristics, they differ seriously in this
respect: that they lack the rigid and mass-produced look which
comes of the near-identities of the most usual forms. The
Gudgers' double-house type, with the open hallway, which in-
cidentally is one of the finest designs I know of, is rare, and
must be derived of the double-houses of square logs which
were the homes of the more substantial frontier and mountain
farmers.* The Woods' house by outward shape, shallow, with
broad façade and leanto, is nearest the standard or class in tenant type; but having begun as a one-room shack it has two
front doors, neither of them at center in the purest boxlike
fashion: and I could wish, too, that its walls were of verticals
and that it was less closely neighbored by trees.

As against other houses in the vicinity: almost no one in the
rural and small-town south lives 'well' or 'handsomely'; the
houses aren't even 'kept up' as they are, for instance, in Ohio
or New England; and by general it would be said that everyone lives in homes equivalent to the homes of those a full
category worse off in the economic-social scale than in the

---

*I remember such square-log double houses in mountain parts of Ten-
nessee. Subsequent to writing this I find them mentioned by Victor Tixier, a
Frenchman traveling in Missouri in the 1830's. If I remember rightly, Huckle-
berry Finn describes one, too.

north: with the rare splendor and size of the pre-war plantation mansions vanished, and with the tenant-style home emerged beneath the scale of northern analogy; and, by lack of upkeep or a tradition or fear enforcing upkeep, with each category looking a full grade 'poorer' again than it was by original design.

Further comments on relations and averages

The tenant house as a shell is, then, a thing to itself, created by the tenant system, but having much in common with southern company houses in general. But beyond that, to talk as if tenantry as such were responsible, as is often done or seldom guarded against, is dishonest or ridiculous or ignorant, or in any case deceptive and dangerous. It is dangerous because by wrong assignment of causes it persuades that the 'cure' is possible through means which in fact would have little effect save to delude the saviors into the comfortable idea that nothing more needed doing, or even looking-to. It is deceptive because, in point of fact, by furnishing, by decoration, by crudeness of physical function as shelter, by nearly all that is held to be 'disgraceful' or 'disadvantageous' in the tenant homes, these homes have any amount more than less in common with the homes of the whole poorest class of the *owning* cotton farmers, and with the whole tribe and twinned race of the poorest human beings in the rural and small town and in considerable degree in the urban south; the economic source is nothing so limited as the tenant system but is the whole world-system of which tenantry is one modification; and there are in the people themselves, and in the land and climate, other sources quite as powerful but less easy to define, far less to go about curing: and they are, to suggest them too bluntly, psychological, semantic, traditional, perhaps glandular. I may as well add here that this spread beyond responsibility of the tenant system is true also of every other aspect of disadvantage in their physical and mental living. Pardon so much repetition of what must be obvious to anyone of any semblance of intelligence, but I understand that this particular subject of tenantry is becoming more and more stylish as a focus of 'reform,'* and

*Now that we are busy buttering ourselves as the last stronghold of democracy, interest in such embarrassments has tactfully slackened off.

in view of the people who will suffer and be betrayed at the hands of such 'reformers,' there could never be enough effort to pry their eyes open even a little wider.

Age

None of the tenants and few landlords have any clear idea of the age of any of the houses, nor can this easily be guessed of the houses themselves, for they have been built in exactly the same patterns and of the same materials for generations: Jesse James' birthplace, for instance (1847), is indistinguishable from tens of thousands of houses all over the south today, Gudger's house is very new (1928), and, excepting the hardness of its wood, is already, in the sense of scale that country imposes, timelessly ancient. The oldest part of Woods' house is I would judge forty to sixty years old; Ricketts', about fifty. But former slave quarters are still used here and there, and from the beginning the tenant types have held a primitive common denominator which has had no reason to change.

General habitability

It is very easy, by mention of, for instance, a fireplace, to make a home or room seem more or less well-appointed than it actually is: also, in my enthusiasm for certain aspects, I have neglected others. I want here briefly to review the houses in terms of their function as shelter.

Even when a wall or roof passes the 'daylight' test, i.e., if, in a darkened room, no light leaks through seams, it is a very poor protection indeed against the weather, particularly the wind wet and coldness of winter: for it is only one thin thickness of wood, surrounding a space which cannot be properly heated. Moreover, a tenant house is open to the weather from all six sides, for the floor is raised, and there are seldom protection boards between floor and earth; and ceilings are not at all common. Holes and broken windows are stopped as well as may be with rags, papers, ropes, raw cotton, and cardboard, but none of this is more than a fraction effective. Only the Ricketts have double walls and, in their bedroom, a big enough fireplace to heat the room. The others are large enough only to heat their immediate vicinity; their chimneys are badly made and do not draw well; the fires cannot be kept going at night;

the bedding is ragged and inadequate; the uncarpeted floors are very cold.* The warmest and best-protected room at the Gudgers' is the kitchen. It is too warm in summer. The worst room at the Woods' is the kitchen. It is too cold in winter. The Ricketts' kitchen is too large for comfort in winter. The only screen on all three farms is one at Gudger's. Aside from this, windows and doors are shut tight at night, in winter against cold, in summer by custom, and against 'the night air,' and against fever mosquitoes. As I have pointed out, two of Gudger's four rooms are so badly made as to be uninhabitable. There is no possibility of privacy at any time for any purpose. The water facilities are such as to hold laundering and personal cleanliness at or beneath its traditional minimum; to virtual nullity during the cold months of the year, and, in the case of the Ricketts and Woods, the water is very probably unhealthful. The beds, the bedding, and the vermin are such a crime against sex and the need of rest as no sadistic genius could much improve on. The furniture in general and the eating implements are all at or very near the bottom of their scale: broken, insecure, uncomfortable, ill-smelling, all that a man without money must constantly accept, when he can get it, and be glad of, or make do. Since I have talked of 'esthetics' the least I can do is to add a note on it in their terms: they live in a steady shame and insult of discomforts, insecurities, and inferiorities, piecing these together into whatever semblance of comfortable living they can, and the whole of it is a stark nakedness of makeshifts and the lack of means: yet they are also, of course, profoundly anesthetized. The only direct opinion I got on the houses as such was from Mrs. Gudger, and it was, with the tears coming to her eyes, 'Oh, I do *hate* this house *so bad*! Seems like they ain't nothing in the whole world I can do to make it pretty.' As for the anesthesia: it seems to me a little more unfortunate, if possible, to be unconscious of an ill than to be conscious of it; though the deepest and most honest and incontrovertible rationalization of the middle-class southerner is that they are 'used' to it.

*I speak here in part by deduction, in part by winter experience of analogous houses.

'Sanitation' and Lighting

I cannot unqualifiedly excite myself in favor of Rural Electrification, for I am too fond of lamplight. Nor in favor of flush
toilets, for I despise and deplore the middle-class American
worship of sterility and worship-fear of its own excrement. Yet
I will grant or for that matter insist it as important that
kerosene light is to electric services what foot and mule travel
is to travel by auto and airplane, or what plowed clay is to
pavement, and that these daily facts and gulfs have incalculably
powerful and in many respects disadvantageous influences
upon the mind and body. Because it is part of a similar gulf and
lag, the lack of a flush toilet is also of great importance. But
here I need not be quite so qualified. These families lack not
only 'plumbing' but the 'privies' which are by jest supposed to
be the property of any American farmer, and the mail-order
catalogues which, again with a loud tee-hee, are supposed to
be this farmer's toilet paper. They retire to the bushes; and
they clean themselves as well as they can with newspaper if
they have any around the house, otherwise with corncobs,
twigs, or leaves. To say they are forced in this respect to live
'like animals' is a little silly, for animals have the advantage of
them on many counts. I will say, then, that whether or not The
Bathroom Beautiful is to be preached to all nations, it is not to
their advantage in a 'civilized' world to have to use themselves
as the simplest savages do.

Recessional and Vortex

Near Woods' barn on the way to the road there is a small wired enclosure of sloping grass, and during this quiet time of the summer three mules, two of them Ricketts', spend most of their time pasturing there. They are bony, very tough, and badly scarred, and have in their eyes and slanted heads the Mongolian look which is common among cruelly used animals. All three show the galled frames of their harness, and large deep red and green sores are eaten against their more prominent bones: one is afflicted all over his back with some festered eruptive disease peculiarly attractive to the largest of the flies, whose stinging is almost as painful as that of hornets, and every three minutes or so, during hour after hour, after trying first to eat, and to walk under low branches, then, after standing twitching all his hide, slashing with his tail, throwing his head around, and stamping and kicking, still trying to chew the sulphur-colored mash, and finally tightening up, trembling all over, with all his strength he bangs himself against the ground in a shock which you think you feel fifty and which you hear two hundred yards away, and hoofs striking loose and wriggling, belly up, grinds his back so hard that the grass in that space is ripped bare.

There is also a cow named Mooly, who, according to Mrs. Woods, would as soon kill the young ones as not, and who one day last winter knocked Mrs. Woods down and stomped on her, cutting her shins badly, the scars still show, and bruising her from head to foot. She is a young cow and has had one calf, and has been crazy in this way since she lost him.

There is also a starved, red young hog, and I remember well how one morning he stood by the front steps fumbling, with his jaws, at the tail of a black kitten, who crouched while this happened, and looked back over his shoulder in apprehension, but who was himself too dazzled with hunger to move or to do more, at length, than spread his red mouth in a scratchy, nearly soundless mew; or even very well to understand that he was being tried out for eating. After a little, though, the hog lost interest and went on, and the kitten sat where he had crouched and licked his thin rat's tail smooth of the jaw slime.

In fact each of the families owns and is drawn-round with animals, for work, for food, or by more vague functions: a mule as one kind of center and leverage, a cow as another, a hog as still another, a dog in different meanings of his own, the tolerated tramp's and robber's life of the cat, the three generations of chickens, the peripheral or parasitic or almost unmagnetized spheres of rats, vermin, insects, and serpents, all in turn sprung round with tended and with random vegetation, and finally, those which lounge in the fields, and the many birds, and those who are hunted; and in any proper account it would be necessary to give such a full record of all these in themselves and in their mutual and human meanings and relationships as is impossible here: for, taking even a single center, the human animals alone, they live in an immediate and most elaborate texture of other forms of existence, of the whole need and fear and spread of nature on their part of the surface of the earth; and this fact is of a significance no less powerful and shaping through the mere impossibility of measuring it. Yet here I can make only the briefest sort of tally.

Gudger: the heavy, deranged yellow rooster of whom I have spoken. A clutter of obese, louse-tormented hens whose bodies end dirtily, like sheaves of barley left in rain. Several neat broilers, a few quilly, half-grown chicks whose heads are still like lizards'. A pair of guineas whose small painted heads and metal bodies thread these surroundings like the exotic glint of naturalistic dreams. A sober, dark-brown, middle-sized dog named Rowdy, who, though he is most strictly suggestible in his resemblance to André Gide, is nevertheless as intensely of his nation, region, and class as Gudger himself. A puppy named Sipco. Two highlegged, rusty, flat-sided young hogs for whom Gudger paid his landlord nine dollars when they were shoats. A cow, tethered from spot to spot in the green stretches, and her calf. A half-grown reptilian cat named Nigger,* so black he is iridescent in the sun. A nameless adolescent tiger cat who just took up with them. And a rented mule, who was not on hand during our time there.

Gudger got the cow in exchange for a grafanola. She has never been much good for milk. The hogs will be fattened and

*My apologies to the more strict left-wingers: the name is Negro.

killed in the fall, for next winter. The hens furnish eggs in season and one of them is eaten every now and then. Once in a while they find guinea eggs but guineas are wild and crafty in hiding their nests. In the fall, Gudger usually affords a box of shells for the possibility of fresh meat and goes out to kill it: rabbits, squirrels, or possum. Rowdy is a fair rabbit dog when he puts his mind to it, but good for nothing else; he is kept because dogs are a habit. Sipco is Louise's pet. She picked him up from some people down across the highway. The cats are good for nothing at all; it isn't often they even kill a rat.

Woods' animals, excepting the chickens, I have mentioned. He has no dog, and this alone would set him apart in that country as an unconventional man. The Ricketts, besides their mules, have a good cow and a bull calf, three dogs, very few chickens in ratio to the size of their family, a cat, and a kitten. The dogs are all mongrel rural hounds with the sycophantic eyes and hula hips of their kind in that country, more hopeful and more pleasantly treated than Rowdy, though hungrier. Indeed, they are almost alarmingly rickety: yet they are fatted to blandness as compared to the black kitten, not much bigger than a beetle, whose motions along the vast floors are those of an impaired clockwork toy, and whose hide is drawn open red along the entire skeleton. The names of two of the dogs are Sport and Queenie. The cat, whose name is Hazel, which perfectly identifies her, is big enough to get what food she needs. Two of the roosters are named Tom and George. Two of the hens are named Ivy and Annie Mae. The naming of poultry is not common and indicates, if you like, the relative 'primitivism' of the Ricketts; though it also indicates less sociological and more attractive things about them; though these in turn are more difficult to define, or even to understand, and would be merely tiresome to those whose intelligence is set entirely on Improving the Sharecropper, and who feel there's no time to waste on petty detail. These same rapid marchers* in the human vanguard will be equally uninterested in the fact that Mrs. Woods' mother calls babies coons and baby chickens sings, or worse still will nod patronizing 'howsweet' approval

*Wearing Enna Jettick and W. L. Douglas shoes by day, Liggett sandals (made in U.S.A.) and Russian Gift Shop Peasant Pantoufles by night.

or somehow manage to capitalize it politically or against landowners as the unvanquishable poetry of the oppressed, but I
will put it on record all the same, and will venture to say that it
is more valuable than they think it is, or, for that matter, than
they are.

Children are strictly trained not to use cows too roughly:
not, for instance, to kick their udders: it is liable to damage the
milk supply. A mule is another matter. Even in harnessing him
his head is knocked around some, and in all his motions relevant to his users he is used with the gratuitous sort of toughness an American policeman uses against anyone (except the
right people) who happens to fall into his power: and this in
part for the same 'reasons': get hard before the victim does; or
before, in the case of the mule, he gets stubborn or tricky. And
in fact mules are in general balky and tricky; I think they are
probably in part extremely intelligent and in part insane, and
are far less pliable to the reaction of the white, which is to beat,
than to that of the negro, which, though with its full share of
cruelty, is to converse. In any case if a mule gets tricky, or still
worse if he balks, he is in for a physical contest and for hell
with any average white farmer; and this farmer is liable to be an
expert within the whole range of bullying, battering, and tor-
turing this particular animal, and to have peculiarly urgent
egoistic and sexual need to exert full violence and domination
over something living, preferably something at least as large
and strong as himself. It should be added, in further suggestion, that the mule stands readier victim than any other animal
because he is used in the main and most hopeless work, because he is an immediate symbol of this work, and because by
transference he is the farmer himself, and in the long tandem
harness wherein members and forces of a whole world beat
and use and drive and force each other, if they are to live at all,
is the one creature in front of this farmer. But any proper set of
suggestions, far less statements about this, and about the
causes and kinds of sadism in the South, would require more
space, time, and understanding than I have at present. Here I
can only say that in the people of this country you care most
for, pretty nearly without exception you must reckon in traits,
needs, diseases, and above all mere natural habits, differing from
our own, of a casualness, apathy, self-interest, unconscious, off-

hand, and deliberated cruelty, in relation toward extra-human life and toward negroes, terrible enough to freeze your blood or to break your heart or to propel you toward murder; and that you must reckon them as 'innocent' even of the worst of this; and must realize that it is at least unlikely that enough of the causes can ever be altered, or pressures withdrawn, to make much difference.

I could tell you details, most of them casual enough, in extension of what I am speaking of, and I could a good deal further explain and guess at the causes, but I think I had better defer all of that until I have more room and understand it better, and here will add only a few short notes.

Animals are fed and cared for in proportion to their usefulness: the cow and mule and hogs first, then the dogs, et cetera. Cats are casually but thoroughly disliked and are given nothing; they are never fed, far less caressed; yet their presence and certain forms of theft are tolerated. Or again: dogs are never kindly touched by adults, unless they are puppies; the children play with them in the usual mixed affection and torture; the Gudgers feed Rowdy rather irregularly from their plates, seldom with a floor plate of his own; the Ricketts put down a plate for their dogs; the cats grab what they can at the end of a meal or from the dogs' plate. Children are very casually reproved, after the screaming has become noisy enough, for mistreatment of kittens; dogs, if they blunder into the way or are slow in obeying an order, are kicked hard enough to crack their ribs, and, in that manner which has inspired man to call them, in competition only with his mother, his best friend, offer their immediate apologies; the sickness or suffering in sickness or death of any animal which has no function as food or power goes almost unnoticed, though not at all unkindly so.

The snakes are blacksnakes, garter snakes, milk snakes, hoop snakes, bull snakes, grass snakes, water moccasins, copperheads, and rattlers. Milk snakes hang around barns and suck the cows' tits; hoop snakes take their tails in their mouths and run off like hoops; bull snakes swell up and roar like a bull when they are cornered; grass snakes are green, small, and pretty; rattlers are used as amulets by whites as well as negroes; copperheads are the worst snakes of all. None of these are common in the sense of daily appearance, but they are by no

means rare, and during the hot months of the year everyone is
reasonably watchful where he walks—— But it is unhappy to
write of animals when there is no time to write of them properly; so likewise with the plants: and so, in only a few more
words, merely the suggestion of what is textured within any
one of these silent and simple-appearing horizons and of what
in and around even one of these blank wood houses is sewn
into these human lives: on the leather land, and sleeping of
swamps, and sliding of streamed water, in light and deep
shade, are poured up hickories, red oaks, cottonwoods, pines,
junipers, cedars, chestnuts, locusts, black walnuts, swamp willow, crabapple, wild plum, holly, laurel, chinaberry, May apple,
arbutus, honeysuckle, trumpet vine, goldenrod, all kinds of
wild daisies, many ferns, corn, cotton, sorghum cane, watermelon vines, muskmelons, peanuts, yams, sweet potatoes, irish
potatoes, three kinds of bean, field peas, okra, tomatoes,
turnips, fennel, ragweed, jimpson weed: and these are netted
through with the traffic and simmering of bees and of wasps
and hornets and snakedoctors, and with the needs and the
leisures of rabbits, red squirrels, gray squirrels, opossums, rac-
coons, wild razorbacks, wildcats, perhaps rare foxes, and spiders spread ghosts of suns between branches and start along
water, and tadpoles and frogs are in the water and frogs on the
earth and trees, and arrowy minnows, and mud turtles, and
land tortoises with their curious odor, and the trees are
glanded with the nests of birds and the air is streamed and
sparkled with their singing, and ribboned and streamered with
their flight, the sparrows, ricebirds, thrushes, catbirds, mock-
ingbirds, jays, red-winged blackbirds, cardinals, and groaning
and flauting doves, the robins and the sharp wrens, the diamond hummingbirds and their wincing song, sustained in
their vibrating spheres, and by night the screechowl and the
whippoorwill, the crickets and the roaring frogs, the luna
dozing in the daylit swamp, the monarchs and the fields flown
low with yellow paper twinkling in the sun, and at the house,
the hens who dab and thud at the mealy dung which the
puppy or, weightily, the littlest child has disposed on the porch
floor, and who, finished, clean their beaks against the oak,
their eyes blue with autoerotism, the clatter of the swift and
afric guineas, the wasps lance in the eaves and the dark, hot

roof, the corn and the trees move as if a great page were being turned, the cat stalks a horned toad who will be too swift, the flies do what they can between now and dinner time, the bedbugs sleep, and so do the rats who tonight will skitter and thump and gnaw and fight the cats, and the dog dozes in shade, and the white puppy, his bowels bursting with petrified food, waddles along the shaded back yard close against the house, his nose to the bare clay, and out toward the spring the cow stands in the shade, working her jaws, and suspending upon creation the wide amber holy lamp of her consciousness, and at a gap in his pen next winter's meat hopefully dilates his slimy disk: and dinner, and they are all drawn into the one and hottest room, the parents; the children; and beneath the table the dog and the puppy and the sliding cats, and above it, a grizzling literal darkness of flies, and spread on all quarters, the simmering dream held in this horizon yet overflowing it, and of the natural world, and eighty miles back east and north, the hard flat incurable sore of Birmingham.

Meanwhile the floor, the roof, the opposed walls, the furniture, in their hot gloom: all watch upon one hollow center. The intricate tissue is motionless. The swan, the hidden needle, hold their course. On the red-gold wall sleeps a long, faded, ellipsoid smear of light. The vase is dark. Upon the leisures of the earth the whole home is lifted before the approach of darkness as a boat and as a sacrament.

(On the Porch: 2

W<small>E LAY</small> on the front porch. The boards were unplaned thick oak, of uneven length, pinned down by twenty-penny nails. A light roof stuck out its tongue above us dark and squarely, sustained at its outward edge by the slippery trunks of four young trees from which the bark had been peeled. There were four steps down, oak two-by-twelves; the fourth, when stepped on, touched the ground. These steps were at the middle of the porch. They led, across the porch, into a roofed doorless hallway, about six feet wide, which ran straight through the house and clove it in half. There was a floor to this hallway, of wide unplaned boards. Laid across beams too wide apart, they sagged beneath a heavy foot. For ten feet toward the rear end they were only an inch from the ground. At the end they lay flush on it.

We lay on the front porch to the left of the hall as you enter. One of us lay on the rear seat of a chevrolet sedan, the other on a piece of thin cotton-filled quilting taken from the seat of a divan made of withes. We exchanged these night by night. The problem with the auto seat was its height on one side and lowness on the other, its shortness, and its texture. By letting the center of your weight fall far enough on the high side it was possible to effect a compromise by which you had the benefit of a fair amount of the width of the seat and yet were not rolled off it. Lying with the head on the seat, the lower end gave out abruptly a few inches above the knee: so you slept best on the back, or, curled, on the side. Sleeping on the belly you made sustaining springs of your feet, and this was slightly and invariably reminiscent of sexual intercourse. A handkerchief or towel under the cheek was helpful while it lasted but generally managed to slip loose while you slept so that, waking, your cheek was red and burnt with the friction of warmed plush. Before long, of course, it occurred to us to level up the seat by stacking books under the low side. That was better; but even so, the springs were strong and large on one side and small and weak on the other. Our bodies learned to adjust

themselves to holding a tension of balance while they were unconscious.

Beyond a not unreasonable phobia that it contained bedbugs, or lice, or both, there was no difficulty about the pallet.
It was thin; the hard boards and their ridges printed themselves on the flesh distinctly through it. It was short, but, being
so thin, offered no inconvenience to the length of legbone. Its
texture was soft and leaky. Here again you spread a handkerchief or shirt or towel for your head; and again it was liable to
get away from you. Waking, feeling on your face the almost
slimy softness of loose cotton lint and of fragile, much washed,
torn cotton cloth, and immediately remembering your fear of
the vermin it might be harboring, your first reactions were of
light disgust and fear, for your face, which was swollen and
damp with sleep and skimmed with lint, felt fouled, secretly
and dirtily bitten and drawn of blood, insulted. This always
wore off within a few moments, but always on first waking you
had it full strength.

We kept exchanging not because one was preferable to the
other but because there was no way of making up our minds
that either was preferable. I perhaps very slightly preferred the
pallet, in part because I like the finality and immediacy of
floors and too because the children were sleeping on pallets.
The auto seat, like virtually everything else about us, was not
so near the norm of what we were living in as we might have
wished. But the feeling and sound of the yielding springs, the
always slightly comic postures of your discommoded legs, and
the texture of plush, like a night on a daycoach, under the lips
and cheeks, made it attractive under the body, and brought
with it, into a time of celibacy, a pleasing, nostalgic drift of
memory and imagination. Even risking the Sportsmanlike way
in which this could be misread, and which I despise, neither of
them was at all a bad bed.

The dead oak and pine, the ground, the dew, the air, the
whole realm of what our bodies lay in and our minds in silence
wandered, walked in, swam in, watched upon, was delicately
fragrant as a paradise, and, like all that is best, was loose, light,
casual, totally *actual*. There was, by our minds, our memories,
our thoughts and feelings, some combination, some general-

izing, some art, and science; but none of the close-kneed prig-gishness of science, and none of the formalism and straining and lily-gilding of art. All the length of the body and all its parts and functions were participating, and were being realized and rewarded, inseparable from the mind, identical with it: and all, everything, that the mind touched, was actuality, and all, everything, that the mind touched turned immediately, yet without in the least losing the quality of its total individuality, into joy and truth, or rather, revealed, of its self, truth, which in its very nature was joy, which must be the end of art, of in-vestigation, and of all anyhow human existence.

This situation is possible at any junction of time, space and consciousness: and just as (at least so far as we can know and can be concerned) it is our consciousness alone, in the end, that we have to thank for joy, so too it is our consciousness alone that is defective when we fall short of it. It is curious, and unfortunate, that we find this luck so rarely; that it is so almost purely a matter of chance: yet that, as matters are, becomes in-extricably a part of the whole texture of the pleasure: at such a time we have knowledge that we are witnessing, taking part in, being, a phenomenon analogous to that shrewd complex of the equations of infinite chance which became, on this early earth, out of lifelessness, life. No doubt we overvalue the dif-ference between life and lifelessness, but there is a certain dif-ference, just as, in the situation we are speaking of, a difference is remarkable: the difference between a conjunction of time, place and unconscious consciousness and a conjunction of time, place and conscious consciousness is, so far as we are concerned, the difference between joy and truth and the lack of joy and truth. Unless wonder is nothing in itself, but only a moon which glows only in the mercy of a sense of wonder, and unless the sense of wonder is peculiar to consciousness and is moreover an emotion which, as it matures, consciousness will learn the juvenility of, and discard, or only gratefully refresh it-self under the power of as under the power of sleep and the healing vitality of dreams, and all this seems a little more likely than not, the materials which people any intersection of time and place are at all times marvelous, regardless of conscious-ness: and in either or any case we may do well to question whether there is anything more marvelous or more valuable in the state of being we distinguish as 'life' than in the state of being of a stone, the brainless energy of a star, the diffuse existence of space. Certainly life is valuable; indispensable to all our personal calculations, the very spine of them: but we should realize that life and consciousness are only the special crutches of the living and the conscious, and that in setting as we do so high a value by them we are in a certain degree making a virtue of necessity; are being provincial; are pleading a local cause: like that small Nevada town whose pride, because it is its chiefly discernible exclusive distinction, is a mineral spring whose water, assisted by salt and pepper, tastes remarkably like chicken soup.

This lucky situation of joy, this at least illusion of personal wholeness or integrity, can overcome one suddenly by any one of any number of unpredictable chances: the fracture of sunlight on the façade and traffic of a street; the sleaving up of chimneysmoke; the rich lifting of the voice of a train along the darkness; the memory of a phrase of an inspired trumpet; the odor of scorched cloth, of a car's exhaust, of a girl, of pork, of beeswax on hot iron, of young leaves, of peanuts; the look of a toy fire engine, or of a hundred agates sacked in red cheesecloth; the oily sliding sound as a pumpgun is broken; the look of a child's underwaist with its bone buttons loose on little cotton straps; the stiffening of snow in a wool glove; the odor of kitchen soap, of baby soap, of scorched bellybands: the flexion of a hand; the twist of a knee; the modulations in a thigh as someone gets out of a chair: the bending of a speeding car round a graded curve: the swollen, blemished feeling of the mouth and the tenacity and thickness of odor of an unfamiliar powder, walking sleepless in high industrial daybreak and needing coffee, the taste of cheap gin mixed with cheap ginger ale without much ice: the taste of turnip greens; of a rotted seed drawn from between the teeth; of rye whiskey in the green celluloid glass of a hotel bathroom: the breath that comes out of a motion-picture theater: the memory of the piccolo notes which ride and transfix Beethoven's pastoral storm: the odor of a freshly printed newspaper; the stench of ferns trapped in the hot sunlight of a bay window; the taste of a mountain summer night: the swaying and shuffling beneath

the body of a benighted train; the mulled and branny earth beneath the feet in fall; a memory of plainsong or of the first half
hour after receiving a childhood absolution; the sudden re-
realization of a light-year in literal, physical terms, or of the
shimmering dance and diffuseness of a mass of granite: aside
from such sudden attacks from unforeseen directions, gifts
which as a rule are as precarious and transient as the returns
and illusions of love for a girl one no longer loves, there are
few ways it can give itself to you. Wandering alone; in sickness;
on trains or busses; in the course of a bad hangover; in any rare
situation which breaks down or lowers our habitual impatience, superficial vitality, overeagerness to clinch conclusions,
and laziness. We were at this time, and in all the time surrounding it, in such a situation; nor could we for an instant
have escaped it, even if we had wished to. At times, exhausted
by it, we did wish to and did try, but even when our minds
were most exhausted and most deafened such breath as we
got, and subsisted on, no matter what its change of constitu-
ence and odor (and it now somewhat falsely seems to me that
this change occurred with every breath drawn) was the breath
of the same continuous excitement; an excitement whose nature seems to me not only finally but essentially beyond the
power of an art to convey.

We lay on our backs about two feet apart in silence, our eyes
open, listening. The land that was under us lay down all
around us and its continuance was enormous as if we were
chips or matches floated, holding their own by their very
minuteness, at a great distance out upon the surface of a tenderly laboring sea. The sky was even larger.

Officially, so far as human beings were concerned; and literally; much of this great surface and space of land had fallen
subject to the instruments and ritual actions of human need.
Much of it was cultivated for immediate subsistence or for
somebody's profit. It was scattered with houses, most of them
more like than unlike the house on whose front porch we lay;
thinly scattered with houses; much more thinly with towns;
very remotely with cities.

Human beings, with the assistance of mules, worked this
land so that they might live. The sphere of power of a single

human family and a mule is small; and within the limits of each of these small spheres the essential human frailty, the ultimately mortal wound which is living and the indignant strength not to perish, had erected against its hostile surroundings this scab, this shelter for a family and its animals: so that the fields, the houses, the towns, the cities, expressed themselves upon the grieved membrane of the earth in the symmetry of a disease: the literal symmetry of the literal disease of which they were literally so essential a part.

The prime generic inescapable stage of this disease is being. A special complication is life. A malignant variant of this complication is consciousness. The most complex and malignant form of it known to us is human consciousness. Even in its simplest form this sore raises its scab: all substance is this scab: the scab and the sore are one. Taking shape and complexity precisely in proportion to the shape and complexity of the disease; identical with it, in fact; this identical wound and scab fills out not merely all substance and all process and contrivance of substance but the most intangible reaches of thought, deduction and imagination; the exactitude of its expression may be seen in the skull that scabs a brain, in the deity the race has erected to shield it from the horror of the heavens, in the pressed tin wall of a small restaurant where some of the Greek disease persists through the persistence of a Renaissance disease: in every thing within and probably in anything outside human conception; and in every combination and mutation of these things: and in a certain important sense let it be remembered that in these terms, in terms, that is to say, of the manifestations of being, taken as such, which are always strict and perfect, nothing can be held untrue. A falsehood is entirely true to those derangements which produced it and which made it impossible that it should emerge in truth; and an examination of it may reveal more of the 'true' 'truth' than any more direct attempt upon the 'true' 'truth' itself.

A few words also on symmetry:

On perfectly regular land, of perfectly regular quality, under perfectly regular weather or rhythms of weather, this symmetry would have the simple absoluteness which in fact it approaches in parts of the middle west of this country, just as by other roads, under other pressures, it approaches simple absoluteness under the imposed rigors of a city, a company town, a series of machines, utter poverty, a flower, a strongly organized religion, a sonata, or a beehive. But it is a symmetry sensitive to shape and quality of land, to irregularities and chances of weather, to the chance strength or weakness and productivity of the individual man or mule, to the chance or lack or efficacy or relative obsolescence of machinery, to meteorological, geological, historic, physical, biologic, mental chance: to other matters which I lack the imagination here to consider. Yet of these irregularities of complex equations, which are probably never repeated, inevitabilities infallibly take their shape. Symmetry as we use it here, then, needs a little further examination. Because it is a symmetry sensitive to so many syncopations of chance (all of which have proceeded inevitably out of chances which were inevitable), it is in fact asymmetrical, like Oriental art.* But also, because it is so pliant, so exquisitely obedient before the infinite irregularities of chance, it reachieves the symmetry it had by that docility lost on a 'higher' plane: on a plane in any case that is more complex, more comprehensive, born of a subtler, more numerous, less obvious orchestration of causes. This asymmetry now seems to us to extend itself into a worrying even of the rigid dances of atoms and of galaxies, so that we can no longer with any certitude picture ourselves as an egregiously complicated flurry and convolved cloud of chance sustained between two simplicities.

This hearing and seeing of a complex music in every effect and in causes of every effect and in the effects of which this effect will be part cause, and the more than reasonable suspicion that there is at all times further music involved there, beyond the simple equipment of our senses and their powers of reflection and deduction to apprehend, 'gets' us perhaps nowhere. One reason it gets us nowhere is that in a very small degree, yet an absolute one so far as each of us is capable, we are already there: and we take another step still closer when we realize that the symmetry and the disease are identical. In this small but absolute degree then, we are already there. That is one strong argument in favor of art which proves and asserts nothing but which exists, as has been dangerously guessed at,

*As I have been told is basic to Chinese art.

for its own sake. (It could also be said of 'problem' art that severe and otherwise insolvable human and spiritual problems are solved in every performance of, or for that matter in the silent existence of, say, Beethoven's quartet Opus 131.) It is a still stronger part of an argument, which, I grant, cannot apply on all 'levels' in all contexts, against art of any sort from the most 'pure' to the most diluted or the most involved in matters supposedly irrelevant to art. How many, not of the salient and obvious but more particularly of the casual passages in our experience, carry a value, joy, strength, validity, beauty, wholeness, radiance, of which we must admit not only that they equal in their worthiness as a part of human experience, and of existence, the greatest works of art but, quite as seriously, that the best art quite as powerfully as the worst manages, in the very process of digesting them into art, to distort, falsify and even to obliterate them.

Without any qualification and if necessary with belligerence I respect and believe in even the most supposedly 'fantastic' works of the imagination. I am indeed ready to say, because with fair consistency I believe, that works of the imagination (chiefly because* in a certain degree they create something which has never existed before, they add to and somewhat clarify the sum total of the state of being, whereas the rest of the mind's activity is merely deductive, descriptive, acquisitive or contemplative), advance and assist the human race, and make an opening in the darkness around it, as nothing else can. But art and the imagination are capable of being harmful, and it is probably neither healthy for them nor, which is more to the point, anywhere near true even to the plainest facts, to rate them so singly high. It seems to me there is quite as considerable value (to say nothing of joy) in the attempt to see or to convey even some single thing as nearly as possible as that thing is. I grant the clarifying power in this effort of the memory and the imagination: but they are quite as capable of muddying as of clearing the water and frequently indeed, so frequently that we may suspect a law in ambush, they do both at the same time, clouding in one way the thing they are clearing in another.

George Gudger is a human being, a man, not like any other

*And for many other still more powerful and less 'useful' reasons.

human being so much as he is like himself. I could invent incidents, appearances, additions to his character, background, surroundings, future, which might well point up and indicate and clinch things relevant to him which in fact I am sure are true, and important, and which George Gudger unchanged and undecorated would not indicate and perhaps could not even suggest. The result, if I was lucky, could be a work of art. But somehow a much more important, and dignified, and true fact about him than I could conceivably invent, though I were an illimitably better artist than I am, is that fact that he is exactly, down to the last inch and instant, who, what, where, when and why he is. He is in those terms living, right now, in flesh and blood and breathing, in an actual part of a world in which also, quite as irrelevant to imagination, you and I are living. Granted that beside that fact it is a small thing, and granted also that it is essentially and finally a hopeless one, to try merely to reproduce and communicate his living as nearly exactly as possible, nevertheless I can think of no worthier and many worse subjects of attempt.

The same seems to me true of every item in the experience of which I am speaking, and I could say it with equal sincerity of conviction of all human experience. Moreover, and especially if you bear in mind such structures as those of disease and symmetry I sketched out a little, I cannot see how such a piece of work could be small in intensity, 'truth,' complex richness and stature of form and nature, as compared with a work of art. Calling for the moment everything except art Nature, it would insist that everything in Nature, every most casual thing, has an inevitability and perfection which art as such can only approach, and shares in fact, not as art, but as the part of Nature that it is; so that, for instance, a contour map is at least as considerably an image of absolute 'beauty' as the counterpoints of Bach which it happens to resemble. I would further insist that it would do human beings, including artists, no harm to recognize this fact, and to bear it in mind in their seining of experience, and to come as closely as they may be able, to recording and reproducing it for its own, not for art's sake.

One reason I so deeply care for the camera is just this. So far as it goes (which is, in its own realm, as absolute anyhow as the traveling distance of words or sound), and handled cleanly and literally in its own terms, as an ice-cold, some ways limited, some ways more capable, eye, it is, like the phonograph record and like scientific instruments and unlike any other leverage of art, incapable of recording anything but absolute, dry truth.

Who, what, where, when, and why (or how) is the primal cliché and complacency of journalism: but I do not wish to appear to speak favorably of journalism. I have never yet seen a piece of journalism which conveyed more than the slightest fraction of what any even moderately reflective and sensitive person would mean and intend by those inachievable words, and that fraction itself I have never seen clean of one or another degree of patient, to say nothing of essential, falsehood. Journalism is true in the sense that everything is true to the state of being and to what conditioned and produced it* (which is also, but less so perhaps, a limitation of art and science): but that is about as far as its value goes. This is not to accuse or despise journalism for anything beyond its own complacent delusion, and its enormous power to poison the public with the same delusion, that it is telling the truth even of what it tells of. Journalism can within its own limits be 'good' or 'bad,' 'true' or 'false,' but it is not in the nature of journalism even to approach any less relative degree of truth. Again, journalism is not to be blamed† for this; no more than a cow is to be blamed for not being a horse. The difference is, and the reason one can respect or anyhow approve of the cow, that few cows can have the delusion or even the desire to be horses, and that none of them could get away with it even with a small part of the public. The very blood and semen of journalism, on the contrary, is a broad and successful form of lying. Remove that form of lying and you no longer have journalism.

Nor am I speaking of 'naturalism,' 'realism': though just here may be the sharpest and most slippery watershed within this first discussion.

Trying, let us say, to represent, to reproduce, a certain city

*Looked at in this way a page of newspaper can have all the wealth of a sheet of fossils, or a painting.

†Why not.

street, under the conviction that nothing is as important, as sublime, as truly poetic about that street in its flotation upon time and space as the street itself. Your medium, unfortunately, is not a still or moving camera, but is words. You abjure all metaphor, symbol, selection and above all, of course, all temptation to invent, as obstructive, false, artistic. As nearly as possible in words (which, even by grace of genius, would not be very near) you try to give the street *in its own terms*: that is to say, either in the terms in which you (or an imagined character) see it, or in a reduction and depersonalization into terms which will as nearly as possible be the 'private,' singular terms of that asphalt, those neon letters, those and all other items combined, into that alternation, that simultaneity, of flat blank tremendously constructed chords and of immensely elaborate counterpoint which is the street itself. You hold then strictly to materials, forms, colors, bulks, textures, space relations, shapes of light and shade, peculiarities, specializations, of architecture and of lettering, noises of motors and brakes and shoes, odors of exhausts: all this gathers time and weightiness which the street does not of itself have: it sags with this length and weight: and what have you in the end but a somewhat overblown passage from a naturalistic novel: which in important ways is at the opposite pole from your intentions, from what you have seen, from the fact itself.

The language of 'reality' (in the sense of 'reality' we are trying to speak of here) may be the most beautiful and powerful but certainly it must in any case be about the heaviest of all languages. That it should have and impart the deftness, keenness, immediacy, speed and subtlety of the 'reality' it tries to reproduce, would require incredible strength and trained skill on the part of the handler, and would perhaps also require an audience, or the illusion of an audience, equally well trained in catching what is thrown: an audience to whom the complex joke can simply be told, without the necessity for a preceding explanation fifteen times the length of the joke which founders every value the joke of itself has. I know of no one with this particular training or interest who is using words, though one man, at least, is doing even more difficult and more valuable things.

For the camera, much of this is solved from the start: is solved so simply, for that matter, that this ease becomes the greatest danger against the good use of the camera.

Words could, I believe, be made to do or to tell anything within human conceit. That is more than can be said of the instruments of any other art. But it must be added of words that they are the most inevitably inaccurate of all mediums of record and communication, and that they come at many of the things which they alone can do by such a Rube Goldberg articulation of frauds, compromises, artful dodges and tenth removes as would fatten any other art into apoplexy if the art were not first shamed out of existence: and which, in two centrally important and inescapable ways: falsification (through inaccuracy of meaning as well as inaccuracy of emotion); and inability to communicate simultaneity with any immediacy; greatly impairs the value and the integrity of their achievement. It may, however, be added: words like all else are limited by certain laws. To call their achievement crippled in relation to what they have tried to convey may be all very well: but to call them crippled in their completely healthful obedience to their own nature is again a mistake: the same mistake as the accusation of a cow for her unhorsiness. And if you here say: 'But the cow words are trying to be a horse,' the answer is: 'That attempt is one of the strongest laws of language, just as it is no law at all so far as cows are concerned.' In obeying this law words are not, then, at all necessarily accusable, any more than in disobeying it. The cleansing and rectification of language, the breakdown of the identification of word and object, is very important, and very possibly more important things will come of it than have ever come of the lingual desire of the cow for the horse: but it is nevertheless another matter whenever words start functioning in the command of the ancient cow-horse law. Human beings may be more and more aware of being awake, but they are still incapable of not dreaming; and a fish forswears water for air at his own peril.

I doubt that the straight 'naturalist' very well understands what music and poetry are about. That would be all right if he understood his materials so intensely that music and poetry seemed less than his intention; but I doubt he does that, too.

That is why his work even at best is never much more than documentary. Not that documentation has not great dignity and value; it has; and as good 'poetry' can be extracted from it as from living itself: but the documentation is not of itself either poetry or music and it is not, of itself, of any value equivalent to theirs. So that, if you share the naturalist's regard for the 'real,' but have this regard for it on a plane which in your mind brings it level in value at least to music and poetry, which in turn you value as highly as anything on earth, it is important that your representation of 'reality' does not sag into, or become one with, naturalism; and in so far as it does, you have sinned, that is, you have fallen short even of the relative truth you have perceived and intended. And if, anti-artistically, you desire not only to present but to talk about what you present and how you try to present it, then one of your first anxieties, in advance of failure foreseen, is to make clear that a sin is a sin.

I feel sure in advance that any efforts, in what follows, along the lines I have been speaking of, will be failures.*

'Description' is a word to suspect.

Words cannot embody; they can only describe. But a certain kind of artist, whom we will distinguish from others as a poet rather than a prose writer, despises this fact about words or his medium, and continually brings words as near as he can to an illusion of embodiment. In doing so he accepts a falsehood but makes, of a sort in any case, better art. It seems very possibly true that art's superiority over science and over all other forms of human activity, and its inferiority to them, reside in the identical fact that art accepts the most dangerous and impossible of bargains and makes the best of it, becoming, as a result, both nearer the truth and farther from it than those things which, like science and scientific art, merely describe, and those things which, like human beings and their creations and the entire state of nature, merely are, the truth.

Most young writers and artists roll around in description like honeymooners on a bed. It comes easier to them than

*Failure, indeed, is almost as strongly an obligation as an inevitability, in such work: and therein sits the deadliest trap of the exhausted conscience.

anything else. In the course of years they grow or discipline themselves out of it. At best they are undoubtedly right in doing so. But again I suspect that the lust for describing, and that lust in action, is not necessarily a vice. Plain objects and atmospheres have a sufficient intrinsic beauty and stature that it might be well if the describer became more rather than less shameless: if objects and atmospheres for the secret sake of which it is customary to write a story or poem, and which are chronically relegated to a menial level of decoration or at best illumination, were handled and presented on their own merits without either distortion or apology. Since when has a landscape painter apologized for painting landscapes;* and since when, again, should a cow put on a false beard and play horse or, on the other hand, blush and dither over the excellent fact of being a good plain cow, a creature no horse can ever be?

George Gudger is a man, et cetera. But obviously, in the effort to tell of him (by example) as truthfully as I can, I am limited. I know him only so far as I know him, and only in those terms in which I know him; and all of that depends as fully on who I am as on who he is.

I am confident of being able to get at a certain form of the truth about him, *only if* I am as faithful as possible to Gudger as I know him, to Gudger as, in his actual flesh and life (but there again always in my mind's and memory's eye) he is. But of course it will be only a relative truth.

Name me one truth within human range that is not relative and I will feel a shade more apologetic of that.

For that reason and for others, I would do just as badly to simplify or eliminate myself from this picture as to simplify or invent character, places or atmospheres. A chain of truths did actually weave itself and run through: it is their texture that I want to represent, not betray, nor pretty up into art. The one deeply exciting thing to me about Gudger is that he is actual, he is living, at this instant. He is not some artist's or journalist's or propagandist's invention: he is a human being: and to what degree I am able it is my business to reproduce him as

*Cocteau, writing of Picasso and of painting, remarks that the subject is merely the excuse for the painting, and that Picasso does away with the excuse.

the human being he is; not just to amalgamate him into some invented, literary imitation of a human being.

The momentary suspension of disbelief is perhaps (and perhaps not) all very well for literature and art: but it leaves literature and art, and it leaves an attempt such as this, in a bad hole. It means that anything set forth within an art form, 'true' as it may be in art terms, is hermetically sealed away from identification with everyday 'reality.' No matter how strong and vivid it may be, its strength and vividness are not of that order which, in the open air of our actual, personal living, we draw in every time we breathe. Even at its very best it is make believe, requiring the killing insult of 'suspension of disbelief,' because it is art. This is in some degree true even of the most 'real' writing I know. It is simply impossible for anyone, no matter how high he may place it, to do art the simple but total honor of accepting and believing it in the terms in which he accepts and honors breathing, lovemaking, the look of a newspaper, the street he walks through. If you think of that a little while, and have any respect for art and for what it is or should be capable of if it is to be held worthy of its own existence, that is a crucially serious matter.

And yet is there any good reason why socalled art cannot, without any complicated wrench of the mind, be accepted as living, as telling of the living 'truth,' so long as art meets you halfway, and tries to tell of nothing else?*

When, in talk with a friend, you tell him, or hear from him, details of childhood, those details are perhaps even more real to you than in your solitary memory; and they are real and exciting to both of you in a way no form of art can be, or anyhow is. He is accepting what you say as truth, not fiction. You in turn, and the truth you are telling, are conditioned in some degree by his personality—you are in part, and he knows you are in part, selecting or inventing toward his color—but your whole effort, at which you both may be willing and interested to spend a great deal of time, is to reduce these half-inventions more and more towards the truth. The centrally exciting and important fact, from which ramify the thousand others which otherwise would have no clear and valid existence, is: that was

*Or even if it is scornful of every such effort.

the way it was. What could be more moving, significant or true: every force and hidden chance in the universe has so combined that a certain thing was the way it was.

And why is it that, written, these facts lose so much of their force and reality. Partly the writer's doing: as part-artist he feels the strength of need to select and invent.* Also, he is not aware that the truth is more important than any pretty lie he may tell. And partly the reader's doing: he is so used to the idea that art is a fiction that he can't shake himself of it. And partly the whole weight of art tradition, the deifying of the imagination. All right, go ahead and deify it: I will grant that it is responsible for every great work in any art. What of it! Must it therefore interfere with still another way of seeing and telling of still another form of the truth which is in its own way at least as sound? Is there such a cleavage between the 'scientific' and the 'artistic'? Isn't every human being both a scientist and an artist; and in writing of human experience, isn't there a good deal to be said for recognizing that fact and for using both methods?

I will be trying here to write of nothing whatever which did not in physical actuality or in the mind happen or appear; and my most serious effort will be, not to use these 'materials' for art, far less for journalism, but *to give them as they were and as in my memory and regard they are.* If there is anything of value and interest in this work it will have to hang entirely on that fact. Though I may frequently try to make use of art devices and may, at other times, being at least in part an 'artist,' be incapable of avoiding their use, I am in this piece of work illimitably more interested in life than in art.

Needless perhaps to say, then, I shall digress, and shall take my time over what may seem to be nonessentials, exactly as seems best.

Make no mistake in this, though: I am under no illusion that I am wringing this piece of experience dry. Nor do I even want to wring it dry. There are reasons of time, judgement and plain desire or, if you like, whim.

*Every deadly habit in the use of the senses and of language; every 'artistic' habit of distortion in the evaluation of experience.

Time: It took a great artist seven years to record nineteen hours and to wring them anywhere near dry. Figure it out for yourself; this lasted several weeks, not nineteen hours. I take what I am trying here seriously but there are other pieces of work I want still more to do.

Judgement: Though I do on the one hand seriously believe that the universe can be seen in a grain of sand and that that is as good a lens as any other and a much more practicable one than the universe, I am again not trying any such job here. On too many other counts I simply do not think the experience was important* enough to justify any such effort; and I will consistently hope to keep the effort and method in strict proportion to my own limited judgement of the importance of the experience as a whole and in its parts.

The plain desire or whim must then be self-evident: all I want to do is tell this as exactly and clearly as I can and get the damned thing done with.† I would again be false to the truth if I were false to that.

Very roughly I know that to get my own sort of truth out of the experience I must handle it from four planes:

That of recall; of reception, contemplation, *in medias res*: for which I have set up this silence under darkness on this front porch as a sort of fore-stage to which from time to time the action may have occasion to return.‡

'As it happened': the straight narrative at the prow as from the first to last day it cut unknown water.

By recall and memory from the present: which is a part of the experience: and this includes imagination, which in the other planes I swear myself against.

As I try to write it: problems of recording; which, too, are an organic part of the experience as a whole.

These are, obviously, in strong conflict. So is any piece of human experience. So, then, inevitably, is any even partially accurate attempt to give any experience as a whole.

It seems likely at this stage that the truest way to treat a

---

*I am no longer so sure of this.

†This is more complicated now.

‡It still may, but not in this volume.

piece of the past is as such: as if it were no longer the present. In other words, the 'truest' thing about the experience is now neither that it was from hour to hour thus and so; nor is it my fairly accurate 'memory' of how it was from hour to hour in chronological progression; but is rather as it turns up in recall, in no such order, casting its lights and associations forward and backward upon the then past and the then future, across that expanse of experience.*

If this is so the book as a whole will have a form and set of tones rather less like those of narrative than like those of music.†

That suits me, and I hope it turns out to be so.

From the amount I am talking about 'this experience' you may have got the idea I think it was of some egregious importance. In that case you will be cheated in proportion to your misapprehension. This 'experience' was just a series of various, fairly complicated, and to me interesting, things which I perceived or which happened to me last‡ summer, that's all. Greater and less things have happened, even to me. And I keep talking so much about it simply because I am respectful of experience in general and of any experience whatever, and because it turns out that going through, remembering, and trying to tell of anything is of itself (not because the Experience was either hot or cold, but of itself, and as a part of the experience) interesting and important to me: and because, as I have said before, I am interested in the actual and in telling of it, and so would wish to make clear that nothing here is invented. The whole job may well seem messy to you. But a part of my point is that experience offers itself in richness and variety and in many more terms than one and that it may therefore be wise to record it no less variously. Much of the time I shall want to tell of particulars very simply, in their own terms: but from any set of particulars it is possible and perhaps useful to generalize. In any case I am the sort of person who general-

*I have still to attempt proper treatment of this sort.

†The forms of this text are chiefly those of music, of motion pictures, and of improvisations and recordings of states of emotion, and of belief.

‡The three sections of *On the Porch* were written in 1937.

izes: and if for your own convenience and mine I left that out, I would be faking and artifacting right from the start.

I think there is at the middle of this sense of the importance and dignity of actuality and the attempt to reproduce and analyze the actual, and at the middle of this antagonism toward art, something of real importance which is by no means my discovery, far less my private discovery, but which is a sense of 'reality' and of 'values' held by more and more people, and the beginnings of somewhat new forms of, call it art if you must, of which the still and moving cameras are the strongest instruments and symbols. It would be an art and a way of seeing existence based, let us say, on an intersection of astronomical physics, geology, biology, and (including psychology) anthropology, known and spoken of not in scientific but in human terms. Nothing that springs from this intersection can conceivably be insignificant: everything is most significant in proportion as it approaches in our perception, simultaneously, its own singular terms and its ramified kinship and probable hidden identification with everything else.

Along the lines of this possible 'art' and attitude toward existence, nothing that follows* can pretend to be anything more advanced than a series of careful but tentative, rudely experimental, and fragmentary renderings of some of the salient aspects of a real experience seen and remembered in its own terms.

But if that is of any interest to you whatever, it is important that you should so far as possible forget that this is a book. That you should know, in other words, that it has no part in that realm where disbelief is habitually suspended. It is much simpler than that. It is simply an effort to use words in such a way that they will tell as much as I want to and can make them tell of a thing which happened and which, of course, you have no other way of knowing. It is in some degree worth your

*I may as well explain that *On the Porch* was written to stand as the beginning of a much longer book, in which the whole subject would be disposed of in one volume. It is here intended still in part as a preface or opening, but also as a frame and as an undertone and as the set stage and center of action, in relation to which all other parts of this volume are intended as flashbacks, foretastes, illuminations and contradictions.

knowing what you can of not because you have any interest in me but simply as the small part it is of human experience in general.

It is one way of telling the truth: the only possible way of telling the kind of truth I am here most interested to tell.

Much of this land that lay out around us had been taken over by human beings, who were under and who will perhaps always remain under the infantile delusion that they own it.

But now, in the short yet extreme winter of that shadow of itself through which a continuous half of the earth twists its surface, this fragile and shallow colonization was reduced to its least, the few chilled embers which cities, thanks to their intense concentration of life, manage steadily fainting to sustain clear into the relief of daybreak, and, on the face of the open earth, only the infinitesimal and starlike infrequent glints of sickness here, death and love there. All normal human life was drained away; all creatures of the day time, under the passage and influence of that shadow, were shriveled as unanimously into sleep as when, in the leaning of the northern tracts of the globe away from the sun, all vegetable nature faints like the fading of a blush, the bees are stunned, and on the cold air in glittering swarms the tribal birds drain southward. This whole area of the planet itself, quite as literally as a weary human head, was loosened on its neck, was nodded and yielded over to the profound influences and memories, unknown to its sun-blind daytime, of its early childhood, before man became a part of its experience. The blind land itself and the blind water, the sky and the dove-light bombardment of its stars, the air, the shadow, the swarming, sleeping civilizations of the vegetable earth, certain frail insects, certain reptiles, birds, and fur-bearing personalities whose sleep is by day and whose business is dark, these were in complete self-possession. They did not even so much as tolerate the great hypnotized existence, the suspended animation, of human life; they simply ignored it, quite as an ocean is casual of the less than toylike traffic upon it.

I know of course: they ignored it no less in the daylight. I know of course: that whatever triumph I smelled, felt, heard in their presence, and whatever fear, was a merely human, merely personal matter. We bask in our lavish little sun as children in the protective sphere of their parents: and perhaps can never outgrow, or can never dare afford to outgrow, our delusions of his strength and wisdom and of our intelligence, competence and safety; and we carry over from him, like a green glow in the eyeballs, these daytime delusions, so inescapably that we can not only never detach ourselves from the earth, even in the perception of our minds, but cannot even face the fact of nature without either stone blindness or sentimentality: and we cannot bear, for any length of time, to carry in our minds in any literalness the fact of our small size and our youth. If this were merely the domestic and personal matter of a father or mother fixation, we would take it very seriously and those of us who could afford it would spend the next two years talking about ourselves in a shaded room.* It is much more serious than that: it affects the deepest feelings and actions of a whole race at the very roots; and beyond a couple of psalms and a few almost accidental artistic trills and semiquavers, what thought have we taken for it: for that basis of our existence which is even simpler and even more literal than the need to eat and sleep.

We have known, or have been told that we know, for some centuries now that the sun does not 'set' or 'rise': the earth twists its surface into and out of the light of the sun.

How many poets have become so aware of this fact that it is natural to them to use it.

In its twisting the earth also cradles back and forth, somewhat like a bobbin, and leans through a very slightly eccentric course, and it is this retirement out of and a return into a certain proximity to the sun which causes the change of seasons. As Canada is retired out of summer, the Argentine is restored into summer, as simultaneously, as literally, as the edge of night is balanced by the edge of day, midnight by noon. Just how much poetry, or art, or plain human consciousness, has taken this into account. You have only to look at all the autumn art about death and at all the spring art about life to get

*Night is, for some, this shaded room; and in this room these talk of themselves to themselves in silence, and may sometimes profit of it, and may somewhat break the paralysis of their parentage. The analyst is the perception toward enigma. Enigma may be called God.

an idea: we are so blindfold by local fact that we cannot even imagine this simultaneity. It is comfortable, and to quite some extent natural, and no doubt to some extent wise, to be local: and yet in for instance politics we flatter ourselves we are outgrowing it.

No doubt we are sensible in giving names to places: Canada; the Argentine. But we would also be sensible to remember that the land we have given these names to, and all but the relatively very small human population, wear these names lightly.

No doubt we have the 'right' to own and use the earth as seems to us best if we can: but we might be thought to qualify a little better for the job if it ever occurred to us in the least to qualify or question that right.

Even what seem to us our present soundest and most final ideas of justice are noticeably cavalier and provincial and self-centered. What would we have to think of hogs who, having managed to secure justice among themselves, still and continuously and without the undertone of a thought to the contrary exploited every other creature and material of the planet, and who wore in their eyes, perfectly undisturbed by any second consideration, the high and holy light of science or religion.

Sure, these things are simple: so simple, God forbid, that they sound merely whimsical. They are, though, literal facts. Our carelessness of them is literal fact. Any child should be able to grasp them. To grasp such facts, to try to understand them and their application, would seem as primal and as relevant to and influential upon the rest of what we are and do as breathing. Our own inability to grasp them or our negligence, which amounts to the same thing, does not qualify us very highly to handle more difficult facts which are of central importance at very least (to remain provincial) to the good of the human race.

I am a Communist by sympathy and conviction.* But it does not appear (just for one thing) that Communists have recognized or in any case made anything serious of the sure fact that

---

* *On the Porch* is used without revision. Discussion of this and other issues is projected but postponed.

the persistence of what once was insufficiently described as Pride, a mortal sin, can quite as coldly and inevitably damage and wreck the human race as the most total power of 'Greed' ever could: and that socially anyhow, the most dangerous form of pride is neither arrogance nor humility, but its mild, common denominator form, complacency.

I am under no delusion that communism can be achieved overnight, if ever; and one's flexibility or patience toward what seem obvious occasions of mishandling should be* as considerable as one's strictness and fearlessness in facing what seem to be the facts of those failures. The fact remains that artists, for instance, should be capable of figuring the situation out to the degree that they would refuse the social eminence and the high pay they are given in Soviet Russia. The setting up of an aristocracy of superior workers is no good sign, either. Certainly, beyond denial, we, human beings, at our best are scarcely entered into the post-diaper stage of our development, and it is common sense to treat us as what we are, and would be as harmful and criminal as it would be foolish to treat ourselves as what we aren't. But it would be bright if the treatment caused us consistently to reach out and grow: you don't clamber out of infantilism by retreating, or staying, or being ordered to retreat, into what any average fool can see is the bedwetting stage.

Certainly we don't know now, and never will, all of even the human truth. But we may as well admit we know a few things, and take full advantage of them. It is probably never really wise, or even necessary, or anything better than harmful, to educate a human being toward a good end by telling him lies.

A couple of hundred yards away I was aware, not by sound but by thinking of it, of the creek bending in the bushes.

We knew this creek a mile away, where it crossed under the highway, and a few yards of it down here near the house. Aside from that we knew nothing of it; it lay only very lightly across our experience and we knew its beginning and course and ending only in a generalized way, a beginning in the sprouting of cold springs, a wandering of the land in sensitive forms, an

*Or should it.

ending, or a change, at that unknown place where at length it
continuously smiled into some stronger stream. These things
we knew in imagination and yet could be sure of, but much
differently and more clearly, as if it stood in the warm light of
a searchlight beam, we knew of our own part of the creek: the
quiet noises and the noiselessnesses with which the burden of
its smooth and brown heavy water lay along the flat stones, the
sudden deeps, the submerged stumps and the sand and the
clay of its patiently fretted trough. The surface of a continent,
condensed here and there by chance into the serious infant
frowning of mountain systems, is drawn away by the action of
water into an enormous and unnaturally slender vine. This
vine takes growth not by the radiant outward energy which
compels a branched tree to burst still further into branches but
always by a sinking away of its energy toward the center, as
leaves are drawn into the wake of an auto, or as if a tree should,
through the energetic contraction of its sap in autumn, still
further pierce the air. As by benefit of that sped-up use of
the moving camera through which it is possible to see the act
of growth continuous from seed through the falling of the
flower, so we may see in five minutes' time the branchings and
searchings and innumerable growth of a river system, like a
vine feeling out and finding its footholds on a wall, or like
those subtlest of all chances which out of the very composture
of an acorn ordain upon the growing action of branches in un-
resisting air certain shapes and not others: this eternal, lithe,
fingering, chiseling, searching out the tender groin of the land
that the water in a river system is carrying on in ten million
parts of a face of earth at once, so that in the least creasing of
the land sucked into scars between two stalks of corn you are
seeing an organic part of the great body of the Mississippi
River. There is no need to personify a river: it is much too literally alive in its own way, and like air and earth themselves is
a creature much more powerful, much more basic, than any
living thing the earth has borne. It is one of those few, huge,
casual and aloof creatures by the mercy of whose existence our
own existence was made possible; and at very least as much as
it is good to hear the whining of dynamos, the artifacted hearts
of our civilization, it is well to hear, to become aware of, the
operations of water among whose spider lacings by chance we

live: and above all it is well to know of it as nearly as possible in its own terms, wherein the crop it brings up, the destruction it is capable of, the dams and the helmeted brains of generators thrown across it and taking a half-hitch on its personal energy, are small, irrelevant, not even noticed incidents in its more serious career, which is by a continual sagging in all parts of its immense branched vine and by a continual searching out of weakness, the ironing flat and reduction to dead sea level of the wrinkled fabric of the earth. How beautifully then it has drawn our country into pleated valleys, in what language it has written upon the genius forehead of the earth the name and destiny of water, how handsome are the meanderings of its dotage through yellow flats across which is seen in the hard sunlight the broken and glass glistering of a city, are matters less truly important than the wrinkling open of a gully in a cornfield, the cellophane crackle of cold mountain branches, the twinkling spiral of sand that stands out of the heart of a spring, the sleeping and high-breasted sliding along of a milewide river, the great, final, digressive rectal discharge which beneath New Orleans yellows the Mexican Gulf: and the knowledge that such actions, going on intimately in every yard of thousands of miles of land beneath the hoverings and discharges of the sky, are all of one thing, one more than beast.

It was good to be doing the work we had come to do and to be seeing the things we cared most to see, and to be among the people we cared most to know, and to know these things not as a book looked into, a desk sat down to, a good show caught, but as a fact as large as the air; something absolute and true we were a part of and drew with every breath, and added to with every glance of the eye. It was good even, to be doing the limited job we had been assigned. We lay thinking of the unprecedented and unrecorded beauty, and sorrow and honor in the existence of, a child who lay sleeping in the room not far from us, and of the family up the road, and of the other family that lived near them, and remembering hours that were still hardly different from the knowledge of the present, and all the things seen and known and wondered over in those hours.

Out in front of the house the ground was tough, and knotty with thin weeds, in a bulge. Rains had taken its slopings-away violently to pieces. After the series of tricks had been learned, the road as far in as the house was a little more than barely passable in good weather, and gave one the pleasure of any newfound skill. Beyond the house it was a hundred yards of falling ditch full of hunched and convulsed muscles of clay whose levels varied suddenly three and five feet. This ditch fell along the side of the cornfield and flattened abruptly into sand as it lay into the woods. They stood up all along the creek and on the low hill on the far side and swung out deep in front of the house at the far side of another corn patch. From these woods a good way out along the hill there now came a sound that was new to us.

CLOTHING

CLOTHING

S UNDAY, George Gudger:
  Freshly laundered cotton gauze underwear.

Mercerized blue green socks, held up over his fist-like calves by scraps of pink and green gingham rag.

Long bulb-toed black shoes: still shining with the glaze of their first newness, streaked with clay.

Trousers of a hard and cheap cotton-wool, dark blue with narrow gray stripes; a twenty-five-cent belt stays in them always.

A freshly laundered and brilliantly starched white shirt with narrow black stripes.

A brown, green, and gold tie in broad stripes, of stiff and hard imitation watered silk.

A very cheap felt hat of a color between that of a pearl and that of the faintest gold, with a black band.

The hat is still only timidly dented into shape. Its lining is still brilliant and pearly, with only a faint shadow of oil. The sweatband, and the bright insole of the shoes, will seem untouched for a long time still, and the scarred soles of the shoes are still yellow.

The crease is still sharp in the trousers.

If he were an older man, and faithful in the rural tradition of dressing well rather than in that of the young men in towns, he would wear, not a belt, but suspenders, striped, or perhaps decorated with rosebuds.

These are the only socks he owns.

He does not wear or own a coat and would not want one. What he would like to wear is a pull-over sweater.

He has two suits of the underwear. He will sleep in this suit tonight and during the rest of the week. The other suit will go into the wash and he will put it on next sunday.

His neck seems violently red against the tight white collar. He is freshly shaven, and his face looks shy and naked.

He wears the hat straight awhile, then draws it down a little, but conservatively, over one eye, then pushes it far back on his head so that it is a halo, then sets it on straight again. He is delicate with his hands in touching it.

He walks a little carefully: the shoes hurt his feet.

Saturday, Mrs. Gudger:

Face, hands, feet and legs are washed.

The hair is done up more tightly even than usual.

Black or white cotton stockings.

Black lowheeled slippers with strapped insteps and single buttons.

A freshly laundered cotton print dress held together high at the throat with a ten-cent brooch.

A short necklace of black glass beads.

A hat.

She has two pairs of stockings. She sometimes goes bare-legged to Cookstown, on saturdays, but always wears stockings on sundays.

The dress is one of two she would not be ashamed to wear away from home: they are not yet worn-down or ineradicably spotted. In other respects it is like all her other dresses: made at home, of carefully selected printed cotton cloth, along narrow variants of her own designing, which differs from some we saw and is probably a modified inheritance from her mother: short sleeves, a rather narrow skirt several inches longer than is ordinary. No kind of flaring collar, but in some of them, an effort to trim with tape. They are all cut deep at the breast for nursing, as all her dresses must have been for ten years now. The lines are all long, straight, and simple.

The hat is small and shallow, crowned with a waved brim. She must have taken care in its choice. It is a distant imitation of 'gay' or 'frivolous' 'trifles.' It is made of frail glazed magenta straw in a wide mesh through which her black hair shows. It has lost its shape a little in rain. She wears it exactly level, on the exact top of her small and beautifully graven head.

No southern country woman in good standing uses rouge or lipstick, and her face is colorless. There are traces of powder at the wings of her nose and in the seamed skin just in front of her left ear.

She is keenly conscious of being carefully dressed, and carries herself stiffly. Her eyes are at once searching, shy, excited, and hopelessly sad.

Saturday is the day of leaving the farm and going to Cookstown, and from the earliest morning on I can see that she is thinking of it. It is after she has done the housework in a little hurry and got the children ready that she bathes and prepares herself, and as she comes from the bedroom, with her hat on, ready to go, her eyes, in ambush even to herself, look for what I am thinking in such a way that I want to tell her how beautiful she is; and I would not be lying.

She will carry herself in this stiff, gravely watchful, and hopeful way all during the day in town, taking care to straighten her hat, and retiring as deeply as possible behind the wagons to nurse her baby. On the way home in the slow, rattling wagon, she will be tired and drooped, her hat crooked, her eyes silent, and once she will take the smallest child intensely against her, very suddenly.

Sunday: it is not very different from saturday, for she has no really 'sunday' dress, no other dress shoes, no other hat, and no other jewelry. If she is feeling happy, though, she will set into her hair the pink celluloid comb I have spoken of, with the glass diamonds.

George, on saturday, dresses not in his dress clothes but in the newest and cleanest of his work clothes; if there is time, if he is not working until noon, away from home, he shaves that morning and washes his feet. When there is no work to do, in winter and midsummer, he shaves twice a week.

Ricketts, on sunday:

No socks.

Old, black sunday shoes, washed off with water, and slashed with a razor at the broadest part of the feet.

Very old dark trousers with the compound creases of two ironings in them; nearly new white suspenders with narrow blue stripes down the sides and brown dots down the centers, the strap at the right attached to the trousers by a rusty nail.

A nearly new blue work shirt, worn perhaps twice before since laundering; the sleeves rolled down, the cuffs buttoned, the collar buttoned; no tie.

An open vest, too wide and short for him, of heavy, worn-out, gray-and-black wool; his watch and chain joining it across the waist.

A very old and carefully kept dark felt hat with a narrow band and a delicate bow.

A pair of horn-rimmed spectacles.

The spectacles are worn only on sunday and are perhaps mainly symbolic of the day and of his dignity as a reader in church; yet, too, they have strong small lenses. He bought them at a five-and-ten-cent store in Cherokee City.

Woods, on sunday:

Of the head covering I have no certain memory, yet two images. A hat of coarse-grained, strongly yellow straw, shaped by machine as felt hats are by the owner's hands, with a striped band. And: a nearly new, sober plaid, flat cap, of the sort which juts wide above the ears, and of a kind of crackling cheapness which one rain destroys.

Shoes: the oxfords which at one time were his dress shoes, and in which his wife has worked during the week.

Trousers such as seventeen-year-old boys of small towns select for best who can spend no money and want what flash they can get: a coarse-meshed and scratchy cotton-wool, stiffened with glue, of a bright and youthful yellow-gray crossed in wide squares by horizontals of blue-green and verticals of green-blue, and thinly pebbled with small nodules of red, orange, and purple wool. They are a little large for him. The original crease is entirely gone at the knee and is very sharp from knee to cuff. The suspenders are printed with spaced knots of small blue flowers; are worn out, and have been laundered.

A white shirt, starched; thin brown stripes. The sleeves have been cut off just above the elbows and coarsely hemmed. There are rust marks all over it, and the image of a flatiron is scorched just beneath the heart. An originally white piqué detachable collar, blue-gray from laundering, the fray scissored clean. A white cotton tie with two narrow black lines along each edge; about an inch wide throughout; both 'ends' out; the end next the body much longer than the outside end, and showing three or four inches of knitting-wear.

One day's beard; the mustache trimmed neat and short; the temples and the slender, corded, behind-head, trimmed nearly naked and showing the criss-crossed, quilting work of the scissors, and the meekness of the pallid scalp; scraped toast.

The children, washed and combed, barefooted, with clean feet and legs; clean clothes on: I will tell more of them later; so, too, of Mrs. Woods, and Mrs. Ricketts, and of the Ricketts girls: at present, more of the daily clothing.

On monday Gudger puts on cleanly washed workclothes; the other two men, whose laundering is done less often, change their clothing in a more casual cycle, two to several weeks long: I want now to try to describe these work clothes: shoes, overalls, shirts, head coverings: variants, general remarks: and to speak here perhaps, not of these three men only, but a little more generally as well.

On all the clothing here to be spoken of there are, within the narrow range of availabilities, so many variants that one cannot properly name anything as 'typical,' but roughly align several 'types.' I could say, for instance:

Of shoes: ordinary work shoes, to be described later, may be called 'typical'; but only if you remember that old sunday shoes, tennis sneakers, high tennis shoes, sandals, moccasins, bare feet, and even boots, are not at all rarely used: it should be known, too, that there are many kinds of further, personal treatment of shoes. Mainly, this: Many men, by no means all, like to cut holes through the uppers for foot-spread and for ventilation: and in this they differ a good deal between utility and art. You seldom see purely utilitarian slashes: even the bluntest of these are liable to be patterned a little more than mere use requires: on the other hand, some shoes have been worked on with a wonderful amount of patience and studiousness toward a kind of beauty, taking the memory of an ordinary sandal for a model, and greatly elaborating and improving it. I have seen shoes so beautifully worked in this way that their durability was greatly reduced. Generally speaking, those who do this really careful work are negroes; but again, by no means all of the negroes are 'artists' in this way.

Of overalls, you could say that they are the standard working garment in the country south, and that blue is the standard color. But you should add that old sunday pants in varying degrees of decay are also perhaps half as much used: that striped and khaki overalls sometimes appear and mechanics' coveralls, and dungarees, and khaki work pants:

And again, speaking now of shirts, that though the blue workshirt is standard, there are also gray and brown workshirts; and besides these, old sunday shirts (white or striped), and now and then a homemade shirt, and undershirts, polo shirts, and jerseys:

And again of these categories of body covering, that, though all the variants appear among whites, they are a good deal more frequent among negroes; and again, too, that among the negroes the original predilections for colors, textures, symbolisms, and contrasts, and the subsequent modifications and embellishments, are much more free and notable.

And of hats, you could say that the standard is the ordinary farmers' straw sold at crossroads stores: but here you would be wrong for several reasons. Perhaps half the tenants wear these straws, but even in that category there are many differences in choice of kind at the same price, ranging from hats as conservative in size and shape as the city felts they imitate, through the whole register of what is supposed to be 'typical' to the american farmer, to hats which are only slight modifications of the ten-gallon and of the sombrero. And besides these straws: again there are all kinds of variants: old sunday hats being one whole class; another, caps emulous of small-town and city and factory men: baseball caps, the little caps which are the gifts of flour and paint companies, factory caps; imitation pith helmets imitative of foremen imitative of landowners imitative of the colonists in pith-helmet melodramas; occasionally, too, a homemade hat or cap: and here again, both in choice and in modification, the negroes are much the richer.

There will be no time, though, to go into these variants beyond their mention, nor any time at all to talk of negro work and sunday clothing, which in every respect seems to me, as few other things in this country do, an expression of a genius distributed among almost the whole of a race, so powerful and of such purity that even in its imitations of and plagiarisms on the white race, it is all but incapable of sterility.*

But now having suggested varieties, I want to lay out and tell of 'types,' speaking of the white race.

In general, then: the shoes are either work shoes of one age or another or worn-out sunday oxfords. The body garments are blue overalls and blue work shirts; again, with a wide range of age. The head coverings are straw hats or old sunday hats, or occasionally some more urban form of cap. These things have been bought ready-made, so consistently that any home-made substitute calls for a note to itself. Now a few further notes, on overalls and work shirts.

So far as I know, overalls are a garment native to this country. Subject to the substitutions I have spoken of, they are, nevertheless, the standard or classical garment at very least (to stay within our frame) of the southern rural American working man: they are his uniform, the badge and proclamation of his peasantry. There seems to be such a deep classicism in 'peasant' clothing in all places and in differing times that, for instance, a Russian and a southern woman of this country, of a deep enough class, would be undistinguishable by their clothing: moreover, it moves backward and forward in time: so that Mrs. Ricketts, for instance, is probably undistinguishable from a woman of her class five hundred years ago. But overalls are a relatively new and local garment.

Perhaps little can be said of them, after all: yet something. The basis: what they are: can best be seen when they are still new; before they have lost (or gained) shape and color and

*There is a large class of sober, respectable, pious, mainly middle-aged ne-groes who in every way react intensely against the others of their race, and as intensely toward imitation of the most respectable whites. Their clothing, for instance, has no color in it anywhere, but is entirely black-and-white; and the patterns are equally severe. But even here, the whites are so blazing and starchedly white, and the blacks so waxed-ironed dead, and the clothes are borne in so profound, delicate, and lovely a sobriety, that I doubt the white race has ever approached it.

In all this on negroes, by the way, I am speaking strictly of small towns and of deep country. City negroes, even in the south, are modified; and those of the north are another thing again.

texture; and before the white seams of their structure have lost their brilliance.

Overalls.

They are pronounced overhauls.

Try—I cannot write of it here—to imagine and to know, as against other garments, the difference of their feeling against your body; drawn-on, and bibbed on the whole belly and chest, naked from the kidneys up behind, save for broad crossed straps, and slung by these straps from the shoulders; the slanted pockets on each thigh, the deep square pockets on each buttock; the complex and slanted structures, on the chest, of the pockets shaped for pencils, rulers, and watches; the coldness of sweat when they are young, and their stiffness; their sweetness to the skin and pleasure of sweating when they are old; the thin metal buttons of the fly; the lifting aside of the straps and the deep slipping downward in defecation; the belt some men use with them to steady their middles; the swift, simple, and inevitably supine gestures of dressing and of un-dressing, which, as is less true of any other garment, are those of harnessing and of unharnessing the shoulders of a tired and hard-used animal.

They are round as stovepipes in the legs (though some wives, told to, crease them).

In the strapping across the kidneys they again resemble work harness, and in their crossed straps and tin buttons.

And in the functional pocketing of their bib, a harness mod-ified to the convenience of a used animal of such high intelli-gence that he has use for tools.

And in their whole stature: full covering of the cloven strength of the legs and thighs and of the loins; then nakedness and harnessing behind, naked along the flanks; and in front, the short, squarely tapered, powerful towers of the belly and chest to above the nipples.

And on this façade, the cloven halls for the legs, the strong-seamed, structured opening for the genitals, the broad hori-zontal at the waist, the slant thigh pockets, the buttons at the point of each hip and on the breast, the geometric structures of the usages of the simpler trades—the complexed seams of utilitarian pockets which are so brightly picked out against darkness when the seam-threadings, double and triple stitched, are still white, so that a new suit of overalls has among its beauties those of a blueprint: and they are a map of a working man.

The shirts too; squarely cut, and strongly seamed; with big square pockets and with metal buttons: the cloth stiff, the sweat cold when it is new, the collar large in newness and standing out in angles under the ears; so that in these new workclothes a man has the shy and silly formal charm of a mail-order-catalogue engraving.

The changes that age, use, weather, work upon these.

They have begun with the massive yet delicate beauty of most things which are turned out most cheaply in great tribes by machines: and on this basis of structure they are changed into images and marvels of nature.

The structures sag, and take on the look, some of use; some, the pencil pockets, the pretty atrophies of what is never used; the edges of the thigh pockets become stretched and lie open, fluted, like the gills of a fish. The bright seams lose their whiteness and are lines and ridges. The whole fabric is shrunken to size, which was bought large. The whole shape, texture, color, finally substance, all are changed. The shape, particularly along the urgent frontage of the thighs, so that the whole structure of the knee and musculature of the thigh is sculptured there; each man's garment wearing the shape and beauty of his induplicable body. The texture and the color change in union, by sweat, sun, laundering, between the steady pressures of its use and age: both, at length, into realms of fine softness and marvel of draping and velvet plays of light which chamois and silk can only suggest, not touch;* and into a region and scale of blues, subtle, delicious, and deft beyond what I have ever seen elsewhere approached except in rare skies, the smoky light some days are filmed with, and some of the blues of Cézanne: one could watch and touch even one such garment, study it, with the eyes, the fingers, and the subtlest lips, almost illimitably long, and never fully learn it; and I saw no two which

*The textures of old paper money.

did not hold some world of exquisiteness of its own. Finally, too; particularly athwart the crest and swing of the shoulders, of the shirts: this fabric breaks like snow, and is stitched and patched: these break, and again are stitched and patched and ruptured, and stitches and patches are manifolded upon the stitches and patches, and more on these, so that at length, at the shoulders, the shirt contains virtually nothing of the original fabric and a man, George Gudger, I remember so well, and many hundreds of others like him, wears in his work on the power of his shoulders a fabric as intricate and fragile, and as deeply in honor of the reigning sun, as the feather mantle of a Toltec prince.

Gudger has three; it is perhaps four changes of overalls and workshirts. They are, set by set, in stages of age, and of beauty, distinctly apart from one another; and of the three I remember, each should at best be considered separately and at full length. I have room here to say only that they represent medium-early, middle, and medium-late stages, and to suggest a little more about these. The youngest are still dark; their seams are still visible; the cloth has not yet lost all of its hardness, nor the buttons their brightness. They have taken the shape of the leg, yet they are still the doing as much of machinery as of nature. The middle-aged are fully soft and elegantly textured, and are lost out of all machinery into a full prime of nature. The mold of the body is fully taken, the seams are those of a living plant or animal, the cloth's grain is almost invisible, the buttons are rubbed and mild, the blue is at the full silent, greatly restrained strength of its range; the patches in the overalls are few and strategic, the right* knee, the two bones of the rump, the elbows, the shoulders are quietly fledged: the garments are still wholly competent and at their fullness of comfort. The old: the cloth sleeps against all salients of the body in complete peace, and in its loose hangings, from the knee downward, is fallen and wandered in the first full loss of form into foldings I believe no sculptor has ever touched. The blue is so vastly fainted and withdrawn it is discernible scarcely more as blue than as that most pacific silver which the

---

*The left knee is rubbed thin and has absorbed irreducibly the gold shadow of the blended colors of the clays of that neighborhood.

bone wood of the houses and the visage of genius seem to shed, and is a color and cloth seeming ancient, veteran, composed, and patient to the source of being, as too the sleepings and the drifts of form. The shoulders are that full net of sewn snowflakes of which I spoke. The buttons are blind as cataracts, and slip their soft holes. The whole of the seat and of the knees and elbows* are broken and patched, the patches subdued in age almost with the original cloth, drawn far forward toward the feathering of the shoulders. There is a more youthful stage than the youngest of these; Ricketts, in his photograph here, wears such overalls; there are many median modulations; and there is a stage later than the latest here, as I saw in the legs of Woods' overalls, which had so entirely lost one kind of tendency to form that they had gained another, and were wrinkled minutely and innumerably as may best be paralleled by old thin oilskin crumpled, and by the skin of some aged faces.

Shoes

They are one of the most ordinary types of working shoe: the blucher design, and soft in the prow, lacking the seam across the root of the big toe: covering the ankles: looped straps at the heels: blunt, broad, and rounded at the toe: broad-heeled: made up of most simple roundnesses and squarings and flats, of dark brown raw thick leathers nailed, and sewn coarsely to one another in courses and patterns of doubled and tripled seams, and such throughout that like many other small objects they have great massiveness and repose and are, as the houses and overalls are, and the feet and legs of the women, who go barefooted so much, fine pieces of architecture.

They are softened, in the uppers, with use, and the soles are rubbed thin enough, I estimate, that the ticklish grain of the ground can be felt through at the center of the forward sole. The heels are deeply biased. Clay is worked into the substance of the uppers and a loose dust of clay lies over them. They have visibly though to the eye subtly taken the mold of the foot,

---

*Much of the time the sleeves are rolled high and tight at the height of the biceps; but not always. Enough that these patchings are by other comparisons slight, but not so little but that there are large and manifold patches.

and structures of the foot are printed through them in dark sweat at the ankles, and at the roots of the toes. They are worn without socks, and by experience of similar shoes I know that each man's shoe, in long enough course of wear, takes as his clothing does the form of his own flesh and bones, and would feel as uneasy to any other as if A, glancing into the mirror, were met by B's eyes, and to their owner, a natural part though enforcement of the foot, which may be used or shed at will. There is great pleasure in a sockless and sweated foot in the fitted leathers of a shoe.

The shoes are worn for work. At home, resting, men always go barefooted. This is no symptom of discomfort, though: it is, insofar as it is conscious, merely an exchange of mutually enhancing pleasures, and is at least as natural as the habituated use and lying by of hats or of 'reading-glasses.'

So far as I could see, shoes are never mended. They are worn out like animals to a certain ancient stage and chance of money at which a man buys a new pair; then, just as old sunday shoes do, they become the inheritance of a wife.

Ricketts' shoes are boldly slashed open to accommodate as they scarcely can the years of pain in his feet. The worst of this pain is in stirrup corns, a solid stripe of stony and excruciating pearls across the ball of each foot; for two years, years ago, he rode mules all of each day. Recognizing my own tendency half-consciously to alter my walk or even to limp under certain conditions of mental insecurity, and believing Ricketts to be one of the most piteously insecure men I have ever known, I suspect, too, that nervous modifications in his walking have had much to do with destroying his feet.

Hats

It happens that not one of the three men uses any form of the farmer's-straw which is popularly thought of as the routine hat; and this may well be, in part (and in many other men), in reaction against a rural-identifying label too glibly applied to them. It is certain of Gudger, anyhow, that his head-covering, like his sunday belt and the pull-over sweater he wants, are city symbols against a rural tradition: indeed, it is industrial, or is the symbol almost of a skilled trade: a handsome twenty-five-cent machinist's cap made of ticking in bold stripes of blue-white and dark blue, drawing all possible elements of his square-chopped, goodlooking, and ineradicably rural face into city and machine suggestions.

Woods wears an exceedingly old felt hat, in which some holes are worn ragged and others cut in diamond shapes for ventilation and in respect for one of the sporty traditions among certain, usually younger, working men—negroes in particular—who reduce hats of a good color to a kind of improved and dashingly worn skullcap, or cut them into the shapes of crowns.

There is greatly among negroes,* and considerably, too, among working-class whites, an apparent reverence for the natural and symbolic dignities of the head (which is generally lost in the softer classes of white): so that, perhaps even more than the rest of the body, it is dressed according to symbolic and imitative enforcements. All symbolisms in clothing are complex and corrupt in this country; they are so specially so in the matter of hats, and the variety of personal choice is so wide, it can easily seem pure casual chance and carelessness, which I am sure it is not. In any case an absolute minimum social and egoistic requirement of a man's hat in this class and country is that it be ready-made and store bought. And so the fact that Ricketts is willing to work and to appear in public in a home made hat is significant of his abandonment 'beneath' the requirements of these symbologies, both toward himself and toward his world. A hat could be bought for fifteen cents. But he, and his family, all wear identical hats, which they casually exchange among themselves. They are made of cornshucks. These are plaited into a long ribbon; the ribbon is then sewn against its own edges from center outward in concentric spirals. Margaret or Paralee can make one in a day. They are the shape of very shallow cones, about eight inches in diameter, light enough in the crown that they do not stay easily on the head. They are not only unmistakably home made, and betraying of the most deeply rural class; they suggest also the orient or what is named the 'savage.' The shucks are of a

*Certain of their sculptures in their native continent seem to me to habitually embody this reverence toward the head as other human work does only sporadically, and more confusedly: and this seems to give background and impulse to the beauty of headdress and head-bearing in american country negroes.

metal-silk brilliance I have never seen in other straw, and in this, its painstaking but unachieved symmetries, and the cone and outward spiral, each hat is an extraordinary and beautiful object: but this is irrelevant to its social meanings, as are nearly all products of honesty, intelligence, and full innocence.

Gudger, then: conventional, middle-aged unslashed work shoes; three suits of overalls and work shirts, all blue, in more uniformity to begin with and in more distinction apart through what is done with them, than any tailor would or could create; a machinist's cap; a modification of the Leyendecker face, brick red, clean shaven; a medium-height, powerful, football player's body modified into the burlings of oak and into slow square qualities blending those of the lion and the ox:

Ricketts: overalls too, I think not more than two suits, one youthful, and one very old; in shirts, a confusion of blues with torn white shirts of sundays ten years foundered; slashed, crippled shoes, standing on the outward rims of his heels; long matted hair on the low forehead, flashing, foxy, crazy eyes, a great frowning scoop of dark mustache; a dirty platinum halo; in all his clothing dirtier; a somehow willowy and part feminine yet powerful body, seeming a little soft at the hips as if he might be girlish white there:

Woods: an old man with a lightly made, still vital and sexually engaging body, the beautiful and light-boned, pleasingly carried, skeptic's unconquered head of those men whose ancestors are birds, not mammals: clothed in fine saggings of blue and flangings of white or, as I will now further indicate:

At home and at leisure, barefooted and naked to the waist, the feet narrow and almost fastidious, showing their bones, the elbows sharp like pulleys, the bones sharp at the peaks of the shoulders, and the ribs; strong clearly made and nearly hairless breasts of the form that seems common in men of India; the muscles of the upper arm weakening; the forearms shaped in ovals; a bandana hung on his sore shoulder; the body freckled and white and firm, then abruptly, at the neck, seamed as a turkey; the weathered face, and the sweated, candy hair, delicate as a baby's, laid on his forehead, and the eyes, glittering with narcotics and intelligence like splintered glass, to which

the fringed lashes, which his daughter Emma inherits, give a
sleepy look of charming innocence:

At work, he puts on his shoes and shirt and hat.

An overall strap would continually torment this sore which
has developed in his shoulder, and may indeed—for in this garment this shoulder is the area of greatest stress and friction in
the body—have helped to create it there: and for this reason
Woods has cut off the bib of his overalls and holds them up at
the waist with a piece of tied harness-leather. They are very
old, and hang in a delicateness of wrinklings I have spoken of,
and appear to be the only work clothes he owns.

The shoes are of the Gudger type: but of a lighter leather,
perhaps two years older, worn through in the soles, and tied
up with snaggled and knotted twine, tight on the ankles, for
they are big for him.

The hat I have spoken of.

The shirt is home made out of a fertilizer sack. The cloth, by
use and washing, is of a heavy and delicious look: as if pure
cream were pressed into a fabric an eighth of an inch thick, and
were cut and sewn into a garment. The faded lettering and
branding is still visible, upside down, in red and blue and black.
It is made in earnest imitation of store shirts but in part by
heaviness of cloth and still more by lack of skill is enlarged in
details such as the collar, and simplified, and improved, and is
sewn with tough hand stitches, and is in fact a much more
handsome shirt than might ever be bought: but socially and
economically, it is of like but less significance with Ricketts'
cornshuck hat.

The men's clothes are all ready-made. Any deviation from
this is notable.

The women's and girls' clothes and those of the children are
made at home, excepting boys' overalls and school clothes,
shoes, and head coverings; and with these exceptions all devia-
tions are notable too for one reason and another.

There are standard cloths, cheap cotton prints mainly, and
thin white cottons, woven and on sale specifically to make
clothing of.

Because there is so exceedingly little money, some wives

make use of still other materials in dressing themselves, their children, and less commonly their men, at least for the week-days, when they are sunken far back in their own country, to be seen by none who differ from themselves. Mrs. Woods has one sort of solution, and Mrs. Ricketts another. It is hard to say what is 'normal' here and what is not. By a general common denominator of memory throughout the summer, I would say it was most nearly 'normal' for there to be about an even mixture, in the week-day clothes, of non-clothing with clothing materials: so that Mrs. Woods, dressing herself and her family in so little that was ever intended from human beings to wear, is 'below normal,' and Mrs. Ricketts 'below' and far aside from it. On the other hand, by the almost complete absence of such adapted materials in her family's outfitting, I am sure that Mrs. Gudger feels intense social and perhaps 'spiritual' distinctions between the kinds of cloth in their meanings: and that with as little money as Mrs. Woods and hardly more than Mrs. Ricketts has, her success in keeping to one side of this line is the result of an effort and strain as intense as her feeling. In this she differs from and is 'above' the 'normal,' as she is too in the designing of the clothes, and in various symbolic reaches into the materials of a 'higher' class.

Three women's dresses

Mrs. Gudger: I have spoken already of her dresses. I think she has at most five, of which two are ever worn further away from home than the Woods'. Three are one-piece dresses; two are in two pieces. By cut they are almost identical; by pattern of print they differ, but are similar in having been carefully chosen, all small and sober, quiet patterns, to be in good taste and to relieve one another's monotony. I think it may be well to repeat their general appearance, since it is of her individual designing, and is so thoroughly a part of the logic of her body, bearing, face and temper. They have about them some shadow of nineteenth century influence, tall skirt, short waist, and a little, too, of imitation of Butterick patterns for housewives' housework-dresses; this chiefly in the efforts at bright or 'cheery,' post-honeymoon-atmosphere trimming: narrow red or blue tape sewn at the cuffs or throat. But by other reasons again they have her own character and function: the lines are tall and narrow, as she is, and little relieved, and seem to run straight from the shoulders to the hem low on the shins, and there is no collar, but a long and low V at the throat, shut narrowly together, so that the whole dress like her body has the long vertical of a Chartres statue.

Mrs. Woods: Two work dresses. They are both made of fertilizer* sacks, one in one piece, the other in two. Except that the one-piece dress hangs unbelted, they are much alike: no sleeves; wide hemmed holes cut for the arms; no collar; a wide triangle cut for nursing, and hemmed, in coarse stitching like the armholes; a broad skirt reaching about two inches below the knee, and falling in thick folds: the grain of the cloth defined here and there in dark grease, the whole garment clayed and sweated; the faded yet bold trademarks showing through in unexpected parts of the material: a garment very little different in some respects from those of the women of the ancient Greeks, and probably very closely matched in Thessaly or on Euboea.

Mrs. Ricketts: I am not sure that she has more than one work dress: in any case there was no change of it during the time that I knew her, and it seemed even at the first to have been worn for a long time. Excepting for the clothes of babies, it is the most primitive sewn and designed garment I have ever seen. It is made of a coarse tan cotton I will speak of later. It is shaped like a straight-sided bell, with a little hole at the top for the head to stick through, the cloth slit from the neck to below the breasts and held together if I remember rightly with a small snarl of shoelace; the bare arms sticking through the holes at the sides, the skirt ending a little below the knee, the whole dress standing out a little from the body on all sides like a child's youngest cartoons, not belted, and too stiffened perhaps with dirt to fall into any folds other than the broadest and plainest, the skirt so broad away from her at the bottom that, with her little feet and legs standing down from inside it, for all their beauty they seem comic sticks, and she, a grievous resemblance to newspaper drawings of timid men in barrels labeled John Q. Public.

*Fertilizer sacks are used a great deal in place of calico. Since our visit at least one company is making its sacks in calico patterns.

Mrs. Ricketts wears one of the corn-shuck hats when she is working. I have never seen her with shoes on.

Mrs. Woods wears a big broken straw when she is working and, occasionally, her husband's oldest shoes.

Mrs. Gudger may have no work shoes; more likely, she uses something cast off by her husband. She worked barefooted most of the time, sometimes in her slippers. She was enough embarrassed to be barefooted that she may well have wished to conceal or avoid the indignity before us of using very old and broken shoes which were twice too big for her. She was shy also of our seeing her in a sunbonnet. I doubt that many head-gears have ever been as good or as handsome.

Louise: the dress she wore most was sewn into one piece of two materials, an upper half of faded yellow-checked gingham, and a skirt made of a half-transparent flour sack, and beneath this, the bulk of a pinned, I presume flour sack, clout; and a gingham bow at the small of the back, and trimming at the neck. She has two other dresses, which are worn to Cooks-town or for sundays, and are, I imagine, being saved for school. They too are made painstakingly to be pretty, and as much as possible like pattern and ready-made dresses. During the week she is always barefooted and wears a wide straw hat in the sun. Her mother dresses her carefully in the idiom of a little girl a year or two littler than she is. On sundays she wears slippers and socks, and a narrow blue ribbon in her hair, and a many times laundered white cloth hat.

Junior: ready-made overalls, one pair old, one not far from new, the newer cuffs turned up; a straw hat; bare feet, which are one crust of dew-poisoned sores; a ready-made blue shirt, a homemade gray shirt; a small straw hat. On sunday, cleaned feet, clean overalls, a white shirt, a dark frayed necktie, a small, frayed, clean, gray cap.

Burt: two changes of clothes. One is overalls and one of two shirts, the other is a suit. The overalls are homemade out of pale tan cotton. One of the shirts is pale blue, the other is white; they are made apparently, of pillowslip cotton. The collars are flared open: 'sport' collars, and the sleeves end nearer the shoulder than the elbow. The suit, which is old and, though carefully kept, much faded, is either a ready-made 'ex-

travagance' or a hard-worked imitation of one. It is sewn together, pants and an upper piece, the pants pale blue, the upper
piece white, with a small rabbit-like collar. There are six large
white non-functional buttons sewn against the blue at the
waistline.

Valley Few: In making inventory of the contents of a table
drawer I described a number of Valley Few's dresses. I would
now wish to remind you in particular of one decorated with
homemade rabbits, and that most of the others are either plain
white or in small utility checks. He also had one of a dark solid
blue with red trim at the collar. Relative to the clothing of the
rest of the family, there are a great many babies' dresses, I believe for two good reasons. One is that they are kept for the
use of one child after another. The other is that there is so
little money to spend. Because there is so little; none at all
really for clothes except by luck in the fall; clothes have to be
an afterthought, and because of that, in turn, they can be a
steady undertone of desire: so that from month to month,
with now a dime and now even a quarter to spare, the first
thing to come to Mrs. Gudger's mind would be what is to her
the most immediate need secondary to food: decent clothes
and enough of them. And because there is so little to be had
for that money, she is best likely to satisfy herself in the purchase of the materials for one complete garment. If this is so,
it is of the pattern of her particular care for clothes; it turns up
in neither of the other families.

Valley Few's dresses are like Ellen Woods' and those of most
babies here. There is ordinarily no genital genteelism. The
dress hangs just to the crotch; it is fastened by one button at
the nape of the neck and is open down the back. Often there is
some attempt to make it pretty with a collar or pockets or
both, or a belt; about as often, it is completely plain. Crawling
along the floor, trailing the whole cape to one side, a baby has
the comic and foolish look of a dog who has been dressed up
by children.

Pearl has a dress made of flour sacks, another made of a fertilizer sack, and a third made of brown-and-blue checked
gingham. This is properly her sunday dress, but she is fond of
clothes, and is allowed to wear it a fair amount on week-days,
along with her brown glass beads, her ring and her white

slippers. There will be no time in this volume to tell much of personalities, but I think I will say a little briefly, here. Pearl is much more conscious of clothes than are Louise, Flora Merry Lee, and Katy, who are all near her age, and her mother's casualness is also significant. Mrs. Woods and her mother are of the sexually loose 'stock' of which most casual country and small-town whoredom comes; and the child, already showing the signs, is effortlessly let drift her own way. I would not suggest that any 'attitude' towards this, on your part or mine, is sound enough to be worth striking; I am merely remarking a detail of the childhood of Pearl's mother and grandmother, who I may add appeared to be by far the best satisfied and satisfying women, of their class or of any other, whom I happened to see during this time in the south.

At home her younger half-brother Thomas goes naked some of the time. More often he wears a wornout undershirt which about covers his ribs, or a dress made by cutting off one end of a broadstriped pillowsack and cutting in the other end holes for his head and arms.

Mrs. Gudger has exceedingly little money and an intense determination to hold her family's clothing within a certain level of respectability; Mrs. Woods has exceedingly little money and is relaxed into a level of improvisations, perhaps more fully, with less mixture of calicos, than is average; Mrs. Ricketts, with exceedingly little money as compared even with them, has done still otherwise.

Several years ago, judging by appearance, she bought a quantity of a cloth which, though not intended or ordinarily used for clothes, seemed feasible to her: a great many yards of coarse and unbleached cotton, the cheapest available material of which sheets and pillowcases are made at home: in a color somewhere between ivory, pale gray and white: and of this sheeting nearly all the clothes are made, varied only once or twice in its own designing, and by a few worn-out home-made sunday clothes, and by a few worn-out store clothes. It seems worth noticing that the old sunday clothes are much more than ordinarily talented, careful, hopeful and ambitious, and that with one or two exceptions the sheeting clothes are almost as if vindictively plain. All this sheeting is deeply grained in the colors and maculations of clay, dark grease and sweat and is stiff with this dirt, and is a good deal patched, in more sheeting, in floursack cloth, and in blue shirttail.

Clair Bell wears a short dress, halfway down the thighs, made of a plain straight sack of this sheeting, frayed holes for the arms and head, and alternate with it, a dress of the same material more tenderly made, with a flared skirt, a belt, and an effort at tucking at the throat, abandoned midway. On sundays, or when she is being taken to town, or sometimes when there is 'company,' she is taken aside and a closefitting pair of pink rayon drawers are drawn onto her. These are among the only three garments which give any evidence of recent purchase: everything else seems at least three or four years old.

Katy and Flora Merry Lee are of the same size and use each other's clothes. They have between them perhaps three dresses made of the sheeting, with short sleeves and widened skirts, and shirts or blouses made of thin washed flour sacking, and each has a pair of sheeting overalls. They wear what I presume are floursack drawers, pinned as a diaper is. They sometimes wear the shirts with the overalls; at other times, excepting the overalls, they go naked. They have no 'sunday' clothes; for sunday they wear the least unclean of these dresses, and a few cheap pins, necklaces and lockets. During the week as well as on sunday they sometimes tie dirty blue ribbons into their hair, and sometimes shoestrings.

Richard and Garvrin have between them a pair of very old ready-made overalls, and three or four shirts made some of sheeting and some of floursacks. Each has a pair of sheeting overalls, and a pair of corduroy pants from which the nap is almost entirely rubbed and washed. They fairly often wear the shirts; more often, they go naked except for the overalls or corduroys. On sundays the corduroys are brushed off and the week's damages are mended, and they wear these with frayed nearly clean white shirts which are saved from week to week, and with frazzled ties.

Paralee, for daily work, usually wears what was once her sunday dress. It is a transparent* blue cotton covered with white and faded gold circles, with a carefully made collar, torn, narrow lace at the sleeves, and at the breast a destroyed ruffle of

*It is worn over a slip.

curtain lace and dirty blue ribbons. The dress is torn at the shoulders and along the sides of the back.

Margaret at her daily work wears sometimes a long wide dark skirt and floursack or sheeting blouse, sometimes a sheeting dress. This latter was, I am quite sure, designed as a 'best' dress. It is carefully made throughout to hang and to fit well, and at the left breast and shoulder and across the back of the shoulders, hanging half down the back, is a broad sort of combined collar-and-cape of faded blue cotton.

Paralee sometimes wears black glass beads on weekdays as well as on sundays. Margaret seldom does.

Their clothing too is I presume interchangeable, though there was no overlapping during the time I knew them.

Margaret has two sunday dresses. One was made at home. It is of thin and very cheap white cotton, unskilfully gathered at the breast to a nakedly plain, round, very carefully hemmed throat. It is belted, but does not fit her or hang successfully, and the coarse and somewhat dirty undergarment shows through. Her other dress must I am sure have been bought ready-made and at terrible expense in their scale of money. It is an imitation of the elaborate sort of dress a 'well-preserved,' dark-haired, elegantly well-to-do, middle aged woman might at some uncertain time during the past twenty years have worn formally: black transparent crêpe, sewn over thickly with a coruscation of small jet beads. But the elaborations are worn down into an almost indistinguishable chaos; the black undergarment is torn in several places; many of the beads are lost, or hang loose on their threads; and the cloth is sweated open irreparably and alarmingly at the armpits, so that when the arms are raised, there is in this somberness the sudden bright dreadfulness of twin yawning cats.

Paralee is much more fortunate. She has a new dress, and it is fully and exactly of the kind which middle class girls of her age wear in town on saturday afternoons. And yet it isn't exactly of that kind. In the wish for brilliance and emphasis and propriety, everything is overstepped. The orange and blue and white stripes are far more anxiously bold than any worn by town girls, save now and then a negress, and the fit is almost too sharp and sporting, and the strength, deftness and flexibility of her body betray her, and the dress, and her deeply

tanned, rural, strongly freckled face, her too-carefully done
hair, the use with this garment of all the jewelery she has, and
above all the excitement, the blend of confidence and terror,
and the desperately searching hope which blaze in her eyes, all
these betray her still more hopelessly, so that she would inspire
the fear inspired by all who are over-eager or who would
'climb,' and seems almost as of she had stolen the dress.

These are the clothes which these girls must wear to attract
men and to qualify as marriageable. Many girls marry at sixteen, not a few at fifteen or even fourteen; nearly all are married by seventeen; by the time they are eighteen, if they are
unmarried, they are drifted towards the spinster class, a trouble
to their parents, an embarrassment to court and be seen with,
a dry agony to themselves: Paralee is nineteen; and Margaret is
twenty. Margaret has already the mannerisms and much of the
psychic balance of a middle-aged woman of the middle class in
the north.

Mrs. Ricketts, sunday:

A long and full skirt of dead black cotton held at the hip by
a safetypin. A blouse of the same material, plain at the throat,
sleeves to the elbows. No trimming nor any kind of surplus
cloth. Spots and streaks, reasserting themselves through the
drying moisture with which she has tried to erase them. The
hem fallen in a part of the skirt. No ornaments of any kind. No
hat, or a straw hat (ready-made). It is thus also that she dressed
to ride to Cookstown when cotton was taken to gin.

Mrs. Woods, in Cookstown:

She stands a little apart from everyone in the dark drugstore
waiting until the doctor shall be ready to attend to her ab-
scessed tooth, while the men at the soda fountain are turned
and watch her. She wears no hat, nor stockings, nor shoes. Her
dress is made at home of thin pillowslip cotton, plain at the
throat, cut deep for nursing, without sleeves, reaching a little
below her knees, belted in with a belt of narrow glazed cracked
scarlet leather, all edges of the material frayed, a deep tear
along the back, another through which her right knee shows,
the design of the whole very much that of the plainest sort of
nightgown, the whole fabric a welter of sweat and dirt. She

rests her weight on one foot and studies the other while they look at her. She is noticeably though not yet heavily pregnant. She wears a 'slip' beneath this dress but the materials of both are so thin that her dark sweated nipples are stuck to them and show through, and it is at her nipples, mainly, that the men keep looking. It is thus also that she is dressed on sundays.

Mrs. Woods' mother:

A wide short striped skirt, the stripes blue and white: thick-ribbed black cotton stockings, wrinkled on her legs: Keds, the ankles patched, the soles worn through: a man's work shirt, so exceedingly old it is almost white: a red bandana tied at the throat: a man's large new yellow straw hat.

Past:

Mrs. Gudger has, besides the magenta straw she wears at present, two other hats.

One: an omelet shape of crimson straw slanted through with a thick stripped white quill, the coloring ruined with rain. It is at fifteenth remove an imitation of those 'smart' hats which set off 'smart,' incisive, leisured, vicious faces.

Two: this I have formerly described. It is the great brimmed, triumphal crown I found ruined yet saved in a table drawer, which had been so patiently home made. I will remark now that in its breadth and elaborateness it is reminiscent of the hats which were stylish around 1900, and that it is of such a particular splendor that I am fairly sure it was her wedding hat, made for her, perhaps as a surprise, by her mother. She was sixteen then; her skin would have been white, and clear of wrinkles, her body and its postures and her eyes even more pure than they are today; and she would have been happy, and confident enough in her beauty, to wear it without fear: and in her long white home made marriage dress and in that glory of a hat, with her sister Emma, seven years old, marveling up at her, and her mother standing away and approving her while her image slowly turned upon itself on blank floor and in a glass, she was such a poem as no human being shall touch.

EDUCATION

EDUCATION

I N EVERY CHILD who is born, under no matter what circumstances, and of no matter what parents, the potentiality of the human race is born again: and in him, too, once more, and of each of us, our terrific responsibility towards human life; towards the utmost idea of goodness, of the horror of error, and of God.

Every breath his senses shall draw, every act and every shadow and thing in all creation, is a mortal poison, or is a drug, or is a signal or symptom, or is a teacher, or is a liberator, or is liberty itself, depending entirely upon his understanding: and understanding,* and action proceeding from understanding and guided by it, is the one weapon against the world's bombardment, the one medicine, the one instrument by which liberty, health, and joy may be shaped or shaped towards, in the individual, and in the race.

This is no place to dare all questions that must be asked, far less to advance our tentatives in this murderous air, nor even to qualify so much as a little the little which thus far has been suggested, nor even either to question or to try to support my qualifications to speak of it at all: we are too near one of the deepest intersections of pity, terror doubt and guilt; and I feel that I can say only, that 'education,' whose function is at the crisis of this appalling responsibility, does not seem to me to be all, or even anything, that it might be, but seems indeed the very property of the world's misunderstanding, the sharpest of its spearheads in every brain: and that since it could not be otherwise without destroying the world's machine, the world is unlikely to permit it to be otherwise.

In fact, and ignorant though I am, nothing, not even law,

*Active 'understanding' is only one form, and there are suggestions of 'perfection' which could be called 'understanding' only by definitions so broad as to include diametric reversals. The peace of God surpasses all understanding; Mrs. Ricketts and her youngest child do, too; 'understanding' can be its own, and hope's, most dangerous enemy.

251

nor property, nor sexual ethics, nor fear, nor doubtlessness, nor even authority itself, all of which it is the business of education to cleanse the brain of, can so nearly annihilate me with fury and with horror; as the spectacle of innocence, of defenselessness, of all human hope, brought steadily in each year by the millions into the machineries of the teachings of the world, in which the man who would conceive of and who would dare attempt even the beginnings of what 'teaching' must be could not exist two months clear of a penitentiary: presuming even that his own perceptions, and the courage of his perceptions, were not a poison as deadly at least as those poisons he would presume to drive out: or the very least of whose achievements, supposing he cared truly not only to hear himself speak but to be understood, would be a broken heart.*

For these and other reasons it would seem to me mistaken to decry the Alabama public schools, or even to say that they are 'worse' or 'less good' than schools elsewhere: or to be particularly wholehearted in the regret that these tenants are subjected only to a few years of this education: for they would be at a disadvantage if they had more of it, and at a disadvantage if they had none, and they are at a disadvantage in the little they have; and it would be hard and perhaps impossible to say in which way their disadvantage would be greatest.

School was not in session while I was there. My research on this subject was thin, indirect, and deductive. By one way of thinking it will seem for these reasons worthless: by another, which I happen to trust more, it may be sufficient.

I saw, for instance, no teachers: yet I am quite sure it is safe to assume that they are local at very least to the state and quite probably to the county; that most of them are women to whom teaching is either an incident of their youth or a poor solution for their spinsterhood; that if they were of much intelligence or courage they could not have survived their training in the State Normal or would never have undertaken it in the first place; that they are saturated in every belief and ignorance which is basic in their country and community; that

---

*It may be that the only fit teachers never teach but are artists, and artists of the kind most blankly masked and least didactic.

any modification of this must be very mild indeed if they are to survive as teachers; that even if, in spite of all these screenings, there are superior persons among them, they are still again limited to texts and to a system of requirements officially imposed on them; and are caught between the pressures of class, of the state, of the churches, and of the parents, and are confronted by minds already so deeply formed that to liberate them would involve uncommon and as yet perhaps undiscovered philosophic and surgical skill. I have only sketched a few among dozens of the facts and forces which limit them; and even so I feel at liberty to suggest that even the best of these, the kindly, or the intuitive, the socalled natural teaches, are exceedingly more likely than not to be impossibly handicapped both from without and within themselves, and are at best the servants of unconscious murder; and of the others, the general run, that if murder of the mind and spirit were statutory crimes, the law, in its customary eagerness to punish the wrong person,* might spend all its ingenuity in the invention of deaths by delayed torture and never sufficiently expiate the enormities which through them, not by their own fault, have been committed.

Or again on the curriculum: it was unnecessary to make even such search into this as I made to know that there is no setting before the students of 'economic' or 'social' or 'political' 'facts' and of their situation within these 'facts,' no attempt made to clarify or even slightly to relieve the situation between the white and negro races, far less to explain the sources, no attempt to clarify psychological situations in the individual, in his family, or in his world, no attempt to get beneath and to revise those 'ethical' and 'social' pressures and beliefs in which even a young child is trapped, no attempt, beyond the most nominal, to interest a child in using or in discovering his senses and judgment, no attempt to counteract the paralytic quality inherent in 'authority,' no attempt beyond the most nominal and stifling to awaken, to protect, or to 'guide' the sense of investigation, the sense of joy, the sense of beauty, no attempt to clarify spoken and written words whose power

---

*This is not to suggest there is a 'right person' or that punishment can ever be better than an enhancement of error.

of deceit even at the simplest is vertiginous, no attempt, or very little, and ill taught, to teach even the earliest techniques of improvement in occupation ('scientific farming,' diet and cooking, skilled trades), nor to 'teach' a child in terms of his environment, no attempt, beyond the most suffocated, to awaken a student either to 'religion' or to 'irreligion,' no attempt to develop in him either 'skepticism' or 'faith,' nor 'wonder,' nor mental 'honesty' nor mental 'courage,' nor any understanding of or delicateness in 'the emotions' and in any of the uses and pleasures of the body save the athletic; no attempt either to relieve him of fear and of poison in sex or to release in him a free beginning of pleasure in it, nor to open within him the illimitable potentials of grief, of danger, and of goodness in sex and in sexual love, nor to give him the beginnings at very least of a knowledge, and of an attitude, whereby he may hope to guard and increase himself and those whom he touches, no indication of the damages which society, money, law, fear and quick belief have set upon these matters and upon all things in human life, nor of their causes, nor of the alternate ignorances and possibilities of ruin or of joy, no fear of doubtlessness, no fear of the illusions of knowledge, no fear of compromise:—and here again I have scarcely begun, and am confronted immediately with a serious problem: that is: by my naming of the lack of such teaching, I can appear too easily to recommend it, to imply, perhaps, that if these things were 'taught,' all would be 'solved': and this I do not believe: but insist rather that in the teaching of these things, infinitely worse damage could and probably would result than in the teaching of those subjects which in fact do compose the curriculum: and that those who would most insist upon one or another of them can be among the deadliest enemies of education: for if the guiding hand is ill qualified, an instrument is murderous in proportion to its sharpness. Nothing I have mentioned but is at the mercy of misuse; and one may be sure a thousand to one it will be misused; and that its misuse will block any more 'proper' use even more solidly than unuse and discrediting could. It could be said, that we must learn a certitude and correlation in every 'value' before it will be possible to 'teach' and not to murder; but that is far too optimistic. We would do better to examine, far beyond their present examination, the extensions within ourselves of doubt, responsibility, and conditioned faith and the possibilities of their more profitable union, to a degree at least of true and constant terror in even our tentatives, and if (for instance) we should dare to be 'teaching' what Marx began to open, that we should do so only in the light of the terrible researches of Kafka and in the opposed identities of Blake and Céline.

All I have managed here, and it is more than I intended, is to give a confused statement of an intention which presumes itself to be good: the mere attempt to examine my own confusion would consume volumes. But let what I have tried to suggest amount to this alone: that not only within present reach of human intelligence, but even within reach of mine as it stands today, it would be possible that young human beings should rise onto their feet a great deal less dreadfully crippled than they are, a great deal more nearly capable of living well, a great deal more nearly aware, each of them, of their own dignity in existence, a great deal better qualified, each within his limits, to live and to take part toward the creation of a world in which good living will be possible without guilt toward every neighbor: and that teaching at present, such as it is, is almost entirely either irrelevant to these possibilities or destructive of them, and is, indeed, all but entirely unsuccessful even within its own 'scales' of 'value.'

Within the world as it stands, however, the world they must live in, a certain form of education is available to these tenant children; and the extent to which they can avail themselves of it is of considerable importance in all their future living.

A few first points about it:

They are about as poorly equipped for self-education as human beings can be. Their whole environment is such that the use of the intelligence, of the intellect, and of the emotions is atrophied, and is all but entirely irrelevant to the pressures and needs which involve almost every instant of a tenant's conscious living: and indeed if these faculties were not thus reduced or killed at birth they would result in a great deal of pain, not to say danger. They learn the work they will spend their lives doing, chiefly of their parents, and from their parents and from the immediate world they take their conduct, their morality, and their mental and emotional and spiritual key. One could hardly say that any further knowledge or consciousness is at all to their use or advantage, since there is nothing to read, no reason to write, and no recourse against being cheated even if one is able to do sums; yet these forms of literacy are in general held to be desirable: a man or woman feels a certain sort of extra helplessness who lacks them: a truly serious or ambitious parent hopes for even more, for a promising child; though what 'more' may be is, inevitably, only dimly understood.

School opens in middle or late September and closes the first of May. The country children, with their lunches, are picked up by busses at around seven-thirty in the morning and are dropped off again towards the early winter darkness. In spite of the bus the children of these three families have a walk to take. In dry weather it is shortened a good deal; the bus comes up the branch road as far as the group of negro houses at the bottom of the second hill and the Ricketts children walk half a mile to meet it and the Gudger children walk three quarters. In wet weather the bus can't risk leaving the highway and the Ricketts walk two miles and the Gudgers a mile and a half in clay which in stretches is knee-deep on a child.

There was talk during the summer of graveling the road, though most of the fathers are over forty-five, beyond roadage. They can hardly afford the time to do such work for nothing, and they and their negro neighbors are in no position to pay taxes. Nothing had come of it within three weeks of the start of school, and there was no prospect of free time before cold weather.

Southern winters are sickeningly wet, and wet clay is perhaps the hardest of all walking. 'Attendance' suffers by this cause, and by others. Junior Gudger, for instance, was absent sixty-five and Louise fifty-three days out of a possible hundred-and-fifty-odd, and these absences were 'unexcused' eleven and nine times respectively, twenty-three of Junior's and a proportionate number of Louise's absences fell in March and April, which are full of work at home as well as wetness. Later in her second year in school Louise was needed at home and missed several consecutive school days, including the final examinations. Her 'marks' had been among the best in her class and she had not known of the examination date, but no chance was given her to make up the examinations and she had to take the whole year over. The Ricketts children have much worse attendance records and Pearl does not attend at all.

School does not begin until the children shall have helped two weeks to a month in the most urgent part of the picking season, and ends in time for them to be at work on the cotton-chopping.

The bus system which is now a routine of country schools is helpful, but not particularly to those who live at any distance from tax-maintained roads.

The walking, and the waiting in the cold and wetness, one day after another, to school in the morning, and home from schools in the shriveling daylight, is arduous and unpleasant.

Schooling, here as elsewhere, is identified with the dullest and most meager months of the year, and, in this class and country, with the least and worst food and a cold noonday lunch: and could be set only worse at a disadvantage if it absorbed the pleasanter half of the year.

The 'attendance problem' is evidently taken for granted and, judging by the low number of unexcused absences, is 'leniently' dealt with: the fact remains, though, that the children lose between a third to half of each school year, and must with this handicap keep up their lessons and 'compete' with town children in a contest in which competition is stressed and success in it valued and rewarded.

The schoolhouse itself is in Cookstown; a recently built, windowy, 'healthful' red brick and white-trimmed structure which perfectly exemplifies the American genius* for sterility, unimagination, and general gutlessness in meeting any opportunity for 'reform' or 'improvement.' It is the sort of building a town such as Cookstown is proud of, and a brief explanation of its existence in such country will be worth while. Of late years Alabama has 'come awake' to 'education,' illiteracy has been reduced; texts have been modernized; a good many old schools have been replaced by new ones. For this latter purpose

---

*So well shown forth in 'low-cost' housing.

the counties have received appropriations in proportion to the size of their school population. The school population of this county is five black to one white, and since not a cent of the money has gone into negro schools, such buildings as this are possible: for white children. The negro children, meanwhile, continue to sardine themselves, a hundred and a hundred and twenty strong, into stove-heated one-room pine shacks which might comfortably accommodate a fifth of their number if the walls, roof, and windows were tight.* But then, as one prominent landlord said and as many more would agree: 'I don't object to nigrah education, not up through foath a fift grade maybe, but not furdern dat: I'm too strong a believah in white syewpremcy.'

This bus service and this building the (white) children are schooled in, even including the long and muddy walk, are of course effete as compared to what their parents had.† The schooling itself is a different matter, too: much more 'modern.' The boys and girls alike are subjected to 'art' and to 'music,' and the girls learn the first elements of tap dancing. Textbooks are so cheap almost anyone who can afford them: that is, almost anyone who can afford anything at all; which means that they are a stiff problem in any year to almost any tenant. I want now to list and suggest the contents of a few textbooks which were at the Gudger house, remembering, first, that they imply the far reaches of the book-knowledge of any average adult tenant.

> *The Open Door Language Series: First Book: Language Stories and Games.*
>
> *Trips to Take.* Among the contents are poems by Vachel Lindsay, Elizabeth Madox Roberts, Robert Louis Stevenson, etc. Also a story titled: 'Brother Rabbit's Cool Air Swing,' and subheaded: 'Old Southern Tale.'
>
> *Outdoor Visits:* Book Two of *Nature and Science*

---

*Aside from discomfort, and unhealthfulness, and the difficulty of concentrating, this means of course that several 'grades' are in one room, reciting and studying by rotation, each using only a fraction of each day's time. It means hopeless boredom and waste for the children, and exhaustion for the teacher.

†Their parents would have walked to one-room wooden schoolhouses. I'm not sure, but think it more likely than not, that many of the white children still do today.

Readers. (Book One is *Hunting.*) Book Two opens: 'Dear Boys and Girls: in this book you will read how Nan and Don visited animals and plants that live outdoors.'

Real Life Readers: New Stories and Old: A Third Reader. Illustrated with color photographs.

The Trabue-Stevens Speller. Just another speller.

Champion Arithmetic. Five hundred and ten pages: a champion psychological inducement to an interest in numbers. The final problem: 'Janet bought 1¼ lbs. of salted peanuts and ½ lb. of salted almonds. Altogether she bought ? lbs. of nuts?'

Dear Boys and Girls indeed!

Such a listing is rich as a poem; twisted full of contents, symptoms, and betrayals, and these, as in a poem, are only reduced and diluted by any attempt to explain them or even by hinting. Personally I see enough there to furnish me with bile for a month: yet I know that any effort to make clear in detail what is there, and why it seems to me so fatal, must fail.

Even so, see only a little and only for a moment.

These are books written by 'adults.' They must win the approval and acceptance of still other 'adults,' members of school 'boards'; and they will be 'taught' with by still other 'adults' who have been more or less 'trained' as teachers. The intention is, or should be, to engage, excite, preserve, or develop the 'independence' of, and furnish with 'guidance,' 'illumination,' 'method,' and 'information,' the curiosities of children.

Now merely re-examine a few words, phrases and facts:

The Open Door: open to whom. That metaphor is supposed to engage the interest of children.

Series: First Book. Series. Of course The Bobbsey Twins is a series; so is The Rover Boys. *Series* perhaps has some pleasure associations to those who have children's books, which no tenant children have: but even so it is better than canceled by the fact that this is so obviously not a pleasure book but a schoolbook, not even well disguised. An undisguised textbook is only a little less pleasing than a sneaking and disguised one, though. *First Book:* there entirely for the convenience of adults; it's only grim to a child.

Language: it appears to be a *modern* substitution for the word 'English.' I don't doubt the latter word has been murdered; the question is, whether the new one has any life whatever to a taught child or, for that matter, to a teacher.

Stories and Games: both, modified by a school word, and in a school context. Most children prefer pleasure to boredom, lacking our intelligence to reverse this preference: but you must use your imagination or memory to recognize how any game can be poisoned by being 'conducted': and few adults have either.

Trips to Take. Trips indeed, for children who will never again travel as much as in their daily bus trips to and from school. Children like figures of speech or are, if you like, natural symbolists and poets: being so, they see through frauds such as this so much the more readily. No poem is a 'trip,' whatever else it may be, and suffers by being lied about.

The verse. I can readily imagine that 'educators' are well pleased with themselves in that they have got rid of the Bivouac of the Dead and are using much more nearly contemporary verse. I am quite as sure, knowing their kind of 'knowledge' of poetry, that the pleasure is all theirs.

These children, both of town and country, are saturated southerners, speaking dialects not very different from those of negroes. *Brother* Rabbit! *Old Southern Tale!*

Outdoor Visits. Nature and Science. Book One: *Hunting.* Dear Boys and Girls. In this book you will read (oh, I will, will I?). Nan and Don. Visit. Animals and Plants that Live Outdoors. Outdoors. You will pay formal calls on Plants. They live outdoors. 'Nature.' 'Science.' Hunting. Dear Boys and Girls. Outdoor Visits.

Real Life. 'Real' 'Life' 'Readers.' Illustrated by *color* photographs.

Or back into the old generation, a plainer title: *The Trabue-Stevens Speller.* Or the *Champion Arithmetic*, weight eighteen pounds, an attempt at ingratiation in the word champion, so broad of any mark I am surprised it is not spelled *Champeen.*

Or you may recall the page of geography text I have quoted elsewhere: which, I must grant, tells so much about education that this chapter is probably unnecessary.

—

I give up. Relative to my memory of my own grade-schooling, I recognize all kinds of 'progressive' modifications: Real Life, color photographs, Trips to Take (rather than Journey, to Make), games, post-kindergarten, 'Language,' Nan and Don, 'Nature and Science,' Untermeyer-vintage poetry, 'dear boys and girls'; and I am sure of only one thing: that it is prepared by adults for their own self-flattery and satisfaction, and is to children merely the old set retouched, of afflictions, bafflements, and half-legible insults more or less apathetically submitted to.

Louise Gudger is fond of school, especially of geography and arithmetic, and gets unusually good 'marks': which means in part that she has an intelligence quick and acquisitive above the average, in part that she has learned to parrot well and to respect 'knowledge' as it is presented to her. She has finished the third grade. In the fourth grade she will learn all about the history of her country. Her father and much more particularly her mother is excited over her brightness and hopeful of it: they intend to make every conceivable effort by which she may continue not only through the grades but clear through high school. She wants to become a teacher, and quite possibly she will; or a trained nurse; and again quite possibly she will.

Junior Gudger is in the second grade because by Alabama law a pupil is automatically passed after three years in a grade. He is still almost entirely unable to read and write, and is physically fairly skilful. It may be that he is incapable of 'learning': in any case 'teaching' him would be a 'special problem.' It would be impossible in a public, competitive class of mixed kinds and degrees of 'intelligence'; and I doubt that most public-school teachers are trained in it anyhow.

Burt and Valley Few are too young for school. I foresee great difficulty for Burt, who now at four is in so desperate a psychological situation that he is capable of speaking any language beyond gibberish (in which he has great rhythmic and syllabic talent) only after he has been given the security of long and friendly attention, of a sort which markedly excludes his brothers.

Pearl Woods, who is eight, may have started to school this

fall (1936); more likely not, though, for it was to depend on whether the road was graveled so she would not have the long walk to the bus alone or within contamination of the Ricketts children. She is extremely sensitive, observant, critical and crafty, using her mind and her senses much more subtly than is ever indicated or 'taught' in school: whether her peculiar intelligence will find engagement or ruin in the squarehead cogs of public schooling is another matter.

Thomas is three years too young for school. As a comedian and narcist dancer he has natural genius; aside from this I doubt his abilities. Natural artists, such as he is, and natural craftsmen, like Junior, should not necessarily have to struggle with reading and writing; they have other ways of learning, and of enlarging themselves, which however are not available to them.

Clair Bell is three years young for school and it seems probable that she will not live for much if any of it, so estimates are rather irrelevant. I will say, though, that I was so absorbed in her physical and spiritual beauty that I was not on the lookout for signs of 'intelligence' or the lack of it, and that education, so far as I know it, would either do her no good or would hurt her.

Flora Merry Lee and Katy are in the second grade. Katy, though she is so shy that she has to write out her reading lessons, is brighter than average; Flora Merry Lee, her mother says, is brighter than Katy; she reads and writes smoothly and 'specially delights in music.' Garvrin and Richard are in the fourth grade. Garvrin doesn't take to schooling very easily though he tries hard; Richard is bright but can't get interested; his mind wanders. In another year or two they will be big enough for full farm work and will be needed for it, and that will be the end of school.

Margaret quit school when she was in the fifth grade because her eyes hurt her so badly every time she studied books. She has forgotten a good deal how to read. Paralee quit soon after Margaret did because she was lonesome. She still reads fairly easily, and quite possibly will not forget how.

The Ricketts are spoken of disapprovingly, even so far away as the county courthouse, as 'problem' children. Their attendance record is extremely bad; their conduct is not at all good;

they are always fighting and sassing back. Besides their long walk in bad weather, here is some more explanation. They are much too innocent to understand the profits of docility. They have to wear clothes and shoes which make them the obvious butts of most of the children. They come of a family which is marked and poor even among the poor whites, and are looked down on even by most levels of the tenant class. They are uncommonly sensitive, open, trusting, easily hurt, and amazed by meanness and by cruelty, and their ostracism is of a sort to inspire savage loyalty among them. They are indeed 'problems'; and the 'problem' will not be simplified as these 'over'-sexed and anarchic children shift into adolescence. The two girls in particular seem inevitably marked out for incredibly cruel misunderstanding and mistreatment.

Mrs. Ricketts can neither read nor write. She went to school one day in her life and her mother got sick and she never went back. Another time she told me that the children laughed at her dress and the teacher whipped her for hitting back at them, but Margaret reminded her that that was the dress she had made for Flora Merry Lee and that it was Flora Merry Lee and Katy who had been whipped, and she agreed that that was the way it was.

Fred Ricketts learned quickly. He claims to have learned how to read music in one night (he does, in any case, read it), and he reads language a little less hesitantly than the others do and is rather smug about it—'I was readn whahl back na Pgressive Fahmuh—' He got as far as the fifth grade and all ways was bright. When his teacher said the earth turned on a axle, he asked her was the axle set in posts, then. She said yes, she reckoned so. He said well, wasn't hell supposed to be under the earth, and if it was wouldn't they be all the time trying to chop the axle post out from under the earth? But here the earth still was, so what was all this talk about axles. 'Teacher never did bring up nothn bout no axles after that. No sir, she never did bring up nothing about no durn axles after that. No sir-ree, she shore never did brang up nufn baout no dad blame axles attah dayut.'

Woods quit school at twelve when he ran away and went to work in the mines. He can read, write, and figure; so can his wife. Woods understands the structures and tintings of rationalization in money, sex, language, religion, law, and general social conduct in a sour way which is not on the average curriculum.

George Gudger can spell and read and write his own name; beyond that he is helpless. He got as far as the second grade. By that time there was work for him and he was slow minded anyway. He feels it is a terrible handicap not to be educated and still wants to learn to read and write and to figure, and his wife has tried to learn him, and still wants to. He still wants to, too, but he thinks it is unlikely that he will ever manage to get the figures and letters to stick in his head.

Mrs. Gudger can read, write, spell, and handle simple arithmetic, and grasps and is excited by such matters as the plainer facts of astronomy and geology. In fact, whereas many among the three families have crippled but very full and real intelligence, she and to a perhaps less extent her father have also intellects. But these intellects died before they were born; they hang behind their eyes like fetuses in alcohol.

It may be that more are born 'incapable of learning,' in this class, or in any case 'incapable of learning,' or of 'using their intelligences,' beyond 'rudimentary' stages, than in economically luckier classes. If this is so, and I doubt the proportion is more than a little if at all greater, several ideas come to mind: Incapable of learning what? And capable of learning what else, which is not available either to them or, perhaps, in the whole field and idea of education? Or are they incapable through incompetent teaching, or through blind standards, or none, on the part of educators, for measuring what 'intelligence' is? Or incapable by what pressures of past causes in past generations? Or should the incapability be so lightly (or sorrowfully) dismissed as it is by teachers and by the middle class in general?

But suppose a portion are born thus 'incapable': the others, nevertheless, the great majority, are born with 'intelligences' potentially as open and 'healthful,' and as varied in pattern and in charge, as any on earth. And by their living, and by their education, they are made into hopeless and helpless cripples, capable exactly and no more of doing what will keep them alive: by no means so well equipped as domestic and free animals: and that is what their children are being made into, more and more incurably, in every year, and in every day.

'Literacy' is to some people a pleasing word: when 'illiteracy' percentages drop, many are pleased who formerly were shocked, and think no more of it. Disregarding the proved fact that few doctors of philosophy are literate, that is, that few of them have the remotest idea how to read, how to say what they mean, or what they mean in the first place, the word literacy means very little even as it is ordinarily used. An adult tenant writes and spells and reads painfully and hesitantly as a child does and is incapable of any save the manifest meanings of any but the simplest few hundred words, and is all but totally incapable of absorbing, far less correlating, far less critically examining, any 'ideas' whether true or false; or even physical facts beyond the simplest and most visible. That they are, by virtue of these limitations, among the only 'honest' and 'beautiful' users of language, is true, perhaps, but it is not enough. They are at an immeasurable disadvantage in a world which is run, and in which they are hurt, and in which they might be cured, by 'knowledge' and by 'ideas': and to 'consciousness' or 'knowledge' in its usages in personal conduct and in human relationships, and to those unlimited worlds of the senses, the remembrance, the mind and the heart which, beyond that of their own existence, are the only human hope, dignity, solace, increasement, and joy, they are all but totally blinded. The ability to try to understand existence, the ability to try to recognize the wonder and responsibility of one's own existence, the ability to know even fractionally the almost annihilating beauty, ambiguity, darkness, and horror which swarm every instant of every consciousness, the ability to try to accept, or the ability to try to defend one's self, or the ability to dare to try to assist others; all such as these, of which most human beings are cheated of their potentials, are, in most of those who even begin to discern or wish for them, the gifts or thefts of economic privilege, and are available to members of these leanest classes only by the rare and irrelevant miracle of born and surviving 'talent.'

Or to say it in another way: I believe that every human being is potentially capable, within his 'limits,' of fully 'realizing' his potentialities; that this, his being cheated and choked of it, is infinitely the ghastliest, commonest, and most inclusive of all the crimes of which the human world can accuse itself; and that the discovery and use of 'consciousness,' which has always been and is our deadliest enemy and deceiver, is also the source and guide of all hope and cure, and the only one.

I am not at all trying to lay out a thesis, far less to substantiate or to solve. I do not consider myself qualified. I know only that murder is being done, against nearly every individual in the planet, and that there are dimensions and correlations of cure which not only are not being used but appear to be scarcely considered or suspected. I know there is cure, even now available, if only it were available, in science and in the fear and joy of God. This is only a brief personal statement of these convictions: and my self-disgust is less in my ignorance, and far less in my 'failure' to 'defend' or 'support' the statement, than in my inability to state it even so far as I see it, and in my inability to blow out the brains with it of you who take what it is talking of lightly, or not seriously enough.

A few notes

Most of you would never be convinced that much can be implied out of little: that everything to do with tenant education, for instance, is fully and fairly indicated in the mere list of textbooks. I have not learned how to make this clear, so I have only myself to thank. On the other hand there are plenty of people who never get anything into their heads until they are brained by twenty years' documentation: these are the same people who so scrupulously obey, insist on, and interpret 'the facts,' and 'the rules.'

I have said a good deal more here on what ought to be than on what is: but God forbid I should appear to say, 'I know what ought to be, and this is it.' But it did and does seem better to shout a few obvious facts (they can never be 'obvious' enough) than to meech. The meechers will say, Yes, but do you realize all (or any) of the obstacles, presuming you are (in general) a little more right than merely raving? The answer is, I am sure I don't realize them all, but I realize more of them, probably, than you do. Our difference is that you accept and respect them. 'Education' as it stands is tied in with every bondage I can conceive of, and is the chief cause of these bondages, including acceptance and respect, which are the worst bondages of all. 'Education,' if it is anything short of crime, is a recognition of these bondages and a discovery of more and a deadly enemy of all of them; it is the whole realm of human consciousness, action, and possibility; it has above all to try to recognize and continuously to suspect and to extend its understanding of its own nature. It is all science and all conduct; it is also all religion. By which I mean, it is all 'good' or 'wise' science, conduct, and religion. It is also all individuals; no less various. It cannot be less and be better than outrageous. Its chief task is fearfully to try to learn what is 'good' and 'why' (and when), and how to communicate, and its own dimensions, and its responsibility.

Oh, I am very well aware how adolescent this is and how easily laughable. I will nevertheless insist that any persons milder, more obedient to or compromising* with 'the obstacles as they are,' more 'realistic,' contented with the effort for less, are dreamy and insufficiently skeptical. Those are the worst of the enemies, and always have been.

I don't know whether negroes or whites teach in the negro schools; I presume negroes. If they are negroes, I would presume for general reasons that many of them, or most, are far superior to the white teachers. By and large only the least capable of whites become teachers, particularly in primary schools, and more particularly in small towns and in the country: whereas with so little in the world available to them, it must be that many of the most serious and intelligent negroes become teachers. But you would have to add: They are given, insofar as they are given any, a white-traditioned education,

*One of the researches most urgently needed is into the whole problem of compromise and non-compromise. I am dangerously and mistakenly much against compromise: 'my kind never gets anything done.' The (self-styled) 'Realists' are quite as dangerously ready to compromise. They seem never sufficiently aware of the danger; they much too quickly and easily respect the compromise and come at rest in it. I would suppose that nothing is necessarily wrong with compromise of itself, except that those who are easy enough to make it are easy enough to relax into and accept it, and that it thus inevitably becomes fatal. Or more nearly, the essence of the trouble is that compromise is held to be a virtue of itself.

and are liable to the solemn, meek piousness of most serious and educated negroes in the south; to a deep respect for knowledge and education as they have worked for it; to a piteous mah-people or Uncle Tom attitude towards all life. Even those who are aware of more dangerous attitudes would in the south have to be careful to the point of impotence. Moreover they would be teaching only very young children, in the earliest years of school, in overcrowded classrooms.

Note on all grade-school teachers: that at best they are exceedingly ill-paid, and have also anxiety over their jobs: with all the nervousness of lack of money and of insecurity even in that little: not a good state of mind for a teacher of the young. Nor is the state of mind resulting of sexlessness, or of carefully spotless moral rectitude, whether it be 'innate,' or self-enforced for the sake of the job. Nearly all teachers and clergymen suffocate their victims through this sterility alone.

It would be hard to make clear enough the deadliness of vacuum and of apathy which is closed over the very nature of teaching, over teachers and pupils alike: or in what different worlds words and processes leave a teacher, and reach a child. Children, taught either years beneath their intelligence or miles wide of relevance to it, or both: their intelligence becomes hopelessly bewildered, drawn off its centers, bored, or atrophied. Carry it forward a few years and recognize how soft-brained an american as against a european 'college graduate' is. On the other side: should there be any such thing as textbooks in any young life: and how many 'should' learn to read at all?

As a whole part of 'psychological education' it needs to be remembered that a neurosis can be valuable; also that 'adjustment' to a sick and insane environment is of itself not 'health' but sickness and insanity.

I could not wish of any one of them that they should have had the 'advantages' I have had: a Harvard education is by no means an unqualified advantage.

—

Adults writing to or teaching children: in nearly every word within these textbooks, for instance, there is a flagrant mistake of some kind. The commonest is this: that they simplify their own ear, without nearly enough skepticism as to the accuracy of the simplification, and with virtually no intuition for the child or children; then write or teach to satisfy that ear; discredit the child who is not satisfied, and value the child who, by docile or innocent distortions of his intelligence, is.

In school a child is first plunged into the hot oil bath of the world as its cruelest: and children are taught far less by their teachers than by one another. Children are, or quickly become, exquisitely sensitive to social, psychologic, and physical meanings and discriminations. The war is bloody and pitiless as that war alone can be in which every combatant is his own sole army, and is astounded and terrified in proportion to the healthfulness of his consciousness. What clothes are worn, for one simple thing alone, is of tremendous influence upon the child who wears them. A child is quickly and frightfully instructed of his situation and meaning in the world; and that one stays alive only by one form or another of cowardice, or brutality, or deception, or other crime. It is all, needless to say, as harmful to the 'winners' (the well-to-do, or healthful, or extraverted) as to the losers.

The 'esthetic' is made hateful and is hated beyond all other kinds of 'knowledge.' It is false-beauty to begin with; it is taught by sick women or sicker men; it becomes identified with the worst kinds of femininity and effeminacy; it is made incomprehensible and suffocating to anyone of much natural honesty and vitality.

The complete acquaintance of a child with 'music' is the nauseating little tunes you may remember from your own schooltime. His 'art' has equally little to do with 'art.' The dancing, as I have said, is taught to girls: it is the beginning of tap dancing. The spectacle of a tenant's little daughter stepping out abysmal imitations of Eleanor Powell has a certain charm, but it is somehow decadent, to put it mildly. This is not at all to say that madrigals, finger-painting, or morris-dancing are to be recommended: I wish to indicate only that in either case the 'teaching' of 'the esthetic' or of 'the arts' in Cookstown leaves, or would leave, virtually everything still to be desired.

It is hardly to Louise's good fortune that she 'likes' school, school being what it is. Dressed as she is, and bright as she is, and serious and dutiful and well-thought-of as she is, she already has traces of a special sort of complacency which probably must, in time, destroy all in her nature that is magical, indefinable, and matchless: and this though she is one of the stronger persons I have ever known.

Perhaps half the people alive are born with the possibility of moral intuitions far more subtle and excellent than those laid down by law and custom, and most of the others might learn a great deal. As it is they are more than sufficiently destroyed. If beginning at the age of six they were subjected to a daily teaching of law, the damage would be so much the worse. There is a fair parallel in 'consciousness,' in 'intelligence': and the standards of education, which seem even more monstrous than those of law, are thus imposed as law is not, and are made identical with knowledge.

No equipment to handle an abstract idea or to receive it: nor to receive or handle at all complex facts: nor to put facts and ideas together and strike any fire or meaning from them. They are like revolutionists who must fight fire and iron and poison gas with barrel staves and with bare hands: except that they lack even the idea of revolution.

It would be the narrative task of many pages even scarcely to suggest how slowed, blinded, and helpless-minded they are made. Just as with food, they cannot conceive of or be interested in what they have never tasted or heard of. All except the simplest knowledge of immediate materials and of the senses, is completely irrelevant to the life they are living. Perhaps fortunately, the one thing the adults could most surely receive and understand is what a good revolutionist could tell them about their immediate situation and what is to be done about it: certainly one would be a fool, and an insulting one, who tried much else, or who tried much else before that was accomplished. The children could learn this and much more.

For various reasons I am not a good revolutionist, and much as I wanted to, could bear in my 'conscience,' or in my respect for what they were as they stood, to do almost none of this, beyond determining what in general they might learn if they were rightly given it. Moreover, though there are revolutionists whom I totally respect, and before the mere thought of whom I hold myself in contempt, I go blind to think what crimes others would commit upon them, and instill into them; and by every appearance and probability these latter, who for all their devotion and courage seem to me among the most dangerous and hideous persons at large, are greatly in the majority, and it is they who own and will always betray all revolutions.

'Sense of beauty': Is this an 'instinct' or a product of 'training.' In either case there appears to be almost no such thing among the members of these three families, and I have a strong feeling that the 'sense of beauty,' like nearly everything else, is a class privilege. I am sure in any case that its 'terms' differ by class, and that the 'sense' is limited and inarticulate in the white tenant class almost beyond hope of description. (This quite aside from the fact that in other classes, where it is less limited, it is almost a hundred per cent corrupted.) They live on land, and in houses, and under skies and seasons, which all happen to seem to me beautiful beyond almost anything else I know, and they themselves, and the clothes they wear, and their motions, and their speech, are beautiful in the same intense and final commonness and purity: but by what chance have I this 'opinion' or 'perception' or, I might say, 'knowledge'? And on the other hand, why do they appear so completely to lack it? This latter, there seem good reasons for. Habit. No basis of comparison. No 'sophistication' (there can be a good meaning of the word). No reason nor glimmer of reason to regard anything in terms other than those of need and use. Land is what you get food out of: houses are what you live in, not comfortably: the sky is your incalculable friend or enemy: all nature, all that is built upon it, all that is worn, all that is done and looked to, is in plain and powerful terms of need, hope, fear, chance, and function. Moreover, the profoundest and plainest 'beauties,' those of the order of the stars and of solitude in darkened and empty land, come at least partly of awe, and such in a simple being is, simply, unformulable fear. It is true that in what little they can obtain of them, they use and respect the rotted prettinesses of 'luckier' classes; in such naïvety that these are given beauty: but by and large it seems fairly accurate to say that being so profoundly members in nature, among man-built things and functions which are almost as scarcely complicated 'beyond' nature as such things can be, and exist on a 'human' plane, they are little if at all more aware of 'beauty,' nor of themselves as 'beautiful,' than any other member in nature, any animal, anyhow. It is very possible, I would believe probable, that many animals are sensitive to beauty in terms of exhilaration or fear or courting or lust; many are, for that matter, accomplished and obvious narcists: in this sense I would also guess that the animals are better equipped than the human beings. I would say too that there is a purity in this existence *in* and *as* 'beauty,' which can so scarcely be conscious of itself and its world as such, which is inevitably lost in consciousness, and that this is a serious loss.

But so are resourcefulness against deceit and against strangling: and so are pleasure, and joy, and love: and a human being who is deprived of these and of this consciousness is deprived almost of existence itself.

WORK

WORK

To come devotedly into the depths of a subject, your respect for it increasing in every step and your whole heart
weakening apart with shame upon yourself in your dealing
with it: To know at length better and better and at length into
the bottom of your soul your unworthiness of it: Let me hope
in any case that it is something to have begun to learn. Let this
all stand however it may: since I cannot make it the image it
should be, let it stand as the image it is: I am speaking of my
verbal part of this book as a whole. By what kind of foreword I
can make clear some essential coherence in it, which I know is
there, balanced of its chaos, I do not yet know. But the time is
come when it is necessary for me to say at least this much: and
now, having said it, to go on, and to try to make an entrance
into this chapter, which should be an image of the very essence
of their lives: that is, of the work they do.

It is for the clothing, and for the food, and for the shelter,
by these to sustain their lives, that they work. Into this work
and need, their minds, their spirits, and their strength are so
steadily and intensely drawn that during such time as they are
not at work, life exists for them scarcely more clearly or in
more variance and seizure and appetite than it does for the
more simply organized among the animals, and for the plants.
This arduous physical work, to which a consciousness beyond
that of the simplest child would be only a useless and painful
encumbrance, is undertaken without choice or the thought of
chance of choice, taught forward from father to son and from
mother to daughter; and its essential and few returns you have
seen: the houses they live in; the clothes they wear: and have
still to see, and for the present to imagine, what it brings them
to eat; what it has done to their bodies, and to their consciousness; and what it makes of their leisure, the pleasures
which are made available to them. I say here only: work as a
means to other ends might have some favor in it, even which

was of itself dull and heartless work, in which one's strength was used for another man's benefit: but the ends of this work are absorbed all but entirely into the work itself, and in what little remains, nearly all is obliterated; nearly nothing is obtainable; nearly all is cruelly stained, in the tensions of physical need, and in the desperate tensions of the need of work which is not available.

I have said this now three times. If I were capable, as I wish I were, I could say it once in such a way that it would be there in its complete awefulness. Yet knowing, too, how it is repeated upon each of them, in every day of their lives, so powerfully, so entirely, that it is simply the natural air they breathe, I wonder whether it could ever be said enough times.

The plainness and iterativeness of work must be one of the things which make it so extraordinarily difficult to write of. The plain details of a task once represented, a stern enough effort in itself, how is it possibly to be made clear enough that this same set of leverages has been undertaken by this woman in nearly every day of the eleven or the twenty-five years since her marriage, and will be persisted in in nearly every day to come in all the rest of her life; and that it is only one among the many processes of wearying effort which make the shape of each one of her living days; how is it to be calculated, the number of times she has done these things, the number of times she is still to do them; how conceivably in words is it to be given as it is in actuality, the accumulated weight of these actions upon her; and what this cumulation has made of her body; and what it has made of her mind and of her heart and of her being. And how is this to be made so real to you who read of it, that it will stand and stay in you as the deepest and most iron anguish and guilt of your existence that you are what you are, and that she is what she is, and that you cannot for one moment exchange places with her, nor by any such hope make expiation for what she has suffered at your hands, and for what you have gained at hers: but only by consuming all that is in you into the never relaxed determination that this shall be made different and shall be made right, and that of what is 'right' some, enough to die for, is clear already, and the vast darkness of the rest has still, and far more passionately and more skeptically than ever before, to be questioned into, defended, and learned toward. There is no way of taking the heart and the intelligence by the hair and of wresting it to its feet, and of making it look this terrific thing in the eyes: which are such gentle eyes: you may meet them, with all the summoning of heart you have, in the photograph in this volume of the young woman with black hair: and they are to be multiplied, not losing the knowledge that each is a single, unrepeatable, holy individual, by the two billion human creatures who are alive upon the planet today; of whom a few hundred thousands are drawn into complications of specialized anguish, but of whom the huge swarm and majority are made and acted upon as she is: and of all these individuals, contemplate, try to encompass, the one annihilating chord.

But I must make a new beginning:

(*Selection from Part I:*

The family exists for work. It exists to keep itself alive. It is a cooperative economic unit. The father does one set of tasks; the mother another; the children still a third, with the sons and daughters serving apprenticeship to their father and mother respectively. A family is called a force, without irony; and children come into the world chiefly that they may help with the work and that through their help the family may increase itself. Their early years are leisurely; a child's life work begins as play. Among his first imitative gestures are gestures of work; and the whole imitative course of his maturing and biologic envy is a stepladder of the learning of physical tasks and skills.

This work solidifies, and becomes steadily more and more, in greater and greater quantity and variety, an integral part of his life.

Besides imitation, he works if he is a man under three compulsions, in three stages. First for his parents. Next for himself, single and wandering in the independence of his early manhood: 'for himself,' in the sense that he wants to stay alive, or better, and has no one dependent on him. Third, for himself and his wife and his family, under an employer. A woman works just for her parents; next, without a transition phase, for her husband and family.

Work for your parents is one thing: work 'for yourself' is another. They are both hard enough, yet light, relative to what is
to come. On the day you are married, at about sixteen if you
are a girl, at about twenty if you are a man, a key is turned,
with a sound not easily audible, and you are locked between
the stale earth and the sky; the key turns in the lock behind
you, and your full life's work begins, and there is nothing conceivable for which it can afford to stop short of your death,
which is a long way off. It is perhaps at its best during the first
two years or so, when you are young and perhaps are still enjoying one another or have not yet lost all hope, and when
there are not yet so many children as to weigh on you. It is
perhaps at its worst during the next ten to twelve years, when
there are more and more children, but none of them old
enough, yet, to be much help. One could hardly describe it as
slackening off after that, for in proportion with the size of the
family, it has been necessary to take on more land and more
work, and, too, a son or daughter gets just old enough to be
any full good to you, and marries or strikes out for himself: yet
it is true, anyhow, that from then on there are a number of
strong and fairly responsible people in the household besides
the man and his wife. In really old age, with one of the two
dead, and the children all married, and the widowed one
making his home among them in the slow rotations of a
floated twig, waiting to die, it does ease off some, depending
more then on the individual: one may choose to try to work
hard and seem still capable, out of duty and the wish to help,
or out of 'egoism,' or out of the dread of dropping out of life;
or one may relax, and live unnoticed, never spoken to, dead
already; or again, life may have acted on you in such a way that
you have no choice in it: or still again, with a wife dead, and
children gone, and a long hard lifetime behind you, you may
choose to marry again and begin the whole cycle over, lifting
onto your back the great weight a young man carries, as Woods
has done.

That is the general pattern, its motions within itself lithe-
unfolded, slow, gradual, grand, tremendously and quietly
weighted, as a heroic dance: and the bodies in this dance, and
the spirits, undergoing their slow, miraculous, and dreadful
changes: such a thing indeed should be constructed of just

these persons: the great, somber, blooddroned, beansprout helmed fetus unfurling within Woods' wife; the infants of three families, staggering happily, their hats held full of freshly picked cotton; the Ricketts children like delirious fawns and panthers; and secret Pearl with her wicked skin; Louise, lifting herself to rest her back, the heavy sack trailing, her eyes on you; Junior, jealous and lazy, malingering, his fingers sore; the Ricketts daughters, the younger stepping beautifully as a young mare, the elder at the stove with her mouth twisted; Annie Mae at twenty-seven, in her angular sweeping, every motion a wonder to watch; George, in his sunday clothes with his cuffs short on his blocked wrists, looking at you, his head slightly to one side, his earnest eyes a little squinted as if he were looking into a light; Mrs. Ricketts, in that time of morning when from the corn she reels into the green roaring glooms of her home, falls into a chair with gaspings which are almost groaning sobs, and dries in her lifted skirt her delicate and reeking head; Miss-Molly, chopping wood as if in each blow of the axe she held captured in focus the vengeance of all time; Woods, slowed in his picking, forced to stop and rest much too often, whose death is hastened against a doctor's warnings in that he is picking at all: I see these among others on the clay in the grave mutations of a dance whose business is the genius of a moving camera, and which it is not my hope ever to record: yet here, perhaps, if not of these archaic circulations of the rude clay altar, yet of their shapes of work, I can make a few crude sketches:

A man: George Gudger, Thomas Woods, Fred Ricketts: his work is with the land, in the seasons of the year, in the sustainment and ordering of his family, the training of his sons:

A woman: Annie Mae Gudger, Ivy Woods, Sadie Ricketts: her work is in the keeping of the home, the preparation of food against each day and against the dead season, the bearing and care of her children, the training of her daughters:

Children: all these children: their work is as it is told to them and taught to them until such time as they shall strengthen and escape, and, escaped of one imprisonment, are submitted into another.

There are times of year when all these three are overlapped and collaborated, all in the field in the demand, chiefly, of cotton; but more largely, the woman is the servant of the day, and of immediate life, and the man is the servant of the year, and of the basis and boundaries of life, and is their ruler; and the children are the servants of their parents: and the center of all their existence, the central work, that by which they have their land, their shelter, their living, that which they must work for no reward more than this, because they do not own themselves, and without hope or interest, that which they cannot eat and get no money of but which is at the center of their duty and greatest expense of strength and spirit, the cultivation and harvesting of cotton: and all this effort takes place between a sterile earth and an uncontrollable sky in whose propitiation is centered their chief reverence and fear, and the deepest earnestness of their prayers, who read in these machinations of their heaven all signs of a fate which the hardest work cannot much help, and, not otherwise than as the most ancient peoples of the earth, make their plantations in the unpitying pieties of the moon.

WORK 2: COTTON

Cotton is only one among several crops and among many labors: and all these other crops and labors mean life itself. Cotton means nothing of the sort. It demands more work of a tenant family and yields less reward than all the rest. It is the reason the tenant has the means to do the rest, and to have the rest, and to live, as a tenant, at all. Aside from a few negligibilities of minor sale and barter and of out-of-season work, it is his one possible source of money, and through this fact, though his living depends far less on money than on the manipulations of immediate nature, it has a certain royalty. It is also that by which he has all else besides money. But it is also his chief contracted obligation, for which he must neglect all else as need be; and is the central leverage and symbol of his privation and of his wasted life. It is the one crop and labor which is in no possible way useful as it stands to the tenant's living; it is among all these the one which must and can be turned into money; it is among all these the one in which the landowner is most interested; and it is among all these the one of which the tenant can hope for least, and can be surest that he is being cheated, and is always to be cheated. All other tasks are inci-

dental to it; it is constantly on everyone's mind; yet of all of
them it is the work in which the tenant has least hope and least
interest, and to which he must devote the most energy. Any
less involved and self-contradictory attempt to understand
what cotton and cotton work 'means' to a tenant would, it
seems to me, be false to it. It has the doubleness that all jobs
have by which one stays alive and in which one's life is made a
cheated ruin, and the same sprained and twilight effect on
those who must work at it: but because it is only one among
the many jobs by which a tenant family must stay alive, and de-
flects all these others, and receives still other light from their
more personal need, reward, and value, its meanings are much
more complex than those of most jobs: it is a strong stale mag-
net among many others more weak and more yielding of life
and hope. In the mind of one in whom all these magnetisms
are daily and habituated from his birth, these meanings are one
somber mull: yet all their several forces are pulling at once, and
by them the brain is quietly drawn and quartered. It seems to
me it is only through such a complex of meanings that a tenant
can feel, toward that crop, toward each plant in it, toward
all that work, what he and all grown women appear to feel, a
particular automatism, a quiet, apathetic, and inarticulate yet
deeply vindictive hatred, and at the same time utter hopeless-
ness, and the deepest of their anxieties and of their hopes: as if
the plant stood enormous in the unsteady sky fastened above
them in all they do like the eyes of an overseer. To do all of the
hardest work of your life in service of these drawings-apart of
ambiguities; and to have all other tasks and all one's consciousness stained and drawn apart in it: I can conceive of little else
which could be so inevitably destructive of the appetite for
living, of the spirit, of the being, or by whatever name the centers of individuals are to be called: and this very literally: for just
as there are deep chemical or electric changes in all the body
under anger, or love, or fear, so there must certainly be at the
center of these meanings and their directed emotions; perhaps
most essentially, an incalculably somber and heavy weight and
dark knotted iron of subnausea at the peak of the diaphragm,
darkening and weakening the whole body and being, the literal feeling by which the words a broken heart are so longer
poetic, but are merely the most accurate possible description.

Yet these things as themselves are withdrawn almost beyond visibility, and the true focus and right telling of it would be in the exact textures of each immediate task.

Of cotton farming I know almost nothing with my own eyes; the rest I have of Bud Woods. I asked enough of other people to realize that every tenant differs a little in his methods, so nothing of this can be set down as 'standard' or 'correct'; but the dissonances are of small detail rather than of the frame and series in the year. I respect dialects too deeply, when they are used by those who have a right to them, not to be hesitant in using them, but I have decided to use some of Woods' language here. I have decided, too, to try to use my imagination a little, as carefully as I can. I must warn you that the result is sure to be somewhat inaccurate: but it is accurate anyhow to my ignorance, which I would not wish to disguise.

From the end of the season and on through the winter the cotton and the corn stand stripped and destroyed, the cotton black and brown, the corn gray and brown and rotted gold, much more shattered, the banks of woodland bare, drenched and black, the clay dirt sombered wet or hard with a shine of iron, peaceful and exhausted; the look of trees in a once full-blown country where such a burning of war has gone there is no food left even for birds and insects, all now brought utterly quiet, and the bare homes dark with dampness, under the soft and mourning midwinter suns of autumnal days, when all glows gold yet lifeless, and under constrictions of those bitter freezings when the clay is shafted and sprilled with ice, and the aching thinly drifted snows which give the land its shape, and, above all, the long, cold, silent, inexhaustible, and dark winter rains:

In the late fall or middle February this tenant, which of the three or of the millions I do not care—a man, dressed against the wet coldness, may be seen small and dark in his prostrated fields, taking down these sometimes brittle, sometimes rotted forests of last year's crops with a club or with a cutter, putting death to bed, cleaning the land: and late in February, in fulfillment of an obligation to his landlord, he borrows a second

mule and, with a two-horse plow, runs up the levees,* that is,
the terraces, which shall preserve his land; this in a softening
mild brightness and odoriferousness of presaging spring, and
a rustling shearing apart of the heavy land, his mules moving
in slow scarce-wakened method as of work before dawn,
knowing the real year's work to be not started yet, only made
ready for. It is when this is done, at about the first of March,
that the actual work begins, with what is planted where, and
with what grade and amount of fertilizer, determined by the
landlord, who will also, if he wishes, criticize, advise, and gov-
ern at all stages of planting and cultivation. But the physical
work, and for that matter the knowledge by which he works, is
the tenant's, and this is his tenth or his fortieth year's beginning of it, and it is of the tenant I want to tell.

How you break the land in the first place depends on
whether you have one or two mules or can double up with another tenant for two mules. It is much better to broadcast if
you can. With two mules you can count on doing it all in that
most thorough way. But if you have only one mule you break
what you have time for, more shallowly, and, for the rest, you
bed, that is, start the land.

To broadcast, to break the land broadcast: take a twister,
which is about the same as a turning plow, and, heading the
mule in concentrics the shape of the field, lay open as broad
and deep a ribbon of the stiff dirt as the strength of the mule
and of your own guidance can manage: eight wide by six deep
with a single-horse plow, and twice that with a double, is
doing well: the operation has the staggering and reeling yet
steady quality of a small sailboat clambering a storm.

Where you have broadcast the land, you then lay out the
furrows three and a half feet apart with a shovel plow; and put
down fertilizer; and by four furrows with a turning plow, twist
the dirt back over the fertilized furrow. But if, lacking mule
power, you have still land which is not broken, and it is near

*These farms are the width of a state and still more from the river. Is levee
originally a land or a river word? It must be a river word, for terracing against
erosion is recent in America. So the Mississippi has such power that men who
have never seen it use its language in their work.

time to plant, you bed the rest. There are two beddings. The first is hard bedding: breaking the hard pan between the rows.

Hard bedding: set the plow parallel to the line of (last year's) stalks and along their right, follow each row to its end and up the far side. The dirt lays open always to the right. Then set the plow close in against the stalks and go around again. The stubble is cleaned out this second time round and between each two rows is a bed of soft dirt: that is to say, the hard pan is all broken. That is the first bedding.

Then drop guano along the line where the stalks were, by machine or by horn. Few tenants use the machine; most of them either buy a horn, or make it, as Woods does. It is a long tin cone, small and low, with a wood handle, and a hole in the low end. It is held in the left hand, pointed low to the furrow, and is fed in fistfuls, in a steady rhythm, from the fertilizer sack, the incipient frock, slung heavy along the right side.

After you have strowed the gyewanner you turn the dirt back over with two plowings just as before: and that is the second bedding. Pitch the bed shallow, or you won't be able to work it right.

If you have done all this right you haven't got a blemish in all your land that is not broke: and you are ready to plant.

But just roughly, only as a matter of suggestion, compute the work that has been done so far, in ten acres of land, remembering that this is not counting in ten more acres of corn and a few minor crops: how many times has this land been retraced in the rolling-gaited guidance and tensions and whippings and orderings of plowing, and with the steadily held horn, the steady arc of the right arm and right hand fisting and opening like a heart, the heavy weight of the sack at the right side?

Broadcasting, the whole unbroken plaque slivered open in rectilinear concenters, eight inches apart and six deep if with one mule, sixteen apart and twelve deep if with two: remember how much length of line is coiled in one reel or within one phonograph record: and then each furrow, each three and a half feet, scooped open with a shovel plow: and in each row the fertilizer laid: and each row folded cleanly back in four transits of its complete length: or bedding, the first bedding in four transits of each length; and then the fertilizer: and four more transits of each length: every one of the many rows of the whole of the field gone eight times over with a plow and a ninth by hand; and only now is it ready for planting.

Planting

There are three harrs you might use but the springtoothed harr is best. The long-toothed section harrow tears your bed to pieces; the short-toothed is better, but catches on snags and is more likely to pack the bed than loosen it. The springtooth moves lightly but incisively with a sort of knee-action sensitiveness to the modulations of the ground, and it jumps snags. You harrow just one row at a time and right behind the harrow comes the planter. The planter is rather like a tennis-court marker: a seed bin set between light wheels, with a little plow protruded from beneath it like a foot from under a hoopskirt. The little beak of the plow slits open the dirt; just at its lifted heel the seed thrills out in a spindling stream; a flat wheel flats the dirt over: a light-traveling, tender, iron sexual act entirely worthy of setting beside the die-log and the swept broad-handed arm.*

Depending on the moisture and the soil, it will be five days to two weeks before the cotton will show.

Cultivating begins as soon as it shows an inch.

Cultivation:

Barring off: the sweepings: chopping: laying by:

The first job is barring off.

Set a five- to six-inch twister, the smallest one you have, as close in against the stalks as you can get it and not damage them, as close as the breadth of a finger if you are good at it, and throw the dirt to the middle. Alongside this plow is a wide

---

*I am unsure of this planting machine; I did not see one there; but what Woods described to me seemed to tally with something I had seen, and not remembered with perfect clearness, from my childhood. The die-log is still used, Woods says, by some of the older-fashioned farmers and by some negroes. I'm not very clear about it either, but I am interested because according to Woods its use goes a *way* on back. My 'impression' is that it's simple enough: a hollow homemade cylinder of wood with a hole in it to regulate and direct the falling stream of seed as would be more difficult by hand.

tin defender, which doesn't allow a blemish to fall on the young plants.

Then comes the first of the four sweepings. The sweeps are blunt stocks shaped a good deal like stingrays. Over their dull foreheads and broad shoulders they neither twist nor roll the dirt, but shake it from the middle to the beds on either side. For the first sweeping you still use the defender. Use a little stock, but the biggest you dare to; probably the eighteen-inch.

Next after that comes the chopping, and with this the whole family helps down through the children of eight or seven, and by helps, I mean that the family works full time at it. Chopping is a simple and hard job, and a hot one, for by now the sun, though still damp, is very strong, hot with a kind of itchy intensity that is seldom known in northern springs. The work is, simply, thinning the cotton to a stand; hills a foot to sixteen inches apart, two to four stalks to the hill. It is done with an eight to ten-inch hoeblade. You cut the cotton flush off at the ground, bent just a little above it, with a short sharp blow of the blade of which each stroke is light enough work; but multiplied into the many hundreds in each continuously added hour, it aches first the forearms, which so harden they seem to become one bone, and in time the whole spine.

The second sweeping is done with the twenty to twenty-two-inch stock you will use from now on; then comes hoeing, another job for the whole family; then you run the middles; that is, you put down soda by hand or horn or machine; soda makes the weed, guano puts on the fruit; then comes the third sweeping; and then another hoeing. The first and second sweepings you have gone pretty deep. The stuff is small and you want to give loose ground to your feed roots. The third sweeping is shallow, for the feed roots have extended themselves within danger of injury.

The fourth sweeping is so light a scraping that it is scarcely more than a ritual, like a barber's last delicate moments with his muse before he holds the mirror up to the dark side of your skull. The cotton has to be treated very carefully. By this last sweeping it is making. Break roots, or lack rain, and it is stopped dead as a hammer.

This fourth sweeping is the operation more properly known as laying by. From now on until picking time, there is nothing more a farmer can do. Everything is up to the sky, the dirt, and the cotton itself; and in six weeks now, and while the farmer is fending off such of its enemies as he can touch, and, lacking rations money to live on, is desperately seeking and conceivably finding work, or with his family is hung as if on a hook on his front porch in the terrible leisure, the cotton is making, and his year's fate is being quietly fought out between agencies over which he has no control. And in this white midsummer, while he is thus waiting however he can, and defending what little he can, these are his enemies, and this is what the cotton is doing with its time:

Each square points up. That is to say: on twig-ends, certain of the fringed leaves point themselves into the sharp form of an infant prepuce; each square points up: and opens a flat white flower which turns pink next day, purple the next, and on the next day shrivels and falls, forced off by the growth, at the base of the bloom, of the boll. The development from square to boll consumes three weeks in the early summer, ten days in the later, longer and more intense heat. The plants are well fringed with pointed squares, and young cold bolls, by the time the crop is laid by; and the blooming keeps on all summer. The development of each boll from the size of a pea to that point where, at the size of a big walnut, it darkens and dries and its white contents silently explode it, takes five to eight weeks and is by no means ended when the picking season has begun.

And meanwhile the enemies: bitterweed, ragweed, Johnson grass; the weevil, the army worm; the slippery chances of the sky. Bitterweed is easily killed out and won't come up again. Ragweed will, with another prong every time. That weed can suck your crop to death. Johnson grass, it takes hell and scissors to control. You can't control it in the drill with your plowing. If you just cut it off with the hoe, it is high as your thumb by the next morning. The best you can do is dig up the root with the corner of your hoe, and that doesn't hold it back any too well.

There is a lot less trouble from the weevils* than there used

*If I remember rightly, people never learned any successful method against him, and it is some insect, whose name and kind I forget, who holds him in check.

to be, but not the army worms. Army worms are devils. The biggest of them get to be the size of your little finger. They eat leaves and squares and young bolls. You get only a light crop of them at first. They web up in the leaves and turn into flies, the flies lay eggs, the eggs turn into army worms by the millions and if they have got this good a start of you you can hear the sound of them eating in the whole field and it sounds like a brushfire. They are a bad menace but they are not as hard to control as the weevil. You mix arsenic poison with a sorry grade of flour and dust the plants late of an evening (afternoon) or soon of a morning (pre-morning); and the dew makes a paste of it that won't blow off.

It is only in a very unusual year that you do well with both of the most important crops, the two life mainly depends on, because they need rain and sun in such different amounts. Cotton needs a great deal less rain than corn; it is really a sun flower. If it is going to get a superflux of rain, that will best come before it is blooming; and if it has got to rain during that part of the summer when a fairsized field is blooming a bale a day, it had best rain late in the evening when the blooms are shutting or at night, not in the morning or the mid day: for then the bloom is blared out flat; rain gets in it easy and hangs on it; it shuts wet, sours, and sticks to the boll; next morning it turns red and falls. Often the boll comes off with it. But the boll that stays on is sour and rotted and good for nothing. Or to put it the other way around, it can take just one rain at the wrong time of day at the wrong time of summer to wreck you out of a whole bale.

It is therefore not surprising that they are constant readers of the sky; that it holds not an ounce of 'beauty' to them (though I know of no more magnificent skies than those of Alabama); that it is the lodestone of their deepest pieties; and that they have, also, the deep stormfear which is apparently common to all primitive peoples. Wind is as terrifying to them as cloud and lightning and thunder: and I remember how, sitting with the Woods, in an afternoon when George was away at work, and a storm was building, Mrs. Gudger and her children came hurrying three quarters of a mile beneath the blackening air to shelter among company. Gudger says: 'You never can tell what's in a cloud.'

Picking season

Late in August the fields begin to whiten more rarely with late bloom and more frequently with cotton and then still thicker with cotton, a sparkling ground starlight of it, steadily bursting into more and more millions of points, all the leaves seeming shrunken smaller; quite as at night the whole frontage of the universe is more and more thoroughly printed in the increasing darkness; and the wide cloudless and tremendous light holds the earth clamped and trained as beneath a vacuum bell and burningglass; in such a brilliance that half and two thirds of the sky is painful to look into; and in this white maturing oven the enlarged bolls are streaked a rusty green, then bronze, and are split and splayed open each in a loose vomit of cotton. These split bolls are now *burrs*, hard and edged as chiseled wood, pointed nearly as thorns, spread open in three and four and five gores or cells. It is slow at first, just a few dozen scattered here and there and then a few tens of dozens, and then there is a space of two or three days in which a whole field seems to be crackling open at once, and at this time it seems natural that it must be gone into and picked, but all the more temperate and experienced tenants wait a few days longer until it will be fully worth the effort: and during this bursting of bolls and this waiting, there is a kind of quickening, as if deep under the ground, of all existence, toward a climax which cannot be delayed much longer, but which is held in the tensions of this reluctance, tightening, and delay: and this can be seen equally in long, sweeping drivings of a car between these spangling fields, and in any one of the small towns or the county seats, and in the changed eyes of any one family, a kind of tightening as of an undertow, the whole world and year lifted nearly upon its crest, and soon beginning the long chute down to winter: children, and once in a while a very young or a very old woman or man, whose work is scarcely entered upon or whose last task and climax this may be, are deeply taken with an excitement and a restlessness to begin picking, and in the towns, where it is going to mean money, the towns whose existence is for it and depends on it, and which in most times of year are sunken in sleep as at the bottom of a sea: these towns are sharpening awake; even the white hot streets of a large city

are subtly changed in this season: but Gudger and his wife
and Ricketts and Woods, and most of the heads of the million
and a quarter families who have made this and are to do the
working of taking it for their own harm and another's use,
they are only a little more quiet than usual, as they might be if
they were waiting for a train to come in, and keep looking at
the fields, and judging them; and at length one morning (the
Ricketts women are already three days advanced in ragged
work), Gudger says, Well:

Well; I reckin tomorrow we'd better start to picking:

And the next morning very early, with their broad hats and
great sacks and the hickory baskets, they are out, silent, their
bodies all slanted, on the hill: and in every field in hundreds of
miles, black and white, it is the same: and such as it is, it is a joy
which scarcely touches any tenant; and is worn thin and
through in half a morning, and is gone for a year.

It is simple and terrible work. Skill will help you; all the endurance you can draw up against it from the roots of your existence will be thoroughly used as fuel to it: but neither skill
nor endurance can make it any easier.

Over the right shoulder you have slung a long white sack
whose half length trails the ground behind. You work with
both hands as fast and steadily as you can. The trick is to get
the cotton between your fingertips at its very roots in the burr
in all three or four or five gores at once so that it is brought
out clean in one pluck. It is easy enough with one burr in perhaps ten, where the cotton is ready to fall; with the rest, the
fibers are more tight and tricky. So another trick is, to learn
these several different shapes of burr and resistance as nearly as
possible by instinct, so there will be no second trying and delay, and none left wasted in the burr; and, too, as quickly to
judge what may be too rotted and dirtied to use, and what is
not yet quite ready to take: there are a lot suspended between
these small uncertainties, and there should be no delay, no
need to use the mind's judgement, and few mistakes. Still another trick is, between these strong pulls of efficiency, proper
judgement, and maximum speed, not to hurt your fingers on
the burrs any worse than you can help. You would have to try
hard, to break your flesh on any one burr, whether on its sharp
points or its edges; and a single raindrop is only scarcely in-

strumental in ironing a mountain flat; but in each plucking of
the hand the fingers are searched deep in along these several
sharp, hard edges. In two hours' picking the hands are just
well limbered up. At the end of a week you are favoring your
fingers, still in the obligation of speed. The later of the three to
fives times over the field, the last long weeks of the season, you
might be happy if it were possible to exchange them for boils.
With each of these hundreds of thousands of insertions of the
hands, moreover, the fingers are brought to a small point, in
an action upon every joint and tendon in the hand. I suggest
that if you will try, three hundred times in succession, the following exercise: touch all five fingertips as closely as possible
into one point, trying meanwhile to hold loose cotton in the
palm of the hand: you will see that this can very quickly tire,
cramp and deteriorate the whole instrument, and will understand how easily rheumatism can take up its strictures in just
this place.

Meanwhile, too, you are working in a land of sunlight and
heat which are special to just such country at just that time of
year: sunlight that stands and stacks itself upon you with the
serene weight of deep sea water, and heat that makes the jointed
and muscled and fine-structured body glow like one indiscriminate oil; and this brilliant weight of heat is piled upon you
more and more heavily in hour after hour so that it can seem
you are a diving bell whose strained seams must at any moment burst, and the eyes are marked in stinging sweat, and the
head, if your health is a little unstable, is gently roaring, like a
private blowtorch, and less gently beating with aching blood:
also the bag, which can hold a hundred pounds, is filling as it
is dragged from plant to plant, four to nine burrs to a plant to
be rifled swiftly, and the load shrugged along another foot or
two and the white row stretched ahead to a blur and innumerably manifolded in other white rows which have not yet been
touched, and younger bolls in the cleaned row behind already
breaking like slow popcorn in the heat, and the sack still
heavier and heavier, so that it pulls you back as a beast might
rather than a mere dead weight: but it is not only this: cotton
plants are low, so that in this heat and burden of the immanent
sun and of the heavying sack you are dragging, you are continuously somewhat stooped over even if you are a child, and are

bent very deep if you are a man or a woman. A strong back is a godsend, but not even the strongest back was built for that treatment, and there combine at the kidneys, and rill down the thighs and up the spine and athwart the shoulders the ticklish weakness of gruel or water, and an aching that is increased in geometric progressions, and at length, in the small of the spine, a literal and persistent sensation of yielding, buckling, splintering, and breakage: and all of this, even though the mercy of nature has hardened your flesh and has anesthetized your nerves and your powers of reflection and of imagination, yet reaches in time the brain and the more mirror-like nerves, and thereby is redoubled upon itself much more powerfully than before: and this is all compounded upon you during each successive hour of the day and during each successive day in a force which rest and food and sleep only partly and superficially refresh: and though, later in the season, you are relieved of the worst of the heat, it is in exchange at the last for a coolness which many pickers like even less well, since it so slows and chills the lubricant garment of sweat they work in, and seriously slows and stiffens the fingers which by then at best afford an excruciation in every touch.

The tenants' idiom has been used ad nauseam by the more unspeakable of the northern journalists but it happens to be accurate: that picking goes on each day from can to can't: sometimes, if there is a feeling of rush, the Ricketts continue it by moonlight. In the blasting heat of the first of the season, unless there is a rush to beat a rain or to make up an almost completed wagonload, it is customary to quit work an hour and a half or even two hours in the worst part of the day and to sit or lie in the shade and possible draft of the hallway or porch asleep or dozing after dinner. This time narrows off as the weeks go by and a sense of rush and of the wish to be done with it grows on the pickers and is tightened through from the landlord. I have heard of tenants and pickers who have no rest-period and no midday meal,* but those I am acquainted with

*On the big plantations, where a good deal of the picking is done by day labor and is watched over by riding bosses, all the equations of speed and unresting steadiness are of course intensified; the whole nature of the work, in the men and women and their children, is somewhat altered. Yet not so much as might at first seem. A man and his family working alone are drawn narrowly

have it. It is of course no parallel in heartiness and variety to the proud and enormous meals which farm wives of the wheat country prepare for harvest hands, and which are so very zestfully regarded by some belated virgilians as common to what they like to call the American Scene. It is in fact the ordinary every day food, with perhaps a little less variety than in the earlier summer, hastily thrown together and heated by a woman who has hurried in exhausted from the field as few jumps as possible ahead of her family, and served in the dishes she hurriedly rinsed before she hurried out on the early morning as few jumps as possible behind them. When they are all done, she hurries through the dish washing and puts on her straw hat or her sunbonnet and goes on back into the field, and they are all at it in a strung-out little bunch, the sun a bitter white on their deeply bent backs, and the sacks trailing, a slow breeze idling in the tops of the pines and hickories along the far side but the leaves of the low cotton scarcely touched in it, and the whole land, under hours of heat still to go, yet listed subtly forward toward the late end of the day. They seem very small in the field and very lonely, and the motions of their industry are so small, in range, their bodies so slowly moving, that it seems less that they are so hard at work than that they are bowed over so deeply into some fascination or grief, or are as those pilgrims of Quebec who take the great flights of stairs upon their knees, slowly, a prayer spoken in each step. Ellen lies in the white load of the cotton-basket in the shade asleep; Squinchy picks the front of his dress full and takes it to his mother; Clair Bell fills a hat time after time in great speed and with an expression of delight rushes up behind her mother and dumps the cotton on all of her she can reach and goes crazy with laughter, and her mother and the girls stop a minute and she is hugged, but they talk more among themselves than the other families, they are much more quiet than is usual to them, and Mrs. Ricketts only pauses a minute, cleaning the cotton

---

together in these weeds even within themselves, and know they are being watched: from the very first, in town, their landlords are observant of which tenants bring their cotton first to gin and of who is slow and late; also, there is nearly always, in the tenant's family, the exceedingly sharp need of cottonseed money.

from her skirts and her hair and putting it in her sack, and then she is bowed over deeply at work again. Woods is badly slowed by weakness and by the pain in his shoulder; he welcomes any possible excuse to stop and sometimes has to pause whether there is any excuse or not, but his wife and her mother are both strong and good pickers, so he is able to get by without a hired hand. Thomas is not old enough yet to be any use. Burt too is very young for it and works only by fits and starts; little is expected of children so small, but it is no harm what little they do; you can't learn them too young. Junior is not very quick with it at best. He will work for a while furiously hard, in jealousy of Louise, and then slacken up with sore hands and begin to bully Burt. Katy is very quick. Last summer, when she was only eight, she picked a hundred and ten pounds in a day in a race with Flora Merry Lee. This summer she has had runarounds and is losing two fingernails but she is picking steadily. Pearl Woods is big for her age and is very steadily useful. Louise is an extraordinarily steady and quick worker for her age; she can pick a hundred and fifty pounds in a day. The two Ricketts boys are all right when their papa is on hand to keep them at their work; as it is, with Ricketts at the sawmills they clown a good deal, and tease their sisters. Mrs. Gudger picks about the average for a woman, a hundred and fifty to two hundred pounds a day. She is fast with her fingers until the work exhausts her; 'last half of the day I just don't see how I can keep on with it.' George Gudger is a very poor picker. When he was a child he fell in the fireplace and burnt the flesh off the flat of both hands to the bone, so that his fingers are stiff and slow and the best he has ever done in a day is a hundred and fifty pounds. The average for a man is nearer two hundred and fifty. His back hurts him badly too, so he usually picks on his knees, the way the others pick only when they are resting. Mrs. Ricketts used to pick three hundred and three hundred and fifty pounds in a day but sickness has slowed her to less than two hundred now. Mrs. Ricketts is more often than not a fantast, quite without realizing, and in all these figures they gave me there may be inaccuracy—according to general talk surrounding the Rust machine a hundred pounds a day is good picking—but these are their own estimates of their own abilities, on a matter in which tenants have some pride, and that seems to me more to the point than their accuracy. There are sometimes shifts into gayety in the picking, or a brief excitement, a race between two of the children, or a snake killed; or two who sit a few moments in their sweat in the shaded clay when they have taken some water, but they say very little to each other, for there is little to say, and are soon back to it, and mainly, in hour upon hour, it is speechless, silent, serious, ceaseless and lonely work along the great silence of the unshaded land, ending each day in a vast blaze of dust on the west, every leaf sharpened in long knives of shadow, the clay drawn down through red to purple, and the leaves losing color, and the wild blind eyes of the cotton staring in twilight, in those odors of work done and of nature lost once more to night whose sweetness is a torture, and in the slow, loaded walking home, whose stiff and gentle motions are those of creatures just awakened.

The cotton is ordinarily stored in a small structure out in the land, the cotton house; but none of these three families has one. The Gudgers store it in one of the chambers of their barn, the Woods on their front porch, raising planks around it, the Ricketts in their spare room. The Ricketts children love to play in it, tumbling and diving and burying each other; sometimes, it is a sort of treat, thy are allowed to sleep in it. Rats like it too, to make nest-es* in, and that draws ratsnakes. It is not around, though, for very long at a time. Each family has a set of archaic iron beam scales, and when these scales have weighed out fourteen hundred pounds of cotton it is loaded, if possible during the first of the morning, onto the narrow and high-boarded wagon, and is taken into Cookstown to gin.

It is a long tall deep narrow load shored in with weathered wagonsides and bulged up in a high puff above these sides, and the mule, held far over to the right of the highway to let the cars go by, steps more steadily and even more slowly

*Mrs. Gudger's word. Her saying of it was, 'rats likes it to make nest-es in.' It is a common pluralization in the south. There is no Cuteness in it, of speaking by diminutives, and I wonder whether this is not Scottish dialect, and whether they, too, are not innocent of the 'itsybitsying' which the middle-class literacy assumes of them. *Later*. On the proof-sheets is the following note, which I use with thanks: 'Isn't it the Middle-English plural? Chaucer used it for this same word and as a usual plural ending.'

than ordinary, with a look almost of pomp, dragging the
hearse-shaped wagon: its iron wheels on the left grince in the
slags of the highway, those on the right in clay: and high upon
the load, the father at the reins, the whole of the family is sitting, if it is a small family, or if it is a large, those children
whose turn it is, and perhaps the mother too. The husband is
dressed in the better of his work clothes; the wife, and the children, in such as they might wear to town on saturday, or even,
some of them, to church, and the children are happy and excited, high on the soft load, and even a woman is taken with it
a little, much more soberly, and even the man who is driving,
has in the tightness of his jaws, and in his eyes, which meet
those of any stranger with the curious challenging and protective, fearful and fierce pride a poor mother shows when her
child, dressed in its best, is being curiously looked at; even he
who knows best of any of them, is taken with something of the
same: and there is in fact about the whole of it some raw, festal
quality, some air also of solemn grandeur, this member in the
inconceivably huge and slow parade of mule-drawn, crawling
wagons, creaking under the weight of the year's bloodsweated
and prayed-over work, on all the roads drawn in, from the utmost runners and ramifications of the slender red roads of all
the south and into the southern highways, a wagon every few
hundred yards, crested this with a white and this with a black
family, all drawn toward those little trembling lodes which are
the gins, and all and in each private and silent heart toward
that climax of one more year's work which yields so little at
best, and nothing so often, and worse to so many hundreds of
thousands:

The gin itself, too, the wagons drawn up in line, the people
waiting on each wagon, the suspendered white-shirted men on
the platform, the emblematic sweep of the grand-shouldered
iron beam scales cradling gently on the dark doorway their
design of justice, the landlords in their shirt-sleeves at the gin
or relaxed in swivels beside the decorated safes in their little
offices, the heavy-muscled and bloodfaced young men in baseball caps who tumble the bales with short sharp hooks, the
loafers drawn into this place to have their batteries recharged
in the violence that is in process here in the bare and weedy
outskirts of this bare and brutal town; all this also in its hard,

slack, nearly speechless, sullen-eyed way, is dancelike and triumphal: the big blank surfaces of corrugated metal, bright and
sick as gas in the sunlight, square their darkness round a shuddering racket that subsumes all easy speaking: the tenant gets
his ticket and his bale number, and waits his turn in the long
quiet line; the wagon ahead is emptied and moves forward
lightly as the mule is cut; he cuts his own load heavily under
as the gin head is hoisted; he reaches up for the suction pipe
and they let it down to him; he swings and cradles its voracity
down through the crest of and round and round his stack of
cotton, until the last lint has leapt up from the wagon bed;
and all the while the gin is working in the deafening appetites
of its metals, only it is his work the gin is digesting now, and
standing so close in next its flank, he is intimate with this noise
of great energy, cost and mystery; and out at the rear, the tin
and ghostly interior of the seed shed, against whose roof and
rafters a pipe extends a steady sleet of seed and upon all whose
interior surfaces and all the air a dry nightmare fleece like the
false snows of Christmas movies hangs shuddering as it might
in horror of its just accomplished parturition: and out in front,
the last of the cotton snowlike relaxing in pulses down a slide
of dark iron into the compress its pure whiteness; and a few
moments merely of pressure under the floor level, the air of an
off-stage strangling; and the bale is lifted like a theater organ,
the presses unlatched, the numbered brass tag attached, the
metal ties made fast: it hangs in the light breathing of the
scales, his bale, the one he has made, and a little is slivered
from it, and its weight and staple length are recorded on his
ginning slip, and it is caught with the hooks and tumbled out
of the way, his bale of cotton, depersonalized forever now,
identical with all others, which shall be melted indistinguish-
ably into an oblivion of fabrics, wounds, bleedings, and wars;
he takes his ginning slip to his landlord, and gets his cottonseed money, and does a little buying; and gathers his family together; and leaves town. The exodus from town is even more
formal than the parade in was. It has taken almost exactly
eighteen minutes to gin each bale, once the waiting was over,
and each tenant has done almost exactly the same amount of
business afterward, and the empty, light grinding wagons are
distributed along the roads in a likewise exact collaboration of

time and space apart, that is, the time consumed by ginning plus business, and the space apart which, in that time, a mule traverses at his classic noctambular pace. It is as if those who were drawn in full by the sun and their own effort and sucked dry at a metal heart were restored, were sown once more at large upon the slow breadths of their country, in the precisions of some mechanic and superhuman hand.

That is repeated as many times as you have picked a bale. Your field is combed over three, four or five times. The height of the ginning season in that part of the country is early October, and in that time the loaded wagons are on the road before the least crack of daylight, the waiting is endless hours, and the gin is still pulsing and beating after dark. After that comes hog-killing, and the gristing of the corn and milling of the sorghum that were planted late to come ready late; and more urgent and specific meditation of whether or not to move to another man, and of whether you are to be kept; and settlement time; and the sky descends, the air becomes like dark glass, the ground stiffens, the clay honeycombs with frost, the corn and the cotton stand stripped to the naked bone and the trees are black, the odors of pork and woodsmoke sharpen all over the country, the long dark silent sleeping rains stream down in such grieving as nothing shall ever stop, and the houses are cold, fragile drums, and the animals tremble, and the clay is one shapeless sea, and winter has shut.

INTERMISSION

CONVERSATION IN THE LOBBY

IN MAY, 1939, the Partisan Review sent to a number of writers the questionnaire on the opposite page. It happened succinctly to represent a good deal that made me angry, and I promptly and angrily replied to it. My anger and speed made my answers intemperate, inarticulate, and at times definitely foolish: but my later attempts to do the same job more reasonably seemed, in the very fact of the reasonableness, to do such questions more honor than they deserved. I decided to let the answers stand and, in so far as they were an image of my foolishness, to let them accuse me.

It was not pleasant to do this, for I knew and liked (and like) some of the editors, and felt, also, some respect for some of what they were doing; and I thought it likely that my reply would be regarded as a personal attack. It was; and the reply was not printed, on the grounds that no magazine is under obligation to print an attack on itself, and that I had not answered the questions. That I differ with both opinions is a point worth mentioning but not worth arguing.

Readers who think that in printing this here I am (*a*) digressing from the subject of this volume, or (*b*) indulging in a literary quarrel, are welcome to their thoughts.

I wish to thank Mr. Dwight Macdonald for his decency in returning the manuscript to me, knowing how I would use it; and to express my regret over every misunderstanding, unpleasantness, and difference of opinion that is implicit in the incident, or that has arisen from it.

SOME QUESTIONS WHICH FACE
AMERICAN WRITERS TODAY

1. Are you conscious, in your own writing, of the existence of a 'usable past'? Is this mostly American? What figures would you designate as elements in it? Would you say, for example, that Henry James's work is more relevant to the present and future of American writing than Walt Whitman's?

2. Do you think of yourself as writing for a definite audience? If so, how would you describe this audience? Would you say that the audience for serious American writing has grown or contracted in the last ten years?

3. Do you place much value on the criticism your work has received? Would you agree that the corruption of the literary supplements by advertising—in the case of the newspapers—and political pressures—in the case of the liberal weeklies—has made serious literary criticism an isolated cult?

4. Have you found it possible to make a living by writing the sort of thing you want to, and without the aid of such crutches as teaching and editorial work? Do you think there is any place in our present economic system for literature as a profession?

5. Do you find, in retrospect, that your writing reveals any allegiance to any group, class, organization, region, religion, or system of thought, or do you conceive of it as mainly the expression of yourself as an individual?

6. How would you describe the political tendency of American writing as a whole since 1930? How do you feel about it yourself? Are you sympathetic to the current tendency toward what may be called 'literary nationalism'—a renewed emphasis, largely uncritical, on the specifically 'American' elements in our culture?

7. Have you considered the question of your attitude toward the possible entry of the United States into the next world war? What do you think the responsibilities of writers in general are when and if war comes?

In reply to your questions:

In your letter you say: 'These questions, we think, are central to any discussion of American literature today.'

Then God help 'American' or any other 'literature.' Or else let both suspect words become your property and that of your inferiors. The good work will meanwhile be done by those who can use neither word.

You are supposed to be and I guess are the best 'American' 'literary' and 'critical' magazine. In other words, these questions, the best you can ask, prove a lot about American literature and criticism and about you, the self-assumed 'vanguard.' They prove you as bad for, or irrelevant to, good work, as The New Masses or The Saturday Review or Clifton Fadiman or all the parlor talkers or the publishers or most of the writers themselves.

It sounds like a meeting of the Junior League of Nations at Wellesley; or the Blairstown Conference; or a debate between an episcopal and a unitarian minister on the meaning of god in human experience.

The questions are so bad and so betraying they are virtually unanswerable; and are indeed more interesting as betrayals, that you only think you know what good work is, and have no right to your proprietary attitude about it.

1. A 'usable past'? (The polite substitute for 'tradition.' Academic; philosophic; critics' language.) Beethoven 'used' the 'past': but do you think he ever sat down to wonder, What am I using: What is useful?

All of the past one finds useful is 'usable' because it is of the present and because both present and past are essentially irrelevant to the whole manner of 'use.' Moreover, things are 'usable' only by second-rate people and worse. To those who really perceive them they are too hot to handle in any utilitarian way. These same things 'use' the good people because they have become a part of their identity.

You want to 'use' these people of the past in the same way you want to 'use' the writers and others of the present. A lot of the imitation good ones love to be used. Some of the better ones use you, but you don't know it: you think you are using them.

Each of these 'usable' people are of their time and place, certainly: but essentially they are timeless (or near it), and international neither in the League-of-Nations nor the Esperanto nor the 'Marxian' sense, but because they recognize themselves as members and liberators of the human race.

'Usable': Every good artist; every record of the past; and more particularly, all of the present and past which exists in the 'actual,' 'unrecreated' world of personal or speculative experience.

Christ: Blake: Dostoyevsky: Brady's photographs: everybody's letters: family albums: postcards: Whitman: Crane: Melville: Cummings: Kafka: Joyce: Malraux: Gide: Mann: Beethoven: Eisenstein: Dovschenko: Chaplin: Griffith: von Stroheim: Miller: Evans: Cartier: Levitt: Van Gogh: race records: Swift: Céline:

Some you 'study'; some you learn from; some corroborate you; some 'stimulate' you; some are gods; some are brothers, much closer than colleagues or gods; some choke the heart out of you and make you dubious of ever reading or looking at work again: but in general, you know yourself to be at least by knowledge and feeling, of and among these, a member in a race which is much superior to any organization or Group or Movement or Affiliation, and the bloody enemy of all such, no matter what their 'sincerity,' 'honesty,' or 'good intentions.'

And all the bad and the confused and self-deceiving stuff: Life; The Reader's Digest; any daily paper; any best-seller; the Partisan Review; the Museum of Modern Art: you learn as much out of corruption and confusion and more, than out of the best work that has ever been done. Only after a while you begin to know certain sectors by heart and in advance, and then they are no further use to you.

And why does it have to do with 'American' writing, present or future, when Whitman, Beethoven, Blake, Christ, Céline, and Tolstoy have so much in common?

2. What do you mean, 'audience'? It draws in to the point of a pin and it spreads out flat like a quoit. Some of the time you are writing for all men who are your equals and your superiors, and some of the time for all the deceived and captured, and some of the time for nobody. Some of the time you are trying to communicate (not necessarily to please); some of the time you are trying to state, communication or none. In the terms you are setting it, no decent writer can possibly be interested in the question. And what sort of conception of 'audience' and of 'serious' writing can you have, that you can wonder, journalistically, whether this past or any other ten years can make any but an illusory and dangerous difference to it?

3. Do I place much value on criticism. I sometimes place value on the criticism of a few whom I respect, in one way or another. Few of these happen to be writing critics. I would agree that the literary supplements and the liberal weeklies are corrupted: but more by the corruption of the minds which hold forth in them than by any amount of advertising or politics. I will have to add that in this respect of unsound mind I think nearly everything I have read in the Partisan Review is quite as seriously corrupting, and able further to corrupt the corruptible.

4. No; no living. Nor do I think there is any place in our etcetera for 'literature' as a 'profession,' unless you mean for professional litterateurs, who are a sort of high-class spiritual journalist and the antichrist of all good work. Nor do I think your implied desire that under a 'good system' there would be such a place for real 'writers' is to be respected or other than deplored. A good artist is a deadly enemy of society; and the most dangerous thing that can happen to an enemy, no matter how cynical, is to become a beneficiary. No society, no matter how good, could be mature enough to support a real artist without mortal danger to that artist. Only no one

need worry: for this same good artist is about the one sort of human being alive who can be trusted to take care of himself.

5. 'I find, in retrospect,' that I have felt forms of allegiance or part-allegiance to catholicism and to the communist party. I felt less and less at ease with them and I am done with them. I feel sufficiently intense allegiance toward certain shapes of fact and toward certain ideas that I prefer not to speak of them here, beyond saying that no organization of thought or of persons has ever held them, that they are antipathetic to any such, and that I feel a rarity but by no means a lack of company, and that this company is made up entirely of men who do not breathe one another's breath nor require anything of one another: but are of the only free human beings (and being such, are the only conceivable liberators of others): and that this freedom appears to me impossible under a 'democracy' or in any self-compromising, 'co-operative' effort. I am most certainly 'for' an 'intelligent' 'communism'; no other form or theory of government seems to me conceivable; but even this is only a part of much more, and a means to an end: and in every concession to a means, the end is put in danger of all but certain death. I feel violent enmity and contempt toward all factions and all joiners. I 'conceive of' my work as an effort to be faithful to my perceptions. I am not interested in 'expressing' 'myself' as an 'individual' except when it is suggested that I 'express' someone else.

6. The political tendency of American writing as a whole since 1930 smells no more nor less to heaven than all the other tendencies of all the tendential sheep who make up the bulk of what they please to call literature and who are perhaps the worst of all poisoners of the air against good writing and the most effective secondary stimulants toward the development of ferocity in personal integrity. No, I don't like 'literary nationalism' either. Nor 'peace,' nor 'democracy,' nor 'war,' nor 'fascism,' nor 'science,' nor 'art,' nor your evident self-assurance that by the act of talking in favor of the 'necessary independence of the revolutionary artist' you know any more about it than Granville Hicks does.

7. I have often considered this question (though I might better respect a writer who hadnt done so in the least); first glibly ('on no condition will I enter a war'); later with more and more perplexity, distress, and immediate interest, fascination, and fear. I think I know that I would do one of the following: 1) Enlist in that part of the war which seemed most dangerous, least glamorous, least relevant to any choice I might have through 'education,' 'class,' 'connections,' or personal craftiness. This either for personal-'religious' reasons or out of an 'artist's' curiosity, or more likely both. 2) Join the stalinist party and do as I was told or Bore from Within it. 3) Stay wherever I happened to be, mind my own business, refuse every order, and take the consequences. 4) Stay wherever I happened to be, and write what I thought of the War, the Pacifists, etc., wherever I could get it printed. 5) Escape from it by whatever means possible and by the same means continue to do my own work. Of these I believe my likeliest efforts would be between 1, 3, and 5. On my 'responsibility *as a writer*,' I suspect 1 or 5 would be my choice, and that the steepest responsibility would favor 5. 2 is least attractive to me. I am worst confused between 'responsibilities' as a 'writer' and as a 'human being'; which I would presume are identical, yet which involve constant 'inhumanity' even in times of no official war. Or, in other words, I consider myself to have been continuously at war for some years, and can imagine no form of armistice. In that war I feel 'responsible.' I doubt any other form of war could make me feel more so.*

---

*I would now (fall of 1940) have to add to this a belief in non-resistance to evil as the only possible means of conquering evil. I am in serious uncertainty about this belief; still more so, of my ability to stand by it. I also uncertainly question whether a draft—or even registration—should not be resisted on still other grounds: i.e., whether the State can properly require the service, or even the registration, of the individual. Or, put more immediately, whether an individual can in good conscience serve, or register, by any requirement other than his own.

April 1941: To leave this whole question so tamely and inadequately dealt with is shameful, but I hope less so than to do in haste what I see no immediate prospect of having time to attempt properly.

PART THREE

INDUCTIONS

I will go unto the altar of God:
Even unto the God of my joy and gladness.

Give sentence with me, O God, that I may hear thee, and defend my cause against the ungodly people: O deliver me from the deceitful and wicked man:

For thou art the God of my strength: why hast thou put me from thee: and why go I so heavily while the enemy oppress me?

O send out thy light and thy truth that they may lead me, and bring me unto thy holy hill and to thy dwelling:

For I will go unto the altar of God, even unto the God of my joy and gladness, and upon the harp will I give thanks unto thee, O God, my God:

Why art thou so heavy, O my soul, and why art thou so disquieted within me?

O put thy trust in God, for I will yet give him thanks, which is the help of my countenance, and my God.

INDUCTIONS

I REMEMBER so well, the first night I spent under one of these roofs:

We knew you already, a little, some of you, most of you:

First

First meetings

Down in front of the courthouse Walker had picked up talk with you, Fred, Fred Ricketts (it was easy enough to do, you talk so much; you are so insecure, before the eyes of any human being); and there you were, when I came out of the courthouse, the two of you sitting at the base of that pedestal wherefrom a brave stone soldier, frowning, blows the silence of a stone bugle searching into the North; and we sat and talked; or rather, you did the talking, and the loudest laughing at your own hyperboles, stripping to the roots of the lips your shattered teeth, and your vermilion gums; and watching me with fear from behind the glittering of laughter in your eyes, a fear that was saying, 'o lord god please for once, just for once, don't let this man laugh at me up his sleeve, or do me any meanness or harm' (I think you never got over this; I suppose you never will); while Walker under the smoke screen of our talking made a dozen pictures of you using the angle finder (you never caught on; I notice how much slower white people are to catch on than negroes, who understand the meaning of a camera, a weapon, a stealer of images and souls, a gun, an evil eye): and then two men came up and stood shyly, a little away; they were you, George, and you, Mr. Woods, Bud; you both stood there a little off side, shy, and taciturn, George, watching us out of your yellow eyes, and you, Woods, quietly modeling the quid between your molars and your cheek; and this was the first we saw of you:

You had come down to see if you could get relief or relief work, but there is none of that for your kind, you are technically

employed; and now we all stood there, having introduced ourselves, talking a little, and the eyes of people on us, and you
gained a little confidence in us when I met these eyes with a
comic-contemptuous stare and a sneering smile; and we drove
you out home: out to your home, Ricketts, the furthest along
that branch road: and there you showed us your droughted
corn, for you could not get it out of your head that we were
Government men, who could help you: and there on the side
porch of the house Walker made pictures, with the big camera; and we sat around and talked, eating the small sweet
peaches that had been heating on a piece of tin in the sun, and
drinking the warm and fever-tasting water from the cistern
sunk beneath the porch; and we kept you from your dinners an
hour at least; and I was very sorry and ashamed of that then,
and am the same at all times since to think of it:

And it was here that we first saw most of you, scarcely knowing you by families apart: I can remember it so clearly, as if it
were five minutes ago, and we were just drawn away from your
company, and were riding the light ridges of the winding road,
in the silence before we were able to speak a word of you,
when the whole time was like one chord and shock of music:
how you, Paralee, came up a path barefooted carrying two
heavy buckets, a cornshuck hat on the back of your head; you
were wearing a dress that had been torn apart a dozen times
and sewn together again with whatever thread was handy; so
far gone, so all-the-way broken down into a work dress, there
had been no sense to wash it in a year; it had a big ruffle of
wrecked curtain lace down the breast; and as you came toward
us you looked at us shyly yet very directly and smiling through
your friendly and beautiful, orange-freckled black eyes; and I
shall not forget you soon, your courtesy, your dreadful and
unanswerable need; your manure-stained feet and legs as you
stood in the path and smiled at us; nor God knows, you, Margaret, a year and a whole world more hopeless; nor you children: you started out from behind bushes and hid behind one
another and flirted at us and ridiculed us like young wild animals, and even then we knew you were wonderful, and yet it is
amazing to me now how relatively lightly we realized you
then: I think it was that there was so much going on, so richly,
and so disturbing: such a strangeness of meaning and precari-

ousness of balance, which I was wishing so much as never before to make secure; chiefly in one: in you, Mrs. Ricketts:

You realized what the poor foolishness of your husband had
let you all in for, shouting to you all to come out, children sent
skinning barefooted and slaver-mouthed down the road and
the path to corral the others, the Woods and the Gudgers, all
to stand there on the porch as you were in the average sorrow
of your working dirt and get your pictures made; and to you it
was as if you and your children and your husband and these
others were stood there naked in front of the cold absorption
of the camera in all your shame and pitiableness to be pried
into and laughed at; and your eyes were wild with fury and
shame and fear, and the tendons of your little neck were tight,
the whole time, and one hand continually twitched and tore in
the rotted folds of your skirt like the hand of a little girl who
must recite before adults, and there was not a thing you could
do, nothing, not a word of remonstrance you could make, my
dear, my love, my little crazy, terrified child; for your husband
was running this show, and a wife does as she is told and keeps
quiet about it: and so there you stood, in a one-piece dress
made of sheeting, that spread straight from the hole where the
head stood through to the knee without belting, so that you
knew through these alien, town-dressed eyes that you stood as
if out of a tent too short to cover your nakedness: and the
others coming up: Ivy, blandly, whom nothing could ever embarrass, carrying her baby, her four-year child in a dress made
of pillow-sack that came an inch below his navel; he was carrying a doll; Pearl, with her elegant skin, her red-brown sexy
eyes; Miss-Molly: and Walker setting up the terrible structure
of the tripod crested by the black square heavy head, dangerous as that of a hunchback, of the camera; stooping beneath
cloak and cloud of wicked cloth, and twisting buttons; a witch-
craft preparing, colder than keenest ice, and incalculably cruel:
and at least you could do, and you did it, you washed the
faces of your children swiftly and violently with rainwater, so
that their faces were suddenly luminous stuck out of the holes
of their clothes, the slightly dampened hair swept clean of
the clear and blessed foreheads of these flowers; and your
two daughters, standing there in the crowding porch, yielding and leaning their heads profound against the pulling and

entanglements, each let down their long black hair in haste
and combed and rearrayed it (but Walker made a picture of
this; you didn't know; you thought he was still testing around;
there you all are, the mother as before a firing squad, the children standing like columns of an exquisite temple, their eyes
straying, and behind, both girls, bent deep in the dark shadow
somehow as if listening and as in a dance, attending like harps
the black flags of their hair): and we, the men meanwhile,
Woods and George and I (Fred was in the lineup, talking over
and over about being in the funny papers and about breaking
the camera with his face, and laughing and laughing and
laughing), we were sitting at the roots of a tree talking slowly
and eating one small peach after another and watching, while I
was spreading so much quiet and casualness as I could; but all
this while it was you I was particularly watching, Mrs. Ricketts;
you can have no idea with what care for you, what need to
let you know, oh, not to fear us, not to fear, not to hate us,
that we are your friends, that however it must seem it is all
right, it is truly and all the way all right: so, continually, I was
watching for your eyes, and whenever they turned upon me,
trying through my own and through a friendly and tender
smiling (which sickens me to disgust to think of) to store into
your eyes some knowledge of this, some warmth, some reas-
surance, that might at least a little relax you, that might conceivably bring you to warmth, to any ease or hope of smiling;
but your eyes upon me, time after time, held nothing but the
same terror, the same feeling at very most, of 'if you are our
friend, lift this weight and piercing from us, from my children'
(for it was of them and of your husband that you had this care,
at all times; I don't believe one could ever persuade you such a
thing can exist as a thought for yourself); and at length, and
just once, a change, a softening of expression; your eyes softened, lost all their immediate dread, but without smiling; but
in a heart-broken and infinite yet timid reproachfulness, as
when, say, you might have petted a little animal in a trap, beyond its thorntoothed fierceness, beyond its fear, to quiet, in
which it knows, of your blandishments: you could spring free
the jaws of this iron from my wrist; what is this hand, what are
these kind eyes; what is this gentling hand on the fur of my forehead: so that I let my face loose of any control and it showed

you just what and all I felt for you and of myself: it must have been an ugly and puzzling grimace, God knows no use or comfort to you; and you looked a moment and withdrew your eyes, and gazed patiently into the ground, in nothing but sorrow, your little hand now loosened in your dress.

If I were going to use these lives of yours for 'Art,' if I were going to dab at them here, cut them short here, make some trifling improvement over here, in order to make you worthy of The Saturday Review of Literature; I would just now for instance be very careful of Anticlimax which, you must understand, is just not quite nice. It happens in life of course, over and over again, in fact there is no such thing as a lack of it, but Art, as all of you would understand if you had had my advantages, has nothing to do with Life, or no more to do with it than is thoroughly convenient at a given time, a sort of fair-weather friendship, or gentleman's agreement, or practical idealism, well understood by both parties and by all readers. However, this is just one of several reasons why I don't care for art, and I shan't much bother, I'm afraid. There was an anticlimax. The picture-making was still going on when your children, George, came along, you, Louise, and you, Junior, and Burt. You had been sent for; there were going to be pictures taken; and you came so late, not only because your house was so far and because Burt was so slow, whimpering and crying trying to keep up with you; but also because your mother had taken time to wash you all and to put a clean dress on you, Louise, and a ribbon in your hair. It was the best dress you had, a prettier one than I was to see you wear again; it looked almost though not quite like the 'party-dress' of a little girl your age in town, of people whose mothers are so nice they would never speak to yours unless about putting less starch in the cuffs, please: white, and standing-out, and so soft, and translucent in the sunshine like your own soul, and one could only tell it from a really good party-dress by the intense sleaziness and fragility of the cloth, through which your body was visible, and the safety-pinned floursack you wore for a clout; and by the ribbling hard narrow cheapness of the ribbon, and meagerness of the sash which was trying to look like a great blown sunlit bow at the small of your back and yet to save five or ten cents: and by the stitching, which was done partly by a sewing-machine with the gallops and partly by hand: and by a sort of uncertain embarrassedness in which this whole sweet artifact set itself around the animal litheness of your country body. And then, too, you yourself gave it away, Louise, for your skin was a special quiet glowing gold color, which can never come upon the skin of nicely made little girls in towns and cities, but only to those who came straight out of the earth and are continually upon it in the shining of the sun, active and sweating, and toughening into work that has already made your clear ten-year-old mouth resolute and unquestioning of personal desire: your skin shines like a sober lamp in outdoor noon in all this whiteness; your feet and legs are bare, they were washed, but already they carry the fine orange pollen of the clay; it is entirely obvious that you are not what this dress is pretending you are, Louise, and that the whole thing is a put-up job. But as a matter of fact I am noticing all this less than your eyes. Again, as with the Ricketts children, I am slow, but even so, it would be hard to see them at all and not have lost at least half your soul to them, even before you knew it: and already, though as yet I scarcely realize it, we have begun this looking-at-each-other of which I am later to become so conscious I am liable to trembling when I am in the same room with you. It is scary: scary as hell, and even more mysterious than frightening; and so tentative as I, who am a painfully tentative person, have never been before: yet somehow there is nothing shy about it, in either of us: it is frequent and, through all its guards, wide open: but what it is open upon, Lord only knows: there is no other blankness like you, like these temperatureless, keen, serene and wise and pure gray eyes of yours, set so wide, between your square young temples: and this as I said I am beginning only very faintly to realize now; so that I have become quiet in your presence and watchful, yet hardly know this beyond some feeling: here is a good child, here is a damned thoroughly good child. And so you three stand there, out at the side, near me, and near your father; Junior flickering glances at me which I fear in another way, shooing the flies from the scabs of one foot with the other foot, which is also scabby; Burt sniffling and beginning to talk to himself a little; and you, Louise, between them solid and stolid, looking straight ahead of you (I can rarely tell where your eyes are focused, save when they look at mine), and; well, there you all are, in good order, under the shade of the tree. Your father will not let you get into the pictures on the porch: your picture will be later, to yourselves. (He is not unfriendly or 'pointed' about this, just open, and quiet.) And Mrs. Ricketts has seen you prepared as you are, and separate from those on the porch, and she is all tightened up again, and I know I have lost whatever shameful little I had gained for her, and it is now hard for me to meet her eyes at all, the whole thing has become so complicated and so shameful. (It occurs to me now as I write that I was as helpless as she; but I must confess I don't want to make anything of it.)

So in the course of time the work is done; they drift apart along the porch and break loose along the dirt of the yard, in a sort of relaxation and loudness after tension: the children, that is; Mrs. Ricketts goes directly into the house; and now George has begun to set things in motion for his picture. He doesn't want it around here at the side of the house where everything is trashed and ugly, but with a good background; and in this and in the posing of the picture he gets his way. It is perfectly in one of the classical traditions: that of family snapshots made on summer sunday afternoons thirty to forty years ago, when the simple eyes of family-amateurs still echoed the daguerreotype studios. The background is a tall bush in disheveling bloom, out in front of the house in the hard sun: George stands behind them all, one hand on Junior's shoulder; Louise (she has first straightened her dress, her hair, her ribbon), stands directly in front of her father, her head about to his breastbone, her hands crossed quietly at the joining of her thighs, looking very straight ahead, her eyes wide open in spite of the sun; Burt sits at her feet with his legs uncrossing and his mind wandering (Louise had helped him cross his legs, but no one can keep either them or his attention in place); and there again they are; the three older of them thoroughly and quietly serious, waiting for the shutter to release them: and it is while I am watching you here, Louise, that suddenly yet very quietly I realize a little more clearly that I am probably going to be in love with you: while I am watching you in this precious imposture of a dress, standing up the strength of your father and looking so soberly and so straight into the plexus of the lens through those paralyzing eyes of yours, and being so careful to hold perfectly still, and under sufficient tension of behavior that twice, and then again, I see you swallow, and your mouth twitch a little, trying very hard first not to do this, then to manage it without appearing to move: and it is this sobriety, and stolidity and resolute dutifulness in the sunshine, and the way your mouth and throat worked, which has done the job on me:

And this was the last we had any particular reason to think we would see either of you or any of these others: yet at the very last, just as we left, the unforgiving face, the eyes, of Mrs. Ricketts at her door: which has since stayed as a torn wound and sickness at the center of my chest, and perhaps more than any other thing has insured what I do not yet know: that we shall have to return, even in the face of causing further pain, until that mutual wounding shall have been won and healed, until she shall fear us no further, yet not in forgetfulness but through ultimate trust, through love.

Second

Gradual

And so it was that during the next days, the next weeks, we found ourselves coming back and back while we worked: it was so that we could not drive along the highway past those wand-like posts between which your road leads off along the hill without during the next mile feeling in our chests a pulling eastward alongside and behind us where you were, and a silence or some comment or questioning upon you: this is not a time to tell of this fully as it happened, and I shall here say only, how several times we visited you, Woods, learning you to be the shrewdest and the wisest, to talk to you, to explain ourselves, to seek your help through others to whom you might direct us in this country, and at length to lay ourselves fully before you and to ask you whether among you all, wherever it might be best convenient, we might live, paying our room and board, but with nothing at all changed because we were there: this is not the place to tell of these negotiations, nor of their subtlety and slowness: of how, long before you ceased to mistrust us, you were liking us, and were looking forward to our

visits; nor of how very much we came to like and to look forward to you, so that you became in what our whole lives were
then involved in a sort of father to us, with this half-recognized
yet never made open among the three of us; nor of how a
strange sort of community and understanding developed
among us which we had with none of the others, in that we
were all three of a reflective and skeptical cast of mind, and
more particularly in our recognition of one another as crimi-
nals: neither these, nor the long and guarded, ironic yet
friendly slowdrawling talks we held along the afternoons where
you sat half naked on your unmade bed and scratched your
body and spoke seditious truths in naïve elaborations of irony
and glittered your eyes at us: none of these things are to be developed here; I can only say here how at length it was you who
helped us arrange it, that we were to stay, not with you but at
your son-in-law's, where there was room, and also because,
well, you fellers know, got me this woman, here, not that I
don't *trust* yuns (glittering merrily) but some way don't look
right, couple young fellers, old man like me; don't know's I
could stick up fer my rights, as you might say, if they turned
out any funny-business, you might say. You understand, taint I
don't *trust* yuns, but I know, young feller git too nigh a womurn, may not know hisself what he's lible to do next. Don't
want to take no chanstes. —Sure; sure: we understand that: lot
rather have it that way ourselves. And meantime Ivy is sitting
on the scrapheap ice cream chair with her hands in her lap and
her thick bare ankles crossed, one foot bent under along the
floor, and she is smiling to herself, wearing also the face of one
who would say, I am not hearing a word: and indeed we are all
smiling back and forth, cautiously and respectfully, and yet
openly. There has really been no need in his putting it so delicately: Ivy is a strong, young, good-looking woman, he is a
weakening and nearly old man, and she knows and he does,
and we do, and we all know of the knowledge of each other,
that she is also a serenely hot and simple nymph, whose eyes
go to bed with every man she sees; and of how he has guarded
her (but of that more in its place). So now, this is all quickly
and simply spoken-of and agreed-upon: we and her husband
understand each other in a thoroughly amused and almost affectionate way: and it is as if to seal the agreement, and the

needlessness of talking further of it, that he purses his mouth,
cocks his body, and baptizes with tobacco-amber the pink half-
naked spine-feathered little abominable subpullet who eight
feet away is scratching the stone fireplace full of trash and the
sourness of dead fire: who, startled, shakes herself squeaking,
lets out a wet weak nervous turd, calms, and goes on eating
quids and meat rinds.

Reversion

But before this there has occurred an incident which helped
determine it: that which I spoke of saying, 'I remember so
well, the first night I spent under one of these roofs,' when
'We knew you already, a little, some of you, most of you': it
was in a time about at the most intense, the most nearly insane, of our frustrations; a time by which already, according to
our employers' standards of speed, I should have been back at
my typewriter and Walker at his tanks, and when we were still
involved to suffocation in the inanities of the 'contacts' and
obligations they had wished on us, and were under the nearly
incommunicable weight of paralysis which constant dissimula-
tion, and slowing to alien pace, beneath the white grates of
that summer sky, can bring upon one: and had not as yet
found anything which could satisfy our hope, our need, our
determination to do truly: so that for the moment we had broken all but entirely and had prescribed ourselves a medicine, a
day or two in Birmingham, where, we said to ourselves and to
each other, there would be a hotel bathroom black enough for
Walker to develop some test interiors; and where we might get
help from a New Deal architect whose goodness and understanding Walker felt some certainty of in advance; and where
we might get help through some communists I had seen in
Tarrant City; but we knew well enough that it was less for
these things we went than that we might have the infinite relief
of talking more nearly in our own language to others, to those
who at least were also spies, and enemies of our enemies; and
that we might at the same time use rooms and beds and bath-
rooms and eat foods and walk through lobbies whose provincial slickness we could simultaneously rest upon and ridicule
and in both ways delight in; and that we might walk in the
dynamic and heartening streets of a populous city, a relatively

condensed and sophisticated civilization, whose ways we might stroll by the hour without the pressure upon us, the following, the swerving, of the slow blue dangerous and secret small-town eyes. We went, we sought out and talked with these people, a regular hemorrhage of talking which must have alarmed them but which also stimulated their own terrific loneliness as well as ours, and which was otherwise useless, we ate bloody foods in chilled rooms and drank liquors, we ate up the streets, their façades, their show-windows, the distributions of traffic and people along these troughs, their lights at night, their odors of soft coal and auto exhausts, the faces and forms of their women, as men starved or dried to husks in a desert might eat and drink, and this cruel great spread-out country town was so grateful a metropolis to me as I had never known since New York was virgin before me at fifteen, and I first walked in the late brilliant June dusk into the blinding marvel of Times Square, watching the Covered Wagon cross the river Platte in electric lights, over and over and over, my heart nearly breaking for joy here where all the shows of every kind on the otherwise rural round planet were spread at once before me, a giant tray of choiring diamonds.

But it is now sunday morning; late; we sit high in the Hotel Tutwiler; behind the gray of an opposite screen two floors beneath us a woman is shifting from nightgown through nakedness to day clothing but the sun is spread strongly enough on that tall windowed wall that we can see scarcely anything; little pennons and serpents of black smoke and white steam wave like handkerchiefs above the complex roofs of the lowspread city; it is transferred to us how hot the tar-paper roofs of these buildings are beneath the sun by a special sort of pallor on their blackness; our fan is drilling a steady hole and column of relative coolness straight from the center of the ceiling to the center of the floor:

We found out what train Walker would follow me down on and drank some more sloe gin tepid while we finished reading the Spanish news and the funny papers. I decided to shave and put on a clean shirt. We tried the radio and all we could get was church services. Down beneath us on the nearly smokeless hot sunlight, some tower of bells was still belting out a hymn tune. I had intended to get away by the middle of the morning but it was hot and we talked a good deal, and by the time we got downstairs I saw that I might as well eat first and get one more good meal inside me before resuming the bad ones that were all I could get where I was going back to.

In the bright sunday noon the airconditioned coffee shop of this business-men's big hotel had the deaf horror of a vacuum. Two sunday-clothed middle-class southerners and their adolescent daughter ate at a hard black table in the dead middle of the room, talking very little. When they spoke it was as if they were embarrassed at the loudness of their quieted voices; and their silver was sharp and loud in the brittle cold of ugly air. Waitresses stood at the walls in pastel-shaded brittle dresses and hard, fresh makeup, useless and restless but restrained, their restraint making them still more angry at spending a sunday this way. We ate a large, cold, expensive lunch slowly and with sick gentleness, the way you might unbandage treat and dress some complicated wound on your body, and it was one-forty before I finally got going.

Twenty-four hours of every day for weeks now I had been in the company of another person, and now I was alone, driving in this bright day. I knew now how much greater the strain had been than I had been able, while under it, to realize; for I have never known more complete pleasure and relief at being alone. Thinking over the good day and night Walker would be spending alone in Birmingham, I was almost equally glad on his account. The heat and the pleasure together softened me all over and made me drowsy and I lay down into the driving as if into a hot bath, paying very little attention to anything except the road in front and in my mirror, and pleasurably holding the car, along these first sixty miles of narrow and twisted concrete, up against the thin margin of danger. Except for tobacco and the pleasure of speed, almost none of my appetites were awake; I was just watching the road disinvolve itself from the concealing country and run under me with its noise and the tires and the motor. From time to time I would go over some part of some piece of music I knew, and I enjoyed it, but without any real edge. I knew I very badly wanted, not to say needed, a piece of tail, and remembered the place ahead of me where we had talked with the whore; but neither the want nor the need nor her proximity much impressed me: I felt only that it is too bad so seldom to feel the want of a thing at its keenest when it is available. As I got nearer the filling-station-lunch-house where we had seen her, my mind ran on ahead and slowed around her. It lounged around and talked dialect with her and made out what it could about her and where she had come from; then it took her out to an iron bed in one of the pine log cabins out back. The sun stenciled an astronomical chart on the drawn, cracked windowshade and slivered through chinks in the logs, and in the odor and shade of heated pine a wasp aligned his nervous noise. I found her body heavy, sour, and wet with the heat on the squealing bed, spongy and so discouraging I was good for nothing, while she grunted lines like got it in good, honey, and, sock it to me, shugah. So, as the place came in sight, sooner than I had expected it, I slowed the car only a little, watching out for her with the tagends of sharp but sleepy appetite on the chance that my eyes would tell me different from my imagination. She was loafed up heavily against the flank of a Plymouth, one thick thigh lifted, lowheeled slipper on the runningboard, loosening out like hair her thick whore's dialect upon the whitehatted driver as he drank his dope, and I was glad for good and all that I was not going to move in on that piece of head-cheese in such a guy's tracks, and stepped up the car again. It was the same with Estelle, thinking of her now: not worth the sacrifice of this solitude however well it probably wouldn't work out, and in spite of the vapor-lamp quality of her lavender and inappeasable eyes. I didn't even slow and go through the street her store was on but went straight on through the middle of town and cut south; and as I drew out fast along the road south of Cherokee City, began to realize where it was I was going in such a hurry and what day it was, and slowed down a little, and then I really did begin to realize it. Of all the christbitten places to spend a few free hours alone, and of all the days to do it on. I thought of driving on back to Cherokee City and putting up at some hotel there, for any town is a pleasure until you know it well enough to hate it or like it, and I knew neither of these towns that well; but I knew I was going to Centerboro and no further, and kept right on going there, on road and through country now that I knew by heart, raising a long ruche of orange dust behind me, and wondering what I might read or write in the hotel room, or whether to get hold of some liquor, or whether I might not go deep enough down into the Prairie to make it safe and manage to get into some negro church meeting; and by now here I was, much sooner than I expected, god knows much sooner than I wanted, already piercing the shallow outskirts of Centerboro, and a little ahead of me would be the main street and all the narrow, mean white faces that turned slowly after me watching me and wishing to God I would do something that would give them the excuse,* and the sun blistering down on the business block: I brought the car down to a slow float and swung into it.

It was different from what I had foreseen, for I had thought of it in terms of weekdays, and this was sunday. There was no one at all in sight in the block, and no cars moving, only two parked cars so cooked in the sun they looked as if they might take fire of it any minute. There are no trees in that block, and not even the shadow of the low buildings even partially shut the wound; the sun was hitting every surface in sight, and all of them were bare and hard, and the street and walks were white. The light shrank my eyes half shut, and in the street between the two lines of buildings it was like lime working in a trough. A small hound took the street, trying to go slow because he felt slow and was born slow, but using his feet staccato because the pavement hurt them. It was as hot as all the days of the week piled one on top of another, or as if they were a series of burning-glasses through which this sunday struck. As soon as I slowed and swung into this street, the sweat sprang out and ran on me, and I suddenly knew what a terrible event a summer sunday is in a southern small town, and how strongly influential on its victims and their civilization, and that for miles and hundreds on hundreds of miles all around me in any direction I cared to think, not one human being or animal in five hundred was stirring, nor even the leaves of the trees and the crops except in the slow twisting of some white and silent nightmare. There was nothing in the air that could be called a wind or even a breeze: the air lay all over this land like flesh, and when it moved at all the movement was sense-

*The excuse to make me trouble, as a northern investigator.

less, without direction and frightening, like the flexions of an amoeba. The sun had lost its edge and size and occupied half the sky with a platinum light that shriveled the eye, and at any horizon along the road I had traveled I now remembered the dry, thin steam that had been drawn in toward the sun.

The wind of the plain speed of movement had walled me away as though with the glass of a bathosphere from the reality of this heat; but now the glass was broken and the deep sea stood in upon me; I was a part once more of the pace and nature of this country.

Slowed a long way down into this nearly noiseless floating at five miles an hour I went both ways the whole length of the main street in the shade of the trees that overhung nearly all but the business block and there was not a stir of life anywhere: every last soul in all these shaded, jigsawed, wooden houses must be dead asleep under the weight of the hot greasy sunday dinner in shaded rooms, not even a sheet over them, whose added weight would break them open; and the houses themselves, withdrawn in their dark green, half-bald, twiggy lawns, were numb with sleep as ruins in the dappling and scarce twisting of their tree shade. All the porches were empty, beyond any idea of emptiness. Their empty rockers stood in them; their empty hammocks hung in them. Through windows could be seen details of rooms furnished twenty to forty years ago, and at the same time the window surfaces gave back pieces of street and patterns of leaves on light. Not even a negress cook stole out delicately by the back way in her white slippers on the lawn and her hat and her white sunday dress; she was gone long ago, or asleep by the simmering of the kitchen range. It was silent as the crossing of an old-fashioned ferryboat, where no motor was used and the flat barge, attached to a rope, is swung on the bias of the flat stream's relaxation. On the cool, gray-painted, shaded boards of one of these middleclass porches my body stretched its length and became the loose and milky flesh of its childhood who listened, hours long in the terrible space and enlargement of silence, while the air lay in the metal magnolia leaves asleep, once in a while moving its dreaming mouth on the shapeless word of a dream or lifting and twisting one heavy thigh and creating in the leaves a chaffering and dry chime, and I, this eleven-year-old, male, half-shaped child, pressing between the sharp hip bone and the floor my erection, and, thinking and imagining what I was able of the world and its people and my grief and hunger and boredom, lay shaded from the bird-stifling brilliance of the afternoon and was sullen and sick, nearly crying, striking over and over again the heel of my bruised hand against the sooty floor and sweating and shaking my head in a sexual and murderous anger and despair: and the thought of my grandfather, whose house this now was, and of his house itself, and of each member of his family, and of all I knew so keenly and could never say and of those I too did damage to, and of the brainless strength and mystery behind all that blaze of brightness, all at once had me so powerfully by the root of the throat that I wished I might never have been born: and then this passed, all this, as quickly as it had come, and I was again in Centerboro driving on the slow flotation of silence, door by door and yard by yard in all its detail home by home in a town I hated that was drained, drenched, drowned in the desperateness of sunday. It held even those who were awake under its power, the few, the few, stragglers in the shaded quarters of the street, whose feet dragged in the rich boredom as if in flypaper, making a loud shuffle or swinging scrape on the silence and whose voices here in the open, white-hot air, were subdued and sick to hear. There was no more reason to be walking than to be on beds in the square shadow of screened and blinded rooms. There was not only nothing to do but nothing to talk about and nothing to think about or to have the vitality to desire; there was not even any reason to exist, nor was there enough energy to care that there was no reason. I knew that miles out the red road at the swimming pool there would be girls whose bright legs, arms and breasts in the thick clay water warmth would be comforting to look at as they lolled or lifted, but I knew too that they would be inaccessible, and that I would hate them, and myself, if they were accessible, and that even in their laughter and flirtation there would be the subdual of this sunday deathliness in whose power was held the whole of the south, everything between Birmingham and the smallest farmhouse, and the whole of a continent, and much of the earth. It was like returning several thousand years after the end of the world, when nothing but the sun was left, faithfully blasting away upon the dead earth as it twisted up, like a drowned body swollen light and lifted to the surface, the surfaces of its body and the exactitudes of those scars and lesions it had sustained in the course of its active life. But it was worse. For this was not the end of the world, it was contemporary, the summer of nineteen-thirty-six, and this dread was imposed by sunday, only for a space, and this was what life was like, the only world we have. Tomorrow of these millions each single, destroyed individual would resume the shape of his living just where he had left off; and there was nothing pleasing in the memory of that sure fact.

I went into Gaffney's Lunch. It was nearly cool and its fan drowsed. At the far end of the counter three hard-built, crazy-eyed boys of eighteen lounged in a slow collapse like dough, talking low in sexual voices and sniggering without enthusiasm; sick and desperate with nothing to do and with the rotting which the rightborn energy of their souls could by no chance have escaped. They looked at me with immediate and inevitable enmity. I looked back impersonally, almost wishing there might for their sake and mine be a fight, though I was unable to hate them and am not yet fully over my physical cowardice. They resumed their talk, glancing at me once in a while. I could not hear what they said but by its tone I knew it had nothing to do with me. I decided to assume no disguise in mannerism, but to be just as I was, which was what they would hate, and to let them make what they wanted of it and to take whatever might come. I ate a tomato sandwich as slowly as I possibly could and then another and drank three coca-colas fast and one slow and smoked three cigarettes, while I looked at all the no-credit wisecrack signs, extinct dance announcements, ads, tobacco cans, and packages of tobacco and candy and fig newtons and cigarettes that I could see in front of me and in the mirror. The tone of the talk was not changing and did not change. I was just as glad as not and then I knew I was a little gladder than not. I had nothing against them, I would have got hell beat out of me by even one of them, to say nothing of three, and after such a fight I could have got nowhere with work from this town. I bought two packs of cigarettes and went out into the silent sun again. There was in the bright light a sensation of shadow and I looked at the sky and it was unchanged, stark naked, and I looked lower. Huge thunderheads were barely lifted on the horizon, their convolutions a scarcely discernible brain-shape of silver in the strength of the light. They were no use; they were a trick a drought sun likes to play; and gets away with over and over again. They ride up looking rich as doom, and darken; the look of the earth is already dark purple, olivegreen and wealthy under their shadow and the air goes cold and waits. They let loose drops as big as teacups, about a dozen to the square rod, of which you hear the palpable splash and break; and list off to one side. The sun, which has meanwhile lowered a very little, shines again and the dirt is hard and blue where the drops have hit it; it steams and stinks as if you had spit on a stove. I got on into the car. It had collected such heat while it stood that my eyes were almost immediately blind with sweat and I could feel the tickling of the sweat like rapid insects as it ran on my belly, but I didn't start the car; I was unable to move. I sat looking out through the windshield at the white concrete in the sun, and did not light the cigarette that grew wet and weak between my fingers. There was nothing in the world I wanted so much as a girl, but she must not be a whore or a bitch, nor any girl I knew well either, but a girl nearly new to me. Between us we had only newly established physical understanding and confidence and much was still exploratory, and she would know enough to be quiet and to talk lazily. We would not try anything drastic but would lie in the shade where the grass was short and cold, and perhaps drink weak drinks slowly, fully clothed but without many clothes on in all this heat, and very lazily meddle around with each other's bodies, and talk some. It would be pleasant if we were in the course of becoming in love with each other, so long as that wasn't too strenuous, and this fact would from time to time overtake our cool and lazy, semierotic talk with its serious and honorable joy. This girl would have a good body in a thin, white cotton dress, and her flesh would have the talent for being cool no matter how closely you touched it, in this hot afternoon, and she would feel as much as I did the seaweight of broad leaves the summer had brought out above us and how they hung on the air, and the sense of the damned south spread under and around us, miles and hundreds of miles, millions and millions of people, in this awful paralysis of sunday, and the sense of death. And if, putting my forehead against her cold throat and feeling against my face through her dress the balance and goodness of her breasts, knowing suddenly my weakness and the effort and ugliness and sorrow of the beautiful world, I should almost in silence cry the living blood out of myself, this girl would not only know what it was about but would know that in the only way I would stand for anyone to know it, and we would still be companions in the fall of the afternoon, though we might never find such good of each other again.

I took the car out the Madrid road, and soon the excessive heat was breezed out of it that had assembled in it while it stood frying, and I was lifting a line of dust again while the sun leaned to my left with all its heat still in it and stood like a poultice on my left face and shoulder. All these houses I hurried past were familiar, uhuh; uhuh; on a few of the front porches there were people. They looked after me and the car, turning their heads very slowly, too far gone even subconsciously to be grateful even for so small and meaningless a variant. God damn such a life. I began thinking of the girl again. She was all right but what the hell, fantast. Where was I going to get her and would I want her if I had her. If I was ever in my life going to do one page of decent writing or one good minute of movies that was all in hell I wanted and I knew I wouldn't; not by any chance; and that didn't make much difference either. Who the hell am I. I don't even want a drink, and I don't even much want to die. I wish there was no one in all my life I had ever come close enough to to harm, or change the life of, the least little bit, and what is there to do about that. There is nothing that exists, or in imagination, that is not much more than beautiful, and a lot I care about that, and existence goes on under pressures more terrible than can ever be done a thing for, and a lot I care again. I could put my foot to the floor right now and when it had built up every possible bit of speed I could twist the car off the road, if possible into a good-sized oak, and the chances are fair that I would kill myself, and I don't care much about doing that either. That would do Via some bad damage, just as continuing to live with her is bound to, and just as leaving her is bound to. My father, my grandfather, my poor damned tragic, not unusually tragic, bitched family and all these millions of each individual people that only want to live in kindness and decency, you never live an inch without involvement and hurting people and ——ing yourself everlastingly and only the hard bastards come through, I'm not born and can't be that hard apparently and God —— Genius and Works of Art anyway and who the hell am I, who in Jesus' name am I. This is a beautiful country. You can take that and good art and love together and stick them up your ——. And if you think da dialectic is going to ring any conceivably worthwhile changes, you can stick that and yourself up after. Just an individualizing intellectual. Bad case of infantilism. And —— you, too.

As soon as I got on the slag above Madrid, I started watching for the church. It turned up a couple of miles later. I slowed down and turned to the right between the two peeled posts and took the sharp little hill in high. The man on the porch of the relatively prosperous little farmhouse on my right turned his head after the car. I had wished for better luck, but all right.

The one I wanted to see was Gudger, to himself, or anyhow just with his family. His yellow eyes and very slow way of talking had stayed with me most and some of the things he had said made it possible that he had at least heard of the union. He was the most direct talker and seemed the sorest and most intelligent and I wanted to learn more about him; but I didn't know where he lived. I wanted to avoid involvement today with the Ricketts and with Woods, and if possible I would be glad if they never knew I was there, for any one of the three families was pretty sure to be sensitive and jealous. If I had to see Gudger at the price of involvement with them or of setting them against me I was not at all sure I wanted to, today.

I went on past the row of gray houses and up the second hill and was on the nearly flat top. Out at a distance I could see Ricketts' house. I went on quietly, not very fast, looking at the cotton and the side of the road and the road, and checking on the thunderheads that now stood up all over the sky on my right.

Some woods ran by on my left and I saw Woods' house, back from the road about a hundred yards; nobody in sight except one of the babies on the porch.

I didn't know about this at all. I didn't feel like meeting people, talking, bothering anyone or myself a bit. I wanted to look around and keep quiet.

Woods' low, dry cotton went by and then his corn. His house fell away behind as I took the curve and reappeared a moment in my mirror, and here was the Ricketts' house right by the road only a hundred yards off, and now, its side porch and all the filthy lard cans and the hard dirt scattered with hen turds; nobody there. I would drive on out the road farther than I had been and see what I could find. I slowed the car a little and lifted my foot and tried to coast by quietly.

Out of the bum, low potatoes on my left one of the Ricketts boys stood up fast and grinning and shouted Hello, grinning with joy all over his face, and sure I had come to see them. The other boy and one of the little girls stood up waving and grinning. I waved and smiled and put on the brakes. They floundered out fast through the plants and ran up to the car close to me at the window, feet on the running-board and quick bodies clamped close against the hot flank of the car, panting with the grinning look of dogs, their eyes looking straight, hard, and happy into mine. (Jesus, what could I ever do for you that would be enough.) For a second I was unable to say anything, and just looked back at them. Then I said, taking care to say it to all three, Is your Daddy around? They said nawsuh he was still to meetnen so was Mama but ParlLee was yer they would git her fer me. I told them, No, thanks, I didn't want to make any bother because I couldn't stay any time today; I just wanted to ask their Daddy would he tell me where Mr. George Gudger lived. They said he didn' live fur, he lived jist a piece down over the heel I could walk it easy. Not wanting to leave the car here to have to come back for, I asked if I could be sure of the path. They told me, You go awn daown the heel twhur Tip Foster's haouse is ncut in thew his barn nfoller the foot paff awn aout thew the corn tell ye come to a woods, take the one awn the right nanexunawn a liyuf nye come aout at the high een un a cotton patch, cut awn thew the cotton patch, you'll see the foot paff, ngo awn daown na heeln he's rat thur, the only haouse. I pretended to be confused more than I was and said, Is they any way of getting an auto in? The other little girl had come up on the other side of the car; she was leaning in the window on her folded, slender arms and looking at me smiling gladly but furtively. They said, Shore, ye tuck it a way awn back most t-tha high way twhur they was a ole gravel pit awn my left that wasn't used no more (I remembered it), turn to the left in round the gravel pit and a-past the nigger haouses and keep on a-goin' tell I couldn' go no furdern I would be thur. I thanked them a lot and told them to tell their Mama and Daddy hello for me and that I hoped I would git up and see them all soon; the little girl on my right was giggling and the other one started to giggle, neither of them in at all an un-friendly way. The towhead of the two boys shook his head and laughed snortily like a horse with pleasure; the other kept his eyes on mine and smiled steadily, and suddenly they all yelled, Yer's Daddy, *Dad Dy!* (O Christ!) and ran to meet him.

He was swinging up the road behind us limping on both his equally sore feet and saw who it was and came faster, and I opened the door and lounged one leg out, waiting to get his eye to nod and grin and say hello. He came on up already talking and we shook hands, and I told and asked him what I had told and asked his children (suddenly and vividly remembering how when I was a child that had been repeated over me, taken out of my hands, and how I had known my childhood was mistrusted; and now knowing the children must feel I mis-trusted their efforts to be accurate). Ricketts was giving me back five words for every one, grinning and gleaming his eyes and wrinkling his forehead like a house afire and, from behind his eyes, watching for his effect and for my true intention, which he feared. He said he would go along in the car and show me, in such a way, and so many times, that I knew I risked the complete loss of any possible confidence or liking, and of any access to his family, if I should refuse, so I exagger-ated the size of the favor he was doing me and thanked him in proportion, and opened the door on his side and turned the car around, waved at the children, and started on back down the road. No distance down the road his wife came toward us barefooted in a black cotton sunday dress. I put my hand up as if to the hat I did not have on and smiled, slowing the car. She saw who I was and made a small smile over a face that had doubt, a little hostility, and two degrees of fear, the tremulous and the dreadful. I told Ricketts how sorry we had been the way it had turned out awhile back, getting her and the children all lined up and taking pictures without giving her any explanation, and keeping them all from their dinners, and he said she didn't keer nothn about none of that, in a tone which without unkindness meant that she didn't have a right to, so if she did it made no difference. I told him I couldn't be a bit sure yet just where our work was going to be taking us, but I hoped we would be seeing them all some more. He said, any time, they were always right there. Then he said, any time, they were always right there. Then he laughed very loudly and said, yes sir, any time at all, they was sure God always right there. Then he laughed very loud and long and said, yes sir, they was always right there all right, any time at all, and kept on laughing while, out of the back of his eyes, he watched me. That is the pattern of almost anything Ricketts says.

Yet all this city-business, you can see; you can see how it was not really satisfactory: it was as alien, indeed as betraying, of the true and only possible satisfaction of our need and purpose as when, unable to sustain any instant longer of the effort, the pain, the loneliness, to do the piece of work you would give all your blood to do, and aside from which no hope of peace can reside, a would-be 'artist' breaks down, plays it out by the hour on a piano, sees a movie, takes sex or alcohol as if an enemy by the throat to devour it, seeks out friends and talks them half dead before they crawl to bed, and the bore, trembling and half crazy with need, self-recrimination, sorrow of what he has betrayed and of the persons he has used, begins that awful stone-heeled peripatation of the enchanted streets, watching lights in unknown windows tall in walls, grieving for an open bar, beating his thigh or the sides of buildings with his fist as he walks, doping himself with memories of music, which ends only in an exhaustion final beyond the lifting of one foot before the other, sometimes still in darkness, sometimes in breaking of the dawn, sometimes in clean full-swollen morning stare with the lamps long shut, or a subway ride, in

barrenness of gold straw seats, among those tin-pailed, each
lonesome soldiers, gentle and as if sorrowful still with sleep,
who have lifted once more the burden whence they drooped it
in the water, with night still streaming from it to the floor: and
so, cold, cold, to coffee and the daylit bed:

All it had brought me, was this terrible frustration, which
had in its turn drawn me along these roads and to this place
scarce knowing why I came, to the heart and heart's blood of
my business and my need: and so was I satisfied, as how can I
dream to tell you, first in one incident, so fully it seemed there
could be no more, then in a second so rich, so plain and fair, so
incalculably peaceful, that the first in retrospect seemed of the
ordinary body of events: it was quite as if again as of Birmingham it was thirst: as if in some inconceivable thirst and blaze of
aridity, you had been satisfied twice over, twice differently,
with the first not in the least detracting from the second; two
'dreams,' 'come true,' true like those that tortured my adolescence, and as if then some one of them for whose shadow I
gnawed at my wrist, had quietly, within the next few moments,
materialized before me, smiling gently yet gaily, abolishing
all fear save that which is in wonder and in joy, that I might
behold and touch and smell and taste her, speak to her, worship her, and hear her words, show her places I had found in
walking, music I knew and loved, find that she, too, in a distant city had seen that movie whom few others had noticed
and no one cared for; and that by some cause inexplicable to
her as well as to me, she too as well as I could never hear in our
heads the words and the music of 'tramp, tramp, tramp, the
boys are marching, cheer up comrades they will come,' without breaking apart inside, I suppose where the heart is, into a
shuddering of sweet tears, though our images were disparate;
hers, she being enough younger, of the World War, and of the
poor soldiers who, imprisoned far from home, among those
who did not even speak their same language, heard their
brothers marching in a band, and could not go out and march
with them, play with them, die with them; mine of that last
war in which there was much nobility, the Civil War, the War
Between the States, when dark-bearded, coal-eyed, narrow-
featured men of it seems a different race, yet who were our
grandparents, whose broken old gentleness still trembles along

the flagged streets of late spring, were meeting in glades in a level sleet of lead to take each other's souls out: of a camp, a prison camp, Andersonville whose pictures I had seen, a great stiff clay in winter, closed in a stockade, tents smoking, the ground striped with shallow snow, the feet, the joints, bandaged in pitiful rags, the eyes like skulls; the guards pacing, meeting, pacing, the odors of southern winter, and all centered upon these captives that slow, keen, special, almost weeping yearning of terror toward brutality, in the eyes, the speech, which is peculiar to the men of the south and is in their speech; and beyond this, north, a continent: a continent of southern clay, stiffgrassed, thin-housed, deep-frozen, down which from sheeted snows advanced a blackness and brave string, earnest and gallant, bugles blithing, the bravery of whose feet is known advancing, a hundred, a thousand miles, oh, kind, brave, resolute, oh, some day, some time, dangers braved, all armies cut through, past, to the rescue: cheer up; comrades: they will come: and beneath the starry flag we shall see our homes again, *and* the loved ones we left so far away: so far away: whom also I know, my soldiers, and their homes, those delicate frames, white in the white light snow, the beaded women, whose jaws like eggs are rounded next the hair, their serious eyes, creatures of a nation which has never learned loving and happy living, seated there waiting in the deepskirted secret whiteness of their sex; and the soft-mouthed children, dark-clothed and ruffed, whose dark jelly eyes regard the camera so mildly, so severely; and thou, deep-crafted, rude-boned, mistaken Christ, who sank in an incongruous pietà before a Good Friday farce, those reins left loose whose raving runs six decades nor shall ever cure: we shall treat them as if they had never been away: 'we have lost our best friend': 'I laugh because I must not cry; that's all; that's all.'

I must excuse myself this apparent digression because you of whom I write are added to the meaning of this song, and its meaning to yours: for here, here, in this time; on this vast continental sorrowful clay it is I see you, encamped, imprisoned, each in your pitiably decorated little unowned ship of home, ten million, patient, ignorant, grievous, ruined, so inextricably trapped, captured, guarded; in the patience of your lives; and though you cannot know it you like these prisoners are constantly waiting; and though you cannot hear it yet like them you do hear; how on the stone of this planet there is a marching and resonance of rescuing feet which shall at length all dangers braved, all armies cut through, past, deliver you freedom, joy, health, knowledge like an enduring sunlight: and not to you alone, whose helpless hearts have been waiting and listening since the human world began, but to us all, those lovable and those hateful all alike. And whether this shall descend upon us over the steep north crown I shall not know, but doubt: and after how many false deliverances there can be no hopeful imagining: but that it shall come at length there can be no question: for this I know in my own soul through that regard of love we bear one another: for there it was proved me in the meeting of the extremes of the race.

But this refreshment was as if, to this thirsting man, without warning or teasing of gradualness the sky became somber and opened its heart upon him, and stood itself forth upon the earth, and more rain fell than heaven might carry, and he stood beneath the roaring of its streaming, head back, eyes on the falling wheaten sky, mouth wide to take its falling, and all the earth yielding up that sound of applause which is beyond politeness, beyond reward, beyond acclaim, beyond all such vulgarity, and is the simple roaring of all souls for joy before God, as I have seen occur a few times when Beethoven through Toscanini has imparted his full mind (he who truly hears my music can never know sorrow again).

And secondly, quite different, quite so silent, and so secret, as the other was wild, it is in this same thirst the sudden transport, the finding of one's self in the depth of woods, beside a spring: a spring so cold, so clean, so living, it breaks on the mouth like glass: whereto I prostrate myself as upon a woman, to take her mouth: and here I see, submerged, stones, the baroque roots of a tree, fine dust of leaves, gray leaves, so delicate, laid and laid among this dust a quilt, the feathering of a bird, whose plumage I cherish nor shall in my drinking disturb: and standing from the heart, a twindling, slender, upward spine (it is a column of gnats at evening, the column of the stars of all universes), that little stream of sand upon whose stalk this clean wide flower has spread herself: or better, since this joy is human, it is not in a woodland I stand, but in a springhouse, of plain boards, straddling a capacious spring, a place such as that which was at my grandfather's farm, with the odor of shut darkness, cold, wet wood, the delighting smell of butter; and standing in this spring, the crocks, brimmed with unsalted butter and with cream and milk; the place is shut behind me, but slit through with daylight, but the lighting comes as from a submerged lamp, that is, from the floor of the spring of which half is beyond shelter of the house: and here on this floor, too, I see these leaves, drifted and deep like snow, and driven, even beneath the house: and between two sweating stones, sitting there, watching me, shining with wet in the dark, with broad affronted eyes, the face and shoulders and great dim belly of a black and jade and golden bullfrog, big as a catcher's mitt, his silver larynx twitching constantly with scarcely controllable outrage.

Introit

All the way down from Ricketts' the wind had been lifting, taking up little spirals of dust among the shaken cotton along our left, twisting and treating them roughly, blowing them to pieces, and by the time we had drawn round the tip of the gravel pit to the left and were taking the car for my first time among the difficulties of that broken little road of which I was to learn each trick, forward and backward, like a piece of music; it was tightened full of clay dust, gravel, splinters, twigs, the meager firstlings of the grand impounded rain which slivered horizontals along the blinded windshield, so that all the left flank of the metal car was steadily bombarded with little sharpnesses so rapidly, so intensely, as by electrons. We sank a rooty slope and crossed a branch (whose thin sheet shimmering was shirred all over the road) and opened on the left in a grim olive light a field of corn all slashed one way, the leaves out level in great loudness, the olive light suffused with a dim red gold, which was the substance of the earth; melons like hogs, their dust backs sliced with water; peanut plants twittering as under the scathe of machine-gun fire, or alternate frames cut from a stretch of film; and among woods again, the sanded road resumed in rooted clay, uphill, ravine-like, wrenching a last hump free (the car listing steep as the Vestris), and delivered in suddenness upon wide space of light on torsive clays where stands, first seen to me, your holy house, George, cloven, expectant of storm, the dust sunken about it like sucked-back smoke of magic, the plants released erect and trembling as flesh at end of shock of surgery, the house quiet save one blind creaking, a bull waiting the hammer: for in this last quarter-mile the wind has suddenly sunken as if cut, the dry storm being over, the orchestra arrested of its bullying *tutti*, and among the quivering flocculence of vegetation, which knows well to expect another blow, no sound as such at all, yet a quality of withdrawal, of tension, which is part smell, part temperature, part sound, a motion of withdrawal as of wide hands armed with cymbals: the exhausting odor that breeds of dynamos, a searching change to coldness, a sound from all the air as of a sizzling fuse, a blind blattering of thunder and brightness, silence again, so steep, and down it, water like trays that bursts four inches wide in a slapping of hands, broad-separate drops; and as we draw up across your yard in rapid second, a new cold rushing in the air, a gray roar that runs out of the woods behind your house and takes the field in a stride to meet us where we stop in such a welter that, in the fifteen feet between the lean-to where we leave the car and the porch we sprint for, the clothing is stuck along shoulders and thighs like tissue paper and we stand on the porch against the wall in a quiet of blockaded wind which feels illegal, and the reeking of rain is so outrageous all round that I can scarcely hear half what Ricketts is saying, though the scare and pleasure of storm has brought his voice into a high shout: and we stand, watching, beneath the field, the embattled trees, which are scarcely visible, all thrashing, yet some struck, each as if singled out for it, a great blow across the shoulders and base of the skull that beats it down with an *oooooh* rather than groan, beaten low among the shoulders of his brethren where, arms stretched, he bruises his forehead among them to weep, and a foam running and skipping as foam on surf along their crests, and a regiment of crests suddenly sprung loose, each leaf a catapult in the bumpy wind, smacking their sheen of water up at a wild angle of which wind shears off the top, and the rigid trunks themselves swaying even from their strong footholds in a strong and vertical oscillation as of wharved masts, and George comes out, to see who is here, not at all exhilarated as we are, yet tense; and is much surprised to see me, and we shake hands; and my natural inclination is to stay and watch the rain, but he is as much ready to draw back into his shell as if we were all standing in it, or as if this were an impropriety he could be courteous but not too patient with; and we go back through the open hall (which frames at its far end a barn-yard one emblazoned blizzard), and stepping quickly into the kitchen he takes a lamp from the table, and at the opposite door he knocks; and the door is unbuttoned from inside which had been secured in a thoughtless reflex of fear, and we all hurry in, and he buttons the door to again as promptly as to shut out a following beast, and here in this room we are in a near dead darkness, in which at first I know, only, that it is full of people, whom I do not yet see. Through two walls of this shuttered room and parts of the ceiling daylight is let in short lead slivers; there is the sound of a loud falling trickle and of many assorted paces of dripping water; and even here in this dry and windless place the air is bristly with sieved rain: I begin to see around me a little; George draws out a chair at the fire-place and I sit down; I see there are on the bed and floor a woman and children, none of whom makes a sound or says a word, nor can I yet make out their faces or their eyes; George is scratching a match; it glints and dies; another; dead wet pulp; another, flares; he guards it in his palm, he touches the wick; the dark flame climbs shapeless in braiding of oleaginous smoke; he sets the chimney round it, brings it trim, the flame pales, takes shape, brightens and swells to level, and stands there in glass; I look around me: the sobriety of its fragrant light is spread not quite to the two far walls but on all surfaces of wood more near, details of furniture, bed iron, bodies, faces:

The wood frame of the fireplace is whitewashed. The white-wash is scarred with matches. The hearth is full of sweepings and char. Water drops in a steady spatter on the middle of this heap, and the broken black stones of the chimney-back are crawled with its shimmering in the lamp. A small outer hearth of foot smoothed sandstone is let into the floor; one leg of my hickory-bottom chair stands in it. The floor is so beautiful in the light of the lamp. The planks are pine; they must be each a foot wide. It is all wood around me, and except for the white-washing it is all bare and untouched; it is all pine; wide boards of it; held together against a structure of two-by-fours, some of them splintery, some smoothed with planes. The door we entered is of broad pine vertical boards nailed together by a transverse and two horizontals, hung from hinges: a thick wood button latch, its edges softened with a knife, a twenty-penny nail stuck through its center has made upon the wood of the solid wall and swinging door a circular shadow of its usage. (Later I am to see on much of the wood of this house the arched breath of the saws.) The foot of the bed is iron; dark; the paint is gone from it; and like moist whetstone to the touch: its several rods stand upward to a curving of iron, a little like a lyre, and the head, in darkness, is the same thing taller. The lamp stands on a little table next the fireplace, and this little table is spread with a piece of floursack whose printing is still faint in it and through which the cheapest available kinds of pink and blue shining threads have been drawn in a designing of embroidery which was not completed. The bed is sheeted white, and beyond, more dimly, is another plain of white, and the iron of a somewhat more ornate bed. Between my feet and George's, at the juncture of outer hearth and floor there is a rapid little splittering of water which I can see falling between our eyesight, a little less swift than a continuous stream. Somewhere behind him a bigger dropping is going on, with the loudness and force exactly of a finger nail struck as hard and rapidly as possible against wood. Back in the darkness there is a folding and glad noise as of a forest brook. By lamplight and by day I see, beneath the door, water slide and spread along the wood floor. A large and slow-collected drop breaks now and then on my right knee. I do not move to avoid it but I shade with my hand so that this foolishness shall not be noticed. I see George's feet in their bluchered workshoes, planted in the boards of the floor. I watch his eyes while he watches mainly at nothing, and at the fear of waiting in them as he tries to create a saving rhythm against the unpredictable thunder. I watch these others who in the dark are drawn into a rondure: Junior, sitting on the floor, at the foot of the bed, his teeth working at the root of his thumb nail, watching me constantly with his hidden look: Louise, sitting straight upright at the edge of a hickory chair by the bed and near me, holding a baby close yet lightly against her prescient body; watching me: Burt, on the bed, on his side, his knees drawn tight, his body drawn in a tight curve round the seated hips of his mother, his face jammed against her thin buttock, crying very quietly, twisting his forehead tighter and tighter against her, chewing the cloth of her skirt: you, Annie Mae, whose name I do not yet know, and whom I have never yet seen, and who I gather, are George's wife (though there has been no foolishness of 'intro-ductions,' nor any word spoken, of any such kind): it is you I was first aware of from when first I came into this room, before you were yet a shadow out of the darkness, and you I have had on my mind while we have sat here, and so much cared toward, how from the first you not only never spoke but have not once lifted your face, your head, where you hold it there bowed deep, your sharp elbows on your sharp knees, the heels of the hands clamped to your ears, your eyes I feel sure through the tension of your body so tightly shut they must ache with it. All that I see now is this posture, the sharpness of your bent spine through your dress, the black top of your head locked in your hands and the white broken part down the cen-ter of the skull, and a little of your forehead: the wincing, and the narrow moan you yield in each bellowing of thunder: at which time George winces too, not at all ashamed of his fear, studious to hold it in bounds only for the sake of his family, that they may have something to count on, to look toward for their own courage. No one has anything to say in all this ab-sorption in terror and patience of waiting except now and again Ricketts who, since he must always talk most when he fears most, finds this silence an unbearably frightening trial: so that now and again, out of a silence in which he has been breathing quicker and quicker, he darts a loud-voiced and trembling, joking comment, to which George makes little or no answer, almost as if it were obscene in this context, and which I try to ease into silence with a 'yeah: sure is,' or a smile or short laugh. He remarks how Annie Mae is all squinched up on the bed like the devil was after her, a-har-har-har-har, devil hisself, and George says yes that she sure is afeared of the thun-der and the lightning; Louise tightens her arms round the baby, looking at me: after a little Ricketts says again, look at

Annie Mae; skeered like devil hisself was after her, yes sir, devil hisself. No one answers him. Yes sir, all squinched up like devil hisself was on her tracks; never seed a woman so skeered a thunder; and he quiets again. There is a scratching at the door, without whimpering; nothing is done about it. It keeps up; pauses; resumes in much more urgency; quits; and is done with. After a minute George says: arn draws lightnin. Arn, and dawgs. I offer them another round of cigarettes. Ricketts as before refuses: he keeps on spitting in the fireplace, stooping forward far in his chair to indicate that he is taking due care in a home not his own and for the same reason spitting quietly and rather delicately. George, as before, takes one with thanks. I realize later that he likes machine-made cigarettes less well than those he rolls for himself, but he is fond of the meaning and distinction which is in their price, and would probably always use them if he could afford them. All this while something very important to me is happening, and this is between me and Louise. She sits squarely and upright in her chair, as I have told, silent, and careful of the child, and apparently no more frightened than I, and scarcely even excited by the storm, watching me, without smiling, whether in her mouth or her eyes: and I come soon to realize that she has not once taken her eyes off me since we entered the room: so that my own are drawn back more and more uncontrollably toward them and into them. From the first they have run chills through me, a sort of beating and ticklish vacuum at the solar plexus, and though already I have frequently met them I cannot look into them long at a time without panic and quick withdrawal, fear, whether for her or for myself I don't know. Inevitably I smile a little, quietly, whenever I meet her eyes, but that is all. I meditate, but cannot dare a full and open smile, in any degree which presupposes or hopes for an answer, not only because I realize how likely she would be not to 're-turn' it, which, needing her liking so much, I could not bear, but because too I feel she is a long way above any such disre-spect, and I want her respect also for myself. There are kinds of friendliness: and of love, and of things a long way beyond them, which are communicable not only without 'smiling,' but without anything denominable as 'warmth' in the eyes, and after thinking a little about it, endeavoring to bring myself to dare to, and to lose my conscience, I let all these elements, in other words all that I felt about her, all I might be able to tell her in hours if words could tell it at all, collect in my eyes, and turned my head, and stood them into hers, and we sat there, with such a vibration increasing between us as drove me half unconscious, so that I persisted rather than ran as one might in war or round a pylon, blindly and deafly, and gained a second strength wherein I felt as of a new level, a new world, and kept looking at her, and she at me, each 'coldly,' 'expressionlessly,' I with a qualifying protectiveness toward her from myself, she without fear nor wonder, but with extraordinary serene reception and shining and studiousness, and yielding of no remotest clue, whether of warmth, hatred or mere curiosity; and at length it was she who let her eyes relax away, slowly, with dignity, and gazed down along the flat chest of her dress, and upon her wrist, and I continue to watch her; and after a little, not long at all, she raises her eyes again, and an almost imperceptibly softened face, shy, as if knowledgeable, but the eyes the same as before; and this time it is I who change, to warmth, so that it is as if I were telling her, good god, if I have caused you any harm in this, if I have started within you any harmful change, if I have so much as reached out to touch you in any way you should not be touched, forgive me if you can, despise me if you must, but in god's name feel no need to feel fear of me; it is as if the look and I had never been, so far as any harm I would touch you with, so far as any way I would not stand shelter to you: and these eyes, receiving this, held neither forgiveness nor unforgiveness, nor heat nor coldness, nor any sign whether she understood me or no, but only this same blank, watchful, effortless excitation; and it was I who looked away.

Every few minutes George would get up and open the door a foot or so, and it showed always the same picture: that end of the hallway mud and under water, where the planks lay flush to the ground: the opposite wall; the open kitchen; blown leaves beyond the kitchen window; a segment of the clay rear yard where rain beat on rain beat on rain beat on rain as would beat out the brains of the earth and stood in a bristling smoky grass of water a foot high; a corner of the henhouse; the palings of the garden; the growth of the garden buffeted; a tree by the palings with shearing of rain through it; open land beyond and beyond that trees in a line; the rain moving along the open land in tall swift columns of smoke, the trees lashing and laboring like rooted waves; and in all this time I have talked of, such steady rave of rain and such breakage of thunder as I shall not try to tell: the thunder, at length, has diminished first, and now after a long time further, the rain too, and now we sit with the door a little ajar and watch it follow itself in a frieze of tall forward-leaning figures on the field, and this smokiness faints slowly out of the air, and the yard dirt is needled, not battered; the thunder is growling well off to the west and the air, though completely clouded, is softly shiny; and there is everywhere such a running and rustling, gargling sound of water as might be heard if the recession of the late parts of a wave were magnified; and in all this I now see Louise's face in the strange blend of lamp with daylight; and Burt relaxes, and looks for a little while as if asleep; and Ricketts begins talking again more steadily; and now for the first time in all this hour we have sat here, Annie Mae takes her stiff hands from her ears and slowly lifts her beautiful face with a long stripe of tears drawn, vertical, beneath each eye, and looks at us gravely, saying nothing. After a minute she leans across toward her daughter (every line of her body sharp and straight as if drawn by a ruler), and asks, how's Squinchy? She is really asking for him. Louise knows this, and gives him over to her, and she takes him against her body and gazes carefully into his face, smoothing on his bulged forehead her russet hand. He is asleep, and has been asleep in all this time, but now beneath her hand he comes awake, and cries a little, and begins to smile, and much more to comfort herself than her child, she turns away from us, and draws her dress away from her breast, and nurses him.

The shutters are opened. The lamp is drawn down, blown out. The room is clear with light and breathes coolness like a lung: it is filled with the odors of the rain on the earth and of wood, pork, bedding, and kerosene, and is cleaned of the exhaustion of our breathing. Our faces are no longer subsumed but are casual and they and I look at each other more casually yet shyly, much more sharply aware than before of the strangeness of my presence here. Our voices and our bodies take shape and loosen, and we get up off our chairs and the bed and the floor, and come out of the room to see what the rain has done. There still are no 'introductions'; there is no kind of social talk at all, but as if a definite avoidance of any of these issues as too complicated to try to cope with; but quietness, casualness, courtesy, friendliness, of a sort that make me feel at ease, only careful: and I see how they are very careful toward me, puzzled by me, yet glad rather than not to see me, and not troubled by me.

But from where I say, 'The shutters are opened,' I must give this up, and must speak in some other way, for I am no longer able to speak as I was doing, or rather no longer able to bear to. Things which were then at least immediate in my senses, I now know only as at some great and untouchable distance; distinctly, yet coldly as through reversed field-glasses, and with no warmth or traction or faith in words: so that at best I can hope only to 'describe' what I would like to 'describe,' as at a second remove, and even that poorly:

The room was all shut-in, full of shut odors. The door let in light, but only across one end of this room; so that as I have told the faces were held in two lights at once, in two temperatures also, and in two kinds of air. With even this amount of the light and odor of day there was change; we were all widened apart, and more aware of each other, in the diminished storm: our ordinary egoism and watchfulness of a curious human situation was somewhat restored in each of us, and with this, something happy that came of the air itself, not very different from the venturing and resumed loudness of small birds on the barnyard air, whose pleated flight and song were brash as with dawn: The letting-open of the blinds in two of the four blind walls then let the room full of this cooled and happy light, wherein each piece of furniture stood completed in its casual personality within these blockaded boards, and where we found ourselves and saw each other hovered, no longer with any reason here to be huddled, and sat a few moments as if blinking, and as if embarrassed to be sitting; so that it was in part this embarrassment which, after those moments of shy glancing at one another, broke us and brought us standing and strolling, chairs drawn back, and broken apart along the porch:

and I would wish most deeply to say, how strange the natural day in a room can be, and how curiously, how secretly, it can disturb those who find it broken upon them, and who find themselves resumed each into his ordinary being, before he is quite ready to reassume it, in a room whose walls have widened, have opened once more their square eyes, upon sectors of country, in steadily thinning satin rain:

But the music of what is happening is more richly scored than this; and much beyond what I can set down: I can only talk about it: the personality of a room, and of a group of creatures, has undergone change, as if of two different techniques or mediums; what began as 'rembrandt,' deeplighted in gold, in each integer colossally heavily planted, has become a photograph, a record in clean, staring, colorless light, almost without shadow, of two iron sheeted beds which stand a little away from the walls; of dislocated chairs; within cube of nailed housewood; a family of tenant farmers, late in a sunday afternoon, in a certain fold of country, in a certain part of the south, and of the lives of each of them, confronted by a person strange to them, whose presence and its motives are so outlandish there is no reason why any of it should be ever understood; almost as if there were no use trying to explain; just say, I am from Mars, and let it go at that: and this, as well as the lifted storm, the resumption of work in lack of fear, is happening in these minutes; each mind disaligned, and busy, in a common human timidity or fear; the fear in which a new acquaintance begins to be made. I wish I might remember the talk, or even the method and direction, the shape of the talk, but I can remember this scarcely at all. I explained myself a little, this single visit, that is, as simply as I might: such as it was it was not difficult to believe, and was well enough accepted; neither I nor either of the other men said much directly to Mrs. Gudger, nor she much to us; though, so far as I felt it would be allowed as proper, I turned what I said or replied to include her, and a few times directly her way. She became able to say a little how frightened she was of storms, but without apology and in next to no humor, just statement, a sort of implied courtesy of explanation to me, if I had thought it strange at all: I gave her indirect reason to know I did not in the least think it strange: I spoke a little to the two older chil-

dren, as if it were natural to speak to children; they were puzzled by this but appeared rather to like it. Mrs. Gudger was
very quietly courteous toward me in a deeply withdrawn way:
as a wife, as a woman, it was not her place to show or even to
feel any question who I was, why I might be there; that was
the business of the man and her greatest courtesy lay in this
observance: the children, though, I felt their eyes on me all the
while. Nothing that was said made any difference of itself, but
in each thing that was said there was all the difference in the
world in the way I should meet or say it: I relied on quietness and occasional volunteering, and improvised on whatever
seemed best to hand, and began to have the pleasure of realizing that though I remained inevitably somewhat mysterious,
I was in each few minutes a little more comfortably accepted as
friendly, as respectful toward them, as candid of my ignorance,
my motives, and my regard, and as a person who need not at
all be feared nor dealt toward in any lack of ease.

The yard dirt had no shape left to it at all; or had the shape
the rain had given it; it looked like a relief map. The hens were
out to their threshold or staggered out from under the house,
talking worriedly, trembling, dry and sopping wet in patches.
The hog was grunting and water swashed in his wallow; the
cow let out a comment like a giant wooden flute: I looked, and
saw her stretched head. Out in the edge of the cotton one of
the three peach trees had been torn in half: we got pieces of
wire and lifted its drenching weight and wired it together: the
grass under these trees was littered full of the whole crop of
peaches; hardly a dozen hung surviving; they were broken apart
and bruised beyond any use. We collected them in buckets and
a tub and with Mrs. Gudger and the children sorted apart
those ripe and sufficiently whole to be used for eating and for
drying, and those fit only for the hogs. Gudger was concerned
that I should not muddy my sunday shoes, and (in re-erecting
the tree) that I should not drench my clothes.

While we sorted peaches, the whole storm sank and the sun
spread above its horizon and sank toward it: you know well
enough how cleansed, and glad, and in what appearance of
health and peace, every twig and leaf and all the shape of a
country shine in such a light, and can fill you with love which
has no traceable basis: well, this beyond such had come at the

end of a long and cruel drought, and there was a movement
and noise all round me of creatures and meanings where at
length I found myself; and that I was not crying for joy was
only that there was so much still to watch, to hear, and to
wonder before, while we stood on the front porch and talked,
George saying, over and over, while we looked out upon the
resplendent country, how good a season it had been, a real
good season, and how it seemed sure enough to have been an
answer to prayer, for they had been praying for rain all these
weeks now, more and more: and over to the left where the hill
sank, there stood up among the tops of the thick woods a long
thin wall of white and curving mist above loud water:

And he invited me, several times, to stay the night; of course
the cooking was pretty plain, but stay the night; and each time
in some paralyzing access of shyness before strong desire I
thanked him and said I had better not, knowing even while I
said it how strongly I risked his misunderstanding, and his
hurt, yet unable to say otherwise: and at length, and sure, and
sick to hell, that I had hurt him, that I had seemed in my refusal to set myself above him, no matter how 'politely'; I told
them good-bye and that I wanted to see them soon again, and
Ricketts and I got into the car; and, dangerous in every moment of bogging in the clay, we took our way across the
changed surface of his front yard and out of sight.

(I take Ricketts home. On the way back toward the highway,
short still of the branch road that leads to the Gudgers':)

Third

Second Introit
Ricketts had shown me tricks of driving I shouldn't have
dared or imagined along the clay, and now retracing it, alone,
with the dark coming on, I followed my own ruts most of the
time, often with my hands off the steering-wheel, holding the
car in a light and somewhat swift second gear so that it seemed
more to float and sail than to go on the ground, catching it
lightly as possible in the instant of slewing and putting on
speed rather than slowing and guiding beforehand, as I should
have been more likely to do of myself. Half a dozen places
we had come very near bogging, and here the clay was so

wrought-up it was necessary each time to guess again. You can't afford to use brakes in this sort of material, and whatever steering you do, it must be as light-handed as possible; about the only thing to say of speed in such situations is to go a full shade faster most of the time than you can imagine is at all safe to go. It is different from snow and from any other mud I know of, and it holds a dozen sudden differences within itself, all requiring quick modifications of technique and all more or less indescribably hidden among one another: driving, you feel less like an 'operator' than like a sort of passive-active brain suspended at the center of a machine, careful to let it take its own way, and to hold it at all in restraint only by little ticklings of an end of a whip: your senses are translated, they pervade the car, so that you are all four wheels as sensitively as if each were a fingertip; and these feel out a safe way through rather by force of will or wish than by any action. The joke of this was that my forces of will or of wish were crossed on themselves between the curiosity to manage this two miles of road, out of amateurish pride, and the regret that I was not at the Gudgers' and the desire to be there and to have a good excuse for being there: so that each time I got through a particularly tough stretch, it was in about as much amused regret as pleasure: so that at length, feeling the right rear wheel slew deeply toward the ditch; well, I didn't know then, and don't now, whether the things I was doing to save it were 'correct' or not, and whether or not it was by my will that I wrung the wheel and drove so deep that there was no longer any hope at all of getting it out: but I do know that as I felt it settle it was a thorough pleasure to me, an added pleased feeling of, well, I did all *I* could: I sat in the steep-tilted car maybe a full minute with the motor idling, feeling a smile all over the bones of my face as strange to me as greasepaint: set it in low, shifted the steering, gave it all modulations of power and of steering I could think of; they only foundered it deeper as I had begun to hope they might: and abruptly shut off the engine and the lights and lighted a cigarette and sat looking out at the country and at the sky, while the vanquished engine cooled with a tin noise of ticking.

There was the very darkest kind of daylight which can be called daylight at all, still on everything, and all through the air, a cold, blue-brown light of agate; and I was stationary in the middle of a world of which all members were stationary, and in this stasis, a sour odor of the earth and of night strengthened into me steadfastly until, at length, I felt an exact traction with this country in each twig and clod of it as it stood, not as it stood past me from a car, but to be stood in the middle of, or drawn through, passed, on foot, in the plain rhythm of a human being in his basic relation to his country. Each plant that fluted up in long rows out of the soil was native to its particular few square inches of rootage, and held relationship among these others to the work and living of some particular man and family, in a particular house, perhaps whose lamp I saw beneath this field; and each tree had now its own particular existence and personality, stood up branching out of its special space in the spreading of its blood, and stayed there waiting, a marked man, a tree: as different as the difference between a conducted tour of a prison and the first hours there as a prisoner: and all the while, it grew darker.

I took off my shoes and changed to sneakers (there was no sense in this, and I don't understand why), rolled the legs of my pants to the knee, took out an extra pack of cigarettes, two pencils, a small notebook, rolled up the windows, and locked the car: looked how deeply to the hub the wheel was sunk, and started off down the road, looking back at the car frequently from changed distances as if at a picture of myself, tilted up there helpless with its headlights and bumper taking what light was left. I began to feel laughter toward it as if it were a new dealer, a county dietitian, an editor of Fortune, or an article in the New Republic; and so, too, at myself, marveling with some scorn by what mixture of things in nature good and beneath nausea I was now where I was and in what purposes: but all the while I kept on walking, and all the while the bone center of my chest was beating with haste and hope, and I was watching for landmarks, less by need (for all I needed was to follow this road to a branching and the branch to its end) than for gratification in feeling them approach me once more in a changed pace and purpose and depth of feeling and meaning: for I now felt shy of them yet somehow as if I newly possessed or was soon to possess them, as if they silently opened and stood quiet before me to watch and evaluate and guard against me,

yet at the same time, in a kind of grave aloofness of the defenseless, to welcome me: and yet again in all this I felt humble, and respectful, careful that I should not so much as set my
foot in this clay in a cheapness of attitude, and full of knowledge, I have no right, here, I have no real right, much as I
want it, and could never earn it, and should I write of it, must
defend it against my kind: but I kept on walking: the crumpled
edge of the gravel pit, the two negro houses I twisted between,
among their trees; they were dark; and down the darkness
under trees, whose roots and rocks were under me in the mud,
and shin-deep through swollen water; and watched the steep-
slanted corn, all struck toward me from my left, and nearly
motionless now, while along my right and all upon me there
was the rustling second rain of a trillion leaves relaxing the
aftermath of storm, and a lithe, loud, rambling noise of replenished branches; thinking, how through this night what
seepage in the porous earth would soon express this storm in
glanded springs, deep wells refreshed; odors all round so
black, so rich, so fresh, they surpassed in fecundity the odors of
a woman; the cold and quiet sweating of hard walking; and so
at last to the darkness of that upward ravine of road beyond
which the land opens in a wave, and floats the house:

Up this ravine, realizing myself now near, I came stealthily,
knowing now I had at least half-contrived this, and after a misunderstood refusal, and for the first time realizing that by
now, a half-hour fully dark, you must likely be in bed, through
supper, done with a day, so that I must surely cause disturbance: slower, and slower, and two thirds ready to turn back,
to spend the night in the car; and out into the cleared yard,
silently, standing vertical to the front center of the house; it is
dead black; not a light; just stands there, darker than its surroundings, perfectly quiet: and standing here, silently, in the
demeanor of the house itself I grow full of shame and of reverence from the soles of my feet up my body to the crest of my
skull and the leaves of my hands like a vessel quietly spread full
of water which has sprung from in the middle of my chest: and
shame the more, because I do not yet turn away, but still stand
here motionless and as if in balance, and am aware of a vigilant
and shameless hope that—not that I shall move forward and
request you, disorder you—but that 'something shall happen,'

as it 'happened' that the car lost to the mud: and so waiting, in doubt, desire and shame, in a drawing-back of these around a vacuum of passive waiting, as the six walls of an empty room might wait for a sound: and this, or my breathing, or the beating of my heart, must have been communicated, for there is a sudden forward rush to the ledge of the porch of bellowing barking, and a dog, shouting his soul out against me: nothing else: and I think how they are roused by it and feel I have done wrong enough already, and withdraw a little, hoping that will quiet him, and in the same hope hold forward my hand and speak very quietly. He subdues to a growled snarling of bragging hate and fear and I am ready to turn and leave when a shadow heavily shuffles behind him, and in a stooped gesture of peering me out, Gudger's voice asks, who is it: ready for trouble. I speak before I move, telling him who I am, then what has happened, why I am here, and walk toward him, and how sorry I am to bother them. It is all right with him; come on in; he had thought I was a nigger.

I come up onto the porch shamefacedly, telling him again how sorry I am to have rousted them out like this. It's all right. They were just got to bed, none of them asleep yet. He has pulled on his overalls over nothing else and is barefooted. In the dark I can see him stooping his square head a little forward to study me. There is still antagonism and fear in his voice and in his eyes, but I realize this is not toward me, but toward the negro he thought I was: his emotions and his mind are slow to catch up with any quick change in the actuality of a situation. In a little more this antagonism has drained away and he is simply a tired and not unkind man taking care of a half-stranger at night who is also an anomaly; and thus he does as he has done before without any affectation of social grace: people plain enough take a much more profoundly courteous care of one another and of themselves without much if any surprise and no flurry of fussiness and a kind of respect which does not much ask questions. So it was there was neither any fake warmth and heartiness nor any coldness in his saying, Sure, come on in, to my asking could he put me up for the night after all, and he added, Better eat some supper. I was in fact very hungry, but I did all I was able to stop this, finally trying to compromise it to a piece of bread and some milk, that needn't be prepared; I'm making you enough bother already; but no; Can't go to bed without no supper; you just hold on a second or two; and he leans his head through the bedroom door and speaks to his wife, explaining, and lights the lamp for her. After a few moments, during which I hear her breathing and a weary shuffling of her heels, she comes out barefooted carrying the lamp, frankly and profoundly sleepy as a child; feeling disgusted to wake her further with so many words I say, Hello, Mrs. Gudger: say I want to tell you I'm *aw*ful sorry to give you all this bother: you just, honest I don't need much of anything, if you'd just tell me where a piece of bread is, it'll be *plenty*, I'd hate for you to bother to cook anything up for me: but she answers me while passing, looking at me, trying to get me into focus from between her sticky eyelashes, that 'tain't no bother at all, and for me not to worry over that, and goes on into the kitchen; and how quickly I don't understand, for I am too much occupied to see, with Gudger, and with holding myself from the cardinal error of hovering around her, or of offering to help her, she has built a pine fire and set in front of me, on the table in the hall, warmed-over biscuit and butter and blackberry jam and a jelly-glass full of buttermilk, and warmed field peas, fried pork, and four fried eggs, and she sits a little away from the table out of courtesy, trying to hold her head up and her eyes open, until I shall have finished eating, saying at one time how it's an awful poor sort of supper and at another how it's awful plain, mean food; I tell her different, and eat as rapidly as possible and a good deal more than I can hold, in fact, all the eggs, a second large plateful of peas, most of the biscuit, feeling it is better to keep them awake and to eat too much than in the least to let them continue to believe I am what they assume I must be: 'superior' to them or to their food, eating only so much as I need to be 'polite'; and I see that they are, in fact, quietly surprised and gratified in my appetite.

But somehow I have lost hold of the reality of all this, I scarcely can understand how; a loss of the reality of simple actions upon the specific surface of the earth. This country, these roads, these odors and noises, the action of walking the dark in mud, the approach, just what a slow succession of certain trees past your walking can implant in you, can mean to you, the house as it stands there dark in darkness, the indecisiveness and the bellowing dog, the conversations of questioning, defense, assurance, acceptance, the subtle yet strong distinctions of attitude, the walking between the walls of wood and the sitting and eating, the tastes of the several foods, the weights of our bodies in our chairs, the look of us in the lamplight in the presence of the walls of the house and of the country night, the beauty and stress of our tiredness, how we held quietness, gentleness, and care toward one another like three mild lanterns held each at the met heads of strangers in darkness: such things, and these are just a few, I have not managed to give their truth in words, which are a soft, plain-featured, and noble music, each part in the experience of it and in the memory so cleanly and so simply defined in its own terms, striking so many chords and relationships at once, which I can but have blurred in the telling at all.

To say, then, how, as I sat between the close walls of this hallway, which opened upon wide night at either end, between these two somberly sleepy people in the soft smile of the light, eating from unsorted plates with tin-tasting implements the heavy, plain, traditional food which was spread before me, the feeling increased itself upon me that at the end of a wandering and seeking, so long it had begun before I was born, I had apprehended and now sat at rest in my own home, between two who were my brother and my sister, yet less that than something else; these, the wife my age exactly, the husband four years older, seemed not other than my own parents, in whose patience I was so different, so diverged, so strange as I was; and all that surrounded me, that silently strove in through my senses and stretched me full, was familiar and dear to me as nothing else on earth, and as if well known in a deep past and long years lost; so that I could wish that all my chance life was in truth the betrayal, the curable delusion, that it seemed, and that this was my right home, right earth, right blood, to which I would never have true right. For half my blood is just this; and half my right of speech; and by bland chance alone is my life so softened and sophisticated in the years of my defenselessness, and I am robbed of a royalty I can not only never claim, but never properly much desire or regret. And so in this quiet introit, and in all the time we have stayed in this house, and in all we have sought, and in each detail of it, there is so keen, sad, and precious a nostalgia as I can scarcely otherwise know; a knowledge of brief truancy into the sources of my life, whereto I have no rightful access, having paid no price beyond love and sorrow.

The biscuits are large and shapeless, not cut round, and are pale, not tanned, and are dusty with flour. They taste of flour and soda and damp salt and fill the mouth stickily. They are better with butter, and still better with butter and jam. The butter is pallid, soft, and unsalted, about the texture of cold-cream; it seems to taste delicately of wood and wet cloth; and it tastes 'weak.' The jam is loose, of little berries, full of light raspings of the tongue; it tastes a deep sweet purple tepidly watered, with a very faint sheen of a sourness as of iron. Field peas are olive-brown, the shape of lentils, about twice the size. Their taste is a cross between lentils and boiled beans; their broth is bright with seasoning of pork, and of this also they taste. The broth is soaked up in bread. The meat is a bacon, granular with salt, soaked in the grease of its frying: there is very little lean meat in it. What there is is nearly as tough as rind; the rest is pure salted stringy fat. The eggs taste of pork too. They are fried in it on both sides until none of the broken yolk runs, are heavily salted and peppered while they fry, so that they come to table nearly black, very heavy, rinded with crispness, nearly as dense as steaks. Of milk I hardly know how to say; it is skimmed, blue-lighted; to a city palate its warmth and odor are somehow dirty and at the same time vital, a little as if one were drinking blood. There is even in so clean a household as this an odor of pork, of sweat, so subtle it seems to get into the very metal of the cooking-pans beyond any removal of scrubbing, and to sweat itself out of newly washed cups; it is all over the house and all through your skin and clothing at all times, yet as you bring each piece of food to your mouth it is so much more noticeable, if you are not used to it, that a quiet little fight takes place on your palate and in the pit of your stomach; and it seems to be this odor, and a sort of wateriness and discouraged tepidity, which combine to make the food seem unclean, sticky, and sallow with some in-visible sort of disease, yet this is the odor and consistency and temper and these are true tastes of home; I know this even of myself; and much as my reflexes are twitching in refusal of each mouthful a true homesick and simple fondness for it has so strong hold of me that in fact there is no fight to speak of and no faking of enjoyment at all. And even later, knowing well enough of such food what an insult it is to those who must spend their lives eating it, and who like it well enough, and when I am sick with it, I have also fondness for it, and when this fails, a funny kind of self-scorning determination that I shall eat for a few weeks what a million people spend their lives eating, and feel that whatever discomfort it brings me is little enough and willingly taken on, in the scale of all it could take to even us up.

All this while we are talking some: short of exact recording, which is beyond my memory, I can hardly say how: the forms of these plainest and most casual actions are the hardest I can conceive of to set down straight as they happen; and each is somewhat more beautiful and more valuable, I feel, than, say, the sonnet form. This form was one in which two plain people and one complex one who scarcely know each other discourse while one eats and the others wait for him to finish so they may get back to bed: it has the rhythms and inflections of this triple shyness, of sleepiness, of fast eating, of minds in the influence of lamplight between pine walls, of talk which means little or nothing of itself and much in its inflections: What is the use? What is there I can do about it? Let me try just a few of the surfaces instead. Just in the fact that they were drawn up out of bed to do me this natural kindness, one in overalls and one in a house dress slid on over nakedness, and were sitting here, a man and his wife, in an hour whose lateness is uncommon to them, there is a particular sort of intimacy between the three of us which is not of our creating and which has nothing to do with our talk, yet which is increased in our tones of voice, in small quiet turns of humor, in glances of the eyes, in ways even that I eat my food, in their knowledge how truly friendly I feel toward them, and how seriously I am concerned to have caused them bother, and to let them be done with this bother as quickly as possible. And the best in this—it will be hard to explain unless you know something of women in this civilization —is the experiencing of warmth and of intimacy toward a man and his wife at the same time (for this would seldom happen, it being the business of a wife to serve and to withdraw). I felt such an honor in her not just staying at more distance, waiting to clear up after me, but sitting near, almost equal in balance with her husband, and actually talking; and I began even through her deep exhaustion to see such pleasant and seldom warmth growing in her, in this shifted status and acceptance in it, and such a kindly and surprised current of warmth increasing through this between her husband and her, a new light and gentle novelty spreading a prettiness in her face that, beyond a first expostulation that she get back to her rest and leave me to clean off the table, I not only scarcely worried for her tiredness, or her husband's, but even somewhat prolonged the while we sat there, shamed though I was to do so, and they wakened, and warmed to talking, even while fatigue so much more heavily weighed them under, till it became in the scale of their sleeping an almost scandalously late-night conversation, in which we were all leaned toward each other in the lamplight secretly examining the growth of friendliness in one another's faces, they opening further speaking as often as I and more often: while nevertheless there stole up my quiet delight from the pit of my stomach a cold and sickening shame to be keeping them up, a feeling I had mistaken their interest and their friendliness, that it was only a desperate and nearly broken patience in a trap I had imposed in abuse of their goodness; and I broke through a little wait in what we were speaking, to say how sorry and ashamed I was, and that we must get to sleep; and this they received so genuinely, so kindly, that even in their exhaustion I was immediately healed, and held no fear of their feelings about it: and we drew back our chairs and got up and she cleared the table (no, beyond quickly stacking my dishes toward her I could not offer even to help her with this) and there followed a simple set of transitions which are beautiful in my remembrance and which I can scarcely set down: a telling me where I would sleep, in the front room; a spreading of pallets on the floor of the back bedroom; a waking and bringing-in of the children from their sleeping on the bed I was to have: they came sleepwalking, along bare floor toward lamplight, framed in the lighted upright planks of the door: the yielding-over to me of the lamp, which I accepted (there are courtesies you accept, though you are ashamed to), provided they should have used it first to get themselves to bed: they give me, meanwhile, their little tin night-light, which looks like the minutest kind of Roman lamp: I say good night to Mrs. Gudger and she to me, smiling sleepily and sadly in a way I cannot deduce, and goes on in; I button my door, that leads into their bedroom, and wait in this front room, new to me, with my night-light, sitting on the edge of the child-warmed bed, looking at the little sketches of carpentry I can see in my faint light, and at the light under their door and through seams in the wall, while in a confusion of shufflings and of muted voices which overspreads the sleeping of children like quiet wings; and rustlings of cloth, and sounding of bedsprings, they restore themselves for sleeping: then a shuffling, a sliding of light, a soft knock at the door; I come to it; Gudger and I exchange our lamps, speaking few words in nearly inaudible voices, while beyond his shoulder I feel the deep dark breathing a soft and quiet prostration of bodies: All right in year hain't you?—Ah, sure, fine. Sure am. —Annie Mae told me to say, she's sorry she ain't got no clean sheet, but just have to (*oh, no!*) make out best way you can.—Oh, no. No. You tell her I certainly do thank her, but, no, I'll be fine like this, *fine* like this—She just don't got none tell she does a warshin.—Sure; sure; I wouldn't want to dirty up a clean sheet for you, one night. Thanks a lot. Door, right head a yer bed, if you want to git out. I look, and nod:

Yeah; thanks.

Night:

Night:

The door draws shut.

I stand alone, and I find that, without my knowledge or will, my left arm has slowly extended, the lamp in the hand at the end of it, as far as I can stretch, and I turn upon the center of the room.

In the room: the Testament

Six sides of me, all pine: Floor supported; walls walled, stood vertical, joined at their four edges, at floor, at one another, and at roof: roof, above rafters, tilted tall, from eaves to crest. Between slats, the undersides of shingles. One wall is lapboard, that one which joins the other bedroom: the others, the skeleton and the inward surface of the outward skin of the house. A door to the bedroom: a door by my bed to the hallway: in the wall at the foot of my bed, a square window, shuttered; another in the wall next at right angles. On the floor beneath this window, a small trunk. To its left, stood across the corner, a bureau and mirror. To its right, stood across the corner, a sewing-machine:

I have told of these: But here, and now, I was first acquainting myself of this room in a silence of wonder to match the silence of sleeping in the next room. Its fragrance was everywhere; its plainness and coloring were beautiful to me. The furniture stood, where I have begun to see, sober and naked to me in the solemn light, and seemed as might the furnishing of a box-car, a barn. This barn and box-car resemblance I use, it occurred to me then and since, as an indication of the bonelike plainness and as if fragility of the place; but I would not mislead or miscolor: this was a room of a human house, of a sort stood up by the hundreds of thousands in the whole of a country; the sheltering and home of the love, hope, ruin, of the living of all of a family, and all the shelter it shall ever know, and since of itself it is so ordinary, so universal, there is no need to name it as a barn, or as a box-car.

But here, I would only suggest how thin-walled, skeletal, and beautiful it seemed in a particular time, as if it were a little boat in the darkness, floated upon the night, far out on the steadiness of a vacant sea, whose crew slept while I held needless watch, and felt the presence of the country round me and upon me. I looked along the walls, how things which were pretty were stuck and pinned to the wood; and at the wood: I should find it hard to tire of watching plain wood which is in some human usage; of running my fingers upon it as it were skin; little tricks of glass and china, and of sewn cloths, which were created to be pretty, to be happy: the restings of furniture on the surface of the naked floor; various reflections of the room in the eaten mirror: the square, useless lamp which stood in the dark corner under the sewing-machine: the iron bed, whose sheets and coverlets Mrs. Gudger had drawn smooth for me, the mark of my butt on its edge, my shoes beside it, crazy with mud, worn out and sleeping as a pair of wrecked horses: how the shutters filled their squares of window and were held shut with strings and nails: crevices in the walls, stuffed with hemp, rags, newsprint, and raw cotton: large damp spots and rivulets on the floor, and on the walls, streams and crooked wetness; and a shivering, how chilly and wet the air is in this room: a shutting-off of these matters and mere 'touch' and listening, how the home was squared on us, and beyond on all sides the billion sleeping of the natural earth: sitting, where the table blocks the fireplace, watching the lamp, how the light stands up and the wick sleeps in the glass, and meditating those who sleep just beyond this wall: it was in this first night that I found, on the bureau, a bible; very cheap; bound in a limp brown fake-leather which was almost slimily damp; a family bible: I opened it up quietly in the lamplight, here and there through it: I quote from notes I made at that time:

The Title Page:

The New Testament

With the words spoken by Christ printed in red
 (printed in red)

Malachi 4, v. 6.
And he shall turn the heart of the fathers to the children, and the heart of the children to their fathers, lest I come and smite the earth with a curse.

And elsewhere, printed in brown ink; the handwriting in pencil:

Presented to ...

.... *George Gudger* ....

by ... *Annie Mae Gudger* ....

Family Record:
Parents' Names

Husband ..... *George Gudger* ....

Born .. *September 11—1904* ....

Wife ... *Annie Mae Gudger* ....

Born .. *October 19. 19.7* ....

Married *George G. and Annie Mae G.*
was married April 19ᵗʰ 1924

Children's Names

..... *Maggie Louise G. was born*
.... *February 2ⁿᵈ 1926* ....

... *George Junior Gudger was born*
.. *Sepenber 4. 1927* ....

...... *Martha Ann G. was born*
..... *March 28. 1931* ....

..... *Burt Westly Gudger* ....
...... *July 14 1932* ....
.... *Valley Few G.* ....
..... *Dec, 26, 1936* .... *

*It was written thus. He was born in 1934.

Marriages:

.... *George* ....

.... ⟨ ....

....

....

Deaths: .*Lulla Woods died* .....

.... *June 7, 19×29* ....

.... *Martha Ann G—* ....

.... *Died September 28, 1931* ...

This bible was of some absorbent paper and lay slack, cold, and very heavy in the hand. It gave out a strong and cold stench of human excrement.

In the Room: In Bed

I put in my hand and it took the last warmth of the sleeping of the children. I sat on the edge of the bed, turned out the lamp, and lay back along the outside of the covers. After a couple of minutes I got up, stripped, and slid in between the sheets. The bedding was saturated and full of chill as the air was, its lightness upon me nervous like a belt too loosely buckled. The sheets were at the same time coarse and almost slimily or stickily soft: much the same material floursacks are made of. There was a ridgy seam down the middle. I could feel the thinness and lumpiness of the mattress and the weakness of the springs. The mattress was rustlingly noisy if I turned or contracted my body. The pillow was hard, thin, and noisy, and smelled as of acid and new blood; the pillowcase seemed to crawl at my cheek. I touched it with my lips: it felt a little as if it would thaw like spun candy. There was an odor something like that

of old moist stacks of newspaper. I tried to imagine intercourse in this bed; I managed to imagine it fairly well. I began
to feel sharp little piercings and crawlings all along the surface
of my body. I was not surprised; I had heard that pine is full of
them anyhow. Then, too, for a while longer I thought it could
be my own nerve-ends; I itch a good deal at best: but it was
bugs all right. I felt places growing on me and scratched at
them, and they became unmistakable bedbug bites. I lay
awhile rolling and tightening against each new point of irrita-
tion, amused and curious how I had changed about bedbugs.
In France I used to wake up and examine a new crop each
morning, with no revulsion: now I was squeamish in spite of
myself. To lie there naked feeling whole regiments of them
tooling at me, knowing I must be imagining two out of three,
became more unpleasant than I could stand. I struck a match
and a half-dozen broke along my pillow: I caught two, killed
them, and smelled their queer rankness. They were full of my
blood. I struck another match and spread back the cover; they
rambled off by dozens. I got out of bed, lighted the lamp, and
scraped the palms of my hands all over my body, then went for
the bed. I killed maybe a dozen in all; I couldn't find the rest;
but I did find fleas, and, along the seams of the pillow and
mattress, small gray translucent brittle insects which I suppose
were lice. (I did all this very quietly, of course, very much
aware I might wake those in the next room.) This going-over
of the bed was only a matter of principle: I knew from the first
I couldn't beat them. I might more wisely not have done so,
for I shouldn't have discovered the 'lice.' The thought of their
presence bothered me much more than the bedbugs. I unbuttoned the door by my bed and went out into the hallway; the
dog woke and sidled toward me on his toenails sniffing and I
put my hand on his head and he wagged from the middle of
his spine on back. I was closely aware of all the bare wood of
the house and of the boards under my bare feet, of the damp
and deep gray night and of my stark nakedness. I went out to
the porch and pissed off the edge, against the wall of the
house, to be silent, and stood looking out. It was dark, and
mist was standing up in streaks, and the woods along my left
and at the bottom of the field in front of me were darkest of
any part of the night. Down under the strongest streak of mist

along my left, in the deep woods, there was a steady thrusting and spreading noise of water. There were a few stars through thin mist, and a wet gray light of darkness everywhere. I went down the steps and out into the yard, feeling the clay slippery and very cold on my feet, and turned round slowly to look at the house. The instant I was out under the sky, I felt much stronger than before, lawless and lustful to be naked, and at the same time weak. I watched the house and felt like a special sort of burglar; but still more I felt as if I trod water in a sea whose floor was drooped unthinkably deep beneath me, and I was unsafely far from the wall of the ship. I looked straight up into the sky, found myself nodding at whatever it was I saw, and came back and scraped my feet on the steps, rubbed them dry with my hands, and, with one more slow look out along the sunken landscape went back into the bedroom. I put on my coat, buttoned my pants outside it, put my socks on, got into bed, turned out the lamp, turned up my coat collar, wrapped my head in my shirt, stuck my hands under my coat at the chest, and tried to go to sleep. It did not work out well. They got in at the neck and along my face and at my ankles, and along the wrists and knuckles. I wanted if I could to keep my hands and face clear. I wasn't used to these bugs. Their bites would show, and it might be embarrassing whether questions or comments were placed or not. After a little while I worked it out all over, bandaging more tightly and carefully at every strategic joint of cloth. This time I put the socks on my hands and wrapped my feet in my shorts, and once I was set, took great care to lie still. But they got in as before, and along my back and up my belly too: through my stiff, starved dozing I could feel them crawling captured under the clothes, safe against my getting at them, pricking and munching away: so in time, I revised my attitude. I stripped once more, scratched and cleaned all over, shook out all my clothes, dressed again, lay down outside all the covers, and let them take their course while I attended as well as I could to other things; that is, to my surroundings, to whatever was on my mind, and to relaxing for sleep. This worked better. I felt them nibbling, but they were seldom in focus, and I lay smoking, using one shoe for an ashtray and looking up at the holes in the roof. Now and then I reached out and touched the rough wood of the wall just be-

hind me and of the wall along my right: or felt the iron rods of
the bed with my hands, my feet, and the crown of my head; or
ran the fingertips of my left hand along the grain of the floor:
or tilting my chin, I looked back beyond my forehead through
the iron at the standing-up of the wall: all the while I would be
rubbing and desperately scratching, but this had become me-
chanical by now. I don't exactly know why anyone should be
'happy' under these circumstances, but there's no use laboring
the point: I was: outside the vermin, my senses were taking in
nothing but a deep-night, unmeditatable consciousness of a
world which was newly touched and beautiful to me, and I
must admit that even in the vermin there was a certain amount
of pleasure: and that, exhausted though I now was, it was the
eagerness of my senses quite as fully as the bugs and the itching
which made it impossible for me to sleep and, sickly as I now
strained toward sleep, it was pleasurable to stay awake. I dozed
off and on, but had no realization of deeper sleep. I must have
been pretty far gone, though, for when Gudger came in barefooted to take up the lamp, I feigned sleeping, and lacked interest to look at the furniture which was now visible by a sort
of sub-daylight: and heard the sounds of dressing and movements in the house, and saw the wall of their room slit with
yellow light, only with a deep and gentle sorrow, in some
memory out of childhood which seemed now restored like the
ghost of one beloved and dead: and was taken out of full sleep
by the sound, a little later, of his shoes on the floor, as he came
to the side of the bed and spoke to me.

The sun was not yet up, but the sky over the hill was like
white china and it was full daylight now, everything hung with
rain and letting it run off in large drops; the grain of wood in
the wall of the house was yellow, red and fading blue-black (as
of wet tortoise shell), which the sun would not bleach for several hours yet; the ground was drawn down close on itself with
a somehow blue-sheened surface that looked hard as iron. The
lamp was no longer giving any light beyond its own daylighted
chimney, and Mrs. Gudger put it out. Even now, with the hot
load of the breakfast inside me, I was stiff with cold and was
not yet well awake.
We cut up across the hill field by the path their walking had

laid in it; the path was all but rained out. In some parts it was packed hard enough to be slippery, the rest of the time it let our feet down as deep as plowed dirt itself and we lifted them out in each step with one to three inches of clay hung on them. The cotton plants brushed us at the knees so that in no time we were drenched there.

It was only a chance that the road and the ditch clay would have hardened enough during the night to make it possible to get the car out. With about ten minutes work, that brought up a shallow, stickily drying sweat in the cool of this morning, we managed to do it, and moving precariously in low and second as if walking a slackwire, with a couple of sideslips that nearly ditched us again, we got the car out to the slag and swung right and made speed on its slow rollercoaster lifts and falls while around us fields, with which I found I felt a strong new kind of familiarity, lilted and relaxed upon our motion.

After not more than three miles, just within first sight of Cookstown, low and diminutive, Gudger told me to turn right just this side of the grismill.

It was dirt road again, but wider, and thick enough with sand to be possible, though it was still good and wet. I managed about thirty-five on it, and the tires were very loud under us. This was new country to me, still totally poor, yet with something loosened and pastoral about it and as if self-sufficient and less hopelessly lonesome and abandoned; the early light and the cleanness and silence after the rain may have been responsible for this impression. There were more small, privately owned farms than on many roads I had driven over, none of them any richer-looking than tenant farms; yet living was a little different on them and a little less pointless. Even in the smoke that wrinkled up out of their chimneys and lavished lazily like the tail of a pleased cat and in the keen odors of fire and breakfast that lay occasionally across the road, there was a little more security than in these same on a tenant farm, and a little more of the sense of a family planted in one place and coming up like a tree, even if it was a starved tree.

Strung along at two out of three mail boxes, thinly along the road, men stood smoking and waited. I started to slow for the first and Gudger said the truck would be along. With all the equipment in the back we had room only for one more anyway. They looked at us coldly and shyly as we went past. To three or four Gudger lifted a hand, and these lifted a hand, not smiling.

We ran sharply up a hill with small black pines on it and at the top a small unpainted church and clay burial ground, and the hill ran down much more slowly. Gudger said turn right down there at the bottom. I swung right through a snowlike sludge of clay and righted the car along a rut between the deep ones and a light rut in the grass. It was harder going again. Wet blackberry brambles laid water on the windshield. In two hundred yards more the woods were up to one side of us, a high field to the other, and the road was sand again, and Gudger said to take the right fork, and it was as subduing as going into a tunnel. The pines and the soft-wooded and high trees and the oaks and hickories were thick all around us and over us now, so that the air was cold, dark and clear, and noisily hushed as I remember when, a child, I used to crawl into a culvert, and sat down and listened. The sand road was drenching wet and there was the mark of one car that had been ahead of us, and ahead there was the rattling of a wagon, and we rounded a heavy bush and saw it and slowed; the men looked round, two black, one white, who lifted his hand as Gudger lifted his; the negroes nodded. The whipped mules dragged the wagon on through a flooded branch that submerged thirty yards of the road and stood up around the bushes and tree-trunks on either side so that they had no rootage, and I watched where and how deep the wheels went while I idled the motor and lighted Gudger's and my own cigarette. It was twenty-one past six. Gudger said, 'We got here in good time.' They got the wagon on through and drew up along a patch of grass and roots at the side of the road. I said thanks with hand and head, put the car into low and then into second and, following their trail, which still creased the water a little, went through pretty fast with a loud cold splitting and crashing noise of the new water and was on solid land again. The white man and I lifted hands as I went by and the negroes nodded again, but more slightly. They were all three looking at us curiously and tentatively. 'Left up yer ahead'; where there was wide light on the wet road. We swung as if into the face of a powerful searchlight into a long grassy clearing stacked down the middle with wet yellow lumber and full of light which had, since we lost it to woods, greatly increased and which came straight and low at us from the far end; we went past another wagon and drew up at the side of the road in the heavy grass halfway down the clearing. The wagon passed alongside and Gudger and the men on the wagon lifted their hands and the men looked back non-committally at me and Gudger and the sedan and the Tennessee license. Gudger's watch made twenty-three past six.

We sat still in the car and finished the things we had been saying, very slowly and shyly on both sides, all through the drive; which were, very carefully keyed, chiefly about what the tenant farmer could do to help himself out of the hole he is in. Gudger made him another cigarette and we smoked, talking very little. We were not by any means at ease with each other, but he now felt he could trust me and we liked each other. While we talked, I was looking around slowly.

The sawmill was at the far end; it was still in the morning shadow of the woods. The sun had just cleared the tops of the pines beyond it so that they were still burnt away. Rising and twisting all through these close-growing pines, and on the high glittering grass and in long streams in the air, was the white smoke of the cold, now swiftly heating, early morning, which the sun drew up, and the sun struck through this smoke and diffused it so that the air was clear, transparent and all but blinding bright, as if it had been polished. The wagon that had drawn aside from us in the woods road had come up and let off its men, and a truckload of negroes and white men arrived from Cookstown, and the clearing was thickening but not by any means crowded with men and the sound of their talk and the noises of the beginning of a day's work: nearly every one of these men glanced at us more than once, carefully and with candor, yet they did not stare, and were only careful, not hostile. Over by the toolshed of fresh pine a negro, harnessing his team, threw back his head and looked into the sun and sang, shouting, a phrase which sprang out of his throat like a wet green branch. Gudger said he was agoin to have to git on to work now. I told him I sure was obliged to him for taking me in last night and he said he was glad to have holp me.

END OF PART THREE

SHADY GROVE

TWO IMAGES

JUST beside it there is a large square white-painted church, which we got into. Bare benches of heavy pine, a lot of windows, partition-curtains of white sheeting run on wires, organ, chairs, and lectern.

The graveyard is about fifty by a hundred yards inside a wire fence. There are almost no trees in it: a lemon verbena and a small magnolia; it is all red clay and very few weeds.

Out at the front of it across the road there is a cornfield and then a field of cotton and then trees.

Most of the headboards are pine, and at the far end of the yard from the church the graves are thinned out and there are many slender and low pine stumps about the height of the headboards. The shadows are all struck sharp lengthwise of the graves, toward the cornfield, by the afternoon sun. There is no one anywhere in sight. It is heavily silent and fragrant and all the leaves are breathing slowly without touching each other.

Some of the graves have real headstones, a few of them so large they must be the graves of landowners. One is a thick limestone log erected by the Woodmen of the World. One or two of the others, besides a headpiece, have a flat of stone as large as the whole grave.

On one of these there is a china dish on whose cover delicate hands lie crossed, cuffs at their wrists, and the nails distinct.

On another a large fluted vase stands full of dead flowers, with an inch of rusty water at the bottom.

On others of these stones, as many as a dozen of them, there is something I have never seen before: by some kind of porcelain reproduction, a photograph of the person who is buried there; the last or the best likeness that had been made, in a small-town studio, or at home with a snapshot camera. I remember one well of a fifteen-year-old boy in sunday pants and a plaid pullover sweater, his hair combed, his cap in his hand, sitting against a piece of farm machinery and grinning. His eyes are squinted against the light and his nose makes a deep shadow down one side of his chin. Somebody's arm, with the sleeve rolled up, is against him; somebody who is almost certainly still alive: they could not cut him entirely out of the picture. Another is a studio portrait, close up, in artificial lighting, of a young woman. She is leaned a little forward, smiling vivaciously, one hand at her cheek. She is not very pretty, but she believed she was; her face is free from strain or fear. She is wearing an evidently new dress, with a mail-order look about it; patterns of beads are sewn over it and have caught the light. Her face is soft with powder and at the wings of her nose lines have been deleted. Her dark blonde hair is newly washed and professionally done up in puffs at the ears which in that time, shortly after the first great war of her century, were called cootie garages. This image of her face is split across and the split has begun to turn brown at its edges.

I think these would be graves of small farmers.

There are others about which there can be no mistake: they are the graves of the poorest of the farmers and of the tenants. Mainly they are the graves with the pine head headboards; or without them.

When the grave is still young, it is very sharply distinct, and of a peculiar form. The clay is raised in a long and narrow oval with a sharp ridge, the shape exactly of an inverted boat. A fairly broad board is driven at the head; a narrower one, sometimes only a stob, at the feet. A good many of the headboards have been sawed into the flat simulacrum of an hourglass; in some of these, the top has been roughly rounded off, so that the resemblance is more nearly that of a head and shoulders sunken or risen to the waist in the dirt. On some of these boards names and dates have been written or printed in hesitant letterings, in pencil or in crayon, but most of them appear never to have been touched in this way. The boards at some of the graves have fallen slantwise or down; many graves seem never to have been marked except in their own carefully made shape. These graves are of all sizes between those of giants and of newborn children; and there are a great many, so many they seem shoals of minnows, two feet long and less, lying near one another; and of these smallest graves, very few are marked with any wood at all, and many are already so drawn into the earth that they are scarcely distinguishable. Some of the largest, on the other hand, are of heroic size, seven and eight feet long, and of these more are marked, a few, even, with the smallest and plainest blocks of limestone, and initials, once or twice a full name; but many more of them have never been marked, and many, too, are sunken half down and more and almost entirely into the earth. A great many of these graves, perhaps half to two thirds of those which are still distinct, have been decorated, not only with shrunken flowers in their cracked vases and with bent targets of blasted flowers, but otherwise as well. Some have a line of white clamshells planted along their ridge; of others, the rim as well is garlanded with these shells. On one large grave, which is otherwise completely plain, a blown-out electric bulb is screwed into the clay at the exact center. On another, on the slope of clay just in front of the headboard, its feet next the board, is a horseshoe; and at its center a blown bulb is stood upright. On two or three others there are insulators of blue-green glass. On several graves, which I presume to be those of women, there at the center the prettiest or the oldest and most valued piece of china: on one, a blue glass butter dish whose cover is a setting hen; on another, an intricate milk-colored glass basket; on others, ten-cent-store candy dishes and iridescent vases; on one, a pattern of white and colored buttons. On other graves there are small and thick white butter dishes of the sort which are used in lunch-rooms, and by the action of rain these stand free of the grave on slender turrets of clay. On still another grave, laid carefully next the headboard, is a corncob pipe. On the graves of children there are still these pretty pieces of glass and china, but they begin to diminish in size and they verge into the forms of animals and into homuncular symbols of growth; and there are toys: small autos, locomotives and fire engines of red and blue metal; tea sets for dolls, and tin kettles the size of thimbles: little effigies in rubber and glass and china, of cows, lions, bulldogs, squeaking mice, and the characters of comic strips; and of these I knew, when Louise told me how precious her china dogs were to her and her glass lace dish, where they would go if she were soon drawn down, and of many other things in that home, to whom they would likely be consigned; and of the tea set we gave Clair Bell, I knew in the buying in what daintiness it will a little while adorn her remembrance when the heaviness has sufficiently grown upon her and she has done the last of her dancing: for it will only be by a fortune which cannot be even hoped that she will live much longer; and only by great chance that they can do for her what two parents have done here for their little daughter: not only a tea set, and a cocacola bottle, and a milk bottle, ranged on her short grave, but a stone at the head and a stone at the foot, and in the headstone her six month image as she lies sleeping dead in her white dress, the head sunken delicately forward, deeply and delicately gone, the eyes seamed, as that of a dead bird, and on the rear face of this stone the words:

> We can't have all things to please us,
> Our little Daughter, Joe An, has gone to Jesus.

It is not likely for her; it is not likely for any of you, my beloved, whose poor lives I have already so betrayed, and should you see these things so astounded, so destroyed, I dread to dare that I shall ever look into your dear eyes again: and soon, quite soon now, in two years, in five, in forty, it will all be over, and one by one we shall all be drawn into the planet beside one another; let us then hope better of our children, and of our children's children; let us know, let us *know* there is cure, there is to be an end to it, whose beginnings are long begun, and in slow agonies and all deceptions clearing; and in the teeth of all hope of cure which shall pretend its denial and hope of good use to men, let us most quietly and in most reverent fierceness say, not by its captive but by its utmost meanings:

Our father, who art in heaven, hallowed be thy name: thy kingdom come: thy will be done on earth as it is in heaven: give us this day our daily bread: and forgive us our trespasses as we forgive those who trespass against us: and lead us not into temptation: but deliver us from evil: for thine is the kingdom: and the power: and the glory: for ever and ever: amen.

T HE LAST WORDS of this book have been spoken and these that follow are not words; they are only descriptions of two images. One is of Squinchy Gudger and his mother as they are in the open hall; one is of Ellen Woods as she lies sleeping at the edge of the front porch: both in a silent, white hour of a summer day.

His mother sits in a hickory chair with her knees relaxed and her bare feet flat to the floor; her dress open and one broken breast exposed. Her head is turned a little slantwise and she gazes quietly downward past her son's head into the junctures of the earth, the floor, the wall, the sunlight, and the shade. One hand lies long and flat along her lap: it is elegantly made of bone and is two sizes too large for the keen wrist. With her other hand, and in the cradling of her arm and shoulder, she holds the child. His dress has fallen aside and he is naked. As he is held, the head huge in scale of his body, the small body ineffably relaxed, spilled in a deep curve from nape to buttocks, then the knees drawn up a little, the bottom small and sharp, and the legs and feet drifted as if under water, he suggests the shape of the word siphon. He is nursing. His hands are blundering at her breast blindly, as if themselves each were a new born creature, or as if they were sobbing, ecstatic with love; his mouth is intensely absorbed at her nipple as if in rapid kisses, with small and swift sounds of moisture; his eyes are squeezed shut; and now, for breath, he draws away, and lets out a sharp short whispered *ahh*, the hands and his eyelids relaxing, and immediately resumes; and in all this while, his face is beatific, the face of one at rest in paradise, and in all this while her gentle and sober, earnest face is not altered out of its deep slantwise gazing: his head is now sunken off and away, grand and soft as a cloud, his wet mouth flared, his body still more profoundly relinquished of itself, and I see how against her body he is so many things in one, the child in the melodies

373

of the womb, the Madonna's son, human divinity sunken from the cross at rest against his mother, and more beside, for at the heart and leverage of that young body, gently, taken in all the pulse of his being, the penis is partly erected.

And Ellen where she rests, in the gigantic light: she, too, is completely at peace, this child, the arms squared back, the palms open loose against the floor, the floursack on her face; and her knees are flexed upward a little and fallen apart, the soles of the feet facing: her blown belly swimming its navel, white as flour; and blown full broad with slumbering blood into a circle: so white all the outward flesh, it glows of blue; so dark, the deep hole, a dark red shadow of life blood: this center and source, for which we have never contrived any worthy name, is as if it were breathing, flowering, soundlessly, a snoring silence of flame; it is as if flame were breathed forth from it and subtly played about it: and here in this breathing and play of flame, a thing so strong, so valiant, so unvanquishable, it is without effort, without emotion, I know it shall at length outshine the sun.

Let us now praise famous men.

LET US now praise famous men, and our fathers that begat us.

The Lord hath wrought great glory by them through his great power from the beginning.

Such as did bear rule in their kingdoms, men renowned for their power, giving counsel by their understanding, and declaring prophecies:

Leaders of the people by their counsels, and by their knowledge of learning meet for the people, wise and eloquent in their instructions:

Such as found out musical tunes, and recited verses in writing:

Rich men furnished with ability, living peaceably in their habitations:

All these were honoured in their generations, and were the glory of their times.

There be of them, that have left a name behind them, that their praises might be reported.

And some there be which have no memorial; who perished, as though they had never been; and are become as though they had never been born; and their children after them.

But these were merciful men, whose righteousness hath not been forgotten.

With their seed shall continually remain a good inheritance, and their children are within the convenant.

Their seed standeth fast, and their children for their sakes. Their seed shall remain for ever, and their glory shall not be blotted out.

Their bodies are buried in peace; but their name liveth for evermore.

NOTES AND APPENDICES

1.

2.

BEETHOVEN SONATA
HELD NO DISTURBANCE

San Francisco, Dec. 6 (A.P.).—'Beethoven,' said Judge Herbert Kaufman, 'cannot disturb the peace.'

So he freed Rudolph Ramat, 69 years old and blind, of a charge of disturbing the peace by playing his accordion on Market Street.

'Your honor,' Ramat pleaded yesterday, 'I have worked

—from the New York *Sun*.*

---

*A conservative newspaper.

3.

A NOTE ON THE PHOTOGRAPHS

Margaret Bourke-White Finds
   Plenty of Time to Enjoy Life
   Along With Her Camera Work

————

Famous Photographer Who Took Pictures for
You Have Seen Their Faces Discusses Experiences
Among Southern Share-Croppers

————

By May Cameron

(*Herschel Brickell's reviews of books appear in this space five days a week.*)

It's difficult to know where to begin on Margaret Bourke-White, because she is so many people rolled into one.

"You can't possibly miss her," Miss Bourke-White's secretary told me, "because she's wearing the reddest coat in the world."

A superior red coat, Miss Bourke-White called it, and such fun. It was designed for her by Howard Greer, and if you're as little up on your movie magazines as I am, I'd better explain that the Greer label is some pumpkins. You'd find it, if you could look, in the more glamorous gowns of Dietrich and, among others, Hepburn.

This famous photographer, just past thirty, can well afford Hollywood's best. In less than eight years she has climbed to the top of the heap in her profession and is now—movie actresses barred—one of the highest-paid women in America. Trying to imagine this made me a little dizzy, but here it is: for every minute—minute, mind you—of her working time today Margaret Bourke-White commands quite a few dollars.

And this is the young lady who spent months of her own time in the last two years traveling the back roads of the deep south bribing, cajoling, and sometimes browbeating her way in to photograph Negroes, share-croppers and tenant farmers in their own environments. Seventy-five of these photographs appear in *You Have Seen Their Faces*, a book for which Erskine Caldwell wrote the text.

.   .   .   .

SNUFF, 'RELIGION' AND PATENT MEDICINE

Ingenuity such as she was never called upon to use in her years of industrial photography went into the making of many of the photographs included in the book. The striking photograph of a Negro preacher caught at the very height of his emotion and oratory Miss Bourke-White took on her knees right in front of the pulpit, the preacher's own emotion making him entirely oblivious to exploding flashlights. Her rare photographs of the "coming through" ritual, if it could be called a ritual, in a white Holiness church were possible only because the minister had never before had a photographer to deal with and he didn't know what to do about it.

The small-town orator-politician had already started talking when Margaret Bourke-White set up her tripod and went to work on him. She is certain that he wouldn't have posed for her, but, once he had started to orate, nothing, not even a strange photographer, could stop him. And to one of the last couples pictured in the book, Miss Bourke-White and Erskine Caldwell had to pay a bribe.

"So far as we could tell, they hadn't any food, but they begged for snuff, two kinds, Buttercup and Rooster snuff," Margaret Bourke-White explained. "They hoped we'd throw in a little coffee and maybe some chewing tobacco, but snuff came first. They tell you snuff's good when you are hungry or when you have a toothache or when you're just feeling generally low. They seem to live on snuff and religion—which has no real relation to religion—and patent medicine.

"Caldwell's new play, *Journeyman*, is concerned with one congregation of a white Holiness church. The Negro churches are not, somehow, so shocking, because you think of Negroes as being actors and emotional, but with the white people the whole business is so sordid and desperate and out of place. It isn't as though their church played any role, as we know religion. It's just a place where people go to shout and scream and roll on the floor. They are so beaten down and their lives are so drab and barren and lonely that they have nothing. This terrible thing every Sunday is their only emotional release."

THE PICTURE OF TODAY'S SETUP

Miss Bourke-White, whose beautiful photographs of dynamos and cranes and turbines and girders and industrial fine points are known to every one, made several trips to Russia and, in observing an agricultural nation being turned into an industrial one, became tremendously interested in the man behind the machine.

"I loved the industrial photographs for their pictorial value and all the excitement of machinery, and I still do; but a couple of years ago I began to feel that if I was worth anything at all I wanted to do something really worth while, something lasting," she said. "In Russia I got the first glimpse of figuring out man's relationship to the machine and to his employer, and my eyes were opened tremendously. It's more complicated in America, of course, but now I am most interested in taking pictures of what's going on, not necessarily news, but just man's place in the whole setup of today.

"I'm tired of glorifying big business, tired of photographing beautiful, empty-headed models stepping into beautiful automobiles. I do only the industrial photographs that are interesting now, as, for example, my trip to Brazil last year to photograph coffee plantations, which had never been done, and to do airplane pictures, of which I do a great many.

"I believe, too, that photographs are a true interpretation. One photograph might lie, but a group of pictures can't. I could have taken one picture of share-croppers, for example, showing them toasting their toes and playing their banjos and being pretty happy. In a group of pictures, however, you would have seen the cracks on the wall and the expressions on their faces. In the last analysis, photographs really have to tell the truth; the sum total is a true interpretation. Whatever facts a person writes have to be colored by his prejudice and bias. With a camera, the shutter opens and it closes and the only rays that come in to be registered come directly from the object in front of you."

In the eight or nine years since she started selling photographs, while still in Columbia, Margaret Bourke-White has had the energy and made the time to find an awful lot of fun in just living. She's a tango expert; crazy about the theater; loves swimming, ice skating, skiing, and adores horseback riding. Sometimes, she explained, when she knows that the light will be right only a few hours of the day for whatever pictures she is taking, she has her horse brought around to "location" and rides until the light is right. Movies occupy whatever weekends she spends in New York, often as many as five a day. Aside from a photographer's interest, she just likes the damn things.*

4.

A DEFINITION

The generic word for tenant is tenant. In the vicinity of which we tell, however, and, it appears, generally throughout the south, the word is used to designate only one of the two chief classes of tenant, that is the man who, as distinguished from the man who owns nothing save, perhaps, some furniture, one or two eating or hunting animals, and the clothes on his back, owns a mule and some farm implements and who, not needing to be furnished these, can arrange to yield less of his two major crops in payment of rent to the landowner.

One name for the other chief sort of tenant, the man who, owning neither mule nor implements, must be furnished these as well as land and shelter, and must pay the landowner half his cotton and a third to half his corn, is sharecropper. He is also called a halvers-hand and is described as working on halves, or halvers. In the vicinity of which we tell and, it appears, generally throughout the south, the word sharecropper and its synonyms are used only of this class of tenant.

These usages do not differ from class to class, but are common to the language of landowner, tenant and sharecropper alike.

Of all the words which may be used to designate any sort of tenant, the word we heard used least frequently throughout our investigation, by landowners, storekeepers, townspeople, small farmers, tenants, sharescroppers, and all local human beings white or black, save only new dealers, communists, and various casts of liberal, was the word sharecropper.

In the north, however, and particularly in the seaboard

*Reprinted by courtesy of the New York *Post*, a liberal newspaper.

north, where most of the writing and printing and reading of the United States is carried on, sharecropper has, through the agencies of print and the lectured word, become the generic term. Literally, of course, it describes both sorts of tenant, for each sort shares his crop: and it may be that through constant usage it will establish itself as generic. At present, however, it is in this generic spread unavailable to the mouth of anyone who would speak at all seriously of cotton tenants, and such a person will use it hesitantly if at all even in its specific and proper sense. For not only is the word inaccurately used save where it is indigenous, and not only is it a dialect word, to which a conscientious 'educated' person knows he has forfeited the right, even should he know its meaning accurately; and not only is it a dialect word inaccurately used by those who have no right to use it; but it has very swiftly, and within a very few years, absorbed every corruptive odor of inverted snobbery, marxian, journalistic, jewish, and liberal logomachia, emotional blackmail, negrophilia, belated transference, penis-envy, gynecological flurry and fairly good will which the several hundred thousand least habitable and scrupulous minds of this peculiarly psychotic quarter of the continent can supply to it: and is one of the words a careful man will be watchful of, and by whose use and inflection he may take clear measurement of the nature, and the stature, and the causes, and the timbre, of the enemy.

Note. Other anglosaxon monosyllables are god, love, loyalty, honor, beauty, duty, integrity, art, artist, religion, truth, science, poetry, culture, fascism, communism, dialectical-materialism, fellow-traveler, anarchist, philosophical-anarchist, marx, freud, semantic, loyalist, franco, hitler, duce, committee, friend, enemy, state, totalitarian state, mental state, statement, education, student, teacher, maestro, woman, man, Woman, Man, humanity, kidnap, vigilante, sex fiend, perversion, normal, genius, guarantee, peaceful-picketing, collective-bargaining, Negro, negro, Jew, jew, dinge, jig, boog, colored, jigaboo, nigger, darky, spade, eph, shine, smoke, hebe, kike, sheeny, eskimo, jewish, jow, joosh, antisemitic, swing, cat, alligator, gator, icky, wacky, lick, hotlick, gutbucket, barrelhouse, bennygoodman, plumbing, stick, tea, lush, godbox, jitterbug, tong, goddam, god damn, god damned, swell, oke, okay, lousy, superb, good, excellent, fine, nice, magnificent, bravo, bis, pooch, virgin, frigid, wife, husband, prick, pricque, box, bubs, jamsession, jive, silicosis, syphilis, wasserman, sex, sexual, sexuality, homosexual, heterosexual, bisexual, asexual, fairy, pansy, flit, headleigh, swish, les, lesbie, lesbian, labor, laborite, writer, author, musician, composer, workshop, studio, den, stuff, shot, pic, pix, angle, contact, leica, candid, Life, margaret bourke-white, maggie berkwitz, surrealism, photography, photographer, documentary, work, van gogh, dali, picasso, shakespeare, critic, reviewer, authority, book, publisher, gallery, show, theater, exhibition, stage, drama, tragedy, satire, sincerity, trotskyite, The Old Man, stalinist, liberal, minicam, henchman, the cape, the vineyard, flying, motoring, bathe, cue, revival, luntnfontanne, group theater, group, group consciousness, movement, john-ford, walt-disney, the dance, balletomane, leftist, editor, cub, hack, shop, inhibition, complex, regionalism, nationalism, jingoism, patriotism, americanism, altruism, schism, jizzum, hizzun, malnutrition, pare-lorentz, capital, thurman-arnold, veblen, mysticism, intellectual, emotional outlet, escapism, ideology, business, big business, big operator, layout, setup, pushover, scientist, scientific, medical, surgical, visceral, fiddle, prostie, frank, honest, incest, sponsor, cinematic, film, movie, talkie, moom pitcher, genitalia, parts, privates, idealist, psychotic, psychic, psyche, psychoanalysis, neothomist, physical, mental, emotional, spiritual, intuitive, esp, stooge, gross, clear, cleaned, communication, literature, understand, howdoyoufeelnow, sympathy, sympathizer, galleys, machine, laugh, sadisticanal, balls, nuts, nerts, bastid, taste, serve, deserve, fault, father, mother, dad, mummy, mumsy, mumpsypum, daddy, daddyboy, chickabiddy, comfy, cute, satisfactory, congratulations, congratters, sexual intercourse, fearful, dreadful, awful, godawful, nasty, nastiness, snotty, ghastly, great, greatness, greatest, best, worst, splendid, i mean, on the other hand, that is, for pete's sake, qxr, capehart, disk, disque, album, Jesus, Jesus Christ, Jesus Christ, Jesus H. Christ, Jeez, jeez fellas, jeez fellas, The Nazarene, The Nazarene Carpenter, The Galilean, Our Lord, Our Savior, Christ, christ, kee-rist, crissake, gawd, sacrosanct, sacrament, sacrilege, development, health, mental health, decadent,

depravity, amoral, amorist, unethical, act of kind, coitus, relations, been with, live with, sleep with, mistress, lover, pubes,
curse, fall off the roof, flagging, courses, unwell, period, friend,
art treasure, American, democracy, munich betrayal, rape-of-
czechoslovakia, battle-of-britain, determinism, guy, gal, person, class-consciousness, early-chaplin, late-beethoven, early-
steinbeck, orson-welles, tom-wolfe, toscanini, fifth-column,
reactionary, demagogue, blitzkrieg, defense.

5.

The tigers of wrath are wiser than the horses of instruction.

The road of excess leads to the palace of wisdom.

Prudence is a rich, ugly old maid courted by Incapacity.

Improvement makes straight roads, but the crooked roads
without improvement are roads of Genius.

The eagle never lost so much time when he submitted to
learn of the crow.

The weak in courage are strong in cunning.

Listen to the fool's reproach; it is a kingly title.

The fox provides for himself, but God provides for the lion.

You never know what is enough until you know what is
more than enough.

The Giants who formed this world into its sensual existence
and now seem to live in it in chains are in truth the causes of its
life and the sources of all activity, but the chains are the cunning of weak and tame minds which have power to resist energy, according to the proverb, the weak in courage are strong
in cunning.

Thus one portion of being is the Prolific, the other the De-
vouring. To the devourer it seems as if the producer was in his
chains; but it is not so, he only takes portions of existence and
fancies that the whole.

But the Prolific would cease to be Prolific unless the Devourer as a sea received the excess of his delights.

Some will say, Is not God alone the Prolific? I answer, God
only Acts and Is, in existing beings or Men.

These two classes of men are always upon earth, and they should be enemies. Whoever tries to reconcile them seeks to destroy existence.

If the fool would persist in his folly he would become wise.

Everything possible to be believed is an image of truth.

One thought fills immensity.

Mutual forgiveness of each vice,
Such are the gates of Paradise.

Truth can never be told so as to be understood, and not be believed.

Everything that is is holy.

(*On the Porch: 3*

F ROM these woods a good way out along the hill there now came a sound that was new to us.

All the darkness in near range of the earth as far as we were able to hear was strung with noises that were all one noise, and to this we had become so accustomed that this new sound came out of silence, and left an even more powerful silence behind it, so that with each return it, and the ensuing silence, gave each other more and more value, like the exchanges of two mirrors laid face to face.

Whereas we had been silent before, this sound immediately stiffened us into much more intense silence. Without exchange of word or glance we each received communication of a new opening of delight: but chiefly we now engaged in mutual listening and in analysis of what we heard, so strongly, that in all the body and in the whole range of mind and memory, each of us became all one hollowed and listening ear.

It was perhaps most nearly like the noise hydrogen makes when a match flame is passed across the mouth of a slanted test-tube. It was about the same height as this sound: soprano, with a strong alto illusion. It was colder than this sound, though: as cold and as chilling as the pupil of a goat's eye, or a low note on the clarinet. It ran eight identical notes to a call or stanza, a little faster than allegretto, in this rhythm and accent:

— — – – : – – : – — :

Every note was sharply, dryly, and cleanly accented, just short of staccato; and each was driven out with such strictness and restraint that there was in the short silence between each note an extreme tightness and mutual, organically shared tension. Each of the first seven notes was given exactly the same force; the seventh, hit harder, splayed open a fraction, and out of two things, the extra, hammer hardness it was hit with, and a barely discernible trailing-down at its end, gave the illusion of being a higher note.

393

This sound, then, started up, with great dramatic suddenness, at some indeterminable distance from us, a distance which
in time became a little more determinable, though it was never
at all possible accurately to locate it; for the ear always needs
the help of the eye. It was from somewhere in the woods out
to the left of the house at the bottom of our hill; and a little
later it became clear that it was not in the low woods, but
somewhere up the opposite slope; and after a little we got it in
range within say twenty degrees of the ninety on the horizontal circle which at first it could have occupied any part of. It
became clear that it would be between an eighth and a quarter
mile away; and this became remarkable to us because at that
considerable distance we could nevertheless hear, or rather by
some equivalent to radioactivity strongly feel, the motions and
tensions of the throat and body, the very tilt of the head, that
discharged it.

Soon we were helped in locating it (as a second point in any
geometry always is helpful, whereas one point alone can run
you crazy) by the opening-up of a second call. This call was
identical with the first but, coming from a good deal farther
away, seemed higher, hollower, and thinner: scarcely more, yet
very definitely more, than a loud clear echo.

Which of these calls seemed the more mysterious, it is not
possible to say. Their quality was very different by virtue both
of their difference in distance and of a distinct though indefinable difference in the personality of the callers. At one moment the more distant call was more exciting simply in its
distance and because, by its secondary appearance and by its
distance beyond the first caller in relation to us, we got the
illusion that it was the thing sought by the other; the next, the
nearer call took all the honors from it, by nearness; by having
become the searcher with whom we had identified ourselves
and taken sides and by having yet at the same time remained so
entirely itself, without regard for us, no part of us, more alien
to us, because it was alive and conscious and within our near
perspective of kinship, than any stone or star. The fact is of
course that these two series of calls, when they had been set
going, enhanced each other quite as richly as each enhanced
and received enhancement from its own, and the other's, interventions of silence, and a littler later from its participation

in, yet aristocratic distinction from, that plebeian, unanimous ringing of the air which had at no time ceased or diminished and which, now that we were listening so intently, became once more a part of the reality of hearing.

By use only of silences, without changing their stanzaic structure, these two calls went through any number of rhythmic-dramatic devices of delays in question and answer, of overlappings, of tricks of delay by which each pretended to show that it had signed off for the night or, actually, that it no longer even existed. There is an old, not specially funny vaudeville act in which the whole troupe builds up and burlesques a dramatic situation simply by different vocal and gesticulative colorations of the word 'you.' I thought of that now: but its present use was any amount better because the artists were subtler and what they had to say was more enigmatic and more exciting to the audience. Neither of them changed a note or a beat of his call; and if either allowed himself any change of tone or color whatever, it was so delicate that it is impossible to assign it to the callers save through the changefulness and human sentimentality of us who were listening and making what we could of it. But certainly, one way or the other, its meanings changed. One time it would be sexual; another, just a casual colloquy; another, a challenge; another, a signal or warning; another, a comment on us; another, some simple and desperate effort at mutual location; another, most intense and masterful irony; another, laughter; another, triumph; another, a masterpiece of parody of any one, any combination, or all of these assigned or implicit tones: but at all times it was beyond even the illusion of full apprehension, and was noble, frightening and distinguished: a work of great, private and unambitious art which was irrelevant to audience.

We were trying hardest of all to make out what animal or bird was making these sounds, but we had no clue, no anchorage in knowledge through whose help we might by comparative projections have taken it. I cannot even try to say how in the long run we concluded (perhaps in part through its sharpness, tightness out of the throat, and carnivorous timbre) that it was the voice of a fur-bearing animal and that the animal was on the small side and that he might most likely, then that he must, be a fox. It is this sort of mystery we should run against in all casual experience if we found ourselves without warning possessed of a new sense.

Now this is one of a universe of things which should be accepted and recorded for its own sake. The first entrance of this call was as perfect a piece of dramatic or musical structure as I know of: the context perfectly prepared, the entrance of the mysterious principal completely unforeseen yet completely casual, with none of the quality of studiousness in its surprise which hurts for instance some of the music of Brahms; and from its first entrance on, the whole world was frozen and fixed under its will as by the introduction of a precipitant; so that the identical entrance of the second voice carried with it an excitement almost beyond what is possible to bear.

When this second voice had spoken, the first did not answer, but froze just as we and our world had frozen. That which had called was listening intently too. And that which had called the caller was waiting and listening. And now after a long space of more and more tremendous silence (into which there arose, but very faintly, loosely, as natural and common as dew, the ramified ringing of frogs, insects, and night birds), after this long space of silence had extended itself beyond any degree of natural endurance, the second voice spoke a second time, identically, yet, because of the silence, the lack of answer, more imperious-sounding than at first. Then there was a wait, in whose first part the call repeated itself on the ear's memory silently yet keenly as print, and in whose latter expansion once again we were intense with waiting; and then, by some rhythmic genius a little, but only a very little, off-beat, off the beat of eccentrics our ear had of the sum of the calls computed, a very little before it was quite possible to expect it, there came the voice of the first creature; and it was with the breaking open of this voice that we too broke open, silently, our whole bodies broke open into a laughter that destroyed and restored us more even than the most absolute weeping ever can. This is a laughter I have experienced only rarely: listening to the genius of Mozart at its angriest and cleanest, most masculine fire; the sudden memory of some line of Shakespeare, 'Nymph, in thine orisons be all my sins remembered'; walking in streets or driving in country; watching negroes; or in that delicate stage of love when a girl, serious and scarcely tinged with smiling, her eyes muted and her head poised most immaculately, first begins, not in pleasure alone, but in a kind of fear and deep gentleness, to use her light, slow, frank hands upon your head and body: a phase so unassailably beyond any meaning of tenderness and of trust, so like the opening of first living upon the shining of the young earth in its first morning, that an overwhelming knowledge of God and of his non-existence fight in you and, all in this same quietness, you feel it impossible that you can look into her eyes one more moment and not be so distended by incredulous joy that you are of one size and ignorance and fleshlessness with space itself.*

And this phase of love, to anyone who holds love in the utmost esteem that is its due, must be beyond all comparison the cruelest and bitterest thing in human experience. Even within its own moments it draws you both irresistibly into those desperate battlings of the body which only in their first few seconds seem the greater joy they are not, and which so soon blunt and blind the delicate munificence of your exchange into their own beautiful but violent, charcoal-drawn terms. Out of this violence of flesh and of total mutual confidence it is not possible many times to withdraw into that quieter sphere of apposition in which the body, brain and spirit of each of you is all one perfectly focused lens and in which these two lenses devour, feed, enrich and honor each other; it is not possible because the violence blurs, feathers and distorts the essential constituency of the lens. And it is then, living in flushes of memory of a thing more excellent than you may much hope to share between you again, that with scarcely conscious bravery and sorrow, and with measureless compassion, love must assume itself to be established and alive between you. There will be goodness and joy between you again, with wisdom and luck a great deal, more than enough, but not all the kind regard nor all the love within the scope of existence will ever restore you what for a while, and only that you might lose it in the blind service of nature, you had.

In the sound of these foxes, if they were foxes, there was

*The essences of anguish and of joy are thus identical: they are the explosion or incandescence resulting from the incontrovertible perception of the incredible.

nearly as much joy, and less grief. There was the frightening joy of hearing the world talk to itself, and the grief of incommunicability. In that grief I am now as then, with the small yet absolute comfort of knowing that communication of such a thing is not only beyond possibility but irrelevant to it; whereas in love, where we find ourselves so completely involved, so completely responsible and so apparently capable, and where all our soul so runs out to the loveliness, strength, and defenseless mortality, plain, common, salt and muscled toughness of human existence of a girl* that the desire to die for her seems the puniest and stingiest expression of your regard which you can, like a proud tomcat with a slain fledgling, lay at her feet; in love the restraint in focus and the arrest and perpetuation of joy seems entirely possible and simple, and its failure inexcusable, even while we know it is beyond the power of all biology and even while, like the fading of flowerlike wonder out of a breast to which we are becoming habituated, that exquisite joy lies, fainting through change upon change, in the less and less prescient palm of the less and less godlike, more and more steadily stupefied, human, ordinary hand.

And so though this incident of the calling of two creatures should by rights be established at very least as a poem, or a piece of music, and though, even, I know that a more gifted human being, and even I myself, could come nearer giving it, I did not relinquish the ultimately hopeless effort with entire grief: simply because that effort would be, above most efforts, so useless.

This calling continued, never repeating a pattern, and always with what seemed infallible art, for perhaps twenty minutes. It was thoroughly as if principals had been set up, enchanted, and left like dim sacks at one side of a stage as enormous as the steadfast tilted deck of the earth, and as if onto this stage, accompanied by the drizzling confabulation of nocturnal-pastoral music, two masked characters, unforetold and perfectly irrelevant to the action, had with catlike aplomb and noiselessness stept and had sung, with sinister casualness, what at length

---

*I would presume this to be quite as possible, and of no less dignity and valor, in homosexual as well as in heterosexual love.

turned out to have been the most significant, but most unfathomable, number in the show; and had then in perfect irony
and silence withdrawn.

It was after the ending of this that we began a little to talk.
Ordinarily we enjoyed talking and of late, each absorbed
throughout most of the day in subtle and painful work that
made even the lightest betrayal of our full reactions unwise, we
had found the fragments of time we were alone, and able to
give voice to them and to compare and analyze them, valuable
and necessary beyond comparison of cocaine. But now in this
structure of special exaltation it was, though not unpleasant,
thoroughly unnecessary, and obstructive of more pleasing
usage. Our talk drained rather quickly off into silence and we
lay thinking, analyzing, remembering, in the human and
artist's sense praying, chiefly over matters of the present and of
that immediate past which was a part of the present; and each
of these matters had in that time the extreme clearness, and
edge, and honor, which I shall now try to give you; until at
length we too fell asleep.

THE MORNING WATCH

I

*My soul fleeth unto the Lord
before the morning watch: I say,
before the morning watch.*
—PSALM CXXX

IN HIDDEN vainglory he had vowed that he would stay awake straight through the night, for he had wondered, and not without scorn, how they, grown men, could give way to sleep on this night of all the nights in their life, leaving Him without one friend in His worst hour; but some while before midnight, still unaware that he was so much as drowsy, he had fallen asleep; and now this listening sleep was broken and instantly Richard lay sharp awake, aware of his failure and of the night.

Too late: already it was time: now it was the deepest hour of the deepest night. Already while he slept, with wrathful torches and with swords and staves they had broken among the branches of the Garden; Judas, gliding, had stretched against that clear Face his serpent's smile; Peter in loyal rage had struck off the dazed servant's ear and He in quiet had healed him: and without struggle had yielded Himself into their hands. Could ye not watch with me one hour? No Lord, his humbled soul replied: not even one: and three times, silently, gazing straight upward into the darkness, he struck his breast while tears of contrition, of humility and of a hunger to be worthy, solaced his eyes, and awakened his heart. O yes it was an hour more deep by far than the Agony and Bloody Sweat: no longer alone, unsure; resolved, and taken. That was already fully begun which could come only to one ending. By now He stood peaceful before Pilate, the one calm and silence amid all that tumult of malice and scorn and guile and hatred and beating of unhabitual light through all the sleepless night of spring; while in the dark porchway, even at this moment, the servant girl persistently enquired of Peter and he in fury and in terror denied his Lord: now the bitter terrible weeping and now, saluting this mortal morning, the cock's triumphal and reproaching cry. A deep, deep hour. Soon now the sentence and the torment, the scourging, the mocking robe, the wreathed, wretched Crown: King of the Jews.

O God, he silently prayed, in solemn and festal exaltation: make me to know Thy suffering this day. O make me to know Thy dear Son's suffering this day.

Within Thy Wounds hide me.

Suffer me not to be separated from Thee.

From the Malicious Enemy defend me.

By a habit of their own, meanwhile, his hands searched and tested along the undersheet, and now they told him that this time he had wet the bed so little that by morning nobody would know. He let out a long thankful breath and looked down along his bed.

All he could see at first throughout the long room was a kind of gelatin glimmer at the alcoved windows, and the aisled ends of the iron cots at right angles to his own: but when the foot which had awakened him lifted from the yielding board and it creaked again he saw in his mind's eye, large and close, the coarse-ribbed shambling stocking, flecked with lint, and knew that Father Whitman must be very tired; for to judge by the hissing sound, his feet scarcely left the floor. He wondered whether Father Whitman was sleeping at all, tonight.

Father Whitman touched a foot and whispered: "Quarter of four."

"Okay Fathuh," Hobe Gillum said in his clear hard voice.

"Quiet," Father Whitman said sharply.

"Okay Fathuh," Hobe whispered.

Now that the priest came nearer as silently as he could between the ends of the cots, Richard could see the tall ghostly moving of his white habit.

Father Whitman stopped at Jimmy Toole's cot, touched his foot, and whispered: "Quarter of four." Jimmy mumbled something in a light sad rapid voice and stuck his head under his pillow.

Father Whitman stepped between the cots and touched his shoulder. "Quarter of four," he whispered more loudly.

"Cut it out," Jimmy whined in his sleep.

Richard heard Hobe's knees hit the floor.

Father Whitman shook Jimmy's shoulder. "Quarter of——"

"*Quit* it you *God damn*—" Jimmy snarled, wrenching aside

the pillow; then, with servile Irish charm: "Aw sure Father, I din know it was *you* Father."

At the far end of the dormitory there was a wild stifled snicker.

"Time to get up," Father Whitman whispered.

The snickering became happier and happier. Father Whitman spoke more loudly into the darkness: "Now cut that out fast or you'll be sorry you ever started it."

The snickering persisted as if uncontrollably, but now it was blunted in a pillow. Father Whitman ignored it. "Better get straight out of bed," he told Jimmy. "You'll go back to sleep."

Hobe was buttoning his shirt.

Without a word Jimmy rolled out of bed onto his knees and buried his head in his arms.

Now that Father Whitman came toward him, Richard shut his eyes. When he knew he was about to be touched he opened his eyes and whispered, "All right Father." He saw the stopped hand and, much nearer and larger than he had expected, the beaten, enduring horse face; he became aware of his deceitfulness and was ashamed of it.

"All right," Father Whitman said. Bet he says quarter of four, Richard thought. "Quarter of four," Father Whitman said.

"Yes Father."

"Put your shoes on downstairs," he whispered, and turned away. "Put your shoes on downstairs," he told Hobe, "and don't let Jimmy go to sleep again."

"Okay Fathuh," Hobe said, gallusing himself into his overalls.

"And don't you dawdle when you're done," Father Whitman told him. "You kids see to it you come right back here to bed."

"Yes suh Fathuh."

"Don't think I won't be watching for you."

"No suh Fathuh."

Richard knelt by his cot and sank his face in his hands. O God, he prayed, I thank Thee that I did not wet the bed this night—enough to get caught, he added carefully, remembering Thou God seest me; for Jesus' sake Amen.

He said swiftly to himself the prayer Father Weiler had taught

them as enough when, for any good reason, you did not have
time enough for more: I praise my God this day I give myself
to God this day I ask God to help me this day Amen.

Gripping his hair and pressing the heels of his hands tightly
against his closed eyes he tried as hard as he could to realize
what was happening as he had in the moment of waking. But
now he could realize only what a special night this was, what
grave and holy hours these were. There seemed to be a strange
stillness and power in the air as there always was on very special
occasions and never at ordinary times; it made him feel dry,
light of weight, very watchful, expectant and still, and it almost
made his scalp tingle. It was something like the feeling of his
birthday, and of Christmas, and of Easter, and it was still more
like the feeling he now seldom and faintly recalled, during the
morning just after he learned of his father's death, and during
the day he was buried. But it was not really like any of these, or
anything else, except itself. These were the hours of Our
Lord's deepest Passion. For almost forty days now this feeling
had grown and deepened, not without interruption, for he
had not managed perfectly to keep either his public or his secret Lenten Rules; yet he had been sufficiently earnest and
faithful, and sufficiently grieved in his failures, that the growth
had been deeper and more cumulative and more rewarding
than he had ever known before; and now he was coming into
the heart of it, the holiest and most solemn of its shrines, with
heart and soul prepared and eager. Already it was no longer
Maundy Thursday, the birthday of the Eucharist; that sorrowfully jubilant magnificence was turned under the world; already
the world was brought a few hours forward into the most
gravely majestic of all days, Good Friday; already the wheel
was so turned that high upon darkened heaven white Easter
dazzled, suspended, the crown of the year, like the already
trembling start of an avalanche. Easter was very soon now, so
soon, with his throat brimming with its hymns and his soul
ardent for release and celebration, that it was difficult to be
patient; yet his faith and absorption were such that at the same
time he came into this day as sorrowing and careful as if Christ
had never been crucified before, and could never rise from the
dead. Yet now that he desired to retrieve his waking awareness
he could not, but only knelt, sad, trying to taste the peculiar

quality of the night and to distinguish it from other auras of momentousness, until, realizing how he had misled himself, he gripped his hair and pressed his eyeballs the more tightly, repeating in his heart: Jesus our Lord is crucified. Jesus our Lord is crucified. He saw the Head.

Thrown with fury, a shoe struck the wall next Jimmy's bed: the noise broke upon Richard with sickening fright. Then Hobe's voice:

"All right some mothuf - - - - - sonofabitch is agoana git the livin s - - t beat outn him if I find out who throwed that!"

"Shet yer God damn mouf," said a coldly intense, deeper voice at the far end of the dormitory.

"Yeah fer Chrise sakes *shut up*," said another voice, as several neutral voices said "Shut up."

In the rigid silence Richard and Jimmy dressed quickly while Hobe waited. Carrying their shoes they stole barefoot on tiptoe from the room and along the hall and past the iron cot which had been set up by the stairhead for this one night for Father Whitman. They could just make out how he lay there in the dark in his long white habit, giving off a current of silent and ominous power because they could not be sure as they passed whether he was asleep or aware of them; the clacking of his tin clock filled the pine stairwell with its flagrant loudness. They tried hard not to creak the stairs. The pit of Richard's stomach still felt as it did when, without being too mad or too desperate to care, he knew it was impossible not to fight. By trying hard he was able to restore whole to his mind the thorn-crowned image of his Lord, but now it was not as he had seen it in prayer beside his cot but was very little different from a pious painting he knew: the eyes rolled up in a way that seemed affected, and in his cold sickness the image meant little to him. It was not until they came onto the back porch that the open night put them once more at their ease.

"Sonofabitchin mothuf - - - - - bastud," Hobe said. "At shoe bettah be gone by mawnin or *some* bastudly cocks - - - - -'s agoana be sorry."

"Aw shut up Hobie," Jimmy said. "This ain't no time to talk like that."

"Hell do *I* keer," Hobe said. "*I* hain't been to Confession yet."

But he started on down the steps without saying anything more.

"What happened?" Richard asked.

"Jis trine wake up Jimmy," Hobe said. "God All Mighty Christ, can't even wake nobody up in this friggin School—"

Richard followed them down the steps. He was glad he had learned hardly even to think of saying anything. If Jimmy told Hobie to shut up and quit cussing Hobie would take it off of him, they were buddies; but by now he knew enough to keep *his* mouth shut. He felt uneasy, though, because he was glad he had not sworn. That was like being thankful you were not as other men and that was one of the worst sins of all; the Pharisee.

He had forgotten all about the shoes he carried and now that unexpectedly, for the first time this year, he felt the ground against the bare soles of his feet it was as if, fumbling among clothes in a dark closet, he had put his hand on living flesh. Even though the ground in this schoolyard was skimmed with dusty gravel, its aliveness soared through him like a sob and lifted his eyes in wonder upon the night. There was no moon and what few stars were out, they were made faint by a kind of smiling universal milky silence, not fog, or even the lightest kind of mist, but as if the whole air and sky were one mild supernal breath. Downhill in the Chapel a line of small windows meekly smoldered, dark orange; he followed his companions and saw that they too were carrying their shoes. When they came to the lawn beyond their building they left the gravel; the ground, with its scarce new grass, felt like a fish. There was a thick oak near the center of the lawn and Hobe and Jimmy, as they passed, stung it several times expertly with gravel. It had not occurred to Richard to pick up gravel and now he was glad, for he was sure he would have missed as often as hit.

II

THE NIGHT smelled like new milk; the air which exhaled upon them when they opened the side door of the Chapel was as numb and remote as the air of a cave. Without knowing it they hesitated, subdued by the stagnant darkness and its smell of waxed pine and spent incense. Across the unlighted nave the open door of the Lady Chapel brimmed with shaken light; but just at their left, through the door to the vestry, came a friendlier and more mundane light, a delicious smell, and the tired grinding of the voice they most admired in the world. When he became aware of their hesitation beside this partly closed door, George Fitzgerald spoke to them with a formality as unaccustomed and gentle as if a dead body lay in the room behind him and they came in, silent and shy. By the loud hurrying little clock it was still only four minutes to four. They squatted on their bare heels against the wall and looked on, their six eyes emphatic in the sleepless light.

The inward wall of this long corridor was hung solid with cassocks and they were of all lengths from a size almost big enough for the giant sad boy they all called Undertaker, to the all but baby size of Dillon Prince. At first Richard wondered where all the cottas were; in the laundry for Easter, he realized. The room was so weakly lighted by candlestubs that at the far end it was hardly possible to distinguish the red cassocks from the black. Just within the surer light, his jaw and his shoulders sloping more heavily even than usual with fatigue and with his low posture, Willard Rivenburg sat on a folding-chair which gave out dangerous splintering noises whenever he stirred. It was he who was talking, aimlessly, quietly, almost in his sleep; and Richard could see that George and Lee Allen answered him only so often as courtesy required, never turning their attention from their work. Not only were they Prefects; it was also believed by some of the older people that they alone among the boys now at the School, might have a Vocation. They were in their last year now and it was generally understood that they were both praying hard for this to be made clear to them before they graduated. It was their privilege,

tonight, to trim and change the candles and to remove and replace the withering flowers, and now white-girdled, incongruous in red cassocks, they stood wearily beside a soup plate,
replying gravely in short words while, their eyes bright with
the lateness of the hour and fixed in the profound attentive-
ness of great scientists, they revolved candlestubs between
thumb and forefinger, just above a flame, and watched the
meltings add themselves to the already considerable cone of
wax and tallow which they had developed on the plate. The
shining melt spilled roundly, rambling and congealing; wherever it ridged, they smoothed it delicately with their fingertips.
From the apex of this rounded cone sprang three long fiery
wicks.

Because they were to be up all night these two had been for-
given the fast and had supplied themselves against possible
hunger. But neither had yet eaten or drunk, nor did either privately intend to unless, as seemed unlikely, he became too faint
or too sleepy to attend properly to his share of the work. Their
coffee frothed so noisily over its can of Sterno rather because
this enhanced their feeling of privilege and maturity; Willard
was drinking some while he talked although, Richard reflected, it was long after midnight, when the fast began. He
had also practically finished off a box of Fig Newtons.

The coffee was so strong that it empurpled the wall of the
cup, and its smell was almost as enviably masculine as that of
white lightning. The three younger boys kept respectfully
quiet and looked on, eagerly and sleepily. They watched now
the lapped purple rings in the slanted cup, now the shining of
the living wax and its satin look where it had slowed and had
been smoothed, now the strong loose smoky flame and the
hypnotized faces which leaned above it, and now the reckless
primitive profile and the slash-lined blue-black cheek of the
great athlete Willard Rivenburg, whom they had never seen in
quite such quiet intimacy. Nobody knew for sure just how old
Willard was, but he looked as many men can only at thirty or
so, and then only if they have been through a war, or years of
the hardest kind of work. Richard tried to imagine why he was
here tonight. He was fairly sure it was not for any kind of religious reason: Willard had been confirmed, and made his Confession and his Communion, but it was obviously just as a

matter of course; when he took his turn serving Mass or swinging the Censer or carrying the Crucifix he was never exactly irreverent yet he always looked as if secretly he might be chewing tobacco; it looked as odd and out of place, somehow, as watching a horse dressed up in cassock and cotta and doing these things. He never even crossed himself at a hard time in a game, the way some of the others did. No, he wouldn't be here because he felt pious. It might be because everybody and everything on the place was thinking about just these things that were happening, and moving around them; a kind of shadow and stillness came over everything during Holy Week and it might be that Willard felt this and was made uneasy by it. But mainly it must be just that he was much too grown-up to be able to stand all the silly rules, and tame hours, and good behavior, that were expected of living in a school; he must be even gladder than the little boys were to grab at any chance to break out of that routine, especially anything that would give him an excuse for staying up so long after hours. And yet, Richard reflected, Willard needed and took an awful lot of sleep, dropping off in dull classrooms or wherever he had to sit still, except for eating, as easily as a colored man or a dog. But maybe all that sleep was why he was able to be awake now, though as a matter of fact he wasn't really more than half awake, not nearly as wide awake as Richard felt. But then probably he had been up all night, and probably it wasn't for the first time in his life either.

In some way which it did not occur to him to think about or try to understand, Richard felt a warm rich comforting kind of pride in him and sense of glory as he watched him, as much, in a far quieter and even happier way, as when he watched his almost magical ability in sports; and he began to feel a sense of honor and privilege in having this surprising chance to be so near him and to watch him so closely, to really see him. For normally, when Willard was not playing or practising or sleeping or eating, he was kidding with somebody, in a loudly reckless, crazy way which was a pleasure to see because everything Willard did was a pleasure to see, but was impossible to see through; but now he wasn't kidding at all, only talking quietly and steadily like a grown man, among others whom he treated as grown men. He was finishing up about his grandfather who had come over from Switzerland to settle way back on the Mountain and who had never bothered to learn much English, and he was saying the few words and phrases of German he himself knew, and Richard was deeply impressed in realizing that Willard, who always seemed to him to know about as little as anyone could, except as an athlete and captain of genius and a powerful and experienced man, actually knew words in a foreign language. He himself was accustomed to feel a good deal of complacency because with Father Fish's help he had learned several hundred words of French, but now he felt ashamed of himself, and resolved to learn German, which seemed to him a much more virile language.

He was watching with shy and particular interest the hump between Willard's heavy shoulders, which he had often wondered about but never yet had the chance to examine so privately. It was almost as if Willard were slightly hunchbacked, the low way he always carried his head and sloped his shoulders and the way this hump bulged out just below the base of his neck; yet if he were deformed, he could not have such ability and strength. It must be a very greatly developed muscle, Richard realized, yet it was a funny place to have a muscle; he felt there now on his own body and there wasn't even the beginning of a muscle there; just bone. Could it be bone? But that would be a deformity; and on Willard, more than any other thing, it was what made him unique among others, and marked his all but superhuman powers. Whenever he had done anything physically creditable Richard carried his head low, let his mouth hang open, and tried to hump his back, scarcely knowing of it any more; and so, though it was not generally realized, did many other boys in this school.

"Hey you," Lee said, and startled, they looked: one minute past four. Richard felt a spasm of shame: could ye not watch with me one hour? Besides, they were keeping somebody over his time. "*Jesus!*" Hobe Gillum said, and they stood up quickly. Both of the boys in cassocks ducked in shocked acknowledgement of the Name and Willard's dark face brightened with his satanic parody of falsetto laughter. Lee Allen said with unusually kind gravity: "I sure would hate to have to report anyone for cussn right in Chapel, and on Good Friday too." Hobe's eyes turned Indian, with pride towards Willard, in defiance towards Lee. "Aw forget about it Lee," George Fitzgerald said, "he just wasn't thinking." "I don't want to report you or nobody else," Lee said. "You just watch your mouth, Hobie." "He didn't mean anything," Richard said; and even before everyone looked at him and said nothing, he was miserable. "Better put your shoes on you kids," George said, and with relief Richard sank his hot face over his shoelaces. They felt contempt for him, he was sure, and he felt contempt for himself. Willard thought better of Hobe for cussing than of him for standing up for him, and so did he. Lee jumped on Hobie because Willard's cackling about it bothered him and he couldn't jump on Willard. If it hadn't been Good Friday and Richard had spoken up like that he knew that somebody would have said coldly, "Well look who's talking." Keep your mouth shut, he kept whispering within himself intensely. Just keep your fool mouth shut. And as they left the room he tried to exorcise the feelings of injustice, self-pity and pain by crossing himself quickly and surreptitiously. Fine time to go worrying about your*self*, he sneered at himself.

The nave replied to their timid noises with the threatening resonance of a drumhead. Not even the sanctuary lamps were lighted, but the night at the windows made just discernible the effigies and the paintings and the crucifix, no longer purple veiled but choked in black, and the naked ravagement of the High Altar. The tabernacle gawped like a dead jaw. By this ruthless flaying and deracination only the skeleton of the Church remained; it seemed at once the more sacred in dishonor, and as brutally secular as a boxcar. To cross its axis without the habitual genuflection felt as uneasy as to swim across a sudden unimaginable depth, and as Richard turned and bowed before the central devastation he realized: nothing there. Nothing at all; and with the breath of the Outer Darkness upon his soul, remembered the words: And the Veil of the Temple was rent in twain.

But here in peace and victory before the adoration of all creatures past and breathing and uncreated, shrined and enthroned, starred round with unabating light and with the stars of all the fields of spring as well, exiled there yet abides throughout this night the soul and substance of the everliving

God Who shall, within these few hours now, be restored to
His High Altar and there devoured, leaving His whole Church
desecrate and unconsoled until the hour of His glorious Res-
urrection from the Dead. Tied in its white veil, stifled, a huge
masked Head, a thinly clouded Sun, the monstrance stood
from the top of the tabernacle and broke at its center a dense
tissue of flowers and light: candles it seemed by thousands,
spear-high and merely tall, and short, and guttering, each an
abiding upright fiery piercing and, crisp and wearying, withering, dying, the frugal harvest of the dawn of the year: from
faint orchards the last apple blossoms, still tenderly raveling
their slow-borne blizzard; branches of mild-starred dogwood
and of the hairy wild azalea, pink and white, from the mulled
gray woods, and little fistfuls of those breathless violets which
break the floor of winter, even the rare mayapple, the twinleaf,
whose bloom stays just a day; and, of the first shivering domestic flowers, cold jonquils, crowds of them, greenish with
chill or butter yellow or flaming gold, and clear narcissus,
reaching, bowing, staring, fainting in vases and jars of metal
and glass and clay and in drinking glasses and mason jars and
in small and large tin cans, all these each in their kind and suf-
ferance bore witness before God while they might. Few of
these early flowers have strong fragrance, or any, yet the heat
and the brightness and the fragrance brought forth by the
burning wax and tallow and by the heat in the closed room,
all one wall of dizzying dazzle, were such that it was at first
almost as difficult to breathe the freighted air as to breathe
water, and this air was enriched the more by the devotions of
those who knelt subsumed within the trembling light; and at
the instant of stepping into this hot and fragrant gold, going
upon one knee and gazing upon the blind rondure of the
monstrance and the thousand-pointed blossoming of fire and
flower, his heart was lifted up and turned vague and shy as the
words broke within him, upon each other, God: Death; so that
the two were one. Death: Dead, the word prevailed; and before him, still beyond all other stillness, he saw as freshly as six
years before his father's prostrate head and, through the efforts to hide it, the mortal blue dent in the impatient chin. He
remembered within this instant how for the first time he had
been convinced, and how eternally convincing it had been,

when he saw how through that first full minute of looking his father had neither stirred nor spoken, and how the powerful right hand had lain half open against the exact center of his body; the cloth of his coat was not moved by any breathing and it was as if the hand were only a magically expert imitation of a hand, a hand of wax and, now looking again at the head, lips and a face of wax, a dent of wax, a head of wax immense upon this whole rich waxen air. Dead, the word came again, and shutting his eyes he prayed swiftly for his father the prayer of all his childhood, God bless daddy and keep him close to Thee and may light perpetual shine upon him, Amen; and casually, obliviously, as a trout into shadow, the image and memory vanished. It is Our Lord's death today, he said to himself, but at this moment he could see neither face, that of his father, or that of his Lord; only the words returned, God: Death.

No praying-benches were available at first, and they knelt where they entered, the waxed floor brutal against their bones. In the Name of the Father and of the Son and of the Holy Ghost, Richard whispered rapidly to himself, moving his lips and closing his eyes again. He crossed himself with care. There was a sound of arising and departure and through his eyelashes he saw Knox Peyton complete his genuflection and step ungainly between him and Jimmy, trying to subdue the reproach and annoyance in his face. They stayed where they knelt, all on their good manners before the one empty bench, and Richard heard the whispered "go on" several times before he realized that it was directed at him. Two worshipers glanced unhappily behind them, shut their eyes, and tucked their chins down, trying hard to pray. "I be damned if I will," Richard thought, and caught himself; he shut his eyes tightly and in despairing shame tucked his own chin down. "Go *on*," he heard. He decided that he ought to make a penance of it. Trying to look and to feel neither humble nor proud he crossed himself, got up, genuflected, tiptoed to the empty bench, genuflected, knelt, and crossed himself. Mr. Bradford closed his eyes, frowned, and deeply bowed his head. Home stretch, Richard said to himself, and quickly begged forgiveness for an irreverence which had not been premeditated but spontaneous. But wasn't it even worse to be so unaware of where you were that such a thought could occur spontaneously? Mr. Bradford completed his devotions and tiptoed towards the door, his eyes downcast. His effort to stay within himself was too successful; Richard heard him bump against one of the two boys, and his whispered accusing apology, and their feckless and ill-subdued reply. Deaconess Spenser, at the desk opposite his own, compressed her lips, crossed herself, got up, genuflected, and stepped behind him; he could hear the harsh whispered reprimand whistling through her false teeth. He looked carefully at his clasped hands, but he heard movement as the door was cleared and along the side of his eye Jimmy advanced and swiftly established himself at the newly empty bench and the Deaconess, her wattles a violent red and her mouth pulled in tight, returned to her own bench, genuflected, knelt, crossed herself, and sank her forehead into her hands. Behind him somebody else stood up and he heard the knee touch the floor and, knowing he ought not to, glanced back; it was Hog Eye Kelsey, one of the littler boys from his own dormitory; already Hobe was standing to replace him. Not Hog Eye, he told himself; he can't help it: Jeff.

Pay attention, he told himself. Mind your own business.

He looked at the veiled monstrance; the brightest threads of the veil sparkled like mica, gold-white on silver-white, and in one place a rigid shaft of metal radiance almost pierced the fabric. One azalea bloom strayed against it as if it were straining to be near it. Tiny threads sprang out of the flare of the blossom, the way small straight lines are drawn in a funny-paper to show music coming out of a horn. An apple-blossom fell. Looking at the tired sleepless flames of the candles, Richard felt as if he could almost hear them burning.

Soul of Christ sanctify me, he prayed silently; Body of Christ save me; but he was just saying it mechanically, and too fast. Slowly now, thinking carefully of each word, he began again.

Soul of Christ sanctify me: make me holy: absolve me from all spot of sin:

Body of Christ save me: save me: Thy Body which has already begun to suffer and die:

He braced his mind.

Blood of Christ inebriate me:

Carefully as he tried, he could not avoid it. Inebriate meant just plain drunken, or meant a drunken person, especially habitual drunkard, and as it was used here, it meant to make drunk, to intoxicate. And inebriety meant drunkenness and the habit of drunkenness. He had been fond of the word for a long time before he knew, or realized that he did not know, its meaning—which must of course be simply what the Blood of Christ might most naturally be expected to do: but what would that be, that sounded as nice as inebriate? During the past winter it had occurred to him to look it up in a dictionary. Since then the correct and disconcerting meanings had been indelible, and that part of the prayer had become thin ice. He could only get past it without irreverent or skeptical thoughts by saying it so fast or so shallowly that it was impossible to bear its meaning in mind, and that was no way to pray. He had asked Father Fish about it and Father Fish had shown him that it was possible to be amused by the word without feeling irreverent. He had said that some of these ancient prayers were rather extravagant in their way of putting things, and that there was no need to take them with absolute literalness. Although he had no way of being sure, Richard had a feeling that Father Fish had been as amused at him, as at the word; once again he wondered why, and stopped himself from wondering why because this was no time to. Don't take it literally, he told himself firmly; but the literal words remained and were even more firm: make drunk. Intoxicate. Good ole whiskey, he suddenly heard in his mind, and he remembered how, drinking sodapop in Knoxville, boys slightly more worldly than he would twist the bottle deep into the mouth and cock it up vertically to drink, and taking it down, breathless, would pat their stomachs or rub them in circles and gasp, "Ahhh, good ole whiskey!" But this wasn't even on whiskey. On blood. Jesus' blood, too. His uncle had once sneered, "There is a pudding filled with blood," scornfully exploding the first syllable of "pudding," and Richard had been both shocked and amused, and he was shocked to find that he remembered it with amusement now. Forgive us our trespasses, he whispered, shutting his eyes tight. It was only a hymn, and so it was not as bad to make fun of as some things were. But the blood was "drawn from Emmanuel's veins," so that did make it pretty awful. And his uncle had said it with a kind of hatred which included much more than the hymn: all of religion, and everybody who was religious, even his own sister, Richard's mother, and his Aunt Patty, and him, Richard, and his own sister. Forgive us our trespasses as we forgive those who trespass against us, he prayed, and pushed the matter out of his mind. He does like us all the same, he reflected, same as grandpa does. They just don't like the Church.

Passion of Ch——

Water from the side of Christ wash me; and he felt that his thoughts badly needed washing:

Passion of Christ strengthen me:

Within Thy Wounds hide me, he thought swiftly and with great uneasiness, hugging the ground and the leaf coverage as if beneath the skimming of a bird of prey: but try as he could, the image plunged and took him. An older boy, the only one Richard knew who also liked to read, had with great sophistication and delight explained to him what was meant, in Shakespeare's *Venus and Adonis*, by the words *he saw more wounds than one*, and this had instantly become identical in his mind with a rawly intimate glimpse he had had, three or four years before, of Minnielee Henley when they were climbing a tree; and now with these words *within Thy Wounds hide me* the image fought in his mind with the image of those small but deadly wounds in the body of Jesus, in which surely nobody could hide, not even the one the spear made in His side. But not there either, he insisted to himself; not even if He wasn't a man. Yet there in his mind's eye, made all the worse by all the most insipid and effeminate, simpering faces of Jesus that he had ever seen in pictures, was this hideous image of a huge torn bleeding gulf at the supine crotch, into which an ant-swarm of the pious, millions of them, all pleading and rolling up their eyes, laden souls, by thousands meekly stealing, struggled to crowd themselves, and lose themselves, and drown, and dissolve.

It was the Devil, that was all. Just the Devil Himself, tempting him.

O good Jesu hear me, he prayed with deep self-loathing, almost aloud: and realized with gratitude that for once he had been able to say these words, which for months now had seemed to him fulsome and insincere, with complete desire and sincerity. You just have to mean it, he thought, for it to mean anything.

Suffer me not to be separated from Thee (a mortal sin is a sin that cuts us off from God):

From the Malicious Enemy defend me:

Of these closing lines he never felt doubt and now he repeated, with reverent emphasis and relish:

From the Malicious Enemy defend me:

In the hour of my death call me and bid me come to Thee:

That with Thy

No there was something really wrong about

He prayed, with fear and determination: That with Thy Saints I may praise Thee, forever and ever, Amen.

All the same it was wrong for people to ask to be saints, as flat as all that. Or even just to be *with* the saints, if that was what it meant. To just barely manage through God's infinite mercy to escape burning eternally in the everlasting fires of Hell ought to be just about as much as any good Catholic could pray for; and now Richard remembered still another prayer at which, when he was serving at Mass, he had for quite a while now been accustomed to keep silence or at most to make approximate sounds of the words, with his fingers crossed: where, in the General Confession, reviewing his iniquities, the penitent cries, "The remembrance of them is grievous unto us, the burden of them is intolerable." As a rule he was able to say "the remembrance of them is grievous unto us" with adequate sincerity; but it was seldom that he could feel, at the particular moment he felt required to feel, that "the burden of them is intolerable." It wasn't anywhere near intolerable, no matter how much it ought to be. At first he had been able to say it in the realization that it was intolerable to his soul, whether or not he in his mind and feelings was capable of feeling it just then, and that prayers are said by and for the soul, not the mind or the feelings; but in this he came to feel that he was mistaken: for it was, he noticed, only when he believed and felt deeply with his mind or his emotions that he was able to be aware that his soul, as such, existed. But that isn't true, he now thought with alarm. No matter what I think or feel, the soul is

always there and always alive unless it has been killed by im-
penitence for mortal sin. The hardening of the heart towards
God. I'm only trying to suit myself, he told himself; not my
soul, and not God.

But how can you say things when you only ought to mean
them and don't really mean them at all?

Have mercy upon us O God have mercy upon us, he found
himself praying. These were the words of the Confession
which followed "the burden of them is intolerable," and always,
as now, he was able to mean them when he spoke them.

But not "that with Thy Saints I may praise Thee."

Now it occurred to Richard that perhaps this prayer had
been written by a saint or by someone near sainthood, who was
able to mean every extreme thing that was said; and he knew
that anyone who could fully mean those things, and who
could mean them every time they were said, was to be humbly
respected. But in that case it was a prayer which was good only
for saints and near saints to say, not for ordinary people, no
matter how good they hoped to be. Nobody's got any business even hoping he can be a saint, he told himself.

God no!, he exclaimed to himself, for now suddenly it became vivid and shameful in his memory that he himself had for
a while cherished, more secretly even than his lust, exactly this
inordinate ambition. Good golly!, he whispered within his
soul, feeling the back of his neck and then his cheeks go hot;
and with a cold and marveling, compassionate contempt for
the child he had so recently been, he lost himself in reflective
remembrance, unaware that it was for the first time in his life.

It was hardly more than a year ago, when he was only
eleven, that the image and meaning of Jesus and the power
and meaning of the Sacraments and of the teachings of the
Church, all embodied and set forth in formalities of language
and of motion whose sober beauties were unique, and in
music which at that time moved and satisfied him as no other
music could, had first and, it had seemed, irreducibly, established upon all his heart and mind their quality, their comfort,
their nobility, their sad and soaring weight; and, entering upon
his desolation of loneliness, had made of suffering a springing
garden, an Eden in which to walk, enjoying the cool of the
evening. It had become a secret kind of good to be punished,

especially if the punishment was exorbitant or unjust; better to be ignored by others, than accepted; better still to be humiliated, than ignored. He remembered how on mornings when he had waked up and found his bed dry, he had felt as much regret as relief. He had begun to take care to read in conspicuous places, where he would be most liable to interruption and contempt. He had pretended not to know lessons he had in fact prepared, in order that even such teachers as thought well of him, or thought "at least he's smart," or "he studies, anyway," might think ill of him. He had continued his solitary wanderings in the woods until it occurred to him that these excursions, for all their solitude and melancholy, were more pleasant than unpleasant; from then on he had put himself into the middle of crowds, especially on the drearier afternoons when even the hardiest boys stayed indoors and the restive, vindictive, bored, mob feelings were at their most sullen and light-triggered. The leaden melodies of the Lenten hymns had appealed to him as never before; lines in certain hymns seemed, during that time, to have been written especially for him. *Jesus, I my Cross have taken*, he would sing, already anticipating the lonely solace of tears concealed in public: *all to leave and follow Thee; destitute, despis'd, forsaken*, were words especially dear to him; *Thou from hence my All shalt be.* As he sang that he felt: nobody else wants me; and did his best to believe it, even of his mother. He remembered now that this kind of singing had satisfied him most at Stations of the Cross, on cold rainy nights. *Perish ev'ry fond ambition*, he would sing magnanimously; (no I *won't* become a naturalist; I'll never explore the sources of the Amazon; I'll never even own a monkey, or be junior tennis champion); *all I've thought or hoped or known*; then tears and their subdual rewarded him: *Yet how rich is my condition* (never to live at home again, never to be loved or even liked), *God and Heaven are still my own*; and he saw crowned God and Heaven shining and felt, in a humble kind of way, that he literally owned them. Now remembering it he shook his head almost as if in disbelief, but he knew it had been so. Everything. He had done just about everything he could think of. He had gone seldom to Father Fish's cottage, for friendliness was certain there, and often cookies and cocoa too, and he had found that these luxuries meant most to him,

in his desire to suffer for religious advantage, only when they
were indulged so rarely that even while they were being enjoyed they enhanced the bleakness of the rest of living. He
even schemed to intensify his always all but annihilating home-
sickness to the utmost possible, asking permission of the Master of the Day the more often, that it be the more curtly or
impatiently or, at best, contemptuously refused; watching his
mother's cottage, the one place he was almost never allowed
to go, sometimes by the hour; sometimes in ambush under
dripping trees, relishing the fact that only he knew of the mis-
erableness of that watch; sometimes openly, hanging against
the fence, relishing the fact that she knew, and others could
see, and that even though she knew, she would try to ignore
him and stay out of his sight, and that when at last she could
ignore him no longer, she would hurt him by trying to be
stern with him as she told him to go away, and would sharpen
his unhappiness into agony by her idea of a sensible explanation why this senseless cruelty had to be law. "Because dear,
mother thinks it's best for you not to be too near her, all the
more because you miss her so much." "Because your father—
isn't with us." "Because mother thinks you need to be among
other boys Richard. In charge of men." And worst of all: "I
know how hard it is now but I know that when you're older
you'll understand why I did it, and thank me for it." *Thank
her!* his heart sneered now, in bitter paroxysm. And for a moment so brief that the realization did not stay with him, he felt
hatred and contempt for his mother, for her belief in submis-
siveness and for her telling him, on certain infuriating occasions, that it is only through submitting bravely and cheerfully
to unhappiness that we can learn God's Will, and how most
truly to be good. God's Will, he thought now: I bet it isn't just
for people to be unhappy! Who wants to be *good*! I do, he answered himself. But not like that. I sure was crazy then, he
thought, pleased that he was now able to recognize the fact.
Just a crazy fool. The whole crazy thing had begun to fade
away soon after Easter, with the good weather, and had vanished so completely during the free summer in Knoxville that
he had forgotten the whole of it until just now: but all through
that dreary winter and increasingly throughout that drizzling
season of penitence, he realized now with incredulous and

amused self-scorn, he had ever more miserly cherished and
elaborated his wretchedness in every one of its sorry ramifications, as indispensable to the secret, the solution, he had
through God's Grace discovered; and had managed easily to
forgive himself those parts of his Lenten Rule which he meekly
enjoyed in public, by inventing still other, harder rules which
were private. His mother had tried uneasily to suggest to him
that there might be a kind of vanity mixed up in his extreme
piety—"not that you *mean* it, of course, dear"—against which
he must be on his guard; but remembering the role of dismayed parents and scornful villagers in the early lives of many
of the saints, he had answered her gently and patiently, with
forbearance, that was the word, as befitted communication between creatures of two worlds so unbridgeably different. He
had been tempted on more than one occasion to say to her,
"Woman, what have I to do with thee? Mine hour is not yet
come"; but he had suspected that this might be thought impudent or absurd or even blasphemous. Nor had he ever said
aloud, when others jeered or tormented, "Father, forgive
them, for they know not what they do"; but had often fortified
himself with the silent words, "And He held His peace."

It had only gradually been borne upon him that he himself
might aspire to actual sainthood; he had quickly realized that if
that was to be his goal it was necessary, starting young, he
might already be too late, to perform in private for God's eyes
alone and in public that others might see, and be edified, and
remember, and revere him, a long and consistent series of remarkable spiritual feats. Let your light so shine before men
that they may see your good works and glorify your Father,
Which is in Heaven. But meditating what these might be, he
had realized that there in truth he did run the danger of sin-
ning through Pride, as those people do who look hungry
when they fast; whereas his own ambitions were prompted (or
so it seemed) by true religious feeling and by nothing else.
These ambitions had crystallized during the late weeks of Lent,
into a desire to do for Jesus as much as Jesus was doing for him
and for all souls. He had experimented with extra fasting, but
it was not possible to carry this far, since it was virtually impossible to be excused from meals without the sin of lying, and
almost as difficult, he found, to sit at the table without eating,

or eating little enough to give the fast any dignity or meaning. So he had chosen self-mortification instead. He had gone into the woods and eaten worms, but this had disgusted him, and he had been even worse disgusted when, on one occasion, he had come near tasting his own excrement. It had suddenly struck him as very doubtful indeed that Jesus would ever have done any such thing, and he had thrown the twig deep into the bushes and had carefully buried the filth. Efforts to scourge himself had been moderately painful but not sufficiently effective to outweigh the sense of bashfulness, even of ridiculousness, which he felt over the clumsiness of the attempt, in relation to the severity of the intention. So he had been reduced, mainly, to keeping very bitter vigil over his thoughts and his language and over his sensuous actions upon himself, and to finding out times and places in which it would be possible to kneel, for much longer than it was comfortable to kneel, without danger of getting caught at it. (He had been as frightened, once, by such an interruption, as if he had been surprised in a sexual act.) It was during one of these protracted and uncomfortable sojourns on his knees that his mind, uneasily strained between its own wanderings and efforts at disciplined meditation, had become absorbed in grateful and overwhelmed imagination of Christ Crucified, and had without warning brought to its surface the possibility of his own crucifixion. He had been wondering with all of a sincere heart how ever he might do enough for the Son of God Who had done so much for him when suddenly, supplanting Christ's image, he saw his own body nailed to the Cross and, in the same image, himself looked down from the Cross and felt his weight upon the nails, and the splintered wood against the whole length of his scourged back; and stoically, with infinite love and forgiveness, gazed downward into the eyes of Richard, and of Roman soldiers, and of jeering Jews, and of many people whom Richard had known. It was a solemn and rewarding moment; but almost within the next breath he recognized that he had no such cause or right as Jesus to die upon the Cross: and turning his head, saw Christ's head higher beside his own and a third head, lower, cursing; and knew that he was, instead, the Penitent Thief.

But it was of course out of the question that in a deep country part of Middle Tennessee, in nineteen twenty-three, he could actually manage to have himself nailed to a Cross; and although (if he should have the courage) he could undoubtedly nail his own feet, and even one hand (if someone else would steady the nail), his right hand would still hang free, and it would look pretty foolish beside a real Crucifixion. With any proper humility he would be content merely to be tied up, as the thieves usually were, and to hang during the three hours of Good Friday that Jesus hung on the Cross. Even that would mean a good deal, if only in token; the widow's mite, only it seemed rather more than the widow had managed; and he realized that many others besides himself would be moved, and impressed, and very likely improved, by the good example. It would be impossible of course to get a Cross without removing the image of Jesus from it, that big life-size one out in the vestibule, and that would be irreverent even if it were allowed. Or someone might make one for him but he doubted it. He might make one for himself if he could sneak into Manual Training Shop and get enough private time, only everybody knew he wasn't any good with his hands and simple as a Cross must be to make, they would just laugh at any that he would be likely to make. One of the school's grid-iron bedsteads would be convenient for tying to, and very likely even more uncomfortable to hang against than a Cross, but he was forced to doubt, as with the nail-holding and the Cross, that he could manage the whole tying-up by himself, and as he thought of asking someone else to help him, he felt extraordinarily shy. As he singled over each of the few whom in any degree he trusted, or on whose affection he could at all depend, he became sure that there was not one who would co-operate in this, or even really understand about it. It would be necessary instead to anger and deceive people he disliked into doing it: but that, he felt, was both unlikely and sinful. If he got them mad they would do what they wanted to him, not what he wanted them to do, and he could not imagine how to suggest to them that the one thing he didn't want was to be stripped of his garments (except for a loincloth) and tied to a bedstead for three hours. And even if he should manage to, he would be tricking them into a sin, and that would be a sin of itself. It was easier just to imagine it as something already

done, and as soon as he forgot about the problems of getting
it done it was better, too.

There he hung, the iron bars and edged slats of the bed
acutely painful against flesh and bone alike; but he made no
complaint. Rather, his eyes were fixed steadfastly upon the expiring eyes of his crucified Lord, and his own suffering was as
naught. There was a steady murmuring of scorn, pity, regard
and amazement beneath him, and now and again a familiar
face and voice was lifted, pleading with him or commanding
him to come down. Father McPhetridge, the Prior, his wide
red face reared up and told him that this was the most outrageous thing that had ever been done by a boy in this School
and that he was to stop it immediately and come down and
take his punishment like a man. He replied, gently and calmly,
his voice all the more effective because of its quietness after all
that indignant roaring, that "punishment" (he smiled at the
word in his suffering) would have to come at its own good time;
he would descend (with their help) promptly at three o'clock
and not before; and would give himself up to his punishers
without making a struggle. Scourge me, he said; paddle me
with the one with holes in it; put me on bounds all the rest of
the year; expel me even; there is nothing you can do that
won't be to the greater glory of God and so I forgive you. The
Prior, abashed, withdrew; Richard saw his whispering among
the other monks and the teachers and his face was redder than
ever, and their whispering eyes were on him. The football
coach Braden Bennett, who had so often sneered at his music
lessons; his face was changed, now: though with a scornful
wonder, men see her sore oppressed. He looked straight back
into those bullying eyes, with such quiet fortitude and forgiveness that the scorn and the wonder deepened, the wonder
even more than the scorn. His mother pled with him to come
down; she was even crying; and he was awfully sorry for her;
but he shook his head slowly and, smiling gently, told her:
"No, Mother, I deeply repent for making you cry, and feel so
badly, but mine hour is not yet come." She collapsed with sobbing and the women of the place crowded around her; they
took her arms and helped her as she walked away, all bent over.
Some day you'll understand, he told her within himself, and
you'll thank me for it; and he knew the happiness that comes

only of returning evil with good. Willard Rivenburg's deep
dark jaw hung open and Richard could overhear his whisper,
to Bennett, "Jesus that kid's got guts." George Fitzgerald,
scarcely able to contain his tears, held up a sponge soaked in
vinegar, which Richard forgivingly refused; and Hobe Gillum
and Jimmy Toole and Parmo Gallatin and Keg Head Hodges
and the others looked at him, glum but respectful; even if it
was no more than politeness, he realized, he would never be
last again, when they chose up sides. Through the half-open
Chapel door he could still hear the voice of the Three Hour
Sermon, Father Ogle's voice, and he realized that the service
had no more than an hour, at the outside, to go; but the voice
sounded half-hearted and sailed hollowly around the almost
empty Church; nearly everyone in the community was gathered here in the vestibule, and there were some even from
nearby towns, and suddenly a photographer climbed onto the
sandstone font and aimed at him and flashed a bulb. STRANGE
RITES AT MOUNTAIN SCHOOL, he read: and, as blood broke
scalding upon his nape, sank his face into his hands and
prayed, in despair, *O God forgive me! forgive me if you can
stand to!*

For, musing upon his past vanities with affectionate scorn or
even as with a scornful wonder, the scorn, the living vanity, of
one who has put away childish things, and dwelling upon
them in remembrance, he had dwelt once more within them
(within Thy Wounds hide me), ensnaring himself afresh. For
these later imaginations were not wholly remembrance; some
were newly his, and only now, even in the very hour of Christ's
own passion, he had yet again seduced his soul. If others, if any
other in the world, should know those absurd imaginations of
his heart: by his dread and horror in the mere thought, he
knew his contemptible silliness. But God of course knew, and
Christ Himself, even now when the Son was suffering and the
Father, grieving that He might not take the Cup from Him,
was hovering in love and sorrow, yes, engulfed, enchanted in
woe though they were, They knew very clearly though, it now
occurred to him, his secret was safe with Them. In insupportable self-loathing he squeezed his eyes so tightly shut that they
ached, and dug his chin as tightly against his throat as it would

lock and in blind vertigo, scarcely knowing his action, struck himself heavily upon his breastbone, groaning within his soul, *the burden of them is intolerable*. With the second blow he realized, in gratitude and in a new flowering of vainglory, that he had been surprised into contrition so true and so deep that beside it every moment of contrition he had ever known before seemed trivial, even false, and for an instant he questioned the validity of every Absolution he had ever been granted. Yet almost before this question could take form, and even while his fist was preparing its third assault against his inordinate heart, this new doubt was supplanted by a recognition that his action was conspicuous and that it must seem to others as affected, as much put on for outward show, as he himself, observing others, had come to feel that various mannerisms in prayer must be. Bringing his fist against his breast in circumspection he opened his eyes, raised his head a little, and without turning his head, glanced narrowly around him through his eyelashes.

Nobody seemed to have noticed anything out of the ordinary although he could not, of course, be sure of those who knelt behind him. He bowed his head again, twisting it a little to the right, lowered his right shoulder and drew it back a little, and observed from nearly closed eyes. He still could not see those who knelt directly behind him but so far as he could see, nobody seemed to have noticed him; then he caught Hobe Gillum's coppery eye, and blushed. He readjusted his head and shoulder and watched Claude Gray, who knelt a little ahead of him and to the right. Claude's head was flung far back and was so twisted in adoration that the point of his left jaw, bright gold in the candlelight, was the most conspicuous and almost the highest part of it. What was more, it was clear that he was praying, not to the Blessed Sacrament, but to the small, shrouded statue of the Blessed Virgin above the lavabo table; and noticing now for the first time that a little cup of violets stood on the plaster ledge at her feet, Richard was sure who had searched them out among the wet dead leaves to honor that place. He looked at Claude again, particularly at the tilted curly back of the head and at the abandoned angle of the brightened jaw, and thought, He may really mean it, he may not even know it but I bet he does, I bet he knows it

makes a picture and I bet he got it from some picture of some
saint or other. But if he did really mean it, and no longer knew
he was doing it, then it was not fair to blame him. He was
probably thinking about his mother. It seemed a long time ago
he had lost his mother to keep on making so much fuss about
it but maybe he took things harder than most people. Richard
suddenly felt deeply ashamed of himself in case Claude really
was grieving and praying for his dead mother, and he began to
feel pity for her and for Claude as well, but then he remembered Claude's voice, which sounded more girlish than a girl's
even though it had changed, reciting to him the Litany of the
Blessed Virgin in impassioned sugary tones; O most clement
O most holy O most sweet Virgin Mary; something of that
sort and a lot more besides. He had felt uneasy about the
whole thing and at the instant that Claude brought such juicy
emphasis to the words *mosst sweett*, with such meticulousness
about both t's and pronouncing *most* like *moused*, Richard
had decided that he definitely disliked the whole prayer; and
looking at Claude now, he disliked it even more thoroughly,
and he decided that even if Claude was genuine now in his
praying, he did not trust that kind of praying. He remembered
his mother's gossiping about Claude once, his desire that the
School should put lace borders on the cottas and his special at-
tentions to the Blessed Virgin, and saying impatiently, "Well
what I can't see is, why doesn't he just—go on over to Rome!"

But now remembering the scorn and impatience which had
been in her voice, and still watching Claude, with the long hair
of the back of his head like a shabby chrysanthemum, tilted
above the weak neck, he felt that Claude was pitiful, and that it
was careless and cruel to think of him contemptuously, and as
shameful to be watching him in this way, so unaware that he
was being watched, or that he might look in the least silly, so
defenseless, as it would be to peer at him through a keyhole.
How do *I* know, he thought; he's probably praying all right,
and even if he isn't I've got no right to look at him like this
and——

With this, something he could not quite remember, which
seemed to be prodding at the edges of his thought, came
abruptly clear. He remembered that he had started looking at
Claude, and speculating with mistrust about the quality of his

praying, because he himself had done something, without affectation, which might easily be misunderstood to be affected.
He could not quite understand it but he was in some ignoble
way trying to put off onto Claude something that was wrong
with himself, or even worse, was assuming that Claude was
doing wrongly what he knew he himself had not done wrongly;
and worse even than that, he had so wandered and so lost himself in speculating about the weakness of another that he had
degraded and lost his own moment of contrition, and had forgotten the very sin for which he was contrite, in committing
still another sin of much the same kind. But now, although
he could see the first sin, and the moment of contrition, and
the second sin, quite clearly, they formed something more like
a picture than a feeling, and there were too many things in the
picture for him to look at any one of them really closely. He
felt shame and a sort of astonishment. He wondered whether
he would ever learn, from committing one sin, how not to
commit another of the same sort even in the very moment of
repenting it; and he felt that it was strange, and terrible, that
repentance so deep and real as he knew that his had been,
could be so fleeting. He felt deeply sorry and was filled with
self-dislike as he saw what he had done, but he knew that the
feeling was of a much shallower kind than that in which, without foreseeing it, he had struck his breast so hard. He thought
of Jesus suffering on the Cross, but that deep and truest contrition was not restored; he looked again at Claude's un-
promising head, and felt a mysterious sadness, which he could
not quite understand, for whatever was imperfect and incompetent: Claude; poor little Dillon Prince, with his square-
bobbed tow hair and his pink lashless eyes, forever crying or
just over crying or just about to cry; a hen, with a wry neck
which could never be straightened, standing as if shyly to herself in one corner of the chicken run, with one wing hunched;
his own imperfect and incontinent mind and spirit; and again
of Jesus upon the Cross, suffering and dying that all such imperfections might be made whole, yes, even the poor darn
hen; and tears came into his eyes, which he relished, but he
knew they had nothing to do with the deep contrition he was
trying to recapture. Ye who do truly and earnestly repent you
of your sins, he whispered almost aloud, and are in love and

charity with your neighbors, draw near with faith and take this
Holy Sacrament to your comfort, and make your humble confession to Almighty God, devoutly kneeling.

His heart opened. Almighty and everlasting God, he prayed,
Maker of all things, Judge of all men (and he saw as in a
wheeling rondure the shining of all things, the shadows of all
men), we acknowledge and bewail our manifold sins and wick-
ednesses (and they manifolded themselves upon the air between earth and heaven like falling leaves and falling snow)
which we from time to time (and over and over, morning and
noon and waking in the night) most grievously have committed in thought (the wandering mind, the lascivious image
which even now flashed before him), word (the words of ob-
scenity and of cursing) and deed (the shame and the violence
of the hands) against Thy Divine Majesty (flung upward like so
many arrows and so much filth against the dying Son upon His
Cross and the invincible Father upon His Throne), provoking
most justly Thy wrath and indignation against us (he bowed
his head deeply, with eyes closed, and the entire sky hardened
into one spear driving downwards upon his bowed neck, yet
Christ upon His Cross merely looked into his eyes without
either wrath or indignation). We are heartily sorry for these
our misdoings. The remembrance of them is grievous unto us
(O yes it is surely grievous), the burden of them is (God, forgive me, forgive me, make them intolerable, intolerable), the
burden of them is intolerable (it is, Lord, Lord God I want
it to be), is intolerable. Have mercy upon us most merciful
Father have mercy upon us (and he pressed his clasped hands
tightly against his forehead), for Thy Son Our Lord Jesus
Christ's sake forgive us all that is past (is past), and grant that
we may ever hereafter serve Thee and please Thee in newness
of life, to the honor and glory of Thy Name, Amen.

That we may ever hereafter. Ever hereafter. Serve Thee and
please Thee. Serve Thee and please Thee in newness of life.
Forgive us all that is past. All. Past. Ever hereafter, in newness
of life. Serve Thee, and please Thee. To the honor and glory of
Thy Name.

He was as peaceful and light almost, as if he had just received Absolution. Keeping his eyes thinly closed, tilting his
head quietly back, he could see the tender light of the candles

against his eyelids, and he became aware once again of the
strong fragrance of all the flowers. Dying, he whispered to
himself. Soon now. For me and for all sinners. O sacred Head.
He heard on his rose-mild blindness the infinitesimal flickering
of the clock like those tiniest of thorns which cannot be taken
out of the skin by thousands, by crown of piercing thorn.
Opening his eyes just enough to see, looking through their
rainbow flickering of little sharpness, sharp flames on the dark,
thorn flames in thousands, each a thorn, a little sword, a
tongue of fire, standing from pentecostal waxen foreheads; go
ye unto all the world, a briar-patch of blessed fires, burning,
just audibly crackling; no; the clock. Now pale flowers, round,
in thousands, stared flatly among the thousands of sharp flames,
as white and lonely on the humming gloom as organstops,
gazed at too fixedly during a stupefying sermon, round and
bright as wafers, consecrated Hosts, in the tiny burning and
prickling of Time. He did not quite conceive of Time except as
a power of measure upon the darkness, yet opened his eyes
now and saw that it was almost twenty-five, twenty-three and a
half, past four. The clock stood on the lowest step of the Altar.
Its leather case was inlaid with silver wire almost as fine as hair,
which outlined intricate flowers and leaves. It was his mother's,
and it had been borrowed for use in the Lady Chapel, as it
always was for this Thursday watch, because it was the most
nearly silent clock on the place. Now that he looked at it he
heard it the more clearly, a sound more avid and delicate than
that of a kitten at its saucer, and now that he heard nothing
else he saw nothing else except the face of the clock, hard,
handless, staring white out of a shadow of trembling gold, like
the great Host in a monstrance; and when once again he saw
the hands, and the numbers, they showed that only two minutes of his watch remained. Could ye not watch with me one
hour? Now he remembered the images and emotions into
which he had awakened, so acutely, that they were almost his
again; but now in some way they had hardened, they stayed at
some distance from him, and he began to realize that during
this entire half-hour his mind had been wandering: there had
been scarcely one moment of prayer or of realization. Hell of a
saint I'd make, he said to himself; and added with cold and
level weary self-disgust to the tally of the sins he must soon

confess, I swore in Lady Chapel in the presence of the Blessed Sacrament. God be merciful unto me a sinner, he whispered in his mind, crossing himself.

Now for the first time he realized that his knees were very sore. The small of his back ached. When he moved, bending his back, shifting his knees, everything whirled hazily for a moment, then, with a kind of sliding or shunting like the falling into plumb of a weighted curtain, came clear and stayed still. I guess that was nearly fainting, he thought, with satisfaction. He searched the deep grooves in his knees along the edge of the board and re-established them exactly as they had been, and bore down on them to make them hurt the more, and he found that it hurt still more to keep his back completely straight and still, than to move it at all. The pain made him feel strong and reverent, and smiling he whispered silently to Jesus, "It's nothing to what You're doing." Our Father Who art in Heaven, he began; he knew now that he would stay another watch through.

Now it was half past four, but nobody moved. Nobody wants to be the first, he thought. No they're all praying, he told himself. I'm the only one noticed what time it is. Behind him he heard a sound of stealthy entering and of knees coming quietly to the floor. Now somebody will give up their place, he thought. It ought to be me.

Claude tilted his head to the other side and now Richard noticed the translucent lavender beads in his hands. He heard somebody stir and stand wearily up and he knew by the rustling starch that it was the Deaconess. She was in when I came. Been an hour. Maybe more. Quit keeping tabs, he told himself sharply. None of your business. There was the sound of her going away and the sound of another entering. Pray, he told himself. I ought to give my place. It was nearly thirty-three minutes after. We beseech Thee O Lord pour Thy Grace into our hearts, that——

The sacristy door opened and there was Lee Allen. He looked more grave and tired than before and he avoided Richard's eyes with an aloofness which abashed him. That as we have known the Incarnation of Thy Son Jesus Christ through the message of an Angel: Lee came silently to the

middle and genuflected; then from where he stood, shifting
the extinguishing cone in exact rhythm, he put out seven
shrunken candles to the left and seven to the right. He genuflected again, and leaned the tall snuffer into the corner, and
returned, and genuflected; then strode to the Altar in a quiet
and mastering way, reached delicately among the interlocked
flowers, and uprooted with each hand a smoking seven-
branched candlestick. He genuflected once again and tiptoed
out, shutting the door to softly with one shoe. Smoke crinkled
from each dark candle as he went. There seemed to be scarcely
fewer candles than before, there were so many. There would
be others to change, five on each side; the rest were still tall
enough. Through the message of an Angel, so by His Cross
and Passion: he heard behind him the prudent raising of a window, and for the first time realized how suffocatingly hot it
was, and that he was sweating. The sacristy door opened and
there was George Fitzgerald. His eyes were softer and brighter
with tiredness than before and his face was white and bright
red in patches. He met Richard's eyes quietly and impersonally. He came to the middle and genuflected, and Richard
could see that he was looking at all the flowers before he
moved. Some still had strength and some were dying, and now
he took two vases of those which were dying, unmeshing them
with great care from among the others, and genuflected, and
tiptoed out, shutting the door to softly with his shoe. Petals
flaked away as he went. The living air touched the back of
Richard's neck; now it even cooled his forehead; and now,
rank on rank, the flames of the candles acknowledged the in-
vading night; more petals fell. Upon the fragrance of fire and
wax and fresh and dying flowers there stole the purity of water
from a spring. Snaffling it desperately in an inept hand, somebody sneezed. Claude tilted his head back the first way and
started his beads all over again. Richard heard the sound of
bare feet withdrawing and knew that it must be Hobe and
Jimmy. I haven't even said my prayers, he realized. I'm going
to stay, he told himself. Give up your place, he told himself.
You got no business hogging it. As much business as: you got
no business thinking that either: as Claude with his head on
one side and those beads. Give up your place. Come back.
Kneel on the floor. The same person sneezed, more violently

but better stifled. Claude, straightening his head, laid his beads
down carefully, got up, stepped to the middle, genuflected,
turned, looking like St. Sebastian, and went to the rear of the
Chapel. Richard heard his careful sliding-shut of the window;
the flames stood straight; Claude returned, and again began
his beads at the beginning. Soul of Christ sanctify me, Richard
began aimlessly; the sacristy door opened and there was Lee
Allen.

Richard shut his eyes. O God forgive me that I can't do it
right, he prayed. O God help me do it better now. Make me to
love Thee and to know Thy suffering this day. For Jesus' sake
Amen. He crossed himself meticulously and got to his feet; he
was dizzy and for a moment his knees hurt very badly. He
stepped out of the desk, genuflected, and turned, and all of a
sudden he knew he would have to go out at least for a minute
or two, he was much too tired to stay. When he turned to
genuflect again at the door, Lee was lighting the second of the
tall new candles.

The darkness was cool and stale. From where he stood beside the door of the Lady Chapel, looking back across the
nave, he saw the spaced badges of blacker darkness where the
Stations of the Cross hung veiled. Tall at his right shoulder, a
Madonna stood, a blind black monolith. He walked silently
towards the middle of the transept, and now he could see the
white stops and keys of the organ. He stood at the center,
facing the stripped Altar; sure that it ought not to be done, but
in an obstinate and loyal reverence, he put down one knee and
then both knees before the desolate shrine: until His coming
again.

He bent his head deep towards the floor and heard his voice
whisper slowly and fearfully within him the words which, he
suspected, only a priest may utter without blasphemy: For in
the night in which He was betrayed:

His skin crawled.

This is the night in which He is betrayed.

He felt the floor, bitter against his knees, and whispered
aloud, "This is the night in which He is betrayed"; and with
the whispering it no longer was, and he whispered within himself, He took bread, and brake it, and gave it unto His disciples,

saying, Take, eat, this is my Body which is given for you; do this in remembrance of me.

He saw, and was himself, grown and vested, genuflecting, raising the consecrated Host, again genuflecting, while a bowed kneeling boy, who was also himself, shook the three bells.

Likewise after supper He took the cup, and when He had given thanks he blessed it, and gave it unto His disciples, saying, Drink ye all of this, for this is my Blood of the New Testament, which is shed for you and for many for the remission of sins. Do this as oft as ye shall drink it, in remembrance of me.

And with the words For this is my Blood of the New Testament, he knelt so deep in burden of blood that no priestly image entered him, and whispered again, Which is shed for you, and for many, for the remission of sins. And slowly one by one, while his hands lifted, the words stood up within his silence,

O Thou Lord God my Saviour: ("my Saviour," he whispered):

Look down on this Thy child.

Lord bless (he tried); O Lord lift up (he tried); O Lord forgive Thy child.

He could just see the empty Altar. There were no more words.

Do this as oft as ye shall drink it, in remembrance of me.

No more.

"Look down on this Thy child," he whispered aloud.

Now his knees hurt very badly.

"For Jesus' sake Amen," he whispered, crossing his breastbone with his thumb. He stood up.

If he went into the vestry they would say, What you doing up? They would tell him to get on back to bed. Not mean about it because of the night it was but they would tell him all the same. Because it was the rule. Or maybe they wouldn't but if they did and he didn't go on back to bed it would be even worse than if they hadn't seen him. "I told him Father," he heard Lee Allen say in his serious hollow voice. "That's right Father," George Fitzgerald said, nodding soberly. And that was always worse when somebody had told you; Prefects. "What did you stay out for then?" "I dunno Father." "Course you

know. Why did you stay out? Why did all of you stay out,
Toole? You heard me tell you all to come straight back to
bed." Where were they? He was suddenly scared. If they had
gone back it would be even worse for him if he didn't go back
too. "Where's Richard?" "I dunno Father." "Course you know,
you all went together. Where is he?" "Honest Father *I* dunno.
Last I seen him he was still in Lady Chapel." That ought to
make it all right. Still in Lady Chapel. He was late but it was
because he was praying. Can't whip anybody for that. "You
know what the rule is." No. He'd say that to him, not them,
him, at Council Meeting; they'd come back in time. "You
know what I told you: come right on back to bed." "But I
was staying a second watch Father. Ask Lee. Ask George if I
wasn't." "I don't care what you were doing I told you to come
straight back to bed and you didn't do any such thing. Now
what have you got to say for yourself?" Or no, maybe he
would look embarrassed and just mutter something about You
see to it you do what you're told, and not punish him. Or no
he would maybe look mad when he heard that about the second watch and say, "And you've got the nerve to use *that* for
an excuse?" And yet the year before he had stayed a second
watch and there had not been any trouble. But that year nobody had told him to come right on back to bed. That was the
year three of the boys had never even showed up for the watch
they signed for but went over to Lost Cove and got some
whiskey.

If they'd gone on back he was in trouble already.

Breathing light, and the breathing shaken by his heart, with
the greatest possible stealth he approached the vestry door
and, stiffening beside the frame like an Indian scout, spied
slopewise between the door and the jamb. George was carefully arranging wild azaleas in a Karo bucket. Lee was not
there. Hobe squatted against the wall; Richard could see only
his cheek, brown-orange in the light of the fiery mount of
wax, which had grown much larger. Willard hung out all over
the folding-chair; the quietly snoring head lay back and the
blue chin was the highest part of it. Jimmy sat on the floor between his thighs; he looked very sleepy. Lee Allen came

quickly out of the back passage at the far end and he seemed to look straight at Richard and Richard flinched away and froze, but it was clear by Lee's voice that he had not actually seen him. "Ought to wake up Burgy and send these kids to bed," he said. "They aren't doing any harm," George said. "*I* don't keer," Lee said, "but I don't want to get in no trouble either, you know what they told us." George said nothing for a little while and then he said, "Me neither," and after a while he said, "I don't want you to get in trouble, count of me, Lee. You send them out if you want to. Don't let me hinder you." After thinking, Lee said, "Nobody hindern me." After a little he said, "Where's Sockertees?" which was one of Richard's nicknames, and Richard felt his breathing go thin. And Hobe said, exactly as Richard had fore-heard him, "Last I seen him he was still in Lady Chapel." "Well he ain't there now," Lee said. "Probly went on back to bed,"

George said. "No," he reflected, "we'd a heard him go out." "Crazy kid," Lee said. Richard tried to be sure whether this was said in affection or dislike, but so far as he could see it was neither, just an indifferent statement of fact. Dislike would almost have been better; and now he knew that he could not go in, right after Lee's saying that, and that although he felt very lonely, and suddenly wanted very much to be in there with them where no fuss was being made about not going to bed, he wanted still more not to be anywhere near them or anywhere near anybody. Crazy kid: crazy kid; yet he could not go away, for they might say more about him. He could hear George saying, "Oh, he's a good kid" or even just "Oh, he's all right," and it made everything much better, he could almost have gone in; but George didn't say anything of the kind, or anything at all, he just seemed to accept it as a fact everybody knew; and after a little Lee said, "I got to thin out them candles some if they're goana last through"; and George did not answer, and Lee said, "I thought there was a whole box more of them," and George said, "Not that I know of": and Lee did not answer, and George said, "If you thin out the candles some, maybe it'll give the flowers a chance, anyhow. I sure do hate to see dead flowers"; and suddenly, frightened because he was spying, Richard shrank as small against the wall as he could, for someone had come out of the Lady Chapel and now he could make out that it was Claude and realized thankfully, He sleeps in St. Joseph's, he'll go out the front. And sure enough Claude came to the middle as if to bow or genuflect and stood there a moment and then tossed his head upward to one side in a peculiar, saucy way, and turned his back on the Altar and walked back up the middle aisle and through the vestibule door; and after a moment Richard could hear the outside door; and then nothing; and after his breathing was quiet again, he crossed the transept without pausing to bow, and went back into the Lady Chapel.

The prayer-desks were all taken; he knelt at the rear on the bare floor and crossed himself, and closed his eyes, and bowed his head. Lord make my mind not to wander, he prayed, successfully driving from his mind Claude's impudent head. This is the last chance, he told himself. By leaning a little he could just see the clock. Already it was nearly quarter of. He felt fury against himself and subdued it, for it was evil. God be merciful unto me a sinner, he prayed, shutting his eyes again.

He waited carefully with his eyes closed but nothing came to him except his emptiness of soul and the pain of his knees and of his back. Hail Mary, he whispered to himself, and went through the prayer twice. He repeated five more Hail Marys rather rapidly and then three very slowly, trying to allow each word its full weight, and still there was nothing, not even through the words Pray for us sinners now and in the hour of our death. What's wrong with me, he wondered. He kept his eyes shut. Perhaps exactly because he had given his knees a rest, they now hurt worse than ever. Or it was because they were now on the flat floor, instead of braced against the edge of a board. The grooves where they had been against the board hurt badly, the bones just below the kneecaps hurt even worse. And within another minute or so, the small of his back ached worse than it had before. He bent over a little, and though that hurt his back in a new way, it also gave it a sort of rest. He let himself slacken down so that his buttocks sat on his heels, and that at least changed the pressure on the bones of his knees. He leaned forward so that his chest almost rested against his knees, and that helped his back. It'll just look like at Adoration, he reflected; and was ashamed of his hypocrisy. All the same, he thought, if it'll help me pray. Hail Mary, he prayed again. But still there was nothing. His heart was empty and his mind was idle, and he could not forget his discomfort.

He opened his eyes and looked around for a kneeling-pad and he saw one, skated against the baseboard, ahead of him and across the Chapel. He would have to get up and go in front of Julian to get it, and Julian was not using one. He hasn't been kneeling as long as I have, he reflected. What of it. He'll think I came in late. Just now. What of it. But the more he thought about it the more clearly he decided he would not go over and get the pad. If I can't say my prayers right, he told himself, why anyhow I can do this. He felt proudly and calmly vindictive against himself. Closely attentive to everything he was doing, he raised himself straight onto his knees and he straightened his spine so that his knees and the small of his back should hurt as much as possible, and he put the heels of his hands together, the fingers extended, edge to edge, tips touching, and the right thumb crossed over the left, as he had been taught when he was learning to be an acolyte. Ordinarily this strange and careful position of the hands embarrassed him, for it seemed sissy. Only a few of the servers kept to it; most of them, like Richard, simply folded their hands, and so did most of the priests; but now it seemed no more sissy than being on your knees in the first place. It was just the right way to hold your hands to pray, that was all. For all the aching in his knees and his back he was now even more clearly aware of his hands in this unaccustomed position, the palps of the fingers touching so lightly and competently, the locked thumbs, the cleanly hollow of shaded light within the palms; his hands felt full of goodness and quiet and they made him think of pictures of Cathedrals.

He tried to breathe so quietly that he could not feel his chest go in and out or even any air moving in his nostrils, and he gazed studiously at the monstrance, visualizing through the veil the spangling sunlike gold and the white center, and upon that center Christ Crucified, Whom he saw first in metal and then in wood and then in flesh; but he began to wonder whether these efforts at visualization were not mere tricks and temptations of emptiness, for still he was empty of prayer and of feeling. Now that he forbade himself images and dwelt within the discipline of his body his knees and his back began to hurt worse than ever and he began to think with quiet and increasing amazement of young men, boys really, hardly older than he was, not much older than George anyway, who knelt like this on Chapel stone the whole night through in prayer and vigil, their weapons and armor blessed and waiting, soberly shining in the lambent gloom, before the Mass and the Communion and before the greatest moment of their lives when their King touched the flat of the sword to the shoulder and the young man stood up and was assisted in putting upon himself the whole armor of God and rode forth into the glittering meadows of daybreak for the first time a knight, a knight errant, seeking whatever wrong God might send him to set right, whatever tests of valor and chastity the huge world might hold in ambush for him. O but I can do better than this, he exclaimed to himself in self-contempt; and he thought with envy and reverence of the early time which had belonged to those shining young men, and he pressed down with all his strength and weight, first on one knee and then on the other, so that it was hard not to cry out, and he held his back still more rigidly upright, and he was pleased to find that now, by the way he held his hands out, even his arms ached, deep into the shoulders. But it's so little to do!, he thought, imagining the first, living Crucifix; and he did his best to imagine one hand, against splintery wood, and the point of a spike against the center of the open hand, and a great hammer, and the spike being driven through, breaking a bone, tight into the wood so that the head was all buried in the flesh and the splintered bone, and then to be able to say, *Father forgive them for they know not what they do.* And that's just one hand, he reminded himself. How about both hands. And both feet. Specially both feet crossed on each other and one spike through both insteps. How about when they raise up the Cross with you on it and drop it deep into the hole they dug for it! And imagining that moment he felt a tearing spasm of anguish in the center of each palm and with an instant dazzling of amazed delight, remembering pictures of great saints, shouted within himself, *I've got the Wounds!* and even as he caught himself opening his palms and his eyes to peer and see if this were so he realized that once again this night, and even more blasphemously and absurdly than before, he had sinned in the proud imagination of his heart. *O my God*, his heart moaned, *O my God! My God how can You forgive me!* I'll have to confess it, he realized. I can't. Not this. How can I confess *this*!

The thing he had most dreaded to confess before, an impure act which in its elaborateness had seemed merely the more exciting in the doing and which was so nearly unbearable to specify to another, and a priest at that, that he had gravely considered the risk to his soul of merely generalizing it: beside this new enormity—and twice over in one night, and both times in the Presence—beside this, that ugly and humiliating lustfulness seemed almost easy to tell of. But I'll tell it all the same, he told himself grimly. Because if I don't I'm in mortal sin. No I'll tell it because I did it and I hate to so much, and I don't care who it is I have to tell it to either, I won't dodge whoever it turns out to be and wait for another, not even if it's Father McPhetridge. I'll tell the whole thing just the way it happened —way I thought it happened, that is. I'll tell it all right. Because I've got to.

He looked proudly at the monstrance and felt strength and well-being stand up straight inside him, and self-esteem as well; for it began to occur to him that not many people would even know this for the terrible sin it was, or would feel a contrition so deep, or would have the courage truly and fully, in all of its awful shamefulness, to confess it: and again the strength and the self-esteem fell from him and he was aghast in the knowledge that still again in this pride and complacency he had sinned and must still again confess; and again that in recognizing this newest sin as swiftly as it arose, and in repenting it and determining to confess it as well, he had in a sense balanced the offense and restored his well-being and his self-esteem; and again in that there was evil, and again in the repenting of it there was good and evil as well, until it began to seem as if he were tempted into eternal wrong by rightness itself or even the mere desire for rightness and as if he were trapped between them, good and evil, as if they were mirrors laid face to face as he had often wished he could see mirrors, truly reflecting and extending each other forever upon the darkness their meeting, their facing, created, and he in the dark middle between them, and there was no true good and no true safety in any effort he might ever make to realize or repent a wrong but only a new temptation which his very soul it-self seemed powerless to resist; for was not this sense of peace, of strength, of well-being, itself a sin? yet how else could a for-given or forgivable soul possibly feel, or a soul in true contri-tion or self-punishment? I'm a fool to even try, he groaned to himself, and he felt contempt for every moment of well-being he could recall, which had come of the goodness of a thought or word or deed. *Everything* goes wrong, he realized. Every-thing anyone can ever do for himself goes wrong. Only His Mercy. That's what He died for. That's what He's dying for today. Only His Mercy can be any help. Nothing anyone can do but pray. O God, he prayed, be *merciful* unto *me*, a *sinner*. Let me not feel good when I am good. *If* I am good. Let me just try to be good, don't let me *feel* good. Don't let me even *know* if I'm good. Just let me try. And in this humility, aware that it was of a true and pure kind which was new to him, he felt a flash of relief, well-being, pride: and tightening his shut eyes, cried out in despair within himself, *There it is again! O God make it go away. Make it not mean anything. O God what I can't help, please forgive it*. He wanted to put himself down on his face on the floor. "*All my trust I put in Thee*," he whis-pered aloud and, aware that he had whispered aloud, opened his eyes in the fear that he had been noticed. Nobody seemed to have noticed. Now Jimmy and Hobe were kneeling a little ahead of him. He found that he was drenched with sweat and as short of breath as if he had been running. He felt weak and quiet. The burden of them is intolerable. He could feel the words sincerely and quietly now yet at the same time they meant nothing to him. All my trust I put in Thee, he repeated silently. O let me not fail Thee.

Tonight.

This very night.

For in the night in which He was betrayed.

Now fragments of his first moment awake returned but now they were dry and tired like dead leaves, as dry and tired as he was. He tried to realize what it all meant. But all that he could realize was dry and tired like the tired dry fire of the candles.

He came into the world to be with us and save us, and this is what happened. This is what it all came to.

The light shineth in darkness and the darkness comprehended it not.

He came unto His own and His own received Him not.

So there He was just sitting there waiting. Just waiting to die.

Words stirred and stood up inside him which lifted his heart: But as many as received Him, to them gave He power to become the sons of God.

And the Word was made Flesh and dwelt among us:

He closed his eyes and bowed his head.

Flesh.

All for us.

All his suffering for all of us.

He remembered the terrible thing his uncle had said: "Well who *asked* him to die for me? *I* didn't. He needn't try and collect on the debt," he had said, "because there's no debt, far's I'm concerned." Nearly always when he thought of this Richard was shocked almost into awe of such blasphemy; and some few times when some priest or his mother was insisting what we all owe Jesus he had been tempted to wonder, wasn't it maybe really so, for it was a fact; Jesus had done it without anybody asking Him to: but now it seemed neither blasphemous nor persuasive but only empty and idle and cruel and as he thought of it he could see the man of whom it had been said, sitting very quietly on a stool or maybe a bench among the iron-breasted helmeted soldiers while they hit him and spat in his face and mocked him. Nobody could come near him or help him or even speak a word of love or thanks or comfort to him now. He could see him only as if he spied down on what was happening through a cellar window and it would be torture and death to dare to even try to get in, and no use could come of it, even if he did. The way, maybe, Peter had stayed. All of Peter's betraying and cowardliness was over and done with now. Nothing could ever wipe out for him what he had done. He wasn't even crying any more because he couldn't even cry any more. He was just hiding around on the outskirts, spying through the window. He was afraid to show himself and he couldn't stand to go away. He must wish he was dead.

Judas, by now, had he hanged himself? Richard couldn't remember for sure when. But if he hadn't yet, that was all there was left for him to do. That was all he was thinking about all the rest of this night, all that was left of his life. *I want to die. O I want to be dead. I can't be dead soon enough to suit me.* Judas didn't feel contrition, Father Weiler said, he felt remorse. Probably he couldn't cry like Peter. Just terrible cold remorse, as cold and bitter as the sound of the word. Remorse is very different from contrition; a deadly sin. A mortal sin is a sin that cuts us off from God. With remorse you don't feel sorry like contrition, you feel, well you just feel remorse, that's all.

These were just the dead hours. The hours between. They must be the worst hours of all for Jesus and for everyone who loved Him. No more doubt now. No more praying to God the Father, *if this Cup can be taken from me:* that's over long ago. *It can't. That's all.* No more judgment, standing trial, answering fool questions. He's already been sentenced to die. He belongs to the Law. Now just the time between. So tired. No sleep all this night. Waiting, getting Himself ready inside, while they mock and sneer and holler at him, and spit in his face, and crown him with thorns, and put the reed in his hand for a scepter, just waiting through the rest of the long night, just getting ready to die, while the night slowly turns into morning, and it's the last morning of all. To suffer so he will cry out, *My God, my God, why hast Thou forsaken me?* And then die. *It is finished.* And then die. And meekly bowing down His head, He gave up the ghost. And then (Richard could remember in advance) the stunned and strange peacefulness, throughout that afternoon and night and through all the next day, and the quiet, almost secret lighting of the tremendous candle in the beginning of the dusk of Holy Saturday, everything still going as if on tiptoe, and then in the first light of morning, the stillest and most wonderful moment of the year, the quietly spoken and simple Mass: "He is risen." And then the rich mid-morning and the blinding blaze of Easter. *'Tis the Spring of Souls today, Christ hath burst His prison, and from three days' sleep in Death, like a Sun hath risen.*

But not yet. That is still not known though at the same time it *is* known. We are all in most solemn sorrow and grief and mourning. We know a secret far inside ourselves but we don't dare tell it, even to ourselves. We don't dare to quite believe it will ever really happen again until it really happens again. Until His coming again. For in the night in which He was betrayed. It has happened over nineteen hundred times now and yet it has never happened before. Not yet. And we don't know if it ever can. Never dreamed it could. Can.

Not yet. Now is just the dead time between and he is waiting. This is his last night and his last daybreak begins soon now. Before this day is over he will be dead.

My Jesus, he whispered, clasping his hands strongly; his throat contracted.

O Saviour of the World Who by Thy Cross and Precious Blood hast redee——

O you are dying my dear Lord for me, his soul whispered, wondering, weeping. For *me*, and I can't do anything for you. I can't even comfort you, or speak to you, or thank you. O my Lord Jesus I can thank you. I can think about you. I can try to know what it is you are going through for me. For me and for all sinners. I can know that every sin I do big or no matter how little is a thorn or a nail or the blow of the hammer or even just a fly that teases and hurts you in your blood, crawling and tickling and sipping and eating at you in the hot day on the Cross with you unable to brush him away or even to move, and every good thing, or true thankfulness or thought of love must make it anyway a little less terrible to suffer. My Lord I love Thee. My Lord I grieve for Thee. My dear Lord I adore Thee. My poor Lord I wish I could suffer for Thee. My Lord I thank Thee. Lord have mercy upon me. Christ have mercy upon me. Lord have mercy upon me.

He opened his eyes in quiet wonder. It was indeed to him the very day. Not just a day in remembrance, but the day. There stood His consecrated Body, veiled among fire and flowers, but also living, in the flesh, on this very morning, at this very moment, He was waiting; and He was now within His last hours.

He won't see the sun go down today.

He looked at all the lights, spearing, aspiring, among the dying flowers. Knobbled and fluted with their own spillings, the candles stood like sheaves; some, bent by the heat, bowed over like winter saplings. Almost all the flowers hung their exhausted faces. They were so shrunken and disheveled now that he could see clearly among them the many shapes and sizes of the vessels which held them, the professional vases and ewers and jars, and the tumblers and tin cans from the poor cabins out the Mountain. He could just hear the clock. Tonight, he whispered, watching that devastation. This night. This minute. He leaned, and looked at the clock. It was one minute after five. Something troubled him which he had done or had left undone, some failure of the soul or default of the heart which he could not now quite remember or was it perhaps foresee; he was empty and idle, in some way he had failed. Yet he was also filled to overflowing with a reverent and marveling peace and thankfulness. My cup runneth over, something whispered within him, yet what he saw in his mind's eye was a dry chalice, an empty Grail. No more I could do, he reflected, if I stayed all night. No more. No use: and he continued merely to look without thought at the emblazoned ruin. "Goodbye," something whispered from incalculably deep within him. *O goodbye, goodbye*, his heart replied. A strange and happy sorrow filled him. *It is finished*, his soul whispered. He looked at the humbled backs ahead of him and prayed: The peace of God which passeth all understanding keep our hearts and minds in the knowledge and love of God, and of His Son Jesus Christ. And the blessing of God Almighty, the Father, the Son and the Holy Ghost, be amongst us and remain with us always.

He opened his eyes; and it was all as it was before. Of course it was. He was light and uneasy and at peace within. There was nothing to do or think or say.

He signed himself carefully with the Cross, got up, genuflected, and left the Chapel; just inside the north door, he took off his shoes. Hobe and Jimmy came up behind him and they took off their shoes too.

III

THEY walked down the sandstone steps into an air so different from the striving candles and the expiring flowers that they were stopped flatfooted on the gravel. Morning had not yet begun but the night was nearly over. The gravel took all the light there was in the perishing darkness and shed it upward, and in the darkness among the trees below the outbuildings a blossoming dogwood flawed like winter breath. In the untouchable silence such a wave of energy swept upward through their bare feet and their three bodies into the sky that they were shaken as if a ghost had touched them. Sharply and almost silently, Hobe laughed.

They looked at the last tired stars and at the dark windows of their dormitory and they wondered what their punishment would be.

"S - - t fahr," Hobe said. "Can't even pray, what the f - - - *kin* ye do!"

Maybe, Richard reflected, they wouldn't say anything. Couldn't be a better excuse than praying. In brainless exaltation he flexed the soles of his feet against the ground. What of it if they do.

Rustily, so far down back of them across the fields they could scarcely hear him, a rooster crowed.

"Let's get the rackets," Richard said.

They took it as naturally as if one of them had said it.

"They'd catch us sure," Jimmy said.

"Hell we keer," Hobe said. "Tan our asses anyhow, now."

Creakily, a little nearer, but very faint, a second rooster answered.

Might not, Richard thought; not *anyhow*. What if they do.

"Let's go to the Sand Cut," Hobe said.

"Freeze yer balls off," Jimmy said.

"Sun-up, time we git thur," Hobe said.

Proud, fierce behind the cook's house, the cry of a third rooster shining sprang, speared, vibrated as gaily and teasingly in the centers of their flesh as a jews-harp.

"Come on," Richard said, and started walking rapidly across the pale gravel.

He was surprised that he had spoken and the more surprised to hear them following. How they do it, he thought, stepping along not quite steadily in silent uneasy elation; all there is to it. He led them down past the cook's house.

Pride, he realized; a mortal sin. How do I confess that?

Through the veering wire net he saw, black in the faintness, how the big rooster darted his vigilant head and shuffled his plumage: in the silence before daylight a priest, vesting himself for Mass. Something heavy struck and the whole body splayed, and chuckled with terror; the coward's wives gabbled along their roost.

Richard felt as if he had been hit in the stomach.

I'm scared of both of them, he reflected, specially Hobe, and they know it whenever they want to.

And bigger than either of them, he forced himself to recognize.

Younger. Big for his age that's why I'm clumsy and soft.

Bigger all the same.

Maybe that makes up for the Pride, he thought, as they walked past the bruising foulness of the back-house.

Privately, safe ahead of them, he struck his breast.

Nothing makes up for anything. Confess you thought it did.

He tried to imagine how to confess it. I have sinned the sin of Pride and some other sin I don't know the name of. I was proud because when I said let's go to the Sand Cut (and it wasn't even me that thought of it first) they came along just as if one of them had said it and all of a sudden I knew that all you have to do is say something and go ahead yourself without waiting and they'll do it. Then something happened that made me know I was scared of them and I admitted to myself I'm : yellow : and then I thought maybe because I made myself admit that, why then I wouldn't have to confess I was proud before. I thought it made up for it.

He tried to imagine the priests to whom he would confess this. Father McPhetridge, Father Whitman, Father Weiler, Father Ogle, Father Fish. Unless maybe if he got Father Fish but even if you tried to dodge and choose which was probably a sin why you couldn't ever tell for sure who you'd get. The others would just think he was crazy or something. Crazy kid. Or trying to get credit. And maybe he would be.

What you say in Confession they never tell because if they do they go straight to Hell. But whoever you confess to, he knows all the same. And if he knows you honestly are trying hard to be good he gives you credit afterwards too, that you sin if you try to get, he can't help himself. And if he thinks you're just trying to get credit why everytime he looks at you from then on you know what he thinks of you.

If he really thought you were, though, probably he wouldn't give you Absolution.

If you know it's a sin why you've got to confess it, no matter what he thinks.

The ferment of the hogpen, deepest of blacks and heaviest of oils, so stuffed and enriched their nostrils that as one they slowed against the fence and looked in. Small as the light was, on all its edges the chopped muck shone like coal. Jimmy slid his hand inside his overalls against his naked body; becoming aware of what he had done, he thoughtfully withdrew it. Straining to see into the darkness of the shed they could just discern the close-lying egglike forms of the hogs.

"Oink: oink," Hobe grunted, in a voice so deep that Richard was surprised.

Crooomphth, a sleeping hog replied.

They crossed the stile and struck into the woods, using their unhardened feet somewhat delicately along the familiar path. It was as thrilling cold and as vague and silent here as leaving a hot morning and stepping into a springhouse, and the smell of dead leaves and decaying wood and of the arising year was as keen as the coldness. A dogwood dilated ahead of them, each separate blossom enlarging like an eye, and swung behind, and deeply retired among the black trees ahead they could see the shining of others in the first light, triumphal and sad, lonesome as nebulae; likewise blind clumps of unawakened laurel; and now as the light became adequate they saw that the floor of the woods was still the leathery color of last year's leaves, meagerly stitched with green. In the deeper distances the woods were neutral as a photograph, as they had been all winter, but nearer by, the trunks of the trees were no longer black. Some were blackish, some were brownish, some were gray and gray green and silver brown and silver green and now the forms and varieties of bark, rugged, mosaic, deeply ribbed and satin sleek, knobbled like lepers and fluted like columns of a temple, became entirely distinct. Some of the twigs looked still as dark and fragile as the middle of winter, many were knobbled and pimpled and swollen as if they were about to break open and bleed, and many were the color of bronze and some were the color of blood; on some there were little buds like the nubbins of young deer and on others new leaves as neatly fledged as the feathering ought to be for the arrows Richard had never been able to make perfectly. They could see a long way into the woods as the morning cleared and everywhere underfoot this leather laid its flat musing waves and everywhere among the retreating trees strayed sober clouds of evergreen and mild clouds of blossom and the dreaming laurels, and everywhere, as deep into the stunned woods as they could see, layer above unwavering layer, the young leaves led like open shale; while, against their walking, apostolically, the trees turned. The path among these winding, dancing trees, new to them since late fall, was supple underfoot, the droning trees against which they laid or slapped their hands felt as alive as the flanks of horses, the air was all one listening joy. While they approached the clearing each held in mind a festival imagination of the plum tree, but it hung black, all crazed elbows, in the widened light. From somewhere, however, the fallen silvers of the ruined house it seemed, they were pursued by the chiding, familiar song of an ambushed bird whose kind they did not know; and at the far side of the clearing Richard stopped short and the others passed him: for here, abject against sharp bark, he found a locust shell, transparent silver breathed with gold, the whole back split, the hard claws, its only remaining strength, so clenched into the bark that it was only with great care and gentleness that he was able to detach the shell without destroying it.

It was as if air had been tightened into substance; only by touch and sight, not at all by weight, could he know he held it. He held it in his cupped hand and looked at the hunched, cloven back, turned it over with one fingertip and examined the brutally elaborate structure of the legs and the little talons.

He tested: they could pierce a finger. He turned it again and held it near his eyes: the eyes looked into his. Yes even the eyes were there, blind silver globes which had so perfectly contained the living eyes: even the small rudimentary face in its convulsed and fierce expression, the face of a human embryo, he could remember the engraving in a book of his grandfather's, a paroxysm of armor, frowning, scowling, glaring, very serious, angry, remote, dead, a devil, older, stranger than devils, as early, ancient of days, primordial, as trilobites. Dinosaurs heaved and strove; a pterodactyl, cold-winged, skated on miasmic air, ferns sprang, to make coal in these very coves, more huge than the grandest chestnuts. Silurian, Mesozoic, Protozoic, Jurassic, all the planet one featureless and smoky marsh, Crowns, Thrones, Dominions, Principalities, Archaeozoic, through all ranks and kingdoms, to the central height, armed in the radiant cruelty of immortal patience, Ages and Angels marched clanging in his soul.

When did he come out? Just now? Just this spring? Or has he stayed all winter. And that would mean all fall and summer before.

I'd have seen him; last fall; last spring.

If he was there all the time and I didn't before, how come I saw him now?

All winter. All year. Or just since the first warm weather. Or just now before I found him.

That whole split back. Bet it doesn't hurt any worse than that to be crucified.

He crossed himself.

He sure did hold on hard.

He tried to imagine gripping hard enough that he broke his back wide open and pulled himself out of each leg and arm and finger and toe so cleanly and completely that the exact shape would be left intact.

With veneration, talon by talon, he re-established the shell in its grip against the rigid bark.

By the time he caught up with Hobe and Jimmy they were almost to the railroad track.

At the far end of the break in the woods along the far side of the track they saw the weathered oak tower and soon, walking more briskly along the ties, the relics of machinery and the dead cones of putty-colored sand and the wrinkled sandstone and, at length, the sullen water itself, untouched in all these cold months. There were black slits along the sides of the tower where planks had fallen during the winter. The water was motionless and almost black. The whole place, familiar as it was, was deadly still, and seemed not at all to welcome them. As they left the track to round the near end of the Sand Cut there was a scuttling among the reddened brambles but although they went as fast as they could on their soft feet and threw rocks where the brambles twitched with noise they got no glimpse of whatever it was, and soon the scuttling stopped.

Now that they had stopped walking and stood in the brightened silence of the open light the day began to look practical; they realized how chilly the air still was, even here out of the woods, and how bitter the water looked, and they no longer felt like going in. But none of them was willing to admit this frankly even to himself, and it was only after they stripped that they became openly hesitant. They took care not to shiver more visibly than they could help or to appear to dawdle, either, but they did all dawdle, and they found that they were looking at each other, in this unhabitual place and hesitant quietness, with more interest than in the dormitory. Although Jimmy was the smallest of the three in every other way, his was much the biggest and during the winter he had grown much more hair than Richard had realized up to now. Hobe still didn't have much but then he was said to be part Indian so of course he wouldn't, yet, and probably never would have a lot. What he did have was dark, though, and showed up well against his dark skin, whereas Richard's was so light and there was so little of it that he realized it could probably not be seen at all, farther away than his own eyes. He suspected, however, that his was really the biggest, because it looked as if Jimmy had at least half a hard-up. Jimmy looked comfortable in his supremacy whether it was real or not (he certainly had more hair, anyhow, there wasn't any getting around that) and seemed to feel none of the embarrassment which Richard always felt acutely if he was seen with even a little bit of a hard-up. He turned partly away, though, in honor of Good Friday, and for the same reason he and Richard glanced at each other with even less candor than they would have at any other time, and Richard the more

uneasily crossed and uncrossed his hands in front of himself.
Only Hobe, of any boy Richard knew, never concealed his own
body or his interest in another, and even now, Good Friday
seemed to mean nothing to him. He looked at them, and
watched them look at him, with a coolness which seemed almost amused. He urinated a few drops onto his belly and
rubbed it in with the palm of his hand, against cramps. He
made no gesture of covering himself and grabbed his testicles
with one hand only at the instant he grabbed his nose with the
other to leap with a spangling splash into the water.

He bounced up with an incredulous strangling yell and began a frenzied dogpaddle and both of them knew the water
must be even colder than they had thought, and that there was
no longer any chance of holding back. Jimmy went in feet first;
Richard dove. The iron water distended enormously just beneath him and for an instant, knowing the brutal shock and
the pain to which he had now inescapably committed himself,
he felt the fatal exhilaration of a falling dream and had just
time to dedicate within himself *for Thee!*, in a silent shout as
deafening bright as a smiting of cymbals; then plunged into
the smashing cold. Still crying *for Thee* within his ringing head,
he slanted his hands to dive as deep as he could go and, though
his eyes were open, could see nothing of the steep sandstone
along which his hands guided him, but only the stifled efful-
gence of light above. It was so much colder than he had been
able to imagine that in the first moment he had felt almost unconscious, but the diver's reflex had locked his breath and now
that he searched from ledge to ledge downward along the
much colder bottom there sprang throughout his flesh such an
ardent and serene energy that he was aware of the entire surface of his body as if it were fire, and every muscle seemed to
feel its own exact shape and weight, and he wished that he
need never come up and lay against the deepest trench of the
bottom, his belly foundering in ooze, his eyes shut, staying his
hands on rocks. He lifted his face free of the ooze and cautiously opened his eyes; he could feel, more clearly than be
sure he saw, the light which enlarged above him. He turned his
head and looked up sidelong; there it was, a pure, heavy slab of
still light which by imperceptible degrees shaded downward
into most deadly darkness. His chest and his head began to

knock, it became harder with every pulse to hold onto the rocks. O Lord let me suffer with Thee this day, he prayed, his lungs about to burst; and took hold more firmly. You got no right, his own voice silently told him, you got no right. No right; but still he fought off his need for air, filling his cheeks with the exhausted air from his lungs and taking it down again in the smallest possible gulps. His head was beating and ringing so fiercely that he could scarcely hear the fragments of his own efforts to dedicate and to reprove himself but blindly, with the last of his strength, held himself down. Then he knew that he had stayed down too long; too deep; he could not possibly reach the air in time. Good. That's fine. *For Thee!* he groaned. *No right! Get out!*, he shouted silently. But even before he could command it or fully decide to command it his body was working for him; his feet braced against a ledge, his knees bent, and he leapt upward through the brightening water with more strength than he had realized he had left although the water seemed interminably tall above him and he knew still that he would never reach the surface in time and cried out to himself, *I didn't have the nerve!* and, *Anyhow I tried*, meaning at once that he had tried to stay down too long as an act of devotion and that he had tried to save himself from the deadliest of sins; and broke the surface in time, head back, gasping, feebly treading water, watching the streaming bruise-colored clamorous and silent whirling of the world and taking in air so deeply that his lungs felt as if they were tearing; and soon the world became stable and all of the coloring and discoloration cleared and stood up strongly through the top of the woods across the tracks and he could realize that except for the remote voices of the two boys and the still more remote voice of a bird the world itself was delicately silent and all the noise was within his own head and was rapidly dying: all that he saw still twitched with his pulse and out of the woods, beating like a heart, the sun stood up.

His teeth still ached at their roots and although he clenched them to keep them from chattering his chin trembled like a rabbit's nose and his breath came out shakily in many small pieces as of glass or ice. From its surface down to about his waist, the water seemed surprisingly warm, but from waist to knees it was grimly cold, and his stony feet trod a mortal

bleakness of cold and dark to which he was thankfully sure
now that he would never go down again. Yet except for his
feet, which no longer seemed to belong to him, his body still
blazed with pleasure in its existence, and it was no longer urgent and rigid but almost sleepy. He slid his slick hands along
his ribs and his sides and found that in his sex he was as tightly
shrunken as if he were a baby. I could have died, he realized almost casually. *Here I am!* his enchanted body sang. I could be
dead right now, he reflected in sleepy awe. *Here I am!* Now
that he had his breath and was quiet he no longer tried to control the rattling of his teeth but hung standing in the water, his
head so turned from the others that they might not see the
silent unexpected tears and, drowsily trying to make himself
aware of the suffering to which at this moment Jesus was submitting Himself, crying for tenderness and thankful wonder,
gazed steadily into the beating sun.

But staying still so long, coldness at length overcame him,
and after swimming as fast as he could twice up and down the
length of the quarry, he stumbled out.

He had all but forgotten them; they were already drying
themselves with their shirts. Hobe's body was purplish; Jimmy
looked as if he had been caught in a blue net.

"What you trine to do?" Hobe asked. "Drownd yourself?"

"I was just swimming under water."

"I was damn near ready to dive in after you," Jimmy said,
"when you come up."

"We began to think you was drownded," Hobe said.

"No, I was all right," Richard said. He reached for his shirt.
"*Heyy!*" he shouted.

Steering, serenely, his sutured brow, the sum of those several
thrusting curves which seemed not of themselves to exert
strength but merely to drink and send backward through them
the energies of the guiding head they guided, a snake more
splendid than Richard had ever seen before was just achieving
a sandstone ledge and the first heat of the risen sun. In every
wheaten scale and in all his barbaric patterning he was new and
clear as gems, so gallant and sporting against the dun, he dazzled, and seeing him, Richard was acutely aware how sensitive,
proud and tired he must be in his whole body, for it was
clear that he had just struggled out of his old skin and was

with his first return of strength venturing his new one. His style and brightness, his princely elegance, the coldness of his eye and the knifelike coldness and sweetness of his continuously altering line, his cold pride in his new magnificence, were not at the first in the least dismayed, not even by Richard's shout; only the little tongue, to Richard's almost worshiping delight and awe, sped like a thready horn of smoke, the eye seemed to meet Richard's and become colder and still more haughty, and the vitality of his elegance advanced him still further along the stone: so that for a few seconds Richard saw perfected before him, royally dangerous and to be adored and to be feared, all that is alien in nature and in beauty: and stood becharmed. But as the others ran up, within an instant so swift that it was impossible to see just what transpired among those curves of liquid paroxysm, with a chilly rasping against stone which excited Richard as nothing he had ever heard before had excited him, drawing a stripe of coldness down his spine, the snake reversed direction and slipped rapidly between the ankles of briars and beneath fallen leaves, his brilliance a constant betrayal. The others were shouting and Jimmy shoved a stick under the snake and flipped him so expertly that for a couple of seconds he sailed on the air in a convulsion of escape, a fluid hieroglyph, and landed on open rock in a humiliating flash of ivory belly before he righted himself and with oily fleetness made once more for the bushes. But now Hobe reared up a rock so heavy he could lift it only clumsily, high above his reeling head; and Richard, standing just behind him, felt himself reach towards the rock to pull it backwards out of his hands. But even as his own hand lifted forward he became aware of Jimmy's astounded eye on him, and thus became aware of what he was doing and caught himself, realizing that they would never understand why he did it, that they would be angry with him and rightly so and might even be mad enough to jump on him; and becoming thus aware, became aware also that it was not only his habit of gentleness to animals which made him want to spare the snake, but something new in him which he could not understand, about which he was profoundly uneasy. These several kinds of awareness came over him with terrible speed and transfixed him into the slowness of a dream, so that the fraction of a second froze the high rock, the incredulous

bystander, the bemused hand, and seemed to last almost interminably, while he strove to stay his hand and to set it free. But
it was after all only an instant, and before he could bring himself out of this hesitation, Hobe brought the rock crashing
down against rock and against one arc of the veering snake
which, angled like a broken whip, continued uselessly to thrust
energy through its ruptured body, its eyes terrible, its tongue
so busy that its speed made the shadow of a blossom. Jimmy
hurried up with his stick and beat at its head but the head was
still alert to dodge under his blows. Richard felt for a moment
as if he had just finished retching. Then he picked up a small
rock and yelling "*Get out of the way,*" squatted beside the snake
and pounded at its head. The head lashed about his fist like
summer lightning as he pounded and in the darkness of his
violence the question darted, over and over, *is he poison? is he
poison?* but he cared only for one thing, to put as quick an end
as he could to all this terrible, ruined, futile writhing and un-
killable defiance, and at length he struck and dazed, and struck
and missed, and struck and broke the head which nevertheless
lifted senilely, the tongue flittering and the one remaining eye
entering his own eye like a needle; and again, and the head lay
smashed and shifting among its debris; and again, and it was
flattened against the stone, though still the body, even out beyond the earlier wound, lashed, lay resting, trembled, lashed.

As he watched this trembling twitching, desperately wishing
that he could so crush the snake that it would never move
again, he realized that it would not die until sundown, and
even as he realized this he heard Hobe say it and became
aware, through something quiet in Hobe's voice and through
Jimmy's shyness, that they respected him; that in putting his
bare hand within range of that clever head and in killing so
recklessly and with such brutality, he had lost their contempt
and could belong among them if he wanted to. He looked
coldly at his trembling hand: bloody at the knuckles and laced
with slime, which seemed to itch and to burn as it dried, it still
held the rock.

"Better warsh that stuff off," Hobe said. "Git in your blood:
boy!"

He still squatted, looking at his hand and wondering. In
their good opinion, and in the rugged feeling of the hand itself

and its ferocious moisture, he began to feel that he had been brave in a way he had never been brave before and he wanted the hand to clear gradually and naturally, the way the smudge clears from the forehead on Ash Wednesday. He could not be sure, in its pristine skin, what kind of snake this was, and the head was wrecked beyond any hope of determining whether it had the coffin shape, or venomous fangs. But it was not a rattler, nor was it likely a copperhead, nor was it striped like a moccasin, so that he had to doubt whether, after all, it had been poisonous. If it had not been poisonous he had not been brave; and if it had not been poisonous he was sorry he had killed it or even been fool enough to yell so the others would see it and so automatically kill it, for he had for a long while been fascinated by snakes and had felt that the harmless ones ought to be let alone, as few people let them alone. He was aware that Hobe had spoken and that he had given no kind of answer, and this made him uneasy. He wanted very much to taste the slime; but they were watching. He turned up the rock and looked at it: the slime and breakage of the snake caught the whitening sunlight like mica. He slammed the rock into the middle of the water (just about where I dove in, he realized upon reflection) and clambered cautiously down to the edge and thrust his hand into the cold water and up to the elbow, beating quietly in the brilliant cold, and watched it in the water; the veins stood out on his forearm almost like a man. He decided that he would only submerge his hand, not wash it, no matter what Hobe advised. But Hobe said nothing.

They dressed thoughtfully and they had very little to say; now that they were on their way back there wasn't much to think about except the trouble which waited for them. There would have been trouble even if they had come straight back from Chapel, for they had outstayed the watch they had signed for by a long time. But they began to realize now that it would not have been as bad as it was bound to be now; maybe they'd even have been let off. If they had gotten back to bed at any time before daylight it wouldn't have been as bad as it would be now. If they had come in just while the sun was rising it would have been bad but not as bad as this. Now it was broad daylight and brighter every minute, and with every minute longer now that they stayed away they were in for worse trouble. They might be kept on bounds, they might have to pull stumps or clean out the pit of the backhouse, they might be whipped, they might even not be let go on the Easter Monday picnic and they had planned to go clear to Wet Cave which had never yet been fully explored, and find new passages and if possible, a new and secret entrance. There was no telling what, for the worst of it was that they had gone against a strict rule so conspicuously on Good Friday, and by taking advantage of a religious event, and there was no way of imagining how much more serious an offense this might seem to priests than to people. The train came down from Coal City and passed them while they dressed, making a great deal of happy and vigorous noise, but it only sharpened their realization that by now everybody was up and around and that certain people would be looking for them and watching for them already, so that they hardly even had the heart to look up at the blank baggage car and the empty coach and to wave at the engineer who saluted them.

Richard didn't even look up as the train passed, nor had the thought of punishment very clearly entered his mind; all the while he dressed, he watched the snake. From the break on back it lay belly up and the pallor of the belly, and the different structure of the scales, so well designed for crawling, were quietly sickening to see. He tried to see all that he could see without looking at the annihilated head, but his eyes kept flicking back to where it lay, mashed almost like soft metal against the rock, almost as flat and ragged as the toadfrogs and pennies they used to put on the tracks in Knoxville, after the streetcar ran over them. The snake moved very weakly now, but strongly enough that Richard could not doubt it would keep moving, and blindly experiencing the agony of death, straight on through the morning and the Three Hour Service and on through the afternoon until, at last, as the top rim of the sun sank out of sight, the tip of the tail would give one last quaver and the snake would lie still forever.

"Well come on," he was startled to hear Hobe's voice at his shoulder. He turned to go.

"Aint you takin him?"

It had not occurred to Richard; now that it did, he certainly did not want him.

"No."

"Hell fahr, you kilt him didn you?"

"I don't want him."

Hobe and Jimmy glanced at each other. "Okay," Hobe said. He took the snake carefully by the tail. The break in the body held firm; the head pulled loose from the rock like adhesive tape. He snapped him like a whip; now most of the head was lost.

"He'll bust in the middle," Jimmy said.

"Hell I keer," Hobe said. But he did not snap the snake again. Half a snake wouldn't be worth showing.

On the far side of the track they fell into single file for the woods path, Hobe ahead, swinging the limpid snake at the new leaves, then Jimmy, then Richard. Without consulting or imitation, all three had put their shoes on when they dressed; they walked rather quickly, and they did not talk.

In refusing the snake, Richard realized, he had lost a considerable portion of their esteem, though not all of it. He was still regarded as the hero of this occasion and he knew he was still one of them in a way he had never been before. He was still pleased to have been accepted and still pleased with his own courage, though he was sorry the snake had been killed, and unhappy and uneasy whenever he caught a glimpse of it ahead. He began to know how very hungry he was and with his hunger he remembered once again, with surprise and shame that he could have forgotten, what Day this was. It must be on past seven o'clock by now. He would not start carrying the Cross until nine. By now He would just be sitting on the stool or the bench in the garrison room, probably sort of like a locker room, while the soldiers paid Him no attention much but just hogged their breakfasts and maybe threw cornbread at Him, no it wouldn't be cornbread; He just sat there with nothing to eat or drink and some of the worst things were already over by now; He sat in the purple robe holding the reed and the blood was drying on His back from the scourges and the torn wounds were itching and the spit was drying on His face (like my hand is drying), not just spit but the nastiest kind of snot, too, if it happened here they'd spit tobacco juice, and down through the drying spit the blood ran from the Crown of Thorns; how did they push those thorns down around His forehead without hurting their hands? And here I am, he thought, suddenly remembering the absoluteness of emotions during the moments just after he woke up that morning. Here I am. He struck his breastbone and tried to imagine how it would feel to be scourged with a cat-o'-nine-tails with lead tips, and to wear a crown of thorns. Busy with twisted and uneven walking, he could not make it very clear to himself. He closed his eyes and almost immediately stumbled on a root. Jesus falls for the first time, he said to himself. God help me. God forgive me I didn't mean it. He kept his eyes open and took care how he walked.

The woods were full of ordinary sunlight now; the colors were no longer strange and the deep perspectives were no longer mysterious, but pleasant and casual. When they came to the clearing it was full of simple light and the bird was no longer singing. When they had come nearly to the other side of this warm open silence Richard hurried back to the tree on which he had left the locust shell, detached it gently, and with great care, scarcely looking at it, settled it into the breast-pocket of his shirt. They were not far into the woods when he caught up. His trotting and quick breathing, now that he slowed again to a walk, made him aware once more of his sharp hunger. It was going to be a long day without food, without, if he could help it, even rinsing his mouth out with water. I'll help it, he told himself, imagining water in his mouth. I'll not do that, anyhow. He thought again of the thorns, and the spittle, and the patience and courage, and of his maculate hand. The least I can do, he told himself. The *least* I can do! The day lifted ahead of him very long and hard, a huge unshaded hill. The climbing of it would go on in the heavy sun without rest throughout this livelong day and forever so long as he might be alive and there at the top there was dying: His; his; so hard and so long. It won't be over till sundown, he said to himself. Such a terrible and cold heaviness distended in the pit of his stomach, and his knees became suddenly so weak, that for a few moments he had to lean against a tree, and found it difficult to breathe. He had never before known such heaviness or such cold, crushing sorrow. "*Forgive!*" he whispered, barely able to bring the word out: "*Forgive! O God forgive!*" But the cold and enormous heaviness only increased, and the sadness now seemed more than his soul could endure.

After a little, however, he regained sufficient strength in his knees, and walked again, by now a good way behind the others. But the heaviness stayed, so that he felt as if he were carrying an all but impossible weight in the middle of his body.

By now they could see the first of the buildings through the lightleaved woods; and now the whole of the School stood up before them and the two boys ahead walked more slowly, wondering what lie, if any, might lighten their trouble. But they could not think of any that would do and when Richard over took them, lingering unhappily at the stile, they were so far beyond hope that they didn't even bother to ask him whether he had any ideas.

Now that he was with them again, the heaviness was somewhat less severe, and he began to wonder what had made him so deeply weak and unhappy, and what kind of trouble they would be in for; now he could clearly foresee Father Whitman's hard sleepless eyes in his first look at them as they would come up from the woods, their hair spiky with incriminating wetness; and much as he dreaded in advance the punishment, which would be a whipping for sure, he told himself, he dreaded even more the first meeting with these eyes, and the first words that would be spoken, though he suspected that these would be tempered to the day. He heard Jimmy say to Hobe that he better get rid of that snake, and he thought that he sure better; and he was neither surprised nor particularly troubled when, a few moments later, Hobe slung the snake in among the hogs. He stood with the other children at the fence and watched with interest while two of the hogs, with snarling squeals, scuffled over the snake, tore it apart at its middle wound and, while the two portions still tingled in the muck, gobbled them down. It occurred to him, with a lancing quailing of horror and pity, that the snake was still alive, and would stay alive in their bellies, however chewed, and mangled, and diffused by acids, until the end of the day; but now, remembering the head, he told himself that the snake was so far gone by now that he must be a way beyond really feeling anything, ever any more (the phrase jumped at him): (Who had said that? His mother. "Daddy was terribly hurt so God has taken him up to Heaven to be with Him and he won't come back to us ever any more.") "Ever any more," he heard his quiet voice repeat within him; and within the next moment he ceased to think of the snake with much pain. When the boys turned from the sty he followed them towards the Main Building carrying, step by step with less difficulty, the diminishing weight in his soul and body, his right hand hanging with a feeling of subtle enlargement at his thigh, his left hand sustaining, in exquisite protectiveness, the bodiless shell which rested against his heart.

A DEATH IN THE FAMILY

Contents

Knoxville: Summer 1915

*W*e are talking now of summer evenings in Knoxville, Tennessee in the time that I lived there so successfully disguised
to myself as a child. It was a little bit mixed sort of block, fairly
solidly lower middle class, with one or two juts apiece on either
side of that. The houses corresponded: middlesized gracefully fretted wood houses built in the late nineties and early nineteen hundreds, with small front and side and more spacious back yards,
and trees in the yards, and porches. These were softwooded trees,
poplars, tulip trees, cottonwoods. There were fences around one or
two of the houses, but mainly the yards ran into each other with
only now and then a low hedge that wasn't doing very well. There
were few good friends among the grown people, and they were not
poor enough for the other sort of intimate acquaintance, but
everyone nodded and spoke, and even might talk short times,
trivially, and at the two extremes of the general or the particular,
and ordinarily nextdoor neighbors talked quite a bit when they
happened to run into each other, and never paid calls. The men
were mostly small businessmen, one or two very modestly execu-
tives, one or two worked with their hands, most of them clerical,
and most of them between thirty and forty-five.

But it is of these evenings, I speak.

Supper was at six and was over by half past. There was still
daylight, shining softly and with a tarnish, like the lining of a
shell; and the carbon lamps lifted at the corners were on in the
light, and the locusts were started, and the fire flies were out, and
a few frogs were flopping in the dewy grass, by the time the fathers
and the children came out. The children ran out first hell bent
and yelling those names by which they were known; then the
fathers sank out leisurely in crossed suspenders, their collars removed and their necks looking tall and shy. The mothers stayed
back in the kitchen washing and drying, putting things away, re-
crossing their traceless footsteps like the lifetime journeys of bees,
measuring out the dry cocoa for breakfast. When they came out

469

they had taken off their aprons and their skirts were dampened and they sat in rockers on their porches quietly.

It is not of the games children play in the evening that I want to speak now, it is of a contemporaneous atmosphere that has little to do with them: that of the fathers of families, each in his space of lawn, his shirt fishlike pale in the unnatural light and his face nearly anonymous, hosing their lawns. The hoses were attached at spiggots that stood out of the brick foundations of the houses. The nozzles were variously set but usually so there was a long sweet stream of spray, the nozzle wet in the hand, the water trickling the right forearm and the peeled-back cuff, and the water whishing out a long loose and low-curved cone, and so gentle a sound. First an insane noise of violence in the nozzle, then the still irregular sound of adjustment, then the smoothing into steadiness and a pitch as accurately tuned to the size and style of stream as any violin. So many qualities of sound out of one hose: so many choral differences out of those several hoses that were in earshot. Out of any one hose, the almost dead silence of the release, and the short still arch of the separate big drops, silent as a held breath, and the only noise the flattering noise on leaves and the slapped grass at the fall of each big drop. That, and the intense hiss with the intense stream; that, and that same intensity not growing less but growing more quiet and delicate with the turn of the nozzle, up to that extreme tender whisper when the water was just a wide bell of film. Chiefly, though, the hoses were set much alike, in a compromise between distance and tenderness of spray, (and quite surely a sense of art behind this compromise, and a quiet deep joy, too real to recognize itself), and the sounds therefore were pitched much alike; pointed by the snorting start of a new hose; decorated by some man playful with the nozzle; left empty, like God by the sparrow's fall, when any single one of them desists: and all, though near alike, of various pitch; and in this unison. These sweet pale streamings in the light lift out their pallors and their voices all together, mothers hushing their children, the hushing unnaturally prolonged, the men gentle and silent and each snail-like withdrawn into the quietude of what he singly is doing, the urination of huge children stood loosely military against an invisible wall, and gentle happy and peaceful, tasting the mean goodness of their living like the last of their suppers in their mouths; while the locusts carry on this noise of hoses on their much higher and sharper key. The noise of the locust is dry, and it seems not to be rasped or vibrated but urged from him as if through a small orifice by a breath that can never give out. Also there is never one locust but an illusion of at least a thousand. The noise of each locust is pitched in some classic locust range out of which none of them varies more than two full tones: and yet you seem to hear each locust discrete from all the rest, and there is a long, slow, pulse in their noise, like the scarcely defined arch of a long and high set bridge. They are all around in every tree, so that the noise seems to come from nowhere and everywhere at once, from the whole shell heaven, shivering in your flesh and teasing your eardrums, the boldest of all the sounds of night. And yet it is habitual to summer nights, and is of the great order of noises, like the noises of the sea and of the blood her precocious grandchild, which you realize you are hearing only when you catch yourself listening. Meantime from low in the dark, just outside the swaying horizons of the hoses, conveying always grass in the damp of dew and its strong green-black smear of smell, the regular yet spaced noises of the crickets, each a sweet cold silver noise threenoted, like the slipping each time of three matched links of a small chain.

But the men by now, one by one, have silenced their hoses and drained and coiled them. Now only two, and now only one, is left, and you see only ghostlike shirt with the sleeve garters, and sober mystery of his mild face like the lifted face of large cattle enquiring of your presence in a pitchdark pool of meadow; and now he too is gone; and it has become that time of evening when people sit on their porches, rocking gently and talking gently and watching the street and the standing up into their sphere of possession of the trees, of birds hung havens, hangars. People go by; things go by. A horse, drawing a buggy, breaking his hollow iron music on the asphalt; a loud auto; a quiet auto; people in pairs, not in a hurry, scuffling, switching their weight of aestival body, talking casually, the taste hovering over them of vanilla, straw-berry, pasteboard and starched milk, the image upon them of lovers and horsemen, squared with clowns in hueless amber. A street car raising its iron moan; stopping, belling and starting; stertorous; rousing and raising again its iron increasing moan and swimming its gold windows and straw seats on past and past and past, the bleak spark crackling and cursing above it like a small malignant spirit set to dog its tracks; the iron whine rises on *rising speed; still risen, faints; halts; the faint stinging bell; rises again, still fainter; fainting, lifting, lifts, faints forgone: forgotten. Now is the night one blue dew.*

Now is the night one blue dew, my father has drained, he has coiled the hose.
Low on the length of lawns, a frailing of fire who breathes.
Content, silver, like peeps of light, each cricket makes his comment over and over in the drowned grass.
A cold toad thumpily flounders.
Within the edges of damp shadows of side yards are hovering children nearly sick with joy of fear, who watch the unguarding of a telephone pole.
Around white carbon corner lamps bugs of all sizes are lifted elliptic, solar systems. Big hardshells bruise themselves, assailant: he is fallen on his back, legs squiggling.
Parents on porches: rock and rock: From damp strings morning glories: hang their ancient faces.
The dry and exalted noise of the locusts from all the air at once enchants my eardrums.

On the rough wet grass of the back yard my father and mother have spread quilts. We all lie there, my mother, my father, my uncle, my aunt, and I too am lying there. First we were sitting up, then one of us lay down, and then we all lay down, on our stomachs, or on our sides, or on our backs, and they have kept on talking. They are not talking much, and the talk is quiet, of nothing in particular, of nothing at all in particular, of nothing at all. The stars are wide and alive, they seem each like a smile of great sweetness, and they seem very near. All my people are larger bodies than mine, quiet, with voices gentle and meaningless like the voices of sleeping birds. One is an artist, he is living at home. One is a musician, she is living at home. One is my mother who is good to me. One is my father who is good to me. By some chance, here they are, all on this earth; and who shall ever tell the sorrow of being on this earth, lying, on quilts, on the grass, in a summer evening, among the sounds of the night. May God bless my people, my uncle, my aunt, my mother, my good father, oh, remember them kindly in their time of trouble; and in the hour of their taking away.

After a little I am taken in and put to bed. Sleep, soft smiling, draws me unto her: and those receive me, who quietly treat me, as one familiar and well-beloved in that home: but will not, oh, will not, not now, not ever; but will not ever tell me who I am.

PART I

Chapter 1

A T SUPPER that night, as many times before, his father said, "Well, spose we go to the picture show."

"Oh, Jay!" his mother said. "That horrid little man!"

"What's wrong with him?" his father asked, not because he didn't know what she would say, but so she would say it.

"He's so *nasty!*" she said, as she always did. "So *vulgar!* With his nasty little cane; hooking up skirts and things, and that nasty little walk!"

His father laughed, as he always did, and Rufus felt that it had become rather an empty joke; but as always the laughter also cheered him; he felt that the laughter enclosed him with his father.

They walked downtown in the light of mother-of-pearl, to the Majestic, and found their way to seats by the light of the screen, in the exhilarating smell of stale tobacco, rank sweat, perfume and dirty drawers, while the piano played fast music and galloping horses raised a grandiose flag of dust. And there was William S. Hart with both guns blazing and his long, horse face and his long, hard lip, and the great country rode away behind him as wide as the world. Then he made a bashful face at a girl and his horse raised its upper lip and everybody laughed, and then the screen was filled with a city and with the sidewalk of a side street of a city, a long line of palms and there was Charlie; everyone laughed the minute they saw him squattily walking with his toes out and his knees wide apart, as if he were chafed; Rufus' father laughed, and Rufus laughed too. This time Charlie stole a whole bag of eggs and when a cop came along he hid them in the seat of his pants. Then he caught sight of a pretty woman and he began to squat and twirl his cane and make silly faces. She tossed her head and walked away with her chin up high and her dark mouth as small as she could make it and he followed her very busily, doing all sorts of things with his cane that made everybody laugh, but she paid no attention. Finally she stopped at a corner to wait for a streetcar, turning her back to him, and pretending he wasn't even there, and after trying to get her attention for a while, and not succeeding, he looked out at the audience, shrugged his shoulders, and acted as if *she* wasn't there. But after tapping his foot for a little, pretending he didn't care, he became interested again, and with a charming smile, tipped his derby; but she only stiffened, and tossed her head again, and everybody laughed. Then he walked back and forth behind her, looking at her and squatting a little while he walked very quietly, and everybody laughed again; then he flicked hold of the straight end of his cane and, with the crooked end, hooked up her skirt to the knee, in exactly the way that disgusted Mama, looking very eagerly at her legs, and everybody laughed very loudly; but she pretended she had not noticed. Then he twirled his cane and suddenly squatted, bending the cane and hitching up his pants, and again hooked up her skirt so that you could see the panties she wore, ruffled almost like the edges of curtains, and everybody whooped with laughter, and she suddenly turned in rage and gave him a shove in the chest, and he sat down straight-legged, hard enough to hurt, and everybody whooped again; and she walked haughtily away up the street, forgetting about the streetcar, and "mad as a hornet!" as his father exclaimed in delight; and there was Charlie, flat on his bottom on the sidewalk, and the way he looked, kind of sickly and disgusted, you could see that he suddenly remembered those eggs, and suddenly you remembered them too. The way his face looked, with the lip wrinkled off the teeth and the sickly little smile, it made you feel just the way those broken eggs must feel against your seat, as queer and awful as that time in the white pekay suit, when it ran down out of the pants-legs and showed all over your stockings and you had to walk home that way with people looking; and Rufus' father nearly tore his head off laughing and so did everybody else, and Rufus was sorry for Charlie, having been so recently in a similar predicament, but the contagion of laughter was too much for him, and he laughed too. And then it was even funnier when Charlie very carefully got himself up from the sidewalk, with that sickly look even worse on his face, and put his cane under one arm, and began to pick at his pants, front and back, very carefully, with his little fingers crooked, as if it were too dirty to touch, picking the sticky cloth away from his skin. Then he reached behind him and took out the wet bag of broken eggs and opened it and peered in; and took out a broken egg and pulled the shell disgustedly apart, letting the elastic yolk slump from one half shell into the other, and dropped it, shuddering. Then he peered in again and fished out a whole egg, all slimy with broken yolk, and polished it off carefully on his sleeve, and looked at it, and wrapped it in his dirty handkerchief, and put it carefully into the vest pocket of his little coat. Then he whipped out his cane from under his armpit and took command of it again, and with a final look at everybody, still sickly but at the same time cheerful, shrugged his shoulders and turned his back and scraped backward with his big shoes at the broken shells and the slimy bag, just like a dog, and looked back at the mess (everybody laughed again at that) and started to walk away, bending his cane deep with every shuffle, and squatting deeper, with his knees wider apart, than ever before, constantly picking at the seat of his pants with his left hand, and shaking one foot, then the other, and once gouging deep into his seat and then pausing and shaking his whole body, like a wet dog, and then walking on; while the screen shut over his small image a sudden circle of darkness: then the player-piano changed its tune, and the ads came in motionless color. They sat on into the William S. Hart picture to make sure why he had killed the man with the fancy vest—it was as they had expected by her frightened, pleased face after the killing; he had insulted a girl and cheated her father as well—and Rufus' father said, "Well, reckon this is where we came in," but they watched him kill the man all over again; then they walked out.

It was full dark now, but still early; Gay Street was full of absorbed faces; many of the store windows were still alight. Plaster people, in ennobled postures, stiffly wore untouchably new clothes; there was even a little boy, with short, straight pants, bare knees and high socks, obviously a sissy: but he wore a cap, all the same, not a hat like a baby. Rufus' whole insides lifted and sank as he looked at the cap and he looked up at his father; but his father did not notice; his face was wrapped in good humor, the memory of Charlie. Remembering his rebuff of a year ago, even though it had been his mother, Rufus was afraid to speak of it. His father wouldn't mind, but she wouldn't want him to have a cap, yet. If he asked his father now, his father would say no, Charlie Chaplin was enough. He watched the absorbed faces pushing past each other and the great bright letters of the signs: "Sterchi's." "George's." I can read them now, he reflected. I even know how to say "Sturkeys." But he thought it best not to say so; he remembered how his father had said, "Don't you brag," and he had been puzzled and rather stupid in school for several days, because of the stern tone in his voice.

What was bragging? It was bad.

They turned aside into a darker street, where the fewer faces looked more secret, and came into the odd, shaky light of Market Square. It was almost empty at this hour, but here and there, along the pavement streaked with horse urine, a wagon stayed still, and low firelight shone through the white cloth shell stretched tightly on its hickory hoops. A dark-faced man leaned against the white brick wall, gnawing a turnip; he looked at them low, with sad, pale eyes. When Rufus' father raised his hand in silent greeting, he raised his hand, but less, and Rufus, turning, saw how he looked sorrowfully, somehow dangerously, after them. They passed a wagon in which a lantern burned low orange; there lay a whole family, large and small, silent, asleep. In the tail of one wagon a woman sat, her face narrow beneath her flare of sunbonnet, her dark eyes in its shade, like smudges of soot. Rufus' father averted his eyes and touched his straw hat lightly; and Rufus, looking back, saw how her dead eyes kept looking gently ahead of her.

"Well," his father said, "reckon I'll hoist me a couple."

They turned in through the swinging doors into a blast of odor and sound. There was no music: only the density of bodies and of the smell of a market bar, of beer, whiskey and country bodies, salt and leather; no clamor; only the thick quietude of crumpled talk. Rufus stood looking at the light on a damp spittoon and he heard his father ask for whiskey, and knew he was looking up and down the bar for men he might know. But they seldom came from so far away as the Powell River Valley; and Rufus soon realized that his father had found, tonight, no one he knew. He looked up his father's length and watched him bend backwards tossing one off in one jolt in a lordly manner, and a moment later heard him say to the man next him, "That's my boy"; and felt a warmth of love. Next moment he felt his father's hands under his armpits, and he was lifted, high, and seated on the bar, looking into a long row of huge bristling and bearded red faces. The eyes of the men nearest him were interested, and kind; some of them smiled; further away, the eyes were impersonal and questioning, but now even some of these began to smile. Somewhat timidly, but feeling assured that his father was proud of him and that he was liked, and liked these men, he smiled back; and suddenly many of the men laughed. He was disconcerted by their laughter and lost his smile a moment; then, realizing it was friendly, smiled again; and again they laughed. His father smiled at him. "That's my boy," he said warmly. "Six years old, and he can already read like I couldn't read when I was twict his age."

Rufus felt a sudden hollowness in his voice, and all along the bar, and in his own heart. But how does he fight, he thought. You don't brag about smartness if your son is brave. He felt the anguish of shame, but his father did not seem to notice, except that as suddenly as he had lifted him up to the bar, he gently lifted him down again. "Reckon I'll have another," he said, and drank it more slowly; then, with a few good nights, they went out.

His father proffered a Life Saver, courteously, man to man; he took it with a special sense of courtesy. It sealed their contract. Only once had his father felt it necessary to say to him, "I wouldn't tell your mama, if I were you"; he had known, from then on, that he could trust Rufus; and Rufus had felt gratitude in this silent trust. They walked away from Market Square, along a dark and nearly empty street, sucking their Life Savers; and Rufus' father reflected, without particular concern, that Life Savers were not quite life saver enough; he had better play very tired tonight, and turn away the minute they got in bed.

The deaf and dumb asylum was deaf and dumb, his father observed very quietly, as if he were careful not to wake it, as he always did on these evenings; its windows showed black in its pale brick, as the nursing woman's eyes, and it stood deep and silent among the light shadows of its trees. Ahead, Asylum Avenue lay bleak beneath its lamps. Latticed in pawnshop iron, an old saber caught the glint of a street lamp, a mandolin's belly glowed. In a closed drug store stood Venus de Milo, her golden body laced in elastic straps. The stained glass of the L&N Depot smoldered like an exhausted butterfly, and at the middle of the viaduct they paused to inhale the burst of smoke from a switch engine which passed under; Rufus, lifted, the cinders stinging his face, was grateful no longer to feel fear at this suspension over the tracks and the powerful locomotives. Far down the yard, a red light flinched to green; a moment later, they heard the thrilling click. It was ten-seven by the depot clock. They went on, more idly than before.

If I could fight, thought Rufus. If I were brave; he would never brag how I could read: Brag. Of course. "Don't you brag." That was it. What it meant. Don't brag you're smart if you're not brave. You've got nothing to brag about. Don't you brag.

The young leaves of Forest Avenue wavered against street lamps and they approached their corner.

It was a vacant lot, part rubbed bare clay, part over-grown with weeds, rising a little from the sidewalk. A few feet in from the sidewalk there was a medium-sized tree and, near enough to be within its shade in daytime, an outcrop of limestone like a great bundle of dirty laundry. If you sat on a certain part of it the trunk of the tree shut off the weak street lamp a block away, and it seemed very dark. Whenever they walked downtown and walked back home, in the evenings, they always began to walk more slowly, from about the middle of the viaduct, and as they came near this corner they walked more slowly still, but with purpose; and paused a moment, at the edge of the sidewalk; then, without speaking, stepped into the dark lot and sat down on the rock, looking out over the steep fall of the hill and at the lights of North Knoxville. Deep in the valley an engine coughed and browsed; couplings rattled their long chains, and the empty cars sounded like broken drums. A man came up the far side of the street, walking neither slow nor fast, not turning his head, as he paused, and quite surely not noticing them; they watched him until he was out of sight, and

Rufus felt, and was sure that his father felt, that though there was no harm in the man and he had as good a right as they did to be there, minding his own business, their privacy was interrupted from the moment they first saw him until they saw him out of sight. Once he was out of sight they realized more pleasure in their privacy than before; they really relaxed in it. They looked across the darkness at the lights of North Knoxville. They were aware of the quiet leaves above them, and looked into them and through them. They looked between the leaves into the stars. Usually on these evening waits, for a few minutes before going on home, Rufus' father smoked a cigarette through, and when it was finished, it was time to get up and go on home. But this time he did not smoke. Up to recently he had always said something about Rufus' being tired, when they were still about a block away from the corner; but lately he had not done so, and Rufus realized that his father stopped as much because he wanted to, as on Rufus' account. He was just not in a hurry to get home, Rufus realized; and, far more important, it was clear that he liked to spend these few minutes with Rufus. Rufus had come recently to feel a quiet kind of anticipation of the corner, from the moment they finished crossing the viaduct; and, during the ten to twenty minutes they sat on the rock, a particular kind of contentment, unlike any other that he knew. He did not know what this was, in words or ideas, or what the reason was; it was simply all that he saw and felt. It was, mainly, knowing that his father, too, felt a particular kind of contentment, here, unlike any other, and that their kinds of contentment were much alike, and depended on each other. Rufus seldom had at all sharply the feeling that he and his father were estranged, yet they must have been, and he must have felt it, for always during these quiet moments on the rock a part of his sense of complete contentment lay in the feeling that they were reconciled, that there was really no division, no estrangement, or none so strong, anyhow, that it could mean much, by comparison with the unity that was so firm and assured, here. He felt that although his father loved their home and loved all of them, he was more lonely than the contentment of this family love could help; that it even increased his loneliness, or made it hard for him not to be lonely. He felt that sitting out here, he was not lonely; or if he was, that he felt on good terms with the loneliness; that he was a homesick man, and that here on the rock, though he might be more homesick than ever, he was well. He knew that a very important part of his well-being came of staying a few minutes away from home, very quietly, in the dark, listening to the leaves if they moved, and looking at the stars; and that his own, Rufus' own presence, was fully as indispensable to this well-being. He knew that each of them knew of the other's well-being, and of the reasons for it, and knew how each depended on the other, how each meant more to the other, in this most important of all ways, than anyone or anything else in the world; and that the best of this well-being lay in this mutual knowledge, which was neither concealed nor revealed. He knew these things very distinctly, but not, of course, in any such way as we have of suggesting them in words. There were no words, or even ideas, or formed emotions, of the kind that have been suggested here, no more in the man than in the boy child. These realizations moved clearly through the senses, the memory, the feelings, the mere feeling of the place they paused at, about a quarter of a mile from home, on a rock under a stray tree that had grown in the city, their feet on undomesticated clay, facing north through the night over the Southern Railway tracks and over North Knoxville, towards the deeply folded small mountains and the Powell River Valley, and above them, the trembling lanterns of the universe, seeming so near, so intimate, that when air stirred the leaves and their hair, it seemed to be the breathing, the whispering of the stars. Sometimes on these evenings his father would hum a little and the humming would break open into a word or two, but he never finished even a part of a tune, for silence was even more pleasurable, and sometimes he would say a few words, of very little consequence, but would never seek to say much, or to finish what he was saying, or to listen for a reply; for silence again was even more pleasurable. Sometimes, Rufus had noticed, he would stroke the wrinkled rock and press his hand firmly against it; and sometimes he would put out his cigarette and tear and scatter it before it was half finished. But this time he was much quieter than ordinarily. They slackened their walking a little sooner than usual and walked a little more slowly, without a word, to the corner; and hesitated, before stepping off the sidewalk into the clay, purely for the luxury of hesitation; and took their place on the rock without breaking silence. As always, Rufus' father took off his hat and put it over the point of his bent knee, and as always, Rufus imitated him, but this time his father did not roll a cigarette. They waited while the man came by, intruding on their privacy, and disappeared, as someone nearly always did, and then relaxed sharply into the pleasure of their privacy; but this time Rufus' father did not hum, nor did he say anything, nor even touch the rock with his hand, but sat with his hands hung between his knees and looked out over North Knoxville, hearing the restive assemblage of the train; and after there had been silence for a while, raised his head and looked up into the leaves and between the leaves into the broad stars, not smiling, but with his eyes more calm and grave and his mouth strong and more quiet, than Rufus had ever seen his eyes and his mouth; and as he watched his father's face, Rufus felt his father's hand settle, without groping or clumsiness, on the top of his bare head: it took his forehead and smoothed it, and pushed the hair backward from his forehead, and held the back of his head while Rufus pressed his head backward against the firm hand, and, in reply to that pressure, clasped over his right ear and cheek, over the whole side of the head, and drew Rufus' head quietly and strongly against the sharp cloth that covered his father's body, through which Rufus could feel the breathing ribs; then relinquished him, and Rufus sat upright, while the hand lay strongly on his shoulder, and he saw that his father's eyes had become still more clear and grave and that the deep lines around his mouth were satisfied; and looked up at what his father was so steadily looking at, at the leaves which silently breathed and at the stars which beat like hearts. He heard a long, deep sigh break from his father, and then his father's abrupt voice: "*Well* . . ." and the hand lifted from him and they both stood up. The rest of the way home they did not speak, or put on their hats. When he was nearly asleep Rufus heard once more the crumpling of freight cars, and deep in the night he heard the crumpling of subdued voices and the words, "Naw: I'll probly be back before they're asleep"; then quick feet creaking quietly downstairs. But by the time he heard the cranking and departure of the Ford, he was already so deeply asleep that it seemed only a part of a dream, and by next morning, when his mother explained to them why his father was not at breakfast, he had so forgotten the words and the noises that years later, when he remembered them, he could never be sure that he was not making them up.

Chapter 2

DEEP in the night they experienced the sensation, in their sleep, of being prodded at, as if by some persistent insect. Their souls turned and flicked out impatient hands, but the tormentor would not be driven off. They both awoke at the same instant. In the dark and empty hall, by itself, the telephone was shrilling fiercely, forlorn as an abandoned baby and even more peremptory to be quieted. They heard it ring once and did not stir, crystallizing their senses into annoyance, defiance and acceptance of defeat. It rang again: at the same moment she exclaimed, "Jay! The children!" and he, grunting, "Lie still," swung his feet thumping to the floor. The phone rang again. He hurried out in the dark, barefooted, tiptoe, cursing under his breath. Hard as he tried to beat it, it rang again just as he got to it. He cut it off in the middle of its cry and listened with savage satisfaction to its death rattle. Then he put the receiver to his ear.

"Yeah?" he said, forbiddingly. "*Hel*lo."

"Is this the res dence of, uh . . ."

"Hello, who is it?"

"Is this the res dence of Jay Follet?"

Another voice said, "That's him, Central, let me talk to um, that's . . ." It was Ralph.

"Hello," he said. "Ralph?"

"One moment please, your party is not connec . . ."

"Hello, Jay?"

"Ralph? Yeah. Hello. What's trouble?" For there was something wrong with his voice. Drunk, I reckon, he thought.

"Jay? Can you hear me all right? I said, 'Can you hear me all right,' Jay?"

Crying, too, sounds like. "Sure, I can hear you. What's the matter?" Paw, he thought suddenly. I bet it's Paw; and he thought of his father and his mother and was filled with cold sad darkness.

"Hit's Paw, Jay," said Ralph, his voice going so rotten with tears that his brother pulled the receiver a little away, his mouth contracting with disgust. "I know I got no business aringin y'up this hour night but I know too you'd never a forgive me if . . ."

"Quit it, Ralph," he said sharply. "Cut that out and tell me about it."

"Hit's only my duty, Jay, God Almighty I . . ."

"All right, Ralph," he said, "I preciate your callin. Now tell me about Paw."

"I just got back from thur, Jay, this minute, hurried home specially to ring you up . . . Course I'm agoan right back, you . . ."

"Listen, Ralph. Listen here. Can you hear me?" Ralph was silent. "Is he dead or alive?"

"Paw?"

Jay started to say, "Yeah, Paw," in tight rage, but he heard Ralph begin again. He can't help it, he thought, and waited.

"Why, naw, he ain't dead," Ralph said, deflated. The darkness lifted considerably from Jay: coldly, he listened to Ralph whickering up his feelings again. Finally, his voice shaking satisfactorily, he said, "But O Lord God, hit looks like the end, Jay!"

"I should come up, huh?" He began to wonder whether Ralph was sober enough to be trusted; Ralph heard, and misunderstood the doubt in his voice.

His own voice became dignified. "Course that's entirely up to you, Jay. I know Paw n all of us would feel it was mighty strange if his oldest boy, the one he always thought the most of . . ."

This new voice and this new tack bewildered Jay for a moment. Then he understood what Ralph was driving at, and had misunderstood, and assumed about him, and was glad that he was not where he could hit him. He cut in.

"Hold on, Ralph, you hold on there. If Paw's that bad you know damn well I'm comin so don't give me none a that . . ." But he realized, with self-dislike, how unimportant it was to argue this matter with Ralph and said, "Listen here, Ralph, now don't think I'm jumping on you, just listen. Do you hear me?" His feet and legs were getting chilly. He warmed one foot beneath the other. "Hear me?"

"I can hear you, Jay."

"Ralph, get it straight I'm not trying to jump on you, but sounds to me like you've had a few. Now . . ."

"I . . ."

"Now hold on. I don't give a damn if you're drunk or sober, far's you're concerned: point is this, Ralph. Anyone that's drunk, I know it myself, they're likely to exaggerate, and . . ."

"You think I'm a lyin to you? You . . ."

"Shut up, Ralph. Course you're not. But if you're drunk you can get an exaggerated idea how serious a thing is. Now you think a minute. Just think it over. And remember nobody's goin to think bad of you if you change your mind, or for calling either. Just how sick is he really, Ralph?"

"Course if you don't want to take my word for . . ."

"Think, Goddamn it!" Ralph was silent. Jay changed his feet around. He suddenly realized how foolish he had been to try to get anything level-headed out of Ralph. "Listen, Ralph," he said, "I know you wouldn't a phoned if you didn't think it was serious. Is Sally there?"

"Why yeah, she . . ."

"Let me talk to her a minute, will you?"

"Why I just told you she's out home."

"Course Mother's out there."

"Why, Jay, she wouldn't never leave his side. Mother . . ."

"Doctor's been out, of course."

"He's with him still. Was when I left."

"What's he say?"

Ralph hesitated. He did not want to spoil his story. "He says he has a chance, Jay."

By the way Ralph said it, Jay suspected the doctor had said, a good chance.

He was at the edge of asking whether it was a good chance or just a chance when he was suddenly overcome by even more disgust for himself, for haggling about it, than for Ralph. Besides, his feet were so chilly they were beginning to itch.

"Look here, Ralph," he said, in a different voice, "I'm talking too much. I . . ."

"Yeah, reckon our time must be about up, but what's a few . . ."

"Listen here. I'm starting right on up. I ought to be there by—what time is it, do you know?"

"Hit's two-thirty-seven, Jay. I *knowed* you'd . . ."

"I ought to be there by daylight, Ralph, you tell Mother I'm coming right on up just quicks I can get there. Ralph. Is he conscious?"

"Awf an' on, Jay. He's been speakin yore name, Jay, hit like to broke muh heart. He'll sure thank his stars that his oldest boy, the one he always thought the most of, that you thought it was worth yer while to . . ."

"Cut it out, Ralph. What the hell you think I am? If he gets conscious just let him know I'm comin'. And Ralph . . ."

"Yeah?"

But now he did not want to say it. He said it anyway. "I know I got no room to talk, but—try not to drink so much that Mother will notice it. Drink some coffee fore you go back. Huh? Drink it black."

"Sure, Jay, and don't think I take offense so easy. I wouldn't add a mite to her troubles, not at this time, not for this world, Jay. You know that. So Jay, I *thank* you. I *thank* you for calling it to my tention. I don't take offense. I *thank* you, Jay. I *thank* you."

"That's all right, Ralph. Don't mention it," he added, feeling hypocritical and a little disgusted again. "Now I'll be right along. So good-bye."

"You tell Mary how it is, Jay. Don't want her thinking bad of me, ringing . . ."

"That's all right. She'll understand. Good-bye, Ralph."

"I wouldn't a rung you up, Jay, if . . ."

"That's all right. Thanks for calling. Good-bye."

Ralph's voice was unsatisfied. "Well, good-bye," he said.

Wants babying, Jay realized. Not appreciated enough. He listened. The line was still open. The hell I will, he thought, and hung up. Of all the crybabies, he thought, and went on back to the bedroom.

"Gracious *sake*," said Mary, under her breath. "I thought he'd talk for*ever*!"

"Oh, well," Jay said. "Reckon he can't help it." He sat on the bed and felt for his socks.

"It is your father, Jay?"

"Yup," he said, pulling on one sock.

"Oh, you're going up," she said, suddenly realizing what he was doing. She put her hand on him. "Then it's very grave, Jay," she said very gently.

He fastened his garter and put his hand over hers. "Lord knows," he said. "I can't be sure enough of anything with Ralph, but I can't afford to take the risk."

"Of course not." Her hand moved to pat him; his hand moved on hers. "Has the doctor seen him?" she asked cautiously.

"He says he has a chance, Ralph says."

"That could mean so many things. It might be all right if you waited till morning. You might hear he was better, then. Not that I mean to . . ."

Because, to his shame, he had done the same kinds of wondering himself, he was now exasperated afresh. The thought even flashed across his mind, That's easy for *you* to say. He's not *your* father, and besides you've always looked down at him. But he drove this thought so well away that he thought ill of himself for having believed it, and said, "Sweetheart, I'd rather wait and see what we hear in the morning, just as much as you would. It may all be a false alarm. I know Ralph goes off his trolley easy. But we just can't afford to take that chance."

"Of course not, Jay." There was a loud stirring as she got from bed.

"What *you* up to?"

"Why, your breakfast," she said, switching on the light. "Sakes *alive*!" she said, seeing the clock.

"Oh, Mary. Get on back to bed. I can pick up something downtown."

"Don't be ridiculous," she said, hurrying into her bathrobe.

"Honest, it would be just as easy," he said. He liked night lunchrooms, and had not been in one since Rufus was born. He was very faintly disappointed. But still more, he was warmed by the simplicity with which she got up for him, thoroughly awake.

"Why, Jay, that is out of the question!" she said, knotting the bathrobe girdle. She got into her slippers and shuffled quickly to the door. She looked back and said, in a stage whisper, "Bring your *shoes*—to the *kit*chen."

He watched her disappear, wondering what in hell she

meant by that, and was suddenly taken with a snort of silent amusement. She had looked so deadly serious, about the shoes. God, the ten thousand little things every day that a woman kept thinking of, on account of children. Hardly even thinking, he thought to himself, as he pulled on his other sock. Practically automatic. Like breathing.

And most of the time, he thought, as he stripped, they're dead right. Course they're so much in the habit of it (he stepped into his drawers) that sometimes they overdo it. But most of the time if you think even a second before you get annoyed (he buttoned his undershirt), there is good common sense behind it.

He shook out his trousers. His moment of reflection and light-heartedness was overtaken by shadow, and he felt a little foolish, for he couldn't be sure there was anything to worry about yet, much less feel solemn about. That Ralph, he thought, hoisting the trousers and buttoning the top button. And he stood a moment looking at the window, polished with light, a deep blue-black beyond. The hour and the beauty of the night moved in him; he heard the flickering of the clock, and it sounded alien and mysterious as a rat in a wall. He felt a deep sense of solemn adventure, whether or not there was anything to feel solemn about. He sighed, and thought of his father as he could first remember him: beak-nosed, handsome, with a great, proud scowl of black mustache. He had known from away back that his father was sort of useless without ever meaning to be; the amount of burden he left to Jay's mother used to drive him to fury, even when he was a boy. And yet he couldn't get around it: he was so naturally gay and so deeply kind-hearted that you couldn't help loving him. And he never meant her any harm. He meant so well. That thought used particularly to enrage Jay, and even now it occurred to him with a certain sourness. But now he reflected also: well, but damn it, he did. He may have traded on it, but he never tried to, never knew it gained him anything. He meant the best in the world. And for a moment as he looked at the window he had no mental image of his father nor any thought of him, nor did he hear the clock. He only saw the window, tenderly alight within, and the infinite dark leaning like water against its outer surface, and even the window was not a window, but only something extraordinarily vivid and senseless which for the moment occupied the universe. A sense of enormous distance stole over him, and changed into a moment of insupportable wonder and sadness.

Well, he thought: we've all got to go sometime.

Then life came back into focus.

Clean shirt, he thought.

He unbuttoned the top buttons of his trousers and spread his knees, squatting slightly, to hold them up. Fool thing to do, he reflected. Do it every time. (He tucked in the deep tails and settled them; the tails of this shirt were particularly long, and this always, for some reason, still made him feel particularly masculine.) If I put on the shirt first, wouldn't have to do that fool squat. (He finished buttoning his fly.) Well (he braced his right shoulder) there's habit for you (he braced his left shoulder and slightly squatted again, readjusting).

He sat on the bed and reached for one shoe.

Oh.

Yup.

He took his shoes, a tie, a collar and collar buttons, and started from the room. He saw the rumpled bed. Well, he thought, I can do *some*thing for her. He put his things on the floor, smoothed the sheets, and punched the pillows. The sheets were still warm on her side. He drew the covers up to keep the warmth, then laid them open a few inches, so it would look inviting to get into. She'll be glad of that, he thought, very well pleased with the looks of it. He gathered up his shoes, collar, tie and buttons, and made for the kitchen, taking special care as he passed the children's door, which was slightly ajar.

She was just turning the eggs. "Ready in a second," he told her, and dodged into the bathroom. Ought to get this upstairs, he reflected for perhaps the five hundredth time.

He thrust his chin at the mirror. Not so bad, he thought, and decided just to wash. Then he reflected: after all, why had he worn a clean shirt? He could hope to God not, all he liked, but the chances were this was going to be a very solemn occasion. I'd do it for a funeral, wouldn't I? he reflected, annoyed at his laziness. He got out his razor and stropped it rapidly.

Mary heard this lavish noise of leather, and with a small spasm of impatience shoved the eggs to the back of the stove.

Ordinarily he took a good deal of time shaving, not because he enjoyed it (he loathed it) but because if it had to be done he wanted to do it well, and because he hated to cut himself. This time, because he was in a hurry, he gave a special cold glance at the lump of chin before he leaned forward and got to work. But to his surprise, everything worked like a charm; he even had less trouble than usual at the roots of his nostrils, and with his chin, and there were no patches left. He felt so well gratified that he dabbed each cheekbone with lather and took off the little half-moons of fuzz. Still no complaints. He cleaned up the basin and flushed the lathery, hairy bits of toilet paper down the water closet. Do I? he wondered, as the water closet gargled. Nope. He reached for the collar buttons.

When Mary came to the door he was flinging over and noosing the four-in-hand, his chin stretched and tilted as it always was during this operation, with the look of an impatient horse.

"Jay," she said softly, a little quelled by this impatient look, "I don't mean to hurry you, but things'll get cold."

"I'll be right out." He set the knot carefully above the button, glaring into his reflected eyes, made an unusually scrupulous part in his hair, and hurried to the kitchen table.

"Aw, *darling*!" There were the bacon and eggs and the coffee, all ready, and she was making pancakes as well.

"Well you got to *eat*, Jay. It'll still be chilly for hours." She spoke as if in a church or library, because of the sleeping children, unconsciously, because of the time of night.

"Sweetheart." He caught her shoulders where she stood at the stove. She turned, her eyes hard with wakefulness, and smiled. He kissed her.

"Eat your eggs," she said. "They're getting cold."

He sat down and started eating. She turned the pancakes. "How many can you eat?" she said.

"Gee, I don't know," he said, getting the egg down (don't talk with your mouth full) before he answered. He was not yet quite awake enough to be very hungry, but he was touched, and determined to eat a big breakfast. "Better hold it after the first two, three."

She covered the pancake to keep it hot and poured another.

He noticed that she had peppered the eggs more heavily than usual. "Good eggs," he said.

She was pleased. Not more than half consciously, she had done this because within a few hours he would doubtless eat again, at home. For the same reason she had made the coffee unusually strong. And for the same reason she felt pleasure in standing at the stove while he ate, as mountain women did.

"Good *coffee*," he said. "Now that's more *like* it." She turned the pancake. She supposed she really ought to make two pots always, one that she could stand to drink and one the way he liked it, new water and a few fresh grounds put in, without ever throwing out the old ones until the pot was choked full of old grounds. But she couldn't stand it; she would as soon watch him drink so much sulfuric acid.

"Don't you worry," she smiled at him. "You won't get any from me that's *all* the way like it!"

He frowned at her.

"Come on sit down, sweetheart," he said.

"In a minute . . ."

"Come on. I imagine two are gonna be enough."

"You think so?"

"If it isn't I'll make the third one." He took her hand and drew her towards her chair. "You'll *sit* here." She sat down. "How about you?"

"I couldn't sleep."

"I know what." He got up and went to the icebox.

"What are you—oh. No, Jay. Well. Thanks."

For before she could prevent him he had poured milk into a saucepan, and now that he put it on the stove she knew she would like it.

"Want some toast?"

"No, thank you, darling. The milk, just by itself, will be just perfect."

He finished off the eggs. She got half out of her chair. He pressed down on her shoulder as he got up. He brought back the pancakes.

"They'll be soggy by now. Let me . . ." She started up again; again he put a hand on her shoulder. "You stay *put*," he said in a mockery of sternness. "They're fine. Couldn't be better."

He plastered on butter, poured on molasses, sliced the pancakes in parallels, gave them a twist with knife and fork and sliced them crosswise.

"There's plenty more butter," she said.

"Got a plenty," he said, spearing four fragments of pancake and putting them in his mouth. "Thanks." He chewed them up, swallowed them, and speared four more. "I bet your milk's warm," he said, putting down his fork.

But this time she was up before he could prevent her. "You eat," she said. She poured the white, softly steaming milk into a thick white cup and sat down with it, warming both hands on the cup, and watching him eat. Because of the strangeness of the hour, and the abrupt destruction of sleep, the necessity for action and its interruptive minutiae, the gravity of his errand, and a kind of weary exhilaration, both of them found it peculiarly hard to talk, though both particularly wanted to. He realized that she was watching him, and watched back, his eyes serious yet smiling, his jaws busy. He was glutted, but he thought to himself, I'll finish up those pancakes if it's the last thing I do.

"Don't stuff, Jay," she said after a silence.

"Hm?"

"Don't eat more than you've appetite for."

He had thought his imitation of good appetite was successful. "Don't worry," he said, spearing some more.

There wasn't much to finish. She looked at him tenderly when he glanced down to see, and said nothing more about it.

"*Mnh*," he said, leaning back.

Now there was nothing to take their eyes from each other; and still, for some reason, they had nothing to say. They were not disturbed by this, but both felt almost the shyness of courtship. Each continued to look into the other's tired eyes, and their tired eyes sparkled, but not with realizations which reached their hearts very distinctly.

"What would you like to do for your birthday?" he asked.

"Why, Jay." She was taken very much by surprise. "Why you nice thing! Why—why . . ."

"You think it over," he said. "Whatever you'd like best—within reason, of course," he joked. "I'll see we manage it. The children, I mean." They both remembered at the same time. He said, "That is, of course, if everything goes the way we hope it will, up home."

"Of course, Jay." Her eyes lost focus for a moment. "Let's hope it will," she said, in a peculiarly abstracted voice.

He watched her. That occasional loss of focus always mystified him and faintly disturbed him. Women, he guessed.

She came back into this world and again they looked at each other. Of course, in a way, they both reflected, there isn't anything to say, or need for us to say it, anyhow.

He took a slow, deep breath and let it out as slowly.

"Well, Mary," he said in his gentlest voice. He took her hand. They smiled very seriously, thinking of his father and of each other, and both knew in their hearts, as they had known in their minds, that there was no need to say anything.

They got up.

"Now where—*ahh*," he said in deep annoyance.

"Coat n vest," he said, starting for the stairs.

"You wait," she said, passing him swiftly. "Fraid you'd wake the children," she whispered over her shoulder.

While she was gone he went into the sitting room, turned on one light, and picked up his pipe and tobacco. In the single quiet light in the enormous quietude of the night, all the little objects in the room looked golden brown and curiously gentle. He was touched, without knowing why.

Home.

He snapped off the light.

She was a little slow coming down; seeing if they're covered, he thought. He stood by the stove, idly watching the flexions of the dark and light squares in the linoleum. He was glad he'd gotten it down, at last. And Mary had been right. The plain black and white did look better than colors and fancy patterns.

He heard her on the stairs. Sure enough, first thing she said when she came in was, "You know, I was almost tempted to wake them. I suppose I'm silly but they're so used to— I'm afraid they're going to be very disappointed you didn't tell them good-bye."

"Good night! Really?" He hardly knew whether he was pleased or displeased. Were they getting spoilt maybe?

"I may be mistaken, of course."

"Be silly to wake em up. You might not get to sleep rest of the night."

He buttoned his vest.

"I wouldn't think of it, except: well" (she was reluctant to remind him), "if worst comes to worst, Jay, you might be gone longer than we hope."

"That's perfectly true," he said, gravely. This whole sudden errand was so uncertain, so ambiguous that it was hard for either of them to hold a focused state of mind about it. He thought again of his father.

"You think praps I should?"

"Let me think."

"N-no," he said slowly; "I don't reckon. No. You see, even, well even at the worst I'd be coming back to take you-all up. Funeral I mean. And these heart things, they're generally decided pretty fast. Chances are very good, either way, I'll be back tomorrow night. That's tonight, I mean."

"Yes, I see. Yes."

"Tell you what. Tell them, don't promise them or anything of course, but tell them I'm practicly sure to be back before they're asleep. Tell them I'll do my best." He got into his coat.

"All right, Jay."

"Yes. That's sensible." She reached so suddenly at his heart that by reflex he backed away; the eyes of both were startled and disturbed. With a frowning smile she teased him: "Don't be *frightened*, little Timid Soul; it's only a clean handkerchief and couldn't possibly hurt you."

"I'm sorry," he laughed, "I just didn't know what you were up to." He pulled in his chin, frowning slightly, as he watched her take out the crumpled handkerchief and arrange the fresh one. Being fussed over embarrassed him; he was still more sharply embarrassed by the discreet white corner his wife took care to leave peeping from the pocket. His hand moved instinctively; he caught himself in time and put his hand in his pocket.

"There. You look very nice," she said, studying him earnestly, as if he were her son. He felt rather foolish, tender towards her innocence of this motherliness, and quite flattered.

He felt for a moment rather vainly sure that he did indeed look very nice, to her anyhow, and that was all he cared about.

"Well," he said, taking out his watch. "Good Lord a mercy!" He showed her. Three-forty-one. "I didn't think it was hardly three."

"Oh yes. It's very late."

"Well, no more dawdling." He put an arm around her shoulder and they walked to the back door. "All right, Mary. I hate to go, but—can't be avoided."

She opened the door and led him through, to the back porch. "You'll catch cold," he said. She shook her head. "No. It feels milder outside than in."

They walked to the edge of the porch. The moistures of May drowned all save the most ardent stars, and gave back to the earth sublimated light of the prostrate city. Deep in the end of the back yard, the blossoming peach tree shone like a celestial sentinel. The fecund air lavished upon their faces the tenderness of lovers' adoring hands, the dissolving fragrance of the opened world, which slept against the sky.

"What a heavenly night, Jay," she said in the voice which was dearest to him. "I almost wish I could come with you"— she remembered more clearly "—in whatever happens."

"I wish you could, dear," he said, though his mind had not been on such a possibility; frankly, he had suddenly looked forward to the solitary drive. But now the peculiar quality of her voice reached him and he said, with love, "I wish you could."

They stood bemused by the darkness.

"Well, Jay," she said abruptly, "I mustn't keep you."

He was silent a moment. "Nope," he said, a curious, weary sadness in his voice. "Time to go."

He took her in his arms, leaning back to look at her. It was not really anything of a separation, yet he was surprised to find that it seemed to him a grave one, perhaps because his business was grave, or because of the solemn hour. He saw this in her face as well, and almost wished they had waked the children after all.

"Good-bye, Mary," he said.

"Good-bye, Jay."

They kissed, and her head settled for a moment against him.

He stroked her hair. "I'll let you know," he said, "quick as I can, if it's serious."

"I pray it won't be, Jay."

"Well, we can only hope." The moment of full tenderness between them was dissolved in their thought, but he continued gently to stroke the round back of her head.

"Give all my love to your mother. Tell her they're both in my thoughts and wishes—constantly. And your father, of course, if he's—well enough to talk to."

"Sure, dear."

"And take care of yourself."

"Sure."

He patted her back and they parted.

"Then I'll hear from you—see you—very soon."

"That's right."

"All right, Jay." She squeezed his arm. He kissed her, just beneath the eye, and realized her disappointed lips; they smiled, and he kissed her heartily on the mouth. In a glimmer of gaiety, both were on the verge of parting with their customary morning farewell, she singing, "Good-bye John, don't stay long," he singing back, "I'll be back in a week or two," but both thought better of it.

"All right, dear. Good-bye."

"Good-bye, my dear."

He turned abruptly at the bottom of the steps. "Hey," he whispered. "How's your money?"

She thought rapidly. "All right, thank you."

"Tell the children good-bye for me. Tell them I'll see them tonight."

"I better not promise that, had I?"

"No, but probably. And Mary: I hope I can make supper, but don't wait it."

"All right."

"Good night."

"Good night." He walked back towards the barn. In the middle of the yard he turned and whispered loudly, "And you think it over about your birthday."

"Thank you, Jay. All right. Thank you."

She could hear him walking as quietly as possible on the

cinders. He silently lifted and set aside the bar of the door, and opened the door, taking care to be quiet. The first leaf squealed; the second, which was usually worse, was perfectly still. Stepping to the left of the car, and assuming the serious position of stealth which the narrowness of the garage made necessary, he disappeared into the absolute darkness.

She knew he would try not to wake the neighbors and the children; and that it was impossible to start the auto quietly. She waited with sympathy and amusement, and with habituated dread of his fury and of the profanity she was sure would ensue, spoken or unspoken.

Uhgh—hy uh yu hy why uhy uh: wheek-uh-wheek-uh:

Ughh—hy wh yuh: wheek:

(now the nearly noiseless, desperate adjustments of spark and throttle and choke)

Ughgh—hyuh yuhyuh wheek yuh yuh wheek wheek wheek yuh yuhyuh: wheek:

(which she never understood and, from where she stayed now, could predict so well):

Ughgh— *Ughgh*—yuhyuh *Ugh* wheek yuh yuh *Ughgh* yuh wheek wheek yuhyuh: wheek wheek: uh:

(like a hideous, horribly constipated great brute of a beast: like a lunatic sobbing: like a mouse being tortured):

Ughgh—*Ughgh*—*Ughgh* (Poor thing, he must be simply furious)   *Ughgh*—wheek—*Whughughy*uh—*Ughwhee*kyuh*uu-ghgyugh*yuhyuhy a a a a a a a h h h h h h R h R h R H R H R H (oh, *stop* it!) R H R H (a window went up) R H R H R H-R H R H R yuhyhhRRHRHRHRHRHRHRHRHRHRH-RH (the door smacked to in rage and triumph) RhRhRh - - - - - - - - (the window went down) RHRHRHRHRH (the machine backed out; crackling on the cinders). RHRH - - - - - (he wrenched it rudely but adroitly in a backward curve, almost to the chicken wire; from between the houses, light from the street caught its black side) rhrh - - - - (and swung as rudely round the corner of the barn and, by opposite turn, into the alley, facing eastward, where it stood) rhrh - - - - - - - - (obedient, conquered, malicious as a mule, while he briefly reappeared, faced towards the house, saw her, waved one hand—she waved, but he did not see her—and drew

the gate shut, disappearing beyond it) rhrhrhrhrhrh
RHRHRHRHR HRH R

H

R

H

R

H

rh

rh

rh

rh

rh

rh

rh

rh

rh

rh

rh

rh

C utta wawwwwk:

Craaawwrk?

Chiquawkwawh.

Wrrawkuhkuhkuh.

Craarrawwk.

rwrwrk?

yrk.

rk:

She released a long breath, very slowly, and went into the house.

There was her milk, untouched, forgotten, barely tepid. She drank it down, without pleasure; all its whiteness, draining from the stringing wet whiteness of the empty cup, was singularly repugnant. She decided to leave things until morning, ran water over the dishes, and left them in the sink.

If the children had heard so much as a sound, they didn't show it now. Catherine, as always, was absolutely drowned in sleep, and both of them, as always, were absolutely drowned.

Really, they are too big for that, she thought. Rufus certainly. She carefully readjusted their covers, against catching cold. They scarcely stirred.

I ought to ask a doctor.

She saw the freshened bed. Why, the *dear*, she thought, smiling, and got in. She was never to realize his intention of holding the warmth in for her; for that had sometime since departed from the bed.

Chapter 3

H E IMAGINED that by about now she would about be getting back and finding the bed. He smiled to think of her finding it.

He drove down Forest, across the viaduct, past the smoldering depot, and cut sharply left beneath the asylum and steeply downhill. The L&N yards lay along his left, faint skeins of steel, blacked shadows, little spumes of steam; he saw and heard the flickering shift of a signal, but he could no longer remember what that one meant. Along his right were dark vacant lots, pale billboards, the darker blocks of small sleeping buildings, an occasional light. He would have eaten in one of these places, small, weakly lighted holes-in-the-wall, opaque with the smoke of overheated lard, some for Negroes, some for whites, which served railroad men and the unexplainable nighthawks you found in any fair-sized town. You never saw a woman there, except sometimes behind a counter or sweating over a stove. He never used to talk when he went to them, but he enjoyed the feeling of conspiracy, and the sound of voices. If you went to the right ones, and if you were known, or looked like you could be trusted, you could get a shot or two of liquor, any hour of the night.

He ran his tongue over his teeth, tasting the last of the molasses and coffee and bacon and eggs.

Before long the city thinned out into the darkened evidences of that kind of flea-bitten semi-rurality which always peculiarly depressed him: mean little homes, and others inexplicably new and substantial, set too close together for any satisfying rural privacy or use, too far, too shapelessly apart to have coherence as any kind of community; mean little pieces of ill-cultivated land behind them, and alongside the road, between them, trash and slash and broken sheds and rained-out billboards: he passed a late, late streetcar, no passengers aboard, far out near the end of its run.

Within two more minutes he had seen the last of this sort of thing. The darkness became at once more intimate and more hollow; the engine sounded different, a smooth, easy drone; budding limbs swelled up and swept with sudden speed through the last of the vivid light; the auto bored through the center of the darkness of the universe; its poring shafts of light, like an insect's antennae, feeling into distinctness every relevant small obstacle and ease of passage, and very little else. He unbuttoned his vest and the top button of his trousers and settled back. After a few moments he wondered about taking off his coat; but the rhythm and momentum of night driving were too strongly persuasive to wish to break. He settled still more deeply, his eyes shifting gear constantly between the farthest reach of his lights and the nearest, and gave himself over entirely to the pleasures of the journey, and to its still undetermined but essentially grave significance.

It was just nearing daybreak when he came to the river; he had to rap several times on the window of the little shanty before the ferryman awoke.

"Have to double the charge, mister, cross at night," he said, intent on lighting his lantern.

"That's all right."

At the voice, he looked up, well awake for the first time. "Oh, howdy thur," he said.

"Howdy."

"You generally always come o' Sundays, yer womurn, couple o' young-uns."

"Yeahp."

He walked away, to the edge of the water, and holding his lantern low, examined the fit of his flatboat against the shore. Then he raised the lantern and swung it, as a railroad man would; Jay, who had left his engine running, braked it carefully down the steep, thickly tracked clay, and carefully aboard. He shut off his engine; the sudden silence was magical. He got out and helped the man block the wheels. "All ready here," he said, straightening; but the man said nothing; he was already casting off. They both watched the brown water widen under the lantern light, apparently with equal appreciation. Must be a nice job, Jay reflected, as he nearly always did; except of course winter.

"Run all winter?"

"Eah," said the man, warping his line.

"Tain't so bad," he added after a moment, "only for sleet. I do mislike them sleety nights."

Both were silent. Jay filled his pipe. As he struck a match he felt a difference in motion, a kind of dilation; the ferry was now warped into the bias of the current, which carried it, and the ferryman worked no more; he merely kept one hand on his line. The flat craft rode against the water like a hand on a breast. The water mumbled a little; during this part of the crossing, that was always the only sound. And by now, the surface of the river gave back light which could not as yet be as clearly discerned in the sky, and along both banks the trees which crowded the water like drinking cattle began to take on distinctness one from another. Far back through the country along both sides of the river, roosters screamed. The violet sky shone gray; and now for the first time both men saw, on the opposite shore, a covered wagon, and a little figure motionless beside it.

"I God," said the ferryman. "Reckon how long *they* ben awaitin!" Suddenly he became very busy with his line; he had to build sufficient momentum in cross-power to carry it past the middle of the stream, where the broadside current, at full strength, could lock both line and craft. Jay hurried to help. "Tsch right," the man called him off, too busy for courtesy. Jay quit. After a moment the man's hauling became more casual. He turned, enough to meet Jay's eye. "F'wrn't man enough to hanl that alone, wouldn't be man enough to hanl the job," he explained.

Jay nodded, and watched the expanding light.

"Hope tain't no trouble, brung ya up hyer sich an hour," the ferryman said.

Jay had realized his curiosity, and respected his silence, at the first, and so, although the question slightly altered this respect, he answered, somehow pleased to be able to communicate it to an agent at once so near his sympathies, and so impersonal: "My Paw. Took at the heart. Don't know yet how bad tis."

The man clacked his tongue like an old woman, shaking his head, and looking into the water. "That's a mean way," he said.

Suddenly he looked Jay in the eyes: his own were strangely shy. Then he looked again into the brown water, and continued to haul at the line.

"Well, good luck," he said.

"Much obliged," said Jay.

The wagon grew larger and larger, and now the dark, deeply lined faces of the man and woman became distinct: the sad, deeply lined faces of the profound country which seemed ancient even in early maturity and which always gave Jay a sense of peace. The woman sat high above the mule; the flare of her deep bonnet had the shape of the flare of the wagon's canopy. The man stood beside his wagon, one clayed boot cocked on the clayed hub. They gazed gravely into the eyes of the men on the ferry, and neither of them moved, or made any sign of salutation, until the craft was made fast.

"Ben here long?" the ferryman asked.

The woman looked at him; after a moment the man, without moving his eyes, nodded.

"Didn't hear yer holler."

After a moment the man said, "I hollered."

The ferryman put out his lantern. He turned to Jay. "Twarn't rightly a dark crossing, mister. I can't charge ye but the daytime toll."

"All right," Jay said, giving him fifteen cents. "And much obliged to you." He put out his headlights and stooped to crank the car.

"Hold awn, bud," the wagoner called. Jay looked up; the man took two quick strides and took control of the mule's head. The wagoner nodded.

The engine was warm, and started easily; and though with every wrench of the crank a spasm of anguish wrenched the mule, once the engine leveled out the mule stood quietly, merely trembling. Jay put it violently into low to get up the steep mud bank, giving the mule and wagon as wide a berth as possible, nodding his regret of the racket and his friendliness as he passed; their heads turned, the eyes which followed him could not forgive him his noise. At the top he filled his pipe and watched while the mule and wagon descended, the mule held at the head, his hocks sprung uneasily, hoofs prodding and finding base in the treacherous clay, rump bunched high, the wagon tilting, the block-brakes screeching on the broad iron rim.

Poor damn devils, he thought. He was sure they were bound for the Knoxville market. They had probably waited for the ferry as much as a couple of hours. They would be hopelessly late.

He waited out the lovely sight of the water gaping. The ferry took on its peculiar squareness, its look of exquisite silence. He looked at his watch. Not so bad. He lighted his pipe and settled down to drive. He always felt different once he was across the river. This was the real, old, deep country, now. Home country. The cabins looked different to him, a little older and poorer and simpler, a little more homelike; the trees and rocks seemed to come differently out of the ground; the air smelled different. Before long now, he would know the worst; if it was the worst. Quite unconsciously he felt much more deeply at leisure as he watched the flowing, freshly lighted country; and quite unconsciously he drove a little faster than before.

Chapter 4

DURING the rest of the night, Mary lay in a "white" sleep. She felt as odd, alone in the bed, as if a jaw-tooth had just been pulled, and the whole house seemed larger than it really was, hollow and resonant. The coming of daylight did not bring things back to normal, as she had hoped; the bed and the house, in this silence and pallor, seemed even emptier. She would doze a little, wake and listen to the dry silence, doze, wake again sharply, to the thing that troubled her. She thought of her husband, driving alone on one of the most solemn errands of his life, and of his father, lying fatally sick, perhaps dying, perhaps dead at this moment (she crossed herself), and she could not bring herself to feel as deeply about it as she felt that she should, for her husband's sake. She realized that if the situation were reversed, and it was her own father who was dying, Jay would feel much as she felt now, and that she could not blame either him or herself, but that did her no good. For she knew that at the bottom of it the trouble was, simply, that she had never really liked the old man.

She was sure that she didn't look down on him, as many of Jay's relatives all but said to her face and as she feared that Jay himself occasionally believed; certainly not; but she could not like him, as almost everyone else liked him. She knew that if it was Jay's mother who lay dying, there would be no question of her grief, or inadequacy to her husband; and that was a fair measure of how little she really cared for his father. She wondered why she liked him so little (for to say that she actually disliked him, she earnestly assured herself, would be putting it falsely). She realized that it was mainly because everyone forgave him so much, and liked him so well in spite of his shortcomings, and because he accepted their forgiveness and liking so casually, as if this were his natural due or, worse, as if he didn't even realize anything about it. And the worst of this, the thing she resented with enduring anger and distaste, was the burden he had constantly imposed on his wife, and her perfect patience with him, as if she didn't even know it was a burden or that he was taking advantage. It was this unconsciousness in both of them that she could not abide, and if only once Jay's mother had shown one spark of anger, of realization, Mary felt she might have begun to be able to like him. But this brought her into a resentment, almost a dislike, of Jay's mother, which she knew was both unjust and untrue to her actual feelings, and which made her uncomfortable; she was shocked also to realize that she was lying awake in the hour which might well be his last, to think ill of him. *Shame on you*, she said to herself, and thought earnestly of all that she knew was good about him.

He was generous, for one thing. Generous to a fault. And she remembered how, time and again, he had given away, "loaned," to the first person who asked him the favor, money or food or things which were desperately needed home to keep body and soul together. Fault, indeed. Yet it was a good fault. It was no wonder people loved him—or pretended to—and took every possible advantage of him. And he was very genuinely kind-hearted. A wonderful virtue. And tolerant. She had never heard him say an unkind or a bitter word of anybody, not even of people who had outrageously abused his generosity—he could not, she realized, bear to believe that they really meant to; and he had never once, of that she was sure, joined with most of the others in their envious, hostile, contemptuous talking about her.

On the other hand she could be equally sure that he had never really stood up for her strongly and bravely, and angrily, against everyone, as his wife had, for he disliked arguments as much as he did unkindness; but she put that out of her mind. He had never, so far as she knew, complained, about his sickness or pain, or his poverty, and chronically, insanely, as he made excuses for others, he had never made excuses for himself. And certainly he had precious little right to complain, or make excuses; but that too she hastened to put out of her mind. She reproached herself by remembering how thoroughly nice and friendly he had always been to her; and if she had to realize that that was not at all for herself but purely because she was "Jay's woman," as he'd probably say, she certainly couldn't hold that against him; her own best feelings towards him came out of her recognition of him as Jay's father. You couldn't like anyone more than you happened to like them; you simply couldn't. And you couldn't feel more about them than that amount of liking made possible to you. There was a special kind of basic weakness about him; that was what she could not like, or respect, or even forgive, or resign herself to accepting, for it was a kind of weakness which took advantage, and heaped disadvantage and burden on others, and it was not even ashamed for itself, not even aware. And worse, at the bottom of it all, maybe, Jay's father was the one barrier between them, the one stubborn, unresolved, avoided thing, in their complete mutual understanding of Jay's people, his "background." Even now she could not really like him much, or feel deep concern. Her thoughts for him were grave and sad, but only as they would be for any old, tired, suffering human being who had lived long and whose end, it appeared, had come. And even while she thought of him her real mind was on his son's grief and her inadequacy to it. She had not even until this moment, she realized with dismay, given Jay's mother a thought; she had been absorbed wholly in Jay. I must write her, she thought. But of course, perhaps, I'll see her soon.

And yet, clearly as she felt that she realized what the bereavement would mean to Jay's mother, and wrong as she was even to entertain such an idea, she could not help feeling that even more, his death would mean great relief and release. And, it occurred to her, he'll no longer stand between me and Jay.

At this, her soul stopped in utter coldness. God forgive me, she thought, amazed; I almost *wished* for his death!

She clasped her hands and stared at a stain on the ceiling.

O Lord, she prayed; forgive me my unspeakable sinful thought. Lord, cleanse my soul of such abominations. Lord, if it be Thy will, spare him long that I may learn to understand and care for him more, with Thy merciful help. Spare him not for me but for himself, Lord.

She closed her eyes.

Lord, open my heart that I may be worthy in realization of this sorrowful thing, if it must happen, and worthy and of use and comfort to others in their sorrow. Lord God, Lord Jesus, melt away my coldness and apathy of heart, descend and fill my emptiness of heart. And Lord, if it be Thy will, preserve him yet a while, and let me learn to bear my burden more lightly, or to know this burden is a blessing. And if he must be taken, if he is already with Thee now (she crossed herself), may he rest in Thy peace (again she crossed herself).

And Lord, if it be Thy will, that this sorrow must come upon my husband, then I most humbly beseech Thee in Thy mercy that through this tribulation Thou openest my husband's heart, and awake his dear soul, that he may find comfort in Thee that the world cannot give, and see Thee more clearly, and come to Thee. For there, Lord, as Thou knowest, and not in his poor father or my unworthy feelings, is the true, widening gulf between us.

Lord, in Thy mercy, Who can do all things, close this gulf. Make us one in Thee as we are one in earthly wedlock. For Jesus' sake, Amen.

She lay somewhat comforted, but more profoundly disturbed than comforted. For she had never before so clearly put into words, into visible recognition, their religious difference, or the importance of the difference to her. And how important is it to him, she wondered. And haven't I terribly exaggerated my feeling of it? A "gulf"? And "widening"? Was it really? Certainly he never said anything that justified her in such a feeling; nor did she feel anything of that largeness. It really was only that both of them said so very little, as if both took care to say very little. But that was just it. That a thing which meant so much to her, so much more, all the time, should be a thing that they could not share, or could not be open about. Where her only close, true intimate was Aunt Hannah, and her chief love and hope had to rest in the children. That was it. That was the way it seemed bound to widen (she folded her hands, and shook her head, frowning): it was the children. She felt sure that he felt none of Andrew's anger and contempt, and none of her father's irony, but it was very clear by his special quietness, when instances of it came up, that he was very far away from it and from her, that he did not like it. He kept his distance, that was it. His distance, and some kind of dignity, which she respected in him, much as it hurt her, by this silence and withdrawal. And it would widen, oh, inevitably, because quiet and gentle as she would certainly try to be about it, they were going to be brought up as she knew she must bring them up, as Christian, Catholic children. And this was bound to come into the home, quite as much as in church. It was bound in some ways, unless he changed; it was bound in some important ways, try as hard and be as good about it as she was sure they both would, to set his children apart from him, to set his own wife apart from him. And not by any action or wish of his, but by her own deliberate will. Lord God, she prayed, in anguish. Am I wrong? Show me if I am wrong, I beseech Thee. Show me what I am to do.

But God showed her only what she knew already: that come what might she must, as a Christian woman, as a Catholic, bring up her children thoroughly and devoutly in the Faith, and that it was also her task, more than her husband's, that the family remain one, that the gulf be closed.

But if I do this, nothing else that I can do will close it, she reflected. Nothing, nothing will avail.

But I must.

I must just: trust in God, she said, almost aloud. Just: do His will, and put all my trust in Him.

A streetcar passed; Catherine cried.

Chapter 5

"DADDY had to go up to see Grandfather Follet," their mother explained. "He says to kiss both of you for him and he'll probably see you before you're asleep tonight."

"When?" Rufus asked.

"Way, early this morning, before it was light."

"Why?"

"Grampa Follet is very sick. Uncle Ralph phoned up very late last night, when all of us were asleep. Grampa has had one of his attacks."

"What's attack?"

"Eat your cereal, Catherine. Rufus, eat yours. His heart. Like the one he had that time last fall. Only worse, Uncle Ralph says. He wanted very much to see Daddy, just as quick as Daddy could come."

"Why?"

"Because he loves Daddy and if . . . *Eat*, wicker, or it'll all be nasty and cold, and *then* you know how you hate to eat it. Because if Daddy didn't see him soon, Grampa might not get to see Daddy again."

"Why not?"

"Because Grampa is getting old, and when you get old, you can be sick and not get well again. And if you can't get well again, then God lets you go to sleep and you can't see people any more."

"Don't you ever wake up again?"

"You wake up right away, in heaven, but people on earth can't see you any more, and you can't see them."

"Oh."

"*Eat*," their mother whispered, making a big, nodding mouth and chewing vigorously on air. They ate.

"Mama," Rufus said, "when Oliver went to sleep did he wake up in heaven too?"

"I don't know. I imagine he woke up in a part of heaven God keeps specially for cats."

"Did the rabbits wake up?"

"I'm sure they did if Oliver did."

512

"All bloody like they were?"

"No, Rufus, that was only their poor little bodies. God wouldn't let them wake up all hurt and bloody, poor things."

"Why did God let the dogs get in?"

"We don't know, Rufus, but it must be a part of His plan we will understand someday."

"What good would it do *Him*?"

"Children, don't dawdle. It's almost school time."

"What good would it do *Him*, Mama, to let the dogs in?"

"I don't know, but someday we'll understand, Rufus, if we're very patient. We mustn't trouble ourselves with these things we can't understand. We just have to be sure that God knows best."

"I bet they sneaked in when He wasn't looking," Rufus said eagerly. "Cause He sure wouldn't have let them if He'd been there. Didn't they, Mama? Didn't they?"

Their mother hesitated, and then said carefully, "No, Rufus, we believe that God is everywhere and knows everything and nothing can happen without His knowing. But the Devil is everywhere too—everywhere except heaven, that is—and he is always tempting us. When we do what he tempts us to do, then God lets us do it."

"What's tempt?"

"Tempt is, we, the Devil tempts us when there is something we want to do, but we know it is bad."

"Why does God let us do bad things?"

"Because He wants us to make up our own minds."

"Even to do bad things, right under His nose?"

"He doesn't *want* us to do bad things, but to know good from bad and be good of our own free choice."

"Why?"

"Because He loves us and wants us to love Him, but if He just *made* us be good, we couldn't really love Him enough. You can't love to do what you are *made* to do, and you couldn't love God if He *made* you."

"But if God can do *any*thing, why can't He do that?"

"Because He doesn't *want* to," their mother said, rather impatiently.

"Why *doesn't* He want to?" Rufus said. "It would be so much easier for Him."

"*God—doesn't—believe—*in*—the—easy—way,*" she said, with a certain triumph, spacing the words and giving them full emphasis. "Not for us, not for anything or anybody, not even for Himself. God wants us to *come* to Him, to *find* Him, the best we can."

"Like hide-and-go-seek," said Catherine.

"What was that?" their mother asked rather anxiously.

"Like hide . . ."

"Aw, it isn't a *bit* like hide-and-seek, *is* it Mama?" Rufus cut in. "Hidenseek's just a *game*, just a *game*. God doesn't fool around playing *games*, *does* He, Mama! *Does* He! *Does* He!"

"*Shame on* you, Rufus," his mother said warmly, and not without relief. "Why, *shame on* you!" For Catherine's face had swollen and her mouth had bunched tight, and she glared from her brother to her mother and back again with scalding hot eyes.

"Well He *does*n't," Rufus insisted, angry and bewildered at the turn the discussion had taken.

"That's *enough*, Rufus," his mother whipped out sternly, and leaned across and patted Catherine's hand, which made Catherine's chin tremble and her tears overflow. "That's *all right*, little wicker! That's *all right*! He doesn't play games. Rufus is right about that, but it *is*, someways it *is* like hide-and-seek. You're ab-so-lootly *right*!"

But with this, Catherine was dissolved, and Rufus sat aghast, less at her crying, which made him angry and jealous, than at his sudden solitude. But her crying was so miserable that, angry and jealous as he was, he became ashamed, then sorry for her, and was trying, helplessly, to find a way of showing that he was sorry when his mother glanced up at him fiercely and said, "*Now you march* and get ready for school. I ought to tell Daddy, you're a *bad boy*!"

At the door, a few minutes later, when she leaned to kiss him good-bye and saw his face, she mistook the cause of it and said, more gently but very earnestly: "Rufus, I can see you're sorry, but you mustn't be mean to Catherine. She's just a little *girl*, your *little sister*, and you mustn't ever be unkind to her and hurt her feelings. Do you understand? *Do* you, Rufus?"

He nodded, and felt terribly sorry for his sister and for himself because of the gentleness in his mother's voice.

"Now you come back and tell her how sorry you are, and *hurry*, or you'll be late for school."

He came in shyly with his mother and came up to Catherine; her face was swollen and red and she looked at him bleakly.

"Rufus wants to tell you how sorry he is, Catherine, he hurt your feelings," their mother said.

Catherine looked at him, brutally and doubtfully.

"I *am* sorry, Catherine," he said. "Honest to goodness I am. Because you're a little, *little girl*, and . . ."

But with this Catherine exploded into a roar of angry tears, and brought both fists down into her plate, and Rufus, dumfounded, was hustled brusquely off to school.

Chapter 6

WHEN Jay found how things were at the farm, he was angry at having been so grieved and alarmed; before long,
he felt it had all happened very much as he had suspected.
Ralph had just lost his head, as usual. Now he was very much
ashamed of himself, though still very defensive, and everyone,
including Jay, tried to assure him that he had done the right
thing. Jay could imagine how much Ralph had needed to feel
useful, to take charge. He couldn't think very well of him, but
he was sorry for him. He felt he understood very well how it
had happened.

Actually, he understood only a little about it, and Ralph
understood very little more.

Late in the evening before, their father had suffered a much
more severe and painful attack than any up to then. After no
more than a few minutes, his wife had realized its terrible gravity, and had woken Thomas Oaks. Thomas had hurried across
the hill and roused up Jessie and George Bailey and, without
waiting for them, had hurried back, saddled the horse, and
whipped it as fast as it would go, into LaFollette. The doctor
was out on a call; he left a message, and hurried on to Ralph's.
Ralph was in a virtual panic of aroused responsibility the instant he heard the news. He asked if the doctor was there yet.
Thomas told him; Ralph realized that his mother had told
Thomas to rush out the doctor even before he called her son to
her side. He put it aside as an ungenerous and mean-spirited
thought, yet it stayed, hurting him like a burr. He felt it was no
time for resentments, though; not only he, but Sally as well,
must come to their help, must be there (Sally'd never forgive
me if she wasn't) if Paw was to die (she'd be the only wife
there, of the only son; his mother would never forget that). He
rushed back and told her what was happening as he hurried
into his clothes, hurried two doors away, banged loudly on the
Felts's door, and apologized for the banging by explaining (his
voice was already damp) that his Paw was at death's door if not
already passed on, and he wouldn't have roused them only he
knew they would be only too willing to help out so Sally could

go too. They were very kind to him; Mrs. Felts arrived before
Sally had finished fixing her hair. While she was doing so, Ralph
sped across the street to his office, unlocked his desk, and took
two choking swallows of whiskey in the dark. He rammed the
bottle into his pocket and hurried down to start his car. They
had been so quick that they overtook Thomas on his horse
when he had scarcely passed the edge of town, going, as Ralph
said to himself, his eyes low and cold above the steering wheel,
"like sixty," or anyhow as fast as it was safe to travel on these awful roads, perhaps a little faster, thinking of Barney Oldfield, in
the Chalmers he had chosen because it was a better class of auto
and a more expensive one than his brother's, a machine people
made no smart jokes about. His first impulse, when he saw the
horse and rider ahead, was to honk, both in self-advertisement,
warning and greeting, but he remembered in time the seriousness of the occasion and did not do so, reflecting, after it was
too late, that Thomas might feel he was snubbed, as if he had
passed him in the street without speaking, and he was angry
with Thomas for possibly having any such feeling about such
petty matters, at such a time.

There were nearly two hours of helpless anguish and fright
before the doctor arrived. During that time it is possible that
Ralph suffered more acutely than anyone else. For besides suffering, or believing that he suffered, all the pains that his father
must be experiencing, and all of his mother's grief and anxiety,
and all of the smaller emotions of all the smaller people who
were present, he suffered deep humiliation. When he rushed in
and swept his mother into his arms he felt that his voice and
his whole manner were all that they ought to be; that he
showed himself to be a man who, despite his own boundless
grief, was capable also of boundless strength to sustain others
in their grief, and to take complete charge of all that needed to
be done. But even in that first embrace he could see that his
mother was only by an effort concealing her desire to draw
away from him. He came near her over and over again, hugging her, sobbing over her, fondling her, telling her that she
must be brave, telling her she must not try to be brave, to lean
on him, and cry her heart out, for naturally at such a time she
would want to feel her sons close around her; but every time,
he felt that same patient stiffening and her voice perplexed

him. Everyone in the room, even Ralph in the long run, knew that he was only making things harder for her; only his mother realized that he was beseeching comfort rather than bringing it. She was not in the least angry with him; she was sorry for him and wished that she could be of more help to him, but her mind was not on him, her heart was not with him, and his sobs and the stench of his breath made her a little sick at her stomach. What perplexed him in her voice was its remoteness. He began to realize that he was bringing her no comfort, that she was not leaning on him, that just as he had always feared, she did not really love him. He redoubled his efforts to soothe her and to be strong for her. The harder he tried, the more remote her voice became. At the end of a half hour her face was no less desperate than it had been when he first saw her. And he began to feel that everyone else was watching him, and knew he was no use, and that his mother did not love him. The women watched him one way, the men watched him another. He felt that his wife was thinking ill of him, that she was not even sorry for him; he felt slobbering and fat, the way she looked at him and suddenly with terrible hatred was sure that she would prefer to sleep with flat-bellied men—what man? *Any* man, so long as his belly don't get in the way. As for Jessie, he knew she had always hated him, as much as he hated her. And George Bailey just sitting there looking serious and barrel-chested and always being careful to look away when their eyes met: George thought he was twice the man that Ralph was and twice as good right at this time, better with his in-laws than Ralph could be with his own flesh and blood; and they all knew that George was twice the man and were just trying not to say it or think it even, or let Ralph know they thought it. And even Thomas Oaks, an ignorant hand, who couldn't even read or write, just setting there with his ropy hands hung between his knees, staring down at a knot in the floor with those washed-out blue eyes, even Tom was more of a man and more good use too. When Tom got up and said if there wasn't nothing he could do he reckoned he would get on up to the loft, but if there was anything, they would just let him know, Ralph understood it. He knew Tom might be ignorant but he wasn't so ignorant but he knew when it was best to leave a family to itself; and when Ralph's mother said, "All right, Tom," Ralph heard more life and kindness, and more gratefulness in her voice, than in every word she'd said to him, the whole night; and as he watched Tom climb the ladder, heavily and quietly, rung by rung, he thought: there goes more of a man than I am, he knows how to take himself out of the way, and he thought: he's doing a power more good by going than I can by staying, and he thought: every soul in this room wishes it was me that was going, instead of him, and he called, in a voice which sounded unfriendly, though he had meant to make it sound friendly to everyone except Tom, "That's right, Tom, get ye some sleep"; and Tom pulled his head back through the ceiling and looked down at him with those empty blue eyes and said, "That's all right, Mr. Ralph," and suddenly Ralph realized that he had no intention of sleeping and would be there alone, not sleeping a wink, just ready in case he was needed; and that Tom had seen his malice, his desire to belittle him, and had belittled him instead, before his mother and his wife and his dying father. "That's all right, Mr. Ralph." What's all right? What's all right? He wanted to yell it at him, "What's all right, you poor-white-trash son-of-a-bitch?" but he restrained himself.

Every time he felt their eyes on him especially strongly he went over to his mother again and hugged her, and held her head tightly against him, and tried to say things that would make her cry, and every time, her voice was a little bit further away from him and her face looked a little older and dryer, and every time, he was still more acutely aware of their eyes on him and of the thoughts behind their eyes, and every time, he would swing away from his mother as if he could bear to leave her uncomforted for a moment only because there were still more important things to do, matters of life and death, which he and only he, the son, the man of the family, now that poor Paw lay there so near to death, could handle. And every time, there was nothing whatever to do except wait for the doctor. They had already given the medicine the doctor had given them to give, and they had already given him so much of the ginseng tea the doctor had said wouldn't anyhow do any harm, that Ralph's mother decided they shouldn't give any more of it. His head was low; his feet were braced against hot stones wrapped in flannel, and Mother kept everyone except herself at the far, lighted end of the room, except for short visits. There was nothing to do, nothing to take charge of, and every time Ralph swung about from his mother with an air of heroic authority and rediscovered this fact, he felt as if a chair had been pulled out from under him, in front of everybody, and he began to think that he would burn up and die if he didn't have another drink. He said, "Scuse me," once in the choked and modest tone which should signify to the women that he had to empty his bladder, and he got a good, hard swig that time, and found when he came back in that he didn't care whether they were looking at him or not, or guessed what he really went out for; for two cents he'd take out the bottle and wave it at them. Sooner than it was possible to use that excuse again, he became even more thirsty than before. At the same time he first realized that he was drunk. He was bitterly ashamed of himself, drunk at this time, at his father's very deathbed, when his mother needed him so bad as never before, and when he knew, for he had learned by now to take people's word for it, that he was really good for nothing when he was drunk. And then to feel so thirsty on top of that. He braced himself with all the sternness and strength he was capable of. By God, he told himself, you'll pull yourself together. By God, or . . . By God, you will. You will. And he got up abruptly and walked straight through them into the dark, and splashed his face and neck with water. He realized then that he could take another, now. Just a little one. To brace him. He cursed himself and splashed his face again, and dried carefully with his handkerchief before he came back in. He realized that to everyone else in the room, those two silences meant two more drinks. He made a cynical grimace. By God, *he* knew better! He felt as if he had great physical strength, and in his feeling of strength his thirst was merely like the bite under a punch bar, a pleasure to feel and to brace against. But within a short while the thirst returned even more fiercely as irresistible pain. No, by God, he said again to himself. But he began to wonder. If they thought he'd had one anyhow—two in fact—why in a way he owed himself a couple. Three, for that matter: a third, because he knew they mistook that cynical face he had made for a drunken shamelessness. After all, it wasn't *he* who didn't want to be drunk. He was being careful for *their* sake. And by God, if he was going to get blamed for it anyhow, what was the good of that. Besides, when he really took care he knew he could hold his liquor good as the next man. He'd show them. But it wasn't so easy, figuring how to get out. Can't go out to pee so soon. Nor dipper of water. He felt a sudden terrible excess of shame. No, *by God*, he wouldn't sit there scheming himself a shot over his own dying father, and his mother looking on at him, knowing his mind, not saying a word. By *God*, he wouldn't! He set himself to put everything out of his mind except his father, not as he had ever feared him, or wished he approved of him, or wished he was dead, but as he lay there now, old and broken, cast aside near the end of the trail, yes sir, the embers fading; and within a short while he was sobbing, and talking of his father through his sobs, and within a short while more he began to realize that he had found his way out. His struggles against this temptation, his iterations of "*I'm* no good," and, "I'm the son he set least store by, but I'm the one that cares for him the most," and the voices of the women, soothing him, trying to quiet him, only added to his tears, the richness of his emotions, and his verbosity, and before long he had realized that this too was useful, and was using it. Toward the end all genuine emotion left him and he had to scrape, tickle and torture himself into sufficient feeling and sufficient evidence of an impending breakdown he would inflict on nobody, but at length he felt he had achieved the proper moment, and rushed headlong from the room, all but upsetting his wife in her rocking chair. The instant he was outside he felt nothing in the world except the ferocity of his thirst. He leaned against the cabin wall, uncorked the bottle, wrapped his mouth over its mouth as ravenously as a famished baby takes the nipple, and tilted straight up.

NNHhhh; with a sobbing groan he struck his temple against the side of the house so violently that he could scarcely keep his feet, flung the bottle as far from him as he was able. "*Oh, God! God! God! God! God!*" he moaned, the tears itching on his cheeks. *Fool! Fool! Fool! Why* hadn't he made sure before he left the office? There couldn't have been more than a half a dram left.

He dabbed at his head with his handkerchief and stole leaning into the path of the lamplight. Blood, all right. He felt sick at his stomach. He dabbed again. Not much. He dabbed again; again. Not running, anyhow. He took a deep breath and went back into the room.

"Stumbled," he said. "Tain't nothin."

But even so, Sally came over, and his mother came over, and they both looked carefully, pretending that it was perfectly natural to stumble in a flat clay dooryard, and when they agreed that it was a mean lump but needed no further attention, he felt, suddenly, sad, and as little as a child, and he wished he were.

His rage and despair and the shock of the blow had so quieted and sobered him that now he was beyond even self-hatred. He felt gentle and clear. The sadness grew and became all but insupportable, and for the first time that evening, one of the few times in his life, he began to see things more or less as they were. Yes, over on that bed beyond the carefully shaded lamp, moaning occasionally, his breathing so shaken and irregular that it was as if sorrow disordered it rather than death, his father, his own father, was indeed coming near his last hour; and his mother, his own mother, sat there as quiet and patient, and so strong. There was not likely anyone in the world enough stronger that she could find comfort in him. And he? Yes, he was here, for what little good that was, and he was the only son who was here. But there was no special virtue in that; he was the only son who lived near enough at hand. And he lived so near at hand because he had no courage, no intelligence, no energy, no independence. That was really it: no independence. He always needed to be near. He always needed to feel their support, their company, very near him. He always lived almost from day to day in the hope that by staying near, by always being on hand if he was needed, by always showing how much he loved them, he might at last be sure he had won their approval, their respect. He did not believe, he couldn't remember, one sober breath he had ever drawn, that he had drawn as if in his own right, feeling, I don't care what anybody thinks of me, this is myself and this is how *I* do it. Everything he did, every tone his voice took, was controlled by his idea of what would make the best impression on others. He was worse a slave to that, to his dread for other people's opinion of him, than any nigger had ever been a slave. And his meanness and recklessness when he was drunk enough, he knew that was no good, no good at all. It wasn't even real. It was just the way he wished he was, and it wasn't even that, for what he wished was not to be reckless, but brave, a very different thing, and not to be mean but proud, a different thing too. And what was the worst of it? Why, the worst of it was, that once in a great while he could see himself for what he really was, and almost believe that now that he saw himself so clearly, he could change, all it took was clearness of head, and patience, and courage; and at the same time he had to know that nothing that was in him to do about it could ever be done; that he would never change, except for the worse; that he had no kind of clearness of head, or patience, or courage, that would last beyond the little it took (and even that was enough to make him shiver all over), to just be able, once in ever so long a time, to sit and look at himself for what he really was. He was just weak: he saw that, clear enough. Just no good. He saw that. Just incomplete some way, like a chicken that comes out of the shell with a wry neck and grows on up like that. Like his own poor little Jim-Wilson, that already showed the weakness, with his poor little washed-out eyes, his clinging to Sally, his terror of his father when his father was drunk or even teased him, his readiness to cry. I ought not ever to have fathered children, Ralph thought. I ought not ever to have been born.

And looking at himself now, he neither despised himself nor felt pity for himself, nor blamed others for whatever they might feel about him. He knew that they probably didn't think the incredibly mean, contemptuous things of him that he was apt to imagine they did. He knew that he couldn't ever really know what they thought, that his extreme quickness to think that he knew was just another of his dreams. He was sure, though, that whatever they might think, it couldn't be very good, because there wasn't any very good thing to think of. But he felt that whatever they thought, they were just, as he was almost never just. He knew he was wrong about his mother. He had no doubt whatever, just now, that she really did love him, had never stopped loving him, and never would. He knew even that she was especially gentle to him, that she loved him in a way she loved nobody else. And he knew why he so often felt that she did not really love him. It was because she was so sorry for him, and because she had never had and never possibly could have, any respect for him. And it was respect he needed, infinitely more than love. Just not to have to worry about whether people respect you. Not ever to have to feel that people are being nice to you because they are sorry for you, or afraid of you. He looked at Sally. Poor girl. Afraid of me. That's Sally. And it is all my own fault. Every bit mine. And I hate her for wanting other men, when I know that unfaithfulness never once came into her head, and when I'm the worst tail-chaser in LaFollette and half of the town knows it, and Sally knows it too, and is too gentle-hearted and too scared ever to reproach me with it. And sure I ought to be able to do something about that, at least about that. Any *man* could. Only I'm no man. So how can I expect that people can ever look up to me, or at least not look down on me? People are fair to me and more than fair. More than fair, if ever they knew me for what I really am.

And here tonight it comes like a test, like a trial, one of the times in a man's life when he is needed, and can be some good, just by being a man. But I'm not a man. I'm a baby. Ralph is the baby. Ralph is the baby.

Chapter 7

H ANNAH LYNCH decided, that day, that she would go shopping and that if Rufus wanted to go, she would like to take him with her. She telephoned Rufus' mother to ask whether she had other plans for Rufus that would interfere, and Mary said no; she asked whether so far as Mary knew, Rufus had planned to do anything else, and Mary, a little surprised, said no, not as far as she knew, and whether he had or not, she was sure he would be glad to go shopping with her. Hannah, in a flicker of anger, was tempted to tell her not to make up children's minds for them, but held onto herself and said, instead, well, we'll see, and that she would be up by the time he came back from school. Mary urgently replied that she mustn't come up—much as she would like to see her, of course —but that Rufus would make the trip instead. Hannah, deciding not to make an issue of it, said very well, she would be waiting, but he wasn't to come unless he really wanted to. Mary said warmly that of course he would want to and Hannah again replied, more coolly, "We'll see; it's no matter"; and, getting off the subject, asked, "Have you had any message from Jay?"

For Mary had telephoned her father, that morning, to explain why Jay could not be at the office. "No," Mary said, with slight defensiveness, for she felt somehow that criticism might be involved; and hadn't expected to unless, of course . . .

"Of course," Hannah replied quickly (for she had intended no criticism) "so no doubt we needn't worry."

"No, I'm sure he would have called if his father had—even if there was any grave *danger*," Mary said.

"Of course he would," Hannah replied. Was there anything she could bring Mary? Let's see, Mary said a little vaguely; why; aah; and she realized that Catherine could well use a new underwaist and that—and—but suddenly recalled, also, that it was sometimes difficult to persuade her aunt to accept money, or even to render account, for things she bought this way; and lied, with some embarrassment, why, no, thank you so much, it's very stupid of me but I just can't think of a thing. All right,

Hannah said, honoring her embarrassment, and resolved to take care to embarrass her less often (but after all, *little gifts* should be possible from time to time without this silly pride); all right; I'll be waiting, till three, and if Rufus has other things to do, just let me know. All right, Aunt Hannah, and it's so nice of you to think of him. Not a bit of it, I *like* to take him shopping. Well that's very nice and I'm sure *he* likes it. Perhaps so. Why *certainly* so, Aunt Hannah. All right. All right; *good*-bye. You'll let us know if you *do* hear from Jay? Of course. Right away. But by now I don't really expect to. He'll very likely be back by supper time, or a little after. He was sure he could—if—everything was, well, relatively all right. All right. All right; *good*-bye. Good-bye. Good-bye, Mary's voice trailed, gently.

"Jay?" Andrew called over the banisters.

"No, just talking to Mary," Hannah said. "I guess it can't be so very serious, after all."

"Let's hope not," said Andrew, and went back to his painting.

Hannah made herself ready for town. When Rufus arrived, all out of breath, he found her on a hard little couch in the living room, sitting carefully, not to rumple her long white-speckled black dress, and poring gravely through an issue of *The Nation* which she held a finger length before her thick glasses.

"Well," she smiled, putting the magazine immediately aside. "You're very prompt" (he was not; his mother had required him to wash and change his clothes) "and" (peering at him closely as he hurried up) "you look very nice. But you're all out of breath. Would you really like to come?"

"Oh, yes," he said, with a trace of falseness, for he had been warned to convince her; "I'm *very glad* to come, Aunt Hannah, and thank you very much for thinking of me."

"Huh . . ." she said, for she knew direct quotation when she heard it, but she was also convinced that in spite of the false words, he really meant it. "That's very nice," she said. "Very well; let's be on our way." She took her hard, plain black straw hat from its place on the sofa beside her and Rufus followed her to the mirror in the dark hallway and watched her careful planting of the hat pin. "Dark as the inside of a cow," she muttered, almost nosing the somber mirror, "as your grandfather would say." Rufus tried to imagine what it would be like, inside a cow. It would certainly be dark, but then it would be dark inside anybody or anything, so why a cow? Grandma came prowling dim-sightedly up the hallway from the dining room, smiling fixedly, even though she fancied she was alone, and the little boy and his great-aunt drew quickly aside, but even so, she collided, and gasped.

"Hello, Grandma, it's me," Rufus shrilled, and his aunt Hannah leaned close across her to her good ear at the same moment and said loudly, "Catherine, hello; it's only Rufus and I"; and as they spoke each laid a reassuring hand on her; and upstairs Rufus heard Andrew bite out, "Oh, *G-godd*"; but his grandmother, used to such frights, quickly recovered, laughed her tinkling ladylike laugh (which was beginning faintly to crack) very sportingly, and cried, "Goodness gracious, how you startled me!" and laughed again. "And there's little *Rufus*!" she smiled, leaning deeply towards him with damaged, merry eyes and playfully patting his cheek.

"So you're ready to go!" she said brightly to Hannah.

Hannah nodded conspicuously and leaning again close across her to get at her good ear, cried, "Yes; all ready!"

"Have a nice time," Grandma said, "and give Grandma a good hug," and she hugged him close, saying "Mum-*mum*; nice little boy," and vigorously slapping his back.

"Good-bye," they shouted.

"*Good*-bye," she beamed, following them to the door.

They took the streetcar and got out at Gay Street. There was no flurry and no dawdling as there would have been with any other woman Rufus knew; none of the ceremony that held his grandmother's shopping habits in a kind of stiff embroidery; none of the hurrying, sheepish refusal to be judicious in which men shopped. Hannah steered her way through the vigorous sidewalk traffic and along the dense, numerous aisles of the stores with quiet exhilaration. Shopping had never lost its charm for her. She prepared her mind and her disposition for it as carefully as she dressed for it, and Rufus had seldom seen her forced to consult a shopping list, even if she were doing intricate errands for others. Her personal tastes were almost as frugal as her needs; hooks and eyes, lengths of black tape and white tape, snappers so tiny it was difficult to handle them, narrow lace, a few yards, sometimes, of black or white cotton cloth, and now and then two pairs of black cotton stockings. But she loved to do more luxurious errands for others, and even when there were no such errands, she would examine a rich variety of merchandise she had no intention of buying, always skillful, in these examinations, never to disturb a clerk, and never to leave disturbed anything that she touched, imposing her weak eyes as intently as a jeweler with his glass and emitting little expletives of irony or admiration. Whenever she did have a purchase to make, she got hold of a clerk and conducted the whole transaction with a graceful efficiency which had already inspired in Rufus a certain contempt for every other woman he had seen shopping. Rufus, meanwhile, paid relatively little attention to what she was saying or buying; words passed above him, merely decorating the world he stared at with as much fascination as his aunt's; and best of all were the clashing, banging wire baskets which hastened along on little trolleys, high over them all, bearing to and fro wrapped and unwrapped merchandise, and hard leather cylinders full of money. Taken shopping with anyone else, Rufus suffered extreme boredom, but Hannah shopped much as a real lover of painting visits a gallery; and her pleasure clarified Rufus' eyes and held the whole merchant world in a clean focus of delight. If his mother or his grandmother was shopping, the tape which hung around the saleswoman's neck and the carbon pad in which she recorded purchases seemed twitchy and clumsy to Rufus; but in his great-aunt's company, the tape and pad were instruments of fascination and skill, and the housewives who ordinarily made the air of the stores heavy with fret and foolishness were like a challenging sea, instead, which his aunt navigated most deftly. She did not talk to him too much, nor did she worry over him, nor was Rufus disposed to wander beyond the range of her weak sight, for he enjoyed her company, and of all grown people she was the most considerate. She would remember, every ten minutes or so, to inquire courteously whether he was tired, but he was seldom tired in her company; with her, he never felt embarrassment in saying if he had to go to the bathroom, for she never seemed annoyed, but in consequence he seldom found it necessary to go when they came together on these downtown trips. Today Hannah bought a few of the simplest of things for herself and several more elaborate things for her sister-in-law and a beautifully transparent, flowered scarf for Mary's birthday, taking Rufus into this surprise; then, in the art store, she inquired whether the *Grammar of Ornament* had arrived. But when they showed her the enormous and magnificently colored volume, she exclaimed with laughter, "Mercy, that is no grammar; it's a whole encyclopedia," and the clerk laughed politely, and she said she was afraid it was larger than she could carry; she would like to have it delivered. She must be sure, though, that it was delivered personally to her, no later than May twenty-first, that's three days, can I be sure of that? No, she interrupted herself, in one of her rare confusions or changes of decision, that won't do. She explained to Rufus, parenthetically, "Suppose there was an accident, and your Uncle Andrew saw it too soon!" She paused. "Do you think you can help me with a few more of these bundles?" she asked him. He replied proudly that of course he could. "Then we'll take it now," his aunt told the clerk, and after careful testing and distribution of the various bundles, they came back into the street. And there his Aunt Hannah made a proposal which astounded Rufus with gratitude. She turned to him and said, "And now if you'd like it, I'd like to give you a cap."

He was tongue-tied; he felt himself blush. His aunt could not quite see the blush but his silence disconcerted her, for she had believed that this would make him really happy. Annoyed with herself, she nevertheless could not help feeling a little hurt.

"Or is there something else you'd rather have?" she asked, her voice a little too gentle.

He felt a great dilation in his chest. "*Oh, no!*" he exclaimed with passion. "*Oh, no!*"

"Very well then, let's see what we can do about it," she said, more than reassured; and suddenly she suspected in something like its full magnitude the long, careless denial, and the importance of the cap to the child. She wondered whether he would speak of it—would try, in any cowardly or goody-goody way, to be "truthful" about his mother's distaste for the idea (though she supposed he *ought* to be—truthful, that is); or,

better, whether he could imagine, and try to warn her that in
buying it for him, she risked displeasing his mother; and realized, then, that she must take care not to set him against his
mother. She waited with some curiosity for what he might say,
and when he found no words, said, "Don't worry about Mar
—about your mother. I'm sure if she knew you *really* wanted
it, you would have had it long ago."

He just made a polite, embarrassed little noise and she realized, with regret, that she did not know how to manage it
properly. But she was certainly not going, on that account, to
deny what she had offered; she compressed her lips and, by
unaccountable brilliance of intuition, went straight past
Miller's, a profoundly matronly store in which Rufus' mother
always bought the best clothes which were always, at best, his
own second choice, and steered round to Market Street and
into Harbison's, which sold clothing exclusively for men and
boys, and was regarded by his mother, Rufus had overheard, as
"tough" and "sporty" and "vulgar." And it was indeed a world
most alien to women; not very pleasant men turned to stare at
this spinster with the radiant, appalled little boy in tow; but
she was too blind to understand their glances and, sailing up to
the nearest man who seemed to be a clerk (he wore no hat)
asked briskly, without embarrassment, "Where do I go, please,
to find a cap for my nephew?" And the man, abashed into
courtesy, found a clerk for her, and the clerk conducted them
to the dark rear of the store. "Well, just see what you like,"
said Aunt Hannah; and still again, the child was astonished.
He submitted so painfully conservative a choice, the first time,
that she smelled the fear and hypocrisy behind it, and said
carefully, "That is very nice, but suppose we look at some
more, first." She saw the genteel dark serge, with the all but
invisible visor, which she was sure would please Mary most,
but she doubted whether she would speak of it; and once
Rufus felt that she really meant not to interfere, his tastes surprised her. He tried still to be careful, more out of courtesy,
she felt, than meeching, but it was clear to her that his heart
was set on a thunderous fleecy check in jade green, canary yellow, black and white, which stuck out inches to either side
above his ears and had a great scoop of visor beneath which his
face was all but lost. It was a cap, she reflected, which even a

colored sport might think a little loud, and she was painfully tempted to interfere. Mary would have conniption fits; Jay wouldn't mind, but she was afraid for Rufus' sake that he would laugh; even the boys in the block, she was afraid, might easily sneer at it rather than admire it—all the more, she realized sourly, if they *did* admire it. It was going to cause no end of trouble, and the poor child might soon be sorry about it himself. But she was switched if she was going to boss him! "That's very nice," she said, as little drily as she could manage. "But think about it, Rufus. You'll be wearing it a long time, you know, with all sorts of clothes." But it was impossible for him to think about anything except the cap; he could even imagine how tough it was going to look after it had been kicked around a little. "You're very sure you like it," Aunt Hannah said.

"Oh, yes," said Rufus.

"Better than this one?" Hannah indicated the discreet serge.

"Oh, yes," said Rufus, scarcely hearing her.

"Or this one?" she said, holding up a sharp little checkerboard.

"I think I like it best of all," Rufus said.

"Very well, you shall have it," said Aunt Hannah, turning to the cool clerk.

*W*aking in darkness, he saw the window. Curtains, a tall, cloven wave, towered almost to the floor. Transparent, manifold, scalloped along their inward edges like the valves of a sea creature, they moved delectably on the air of the open window.

Where they were touched by the carbon light of the street lamp, they were as white as sugar. The extravagant foliage which had been wrought into them by machinery showed even more sharply white where the light touched, and elsewhere was black in the limp cloth.

The light put the shadows of moving leaves against the curtains, which moved with the moving curtains and upon the bare glass between the curtains.

Where the light touched the leaves they seemed to burn, a bitter green. Elsewhere they were darkest gray and darker. Beneath each of these thousands of closely assembled leaves dwelt either no natural light or richest darkness. Without touching each other these leaves were stirred as, silently, the whole tree moved in its sleep.

Directly opposite his window was another. Behind this open window, too, were curtains which moved and against them moved the scattered shadows of other leaves. Beyond these curtains and beyond the bare glass between, the room was as dark as his own.

He heard the summer night.

All the air vibrated like a fading bell with the latest exhausted screaming of locusts. Couplings clashed and conjoined; a switch engine breathed heavily. An auto engine bore beyond the edge of audibility the furious expletives of its incompetence. Hooves broached, along the hollow street, the lackadaisical rhythms of the weariest of clog dancers, and endless in circles, narrow iron tires grinced continuously after. Along the sidewalks, with incisive heels and leathery shuffle, young men and women advanced, retreated.

A rocking chair betrayed reiterant strain, as of a defective lung; like a single note from a stupendous jew's-harp, the chain of a porch swing twanged.

Somewhere very near, intimate to some damp inch of the grass between these homes, a cricket peeped, and was answered as if by his echo.

Humbled beneath the triumphant cries of children, which tore the whole darkness like streams of fire, the voices of men and women on their porches rubbed cheerfully against each other, and in the room next his own, like the laboring upward of laden windlasses and the mildest pouring out of fresh water, he heard the voices of men and women who were familiar to him. They groaned, rewarded; lifted, and spilled out: and watching the windows, listening at the heart of the proud bell of darkness, he lay in perfect peace.

Gentle, gentle dark.

My darkness. Do you listen? Oh, are you hollowed, all one taking ear?

My darkness. Do you watch me? Oh, are you rounded, all one guardian eye?

Oh gentlest dark. Gentlest, gentlest night. My darkness. My dear darkness.

Under your shelter all things come and go.

Children are violent and valiant, they run and they shout like the winners of impossible victories, but before long now, even like me, they will be brought into their sleep.

Those who are grown great talk with confidence and are at all times skillful to serve and to protect, but before long now they too, before long, even like me, will be taken in and put to bed.

Soon come those hours when no one wakes. Even the locusts, even the crickets, silent shall be, as frozen brooks

In your great sheltering.

I hear my father; I need never fear.

I hear my mother; I shall never be lonely, or want for love.

When I am hungry it is they who provide for me; when I am in dismay, it is they who fill me with comfort.

When I am astonished or bewildered, it is they who make the weak ground firm beneath my soul: it is in them that I put my trust.

When I am sick it is they who send for the doctor; when I am well and happy, it is in their eyes that I know best that I am loved; and it is towards the shining of their smiles that I lift up my heart and in their laughter that I know my best delight.

I hear my father and my mother and they are my giants, my king and my queen, beside whom there are no others so wise or worthy or honorable or brave or beautiful in this world.

I need never fear: nor ever shall I lack for lovingkindness.

And those also who talk with them in that room beneath whose door the light lies like a guardian slave, a bar of gold, my witty uncle, and my girlish aunt: I have yet to know them well, but they and my father and my mother are all fond of each other, and I like them, and I know that they like me.

I hear the easy chiming of their talk and their laughter.

But before long now they too will leave and the house will become almost silent and before long the darkness, for all its leniency, will take my father and my mother and will bring them, even as I have been brought, to bed and to sleep.

You come to us once each day and never a day rises into brightness but you stand behind it; you are upon us, you overwhelm us, all of each night. It is you who release from work, who bring parted families and friends together, and people for a little while are calm and free, and all at ease together; but before long, before long, all are brought down silent and motionless

Under your sheltering, your great sheltering, darkness.

And all through that silence you walk as if none but you had ever breathed, had ever dreamed, had ever been.

My darkness, are you lonely?

Only listen, and I will listen to you.

Only watch me, and I will watch into your eyes.

Only know that I am awake and aware of you, only be my friend, and I will be your friend.

You need never fear; or ever be lonely; or want for love.

Tell me your secrets; you can trust me.

Come near. Come very near.

Darkness indeed came near. It buried its eye against the eye of the child's own soul, saying:

Had ever breathed, had ever dreamed, had ever been.

And somewhat as in blind night, on a mild sea, a sailor may be made aware of an iceberg, fanged and mortal, bearing invisibly near, by the unwarned charm of its breath, nothingness now revealed itself: that permanent night upon which the stars in their expiring generations are less than the glinting of gnats, and nebulae, more trivial than winter breath; that darkness in which eternity lies bent and pale, a dead snake in a jar, and infinity is the sparkling of a wren blown out to sea; that inconceivable chasm of invulnerable silence in which cataclysms of galaxies rave mute as amber.

Darkness said:

When is this meeting, child, where are we, who are you, child, who are you, do you know who you are, do you know who you are, child; are you?

He knew that he would never know, though memory, almost captured, unrecapturable, unbearably tormented him. That this little boy whom he inhabited was only the cruelest of deceits. That he was but the nothingness of nothingness, condemned by some betrayal, condemned to be aware of nothingness. That yet in that desolation, he was not without companions. For featureless on the abyss, invincible, moved monstrous intuitions. And from the depth and wide throat of eternity burned the cold, delirious chuckle of ravenousness beyond ravenousness, cruelty beyond cruelty.

Darkness said:

Under my sheltering: in my great sheltering.

In the corner, not quite possible to detach from the darkness, a creature increased, which watched him.

Darkness said:

You hear the man you call your father: how can you ever fear?

Under the washstand, carefully, something moved.

You hear the woman who thinks you are her child.

Beneath his prostrate head, eternity opened.

Hear how he laughs at you; in what amusement she agrees.

The curtain sighed as powers unspeakable passed through it.

Darkness purred with delight and said:

What is this change your eye betrays?

Only a moment ago, I was your friend, or so you claimed; why this sudden loss of love?

Only a moment ago you were all eagerness to know my secrets; where is your hunger now?

Only be steadfast: for now, my dear, my darling, the moment comes when hunger and love will be forever satisfied.

And darkness, smiling, leaned ever more intimately inward upon him, laid open the huge, ragged mouth—

Ahhhhh . . . !

Child, child, why do you betray me so?
Come near. Come very near.

Ohhhhhh . . . !

Must you be naughty? It would grieve me terribly to have to force you.

You know that you can never get away: you don't even want to get away.

But with that, the child was torn into two creatures, of whom one cried out for his father.

The shadows lay where they belonged, and he lay shaken in his tears. He saw the window; waited.

Still the cricket struck his chisel; the voices persisted, placid as bran.

But behind his head, in that tall shadow which his eyes could never reach, who could dare dream what abode its moment?

The voices chafed, untroubled: grumble and babble.

He cried out again more fiercely for his father.

There seemed a hollowing in the voices, as if they crossed a high trestle.

Serenely the curtain dilated, serenely failed.

The shadows lay where they belonged, but strain as he might, he could not descry what lay in the darkest of them.

The voices relaxed into their original heartlessness.

He swiftly turned his head and stared through the bars at the head of the crib. He could not see what stood there. He swiftly turned again. Whatever it might be had dodged, yet more swiftly: stood once more, still, forever, beyond and behind his hope of seeing.

He saw the basin and that it was only itself; but its eye was wicked ice.

Even the sugar curtains were evil, a senselessly fumbling mouth; and the leaves, wavering, stifled their tree like an infestation.

Near the window, a stain on the wallpaper, pale brown, a serpent shape.

Deadly, the opposite window returned his staring.

The cricket cherished what avaricious secret: patiently sculptured what effigy of dread?

The voices buzzed, pleased and oblivious as locusts. They cared nothing for him.

He screamed for his father.

And now the voices changed. He heard his father draw a deep breath and lock it against his palate, then let it out harshly against the bones of his nose in a long snort of annoyance. He heard the Morris chair creak as his father stood up and he heard sounds from his mother which meant that she was disturbed by his annoyance and that she would see to him, Jay; his uncle and his aunt made quick, small, attendant noises and took no further part in the discussion and his father's voice, somewhat less unkind than the snort and the way he had gotten from his chair but still annoyed, saying, "No, he hollered for me, I'll see to him"; and heard his mastering, tired approach. He was afraid, for he was no longer deeply frightened; he was grateful for the evidence of tears.

The room opened full of gold, his father stooped through the door and closed it quietly; came quietly to the crib. His face was kind.

"Wuzza matter?" he asked, teasing gently, his voice at its deepest.

"Daddy," the child said thinly. He sucked the phlegm from his nose and swallowed it.

His voice raised a little, "Why, what's the trouble with my little boy," *he said, and fumbled and got out his handkerchief.* "What's *the* trouble! What's *he* crine *about!" The harsh cloth* smelt of tobacco; with his fingertips, his father removed crumbs of tobacco from the child's damp face.

"Blow," he said. "You know your mamma don't like you to swallah that stuff." He felt the hand strong beneath his head and a sob overtook him as he blew.

"Why, what's wrong?" his father exclaimed; and now his voice was entirely kind. He lifted the child's head a little more, knelt and looked carefully into his eyes; the child felt the strength of the other hand, covering his chest, patting gently. He endeavored to make a little more of his sobbing than came out, but the moment had departed.

"Bad dream?"

He shook his head, no.

"Then what's the trouble?"

He looked at his father.

"Feared a—fraid of the dark?"

He nodded; he felt tears on his eyes.

"Noooooooooo," his father said, pronouncing it like do. "You're a big boy now. Big boys don't get skeered of a little dark. Big boys don't cry. Where's the dark that skeered you? Is it over here?" With his head he indicated the darkest corner. The child nodded. He strode over, struck a match on the seat of his pants.

Nothing there.

"Nothing there that oughtn't to be. . . . Under here?" He indicated the bureau. The child nodded, and began to suck at his lower lip. He struck another match, and held it under the bureau, then under the washstand.

Nothing there. There either.

"Nothing there but an old piece a baby-soap. See?" He held the soap close where the child could smell it; it made him feel much younger. He nodded. "Any place else?"

The child turned and looked through the head of the crib; his father struck a match. "Why, there's poor ole Jackie," he said. And sure enough, there he was, deep in the corner.

He blew dust from the cloth dog and offered it to the child. "You want Jackie?"

He shook his head.

"You don't want poor little ole Jackie? So lonesome? Alayin back there in the corner all this time?"

He shook his head.

"Gettin too big for Jackie?"

He nodded, uncertain that his father would believe him.

"Then you're gettin too big to cry."

Poor ole Jackie.

"Pore ole Jackie."

"Pore little ole Jackie, so lonesome."

He reached up for him and took him, and faintly recalled, as he gave him comfort, a multitude of fire-tipped candles (and bristling needles) and a strong green smell, a dog more gaily colored and much larger, over which he puzzled, and his father's huge face, smiling, saying, "It's a dog." His father too remembered how he had picked out the dog with great pleasure and had given it too soon, and here it was now too late. Comforting gave him comfort and a deep yawn, taking him by surprise, was half out of him before he could try to hide it. He glanced anxiously at his father.

"Gettin sleepy, uh?" his father said; it was hardly even a question.

He shook his head.

"Time you did. Time we all got to sleep."

He shook his head.

"You're not skeered any more are you?"

He considered lying, and shook his head.

"Boogee man, all gone, scared away, huh?"

He nodded.

"Now go on to sleep then, son," his father said. He saw that the child very badly did not want him to go away, and realized suddenly that he might have lied about being scared, and he was touched, and put his hand on his son's forehead. "You just don't want to be lonesome," he said tenderly; "just like little ole Jackie. You just don't want to be left alone." The child lay still.

"Tell you what I'll do," his father said, "I'll sing you one song, and then you be a good boy and go on to sleep. Will you do that?" The child pressed his forehead upward against the strong warm hand and nodded.

"What'll we sing?" his father asked.

"Froggy would a wooin go," said the child; it was the longest.

"At's a long one," his father said, "at's a long old song. You won't ever be awake that long, will you?"

He nodded.

"Ah right," said his father; and the child took a fresh hold on Jackie and settled back looking up at him. He sang very low and very quietly: Frog he would a wooin' go uh-hoooo!, Frog he would a wooin' go uh-*hooooo, uh-hoooooo, and all about the courting-clothes the frog wore, and about the difficulties and ultimate success of the courtship and what several of the neighbors said and who the preacher would be and what he said about the match, uh-hoooo, and finally, what will the weddin supper be uhooooo, catfish balls and sassafras tea uh-hoooo, while he gazed at the wall and the child gazed up into the eyes which did not look at him and into the singing face in the dark. Every couple of verses or so the father glanced down, but the child's eyes were as darkly and steadfastly open at the end of the long song as at the beginning, though it was beginning to be an effort for him.*

He was amused and pleased. Once he got started singing, he always loved to sing. There were ever so many of the old songs that he knew, which he liked best, and also some of the popular songs; and although he would have been embarrassed if he had been made conscious of it, he also enjoyed the sound of his own voice. "Ain't you asleep yet?" *he said, but even the child felt there was no danger of his leaving, and shook his head quite frankly.*

"Sing gallon," he said, for he liked the amusement he knew would come into his father's face, though he did not understand it. It came, and he struck up the song, still more quietly because it was a fast, sassy tune that would be likely to wake you up. He was amused because his son had always mistaken the words "gal and" for "gallon," and because his wife and to a less extent her relatives were not entirely amused by his amusement. They felt, he knew, that he was not a man to take the word "gallon" so purely as a joke; not that the drinking had been any sort of problem, for a long time now. He sang:

I got a gallon an a sugarbabe too, my honey, my baby,
I got a gallon an a sugarbabe too, my honey, my sweet thing.
I got a gallon an a sugarbabe too,
Gal don't love me but my sugarbabe do
       This mornin,
       This evenin,
         So soon.

When they kill a chicken, she saves me the wing, my honey, my
   baby,
When they kill a chicken, she saves me the wing, my honey, my
   sweet thing,
When they kill a chicken, she saves me the wing, my honey
Think I'm aworkin ain't adoin a thing
         This mornin,
         This evenin,
            So soon.

Every night about a half past eight, my honey, my baby,
Every night about a half past eight, my honey, my sweet
   thing
Every night about a half past eight, my honey
Ya find me awaitin at the white folks' gate
         This mornin,
         This evenin,
            So soon.

*The child still stared up at him; because there was so little light
or perhaps because he was so sleepy, his eyes seemed very dark, although the father knew they were nearly as light as his own. He
took his hand away and blew the moisture dry on the child's forehead, smoothed his hair away, and put his hand back:*

*What in the world you doin, Google Eyes? he sang, very slowly,
while he and the child looked at each other,*
         What in the world you doin, Google Eyes?
         What in the world you doin, Google Eyes?
         What in the world you doin, Google Eyes?

*His eyes slowly closed, sprang open, almost in alarm, closed
again.*

         Where did you get them great big Google Eyes?
         Where did you get them great big Google Eyes?
         You're the best there is and I need you in my biz,
         Where in the world did you get them Google Eyes?

*He waited. He took his hand away. The child's eyes opened and
he felt as if he had been caught at something. He touched the forehead again, more lightly. "Go to sleep, honey," he said. "Go on to
sleep now." The child continued to look up at him and a tune
came unexpectedly into his head, and lifting his voice almost to
tenor he sang, almost inaudibly:*

> *Oh, I hear them train car wheels arumblin,*
> *Ann, they're mighty near at hand,*
> *I hear that train come arumblin,*
> *Come arumblin through the land.*
> > *Git on board, little children,*
> > *Git on board, little children,*
> > *Git on board, little children,*
> > *There's room for many and more.*

*To the child it looked as if his father were gazing off into a
great distance and, looking up into these eyes which looked so far
away, he too looked far away:*

> *Oh, I look a way down yonder,*
> *Ann, uh what d'you reckon I see,*
> *A band of shinin angels,*
> *A comin' after me.*
> > *Git on board, little children,*
> > *Git on board, little children,*
> > *Git on board, little children,*
> > *There's room for many and more.*

*He did not look down but looked straight on into the wall in
silence for a good while, and sang:*

> *Oh, every time the sun goes down,*
> *There's a dollar saved for Betsy Brown,*
> > *Sugar Babe.*

*He looked down. He was almost certain now that the child was
asleep. So much more quietly that he could scarcely hear himself,
and that the sound stole upon the child's near sleep like a band of
shining angels, he went on:*

There's a good old sayin, as you all know,
That you can't track a rabbit when there ain't no snow
Sugar Babe.

Here again he waited, his hand listening against the child, for he was so fond of the last verse that he always hated to have to come to it and end it; but it came into his mind and became so desirable to sing that he could resist it no longer:

Oh, tain't agoin to rain on, tain't agoin to snow:

He felt a strange coldness on his spine, and saw the glistening as a great cedar moved and tears came into his eyes:
But the sun's agoin to shine, an the wind's agoin to blow

Sugar Babe.

A great cedar, and the colors of limestone and of clay; the smell of wood smoke and, in the deep orange light of the lamp, the silent logs of the walls, his mother's face, her ridged hand mild on his forehead: Don't you fret, Jay, don't you fret. *And before his time, before ever he was dreamed of in this world, she must have lain under the hand of her mother or her father and they in their childhood under other hands, away on back through the mountains, away on back through the years, it took you right on back as far as you could ever imagine, right on back to Adam, only no one did it for him; or maybe did God?*

How far we all come. How far we all come away from ourselves. So far, so much between, you can never go home again. You can go home, it's good to go home, but you never really get all the way home again in your life. And what's it all for? All I tried to be, all I ever wanted and went away for, what's it all for?

Just one way, you do get back home. You have a boy or a girl of your own and now and then you remember, and you know how they feel, and it's almost the same as if you were your own self again, as young as you could remember.

And God knows he was lucky, so many ways, and God knows he was thankful. Everything was good and better than he could have hoped for, better than he ever deserved; only, whatever it was and however good it was, it wasn't what you once had been, and had lost, and could never have again, and once in a while, once in a long time, you remembered, and knew how far you were away, and it hit you hard enough, that little while it lasted, to break your heart.

He felt thirsty, and images of stealthiness and deceit, of openness, anger and pride, immediately possessed him, and immediately he fought them off. If ever I get drunk again, he told himself proudly, I'll kill myself. And there are plenty good reasons why I won't kill myself. So I won't ever get drunk again.

He felt consciously strong, competent both for himself and against himself, and this pleasurable sense of firmness contended against the perfect and limpid remembrance he had for a moment experienced, and he tried sadly, vainly, to recapture it. But now all that he remembered, clear as it was to him, and dear to him, no longer moved his heart, and he was in this sadness, almost without thought, staring at the wall, when the door opened softly behind him and he was caught by a spasm of rage and alarm, then of shame for these emotions.

"Jay," his wife called softly. "Isn't he asleep yet?"

"Yeah, he's asleep," he said, getting up and dusting his knees. "Reckon it's later than I knew."

"Andrew and Amelia had to go," she whispered, coming over. She leaned past him and straightened the sheet. "They said tell you good night." She lifted the child's head with one hand, while her husband, frowning, vigorously shook his head; "It's all right, Jay, he's sound *asleep;" she smoothed the pillow, and drew away: "They were afraid if they disturbed you they might wake Rufus."*

"Gee. I'm sorry not to see them. Is it so late?"

"You must have been in here nearly an hour*! What was the matter with him?"*

"Bad dream, I reckon; fraid of the dark."

"He's all right? Before he went to sleep, I mean?"

"Sure; he's *all right." He pointed at the dog. "Look what I found."*

"Goodness sake, where was it?"

"Back in the corner, under the crib."

"Well shame on me*! But Jay, it must be awfully dirty!"*

"Naww; I dusted it off."

She said, shyly, "I'll be glad when I can stoop again."

He put his hand on her shoulder. "So will I."

"Jay!" she drew away, really offended.

"Honey!" he said, amused and flabbergasted. He put his arm around her. "I only meant the baby! I'll be glad when the baby's here!"

She looked at him intently (she did not yet realize that she was near-sighted), understood him, and smiled and then laughed softly in her embarrassment. He put his finger to her lips, jerking his head towards the crib. They turned and looked down at their son.

"So will I, Jay darling," she whispered. "So will I."

*H*is mother sang to him too. Her voice was soft and shining gray like her dear gray eyes. She sang, "Sleep baby sleep, Thy father watches the sheep," and he could see his father sitting on a hillside looking at a lot of white sheep in the darkness but why; "thy mother shakes the dreamland tree and down fall little dreams on thee," and he could see the little dreams floating down easily like huge flakes of snow at night and covering him in the darkness like babes in the wood with wide quiet leaves of softly shining light. She sang, "Go tell Aunt Rhoda," three times over, and then, "The old gray goose is dead," and then "She's worth the saving," three times over, and then "To make a featherbed," and then again. Three times over. Go tell Aunt Rhoda; and then again the old gray goose is dead. He did not know what "she's worth the saving" meant, and it was one of the things he always took care not to ask, because although it sounded so gentle he was also sure that somewhere inside it there was something terrible to be afraid of exactly because it sounded so gentle, and he would become very much afraid instead of only a little afraid if he asked and learned what it meant. All the more, because when his mother sang this song he could always see Aunt Rhoda, and she wasn't at all like anybody else, she was like her name, mysterious and gray. She was very tall, as tall even as his father. She stood near a well on a big flat open place of hard bare ground, quite a way from where he saw her from, and even so he could see how very tall she was. Far back behind her there were dark trees without any leaves. She just stood there very quiet and straight as if she were waiting to be gone and told that the old gray goose is dead. She wore a long gray dress with a skirt that touched the ground and her hands were hidden in the great falling folds of the skirt. He could never see her face because it was too darkly within the shadow of the sunbonnet she wore, but from within that shadow he could always just discern the shining of her eyes, and they were looking straight at him, not angrily, and not kindly either, just looking and waiting. She is worth the saving.

She sang, "Swing low, sweet cherryut," and that was the best song of all. "Comin for to care me home." So glad and willing and peaceful. A cherryut was a sort of a beautiful wagon because home was too far to walk, a long, long way, but of course it was like a cherry, too, only he could not understand how a beautiful wagon and a cherry could be like each other, but they were. Home was a long, long way. Much too far to walk and you can only come home when God sends the cherryut for you. And it would care him home. He did not even try to imagine what home was like except of course it was even nicer than home where he lived, but he always knew it was home. He always especially knew how happy he was in his own home when he heard about the other home because then he always felt he knew exactly where he was and that made it good to be exactly there. His father loved to sing this song too and sometimes in the dark, on the porch, or lying out all together on a quilt in the back yard, they would sing it together. They would not be talking, just listening to the little sounds, and looking up at the stars, and feeling ever so quiet and happy and sad at the same time, and all of a sudden in a very quiet voice his father sang out, almost as if he were singing to himself, "Swing low," and by the time he got to "cherryut" his mother was singing too, just as softly, and then their voices went up higher, singing "comin for to carry me home," and looking up between their heads from where he lay he looked right into the stars, so near and friendly, with a great drift of dust like flour across the tip of the sky. His father sang it differently from his mother. When she sang the second "Swing" she just sang "swing low," on two notes, in a simple, clear voice, but he sang "swing" on two notes, sliding from the note above to the one she sang, and blurring his voice and making it more forceful on the first note, and springing it, dark and blurry, off the "l" in "low," with a rhythm that made his son's body stir. And when he came to "Tell all my friends I'm comin too," he started four full notes above her, and slowed up a little, and sort of dreamed his way down among several extra notes she didn't sing, and some of these notes were a kind of blur, like hitting a black note and the next white one at the same time on Grandma's piano, and he didn't sing "I'm comin'" but "I'm uh-comin," and there too, and all through his singing, there was that excitement of rhythm that often made him close his eyes and move his head in contentment.

But his mother sang the same thing clear and true in a sweet, calm voice, fewer and simpler notes. Sometimes she would try to sing it his way and he would try to sing it hers, but they always went back pretty soon to their own way, though he always felt they each liked the other's way very much. He liked both ways very much and best of all when they sang together and he was there with them, touching them on both sides, and even better, from when they sang "I look over Jordan what do I see," *for then it was so good to look up into the stars, and then they sang* "A band of angels comin after me" *and it seemed as if all the stars came at him like a great shining brass band so far away you weren't quite sure you could even hear the music but so near he could almost see their faces and they all but leaned down deep enough to pick him up in their arms.* Come for to care me home.

They sang it a little slower towards the end as if they hated to come to the finish of it and then they didn't talk at all, and after a minute their hands took each other across their child, and things were even quieter, so that all the little noises of the city night raised up again in the quietness, locusts, crickets, footsteps, hoofs, faint voices, the shufflings of a switch engine, and after awhile, while they all looked into the sky, his father, in a strange and distant, sighing voice, said "Well . . ." *and after a little his mother answered, with a quiet and strange happy sadness,* "Yes . . ." *and they waited a good little bit longer, not saying anything, and then his father took him up into his arms and his mother rolled up the quilt and they went in and he was put to bed.*

He came right up to her hip bone; not so high on his father.

She wore dresses, his father wore pants. Pants were what he wore too, but they were short and soft. His father's were hard and rough and went right down to his shoes. The cloths of his mother's clothes were soft like his.

His father wore hard coats too and a hard celluloid collar and sometimes a vest with hard buttons. Mostly his clothes were scratchy except the striped shirts and the shirts with little dots or diamonds on them. But not as scratchy as his cheeks.

His cheeks were warm and cool at the same time and they scratched a little even when he had just shaved. It always tickled, on his cheek or still more on his neck, and sometimes hurt a little, too, but it was always fun because he was so strong.

He smelled like dry grass, leather and tobacco, and sometimes a different smell, full of great energy and a fierce kind of fun, but also a feeling that things might go wrong. He knew what that was because he overheard them arguing. Whiskey.

For awhile he had a big mustache and then he took it off and his mother said, "Oh Jay, you look just worlds *nicer, you have such a* nice *mouth, it's a* shame *to hide it." After awhile he grew the mustache again. It made him look much older, taller and stronger, and when he frowned the mustache frowned too and it was very frightening. Then he took it off again and she was pleased all over again and after that he kept it off.*

She called it mustásh. He called it must'ash and sometimes mush'tash but then he was joking, talking like a darky. He liked to talk darky talk and the way he sang was like a darky too, only when he sang he wasn't joking.

His neck was dark tan and there were deep crisscross cracks all over the back of it.

His hands were so big he could cover him from the chin to his bath-thing. There were big blue strings under the skin on the backs of them. Veins, those were. Black hair even on the backs of the fingers and ever so much hair on the wrists; big veins in his arms, like ropes.

*F*or some time now his mother had seemed different. Almost always when she spoke to him it was as if she had something else very much on her mind, and so was making a special effort to be gentle and attentive to him. And it was as if whatever it was that was on her mind was very momentous. Sometimes she looked at him in such a way that he felt that she was very much amused about something. He did not know how to ask her what she was amused by and as he watched her, wondering what it was, and she watched his puzzlement, she sometimes looked more amused than ever, and once when she looked particularly amused, and he looked particularly bewildered, her smile became shaky and turned into laughter and, quickly taking his face between her hands, she exclaimed, "I'm not laughing at you, darling!" and for the first time he felt that perhaps she was.

There were other times when she seemed to have almost no interest in him, but only to be doing things for him because they had to be done. He felt subtly lonely and watched her carefully. He saw that his father's manner had changed towards her ever so little; he treated her as if she were very valuable and he seemed to be conscious of the tones of his voice. Sometimes in the mornings Grandma would come in and if he was around he was told to go away for a little while. Grandma did not hear well and carried a black ear trumpet which was sticky and sour on the end that she put in her ear; but try as he would they talked so quietly that he could hear very little, and none of it enlightened him. There were special words which were said with a special kind of hesitancy or shyness, such as "pregnancy" and "kicking" and "discharge," but others, which seemed fully as strange, such as "layette" and "basinette" and "bellyband," seemed to inspire no such fear. Grandma also treated him as if something strange was going on, but whatever it was, it was evidently not dangerous, for she was always quite merry with him. His father and his Uncle Andrew and Grandpa seemed to treat him as they always had, though there seemed to be some hidden kind of strain in Uncle Andrew's *feeling for his mother. And Aunt Hannah was the same as ever with him, except that she paid more attention to his mother, now. Aunt Amelia looked at his mother a good deal when she thought nobody else was watching, and once when she saw him watching her she looked quickly away and turned red.*

Everyone seemed either to look at his mother with ill-concealed curiosity or to be taking special pains not to look anywhere except, rather fixedly and cheerfully, into her eyes. For now she was swollen up like a vase, and there was a peculiar lethargic lightness in her face and in her voice. He had a distinct feeling that he should not ask what was happening to her. At last he asked Uncle Andrew, "Uncle Andrew, why is Mama so fat?" and his uncle replied, with such apparent anger or alarm that he was frightened, "Why, don't you know?" *and abruptly walked out of the room.*

Next day his mother told him that soon he was going to have a very wonderful surprise. When he asked what a surprise was she said it was like being given things for Christmas only ever so much nicer. When he asked what he was going to be given she said that she did not mean it was a present, specially for him, or for him to have, or keep, but something for everybody, and especially for them. When he asked what it was, she said that if she told him it wouldn't be a surprise any more, would it? When he said that he wanted to know anyway, she said that she would tell him, only it would be so hard for him to imagine what it was before it came that she thought it was better for him to see it first. When he asked when it was coming she said that she didn't know exactly but very soon now, in only a week or two, perhaps sooner, and she promised him that he would know right away when it did come.

He was aflame with curiosity. He had been too young, the Christmas before, to think of looking for hidden presents, but now he looked everywhere that he could imagine to look until his mother understood what he was doing and told him there was no use looking for it because the surprise wouldn't be here until exactly when it came. He asked where was it, then, and heard his father's sudden laugh; his mother looked panicky and cried, "Jay!" all at once, and quickly informed him, "In heaven; still up in heaven."

He looked quickly to his father for corroboration and his father, who appeared to be embarrassed, did not look at him. He knew about heaven because that was where Our Father was, but that was all he knew about it, and he was not satisfied. Again, however, he had a feeling that he would be unwise to ask more. "Why don't you tell him, Mary?" his father said.

"Oh, Jay," she said in alarm; then said, by moving her lips, "Don't talk of it in front of him!"

"Oh, I'm sorry," and he, too, said with his lips—only a whisper leaked around the silence, "but what's the good? Why not get it over with?"

She decided that it was best to speak openly. "As you know, Jay, I've told Rufus about our surprise that's coming. I told him I'd be glad to tell him what it was, except that it would be so very hard for him to imagine it and such a lovely surprise when he first sees it. Besides, I just have a feeling he might m-make see-oh-en-en-ee-see-tee-eye-oh-en-ess, between—between one thing and another."

"Going to make them, going to make em anyhow," his father said.

"But Jay, there's no use simply forcing it on his att-eigh-ten-ten, his attention, now, is there? Is there, Jay!"

She seemed really quite agitated, he could not understand why.

"You're right, Mary, and don't you get excited about it. I was all wrong about it. Of course I was." And he got up and came over to her and took her in his arms, and patted her on the back.

"I'm probably just silly about it," she said.

"No, you're not one bit silly. Besides, if you're silly about that, so am I, some way. That just sort of caught me off my guard, that about heaven, that's all."

"Well what can you say?"

"I'm Godd—I can't imagine, sweetheart, and I better just keep my mouth shut."

She frowned, smiled, laughed through her nose and urgently shook her head at him, all at once.

And then one day without warning the biggest woman he had ever seen, shining deep black and all in magnificent white with bright gold spectacles and a strong smile like that of his Aunt Hannah, entered the house and embraced his mother and swept down on him crying with delight, "Lawd, chile, how mah baby has growed!", and for a moment he thought that this must be the surprise and looked inquiringly at his mother past the onslaught

*of embraces, and his mother said, "Victoria; Victoria, Rufus!";
and Victoria cried, "Now bless his little heart, how would he remembuh," and all of a sudden as he looked into the vast shining
planes of her smiling face and at the gold spectacles which perched
there as gaily as a dragonfly, there was something that he did remember, a glisten of gold and a warm movement of affection,
and before he knew it he had flung his arms around her neck and
she whooped with astonished joy, "Why God bless him, why chile,
chile," and she held him away from her and her face was the hap-
piest thing he had ever seen, "ah believe you* do *remembuh! Ah
sweah ah believe you* do! Do you?" *She shook him in her happiness.
"Do you remembuh y'old Victoria?" She shook him again. "Do
you, honey?" And realizing at last that he was specifically being
asked, he nodded shyly, and again she embraced him. She smelled
so good that he could almost have leaned his head against her and
gone to sleep then and there.*

"Mama," *he said later, when she was out shopping,* "Victoria
smells awful good."

"Hush, *Rufus," his mother said.* "Now you listen *very carefully* to me, do you hear? Say yes if you hear."

"Yes."

"Now you be *very careful* that you never say anything about
how she smells where Victoria can hear you. Will you? Say yes if
you will."

"Yes."

"Because even though you* like *the way she smells, you might
hurt her feelings terribly if you said any such thing, and you
wouldn't want to hurt dear old Victoria's feelings, I know.
Would you, would* you, *Rufus?"

"No."

"Because Victoria is—is colored, Rufus. That's why her skin is
so dark, and colored people are very sensitive about the way they
smell. Do you know what sensitive means?"

He nodded cautiously.

"It means there are things that hurt your feelings so badly,
things you can't help, that you feel like crying, and nice colored
people feel that way about the way they smell. So you be very careful. Will you? Say yes if you will?"

"Yes."

"Now tell me what I've asked you to be careful about, Rufus."

"*Don't tell Victoria she smells.*"

"*Or say anything about it where she can hear.*"

"*Or say anything about it where she can hear.*"

"*Why not?*"

"*Because she might cry.*"

"*That's right. And Rufus, Victoria is very* very clean. *Absolutely spic and span.*"

Spic an span.

Victoria would not allow his mother to get dinner and after they had eaten she also took entire charge of packing some of his clothes into a box, asking advice, however, on each thing that she took out of the drawer. Then Victoria bathed him and dressed him in clean clothes from the skin out, much to his mystification, and once he was ready, his mother called him to her and told him that Victoria was going to take him on a little visit to stay a few days with Granpa and Granma and Uncle Andrew and Aunt Amelia, and he must be a very good boy and do his very best not to wet the bed because when he came back, very soon now, in only a few more days, the surprise would be there and he would know what it was. He said that if the surprise was coming so soon he wanted to stay and see it, and she replied that that was just why he was going away to Granma's, so the surprise could come all by itself. He asked why it couldn't come if he was there and she said because he might frighten it away because it would still be very tiny and very much afraid, so if he really wanted the surprise to come, he could help more than anything else by being a good boy and going right along to Granma's. Victoria would come and bring him home again just as soon as the surprise was ready for him; "Won't you, Victoria?" And Victoria, who throughout this conversation had appeared to be tremendously amused about something, giving tight little cackles of swallowed laughter and murmuring, "Bless his heart," whenever he spoke, said that indeed she most certainly would.

"*And say your prayers,*" *his mother said, looking at him suddenly with so much love that he was bewildered.* "*You're a big boy now, and you can say them by yourself; can't you?*" *He nodded. She took him by the shoulders and looked at him almost as if she were threading a needle. As she looked at him, some kind of astonishment and some kind of fear grew in her face. Her face began to shine; she smiled; her mouth twitched and trembled. She* took him close to her and her cheek was wet. "God bless my dear little boy," she whispered, "for ever and ever! Amen," and again she held him away; her face looked as if she were moving through space at extraordinary speed. "Good-bye, my darling; oh, good-bye!"

"Now you keep aholt a my hand," Victoria told him, the sun flashing her lenses as she looked both ways from the curb. Arching his neck and his forelegs, a bright brown horse drew a buggy crisply but sedately past; in the washed black spokes, sunlight twittered. Far down the sunlight, like a bumblebee, a yellow streetcar buzzed. The trees moved. They did not wait.

"Victoria," he said.

"Wait, chile," said Victoria, breathing hard. "You wait till we're safe across."

"Now what is it, honey?" she asked, once they had attained the other curb.

"Why is your skin so dark?"

He saw her bright little eyes thrust into him through the little lenses and he felt a strong current of pain or danger. He knew that something was wrong. She did not answer him immediately but peered down at him sharply. Then the current passed and she looked away from him, readjusting her fingers so that she took his hand. Her face looked very far away, and resolute. "Just because, chile," she said in a stern and gentle voice. "Just because that was the way God made me."

"Is that why you're colored, Victoria?"

He felt a change in her hand when he said the word "colored." Again she did not answer immediately, nor would she look at him. "Yes," she said at length, "that's why I'm colored."

He felt deeply sad as they walked along, but he did not know why. She seemed to have no more to say, and he had a feeling that it was not proper for him to say anything either. He watched her great, sad face beneath its brilliant cap, but she did not seem to know that he was watching her or even that he was there. But then he felt the pressure of her hand, and squeezed her hand, and he felt that whatever had been wrong was all right again.

After quite a little while Victoria said, "Chile, I want to tell you sumpn." He waited; they walked. "Victoria don't pay it no mind, because she knows you. She knows you wouldn't say a mean thing to nobody, not for this world. But dey is lots of other colored *folks dat don't know you, honey. And if you say that, you know, about their skins, about their coloh, they goan think you're trying to be mean to em. They goan to feel awful bad and maybe they be mad at you too, when Victoria knows you doan mean nuthin by it, cause they don't know you like Victoria do. Do you understand me, chile?" He looked earnestly up at her. "Don't say nuthin bout skins, or coloh, wheah colored people can heah you. Cause they goana think you're mean to em. So you be careful." And again she squeezed his hand.*

He thought about Victoria while they walked and he wished that she was happy, and he felt that it was because of him that she was not happy. "Victoria," he said.

"What is it, honey?"

"I didn't want to be mean to you."

She stopped abruptly and with creaking and difficulty squat-ted down in the middle of the sidewalk so that a man who was passing stepped suddenly aside and looked coldly down as he went by. She put both hands on his shoulders and her large, kind face and her kind smell were close to him. "Lord bless you, baby, Victo-ria knows you didn't! Victoria knows you is de goodest little boy in all dis world! She just had to tell you, you see. Cause colored folks has a hard time in dis world and she knows you wouldn't want to make em feel bad, not even if you didn't mean to."

"I didn't want to make you feel bad."

"Bless your little heart. I don't feel bad, not one bit. You make me feel happy, and your mama makes me feel happy, and there's not one thing in dis world I wouldn't do for de bofe a you, honey, and dat you know. Dat you know," she said again, rocking her head and smiling and patting both his shoulders. "I missed you terrible, honey," she said, but somehow he felt that she was not talking exactly to him. "I couldn't hardly love you more if you was my own baby." A silence opened around them in which he felt at once great space, the space almost of darkness itself, and great peace and comfort; and the whole of this immensity was pervaded by her vague face and by the waving light of leaves. "Now let's git along," she said, creaking upright and smoothing her starched garments. "We don't want to keep your granmaw waitin."

And there was the dusty ivy on the wall, the small glass-house in front, and on the porch, Aunt Amelia and his grandma. Even when they were still across the street he saw his Aunt Amelia wave and Victoria waved gaily back, chuckling and croaking, "Hello," and he waved too; and Amelia leaned towards his grandmother who sought out and tilted her little trumpet and Amelia leaned close to it and then they both turned to look and Grandma got up and he could hear her high, "Hello," and they were at the front steps, and Grandma came cautiously down the steps from the porch, and they all met on the brick walk in the shade of the magnolia, while Aunt Amelia came up smiling from behind her mother. And soon Victoria left; she disappeared around a corner, a few blocks up the street, handsomely and gradually as a sailboat.

PART II

Chapter 8

A FEW MINUTES before ten, the phone rang. Mary hurried to quiet it. "Hello?"

The voice was a man's, wiry and faint, a country voice. It was asking a question, but she could not hear it clearly.

"Hello?" she asked again. "Will you please talk a little louder? I can't hear. . . . I said I can't hear you! Will you talk a little louder please? Thank you."

Now, straining and impatient, she could hear, though the voice seemed still to come from a great distance.

"Is this Miz Jay Follet?"

"Yes; what is it?" (for there was a silence); "yes, this is she."

After further silence the voice said, "There's been a slight—your husband has been in a accident."

His head! she told herself.

"Yes," she said, in a caved-in voice. At the same moment the voice said, "A serious accident."

"Yes," Mary said more clearly.

"What I wanted to ask, is there a man in his family, some kin, could come out? We'd appreciate if you could send a man out here, right away."

"Yes; yes, there's my brother. Where should he come to?"

"I'm out at Powell Station, at Brannick's Blacksmith Shop, bout twelve miles out the Ball Camp Pike."

"Brannick's bl—"

"B-r-a-n-n-i-c-k. It's right on the left of the Pike comin out just a little way this side, Knoxvul side of Bell's Bridge." She heard muttering, and another muttering voice. "Tell him he can't miss it. We'll keep the light on and a lantern out in front."

"Do you have a doctor?"

"How's that again, ma'am?"

"A doctor, do you have one? Should I send a doctor?"

"That's all right, ma'am. Just some man that's kin."

"He'll come right out just as fast as he can." Walter's auto, she thought. "Thank you very much for calling."

"That's all right, ma'am. I sure do hate to give you bad news."

"Good night."

"Good-bye, ma'am."

She found she was scarcely standing, she was all but hanging from the telephone. She stiffened her knees, leaned against the wall, and rang.

"Andrew?"

"Mary?"

She drew a deep breath.

"Mary."

She drew another deep breath; she felt as if her lungs were not large enough.

"Mary?"

Dizzy, seeing gray, trying to control her shaking voice, she said, "Andrew, there's been an—a man just phoned, from Powell's Station, about twelve miles out towards LaFollette, and he says—he says Jay—has met with a very serious accident. He wants . . ."

"Oh, my God, Mary!"

"He said they want some man of his family to come out just as soon as possible and, help bring him in, I guess."

"I'll call Walter, he'll take me out."

"Yes do, will you, Andrew?"

"Of course I will. Just a minute."

"What?"

"Aunt Hannah."

"May I speak to her when you're through?"

"Certainly. Where is he hurt, Mary?"

"He didn't say."

"Well, didn't you—no matter."

"No I didn't," she said, now realizing with surprise that she had not, "I guess because I was so sure. Sure it's his head, that is."

"Do they—shall I get Dr. Dekalb?"

"He says no; just you."

"I guess there's already a doctor there."

"I guess."

"I'll call Wa—wait, here's Aunt Hannah."

"Mary."

"Aunt Hannah, Jay is in a serious accident, Andrew has to go out. Would you come up and wait with me and get things ready just in case? Just in case he's well enough to be brought home and not the hospital?"

"Certainly, Mary. Of course I will."

"And will you tell Mama and Papa not to worry, not to come out, give them my love. We might as well just be calm as we can, till we know."

"Of course we must. I'll be right up."

"Thank you, Aunt Hannah."

She went into the kitchen and built a quick fire and put on a large kettle of water and a small kettle, for tea. The phone rang.

"Mary! Where do I go!"

"Why, Powell's Station, out the Pike towards . . ."

"I know, but exactly where? Didn't he say?"

"He said Brannick's blacksmith shop. B-r-a-n-n-i-c-k. Do you hear?"

"Yes. Brannick."

"He said they'll keep the lights on and you can't miss it. It's just to the left of the Pike just this side of Bell's Bridge. Just a little way this side."

"All right, Mary, Walter will come by here and we'll bring Aunt Hannah on our way."

"All right. Thank you, Andrew."

She put on more kindling and hurried into the downstairs bedroom. How do I know, she thought; he didn't even say; I didn't even ask. By the way he talks he may be—she whipped off the coverlet, folded it, and smoothed the pad. I'm just simply not going to think about it until I know more, she told herself. She hurried to the linen closet and brought clean sheets and pillowcases. He didn't say whether there was a doctor there or not. She spread a sheet, folded it under the foot of the mattress, pulled it smooth, and folded it under all around. Then she spread her palms along it; it was cold and smooth beneath her hands and it brought her great hope. Oh God, let him be well enough to come home where I can take care of

him, where I can take *good* care of him. How good to rest!
That's all right, ma'am. Just some man that's kin. She spread
the top sheet. That's all right, ma'am. That can mean anything. It can mean there's a doctor there and although it's
serious he has it in hand, under control, it isn't so dreadfully
bad, although he did say it's serious or it can . . . A light
blanket, this weather. Two, case it turns cool. She hurried and
got them, unaware whether she was making such noise as
might wake the children and unaware that even in this swift-
ness she was moving, by force of habit, almost silently. Just
some man that's kin. That means it's bad, or he'd ask for me.
No, I'd have to stay with the children. But *he* doesn't know
there are children. My place'd be home anyhow, getting things
ready, he knows that. He didn't suggest getting anything
ready. He knew I'd know. He is a man, wouldn't occur to him.
She took the end of a pillow between her teeth and pulled the
slip on and plumped it and put it in place. She took the end of
the second pillow between her teeth and bit it so hard the
roots of her teeth ached, and pulled the slip on and plumped
it. Then she set the first pillow up on edge and set the second
pillow on edge against it and plumped them both and
smoothed them and stood away and looked at them with her
head on one side, and for a moment she saw him sitting up in
bed with a tray on his knees as he had sat when he strained his
back, and he looked at her, almost but not quite smiling, and
she could hear his voice, grouchy, pretending to be for the fun
of it. If it's his head, she remembered, perhaps he'll have to lie
very flat.

How do I know? How do I know?

She left the pillows as they were, and turned down the bed
on that side, next the window, and smoothed it. She carefully
refolded the second blanket and laid it on the lower foot of the
bed, no, it would bother his poor feet. She hung it over the
footboard. She stood looking at the carefully made bed, and,
for a few seconds, she was not sure where she was or why she
was doing this. Then she remembered and said, "oh", in a
small, stupefied, soft voice. She opened the window, top and
bottom, and when the curtains billowed she tied them back
more tightly. She went to the hall closet and brought out the
bedpan and rinsed and dried it and put it under the bed. She

went to the medicine chest and took out the thermometer, shook it, washed it in cool water, dried it, and put it beside the bed in a tumbler of water. She saw that the hand towel which covered this table was dusty, and threw it into the dirty-clothes hamper, and replaced it with a fresh one, and replaced that with a dainty linen guest towel upon the border of which pansies and violets were embroidered. She saw that the front pillow had sagged a little, and set it right. She pulled down the shade. She turned out the light and dropped to her knees, facing the bed, and closed her eyes. She touched her forehead, her breastbone, her left shoulder and her right shoulder, and clasped her hands.

"O God, if it be Thy will," she whispered. She could not think of anything more. She made the sign of the Cross again, slowly, deeply, and widely upon herself, and she felt something of the shape of the Cross; strength and quiet.

Thy will be done. And again she could think of nothing more. She got from her knees and without turning on the light or glancing towards the bed, went into the kitchen. The water for tea had almost boiled away. The water in the large kettle was scarcely tepid. The fire was almost out. While she was putting in more kindling, she heard them on the porch.

Hannah came in with her hands stretched out and Mary extended her own hands and took them and kissed her cheek while at the same instant they said, "Mary" and, "my dear"; then Hannah hurried to put her hat on the rack. Andrew stayed at the open door and did not speak but merely kept looking into her eyes; his own eyes were as hard and bright as those of a bird and they spoke to her of a cold and bitter sardonic incredulity, as if he were accusing something or someone (even perhaps his sister) which it was useless beyond words to accuse. She felt that he was saying, "And you can still believe in that idiotic God of yours?" Walter Starr stayed back in the darkness; Mary could just see the large lenses of his glasses, and the darkness of his mustache and of his heavy shoulders.

"Come in, Walter," she said, and her voice was as over-warm as if she were coaxing a shy child.

"We can't stop," Andrew said sharply.

Walter came forward and took her hand, and gently touched her wrist with his other hand. "We shan't be long," he said.

"Bless you," Mary murmured, and so pressed his hand that her arm trembled.

He patted her trembling wrist four times rapidly, turned away saying, "Better be off, Andrew," and went towards his automobile. She could hear that he had left the engine running, and now she realized all the more clearly how grave matters were.

"Everything's ready here in case—you know—he's—well enough to be brought home," Mary told Andrew.

"Good. I'll phone, the minute I know. Anything."

"Yes, dear."

His eyes changed, and abruptly his hand reached out and caught her shoulder. "Mary, I'm so sorry," he said, almost crying.

"Yes, dear," she said again, and felt that it was a vacuous reply; but by the time this occurred to her, Andrew was getting into the automobile. She stood and watched until it had vanished and, turning to go in, found that Hannah was at her elbow.

"Let's have some tea," she said. "I've hot water all ready," she said over her shoulder as she hurried down the hall.

Let her, Hannah thought, following. By all means.

"Goodness no, it's boiled away! Sit down, Aunt Hannah, it'll be ready in a jiff." She hustled to the sink.

"Let me . . ." Hannah began; then knew better, and hoped that Mary had not heard.

"What?" She was drawing the water.

"Just let me know, if there's anything I can help with."

"Not a thing, thank you." She put the water on the stove. "Goodness, sit down." Hannah took a chair by the table. "Everything is ready that I can think of," Mary said. "That we can know about, yet." She sat at the opposite side of the table. "I've made up the downstairs bedroom" (she waved vaguely towards it), "where he stayed when his poor back was sprained, you remember." (Of course I do, Hannah thought; let her talk.) "It's better than upstairs. Near the kitchen and bathroom both and no stairs to climb and of course if need be, that is, if he needs a nurse, night nursing, we can put her in the dining room and eat in the kitchen, or even set up a cot right in the room with him; put up a screen; or if she minds that, why she can just sleep on the living-room davenport and keep the door open between. Don't you think?"

"Certainly," Hannah said.

"I think I'll see if I can possibly get Celia, Celia Gunn, if she's available, or if she's on a case she can possibly leave, it'll be so much nicer for everyone to have someone around who is an old friend, really one of the family, rather than just a complete stranger, don't you think?"

Hannah nodded.

"Even though of course Jay doesn't specially, of course she's really an old friend of mine, rather than Jay's, still, I think it would be more, well, harmonious, don't you think?"

"Yes indeed."

"But I guess it's just as well to wait till we hear from Andrew, not—create any needless disturbance, I guess. After all, it's very possible he'll have to be taken straight to a hospital. The man *did* say it was serious, after all."

"I think you're wise to wait," Hannah said.

"How's that water?" Mary twisted in her chair to see. "Sakes alive, the watched pot." She got up and stuffed in more kindling, and brought down the box of tea. "I don't know's I really want any tea, anyway, but I think it's a good idea to drink something warm while we're waiting, don't you?"

"I'd like some," said Hannah, who wanted nothing.

"Good, then we'll have some. Just as soon as the water's ready." She sat down again. "I thought one light blanket would be enough on a night like this but I've another over the foot of the bed in case it should turn cool."

"That should be sufficient."

"Goodness knows," Mary said, vaguely, and became silent. She looked at her hands, which lay loosely clasped on the table. Hannah found that she was watching Mary closely. In shame, she focused her sad eyes a little away from her. She wondered. It was probably better for her not to face it if she could help until it had to be faced. If it had to be. Just quiet, she said to herself. Just be quiet.

"You know," Mary said slowly, "the queerest thing." She began slowly to turn and rub her clasped fingers among each other. Hannah waited. "When the man phoned," she said, gazing quietly upon her moving fingers, "and said Jay had been in a—serious accident"; and now Hannah realized that Mary was looking at her, and met her brilliant gray eyes; "I felt it just as certainly as I'm sitting here now, 'It's his head.' What do you think of that?" she asked, almost proudly.

Hannah looked away. What's one to say, she wondered. Yet Mary had spoken with such conviction that she herself was half convinced. She looked into an image of still water, clear and very deep, and even though it was dark, and she had not seen so clearly since her girlhood, she could see sand and twigs and dead leaves at the bottom of the water. She drew a deep breath and let it out in a long slow sigh and clucked her tongue once. "We never know," she murmured.

"Of course we just have to wait," Mary said, after a long silence.

"Hyesss," Hannah said softly, sharply inhaling the first of the word, and trailing the sibilant to a hair.

Through their deep silence, at length, they began to be aware of the stumbling crackle of the water. When Mary got up for it, it had boiled half away.

"There's still plenty for two cups," she said, and prepared the strainer and poured them, and put on more water. She lifted the lid of the large kettle. Its sides, below the water line, were richly beaded; from the bottom sprang a leisured spiral of bubbles so small they resembled white sand; the surface of the water slowly circled upon itself. She wondered what the water might possibly be good for.

"Just in case," she murmured.

Hannah decided not to ask her what she had said.

"There's ZuZus," Mary said, and got them from the cupboard. "Or would you like bread and butter? Or toast. I could toast some."

"Just tea, thank you."

"Help yourself to sugar and milk. Or lemon? Let's see, do I have le . . ."

"Milk, thank you."

"Me too." Mary sat down again. "My, it's frightfully *hot* in here!" She got up and opened the door to the porch, and sat down again.

"I wonder what ti . . ." She glanced over her shoulder at the kitchen clock. "What time did they leave, do you know?"

"Walter came for us at quarter after ten. About twenty-five after, I should think."

"Let's see, Walter drives pretty fast, though not so fast as Jay, but he'd be driving faster than usual tonight, and it's just over twelve miles. That would be, supposing he goes thirty miles an hour, that's twelve miles in, let's see, six times four is twenty-four, six times five's thirty, twice twelve is twenty-four, sake's alive, I was always dreadful at arithmetic . . ."

"Say about half an hour, allowing for darkness, and Walter isn't familiar with those roads."

"Then we ought to be hearing pretty soon. Ten minutes. Fifteen at the outside."

"Yes, I should think."

"Maybe twenty, allowing for the roads, but that is a good road out that far as roads go."

"Maybe."

"Why didn't he *tell* me!" Mary burst out.

"What is it?"

"Why didn't I *ask*?" She looked at her aunt in furious bewilderment. "I didn't even *ask*! *How* serious! *Where* is he hurt! Is he living or *dead*!"

There it is, Hannah said to herself. She looked back steadily into Mary's eyes.

"That we simply have to wait to find out," she said.

"Of *course* we have," Mary cried angrily. "That's what's so *unbearable*!" She drank half her tea at a gulp; it burned her painfully but she scarcely noticed. She continued to glare at her aunt.

Hannah could think of nothing to say.

"I'm sorry," Mary said. "You're perfectly right. I've just got to hold myself together, that's all."

"Never mind," Hannah said, and they fell silent.

Hannah knew that silence must itself be virtually unbearable for Mary, and that it would bring her face to face with likelihoods still harder to endure. But she has to, she told herself; and the sooner the better. But she found that she herself could not bear to be present, and say nothing which might in some degree protect, and postpone. She was about to speak when

Mary burst out: "In heaven's *name*, why didn't I ask him! *Why* didn't I? Didn't I *care*?"

"It was so sudden," Hannah said. "It was such a shock."

"You *would* think I'd *ask*, though! Wouldn't you?"

"You thought you knew. You told me you were sure it was his—in the head."

"But how *bad*? *What!*"

We both know, Hannah said to herself. But it's better if you bring yourself to say it. "It certainly wasn't because you didn't care, anyway," she said.

"No. No it certainly wasn't that, but I think I do know what it was. I think, I think I must have been too afraid of what he would have to say."

Hannah looked into her eyes. Nod, she told herself. Say yes I imagine so. Just say nothing and it'll be just as terrible for her. She heard herself saying what she had intended to venture a while before, when Mary had interrupted her: "Do you understand why J—your father stayed home, and your mother?"

"Because I asked them not to come."

"Why did you?"

"Because if all of you came up here in a troop like that, it would be like assuming that—like assuming the very worst before we even know."

"That's why they stayed home. Your father said he knew you'd understand."

"Of course I do."

"We just must try to keep from making any assumptions— *good* or bad."

"I know. I know we must. It's just, this waiting in the dark like this, it's just more than I can stand."

"We ought to hear very soon."

Mary glanced at the clock. "Almost any minute," she said.

She took a little tea.

"I just can't help wondering," she said, "why he didn't say *more*. 'A serious accident,' he said. Not a 'very' serious one. Just 'serious.' Though, goodness knows, that's serious enough. But why couldn't he *say*?"

"As your father says, it's ten to one he's just a plain damned fool," Hannah said.

"But it's such an *important* thing to say, and so *simple* to say, at least to give some general idea about. At least whether he could come home, or go to a hospital, or . . . He didn't say anything about an ambulance. An ambulance would mean hospital, almost for sure. And surely if he meant the—the *very* worst, he'd have just said so straight out and not leave us all on tenterhooks. I know it's just what we have no earthly business guessing about, good *or* bad, but really it does seem to me there's every good reason for hope, Aunt Hannah. It seems to me that if . . ."

The telephone rang; its sound frightened each of them as deeply as either had experienced in her lifetime. They looked at each other and got up and turned towards the hall. "I . . ." Mary said, waving her right hand at Hannah as if she would wave her out of existence.

Hannah stopped where she stood, bowed her head, closed her eyes, and made the sign of the Cross.

Mary lifted the receiver from its hook before the second ring, but for a moment she could neither put it to her ear, nor speak. God *help me, help me*, she whispered. "Andrew?"

"Poll?"

"Papa!" Relief and fear were equal in her. "Have you heard anything?"

"You've heard?"

"No, I said: *Have you heard from Andrew?*"

"No. Thought you might have by now."

"No. Not yet. Not yet."

"I must have frightened you."

"Never mind, Papa. It's all right."

"Sorry as hell, Poll, I shouldn't have phoned."

"Never mind."

"Let us know, quick's you hear anything."

"Of course I will, Papa. I promise. Of course I will."

"Shall we come up?"

"No, bless you, Papa, it's better not, yet. No use getting all worked up till we *know*, is there?"

"That's my girl!"

"My love to Mama."

"Hers to you. Mine, too, needless to say. You let us know."

"Certainly. Good-bye."

"Poll."

"Yes?"

"You know how I feel about this."

"I do, Papa, and thank you. There's no need to say it."

"Couldn't if I tried. Ever. And for Jay as much as you, and your mother too. You understand."

"I do understand, Papa. Good-bye."

"It's only Papa," she said, and sat down, heavily.

"Thought Andrew had phoned."

"Yes . . ." She drank tea. "He scared me half out of my wits."

"He had no business phoning. He was a perfect fool to phone."

"I don't blame him. I think it's even worse for them, sitting down there, than for us here."

"I've no doubt it is hard."

"Papa feels things a lot more than he shows."

"I know. I'm glad you realize it."

"I realize how very much he really does think of Jay."

"Great—heavens, I should hope you do!"

"Well, for a long time there was no reason to be sure," Mary retorted with spirit. "Or Mama either." She waited a moment. "You and her, Aunt Hannah," she said. "You know that. You tried not to show it, but I knew and you knew I did. It's all right, it has been for a long time, but you do know that."

Hannah continued to meet her eyes. "Yes, it's true, Mary. There were all kinds of—terrible misgivings; and not without good reason, as you both came to know."

"Plenty of good reasons," Mary said. "But that didn't make it any easier for us."

"Not for any of us," Hannah said. "Particularly you and Jay, but your mother and father too, you know. Anyone who loved you."

"I know. I *do* know, Aunt Hannah. I don't know how I got onto this tack. There's nothing there to resent any more, or worry over, or be grieved by, for any of us, and hasn't been for a long time, thank God. Why on earth did I get *off* on such a tangent! Let's not say another word about it!"

"Just one word more, because I'm not sure you've ever quite known it. Have you ever realized how very highly your father *always* thought of Jay, right from the very beginning?"

Mary looked at her, sensitively and suspiciously. She thought carefully before she spoke. "I know he's *told* me so. But every time he told me he was warning me, too. I know that, as time passed, he came to think a great deal of Jay."

"He thinks the world of him," Hannah rapped out.

"But, no, I never quite believed he really liked him, or respected him from the first and I never will. I think it was just some kind of soft soap."

"Is Joel a man for soft soap?"

"No," she smiled a little, "he certainly isn't, ordinarily. But what *am* I to make of it? Here he was praising Jay to the skies on the one hand and on the other, why practically in the same breath, telling me one reason after another why it would be plain foolhardiness to marry him. What would *you* think!"

"Can't you see that both things might be so—or that he might very sincerely have felt that both things were so, rather?"

Mary thought a moment. "I don't know, Aunt Hannah. No, I don't see quite how."

"You learned how yourself, Mary."

"Did I!"

"You learned there was a lot in what your father—in all our misgivings, but learning it never changed your essential opinion of him, did it? You found you could realize both things at once."

"That's true. Yes. I did."

"We had to learn more and more that was good. You had to learn more and more that wasn't so good."

Mary looked at her with smiling defiance. "All the same, blind as I began it," she said, "I was more right than Papa, wasn't I? It wasn't a *mistake*. Papa was right there'd be trouble —more than he'll ever know or any of you—but it *wasn't* a mistake. Was it?"

Don't *ask* me, child, *tell* me, Hannah thought. "Obviously not," she said.

Mary was quiet a few moments. Then she said, shyly and proudly, "In these past few months, Aunt Hannah, we've come to a—kind of harmoniousness that—that," she began to shake her head. "I've no business talking about it." Her voice trembled. "Least of all right now!" She bit her lips together, shook her head again, and swallowed some tea, noisily. "The way we've been talking," she blurted, her voice full of tea, "it's just like a post-mortem!" She struck her face into her hands and was shaken by tearless sobbing. Hannah subdued an impulse to go to her side. God help her, she whispered. God keep her. After a little while Mary looked up at her; her eyes were quiet and amazed. "If he dies," she said, "if he's dead, Aunt Hannah, I don't know what I'll do. I just don't know what I'll do."

"God help you," Hannah said; she reached across and took her hand. "God keep you." Mary's face was working. "You'll do well. Whatever it is, you'll do well. Don't you doubt it. Don't you fear." Mary subdued her crying. "It's well to be ready for the worst," Hannah continued. "But we mustn't forget, we don't know yet."

At the same instant, both looked at the clock.

"Certainly by very soon now, he should phone," Mary said. "Unless *he's* had an accident!" she laughed sharply.

"Oh soon, I'm sure," Hannah said. Long before now, she said to herself, if it were anything but the worst. She squeezed Mary's clasped hands, patted them, and withdrew her own hand, feeling, there's so little comfort anyone can give, it'd better be saved for when it's needed most.

Mary did not speak, and Hannah could not think of a word to say. It was absurd, she realized, but along with everything else, she felt almost a kind of social embarrassment about her speechlessness.

But after all, she thought, what *is* there to say! What earthly help am I, or anyone else?

She felt so heavy, all of a sudden, and so deeply tired, that she wished she might lean her forehead against the edge of the table.

"We've simply got to wait," Mary said.

"Yes," Hannah sighed.

I'd better drink some tea, she thought, and did so. Lukewarm and rather bitter, somehow it made her feel even more tired.

They sat without speaking for fully two minutes.

"At least we're given the mercy of a little time," Mary said

slowly, "awful as it is to have to wait. To try to prepare ourselves for whatever it may be." She was gazing studiously into
her empty cup.

Hannah felt unable to say anything.

"Whatever is," Mary went on, "it's already over and done
with." She was speaking virtually without emotion; she was
absorbed beyond feeling, Hannah became sure, in what she
was beginning to find out and to face. Now she looked up at
Hannah and they looked steadily into each other's eyes.

"One of three things," Mary said slowly. "Either he's badly
hurt but he'll live, and at best even get thoroughly well, and at
worst be a helpless cripple or an invalid or his mind impaired."
Hannah wished that she might look away, but she knew that
she must not. "Or he is so terribly hurt that he will die of it,
maybe quite soon, maybe after a long, terrible struggle, maybe
breathing his last at this very minute and wondering where I
am, why I'm not beside him." She set her teeth for a moment
and tightened her lips, and spoke again, evenly: "Or he was
gone already when the man called and he couldn't bear to be
the one to tell me, poor thing.

"One, or the other, or the other. And no matter what,
there's not one thing in this world *or* the next that we can do
or hope or guess at or wish or pray that can change it or help it
one iota. Because whatever is, is. That's all. And all there is
now is to be ready for it, strong enough for it, whatever it may
be. That's all. That's all that matters. It's all that matters because it's all that's possible. Isn't that so?"

While she was speaking, she was with her voice, her eyes and
with each word opening in Hannah those all but forgotten
hours, almost thirty years past, during which the iron of living
had first nakedly borne in upon her being, and she had made
the first beginnings of learning how to endure and accept it.
Your turn now, poor child, she thought; she felt as if a prodigious page were being silently turned, and the breath of its
turning touched her heart with cold and tender awe. Her soul
is beginning to come of age, she thought; and within those
moments she herself became much older, much nearer her
own death, and was content to be. Her heart lifted up in a
kind of pride in Mary, in every sorrow she could remember,
her own or that of others (and the remembrances rushed upon

her); in all existence and endurance. She wanted to cry out *Yes! Exactly! Yes. Yes. Begin to see. Your turn now.* She wanted to hold her niece at arms' length and to turn and admire this blossoming. She wanted to take her in her arms and groan unto God for what it meant to be alive. But chiefly she wanted to keep stillness and to hear the young woman's voice and to watch her eyes and her round forehead while she spoke, and to accept and experience this repetition of her own younger experience, which bore her high and pierced like music.

"Isn't that so?" Mary repeated.

"That and much more," she said.

"You mean God's mercy?" Mary asked softly.

"Nothing of the kind," Hannah replied sharply. "What I mean, I'd best not try to say." (I've begun, though, she reflected; and I startled her, I hurt her, almost as if I'd spoken against God.) "Only because it's better if you learn it for yourself. *By* yourself."

"What do you mean?"

"Whatever we hear, learn, Mary, it's almost certain to be hard. Tragically hard. You're beginning to know that and to face it: very bravely. What I mean is that this is only the beginning. You'll learn much more. Beginning very soon now."

"Whatever it is, I want so much to be *worthy* of it," Mary said, her eyes shining.

"Don't try too hard to be worthy of it, Mary. Don't think of it that way. Just do your best to endure it and let any question of worthiness take care of itself. That's more than enough."

"I feel so utterly unprepared. So little time to prepare *in.*"

"I don't think it's a kind of thing that can be prepared for; it just has to be lived through."

There was a kind of ambition there, Hannah felt, a kind of pride or poetry, which was very mistaken and very dangerous. But she was not yet quite sure what she meant; and of all the times to become beguiled by such a matter, to try to argue it, or warn about it! She's so young, she told herself. She'll learn; poor soul, she'll learn.

Even while Hannah watched her, Mary's face became diffuse and humble. *Oh, not yet*, Hannah whispered desperately to herself. *Not yet.* But Mary said, shyly, "Aunt Hannah, can we kneel down for a minute?"

Not yet, she wanted to say. For the first time in her life she suspected how mistakenly prayer can be used, but she was unsure why. *What can I say*, she thought, almost in panic. *How can I judge?* She was waiting too long; Mary smiled at her, timidly, and in a beginning of bewilderment; and in compassion and self-doubt Hannah came around the table and they knelt side by side. We can be seen, Hannah realized; for the shades were up. *Let us*, she told herself angrily.

"In the name of the Father and of the Son and of the Holy Ghost, Amen," Mary said in a low voice.

"Amen," Hannah trailed.

They were silent and they could hear the ticking of the clock, the shuffling of fire, and the yammering of the big kettle.

God is not here, Hannah said to herself; and made a small cross upon her breastbone, against her blasphemy.

"O God," Mary whispered, "strengthen me to accept Thy will, whatever it may be." Then she stayed silent.

God hear her, Hannah said to herself. God forgive me. God forgive me.

What can I know of the proper time for her, she said to herself. God forgive me.

Yet she could not rid herself: something mistaken, unbearably piteous, infinitely malign was at large within that faithfulness; she was helpless to forfend it or even to know its nature.

Suddenly there opened within her a chasm of infinite depth and from it flowed the paralyzing breath of eternal darkness.

I believe nothing. Nothing whatever.

"Our Father," she heard herself say, in a strange voice; and Mary, innocent of her terror, joined in the prayer. And as they continued, and Hannah heard more and more clearly than her own the young, warm, earnest, faithful, heartsick voice, her moment of terrifying unbelief became a remembrance, a temptation successfully resisted through God's grace.

Deliver us from evil, she repeated silently, several times after their prayer was finished. But the malign was still there, as well as the mercifulness.

They got to their feet.

As it became with every minute and then with every flickering of the clock more and more clear that Andrew had had far more than enough time to get out there, and to telephone, Mary and her aunt talked less and less. For a little while after their prayer, in relief, Mary had talked quite volubly of matters largely irrelevant to the event; she had even made little jokes and had even laughed at them, without more than a small undertone of hysteria; and in all this, Hannah had thought it best (and, for that matter, the only thing possible), to follow suit; but that soon faded away; nor was it to return; now they merely sat in quietness, each on her side of the kitchen table, their eyes cast away from each other, drinking tea for which they had no desire. Mary made a full fresh pot of tea, and they conversed a little about that, and she heated water with which to dilute it, and they discussed that briefly; but such little exchanges wore quickly down into silence. Mary, whispering, "Excuse me," retired to the bathroom, affronted and humbled that one should have to obey such a call at such a time; she felt for a few moments as stupid and enslaved as a baby on its potty, and far more ungainly and vulgar; then, with her wet hands planted in the basin of cold water she stared incredulously into her numb, reflected face, which seemed hardly real to her, until, with shame, she realized that at this of all moments she was mirror gazing. Hannah, left alone, was grateful that we are animals; it was this silly, strenuous, good, humble cluttering of animal needs which saw us through sane, fully as much as prayer; and towards the end of these moments of solitude, with her mind free from the subtle deceptions of concern, she indulged herself in whispering, aloud, "He's dead. There's no longer the slightest doubt of it;" and began to sign herself with the Cross in prayer for the dead, but sharply remembering *we do not know*, and feeling as if she had been on the verge of exercising malign power against him, deflected the intention of the gesture towards God's mercy upon him, in whatsoever condition he might now be. When Mary returned, she put more wood on the fire, looked into the big kettle, saw that a third of the water had boiled away, and refilled it. Neither of them said anything about this, but each knew what the other was thinking, and after they had sat again in silence for well over ten minutes, Mary looked at her aunt who, feeling the eyes upon her, looked into them; then Mary said, very quietly, "I only wish we'd hear now, because I am ready."

Hannah nodded, and felt: you really are. How good it is that you don't even want to touch my hand. And she felt something shining and majestic stand up within her darkness as if to say before God: Here she is and she is adequate to the worst and she has done it for herself, not through my help or even, particularly, through Yours. See to it that You appreciate her.

Mary went on: "It's just barely conceivable that the news is so much less bad than we'd expected, that Andrew is simply too overjoyed with relief to bother to phone, and is bringing him straight home instead, for a wonderful surprise. That would be like him. If things were that way. And like Jay, if they were, if he were, conscious enough, to go right along with the surprise and enjoy it, and just *laugh* at how scared we've been." By her shining eyes, and her almost smiling face, she seemed almost to be believing this while she said it; almost to be sure that within another few minutes it would happen in just that way. But now she went on, "That's just barely conceivable, just about one chance in a million, and so long as there *is* that chance, so long as we don't absolutely know to the contrary, I'm not going to dismiss the possibility entirely from my mind. I'm not going to say he's dead, Aunt Hannah, till I know he is," she said as if defiantly.

"Certainly *not*!"

"But I'm all but certain he is, all the same," Mary said; and saying so, and meeting Hannah's eyes, she could not for a few moments remember what more she had intended to say. Then she remembered, and it seemed too paltry to speak of, and she waited until all that she saw in her mind was again clear and full of its own weight; then again she spoke, "I think what's very much more likely is, that he was already dead when the man just phoned, and that he couldn't bear to tell me, and I don't blame him, I'm grateful he didn't. It ought to come from a man in the family, somebody—close to Jay, and to me. I think Andrew was pretty sure—what was up—when he went out, and had every intention not to leave us in mid-air this way. He meant to phone. But all the time he was hoping against hope, as we all were, and when—when he *saw* Jay—it was more than he could do to phone, and he knew it was more than I could stand to *hear* over a phone, even from him, and so he didn't, and I'm infinitely grateful he didn't. He must have known that as time kept—wearing on in this terrible way, we'd draw our own conclusions and have time to—time. And that's best. He wanted to be with me when I heard. And that's right. So do I. Straight from his lips. I think what he did— what he's doing, it's . . ."

Hannah saw that she was now nearer to breaking than at any time before, and she could scarcely resist her impulse to reach for her hand; she managed, with anguish, to forbid herself. After a moment Mary continued, quietly and in control, "What he's doing is to come in with Jay's poor body to the undertaker's, and soon now he'll come home to us and tell us."

Hannah continued to look into her gentle and ever more incredulous and shining eyes; she found that she could not speak and that she was nodding, as curtly, and rapidly, almost as if she were palsied. She made herself stop nodding.

"That's what I think," Mary said, "and that's what I'm ready for. But I'm not going to say it, or accept it, or do my husband any such dishonor or danger—not until I know beyond recall that it's so."

They continued to gaze into the other's eyes; Hannah's eyes were burning because she felt she must not blink; and after some moments a long, crying groan broke from the younger woman and in a low and shaken voice she said, "Oh I do beseech my God that it not be so," and Hannah whispered, "So do I"; and again they became still, knowing little and seeing nothing except each other's suffering eyes; and it was thus that they were when they heard footsteps on the front porch. Hannah looked aside and downward; a long, breaking breath came from Mary; they drew back their chairs and started for the door.

Chapter 9

S HE was watching for him anxiously as he came back into the living room; he bent to her ear and said, "Nothing."

"No word yet?"

"No." He sat down. He leaned towards her. "Probably too soon to expect to hear," he said.

"Perhaps." She did not resume her mending.

Joel tried again to read *The New Republic*.

"Does she seem well?"

Good God, Joel said to himself. He leaned towards her, "Well's can be expected."

She nodded.

He went back to *The New Republic*.

"Shouldn't we go up?"

That's about all it would need, Joel thought, to have to bellow at us. He leaned towards her and put his hand on her arm. "Better not," he said, "till we know what's what. Too much to-do."

"Too much what?"

"*To-do*. Fuss. Too many people."

"Oh. Perhaps. It does seem our place to, Joel."

Rot! he said to himself. "Our place," he said rather more loudly, "is to stay where she prefers us to be." He began to realize that she had not meant *our place* in mere propriety. Goddamn it all, he thought, why *can't* she be there! He touched her shoulder. "Try not to mind it, Catherine," he said. "I asked Poll, and she said, better not. She said, there's no use our getting all wrought up until we know."

"Very sensible," she said, dubiously.

"*Damned* sensible," he said with conviction. "She's just trying her best to hold herself together," he explained.

Catherine turned her head in courteous inquiry.

"Trying—to hold—herself—together!"

She winced. "Don't—shout at me, Joel. Just speak distinctly and I can hear you."

"I'm sorry," he said; he knew she had not heard. He leaned

close to her ear. "I'm sorry," he said again, carefully and not too loudly. "Jumpy, that's all."

"No matter," she said in that level of her voice which was already old.

He watched her a moment, and sighed with sorrow for her, and said, "We'll know before long."

"Yes," she said. "I presume." She relaxed her hands in her sewing and gazed out across the shadowy room.

It became mere useless torment to watch her; he went back to *The New Republic*.

"I wonder how it happened," she said, after a while. He leaned towards her: "So do I."

"There must have been others injured, as well."

Again he leaned towards her. "Maybe. We don't know."

"Even killed, perhaps."

"We don't—know, Catherine."

"No."

Jay drives like hell broken loose, Joel thought to himself; he decided not to say it. Whatever's happened, he thought, one thing he doesn't need is that kind of talk about him. Or even thinking.

He began to realize, with a kind of sardonic amusement, that he was being superstitious as well as merely courteous. Why I don't want to go up till we hear, too, he said to himself. Hands off. Lap of the gods. Don't rock the boat.

Particularly not a wrecked boat.

"Of course, it does seem to me, Jay drives rather recklessly," Catherine said, carefully.

"*Everybody* does," he told her. *Rather*, indeed!

"I remember I was *most uneasy* when they decided to purchase it."

Well, you're vindicated.

"Progress," he told her.

"Beg pardon?"

"*Progress*. We mustn't—stand—in the way—of Progress."

"No," she said uneasily, "I suppose not."

Good—God, woman!

"That's a joke, Catherine, a very—poor—joke."

Oh.

"I don't think it's a time for levity, Joel."

"Nor do I."

She tilted her head courteously. Taking care not to yell, he said, "You're right. Neither—do—I."

She nodded.

Working his way through another editorial as through barbed wire, Joel thought: I had no business calling her. Why couldn't I trust her to let me know, quick's she heard. Hannah, anyhow.

He pushed ahead with his reading.

A heaviness had begun in him from the moment he had heard of the accident; he had said to himself, *uh-huh*, and without expecting to, had nodded sharply. It had been as if he had known that this or something like it was bound to happen, sooner or later; and he was hardly more moved than surprised. This heaviness had steadily increased while he sat and waited and by now the air felt like iron and it was almost as if he could taste in his mouth the sour and cold, taciturn taste of iron. Well what else are we to expect, he said to himself. What life is. He braced against it quietly to accept, endure it, relishing not only his exertion but the sullen, obdurate cruelty of the iron, for it was the cruelty which proved and measured his courage. Funny I feel so little about it, he thought. He thought of his son-in-law. He felt respect, affection, deep general sadness. No personal grief whatever. After all that struggle, he thought, all that courage and ambition, he was getting nowhere. Jude the Obscure, he suddenly thought; and then of the steady thirty-years' destruction of all of his own hopes. If it has to be a choice between crippling, invalidism, death, he thought, let's hope he's out of it. Even just a choice between that and living on another thirty or forty years; he's well out of it. In my opinion, damn it; not his. He thought of his daughter: all her spirit, which had resisted them so admirably to marry him, then only to be broken and dissolved on her damned piety; all her intelligence, hardly even born, came to nothing in the marriage, making ends meet and again above all, the Goddamned piety; all her innocent eagerness, which it looked as if nothing could ever kill, still sticking its chin out for more. And again, he could feel very little personal involvement. She made her bed, he thought, and she's done a damned creditable job of lying in it; not one whine. And if he's—if that's—finished now, there's hell to pay for her, and little if anything I can do. Now he remembered vividly, with enthusiasm and with sadness, the few years in which they had been such good friends, and for a moment he thought *perhaps again*, and caught himself up in a snort of self-contempt. Bargaining on his death, he thought, as if I were the rejected suitor, primping up for one more try: *once more unto the breach*. Besides, that had never been the real estrangement; it was the whole stinking morass of churchiness that really separated them, and now that was apt to get worse rather than better. Apt? Dead certain to.

And his wife, while she mended, was thinking: such a tragedy. Such a burden for her. Poor dear Mary. How on earth is she to manage. Of course it's still entirely possible that he isn't—passed away. But that could make matters even more— tragic, for both of them. Such an active man, unable to support his family. How dreadful, in any event. Of course, we can help. But not with the hardest of the burden. Poor dear child. And the poor children. And beneath such unspoken words, while with her weak eyes she bent deeply to her mending, her generous and unreflective spirit was more deeply grieved than she could find thought for, and more resolute than any thought for resoluteness could have made it. How very swiftly life goes! she thought. It seems only yesterday that she was my little Mary, or that Jay first came to call. She looked up from her mending into the silent light and shadow, and the kind of long and profound sighing of the heart flowed out of her which, excepting music, was her only way of yielding to sadness.

"We must be very good to them, Joel," she said.

He was startled, almost frightened, by her sudden voice, and he wanted, in some vengeful reflex of exasperation, to ask her what she had said. But he knew he had heard her and, leaning towards her, replied, "Of course we must."

"Whatever has happened."

"Certainly."

He began to realize the emotion, and the loneliness, behind the banality of what she had said; he was ashamed of himself to have answered as if it were merely banal. He wished he could think what to say that would make up for it, but he could not think of what to say. He knew of his wife, with tender amusement, that she almost certainly had not realized his un-kindness, and that she would be hopelessly puzzled if he tried to explain and apologize. Let it be, he thought.

He feels much more than he says, she comforted herself; but she wished that he might ever say what he felt. She felt his hand on her wrist and his head close to hers. She leaned towards him.

"I understand, Catherine," he said.

What does he mean that he understands, Catherine won-dered. Something I failed to hear, no doubt, she thought, though their words had been so few that she could not imag-ine what. But she quickly decided not to exasperate him by a question; she was sure of his kind intention, and deeply touched by it.

"Thank you, Joel," she said, and putting her other hand over his, patted it rapidly, several times. Such endearments, ex-cept in their proper place, embarrassed her and, she had always feared, were still more embarrassing to him; and now, though she had been unable to resist caressing him, and take even greater solace from his gentle pressing of her wrist, she took care soon to remove her hand, and soon after, he took his own away. She felt a moment of solemn and angry gratitude to have spent so many years, in such harmony, with a man so good, but that was beyond utterance; and then once more she thought of her daughter and of what she was facing.

Joel, meanwhile, was thinking: she needs that (pressing her wrist), and, as she shyly took her hand away, I wish I could do more; and suddenly, not for her sake but by an impulse of his own, he wanted to take her in his arms. Out of the question. Instead, he watched her dim-sighted, enduring face as she gazed out once more across the room, and felt a moment of incredulous and amused pride in her immense and unbreak-able courage, and of proud gratitude, regardless of and includ-ing all regret, to have had so many years with such a woman; but that was beyond utterance; and then once more he thought of his daughter and of what she had been through and now must face.

"Sometimes life seems more—cruel—than can be borne," she said. "Theirs, I'm thinking of. Poor Jay's, and poor dear Mary's."

She felt his hand and waited, but he did not speak. She looked toward him, apprehensively polite, her beg-pardon smile, by habit, on her face; and saw his bearded head, unexpectedly close and huge in the light, nodding deeply and slowly, five times.

Chapter 10

ANDREW did not bother to knock, but opened the door and closed it quietly behind him and, seeing their moving shadows near the kitchen threshold, walked quickly down the hall. They could not see his face in the dark hallway but by his tight, set way of walking, they were virtually sure. They were all but blocking his way. Instead of going into the hall to meet him, they drew aside to let him into the kitchen. He did not hesitate with their own moment's hesitation but came straight on, his mouth a straight line and his eyes like splintered glass, and without saying a word he put his arms around his aunt so tightly that she gasped, and lifted her from the floor. "Mary," Hannah whispered, close to his ear; he looked; there she stood waiting, her eyes, her face, like that of an astounded child which might be pleading, Oh, don't hit me; and before he could speak he heard her say, thinly and gently, "He's dead, Andrew, isn't he?" and he could not speak, but nodded, and he became aware that he was holding his aunt's feet off the floor and virtually breaking her bones, and his sister said, in the same small and unearthly voice, "He was dead when you got there"; and again he nodded; and then he set Hannah down carefully on her feet and, turning to his sister, took her by her shoulders and said, more loudly than he had expected, "He was instantly killed," and he kissed her upon the mouth and they embraced, and without tears but with great violence he sobbed twice, his cheek against hers, while he stared downwards through her loose hair at her humbled back and at the changeful blinking of the linoleum; then, feeling her become heavy against him, said, "Here Mary," catching her across the shoulders and helping her to a chair, just as she, losing strength in her knees, gasped, "I've got to sit down," and looked timidly towards her aunt, who at the same moment saying, in a broken voice, "Sit down, Mary," was at her other side, her arm around her waist and her face as bleached and shocking as a skull. She put an arm tightly around each of them and felt gratitude and pleasure, in the firmness and warmth of their moving bodies, and they walked three abreast (like bosom friends, it occurred to her, the three Musketeers) to the nearest chair; and she could see Andrew twist it towards her with his outstretched left hand, and between them, slowly, they let her down into it, and then she could see only her aunt's face, leaning deep above her, very large and very close, the eyes at once intense and tearful behind their heavy lenses, the strong mouth loose and soft, the whole face terrible in love and grief, naked and undisciplined as she had never seen it before.

"Let Papa know and Mama," she whispered. "I promised."

"I will," Hannah said, starting for the hall.

"Walter's bringing them straight up," Andrew said. "They know by now." He brought another chair. "Sit down, Aunt Hannah." She sat and took both Mary's hands in her own, on Mary's knees, and realized that Mary was squeezing her hands with all her strength, and as strongly as she was able. She replied in kind to this constantly, shifting, almost writhing pressure.

"Sit with us, Andrew," Mary said, a little more loudly; he was already bringing a third chair and now he sat, and put his hands upon theirs, and, feeling the convulsing of her hands, thought, Christ, it's as if she were in labor. *And she is.* Thus they sat in silence a few moments while he thought: now I've got to tell them how it happened. In God's name, how can I begin!

"I want whiskey," Mary said, in a small, cold voice, and tried to get up.

"I'll get it," Andrew said, standing.

"You don't know where it is," she said, continuing to put aside their hands even after they were withdrawn. She got up and they stood as if respectfully aside and she walked between them and went into the hall; they heard her rummaging in the closet, and looked at each other. "She needs it," Hannah said.

He nodded. He had been surprised, because of Jay, that there was whiskey in the house; and he was sick with self-disgust to have thought of it. "We all do," he said.

Without looking at them Mary went to the kitchen closet and brought a thick tumbler to the table. The bottle was almost full. She poured the tumbler full while they watched her, feeling they must not interfere, and took a deep gulp and choked on it, and swallowed most of it.

"Dilute it," Hannah said, slapping her hard between the

shoulders and drying her lips and her chin with a dish towel. "It's much too strong, that way."

"I will," Mary croaked, and cleared her throat, "I will," she said more clearly.

"Just sit down, Mary," Andrew and Hannah said at the same moment, and Andrew brought her a glass of water and Hannah helped her to her chair.

"I'm going to have some, too," Andrew said.

"Goodness, do!" said Mary.

"Let me fix us a good strong toddy," Hannah said. "It'll help you to sleep."

"I don't want to sleep," Mary said; she sipped continuously at her whiskey and took plenty of the water. "I've got to learn how it happened."

"Aunt Hannah," Andrew asked quietly, motioning towards the bottle.

"Please."

While he broke ice and brought glasses and a pitcher of water, none of them spoke; Mary sat in a distorted kind of helplessness at once meek and curiously sullen, waiting. Months later, seeing a horse which had fallen in the street, Andrew was to remember her; and he was to remember it wasn't drunkenness, either. It was just the flat of the hand of Death.

"Let me pour my own," Mary said. "Because," she added with deliberation while she poured, "I want it just as strong as I can stand it." She tasted the dark drink, added a little more whiskey, tasted again, and put the bottle aside. Hannah watched her with acute concern, thinking, if she gets drunk tonight, and if her mother sees her drunk, she'll half die of shame, and thinking, nonsense. It's the most sensible thing she could do.

"Drink it very slowly, Mary," Andrew said gently. "You aren't used to it."

"I'll take care," Mary said.

"It's just the thing for shock," Hannah said.

Andrew poured two small straight drinks and gave one to his aunt; they drank them off quickly and took water, and he prepared two pale highballs.

"Now, Andrew, I want to hear all about it," Mary said.

He looked at Hannah.

"Mary," he said. "Mama and Papa'll be here any minute. You'd just have to hear it all over again. I'll tell you, of course, if you prefer, right away but—could you wait?"

But even as he was speaking she was nodding, and Hannah was saying, "Yes, child," as all three thought of the confusions and repetitions which were, at best, inevitable. Now after a moment Mary said, "Anyway, you say he didn't have to suffer. *Instantly*, you said."

He nodded, and said, "Mary, I saw him—at Roberts'. There was just one mark on his body."

She looked at him. "His head."

"Right at the exact point of the chin, a small bruise. A cut so small—they can close it with one stitch. And a little blue bruise on his lower lip. It wasn't even swollen."

"That's all," she said.

"All," Hannah said.

"That's all," Andrew said. "The doctor said it was concussion of the brain. It was instantaneous."

She was silent; he felt that she must be doubting it. Christ, he thought furiously, at least she could be spared *that*!

"He can't have suffered, Mary, not even for a fraction of a second. Mary, I saw his face. There wasn't a glimmer of pain in it. Only—a kind of surprise. Startled."

Still she said nothing. I've got to make her sure of it, he thought. How in heaven's name can I make it clearer? If necessary, I'll get hold of the doctor and make him tell her hims . . .

"He never knew he was dying," she said. "Not a minute, not one moment, to know, 'my life is ending.'"

Hannah put a quick hand to her shoulder; Andrew dropped to his knees before her; took her hands and said, most earnestly, "Mary, in God's name be thankful if he didn't! That's a hideous thing for a man in the prime of life to have to know. He wasn't a *Christian*, you know," he blurted it fiercely. "He didn't have to make his peace with God. He was a man, with a wife and two children, and I'd say that sparing him *that* horrible knowledge was the one thing we can thank God for!" And he added, in a desperate voice, "I'm so terribly sorry I said that, Mary!"

But Hannah, who had been gently saying, "He's right,

Mary, he's right, be thankful for that," now told him quietly, "It's all right, Andrew"; and Mary, whose eyes fixed upon his, had shown increasing shock and terror, now said tenderly, "Don't mind, dear. Don't be sorry. I understand. You're right."

"That venomous thing I said about Christians," Andrew said after a moment. "I can never forgive myself, Mary."

"Don't grieve over it, Andrew. Don't. Please. Look at me, please." He looked at her. "It's true I was thinking as I was bound to as a Christian, but I was forgetting we're human, and you set me right and I'm thankful. You're right. Jay wasn't —a religious man, in that sense, and to realize could have only been—as you said for him. Probably as much so, even if he were religious." She looked at him quietly. "So just please know I'm not hurt or angry. I needed to realize what you told me and I thank God for it."

There was a noise on the porch; Andrew got from his knees and kissed his sister on the forehead. "Don't be sorry," she said. He looked at her, tightened his lips, and hurried to the door.

"Papa," he said, and stood aside to let him past. His mother fumbled for his arm, and gripped it hard. He put his hand gently across her shoulders and said, next her ear, "They're back in the kitchen"; she followed her husband. "Come in, Walter."

"Oh no. Thank you," Walter Starr said. "These are family matters. But if there's . . ."

Andrew took him by the arm. "Come in a minute, anyway," he said. "I know Mary'll want to thank you."

"Well now . . ." Andrew led him in.

"Papa," Mary said, and got up and kissed him. He turned with her towards her mother. "Mama?" she said in a pinched, almost crying voice, and they embraced. "There, there, there," her mother said in a somewhat cracked voice, clapping her loudly on the back. "Mary, dear. There, there, there!"

She saw Walter Starr, looking as if he were sure he was unwelcome. "Why, Walter!" she whispered, and hurried to meet him. He put out his hand, looking frightened, and said, "Mrs. Follet, I just couldn't ever . . ."

She threw her arms around him and kissed him on the cheek. "Bless you," she whispered, crying softly.

"There now," he said, blushing deeply and trying to embrace

and to sustain her without touching her too closely. "There now," he said again.

"I must stop this," she said, drawing away from him and looking about wildly for something.

"Here," said Andrew and her father and Walter Starr, each offering a handkerchief. She took her brother's, blew her nose, dried her eyes, and sat down. "Sit down, Walter."

"Oh thank you, no. I don't think," Walter said. "Only dropped in a moment; really must be off."

"Why Walter, what nonsense, you're one of the family," Mary said, and those who could hear nodded and murmured "Of course," although they knew this was embarrassing for him, and hoped he would go home.

"Now that's ever so kind," Walter said, "but I can't stay. Really must be off. Now if . . ."

"Walter, I want to thank you," she said; for now she too had reconsidered.

"So do we all," Andrew said.

"More than I can say," Mary finished.

He shook his head. "Nothing. Nothing," he said. "Now I just want you to know, if there's anything in the world I can do, be of help in any way, let me please, don't hesitate to tell me."

"Thank you, Walter. And if there is, we certainly will. Gratefully."

"Good night then."

Andrew walked with him to the front door. "Just let me know, Andrew. *Anything*," Walter said.

"I will and thank you," Andrew replied. Their eyes met, and for a moment both were caught in astonishment. *He wishes it was me!* Andrew thought. *He wishes it was himself!* Walter thought. *Perhaps I do, too*, Andrew thought, and once again, as he had felt when he first saw the dead body, he felt absurd, ashamed, guilty almost of cheating, even of murder, in being alive.

"Why Jay, of all people?" Andrew said, in a low voice.

Still watching his splintered eyes, Walter heavily shook his head.

"Good night, Andrew."

"Good night, Walter."

He shut the door.

Mary's father caught her eye; with his chin he beckoned her to a corner of the kitchen. "I want to talk to you alone a minute," he said in a low voice.

She looked at him thoughtfully, then took her glass from the table, said, "Excuse us a minute," over her shoulder, and ushered him into the room she had prepared for her husband. She turned on the bedside lamp, quietly closed both doors, and stood looking at him, waiting.

"Sit down, Poll," he said.

She looked about. One of them would have to sit on the bed. It was neatly laid open, cool and pleasant below the plumped pillows.

"I had it all ready," she said, "but he never came back."

"What's that?"

"Nothing, Papa."

"Don't stay on your feet," he said. "Let's sit down."

"I don't care to."

He came over to her and took her hand and looked at her searchingly. Why he's just my height, she realized again. She saw how much his eyes, in sympathy and pain, were like his sister's, tired, tender and resolute beneath the tired, frail eyelids. He could not speak at first.

You're a *good* man, she said to herself, and her lips moved. A good, good man. My father. In an instant she experienced afresh the whole of their friendship and estrangement. Her eyes filled with tears and her mouth began to tremble. "Papa," she said. He took her close to him and she cried quietly.

"It's hell, Poll," she heard him say. "Just hell. It's just plain hell." For a few moments she sobbed so deeply that he said nothing more, but only stroked the edge of her back, over and over, from her shoulder to her waist, and cried out within himself in fury and disgust, God*damn* it! God *damn* such a life! She's too young for this. And thinking of that, it occurred to him that it was at just her age that his own life had had its throat twisted, and not by death, but by her own birth and her brother's.

"But you gotta go through with it," he said.

Against his shoulder he could feel her vigorous nodding. You will, he thought; you've got spunk.

"No way out of it," he said.

"I think I *will* sit down." She broke from him and with an almost vindictive sense of violation sat heavily at the edge of the bed, just where it was turned down, next the plumped pillows. He turned the chair and sat with her knee to knee.

"Something I've got to tell you," he said.

She looked at him and waited.

"You remember what Cousin Patty was like? When she lost George?"

"Not very well. I wasn't more than five or six."

"Well, I do. She ran around like a chicken with its head off. 'Oh, why does it have to be *me*? What did *I* ever do that it happened to *me*?' Banging her head against the furniture, trying to stab herself with her scissors, yelling like a stuck pig: you could hear her in the next block."

Her eyes became cold. "You needn't worry," she said.

"I don't, because you're not a fool. But *you'd* better, and that's what I want to warn you about."

She kept looking at him.

"See here, Poll," he said. "It's bad enough right now, but it's going to take a while to sink in. When it really sinks in it's going to be any amount worse. It'll be so much worse you'll think it's more than you can bear. Or any other human being. And worse than that, you'll have to go through it alone, because there isn't a thing on earth any of us can do to help, beyond blind animal sympathy."

She was gazing slantwise towards the floor in some kind of coldly patient irony; he felt sick to death of himself.

"Look at me, Poll," he said. She looked at him. "That's when you're going to need every ounce of common sense you've got," he said. "Just spunk won't be enough; you've got to have gumption. You've got to bear it in mind that nobody that ever lived is specially privileged; the axe can fall at any moment, on any neck, without any warning or any regard for justice. You've got to keep your mind off pitying your own rotten luck and setting up any kind of a howl about it. You've got to remember that things as bad as this and a hell of a lot worse have happened to millions of people before and that they've come through it and that you will too. You'll bear it because there isn't any choice—except to go to pieces. You've got two children to take care of. And regardless of that you owe it to yourself and you owe it to him. You understand me."

"Of course."

"I know it's just unmitigated tommyrot to try to say a word about it. To say nothing of brass. All I want is to warn you that a lot worse is yet to come than you can imagine yet, so for God's sake brace yourself for it and try to hold yourself together." He said, with sudden eagerness, "It's a kind of test, Mary, and it's the only kind that amounts to anything. When something rotten like this happens. Then you have your choice. You start to really be alive, or you start to die. That's all." Watching her eyes, he felt fear for her and said, "I imagine you're thinking about your religion."

"I am," she said, with a certain cool pride.

"Well, more power to you," he said. "I know you've got a kind of help I could never have. Only one thing: take the greatest kind of care you don't just—crawl into it like a hole and hide in it."

"I'll take care," she said.

She means there is nothing I can tell her about that, he thought; and she is right.

"Talk to Hannah about it," he said.

"I will, Papa."

"One other thing."

"Yes?"

"There are going to be financial difficulties. We'll see just what, and just how to settle them, course of time. I just want to *take* that worry off your hands. Don't worry. We'll work that out."

"Bless you, Papa."

"Rats. Drink your drink."

She drank deeply and shuddered.

"Take all you can without getting drunk," he said. "I wouldn't give a whoop if you got blind drunk, best thing you could do. But you've got tomorrow to reckon with." And tomorrow and tomorrow.

"It doesn't seem to have any effect," she said, her voice still liquid. "The only times I drank before I had a terribly weak head, just one drink was enough to make me absolutely squiffy.

But now it doesn't seem to have any effect in the slightest."
She drank some more.

"Good," he said. "That can happen. Shock, or strain. I
know once when your mother was very sick I . . ." They both
remembered her sickness. "No matter. Take all you want and
I've more if you want it, but keep an eye on yourself. It can hit
you like a ton of bricks."

"I'll be careful."

"Time we went back to the others." He helped her to her
feet, and put a hand on her shoulder. "Just bear in mind what
I said. It's just a test, and it's one that good people come
through."

"I will, Papa, and thank you."

"I've got absolute confidence in you," he said, wishing that
this was entirely true, and that she could entirely care.

"Thank you, Papa," she said. "That's going to be a great
help to know."

Her hand on the doorknob, she turned off the light and
preceded him into the kitchen.

Chapter 11

"WHY WHERE . . ." Mary began, for there was nobody in the kitchen.

"Must be in the living room," her father said, and took her arm.

"There's more room here," Andrew told her, as they came in. Although the night was warm, he was nursing a small fire. All the shades, Mary noticed, were drawn to the window sills.

"Mary," her mother said loudly, patting a place beside her on the sofa. Mary sat beside her and took her hand. Her mother took Mary's left hand in both of her hands, drew it into her lap, and pressed it against her thin thighs with all her strength.

Her aunt sat to one side of the fireplace and now her father took a chair at the other side. The Morris chair just stood there empty beside its reading lamp. Even after the fire was going nicely, Andrew squatted before it, making small adjustments. Nobody spoke, and nobody looked at the Morris chair or at another person. The footsteps of a man, walking slowly, became gradually louder along the sidewalk, and passed the house, and diminished into silence; and in the silence of the universe they listened to their little fire.

Finally Andrew stood up straight from the fire and they all looked at his despairing face, and tried not to demand too much of him with their eyes. He looked at each of them in turn, and went over and bent deeply towards his mother.

"Let me tell you, Mama," he said. "That way, we can all hear. I'm sorry, Mary."

"Dear," his mother said gratefully, and fumbled for his hand and patted it. "Of course," Mary said, and gave him her place beside the "good" ear. They shifted to make room, and she sat at her mother's deaf side. Again her mother caught her hand into her lap; with the other, she tilted her ear trumpet. Joel leaned toward them, his hand behind his ear; Hannah stared into the wavering hearth.

"He was all alone," Andrew said, not very loudly but with

the most scrupulous distinctness. "Nobody else was hurt, or even in the accident."

"That's a mercy," his mother said. It was, they all realized; yet each of them was shocked. Andrew nodded sharply to silence her.

"So we'll never know exactly how it happened," he went on. "But we know *enough*," he said, speaking the last word with a terrible and brutal bitterness.

"*Mmh*," his father grunted, nodding sharply; Hannah drew in and let out a long breath.

"I talked with the man who found him. He was the man who phoned you, Mary. He waited there for me all that time because he thought it would help if—if the man who first saw Jay was there to tell one of us all he could. He told me all he knew of course," he said, remembering, with the feeling that he would never forget it, the awed, calm, kind, rural face and the slow, careful, half-literate voice. "He was just as fine as a human being can be." He felt a kind of angry gratitude that such a man had been there, and had been there first. Jay couldn't have asked for anyone better, he said to himself. Nobody could.

"He said he was on his way home, about nine o'clock, coming in towards town, and he heard an auto coming up from behind, terrifically fast, and coming nearer and nearer, and he thought, There's somebody that's sure got to get some place in a bad hurry" ("He was hurrying home," Mary said) "or else he's crazy" (he had said "crazy drunk").

"He wasn't crazy," Mary said. "He was just trying to get home (bless his heart), he was so much later than he'd said."

Andrew looked at her with dry, brilliant eyes and nodded.

"He'd told me not to wait supper," she said, "but he wanted to get home before the children were asleep."

"What is it?" her mother asked, with nervous politeness.

"Nothing important, Mama," Andrew said gently. "I'll explain later." He drew a deep breath in very sharply, and felt less close to tears.

"All of a sudden, he said, he heard a perfectly terrifying noise, just a second or two, and then dead silence. He knew it must be whoever was in that auto and that they must be in bad trouble, so he turned around and drove back, about a quarter of a mile, he thinks, just the other side of Bell's Bridge. He told me he almost missed it altogether because there was nothing on the road and even though he'd kind of been expecting that and driving pretty slowly, looking off both sides of the road, he almost missed it because just next the bridge on that side, the side of the road is quite a steep bank."

"I know," Mary whispered.

"But just as he came off the far end of the bridge—you come down at a sort of angle, you know . . ."

"I know," Mary whispered.

"Something caught in his lights and it was one of the wheels of the automobile." He looked across his mother and said, "Mary, it was still turning."

"Beg pardon?" his mother said.

"It was still, turning," he told her. "The wheel he saw."

"Mercy, Andrew," she whispered.

"*Hahh!*" her husband exclaimed, almost inaudibly.

"He got out right away and hurried down there. The auto was upside down and Jay . . ."

Although he did not feel that he was near weeping he found that for a moment he could not speak. Finally he said, "He was just lying there on the ground beside it, on his back, about a foot away from it. His clothes were hardly even rumpled."

Again he found that he could not speak. After a moment he managed to force himself to.

"The man said somehow he was sure he was—dead—the minute he saw him. He doesn't know how. Just some special kind of stillness. He lighted matches though, of course, to try and make sure. Listened for his heartbeat and tried to feel for his pulse. He moved his auto around so he could see by the headlights. He couldn't find anything wrong except a little cut, exactly on the point of his chin. The windshield of Jay's car was broken and he even took a piece of it and used it like a mirror, to see if there was any breath. There wasn't. After that he just waited a few minutes until he heard an auto coming and stopped them and told them to get help as soon as possible."

"Did they get a doctor?" Mary asked.

"Mary says, 'Did they get a doctor,'" Andrew said to his mother. "Yes, he told them to and they did. And other people.

Including—Brannick, Papa," he said; "that blacksmith you know. It turns out he lives quite near there."

"*Huh!*" said Joel.

"The doctor said the man was right," Andrew said. "He said he must have been killed instantly. They found who he was, by papers in his pocket, and that was when he phoned you, Mary.

"He asked me if I'd please tell you how dreadful he felt to give you such a message, leaving you uncertain all this time. He just couldn't stand to be the one to tell you the whole thing— least of all just bang like that, over a phone. He thought it ought to be somebody in the family."

"That's what I imagined," Mary said.

"He was right," Hannah said; and Joel and Mary nodded and said, "Yes."

"By the time Walter and I got there, they'd moved him," Andrew said. "He was at the blacksmith shop. They'd even brought in the auto. You know, they say it ran perfectly. Except for the top, and the windshield, it was hardly even damaged."

Joel asked, "Do they have any idea what happened?"

Andrew said to his mother, "Papa says, 'Do they have any idea how it happened?' " She nodded, and smiled her thanks, and tilted her trumpet nearer his mouth.

"Yes, some idea," Andrew said. "They showed me. They found that a cotter pin had worked loose—that is, it had fallen all the way out—this cotter pin had fallen out, that held the steering mechanism together."

"*Hahh?*"

"Like this, Mama—*look*," he said sharply, thrusting his hands under her nose.

"Oh *excuse* me," she said.

"See here," he said; he had locked a bent knuckle between two bent knuckles of the other hand. "As if it were to hold these knuckles together—see?"

"Yes."

"There would be a hole right through the knuckles and that's where the cotter pin goes. It's sort of like a very heavy hairpin. When you have it all the way through, you open the two ends flat—spread them—like this . . ." he showed her his thumb and forefinger, together, then spread them as wide and flat as he could. "You understand?"

"No matter."

"Let it go, son," his father said.

"It's all right, Mama," Andrew said. "It's just something that holds two parts together—in this case, his steering gear—what he guided the auto with. Th . . ."

"*I understand*," she said impatiently.

"*Good*, Mama. Well this cotter pin, that held the steering mechanism together down underneath the auto, where there was no chance of seeing it, had fallen out. They couldn't find it anywhere, though they looked all over the place where it happened and went over the road for a couple of hundred yards with a fine-tooth comb. So they think it may have worked loose and fallen out quite a distance back—it could be, even miles, though probably not so far. Because they showed me," again he put his knuckles where she could see, "even without the pin, those two parts might hang together," he twisted them, "you might even steer with them, and not have the slightest suspicion there was anything wrong, if you were on fairly smooth road, or didn't have to wrench the wheel, but if you hit a sharp bump or a rut or a loose rock, or had to twist the wheel very hard very suddenly, they'd come apart, and you'd have no control over anything."

Mary put her hands over her face.

"What they think is that he must have hit a loose rock with one of the front wheels, and that gave everything a jolt and a terrific wrench at the same time. Because they found a rock, oh, half the size of my head, down in the ditch, very badly scraped and with tire marks on it. They showed me. They think it must have wrenched the wheel right out of his hands and thrown him forward very hard so that he struck his chin, just one sharp blow against the steering wheel. And that must have killed him on the spot. Because he was thrown absolutely clear of the car as it ran off the road—they showed me. I never saw anything to equal it. Do you know what happened? That auto threw him out on the ground as it careened down into that sort of flat, wide ditch, about five feet down from the road; then it went straight on up an eight-foot embankment. They showed me the marks where it went, almost to the top, and then toppled backward and fell bottom side up right beside him, without even grazing him!"

"Gracious," Mary whispered; "*Tst*," Hannah clucked.

"How are they so sure it was—instant, Andrew?" Hannah asked.

"Because if he'd been conscious they're sure he wouldn't have been thrown out of the auto, for one thing. He'd have grabbed the wheel, or the emergency brake, still trying to control it. There wasn't time for that. There wasn't any time at all. At the most there must have been just the tiniest fraction of a second when he felt the jolt and the wheel was twisted out of his hand, and he was thrown forward. The doctor says he probably never even knew what hit him—hardly even felt the impact, it was so hard and quick."

"He may have just been unconscious," Mary groaned through her hands. "Or conscious and—pparalyzed; unable to speak or even seem to breathe. If only there'd been a doctor, right there, mayb . . ."

Andrew reached across his mother and touched her knees. "No, Mary," he said. "I have the doctor's word for that. He says the only thing that could have caused death was concussion of the brain. He says that when that—happens to kill, it—does so instantly, or else takes days or weeks. I asked him about it very particularly because—I knew you'd want to be sure just how it was. Of course I wondered the same thing. He said it couldn't have been even a few seconds of unconsciousness, and then death, because nothing more happened, after that one blow, that could have added to what it did. He said it's even more sudden than electrocution. Just an enormous shock to the brain. The quickest death there is." He returned to his mother. "I'm sorry, Mama," he said. "Mary was saying, perhaps he was only unconscious. That maybe if the doctor had been there right on the spot, he could have been saved. I was telling her, no. Because I asked the doctor everything I could think to, about that. And he said no. He says that when a concussion of the brain—is fatal—it's the quickest death there is."

He looked at each of them in turn. In a light, vindictive voice he told them, "He says it was just a chance in a million."

"Good God, Andrew," his father said.

"Just that one tiny area, at just a certain angle, and just a certain sharpness of impact. If it had been even a half an inch to one side, he'd be alive this minute."

"Shut up, Andrew," his father said harshly; for with the last few words that Andrew spoke, a sort of dilation had seized Mary, so that she had almost risen from her place, seeming larger than herself, and then had collapsed into a shattering of tears.

"Oh Mary," Andrew groaned, and hurried to her, while her mother took her head against her breast. "I'm so sorry. God, what possessed me! I must be out of my mind!" And Hannah and Joel had gotten from their chairs and stood nearby, unable to speak.

"Just—have a little *mercy*," she sobbed. "A little *mercy*."

Andrew could say only, "I'm so sorry. I'm *so* sorry, Mary," and then he could say nothing.

"Let her cry," Joel said quietly to his sister, and she nodded. As if anything on earth could stop her, he said to himself.

"O God, *forgive* me," Mary moaned. "*Forgive* me! *Forgive* me! It's just more than I can bear! Just more than I can bear! *Forgive* me!" And Joel, with his mouth fallen open, wheeled upon his sister and stared at her; and she avoided his eyes, saying to herself, *No, No*, and *protect her, O God, protect Thy poor child and give her strength*; and Andrew, his face locked in a murderer's grimace, contained the furious and annihilating words which were bursting within him to be spoken, groaned within himself, *God, if You exist, come here and let me spit in Your face. Forgive her, indeed!*

Then Hannah moved him aside and stooped before Mary, taking her wrists and talking earnestly into her streaming hands: "Mary, listen to me. Mary. There's nothing to ask forgiveness for. There's nothing to ask forgiveness for, Mary. Do you hear me? Do you hear me, Mary?" Mary nodded within her hands. "God would never ask of you not to grieve, not to cry. Do you hear? What you're doing is absolutely natural, absolutely right. Do you hear! You wouldn't be human if you did otherwise. Do you hear me, Mary? You're not human to ask His forgiveness. You're wrong. You're terribly mistaken. Do you hear me, my dear? Do you hear me?"

While she was speaking, Mary, within her hands, now nodded and now shook her head, always in contradiction of what her aunt was saying, and now she said, "It isn't what you think. I spoke to Him as if He had no mercy!"

"Andrew? Andrew was ju . . ."

"No: to God. As if He were trying to rub it in. Torment me. That's what I asked forgiveness for."

"There, Mary," her mother said; she could hear virtually nothing of what was said, but she could feel that the extremity of the crying had passed.

"Listen, Mary," Hannah said, and she bent so close to her that she could have whispered. "Our Lord on the Cross," she said, in a voice so low that only Mary and Andrew could hear, "do you remember?"

"My God, my God, why hast Thou forsaken me?"

"Yes. And then did He ask forgiveness?"

"He was God. He didn't have to."

"He was human, too. And He didn't ask it. Nor was it asked of Him to ask it, no more are you. And no more *should* you. What was it He said, instead? The very next thing he said."

"Father, into Thy hands I commend my spirit," she said, taking her hands from her face and looking meekly at her aunt.

"Into Thy hands I commend my spirit," her aunt said.

"There, dear," her mother said, and Mary sat upright and looked straight ahead.

"Please don't feel sorry, Andrew," she said. "You're right to tell me every last bit you know. I want to know—all of it. It was just—it just overwhelmed me for a minute."

"I shouldn't tell you so much all in a heap."

"No, that's better. Than to keep hearing—horrible little new things, just when you think you've heard the worst and are beginning to get used to it."

"That's right, Poll," her father said.

"Now just go straight on telling me. Everything there is to tell. And if I do break down, why don't reproach yourself. Remember I *asked* you. But I'll try to not. I think I'll be all right."

"All right, Mary."

"Good, Poll," her father said. They all sat down again.

"And Andrew, if you'll get it for me, I think I'd like some more whiskey."

"Of course I will." He had brought the bottle in; he took her glass to the table.

"Not quite so strong as last time, please. Pretty strong, but not so strong as that."

"This all right?"

"A little more whiskey, please."

"Certainly."

"That looks all right."

"You all right, Poll?" her father asked. "Isn't going to your head too much?"

"It isn't going anywhere so far as I can tell."

"Good enough."

"I think perhaps it would be best if we didn't—prolong the discussion any further tonight," Catherine said, in her most genteel manner; and she patted Mary's knee.

They looked at her with astonishment and suddenly Mary and then Andrew began to laugh, and then Hannah began to laugh, and Joel said, "What's up? What's all the hee-hawing about?"

"It's Mama," Andrew shouted joyfully, and he and Hannah explained how she had suggested, in her most ladylike way, that they adjourn the discussion for the evening when all they were discussing was how much whiskey Mary could stand, and it was as if she meant that Mary was much too thirsty to wait out any more of it; and Joel gave a snort of amusement and then was caught into the contagion of this somewhat hysterical laughter, and they all roared, laughing their heads off, while Catherine sat there watching them, disapproving such levity at such a time, and unhappily suspecting that for some reason they were laughing at her; but in courtesy and reproof, and an expectation of hearing the joke, smiling and lifting her trumpet. But they paid no attention to her; they scarcely seemed to know she was there. They would quiet down now and then and moan and breathe deeply, and dry their eyes; then Mary would remember, and mimic, precisely the way her mother had patted her knee with her ringed hand, or Andrew would mimic her precise intonation as she said "*prolong*," or any of the four of them would roll over silently upon the tongue of the mind some particularly ticklish blend of the absurdity and horror and cruelty and relief, or would merely glance at Catherine with her smile and her trumpet, and would suddenly begin to bubble and then to spout with laughter, and another would be caught into the machinery, and then they would start all over again. Some of the time they deliberately strained for more laughter, or to prolong it, or to revive it if it had died; some of the time they tried just as hard to stop laughing or, having stopped, not to laugh any more. They found that on the whole they laughed even harder if they tried hard not to, so they came to favor that technique. They laughed until they were weak and their bellies ached. Then they were able to realize a little more clearly what a poor joke they had all been laughing at, and the very feebleness of the material and outrageous disproportion of their laughter started them whooping again; but finally they quieted down, because they had no strength for any more, and into this nervous and somewhat aborted silence Catherine spoke, "Well, I have never in my life been so thoroughly shocked and astonished," and it began all over again.

But by now they were really worn out with laughter; moreover, images of the dead body beside the capsized automobile began to dart in their minds, and then to become cold, immense, and immovable; and they began fully to realize, as well, how shamefully they had treated the deaf woman.

"Oh, *Mama*," Andrew and Mary cried out together, and Mary embraced her and Andrew kissed her on the forehead and on the mouth. "It was awful of us," he said. "You've just got to try to forgive us. We're all just a little bit hysterical, that's all."

"Better tell her, Andrew," his father said.

"Yes, poor thing," Hannah said; and he tried as gently as he could to explain it to her, and that they weren't really laughing at her expense, or even really at the joke, such as it was, because it wasn't really very funny, he must admit, but it had simply been a Godsend to have something to laugh about.

"I see," she said ("I see, said the blindman," Andrew said), and gave her polite, tinkling, baffled little laugh. "But of course it wasn't the—question of spirits that I meant. I just felt that perhaps for poor dear Mary's sake we'd better . . ."

"Of course," Andrew shouted. "We understand, Mama. But Mary'd rather hear now. She'd already said so."

"Yes, Mama," Mary screamed, leaning across towards her "good" ear.

"Well in that case," Catherine said primly, "I think it would have been kind so to inform me."

"I'm awfully sorry, Mama," Andrew said. "We would have. We really would have. In about another minute."

"Well," Catherine said; "no matter."

"Really we would, Mama," Mary said.

"Very well," Catherine said. "It was just a misfortune, that's all. I know I make it—very difficult, I try not to."

"Oh, Mama, no."

"No, I'm not hurt. I just suggest that you ignore me now, for everybody's convenience. Joel will tell me, later."

"She means it," Joel said. "She's not hurt any more."

"I know she does," Andrew said. "That's why I'm *God*-damned if I'll leave her out. Honestly, Mama," he told her, "just let me tell you. Then we can all hear. Don't you see?"

"Well, if you're sure; of course I'd be most grateful. Thank you." She bowed, smiled, and tilted her trumpet.

It required immediate speech. That trumpet's like a pelican's mouth, he thought. Toss in a fish. "I'm sorry, Mama," he said. "I've got to try to collect my wits."

"That's perfectly all right," his mother said.

What was I—oh. Doctor. Yes.

"I was telling you what the doctor said."

Mary drank.

"Yes," Catherine replied in her clear voice. "You were saying that it was only by merest chance, where the blow was struck, a chance in a million, that . . ."

"Yes, Mama. It's just unbelievable. But there it is."

"Hyesss," Hannah sighed.

Mary drank.

"It does—beat—all—hell," Joel said. He thought of Thomas Hardy. There's a man, he thought, who knows what it's about. (And *she* asks God to forgive *her*!) He snorted.

"What is it, Papa?" Mary asked quietly.

"Nothing," he said, "just the way things go. As flies to wanton boys. That's all."

"What do you mean?"

"As flies to wanton boys are we to the gods; they kill us for their sport."

"No," Mary said; she shook her head. "No, Papa. It's not that way."

He felt within him a surge of boiling acid; he contained

himself. If she tries to tell me it's God's inscrutable mercy, he said to himself, I'll have to leave the room. "Ignore it, Poll," he said. "None of us knows one damned thing about it. Myself least of all. So I'll keep my trap shut."

"But I can't bear to have you even *think* such things, Papa."

Andrew tightened his lips and looked away.

"Mary," Hannah said.

"I'm afraid that's something none of us can ask—or change," her father said.

"Yes, Mary," Hannah said.

"But I can assure you of this, Poll. I have very few thoughts indeed and none of 'em are worth your minding about."

"Is there something perhaps I should be hearing?" Catherine asked.

They were silent a moment. "Nothing, Mama," Andrew said. "Just a digression. I'd tell you if it was important."

"You were about to continue, with what the doctor told you."

"Yes I was. I will. He told me a number of other things and I can—assure—everybody—that such as they are, at least they're some kind of cold comfort."

Mary met his eyes.

"He said that if there had to be such an accident, this was pretty certainly the best way. That with such a thing, a concussion, he might quite possibly have been left a hopeless imbecile."

"Oh, Andrew," Mary burst out.

"The rest of his life, and that could have been another forty years as easily as not. Or maybe only a semi-invalid, laid up just now and then, with terrific recurrent headaches, or spells of amnesia, of feeble-mindedness. Those are the things that *didn't* happen, Mary," he told her desperately. "I think I'd just better get them over and done with right now."

"Yes," she said through her hands. "Yes, you had. Go on, Andrew. Get it over."

"He pointed out what would have happened if he'd stayed conscious, if he hadn't been thrown clear of the auto. Going fast, hopelessly out of control, up that eight-foot embankment and then down. He'd have been crushed, Mary. Horribly mangled. If he'd died it would have been slowly and agonizingly. If he'd lived, he'd have probably been a hopeless cripple."

"Dreadful," Catherine cried loudly.

"An idiot, or a cripple, or a paralytic," Andrew said. "Because another thing a concussion can do, Mary, is paralyze. Incurably. Those aren't fates you can prefer for anyone to dying. Least of all a man like Jay, with all his vigor, of body and mind too, his independence, his loathing for being laid up even one day. You remember how impossible it was to keep him quiet enough when his back was strained."

"Yes," she said. "Yes, I do." Her hands were still to her face and she was pressing her fingers tightly against her eyeballs.

"Instead . . ." Andrew began; and he remembered his face in death and he remembered him as he lay on the table under the glare. "Instead of that, Mary, he died the quickest and most painless death there is. One instant he was fully alive. Maybe more alive than ever before for that matter, for something had suddenly gone wrong and everything in him was roused up and mad at it and ready to beat it—because you know that of Jay, Mary, probably better than anyone else on earth. He didn't know what fear was. Danger only made him furious—and tremendously alert. It made him every inch of the man he was. And the next instant it was all over. Not even time to know it was hopeless, Mary. Not even one instant of pain, because that kind of blow is much too violent to give pain. Immediate pain. Just an instant of surprise and every faculty at its absolute height, and then just a tremendous blinding shock, and then nothing. You see, Mary?"

She nodded.

"I saw his face, Mary. It just looked startled, and resolute, and mad as hell. Not one trace of fear or pain."

"There wouldn't have been any fear, anyway," she said.

"I saw him—stripped—at the undertaker's," Andrew said. "Mary, there wasn't a mark on his body. Just that little cut on the chin. One little bruise on his lower lip. Not another mark on his body. He had the most magnificent physique I've ever seen in a human being."

Nobody spoke for a long while; then Andrew said, "All I can say is, when my time comes, I only hope I die half as well."

His father nodded; Hannah closed her eyes and bowed her head. Catherine waited, patiently.

"In his strength," Mary said; and took her hands from her face. Her eyes were still closed. "That's how he was taken," she said very tenderly; "in his strength. Singing, probably"— her voice broke on the word—"happy, all alone, racing home because he loved so to go fast and couldn't except when he was alone, and because he didn't want to disappoint his children. And then just as you said, Andrew. Just one moment of trouble, of something that might be danger—and was; it was death itself—and everything in his nature springing to its full height to fight it, to get it under control, not in fear. Just in bravery and nobility and anger and perfect confidence he could. It's how he'd look Death itself in the face. It's how he did! In his strength. Those are the words that are going to be on his gravestone, Andrew."

That's what they're for, epitaphs, Joel suddenly realized. So you can feel you've got some control over the death, you *own* it, you choose a name for it. The same with wanting to know all you can about how it happened. And trying to imagine it as Mary was. Andrew, too. Any poor subterfuge'll do; and welcome to 'em.

"Don't you think?" Mary asked shyly; for Andrew had not replied.

"Yes I do," he said, and Hannah said, "Yes, Mary," and Joel nodded.

Hannah: I want to *know* when I die, and not just for religious reasons.

"Mama," Mary called, drawing at her arm. Her mother turned eagerly, thankfully, with her trumpet. "I was telling Andrew," Mary told her, "I think I know the words, the epitaph, that ought to go on Jay's—on the headstone." Her mother tilted her head politely. "In his strength," Mary said. Her mother looked still more polite. "In—his—*strength*," Mary said, more loudly. Christ, I don't think I can stand this, Andrew thought. "Because that was the way it happened. Mama. Just so suddenly, without any warning, or suffering, or weakness, or illness. Just—instantly. In the very prime of his life. Do you see?"

Her mother patted her knee and took her hand. "Very appropriate, dear," she said.

"*I* think so," Mary said; she wished she had not spoken of it.

"It is, Mary," Andrew assured her.

"Why didn't you answer when I asked you?"

"I was just thinking about him."

There was a silence; Catherine who had still held her trumpet hopefully extended, turned away.

"He was thirty-six," Mary said. "Just exactly a month and a day ago."

Nobody spoke.

"And last night—great, *goodness* it was only last night! Just think of that. Less than twenty-four hours ago, that awful phone ringing and we sat in the kitchen together—thinking of *his father*! We both thought it was his father who was at death's door. That's why he went up there. That's why it happened! And that miserable Ralph was so drunk he couldn't even be sure of the need. He just had to go *in case*. Oh, it's just beyond words!"

She finished her drink and stood up to get more.

"I'll get it," Andrew said quickly, and took her glass.

"Not quite so strong," she said. "Thank you."

"It's like a checkerboard," her father said.

"*What* is?"

"What you were saying. You think everything bears on one person's dying, and b'God it's another who does. One instant you see the black squares against the red and the next you see the red against the black."

"Yes," Mary said, somewhat in her mother's uncertain tone.

"None of us know what we're doing, any given moment."

How you manage not to have religious faith, Hannah wanted to tell him, is beyond me. She held her tongue.

"A tale told by an idiot . . . signifying nothing."

"Signifying something," Andrew said, "but we don't know what."

"Just as likely. Choice between rattlesnake and skunk."

"Jay knows what; now," Mary said.

"I certainly won't swear he doesn't," her father said.

"He does, Mary," her aunt said.

"Of course he does," Mary said.

Child, you'd better believe it, her aunt thought, disturbed by the "of course."

"I wonder," Catherine said; everyone turned towards her. "Mary's suggestion—for—an epitaph—is very lovely and appropriate, but I *wonder*, whether people will quite—*understand* it."

"*Agh*," Joel growled.

"What if they don't?" Andrew said.

Mary leaned across her. "Yes, Mama! What if they *don't*! *We* understand it. *Jay* understands it. What do *we* care if they *don't*!"

She was surprised and somewhat hurt by the violence of this attack. "It was merely something to be considered," she said with dignity. "After all, it will be in a *public place*. Many people will see it besides ourselves. I've always, supposed, it was the business of *words*—to *communicate*—*clearly*."

"Oh Mama, don't be mad," Mary cried. "I understand. I appreciate the suggestion. I just can't see that in a—that in this particular case, it's anything to be seriously concerned about. It's Jay we're thinking of. Not other people."

"I see; perhaps you're right. Praps I shouldn't have me . . ."

"We're very glad you mentioned it, Mama. We appreciate you mentioning it. It hadn't even occurred to me and it ought to of. Only now that it does, now that you've told me, why, well, I just still think it's all right as it is. That's all."

"*Let it go, Catherine, for God's sake let it go!*" Joel was saying in a low voice; but now she nodded and became quiet.

"I hate to hurt Mama's feelings," Mary said, "but *really*!"

"It's all right, Mary," Andrew said.

"Let it go, Poll," her father said.

"I am," Mary said; she took a drink.

"We've got to let them know," she said. "His mother. We'll have to phone Ralph. Andrew, will you do that?"

"Of course I will." He got up.

"Just tell them I'm sorry, I couldn't come to the phone. Will you, Andrew? I'm sure they'll understand."

"Of course they will."

"Just tell them—how it happened. Tell Ralph I send his mother all my love." He nodded. "And Andrew. Be sure and ask how Jay's father is." He nodded. "And let them know when

—why; why we don't even *know*, do we? When the—what day he'll—be—the *funeral*, Andrew!"

"Not for sure. I told them I'd see them in the morning about all that."

"Well you'll just have to tell them we'll let them know as soon as we do. In plenty of time. To get here I mean."

"What's the number, Mary?"

"Number?"

"What is Ralph's telephone number?"

"I—can't remember. I guess I don't know for sure. You'll have to ask Central. It's always Jay who called."

"All right."

"It's LaFollette," she called, as he went into the hall.

"All right, Mary." He went out.

"And, Andrew."

"Yes, Mary?" He put his head in.

"Talk as quietly as you can. We don't want to wake the children."

"Yes, Mary."

"It's queer I don't know," she told the others. "But it was always Jay who called."

"Tell your mother what's up," her father advised, for she was looking inquiring. Mary leaned across her.

"Bathroom?" her mother whispered discreetly.

"No, Mama. He's gone to telephone Jay's brother."

Her mother nodded, and still extended her trumpet, but Mary had nothing to say.

"I hope he will extend all our most—heartfelt—sympathies," her mother said.

Mary nodded conspicuously. "I specially asked him to," she lied.

After a few moments Catherine gave up, and relaxed her trumpet between her withered hands into her lap.

Chapter 12

ANDREW had shut the door but they could hear him, trying to talk quietly. He was talking, indeed, very quietly, close to the mouthpiece with his hand around it; even so, Mary and Hannah could hear most of what he said. They did not want to listen, but they couldn't help it.

He said, "I want to make a long-distance call, please," and the quietness of his voice made them listen the more carefully. It was full of covered danger.

"Hello? Hello, is this long distance? Long distance I want to call Ralph Follet, Ralph, Follet, F, O, L, L, E, T, no, Central, F, as in father—F, O,—have you got that?—L, L, ET. FOLLET. At LaFollette, Tennessee. No, I haven't. Thank you. I said, thank you."

"I don't see how his mother's going to bear it," Mary said, in a subdued voice. "I said I just don't see how Jay's mother is going to bear it," she told her mother.

"Her own husband right at death's door," she said to Hannah, "and now this. He was just the apple of her eye, that's all."

"Hello?"

"She has a world of grit," Hannah said.

"Ralph? Is this Ralph Follet?"

"If she hadn't she wouldn't be alive today," Mary said.

"Ralph, this is Andrew Lynch." They sat very still and made no pretense of not listening.

"Yes. Andrew. Ralph, I have to tell you about Jay." Hannah and Mary looked at each other. With everything that Andrew said, from then on, they realized in a sense which they had failed to before, that it had really happened and that it was final.

"Jay died tonight, Ralph.

"He's dead.

"He died in an auto accident, on the way home, out near Powell's Station. He was instantly killed."

Mary looked down into the whiskey and began to tremble.

"Instantly. I have a doctor's word for it. He couldn't even have known what hit him.

"It was concussion of the brain, Ralph. Concussion—of the brain. Just so hard a shock to the brain that it killed him instantly."

"They mustn't tell his father," Mary said suddenly. "It'll just kill his father."

"I don't see how they can avoid it," Hannah said. "Mary says they mustn't tell his, Jay's, father," Hannah told her brother. "In his condition the news might kill him. I told her I simply don't see how they can avoid it. They'll have to account for coming away to the funeral, after all."

"Just tell him he's hurt," Joel said.

Mary hurried into the hall. "Andrew," she whispered loudly. With a contortion of the face which terrified her he slapped his hand through the air at her as if she had been a mosquito. "Just that one place, on the point of the chin," he was saying. He turned to Mary, but the voice held him and he turned away. "He may have driven for miles that way. They don't know. They looked all around and quite a distance up the road —yes, of course with flashlights—and they couldn't find it." Again she heard the voice, squirming like a wire. "No, they haven't any idea. Except that there are some very rough stretches in those roads and Jay was driving very fast. Just a minute, Ralph." He covered the mouthpiece. "What is it, Mary?"

She could hear the distraught and squirming voice. Like a worm on a hook, she thought. Poor nasty fat thing! "Tell Ralph not to tell his father," she whispered. "In his condition it might kill him. If they have to say anything, about—coming down—tell him he's hurt." Andrew nodded.

"Ralph," he said. "Go away," he whispered, for she was lingering. "We just want to remind you, it might be very dangerous to your father" (by now Mary heard him through the door; she took her seat) "if he heard this now. Of course you and your mother'll know best but in case you have to explain, when you come away to the funeral, it might be better just to say that Jay's been hurt; not in danger. Don't you think?

"What did you say?

"Why no, we . . .

"He's at Roberts'. I came in with him tonight.

"Why I'd suppose that . . ."

"Oh *heavens*!" Mary said, loudly enough that her father jumped. "Ralph's an undertaker!"

"Of course, I see your point, Ralph.

"No. Not yet.

"Well the saving of money is not a question in this . . .

"Look here, Ralph will you just . . .

"Will you just hold the phone a minute, please? I really think we should leave this up to Mary, don't you?

"Of course she does. You too. I . . .

"I don't doubt it at all.

"No, I appreciate it very deeply, Ralph, and I know Mary will, but just let me consult her wishes on it, please. Just wait."

They heard his rapid walk and he thrust his infuriated face into the room.

"Ralph," he announced, "is an undertaker. I imagine you know what he wants. I told him it was up to you to decide."

"Good—God!" Joel exclaimed.

"Andrew, you'll have to tell him—I—just simply can't."

"He's blaming himself for Jay's . . . He wants to try to make up for it."

"How on earth can he blame himself!"

"For phoning Jay in the first place."

"What nonsense," Hannah said.

"But Jay's already at Ro . . ."

"Ralph says that's easily arranged. He can come down first thing tomorrow."

"Well, then we just can't. We just won't, no matter what. Tell him how very *very* much I appreciate it and thank him, but I just can't. Tell him I'm prostrated. I don't care what you tell him, you handle it, Andrew."

"I'll handle it." He went back to the phone.

"Seems downright incestuous," Joel said.

His sister laughed harshly.

"Nothing important, Mama," Mary said. "Just—arrangements about the funeral."

Nothing important! Joel thought. People can only get through these things by being blind at least half the time. No: she was just cutting a corner for Catherine.

"When will the ceremony be held?"

Hannah stifled a laugh and Joel did not. Mary's face worked

curiously with a smile as she told her mother, "We don't know yet. This was a question of where. Here or LaFollette?"

"I would have supposed that his home was Knoxville."

"We think so, too. That's how it's settled."

"That seems as it should be."

Andrew came in. "Well," he said, "it was either Ralph or you and I chose you."

"Oh, Andrew, you must have hurt him."

"There wasn't any way out. He just wouldn't take no for an answer."

"He's going to make an awful case of it to his mother."

"Well he'll just have to, then."

"She's got sense, Mary," Hannah said.

"I'm going to have a drink," Andrew said. "*God!*" he groaned. "Talking to that fool is like trying to put socks on an octopus!"

"Why, Andrew," Mary laughed; she had never heard the expression. "I'm very grateful to you, dear," she said. "You must be worn to a frazzle."

"We all are," Hannah said. "You most of all, Mary. We better think about getting some sleep."

"I suppose we must, but I really don't feel as if I *could* sleep. *You*-all better though."

"We're all right," Andrew said. "Except maybe Mama. And Papa, you'd b . . ."

"Never sleep before two in the morning," Joel said. "You know that."

"Let me fix you a good stiff hot toddy," Hannah said. "It'll help you sleep."

"It all just seems to wake me up."

"Hot."

"Maybe just some hot milk. *No I won't, either*," she cried out, with sudden tears; they looked at her and looked away; she soon had control of herself.

"One of the last things Jay did for me," she explained, "way early in the morning before he—went away. He fixed me some hot milk to help me sleep." She began to cry again. "Bless his heart," she said. "Bless his dear heart."

"You know almost the last thing he said to me?

"He asked me to think what I wanted for my birthday.

" 'Within reason,' he said. He was just joking.

"And he said not to wait supper, but he'd—he'd try to be back before the children were asleep, for sure."

She'd feel better later on if she'd kept a few of these things to herself, Joel thought.

Or would she. I would. But I'm not Poll.

"Rufus just—*wouldn't* give up. He just *wouldn't* go to sleep. He was so proud of that cap, Aunt Hannah. He wanted *so much* to show it to his father."

Hannah came over to her and leaned to her, an arm around her shoulder.

"Talk if you want to, Mary," she said. "If you think it does you good. But try not to harp on these things."

"And I was so mad at him, only a few hours ago, for not phoning all day, and because of Rufus. I had such a good supper ready, and I *did* wait it, and . . ."

"It wasn't *his* fault it was good," Hannah said.

"Of *course* it isn't his fault and I had no *business* waiting it but I *did*, and I was so angry with him—why I even—I even . . ."

But this she found she would not tell them. I even thought he was drunk, she said to herself. And if he was, why what in the world of it. Let's hope if he was he really loved being, God bless him always. *Always*.

And then a terrifying thought occurred to her, and she looked at Andrew. No, she thought, he wouldn't lie to me if it were so. No, I won't even ask it. I won't even imagine it. I just don't see how I could bear to live if that were so.

But there he was, all that day, with Ralph. He *must* have. Well he probably did. That was no part of the promise. But not really *drunk*. Not so he couldn't—navigate. Drive well.

No.

Oh, no.

No I won't even dishonor his dear memory by asking. Not even Andrew in secret. No, I won't.

And she thought with such exactness and with such love of her husband's face, and of his voice, and of his hands, and of his way of smiling so warmly even though his eyes almost never lost their sadness, that she succeeded in driving the other thought from her mind.

"Hark!" Hannah whispered.

"What *is* it?"

"*Ssh!* Listen."

"What's up?" Joel asked.

"Be quiet, Joel, *please*. There's something."

They listened most intently.

"I can't hear anything," Andrew whispered.

"Well *I* do," Hannah said, in a low voice. "Hear it or feel it. There's *something*."

And again in silence they listened.

It began to seem to Mary, as to Hannah, that there was someone in the house other than themselves. She thought of the children; they might have waked up. Yet listening as intently as she could, she was not at all sure that there was any sound; and whoever or whatever it might be, she became sure that it was no child, for she felt in it a terrible forcefulness, and concern, and restiveness, which were no part of any child.

"There *is* something," Andrew whispered.

Whatever it might be, it was never for an instant at rest in one place. It was in the next room; it was in the kitchen; it was in the dining room.

"I'm going out to see," Andrew said; he got up.

"Wait, Andrew, don't, not yet," Mary whispered. "No; no"; now it's going upstairs, she thought; it's along the—it's in the children's room. It's in *our* room."

"Has somebody come into the house?" Catherine inquired in her clear voice.

Andrew felt the flesh go cold along his spine. He bent near her. "What made you think so, Mama?" he asked quietly.

"It's right here in the room with us," Mary said in a cold voice.

"Why, how very stupid of me, I *thought* I *heard*. Footsteps." She gave her short, tinkling laugh. "I must be getting old and dippy." She laughed again.

"*Sshh!*"

"It's Jay," Mary whispered. "I know it now. I was so wrapped up in wondering *what* on earth . . . Jay. Darling. Dear heart, can you hear me?

"Can you tell me if you hear me, dearest?

"Can you?

"Can't you?

"Oh try your best, my dear. Try your *very* hardest to let me know.

"You can't, can you? You can't, no matter *how* hard.

"But O, do hear me, Jay. I do pray God with all my heart you can hear me, I want so to assure you.

"Don't be troubled, dear one. Don't you worry. Stay near us if you can. *All* you can. But let not your heart be troubled. They're all right, my sweetheart, my husband. I'm going to be all right. Don't you worry. We'll make out. Rest, my dear. Just rest. Just rest, my heart. Don't ever be troubled again. Never again, darling. Never, never again."

"May the souls of the faithful through the mercy of God rest in peace," Hannah whispered. "Blessed are the dead."

"Mary!" her brother whispered. He was crying.

"He's not here any more now," she said. "We can talk."

"Mary, in God's name what was it?"

"It was Jay, Andrew."

"It was *something*. I haven't any doubt of that, but—good God, Mary."

"It was Jay, all right. I *know*! Who else would be coming here tonight, so terribly worried, so terribly concerned for us, and restless! Besides, Andrew, it—it simply *felt* like Jay."

"You mean . . ."

"I just mean it felt like his *presence*."

"To me, too," Hannah said.

"I don't like to interrupt," Joel said, "but would you mind telling me, please, what's going on here?"

"You felt it too, Papa?" Mary asked eagerly.

"Felt what?"

"You remember when Aunt Hannah said there was something around, someone or something in the house?"

"Yes, and she told me to shut up, so I did."

"I simply asked you please to be quiet, Joel, because we were trying to hear."

"Well, what did you hear?"

"I don't know's I *heard* anything, Joel. I'm not a bit sure. I don't think I did. But I *felt* something, very distinctly. So did Andrew."

"Yes I did, Papa."

"And Mary."

"Oh, very much so."

"What do you mean you *felt* something?"

"Then you didn't, Papa?"

"I got a feeling there was some kind of a strain in the room, something or other was up among you; Mary looking as if she'd seen a ghost; *all* of you . . ."

"She did," Andrew said. "That is, she didn't actually see anything, but she felt it. She knew something was there. She says it was Jay."

"*Hahh?*"

"Jay. Aunt Hannah thinks so too."

"Hannah?"

"Yes I do, Joel. I'm not as sure as Mary, but it did seem like him."

"What's 'it'?"

"The thing, Papa, whatever it was. The thing we all felt."

"What did it feel like?"

"Just a . . ."

"You think it was Jay?"

"No, I had no idea *what* it was. But I know it was *something*. Mama felt it too."

"Catherine?"

"Yes. And it couldn't have been through us because she didn't even know what we were doing. All of a sudden she said, 'Has somebody come into the house?' and when I asked her why she thought so she said she thought she'd heard footsteps."

"Could be thought transference."

"None of the rest of us thought we heard footsteps."

"All the same. It can't be what you think."

"I don't know what it was, Papa, but there are four of us here independently who are sure there was something."

"Joel, I know that God in a wheelbarrow wouldn't convince you," his sister said. "We aren't even trying to convince you. But while you're being so rational, why at least please be rational enough to realize that we experienced what we experienced. "

"The least I can do is accept the fact that three people had a hallucination, and honor their belief in it. That I can do, too, I guess. I believe you, for yourself, Hannah. All of you. I'd have to have the same hallucination myself to be convinced. And even then I'd have my doubts."

"What on earth do you mean, *doubts*, Papa, if you had it yourself?"

"I'd suspect it was just a hallucination."

"Oh, good Lord! You've got it going and coming, haven't you!"

"Is this a dagger that I see before me? Wasn't, you know. But you could never convince Macbeth it wasn't."

"Andrew," Mary broke in, "tell Mama. She's just dying to know what we're . . ." she trailed off. I must be out of my mind, she said to herself. *Dying!* And she began to think with astonishment and disgust of the way they had all been talking —herself most of all. How can we bear to chatter along in normal tones of voice! she thought; how can we even use ordinary words, or say words at all! And now, picking his poor troubled soul to pieces, like so many hens squabbling over—she thought of a worm, and covered her face in sickness. She heard her mother say, "Why, Andrew, how perfectly *extraordinary!*" and then she heard Andrew question her, had she had any special *feeling* about what *kind* of a person or thing it was, that is, was it quiet or active, or young or old, or disturbed or calm, or was it anything: and her mother answered that she had had no particular impression except that there was someone in the house besides themselves, not the children either, somebody mature, some sort of intruder; but that when nobody had troubled to investigate, she had decided that it must be an hallucination—all the more so because, as she'd said, she thought she'd actually *heard* someone, whereas with her poor old ears (she laughed gracefully) that was simply out of the question, of course. Oh, I do wish they'd leave him in peace, she said to herself. A thing so wonderful. Such a *proof!* Why can't we just keep a reverent silence! But Andrew was asking his mother, had she, a little later than that, still felt even so that there was somebody? or not. And she said that indeed she had had such an *impression*. Where? Why she couldn't say where, except that the *impression* was even stronger than before, but, of course, by then she realized it was an hallucination. But they felt it too! Why how perfectly uncanny!

"Mary thinks it was Jay," Andrew told her.

"Why, I . . ."

"So does Aunt Hannah."

"Why how—how perfectly extraordinary, Andrew!"

"She thinks he was worried about . . ."

"Oh, Andrew!" Mary cried. "Andrew! *Please* let's don't *talk* about it any more! Do you mind?"

He looked at her as if he had been slapped. "Why, Mary, of course not!" He explained to his mother: "Mary'd rather we didn't discuss it any more."

"Oh, it's not that, Andrew. It just—means so much more than anything we can *say* about it or even think about it. I'd give anything just to sit quiet and think about it a little while! Don't you see? It's as if we were driving him away when he wants so much to be here among us, with us, and can't."

"I'm *awfully* sorry, Mary. Just *awfully* sorry. Yes, of *course* I *do* see. It's a kind of sacrilege."

So they sat quietly and in the silence they began to listen again. At first there was nothing, but after a few minutes Hannah whispered, "He's there," and Andrew whispered, "Where?" and Mary said quietly, "With the children," and quietly and quickly left the room.

When she came through the door of the children's room she could feel his presence as strongly throughout the room as if she had opened a furnace door: the presence of his strength, of virility, of helplessness, and of pure calm. She fell down on her knees in the middle of the floor and whispered, "Jay. My dear. My dear one. You're all right now, darling. You're not troubled any more, are you, my darling? Not any more. Not ever any more, dearest. I can feel how it is with you. I know, my dearest. It's terrible to go. You don't want to. Of *course* you don't. But you've got to. And you know they're going to be all right. Everything is going to be all right, my darling. God take you. God keep you, my own beloved. God make His light to shine upon you." And even while she whispered, his presence became faint, and in a moment of terrible dread she cried out "Jay!" and hurried to her daughter's crib. "Stay with me just one minute," she whispered, "just one minute, my dearest"; and in some force he did return; she felt him with her, watching his child. Catherine was sleeping with all her might and her thumb was deep in her mouth; she was scowling fiercely. "Mercy, child," Mary whispered, smiling, and touched her hot forehead to smooth it, and she growled. "God bless you, God keep you," her mother whispered, and came silently to her son's bed. There was the cap in its tissue paper, beside him on the floor; he slept less deeply than his sister, with his chin lifted, and his forehead flung back; he looked grave, serene and expectant.

"Be with us all you can," she whispered. "This is good-bye." And again she went to her knees. Good-bye, she said again, within herself; but she was unable to feel much of anything. "God help me to *realize* it," she whispered, and clasped her hands before her face: but she could realize only that he was fading, and that it was indeed good-bye, and that she was at that moment unable to be particularly sensitive to the fact.

And now he was gone entirely from the room, from the house, and from this world.

"Soon, Jay. Soon, dear," she whispered; but she knew that it would not be soon. She knew that a long life lay ahead of her, for the children were to be brought up, and God alone could know what change and chance might work upon them all, before they met once more. She felt at once calm and annihilating emptiness, and a cold and overwhelming fulness.

"God help us all," she whispered. "May God in His loving mercy keep us all."

She signed herself with the Cross and left the room.

She looks as she does when she has just received, Hannah thought as she came in and took her old place on the sofa; for Mary was trying, successfully, to hide her desolation; and as she sat among them in their quietness it was somewhat diminished. After all, she told herself, he *was there*. More strongly even than when he was here in the room with me. Anyhow. And she was grateful for their silence.

Finally Andrew said, "Aunt Hannah has an idea about it, Mary."

"Maybe you'd prefer not to talk about it," Hannah said.

"No; it's all right; I guess I'd rather." And with mild surprise she found that this was true.

"Well, it's simply that I thought of all the old tales and beliefs about the souls of people who die sudden deaths, or violent deaths. Or as Joel would prefer it, not souls. Just their life force. Their consciousness. Their life itself."

"Can't get around that," Joel said. "Hannah was saying that everything of any importance leaves the body then. I certainly have to agree with that."

"And that even whether you believe or not in life after death," Mary said, "in the soul, as a living, immortal thing, creature, why it's certainly very believable that for a little while afterwards, this force, this life, stays on. Hovers around."

"Sounds highly unlikely to me, but I suppose it's conceivable."

"Like looking at a light and then shutting your eyes. No, not like that but—but it does stay on. Specially when it's someone very strong, very vital, who hasn't been worn down by old age, or a long illness or something."

"That's exactly it," Andrew said. "Something that comes out whole, because it's so quick."

"Why they're as old as the hills, those old beliefs."

"I should imagine they're as old as life and death," Andrew said.

"The thing I mean is, they aren't taken straight to God," Hannah said. "They've had such violence done them, such a shock, it takes a while to get their wits together."

"That's why it took him so long to come," Mary said. "As if his very *soul* had been struck unconscious."

"I should think maybe."

"And above all with someone like Jay, young, and with children and a wife, and not even dreaming of such a thing coming on him, no time to adjust his mind and feelings, or prepare for it."

"That's just it," Andrew said; Hannah nodded.

"Why he'd feel, 'I'm worried. This came too fast without warning. There are all kinds of things I've got to tend to. I can't just leave them like this.' *Wouldn't* he! And that's just how he was, how we felt he was. So *anxious*. So awfully concerned, and disturbed. Why yes, it's just exactly the way it was!

"And only when they feel convinced you know they care, and everything's going to be taken good care of, just the very best possible, it's only then they can stop being anxious and begin to rest."

They nodded and for a minute they were all quiet.

Then Mary said tenderly, "How awful, pitiful, beyond words it must be, to be so terribly anxious for others, for others' good, and not be able to do anything, even to say so. Not even to help. Poor things.

"Oh, they *do* need reassuring. They *do* need rest. I'm *so grateful* I could assure him. It's so good he can rest at last. I'm *so glad*." And her heart was restored from its desolation, into warmth and love and almost into wholeness.

Again they were all thoughtfully silent, and into this silence Joel spoke quietly and slowly, "I *don't—know*. I *just—don't—know*. Every bit of gumption I've got tells me it's impossible, but if this kind of thing is so, it isn't with gumption that you see it is. I *just—don't—know*.

"If you're right, and I'm wrong, then chances are you're right about the whole business, God, and the whole crew. And in that case I'm just a plain damned fool.

"But if I can't trust my common sense—I know it's nothing much, Poll, but it's all I've got. If I can't trust that, what in hell *can* I trust!

"God, you'n Hannah'd say. Far's I'm concerned, it's out of the question."

"Why, Joel?"

"It doesn't seem to embarrass your idea of common sense, or Poll's, and for that matter I'm making no reflections. You've got plenty of gumption. But how you can reconcile the two, I can't see."

"It takes faith, Papa," Mary said gently.

"That's the word. That's the one makes a mess of everything, far's I'm concerned. Bounces up like a jack-in-the-box. Solves everything.

"Well it doesn't solve anything for me, for I haven't got any.

"Wouldn't hurt it if I had. Don't believe in it.

"Not for me.

"For you, for anyone that can manage it, all right. More power to you. Might be glad if I could myself. But I can't.

"I'm not exactly an atheist, you know. Least I don't suppose

I am. Seems as unfounded to me to say there isn't a God as to say there is. You can't prove it either way. But that's it: I've got to have proof. And on anything can't be proved, be damned if I'll jump either way. All I can say is, I hope you're wrong but I just don't know."

"I don't, either," Andrew said. "But I hope it's so."

He saw Mary and Hannah look at him hopefully.

"I don't mean the whole business," he said. "I don't know anything about that. I just mean tonight."

Can't eat your cake and have it, his father thought.

Like slapping a child in the face, Andrew thought; he had been rougher than he had intended.

"But, Andrew dear," Mary was about to say, but she caught herself. What a thing to argue about, she thought; and what a time to be wrangling about it!

Each of them realized that the others felt something of this; for a little while none of them had anything to say. Finally Andrew said, "I'm sorry."

"Never mind," his sister said. "It's all right, Andrew."

"We just each believe what we're able," Hannah said, after a moment.

"Even you, Joel. You have faith in your mind. Your reason."

"Not very much: all I've got, that's all. All I can be sure of."

"That's all I mean."

"Let's not talk about it any more," Mary said. "Tonight," she added, trying to make her request seem less peremptory.

The word was a reproach upon them all, much more grave, they were sure, than Mary had intended, so that to spare her regret they all hastened to say, kindly and as if somewhat callously, "No, let's not."

In the embarrassment of having spoken all at once they sat helpless and sad, sure only that silence, however painful to them all and to Mary, was less mistaken than trying to speak. Mary wished that she might ease them; her continued silence, she was sure, intensified their self-reproach; but she felt, as they did, that an attempt to speak would be worse than quietness.

In this quietness their mother sat, and smiled nervously and politely, and tilted her trumpet in a generalized way towards all of them. She realized that nobody was speaking and it was at such times, ordinarily, that she felt sure that she could speak without interrupting anyone, but she feared that anything that she might say might brutally or even absurdly disrupt a weaving of thought and feeling whose motions within the room she could most faintly apprehend.

After a little while it occurred to her that even to hold out her trumpet might seem to require something of them; she held it in her lap. But lest any of them should feel that this was in any sense a reproach, or should in the least feel sorry for her, she kept her little smile, thinking, how foolish, how very foolish, to smile.

Smiling at grief, Joel thought. He wondered whether his sister and his son and his daughter, if they were thinking of it at all, understood the smile as he was sure he did. He wished that he could pat her hand. By God, they'd better, he thought.

Andrew could not get out of his mind the image of his brother-in-law as he had first seen him that night. By the mere shy, inactive way the men stood who, as he and Walter first came up, stood between them and Jay, he had realized, instantly, before anyone spoke, "He's dead." Somebody had murmured something embarrassed about identification and he had answered sharply that they'd managed to phone the family, hadn't they?, and again they had murmured embarrassedly, and ashamed of his sharpness he had assented, and there in the light of the one bulb one of the men had gently turned down the sheet (for he gathered a little later that the blacksmith's wife, finding him covered with a reeking horse blanket, had hurried to bring this sheet) and there he was; and Andrew nodded, and made himself say, "Yes," and he heard Walter's deep, quiet breathing at his shoulder and heard him say, "Yes," and he stood a little aside in order that Walter might have room, and together they stood silent and looked at the uncovered head. The strong frown was still in the forehead but, even as they watched, it seemed to be fading very slowly; already the flesh had settled somewhat along the bones of the prostrate skull; the temples, the forehead and the sockets of the eyes were more subtly molded than they had been in life and the nose was more finely arched; the chin was thrust upward as if proudly and impatiently, and the small cut at its point was as neat and bloodless as if it had been made by a chisel in soft wood. They watched him with the wonder which is felt in the presence of anything which is great and new, and, for a little while, in any place where violence has recently occurred; they were aware, as they gazed at the still head, of a prodigious kind of energy in the air. Without turning his head, Andrew became aware that tears were running down Walter's cheeks; he himself was cold, awed, embittered beyond tears. After perhaps a half minute he said coldly, "Yes, that's he," and covered the face himself and turned quickly away; Walter was drying his face and his glasses; aware of some obstacle, Andrew glanced quickly down upon a horned, bruised anvil; and laid his hand flat against the cold, wheemed iron; and it was as if its forehead gave his hand the stunning shadow of every blow it had ever received.

Now these images manifolded upon each other with great rapidity, at their constant center, the proud, cut chin, and could be driven from his mind's eye only by two others, Jay as he felt he had seen him, the instant after the accident, lying, they had told him, so straight and unblemished beside the car, the dead eyes shining with starlight and the hand still as if ready to seize and wrestle; and as he had last actually seen him, naked on the naked table, a block beneath his nape.

Somebody sighed, from the heart; he looked up; it was Hannah. They were all looking downward and sidelong. His sister's face had altered strangely during this silence; it had become thin, shy and somehow almost bridal. He remembered her wedding in Panama; yes, it was much the same face. He looked away.

"Aunt Hannah, will you please stay with me here tonight?" Mary asked.

Mama, Andrew thought, and his heart went out to her as he looked at her deaf, set smile.

"Why certainly, Mary."

Joel decided not to look at his watch. Andrew covertly glanced at the mantel clock. It was. . . .

"I hope Mama won't mind too much. I hope she'll understand. Poor thing. Mama," she suddenly called, and put her hand on her mother's hand and on the trumpet. Her mother eagerly tilted it. "I think it's about time we all tried to get some sleep." Her mother nodded, and seemed to be about to speak; Mary pressed her hand for silence and continued,

"Mama, I've asked Aunt Hannah if she'll stay here tonight with me." Her mother nodded and again seemed to be about to speak. Again Mary pressed her hand: "I'd love it if you could, but I know how it would disrupt things at eleven-fifteen,"— "*Hahh*," her father exclaimed—"and I just . . ."

"*Tell* her, Poll!"

"Also, Mama. Also it's just—I hope you'll understand and not mind, Mama dear—it's just it would be so very hard for us to *talk, quietly*, and with the children and all, why I just sort of think . . ."

"Why certainly, Mary," her mother interrupted, in her somewhat ringing voice. "I absolutely agree with you. I think it's so nice that Hannah can stay!" she added, almost as if Mary and Hannah were little girls.

"I hope you know, Mama, how *very much!*—I hope you don't mind. I just appreciate it so much, I . . ."

Her mother patted her hand rapidly. "It's perfectly all right, Mary. It's very *sensible*." She smiled.

Mary put an arm around her and hugged her; she turned her aging face and smiled very brightly and Mary could see the tears in her eyes. She was speechless and her head was shaking in her effort to convey her love and the entirety of her feeling. "*Anything* I can do, dear child," she said after a few moments. "*Anything!*"

"Bless you, Mama!"

"Beg pardon?"

"I said *bless* you, dear!"

Catherine patted her hand on the back and smiled even more tightly.

I love you so much! Mary exclaimed within herself.

"Praps the children," Catherine said. "I could take care, if—it would be more, *convenient* . . ."

"Oh, I don't think we should wake them up!" Mary said.

"She doesn't mean . . ." Andrew began.

"Tomorrow," her mother said. "Just, perhaps, during the—interim . . ."

"That's wonderful, Mama, that may turn out to be just the thing and if it is I most certainly will. *Most gratefully*. It's just, I'm in such a spin it's just too soon to quite know yet, make any plans. Anything. Tomorrow."

"Tomorrow then."

"Thank you, Mama."

"Not at all."

"Thank you all the same."

Her mother smiled and shook her head.

Joel and his sister stood up.

"Mary, before we go," Andrew said.

"?"

"It's much too late, Mary, you're much too tired."

"Not if it's important, Andrew."

"Let's let it go till morning."

"What is it, Andrew?"

"Just—various things we'll have to discuss pretty soon." He took a deep breath and said in a loud voice. "Getting a plot, making arrangements about the funeral; seeing about a headstone. Let's wait till morning."

Earth, stone, a coffin. The ugly craft of undertakers became real and tangible to her, but as if she touched them with frozen hands. She looked at him with glazed eyes.

"That'll be plenty of time, Mary," she heard her aunt say.

"Of course it will," Andrew said. "It was foolish of me to even speak of it tonight."

"Well if there's time," she said vaguely. "Yes *if* there's time, Andrew," she said more distinctly. "Yes, then I'd rather, if you don't mind. Tomorrow in the morning." She glanced at the clock. "Goodness *this* morning," she exclaimed.

"Of course not," Andrew said. He turned to his aunt and said in a low voice, as one speaks before an invalid, "Let her sleep if she can. You phone me."

Hannah nodded.

"Must've . . ." Joel said, and went into the hall.

"What's . . ." Hannah began.

"Hat I guess. Mine too." Andrew left the room; in the hall he met his father, carrying his own hat, his wife's, and Andrew's.

"Left them in the kitchen," his father said.

"Thank you, Papa." Andrew took his hat.

Catherine was standing uneasily in the middle of the room, holding her trumpet and her purse and looking towards the hall door. "Thank you, Joel," she said. She settled and pinned her hat by touch, a little crooked, and looked at Hannah inquiringly.

"It's all right, Catherine," her husband said.

Andrew was watching his sister. It seemed to him that these preparations for departure put her into some kind of silent panic. Maybe we should stay, he thought. All night. I could. But Mary was chiefly watching her mother's difficulties with the hat. No, it's the slowness, he corrected himself. Sooner the better.

"Well, Mary," he said, and stepped to her and put his arms around her. He saw that her eyes were speckled; it was as if the irises had been cracked into many small fragments; and in her eyes and her presence he felt something of the shock and energy which had radiated so strongly from the dead body. She was new; changed. Nothing I can do, he thought.

"Thank you for everything," she said. "I'm so sorry you had it to do."

He could not answer or continue to look into her eyes; he embraced her more closely. "Mary," he said finally.

"I'm all right, Andrew," she said quietly. "I've got to be."

He nodded sharply.

"You come up in the morning. We'll—make our plans."

"Sleep if you can."

"Just come up first thing because I know there's an awful lot to do and not much time."

"All right."

"Good night, Andrew."

"Good night, Mary."

"*Bless you*," her mother exploded, almost as if she were cursing; deaf, near-sighted, she caught her daughter in her arms with all her strength and patted her back with both hands, thinking: how young and good she smells!

She wants so to help, Mary realized. To stay! Under her caress she felt the hard, round shoulders, sharp backbone, already hunching with age. Leaning back in her mother's embrace, she straightened the hat, looked into the trembling face, and kissed her hard on the mouth. Her mother twice returned the kiss, then stood aside, gathering her long skirt for the porch steps.

"Poll," her father said; she felt the beard against her cheek and heard his whisper: "Good girl. Keep it up."

She nodded.

"Good night," Hannah said.

"Good night, Aunt Hannah," Andrew replied.

"Night, Hannah," her brother said. He steered Catherine by one elbow, Andrew by the other; they went onto the porch.

"Light!" Mary exclaimed.

"What?" Andrew and Hannah asked, startled.

Mary switched on the porch light. "Tsall right," her father said in mild annoyance; "Thank you," her mother chimed, politely. Mary and Hannah stood at the door while they carefully descended the porch steps, and they watched them until they reached the corner and then until they had safely crossed the street. Under the corner lamp, Andrew turned his head and lifted and let fall his hand in something less than a wave. The others did not turn; and now Andrew also had turned away, and they went carefully away along the sidewalk, and Mary switched off the light, and still watched. Hannah could no longer see them now, and after a few moments, gave up pretending to watch them and watched Mary as she looked after them, as intently, Hannah felt, as if it were of more importance than anything else, to see them until the last possible instant. And still Mary could see them, somewhat darker against the darkness and of uneven heights, growing smaller, so that it was not finally the darkness which made them impossible to see, but the corner of the Biddles' house.

When they were gone she continued to look up and down the street as far as she could see. There was the strong carbon light at the corner, and there was the glow of an unseen light at a more distant corner to the west; and of another, still more distant, to the east. There was no sound, and there were no lights on in any of the houses. The air moved mildly on her forehead. She turned, and saw that her aunt was watching her, and looked into her eyes.

"Time to sleep," she said.

She closed the door; they continued to look at each other.

"It was just about this time last night," she said.

Hannah sighed, very low; after a moment she touched Mary's hand. Still they stood and looked at each other.

"Yes, just about," Mary whispered strangely.

Through the silence they began to hear the kitchen clock.

"Let's not even *try* to talk now," Mary said. "We're both worn out."

"Let me fix you a good hot toddy," Hannah said, as they turned towards the living room. "Help you sleep."

"I honestly don't think I'll *need* it, Aunt Hannah."

I'll make one and you take it or not as you like, Hannah wanted to say; suddenly she realized: I'm only trying to think I'm useful. She said nothing.

There was an odd kind of shyness or constraint between them, which neither could understand. They stood still again, just inside the living room; the silence was somewhat painful for both of them, each on the other's account. Does she really *want* me to stay, Hannah wondered; what earthly use am I! Does she think I don't *want* her to stay, Mary wondered, just because I can't talk? No, she's no talker.

"I just can't talk just now," she said.

"Of course you can't, child."

Hannah felt that she probably ought to take charge of everything, but she felt still more acutely that she should be at the service of Mary's wishes, or lack of them for that matter, she told herself.

I can't stand to *send* her to bed, Mary thought.

"It's all ready," she said abruptly and, she feared, rather ruthlessly, and walked quickly across to the downstairs bedroom door and opened it. "See?" She walked in and turned on the light and faced her aunt. "I got it ready in case Jay," she said, and absently smoothed the pillow. "Just as well I did."

"You go straight to bed, Mary," Hannah said. "Let me help if I . . ."

Mary went into the kitchen; then Hannah could hear her in the hall; after a moment she came back. "Here's a clean nightgown," she said, "and a wrapper," putting them across her aunt's embarrassed hands. "It'll be big, I'm afraid, the wrapper, it's—was—it's Jay's, but if you'll turn up the sleeves it'll do in a pinch, I guess." She went past Hannah into the living room.

"I'll see to that, Mary," Hannah hurried after her; she was already gathering tumblers towards the tray.

"Great—goodness!" Mary exclaimed. She lifted the bottle. "Do you mean to say *I* drank all *that*?" It was three-quarters empty.

"No. Andrew had some, so did I, so did J— your father."

"But—just one apiece, Aunt Hannah. I *must* have. Nearly all of it."

"It hasn't had any effect."

"How on earth!" She held the low whiskey close to her eyes and looked at it as if she were threading a needle. "Well I most *certainly* don't need a *hot toddy*," she said.

"I never *heard* of such a thing!" she exclaimed quietly.

"Aspirin, perhaps."

"Aspirin?"

"You might wake up with a headache."

"It must just, Papa, Papa says, he said it sometimes doesn't, in a state of shock or things . . . Aunt Hannah?" She called more loudly. "Aunt Hannah?" Mustn't wake them, she remembered. She waited. Her aunt came in from the hall with a glass of water and two aspirins.

"Here," she said, "you take these."

"But I . . ."

"Just swallow them. You don't want to wake up with a headache and they'll help you sleep, too."

She took them docilely; Hannah loaded and lifted the tray.

Chapter 13

ALONG Laurel, it was much darker; heavy leaves obscured the one near street lamp. Andrew could hear only their footsteps; his father and mother, he realized, could hear nothing even of that. How still we see thee lie. Yes, and between the treetops; the pale scrolls and porches and dark windows of the homes drifting past their slow walking, and not a light in any home, and so for miles, in every street of home and of business; above thy deep and dreamless sleep, the silent stars go by.

He helped his mother from the curb; this slow and irregular rattling of their little feet.

The stars are tired by now. Night's nearly over.

He helped her to the opposite curb.

Upon their faces the air was so marvelously pure, aloof and tender; and the silence of the late night in the city, and the stars, were secret and majestic beyond the wonder of the deepest country. Little houses, bigger ones, scrolled and capacious porches, dark windows, leaves of trees already rich with May, homes of rooms which chambered sleep as honey is cherished, drifted past their slow walking and were left behind, and not a light in any home. Along Laurel Avenue it was still darker. The lamp behind them no longer cast their shadows; in the light of the lamp ahead, a small and distant bit of pavement looked scalded with emptiness, a few leaves were touched to acid flame, the spindles and turned posts of one porch were rigidly white. Helping his mother along through the darkness, Andrew was walking much more slowly than he was used to walking, and all these things entered him calmly and thoroughly. Full as his heart was, he found that he was involved at least as deeply in the loveliness and unconcern of the spring night, as in the death. It's as if I didn't even care, he reflected, but he didn't mind. He knew he cared; he felt gratitude towards the night and towards the city he ordinarily cared little for. *How still we see thee lie*, he heard his mind say. He said the words over, drily within himself, and heard the melody; a child's voice, his own, sang it in his mind.

Hm.

He tried to remember when he had last walked in the open night at such an hour. He wasn't sure he even . . . God, years. Seven—about sixteen, when he still thought he was Shelley, watching the river. Leaning on the bridge rail and literally praying with gratitude for being alive.

Instinctively, he turned his head so that his parents could not see his face.

I don't want to see it, either, he thought.

By that time, Jay was trying to teach himself law.

Above thy deep and dreamless sleep, the silent stars go by.

The words had always touched him; every year they still brought back Christmas to him, for some reason, as nothing else could. Now they seemed to him as beautiful as any poetry he had ever known.

He said them over to himself very slowly and calmly: just a statement.

They do indeed, he thought, looking up. They do indeed. And God, how tired they look!

It's the time of night.

The silent stars go by, he said aloud, not whispering, but so quietly he was sure they would not hear.

His eyes sprang full of tears; his throat, his chest knotted into a deep sob which he subdued, and the tears itched on his cheeks.

Yet in thy dark streets shineth, he sang loudly, almost in fury, within himself: *the everlasting light!* and upon these words a sob leapt up through him which he could not subdue but could only hope to conceal.

They did not notice.

This is crazy, he told himself incredulously. *No sense in this at all!*

Everlasting light!

The hopes and fears, a calm and implacable voice continued within him; he spoke quietly: *Of all the years.*

Are met in thee tonight, he whispered: and in the middle of a wide plain, the middle of the dark and silent city, slabbed beneath shadowless light, he saw the dead man, and struck his thigh with his fist with all his strength.

All he could hear in this world was only their footsteps; his father and mother, he realized, could hear nothing even of that.

He helped her from the curb; this slow and irregular rattling of their little feet; and across the space of bitter light.

He helped her to the opposite curb; they followed their absurd shadows until all was once more one shadow.

None of the three of them spoke, throughout their walk; when they came to the corner at which they would turn for home, it was as if all three spoke, accepting the fact: for each man tightened his hand gently at the woman's elbows and, bowing her head, she pressed their hands against her sides. They turned down the steep hill, walking still more slowly and tightening their knees, and saw the one light which had been left burning, and entered their home, quietly as burglars, by the back way.

They stopped at the foot of the stairs.

"Mary," Hannah asked, "is there anything I can do?"

You want to come up with me, Mary realized. "I think I just better be alone," she said. "But thank you. Thank you, Aunt Hannah."

"Just call if you want me. You know how lightly I sleep."

"I'll be all right, I really will."

"You rest in the morning. I'll take care of the children."

Mary looked at her with brightened eyes, and said, "Aunt Hannah, I'll have to tell them."

Hannah nodded, and sighed: "Yesss. Good night then," she said, and kissed her niece. "God bless you," she said, in a broken voice.

Mary looked at her carefully and said, "God help us all."

She turned and went up the stairs, and leaned, smiling, just before she disappeared, and whispered, "Good night."

"Good night, Mary," Hannah whispered.

She turned off the hall light and the light in the living room and went into the lighted bedroom and pulled down the shade and shut the doors to the kitchen and the living room. She took off her dress and laid it over the back of a chair and sat on the edge of the bed to unlace her shoes, and hesitated, until she was certain that she remembered, clearly, putting out the lights in the kitchen and bathroom. She put on the nightgown except for the sleeves and finished undressing under the nightgown; it was rather large for her and she gathered and lifted it about her. She knelt beside the bed and said an Our Father and a Hail Mary, and found that her heart and mind were empty of further prayer or even of feeling. May the souls of the faithful, she tried; she clamped her teeth and, after a moment, prayed angrily: May the souls of everyone who has ever had to live and die, in the Faith or outside it, rest in peace. And especially his!

Strike me down, she thought. Visit upon me Thy lightnings. I don't care. I can't care.

Forgive me if I'm wrong, she thought. If You can. If You will. But that's how I feel, and that's all there is to it.

Again her heart and mind were empty; even now, feeling the breath of the abyss, she could not feel otherwise, or even care or fear.

Lord, I believe. Help Thou mine unbelief.

But I don't really know's I do.

I can't pray, God. Not now. Try to forgive me. I'm just too tired and too appalled.

Thirty-six years old.

Thirty-six.

Well, why not? Why one time worse than another? God knows it's no picnic or ever was intended as such.

Into Thy hands I commend my spirit.

She made the sign of the Cross, raised the shade, opened the window, and got into bed. As her bare feet slid along the cold, clean linen and she felt its cold, clean blandness beneath her and above her, she was taken briefly by trembling and by loneliness, and remembered touching her dead mother's cheek.

Oh, why am I alive!

She took off her glasses and laid them carefully in reach at the foot of the lamp, and turned out the light. She straightened formally on her back, folded her hands upon her breast, and shut her eyes.

I can't worry any more about anything tonight, she said to herself. He'll just have to take care of it.

Till morning.

*

Mary did not bother to turn on the light; she could see well enough by the windows. She put on her nightgown and undressed beneath it, and saw to it that the door was left ajar for the children, and climbed into bed before she realized that these were the same sheets and before it occurred to her that she had not said her prayers; and for such a while now she had felt that if only she could be alone, only for that!

It's all right, she whispered to herself; it's all right, she whispered aloud. She had meant that she was sure that God would understand and forgive her inability to pray, but she found that she meant too that it really was all right, everything, the whole thing, really all right. Thy will be done. All right. Truly all right. She lay straight on her back with her hands open, upward at her sides and could just make out, in the subtly diminished darkness, a familiar stain which at various times had seemed to resemble a crag, a galleon, a fish, a brooding head. Tonight it was just itself, with one meaningless eye. It seemed to her that she was falling backward and downward, prostrate, through eternity; she felt no concern. Without concern she heard a voice speak within her: Out of the deep have I called unto Thee, O Lord; Lord, hear my voice, she joined in. O let Thine ears consider well the voice of my complaint. And now the first voice said no more and, aware of its silent presence, Mary continued, whispering aloud: If Thou, Lord, wilt be extreme to mark what is done amiss O Lord, who may abide it? And with these last words she began to cry freely and quietly, her hands turned downward and moved wide on the bed.

Oh, Jay! Jay!

Under the lid of the large kettle the low water was lukewarm; one by one, along the curved firmament, the last of the bubbles broke and vanished.

Hannah lay straight on her back with her hands folded: in their deep sockets, beneath lids as frail as membranes, her eyeballs were true spheres. No lines were left in her face; she might have been a young woman. Her lips were parted, and each breath was a light sigh.

Mary lay watching the ceiling: Who may abide it, she whispered.

Silently.

One by one, million by million, in the prescience of dawn, every leaf in that part of the world was moved.

*R*ufus' house was on the way to school for a considerable neighborhood, and within a few minutes after his father had
waved for the last time and disappeared, the walks were filled
with another exciting thing to look at as the boys and girls who
were old enough for school came by. At first he was content to
watch them through the front window; they were creatures of an
all but unimaginable world; he personally knew nobody who was
big enough even for kindergarten. Later he felt more kinship with
them, more curiosity, great envy, and considerable awe. It did
not yet occur to him that he could ever grow up to be one of them,
but he began to feel that in any case they were somehow of the
same race. He wandered out into the yard, even to the sidewalk,
even, at length, to the corner, where he could see them coming
from three ways at once. He was fascinated by the way they looked,
the boys so powerfully dressed and the girls almost as prettily as if
they were going to a party. Nearly all of them walked in two's
and three's, and members of these groups often called to others of
the groups. You could see how well they all knew each other; any
number of people; a whole world. And they all carried books of
different colors and thicknesses, and lunches done up in packages
or boxes, and pencils in still other boxes; or carried all these things
together in a satchel. He loved the way they carried these things, it
seemed to give them wonderful dignity and purpose, to be the
mark that set them apart in their privileged world. He particularly admired and envied the way the boys who carried their books
in brown canvas straps could swing them, except when they
swung them at his head. Then he was at the same time frightened
and very much surprised, and the boy who had pretended he
meant to hit him, and anyone else who saw, would laugh to see
that look of fear and surprise on his face, and he felt puzzled and
unhappy because they laughed.

But this did not happen often enough to discourage him, and
going to the corner at the time they went to school, and at the time
they could be expected back again, became quite a habit with

him, almost as happy and exciting, in its way, as watching for the first glimpse of his father, late in the afternoon. Sometimes when he caught an eye he would even say, "Hello," as much out of embarrassment as eagerness to communicate. Of course he was very seldom answered; the boys would merely stare at him for a second or so, with the stare turning hot or more often cold, and the girls, depending on age or disposition, either giggled in a way that made him look quickly away, or pretended that they had not even seen or heard him. But since he did not, after all, expect any answer, it was wonderfully pleasant when, occasionally, a much older boy would smile and say, "Hello there"; a few times they even reached out and mussed up his hair. Once, too, when he had said hello to some much older girls, one of them cried out in the strange, sticky voice he had heard grown women use, "Ooh, just look at the darlin little boy!"

He had felt embarrassed but pleasantly flattered for a moment; then he heard several boys squealing the same words, but insincerely, in fact with a hatred and scorn which appalled him, and he had wished that he could not be seen.

He never learned the names of more than two or three of these boys, for most of them lived several blocks away; but quite a few of them, in time, knew him very well. They would come up, nearly always, with the same question: "What's your name?" It seemed strange to him that they could not remember his name from one day to the next, for he always told it to them perfectly clearly, but he felt that if they forgot, and asked again, he ought to tell them again, and when he told them, politely, they all laughed. After a while he began to realize that they only asked him, day after day, not because they had really forgotten, but only to tease him. So he became more careful. When they asked, "What's your name?" he would feel embarrassed and say, "Oh, you know my name, you're only trying to tease me."

And some of them would snicker, but invariably the boy who had asked it this time would say very seriously and politely, "No, I don't know your name, you never told me your name," and he would begin to wonder; had he or hadn't he.

"Yes I did, too," he would say, "I remember. It was only day before yesterday."

And again there would be snickering, but the questioner looked even more serious and kind, and one or two of the boys next him looked equally serious, and he would say, "No, honest. Honest, it couldn't have been me. I don't know your name."

And one of the other boys would say, very reasonably, "Gee, he wouldn't ast you if he knowed it already, would he?"

And Rufus would say, "Aw, you're just trying to tease me. You all know my name."

And one of the other boys would say, "I've forgot it. I knew it but I've plumb forgot it. I'd tell him if I could but I just can't remember it."

And he too would look very sincere. And the first questioner would say, almost pleading, and very kind-looking, "Come on, tell us your name. Maybe you told it to him but he don't remember. If he could remember he'd tell me, now wouldn't he? Wouldn't you tell me?"

"Sure I'd tell you if I could remember it. Wisht you'd tell it to me again."

And two or three other boys, in similar tones of kindness, respect and concern, would chime in, "Aw come on, tell us your name."

And he was taken aback by all this kindness and concern, for they did not seem to act in that way towards him at any other time, and yet it did seem real. And after thinking a moment he would say, looking cautiously and earnestly, at the boy who had forgotten, "Do you promise you really honestly forgot?"

And looking back just as earnestly the boy said, "Cross my heart and body," and did so.

Then there was a snicker again from somebody, and Rufus realized that some of them were undoubtedly teasing; but he felt that he did not much mind, if these central boys were not. So he paid no attention to the snickering and said to every one of the kind-looking, serious boys, "You promise you honestly aren't teasing this time?" and they promised. Then he said, "If I tell you this time will you promise to do your very best to remember, and not ask me again?" and they said that they sure would, they crossed their hearts and bodies. At the last moment, just as he was beginning to tell them, he always felt such sudden, profound doubt of their sincerity that he did not want to go ahead, but he always felt, too, Maybe they mean it. If they do, it would be mean not to tell them. So he always told them. "Well," he always said rather doubtfully, and brought out his name in a peculiarly *muffled and shy way (he had come almost to feel that the name itself was being physically hurt, and he did not want it to be hurt again); "Well, it's Rufus."*

And the instant it was out of his mouth he knew that he had been mistaken once again, that not a single soul of them had meant one thing that he had said, for with that instant every one of them screamed as loudly as he could with a ferocious kind of joy, and it was as if the whole knot exploded and sent its fragments tearing all over the neighborhood, screaming his name with amusement and apparently with some kind of contempt; and many of them screamed, as well, a verse which they seemed to think very funny, though Rufus could not understand why.

> *Uh-Rufus, Uh-Rastus, Uh-Johnson, Uh-Brown,*
> *uh-What ya gonna do when the rent comes roun?*

and others yelled, "Nigger's name, nigger's name," and chanted a verse that he had often heard them yell after the backs of colored children and even grown-up colored people,

> *Nigger, nigger, black as tar,*
> *Tried to ride a lectric car,*
> *Car broke down an broke his back*
> *Poor nigger wanted his nickel back.*

Three or four, instead of running, stood screaming his name and these verses at him, and the word, "nigger," jumping up and down and shoving their fingers at his chest and stomach and face while he stood in abashment, and followed by these, he would walk unhappily home.

It puzzled him very deeply. If they knew his name all the time, as apparently they did, then why did they keep on asking as if they had never heard it, or as if they couldn't remember it? It was just to tease. But why did they want to tease? Why did they get such fun out of it? Why was it so much fun, to pretend to be so nice and so really interested, to pretend it so well that somebody else believed you in spite of himself, just so that he would show that he was deceived once again, because if you honestly did *mean it, this time, he didn't want to not tell you when you honestly seemed to want so much to know. Why was it that when some of them were asking him, and others were backing them up or just looking on, there was some kind of a strange, tight force in the air all around*

them that made them all seem very much together and that made
him feel very much alone and very eager to be liked by them, together with them? Why did he keep on believing them? It happened over and over and he could not think of a single time that
they had looked so interested, and friendly, and kind, but what it
had turned out that they didn't really mean one bit of it. The
ones who were really nice, the ones who never deceived him or
teased him, were a few of the much bigger boys, who were never so
attentive or kind as this, but just said, "Hello, there," and smiled
as they went by, or maybe mussed up his hair or gave him a little
punch, not to hurt or scare him, but only in play. They were very
different from these, they never paid him such close attention or
looked so affectionate, but they were the nice ones and these were
mean to him, every time. But every time, it was the same. When
they started he was always absolutely sure they were teasing, and
he was always absolutely sure that this time, he would not give in
to them; but every time, as they kept talking, he became less sure.
At the same time that he became less sure, he became more sure,
but that confused and troubled him, and the more sure he was
that all this apparent kindness was merely deception and meanness, the more eagerly he studied their faces in the hope that this
time they really meant it. The less he believed them, the more he
was led to believe them, and the easier it was for him to believe
them. The more alone he felt, the more he wanted to feel that he
was not alone, but one of them. And every time he finally gave in,
he became a little more sure, just before he gave in, that he would
not take this chance again. And every time he finally spoke his
name, he spoke it a little more shyly, a little more in shame, until
he began to feel some kind of shame about the name itself. The
way they all screamed it at him, and screamed that rhyme they
all laughed at, the more he came to feel that there must be something wrong with the name itself, so that even at home sometimes,
even when Mama said it, if he heard it without expecting it, he
felt some kind of obscure, wincing shock and shame. But when he
asked her if Rufus was really a nigger's name, and why that
made everybody laugh at it, she turned to him sharply and said to
him in a sharp voice, as if she were accusing him of something,
"Who told you that?", and he had answered, in fear, that he did
not know who, and she had said, "Don't you just pay any attention to them. It's a very fine old name. Some colored people take it

too, but that is perfectly all right and nothing for them to be ashamed of or for white people to be ashamed of who take it. You were given that name because it was your great-grandfather Lynch's name, and it's a name to be proud of. And Rufus: don't ever speak that word 'nigger'."

But he had felt that although maybe she was proud of the name, he was not. How could you be proud of a name that everybody laughed at? Once when they were less noisy, and one of them said to him, quietly, "That's a nigger's name," he had tried to feel proud and had said, "It is not either, it's a very fine old name and I got it from my Great-granpa Lynch," they yelled, "Then your granpa's a nigger too," and ran off down the street yelling, "Rufus is a nigger, Rufus' granpa's a nigger, he's a ning-ger, he's a nin-ger," and he had yelled after them, "He is not, either, it's my great-granpa *and he is* not!*"; but after that they sometimes opened a conversation by asking, "How's your nigger granpaw?" and he had to try to explain all over again that it was* his *great-grandpa and he was* not *colored, but they never seemed to pay any attention.*

He could not understand what amused them so much about this game, or why they should pretend to be all kindness and interest for the sake of deceiving him into doing something still again that he knew they knew better than to do, but it gradually became clear to him that no matter how much they pretended good, they always meant meanness, and that the only way to guard against this was never to believe them, and never to do what they asked him to. And so in time he found that no matter how nice they acted, he was not deceived by them and would not tell them his name, and this made him feel much better, except that now they seemed to have much less interest in him. He did not want them to go by without even looking at him, or just saying something mean or sneering as they passed, pretending so successfully that they meant to hit him with their books, that he had to duck; he only wanted them not to tease and fool him; he only wanted them to be nice to him and like him. And so he remained very ready to do whatever seemed necessary to be liked, except that one thing, telling his name, which was clearly not ever a good thing to do. And so, as long as they didn't ask him his name (and they soon knew that this joke was no good any more), he continued to hope against hope that in every other way, they were not trying to tease or fool him. Now they would come up to him looking quite serious, the older boys, and say, as if it were a very serious question,

> *Rufus Rastus Johnson Brown*
> *What you gonna do when the* rent *comes roun?*

He always felt that they were still teasing him about his name, when they said that; there was something about the word "Rastus" that they said in such a tone that he knew they disliked both names and held both in contempt, and he could not understand why they gave him so many names when only one was really his and his last name was really Follet. But at least they knew what his name was now, even if most of them pronounced it "Roofeass"; at least they weren't pretending they didn't know; it wasn't as bad as that. Besides, what they were really doing was asking him a question, "What you gonna do when the rent comes roun?" Though they asked it every time and it seemed a nonsensical question. They seemed to really want to know, and if he could answer them, then he could really tell them something they really didn't know and then maybe they would really like him and not tease him. Yet he realized that this too must be teasing. They did not really want to know. How could they, when the question had no meaning? What was the rent? What did it look like when it came roun? It probably looked very mean or maybe it looked nice but was mean when you got to know it. And what would you do when it came roun? What could you do if you didn't even know what it was? Or if it was just something they made up, that wasn't really alive, just a story? He wanted to ask what the rent was, but he suspected that that was exactly what they wanted him to ask, and that if or when he asked it, it would turn out that the whole thing was a trap of some kind, a joke, and that he had done something shameful or ridiculous in asking. So that was one thing he was now wise enough never to do: he never asked what the rent was, and this was one of the things he felt sure that somehow he had better not ask his mother or his father, either. So when they came up to him now, he always knew they were going to ask this foolish question, and when they asked it he felt stubborn and shy, determined not to ask what the rent was; and once they had asked it, and stood looking at him with a curious, cold look as if they were hungry, he looked back at them until he felt too embarrassed, and saw them start to smile in a way that might be mean or might possibly be friendly, and on the possibility that they were friendly, smiled unsurely too, and looked down at the pavement, and muttered, "I don't know"; which seemed to amuse them almost as much as when he had told what his name was, though not so loudly; and then sometimes he would walk away from them, and after a while he learned that he should not answer this question any more than he should answer the question about his name.

When he walked away, or when he refused to answer, he always realized that in some way he had defeated them, but he also always felt disconsolate and lonely, and sometimes because of this he would turn around after he had gone a little way, and look and they would come up and go round him again, and other times, when he kept on walking away, he felt even more lonely and unhappy, so much so that he went down between the houses into the back yard and stayed for a while because he felt uneasy about being seen, yet, by his mother. He began to anticipate going out to the corner with as much unhappiness as hope, and sometimes he did not go at all; but when he went again, after not going at all, he was asked where he had been and why he had not been there the day before, and he had not known what to answer, and had been much encouraged because they spoke in such a way that they really seemed to care where he had been. And within the next days things did seem to change. The older and more perceptive of the boys realized that the shape of the game had shifted and that if they were to count on him to be there, and to be such a fool as always before, they had to act much more friendly; and the more stupid boys, seeing how well this worked, imitated them as well as they could. Rufus quickly came to suspect the more flagrant exaggerations of friendliness, but the subtler boys found, to their intense delight, that if only they varied the surface, the bait, from time to time, they would almost always deceive him. He was ever so ready to oblige. How it got started none of them remembered or cared, but they all knew that if they kept at him enough he would sing them his song, and be fool enough to think they actually liked it. They would say, "Sing us a song, Roofeass," and he would look as if he knew they were teasing him and say, "Oh, you don't want to hear it."

And they would say that they sure did want to hear it, it was a real pretty song, better than they could sing, and they liked the *way he danced when he sang it, too. And since they had very early learned to take pains to listen to the song with apparent respect and friendliness, he was very soon and easily persuaded. And so, feeling odd and foolish not because he felt they were really deceiving him or laughing at him, but only because with each public repetition of it he felt more silly, and less sure that it was really as pretty and enjoyable as he liked to think it was, he would give them one last anxious look, which always particularly tickled them, and would then raise his arms and turn round and round, singing,*

I'm a little busy bee, busy bee, busy bee,
I'm a little busy bee, singing in *the clover.*

As he sang and danced he could hear through his own verses a few obscure, incredulous cackles, but nearly all of the faces which whirled past him, those of the older boys, were restrained, attentive and smiling, and this made up for the contempt he saw on the faces of the middle-sized boys; and when he had finished, and was catching his breath, these older boys would clap their hands in real approval, and say, "That's an awful pretty song, Rufus, where did you learn that song?"

And again he would suspect some meanness behind it and so would refuse to say until they had coaxed him sufficiently and then out it came, "My mama"; and at that point some of the smaller boys were liable to spoil everything by yelling and laughing, but often even if they did, the older boys could save it all by sternly crying, "You shut up! Don't you know a pretty song when you hear it?" and by turning to him, with faces which shut out those boys and included him among the big boys, and saying, "Don't you care about them, Rufus, they're just ignorant and don't know nothing. You sing your song." And another would chime in, "Yeah, Rufus, sing it again. Gee, that's a pretty song"; and a third would say, "And don't forget to dance"; and for this reduced but select audience he would do the whole thing over again.

At that point someone usually said, abruptly, "Come on, we got to go," and as suddenly as if a chair had been pulled from under him, he would be left by himself; they hardly even clapped their hands before they walked away. But some of the boys with the nicest faces always took care, before they left, to tell him, "Gee, thanks, Rufus, that was mighty *pretty," and to say, "Don't you forget, you be here tomorrow"; and this more than made up for the thing which never failed to perplex him. Why did they walk off, so suddenly as all that? Why did they all keep looking back and laughing in that queer way; subdued talk, their heads close together, and then those sudden whoops of laughter? It almost seemed as if they were laughing at him. And once when one of the bigger boys suddenly flung up his arms and whirled into the street, piping in a high, squeaky voice,* "I'm a little busy bee," *he was quite sure that they had not really liked the song, or him for singing it. But if they didn't, then why did they ask him to sing it? And then once he heard one of them, far down the block, squeak,* "My mama," *and he felt as if something went straight through his stomach, and they all laughed, and he was practically certain that to those boys at least, the whole thing was just some kind of mean joke. But then he remembered how nice the boys he liked best and trusted most had been, and he knew that anyway the boys he liked best were not in any way trying to tease him.*

After a while, however, he began to wonder even about them. Maybe their being so extra nice was just their way of getting him to do things he would never do if they were only nice part of the time and then laughed at him. Yet if they were nice all the time, it must be because they honestly meant it. And yet the way some of the others laughed, what he was doing must be wrong or silly somehow. He would be much more careful. He would be careful not to do anything or say anything anybody asked him to, unless he was sure they were really nice and really meant it. He now watched even the boys he liked best with very particular caution, and they saw that unless they were much more shrewd the game was likely to be spoiled again. They began to promise him rewards, a stick of chewing gum, the stub of a pencil, chalk, a piece of candy, and this seemed to convince him. The less shrewd of the boys often did not give him the promised reward, and this of course was more fun, but the smarter ones were always consistent, so that he never refused them. It was all so easy, in fact, that it began to bore them. They began to appreciate the tricks the more stupid boys played, one getting down behind him while he danced and another pushing him over backwards, but they were intelligent enough never to take part in this, always to pretend thorough disapproval, always to help him to his feet and brush him off and console him if he had struck his head hard and was crying, and always to conceal their astonished delight at his utter bewilderment and gullibility and their astonished contempt at his complete lack of spirit to strike out against his tormentors, his lack of ability, even, for real solid anger. And because they were always there, and always seemed to be on his side, they could always keep him sufficiently deceived to come back for more than anyone in his right senses would come back for.

The oldest of them began to be obscurely ashamed, as well as bored. They were all much older and smarter than he was; even the youngest of the boys who went to school were enough older than he was that it seemed no wonder that he was continually fooled, and that he never fought back. They felt that this little song, for instance, was too sissy to be fun for much longer. They felt that more violent things should be done. But they themselves could not do such things. If they showed him they were not on his side, the fun would all be over. And even if it were not, they knew that it would be unfair of them to do the really violent things, which absolutely required violence in return, to anyone so much younger and smaller, no matter how big a fool he was. Besides, they had received more than enough hints that even if he were driven to fight, he would not have the nerve to, probably wouldn't even know he had to. They were curious to see what would happen. They left the game wider and wider open to the smaller, crueler and more simple boys. But it was no good. He would just look at them with surprise, pain and reproach, and get up and walk away; and if any of these older, normally friendly boys consoled him too closely, he would burst into sobs which disgusted as well as delighted them.

At length they found the right formula. They would put some boys as small as he was, up to some trick which nobody bigger would have any right to do.

*A*fter dinner the babies and all the children except Rufus were laid out on the beds to take their naps, and his mother thought he ought to lie down too, but his father said no, why did he need to, so he was allowed to stay up. He stayed out on the porch with the men. They were so full up and sleepy they hardly even tried to talk, and he was so full up and sleepy that he could hardly see or hear, but half dozing between his father's knees in the thin shade, trying to keep his eyes open, he could just hear the mild, lazy rumbling of their voices, and the more talkative voices of the women back in the kitchen, talking more easily, but keeping their voices low, not to wake the children, and the rattling of the dishes they were doing, and now and then their walking here or there along the floor; and mused with half-closed eyes which went in and out of focus with sleepiness, upon the slow twinkling of the millions of heavy leaves on the trees and the slow flashing of the blades of the corn, and nearer at hand, the hens dabbing in the pecked dirt yard and the ragged edge of the porch floor, and everything hung dreaming in a shining silver haze, and a long, low hill of blue silver shut off everything against a blue-white sky, and he leaned back against his father's chest and he could hear his heart pumping and his stomach growling and he could feel the hard knees against his sides, and the next thing he knew his eyes opened and he was looking up into his mother's face and he was lying on a bed and she was saying it was time to wake up because they were going on a call and see his great-great-grandmother and she would most specially want to see him because he was her oldest great-great-grandchild. And he and his father and mother and Catherine got in the front seat and his Granpa Follet and Aunt Jessie and her baby and Jim-Wilson and Ettie Lou and Aunt Sadie and her baby got in the back seat and Uncle Ralph stood on the running board because he was sure he could remember the way, and that was all there was room for, and they started off very carefully down the lane, so nobody would be jolted, and even *before they got out to the road his mother asked his father to stop a minute, and she insisted on taking Ettie Lou with them in front, to make a little more room in back, and after she insisted for a while, they gave in, and then they all got started again, and his father guided the auto so very carefully across the deep ruts into the road, the other way from LaFollette as Ralph told him to ("Yeah, I know," his father said, "I remember that much anyhow."), that they were hardly joggled at all, and his mother commented on how* very *nicely and carefully his father always drove when he didn't just forget and go too fast, and his father blushed, and after a few minutes his mother began to look uneasy, as if she had to go to the bathroom but didn't want to say anything about it, and after a few minutes more she said, "Jay, I'm awfully sorry but now I really think you* are *forgetting."*

"Forgetting what?" he said.

"I mean a little too fast, dear," she said.

"Good road along here," he said. "Got to make time while the road's good." He slowed down a little. "Way I remember it," he said, "there's some stretches you can't hardly ever get a mule through, we're coming to, ain't they Ralph?"

"Oh mercy," his mother said.

"We are just raggin you," he said. "They're not all that *bad. But all the same we better make time while we can." And he sped up a little.*

After another two or three miles Uncle Ralph said, "Now around this bend you run through a branch and you turn up sharp to the right," and they ran through the branch and turned into a sandy woods road and his father went a little slower and a cool breeze flowed through them and his mother said how lovely this shade was after that terrible hot sun, wasn't it, and all the older people murmured that it sure was, and almost immediately they broke out of the woods and ran through two miles of burned country with stumps and sometimes whole tree trunks sticking up out of it sharp and cruel, and blackberry and honeysuckle all over the place, and a hill and its shadow ahead. And when they came within the shadow of the hill, Uncle Ralph said in a low voice, "Now you get to the hill, start along the base of it to your left till you see your second right and then you take that," but when they got there, there was only the road to the left and none to the right and his father took it and nobody said anything, and after a minute Uncle Ralph said, "Reckon they wasn't much to choose from there, was they?" and laughed unhappily.

"That's right," his father said, and smiled.

"Reckon my memory ain't so sharp as I bragged," Ralph said.

"You're doin fine," his father said, and his mother said so too.

"I could a swore they was a road both ways there," Ralph said, "but it was nigh on twenty years since I was out here." Why for goodness sake, his mother said, then she certainly *thought he had a wonderful memory.*

"How long since you were here, Jay?" He did not say anything. "Jay?"

"I'm a-studyin it," he said.

"There's your turn," Ralph said suddenly, and they had to back the auto to turn into it.

They began a long, slow, winding climb, and Rufus half heard and scarcely understood their disjointed talking. His father had not been there in nearly thirteen years; the last time was just before he came to Knoxville. He was always her favorite, Ralph said. Yes, his grandfather said, he reckoned that was a fact, she always seemed to take a shine to Jay. His father said quietly that he always did take a shine to her. It turned out he was the last of those in the auto who had seen her. They asked how she was, as if it had been within a month or two. He said she was failing lots of ways, specially getting around, her rheumatism was pretty bad, but in the mind she was bright as a dollar, course that wasn't saying how they might find her by now, poor old soul; no use saying. Nope, Uncle Ralph said, that was a fact; time sure did fly, didn't it; seemed like before you knew it, this year was last year. She had never yet seen Jay's children, or Ralph's, or Jessie's or Sadie's, it was sure going to be a treat for her. A treat and a surprise. Yes it sure would be that, his father said, always supposing she could still recognize them. Mightn't she even have died? his mother wanted to know. Oh no, all the Folletts said, they'd have heard for sure if she'd died. Matter of fact they had heard she had failed a good bit. Sometimes her memory slipped up and she got confused, poor old soul. His mother said well she should think so, poor old lady. She asked, carefully, if she was taken good care of. Oh, yes, they said. That she was. Sadie's practically given up her life to her. That was Grandpa Follett's oldest *sister and young Sadie was named for her. Lived right with her tending to her wants, day and night. Well, isn't that just wonderful, his mother said. Wasn't anybody else could do it, they agreed with each other. All married and gone, and she wouldn't come live with any of them, they all offered, over and over, but she wouldn't leave her home. I raised my family here, she said, I lived here all my life from fourteen years on and I aim to die here, that must be a good thirty-five, most, a good near forty year ago, Grampaw died. Goodness sake, his mother said, and she was an old* old *woman then!* His father said soberly, "She's a hundred and three years old. Hundred and three or hundred and four. She never could remember for sure which. But she knows she wasn't born later than eighteen-twelve. And she always reckoned it might of been eighteen-eleven.*

"Great heavens, *Jay! Do you* mean *that?*" He just nodded, and kept his eyes on the road. "*Just* imagine that, *Rufus,*" she said. "*Just* think *of* that! "

"*She's an old, old lady,*" his father said gravely; and Ralph gravely and proudly concurred.

"*The things she must have seen!*" Mary said quietly. "*Indians. Wild animals.*" Jay laughed. "*I mean* man-*eaters, Jay. Bears, and wildcats—terrible things.*"

"*There were cats back in these mountains, Mary—we called em painters, that's the same as a panther—they were around here still when I was a boy. And there is still bear, they claim.*"

"*Gracious Jay, did you ever* see *one? A panther?*"

"*Saw one'd been shot.*"

"*Goodness,*" Mary said.

"*A mean-lookin varmint.*"

"*I know,*" she said. "*I mean, I* bet *he was. I just can't get over—why she's almost as old as the country, Jay.*"

"Oh, *no,*" he laughed. "*Ain't nobody* that *old. Why I read somewhere, that just these mountains here are the oldest . . .*"

"*Dear, I meant the nation,*" she said. "*The United States, I mean. Why let me see, why it was hardly as old as I am when she was born.*" They all calculated for a moment. "Not *even as old,*" she said triumphantly.

"*By golly,*" his father said. "*I never thought of it like that.*" He shook his head. "*By golly,*" he said, "*that's a fact.*"

"*Abraham Lincoln was just two years old,*" she murmured.

"*Maybe three,*" *she said grudgingly.* "*Just try to* imagine *that, Rufus,*" *she said after a moment.* "*Over a hundred years.*" *But she could see that he couldn't comprehend it.* "*You know what she is?*" *she said,* "*she's Granpa Follet's* grandmother!"

"*That's a fact, Rufus,*" *his grandfather said from the back seat, and Rufus looked around, able to believe it but not to imagine it, and the old man smiled and winked.* "*Woulda never believed you'd hear* me *call nobody 'Granmaw,' now would you?*"

"*No sir,*" *Rufus said.*

"*Well, yer goana,*" *his grandfather said,* "*quick's I see her.*"

Ralph was beginning to mutter and to look worried and finally his brother said, "*What's eaten ye, Ralph? Lost the way?*" *And Ralph said he didn't know for sure as he had lost it exactly, no, he wouldn't swear to that yet, but by golly he was damned if he was sure this was* hit *anymore, all the same.*

"*Oh dear, Ralph how too bad,*" *Mary said,* "*but don't you mind. Maybe we'll find it. I mean maybe soon you'll recognize landmarks and set us all straight again.*"

But his father, looking dark and painfully patient, just slowed the auto down and then came to a stop in a shady place. "*Maybe we better figure it out right now,*" *he said.*

"*Nothin round hyer I know,*" *Ralph said, miserably.* "*What I mean, maybe we ought to start back while we still know the way back. Try it another Sunday.*"

"*Oh, Jay.*"

"*I hate to but we got to get back in town tonight, don't forget. We could try it another Sunday. Make an early start.*" *But the upshot of it was that they decided to keep on ahead awhile, anyway. They descended into a long, narrow valley through the woods of which they could only occasionally see the dark ridges and the road kept bearing in a direction Ralph was almost sure was wrong, and they found a cabin, barely even cut out of the woods, they commented later, hardly even a corn patch, big as an ordinary barnyard; but the people there, very glum and watchful, said they had never even heard of her; and after a long while the valley opened out a little and Ralph began to think that perhaps he recognized it, only it sure didn't look like itself if it* was *it, and all of a sudden a curve opened into half-forested meadow and there were glimpses of a gray house through swinging vistas of saplings and Ralph said,* "*By golly,*" *and again,* "*By golly, that is* hit. *That's hit all right. Only we come on it from behind!"* And his father began to be sure too, and the house grew larger, and they swung around where they could see the front of it, and his father and his Uncle Ralph and his Grandfather all said, "Why sure enough," and sure enough it was: and, "There she is," and there she was: it was a great, square-logged gray cabin closed by a breezeway, with a frame second floor, and an enormous oak plunging from the packed dirt in front of it, and a great iron ring, the rim of a wagon wheel, hung by a chain from a branch of the oak which had drunk the chain into itself, and in the shade of the oak, which was as big as the whole corn patch they had seen, an old woman was standing up from a kitchen chair as they swung slowly in onto the dirt and under the edge of the shade, and another old woman continued to sit very still in her chair.

The younger of the two old women was Great Aunt Sadie, and she knew them the minute she laid eyes on them and came right on up to the side of the auto before they could even get out. "Lord God," she said in a low, hard voice, and she put her hands on the edge of the auto and just looked from one to the other of them. Her hands were long and narrow and as big as a man's and every knuckle was swollen and split. She had hard black eyes, and there was a dim purple splash all over the left side of her face. She looked at them so sharply and silently from one to another that Rufus thought she must be mad at them, and then she began to shake her head back and forth. "Lord God," she said again. "Howdy, John Henry," she said.

"Howdy, Sadie," his grandfather said.

"Howdy, Aunt Sadie," his father and his Aunt Sadie said.

"Howdy, Jay," she said, looking sternly at his father, "howdy, Ralph," and she looked sternly at Ralph. "Reckon you must be Jess, and yore Sadie. Howdy, Sadie."

"This is Mary, Aunt Sadie," his father said. "Mary, this is Aunt Sadie."

"I'm proud to know you," the old woman said, looking very hard at his mother. "I figured it must be you," she said, just as his mother said, "I'm awfully glad to know you too." "And this is Rufus and Catherine and Ralph's Jim-Wilson and Ettie Lou and Jessie's Charlie after his daddy and Sadie's Jessie after her Granma and her Aunt Jessie," his father said.

"Well, Lord God," the old woman said. "Well, pile on out."

"How's Granmaw?" his father asked, in a low voice, without moving yet to get out.

"Good as we got any right to expect," she said, "but don't feel put out if she don't know none-a-yews. She mought and she mought not. Half the time she don't even know me."

Ralph shook his head and clucked his tongue. "Pore old soul," he said, looking at the ground. His father let out a slow breath, puffing his cheeks.

"So if I was you-all I'd come up on her kind of easy," the old woman said. "Bin a coon's age since she seen so many folks at onct. Me either. Mought skeer her if ye all come a whoopin up at her in a flock."

"Sure," his father said.

"Ayy," his mother whispered.

His father turned and looked back. "Whyn't you go see her the first, Paw?" he said very low. "Yore the eldest."

"Tain't me she wants to see," Grandfather Follet said. "Hit's the younguns ud tickle her most."

"Reckon that's the truth, if she can take notice," the old woman said. "She shore like to cracked her heels when she heared yore boy was born," she said to Jay, "Mary or no Mary. Proud as Lucifer. Cause that was the first," she told Mary.

"Yes, I know," Mary said. "Fifth generation, that made."

"Did you get her postcard, Jay?"

"What postcard?"

"Why no," Mary said.

"She tole me what to write on one a them postcards and put hit in the mail to both a yews so I done it. Didn't ye never get it?"

Jay shook his head. "First I ever heard tell of it," he said.

"Well I shore done give hit to the mail. Ought to remember. Cause I went all the way into Polly to buy it and all the way in again to put it in the mail."

"We never did get it," Jay said.

"What street did you send it, Aunt Sadie?" Mary asked. "Because we moved not long be . . ."

"Never sent it to no street," the old woman said. "Never knowed I needed to, Jay working for the post office."

"Why, I quit working for the post office a long time back, Aunt Sadie. Even before that."

"Well I reckon that's how come then. Cause I just sent hit to 'Post Office, Cristobal, Canal Zone, Panama,' and I spelt hit right, too. C-r-i . . ."

"Oh," Mary said.

"Aw," Jay said. "Why, Aunt Sadie, I thought you'd a known. We been living in Knoxvul since pert near two years before Rufus was born."

She looked at him keenly and angrily, raising her hands slowly from the edge of the auto, and brought them down so hard that Rufus jumped. Then she nodded, several times, and still she did not say anything. At last she spoke, coldly, "Well, they might as well just put me out to grass," she said. "Lay me down and give me both barls threw the head."

"Why, Aunt Sadie," Mary said gently, but nobody paid any attention.

After a moment the old woman went on solemnly, staring hard into Jay's eyes: "I knowed that like I know my own name and it plumb slipped my mind."

"Oh what a shame," Mary said sympathetically.

"Hit ain't shame I feel," the old woman said, "hit's sick in the stummick."

"Oh I didn't m . . ."

"Right hyer!" and she slapped her hand hard against her stomach and laid her hand back on the edge of the auto. "If I git like that too," she said to Jay, "then who's agonna look out fer her?"

"Aw, tain't so bad, Aunt Sadie," Jay said. "Everybody slips up nown then. Do it myself an I ain't half yer age. And you just ought see Mary."

"Gracious, yes," Mary said. "I'm just a perfect scatterbrain."

The old woman looked briefly at Mary and then looked back at Jay. "Hit ain't the only time," she said, "not by a long chalk. Twarn't three days ago I . . ." she stopped. "Takin on about yer troubles ain't never holp nobody," she said. "You just set hyer a minute."

She turned and walked over to the older woman and leaned deep over against her ear and said, quite loudly, but not quite shouting, "Granmaw, ye got company." And they watched the old woman's pale eyes, which had been on them all this time in the light shadow of the sunbonnet, not changing, rarely ever blinking, to see whether they would change now, and they did not *change at all, she didn't even move her head or her mouth. "Ye hear me, Granmaw?" The old woman opened and shut her sunken mouth, but not as if she were saying anything. "Hit's Jay and his wife and younguns, come up from Knoxvul to see you," she called, and they saw the hands crawl in her lap and the face turned towards the younger woman and they could hear a thin, dry crackling, no words.*

"She can't talk any more," Jay said, almost in a whisper.

"Oh no," Mary said.

But Sadie turned towards them and her hard eyes were bright. "She knows ye," she said quietly. "Come on over." And they climbed slowly and shyly out onto the swept ground. "I'll tell her about the rest a yuns in a minute," Sadie said.

"Don't want to mix her up," Ralph explained, and they all nodded.

It seemed to Rufus like a long walk over to the old woman because they were all moving so carefully and shyly; it was almost like church. "Don't holler," Aunt Sadie was advising his parents, "hit only skeers her. Just talk loud and plain right up next her ear."

"I know," his mother said. "My mother is very deaf, too."

"Yeah," his father said. And he bent down close against her ear. "Granmaw?" he called, and he drew a little away, where she could see him, while his wife and his children looked on, each holding one of the mother's hands. She looked straight into his eyes and her eyes and her face never changed, a look as if she were gazing at some small point at a great distance, with complete but idle intensity, as if what she was watching was no concern of hers. His father leaned forward again and gently kissed her on the mouth, and drew back again where she could see him well, and smiled a little, anxiously. Her face restored itself from his kiss like grass that has been lightly stepped on; her eyes did not alter. Her skin looked like brown-marbled stone over which water has worked for so long that it is as smooth and blind as soap. He leaned to her ear again. "I'm Jay," he said. "John Henry's boy." Her hands crawled in her skirt: every white bone and black vein showed through the brown-splotched skin; the wrinkled knuckles were like pouches; she wore a red rubber guard ahead of her wedding ring. Her mouth opened and shut and they heard her low, dry croaking, but her eyes did not change. They were bright in their

*thin shadow, but they were as impersonally bright as two perfectly
shaped eyes of glass.*

"I figure she knows you," Sadie said quietly.

*"She can't talk, can she?" Jay said, and now that he was not
looking at her, it was as if they were talking over a stump.*

*"Times she can," Sadie said. "Times she can't. Ain't only so sel-
dom call for talk, reckon she loses the hang of it. But I figger she
knows ye and I am tickled she does."*

*His father looked all around him in the shade and he looked
sad, and unsure, and then he looked at him. "Come here, Rufus," he said.*

*"Go to him," his mother whispered for some reason, and she
pushed his hand gently as she let it go.*

*"Just call her Granmaw," his father said quietly. "Get right up
by her ear like you do to Granmaw Lynch and say, 'Granmaw,
I'm Rufus.'"*

*He walked over to her as quietly as if she were asleep, feeling
strange to be by himself, and stood on tiptoe beside her and looked
down into her sunbonnet towards her ear. Her temple was deeply
sunken as if a hammer had struck it and frail as a fledgling's
belly. Her skin was crosshatched with the razor-fine slashes of innumerable square wrinkles and yet every slash was like smooth
stone; her ear was just a fallen intricate flap with a small gold
ring in it; her smell was faint yet very powerful, and she smelled
like new mushrooms and old spices and sweat, like his fingernail
when it was coming off. "Granmaw, I'm Rufus," he said carefully, and yellow-white hair stirred beside her ear. He could feel
coldness breathing from her cheek.*

*"Come out where she can see you," his father said, and he drew
back and stood still further on tiptoe and leaned across her, where
she could see. "I'm Rufus," he said, smiling, and suddenly her eyes
darted a little and looked straight into his, but they did not in
any way change their expression. They were just color: seen close as
this, there was color through a dot at the middle, dim as blue-
black oil, and then a circle of blue so pale it was almost white,
that looked like glass, smashed into a thousand dimly sparkling
pieces, smashed and infinitely old and patient, and then a ring
of dark blue, so fine and sharp no needle could have drawn it,
and then a clotted yellow full of tiny squiggles of blood, and then
a wrong-side furl of red-bronze, and little black lashes. Vague*

light sparkled in the crackled blue of the eye like some kind of remote ancestor's anger, and the sadness of time dwelt in the blue-breathing, oily center, lost and alone and far away, deeper than the deepest well. His father was saying something, but he did not hear and now he spoke again, careful to be patient, and Rufus heard, "Tell her 'I'm Jay's boy.' Say, 'I'm Jay's boy Rufus.'"

And again he leaned into the cold fragrant cavern next her ear and said, "I'm Jay's boy Rufus," and he could feel her face turn towards him.

"Now kiss her," his father said, and he drew out of the shadow of her bonnet and leaned far over and again entered the shadow and kissed her paper mouth, and the mouth opened, and the cold sweet breath of rotting and of spice broke from her with the dry croaking, and he felt the hands take him by the shoulders like knives and forks of ice through his clothes. She drew him closer and looked at him almost glaring, she was so filled with grave intensity. She seemed to be sucking on her lower lip and her eyes filled with light, and then, as abruptly as if the two different faces had been joined without transition in a strip of moving-picture film, she was not serious any more but smiling so hard that her chin and her nose almost touched and her deep little eyes giggled for joy. And again the croaking gurgle came, making shapes which were surely words but incomprehensible words, and she held him even more tightly by the shoulders, and looked at him even more keenly and incredulously with her giggling, all but hidden eyes, and smiled and smiled, and cocked her head to one side, and with sudden love he kissed her again. And he could hear his mother's voice say, "Jay," almost whispering, and his father say, "Let her be," in a quick, soft, angry voice, and when at length they gently disengaged her hands, and he was at a little distance, he could see that there was water crawling along the dust from under her chair, and his father and his Aunt Sadie looked gentle and sad and dignified, and his mother was trying not to show that she was crying, and the old lady sat there aware only that something had been taken from her, but growing quickly calm, and nobody said anything about it.

*L*ate one afternoon Uncle Ted and Aunt Kate came, all the way from Michigan. Aunt Kate had red hair. Uncle Ted had glasses and he could make faces. They brought him a book and what he liked best was a picture of a fat man with a cloth around his head, sitting on a tasseled cushion with a long snakey tube in his mouth, and it said:

> There was a fat man of Bombay
> Who was smoking his pipe one fine day
> When a bird called a snipe
> Flew away with his pipe,
> Which vexed that fat man of Bombay.

But there wasn't any bird in the picture. His father said he reckoned it was still out snipe-hunting.

They weren't really his uncle and aunt, it was like Aunt Celia. Just a friend. But Aunt Kate was a kind of cousin. She was Aunt Carrie's daughter and Aunt Carrie was Granma's half-sister. You were a half-sister if you had the same father or mother but not the same other one, and they had the same mother.

They slept on the brand-new davenport in the sitting room.

Next morning before daylight they all got up and went to the L&N depot. A man came for them in an auto because there was no streetcar to the L&N. They had so much to carry that even he was given a box to carry. They sat in the big room and it was full of people. His mother told his Uncle Ted she liked it better than the Southern depot because there were so many country folks and his father said he did too. It smelled like chewing tobacco and pee, and like a barn. Some of the ladies wore sunbonnets and lots of the men wore old straw hats, not the flat kind. One lady was nursing her baby. They had a long time to wait for their train; his father said, "Count on Mary and you won't never miss a train, but you may get the one the day before you aimed to," and his mother said, "Jay," and Uncle Ted laughed; so he heard the man call several trains in his fine, echoing voice, and finally he started

661

calling out a string of stations and his father got up saying, "That's us," and they got everything together and as soon as the man called the track they hurried fast, so they got two seats and turned them to face each other, and afterwhile the train pulled out and it was already broad daylight. The older people were all kind of sleepy and didn't talk much, though they pretended to, and afterwhile Aunt Kate dropped off to sleep and leaned her head against his mother's shoulder and the men laughed and his mother smiled and said, "Let her, the dear."

The news butcher came through and in spite of his mother, Uncle Ted bought him a glass locomotive with little bright-colored pieces of candy inside and Catherine a glass telephone with the same kind of candy inside, which his father had never done. His father and Uncle Ted spent a good deal of time in the smoking car, to smoke, and to make more room. It got hot and dull. But after quite a while his father came hurrying back down the aisle and told his mother to look out the window and she did and said, "Well what?" and he said, "No—up ahead," and they all three looked up ahead and there on the sky above the scrubby hill, there was a grand great lift of grayish blue that looked as if you could see the light through it, and then the train took a long curve and these liftings of gray blue opened out like a fan and filled the whole country ahead, shouldering above each other high and calm and full of shadowy light, so that he heard his mother say, "Ohhh! How perfectly glorious!", and his father say shyly, a little as if he owned them and was giving them to her, "That's them. That's the Smokies all right," and sure enough they did look smoky, and as they came nearer, smoke and great shadows seemed to be sailing around on them, but he knew that must be clouds. After a while he could begin to see the shapes of them clearly, great bronzy bulges that looked as if they were blown up tight like balloons, and solemn deep scoops of shady blue that ran from the tops on down below the tops of the near hills, deeper than he could see; "They're just like huge waves, Jay," his mother said with awe; "That's right," he said; "you remember?"; "Sure I do," he said; "just like seeing sunlight striking through waves, just before they topple."

"Yeah," his father said.

"Kate mustn't miss this," his mother said; "Kate!", and she took Aunt Kate by the shoulder.

"Sssh!" *his father hissed, and he frowned.* "Let her alone!" *But Aunt Kate was already waked up, though she was still very sleepy, wondering what it was all about.*

"Just look, *Kate," his mother said.* "Out there!" *Aunt Kate looked.* "See?" *his mother said.*

"Yes," Aunt Kate said.

"That's where we're going," his mother said.

"Yes," Aunt Kate said.

"Aren't they grand?" *his mother said.*

"Yes," Aunt Kate said.

"Well I think they're absolutely breath*taking," his mother said.*

"So do I," Aunt Kate said, and went back to sleep.

His mother made one of the funniest faces he had ever seen, looking at his father all bewildered and surprised and holding in her laughter, and his father laughed out loud but Aunt Kate didn't wake up. "Just like Catherine," *his mother whispered, laughing, and they all looked at Catherine, who was staring out at the mountains and looking very heavy and earnest; and they laughed and Catherine looked at them and began to realize they were laughing at her, and that made her face get red and that made them laugh some more, and even Rufus joined in, and they only stopped when Catherine began to stick out her lower lip and her mother said,* "Mercy, child, you've got to learn to take a joke."

But her father said, "Doesn't anybody like to be laughed at," *and took her on his lap, and she pulled her lip in and looked out the window again. Now they could even see the separate trees all over the sides of the mountains like rice, all shades of green and some almost black, and before much longer they were climbing more slowly past the feathery tops of trees and the high shoulders of the mountains and the great deep scoops were turning past them and beneath them as if they were very slowly and seriously dancing in sunlight and in cloud and in shadows almost of night, and now and then they could see a tiny cabin and a corn patch far off on the side of a mountain, and twice they even saw a tinier mule and a man with it, one of the men waved; and high above them in the changing sunlight, slowest of all, the tops of the mountains twisted and changed places. And after quite a while his father said he reckoned they better start getting their stuff together, and before much longer they got off.*

That night at supper when Rufus asked for more cheese Uncle Ted said, "Whistle to it and it'll jump off the table into your lap."

"Ted!" his mother said.

But Rufus was delighted. He did not know very well how to whistle yet, but he did his best, watching the cheese very carefully: it didn't jump off the table into his lap; it didn't even move.

"Try some more," Uncle Ted said. "Try harder."

"Ted!" his mother said.

He tried his very best and several times he managed to make a real whistle, but the cheese didn't even move, and he began to realize that Uncle Ted and Aunt Kate were shaking with laughter they were trying to hold in, though he couldn't see what there was to laugh about in a cheese that wouldn't even move when you whistled even when Uncle Ted said it would and he was really whistling, not just trying to whistle.

"Why won't it jump to me, Daddy?" he asked, almost crying with embarrassment and impatience, and at that Uncle Ted and Aunt Kate burst out laughing out loud, but his father didn't laugh, he looked all mixed up, and mad, and embarrassed, and his mother was very mad and she said, "That's just about enough of that, Ted. I think it's just a perfect shame, deceiving a little child like that who's been brought up to trust people, and laughing right in his face!"

"Mary," his father said, and Uncle Ted looked very much surprised and Aunt Kate looked worried, though they were still laughing a little, as if they couldn't stop yet.

"Now, Mary," his father said again, and she turned on him and said angrily, "I don't care, Jay! I just don't care a hoot, and if you won't stand up for him, I will, I can promise you that!"

"Ted didn't mean any harm," his father said.

"Course I didn't, Mary," Uncle Ted said.

"Of course not," Aunt Kate said.

"It was just a joke," his father said.

"That's all it was, Mary," Uncle Ted said.

"He just meant it for a joke," his father and Aunt Kate said together.

"Well, it's a pretty poor kind of a joke, if you ask me," his mother said, "violating a little boy's trust."

"*Why, Mary, he's got to learn what to believe and what not to,*" Uncle Ted said, *and Aunt Kate nodded and put her hand on Uncle Ted's knee.* "*Gotta learn common sense.*"

"*He's got* plenty *of common sense,*" *his mother flashed.* "*He's a very bright child* indeed, *if you must know. But he's been brought up to* trust *older people when they tell him something. Not be* suspicious *of everybody. And so he trusted* you. *Because he likes you, Ted. Doesn't that make you ashamed?*"

"*Come on, Mary, cut it out,*" *his father said.*

"*But Mary, you wouldn't think* anybody'd *believe what I said about the* cheese," *Uncle Ted said.*

"*Well you certainly* expected *him to believe it,*" *she said, with fury,* "*otherwise why'd you ever* say *it?*"

Uncle Ted looked puzzled, and his father said, trying to laugh, "*Reckon she cornered you there, Ted,*" *and Uncle Ted smiled uncomfortably and said,* "*I guess that's so.*"

"*Of* course *it's so,*" *his mother blazed, though his father frowned at her and said* "Ssh!"

PART III

Chapter 14

WHEN he woke it was already clear daylight and the sparrows were making a great racket and his first disappointed thought was that he was too late, though he could not yet think what it was he was too late for. But something special was on his mind which made him eager and happy almost as if this were Christmas morning and within a second after waking he remembered what it was and, sitting up, his lungs stretching full with anticipation and pride, he put his hand into the crisp tissue paper with a small smashing noise and took out the cap. There was plenty of light to see the colors well; he quickly turned it around and over, and smelled of the new cloth and of the new leather band. He put it on and yanked the bill down firmly and pelted down the hallway calling "*Daddy! Daddy!*", and burst through the open door into their bedroom; then brought up short in dismay, for his father was not there. But his mother lay there, propped up on two pillows as if she were sick. She looked sick, or very tired, and in her eyes she seemed to be afraid of him. Her face was full of little lines he had never seen before; they were as small as the lines in her mended best teacup. She put out her arms towards him and made an odd, kind noise. "Where's Daddy?" he shouted, imperiously ignoring her arms. "Daddy—isn't here yet," she told him, in a voice like hot ashes, and her arms sank down along the sheet.

"Where *is* he, then!" he demanded, in angry disappointment, but she thrust through these words with her own: "Go wake—little Catherine and bring her straight here," she said in a voice which puzzled him; "there's something I must tell you both together."

He was darting his eyes everywhere for clues of his father: clothes? watch? tobacco? nightshirt? "*Right away*," she said, in a desperate voice.

Startled by its mysterious rebuke, and uneasy in his stomach because she had said "little Catherine," he hurried out—and all but collided with his Aunt Hannah. Her mouth was strong and tightly pressed together beneath her glittering spectacles as she stooped, peering forward.

"Hello, Aunt Hannah," he called with astonishment, as he sped around and past her; he saw her go into the bedroom, her hair sticking out from her thin neck in two twiggy gray braids; he hurried to Catherine's crib.

"Wake *up*, Catherine!" he yelled, "Mama says wake *up!* Right *away!*" He shook her.

"*Stob*bit," she bawled, her round, red face glaring.

"Well Mama *said* so, Mama *said* so, wake *up!*"

And a few moments later he hurried back ahead of her and hollered breathlessly, "She's coming!" and she trailed in, two-thirds asleep, snuffling with anger, her lower lip stuck out.

"*Take off that cap!*" his Aunt Hannah snapped with frightening sternness, and his hands only just caught it against her snatching. He was appalled by this inexplicable betrayal, and the hardness of her mouth as she struggled with self-astonishment and repentance was even more ominous.

"Oh, Hannah, no, let him," his mother said in her strange voice, "he was so crazy for Jay to see it," and even as she said it he was surprised all over again for his aunt, whispering something inaudible, touched his cheek very gently. And now as she had done before, his mother lifted forward her hands and her kind arms; "Children, come close," she said.

Aunt Hannah went silently out of the room.

"Come close"; and she touched each of them. "I want to tell you about Daddy." But upon his name her voice shook and her whole dry-looking mouth trembled like the ash of burned paper in a draft. "Can you hear me, Catherine?" she asked, when she had recovered her voice. Catherine peered at her earnestly as if through a thick fog. "Are you waked up enough yet, my darling?" And because of her voice, in sympathy and for her protection, they both came now much nearer, and she put her arms around both of them, and they could smell her breath, a little like sauerkraut but more like a dried-up mouse. And now even more small lines like cracked china branched all over her face. "Daddy," she said, "your father, children": and this time she caught control of her mouth more quickly, and a single tear spilled out of her left eye and slid jaggedly down all the jagged lines: "Daddy didn't come home. He isn't going to come home ever any more. He's—gone away to heaven and he isn't ever coming home again. Do you hear me, Catherine? Are you awake?" Catherine stared at her mother. "Do *you* understand, Rufus?"

He stared at his mother. "Why not?" he asked.

She looked at him with extraordinary closeness and despair, and said, "Because God wanted him." They continued to stare at her severely and she went on: "Daddy was on his way home last night—and he was—he—got hurt and—so God let him go to sleep and took him straight away with Him to heaven." She sank her fingers in Catherine's springy hair and looked intently from one to the other. "Do you see, children? Do you understand?" They stared at her, and now Catherine was sharply awake.

"Is Daddy *dead*?" Rufus asked. Her glance at him was as startled as if he had slapped her, and again her mouth and then her whole face began to work, uncontrollably this time, and she did not speak, but only nodded her head once, and then again, and then several times rapidly, while one small, squeaky "*yes*" came out of her as if it had been squeezed out; then suddenly sweeping both of them close against her breasts, she tucked her chin down tightly between the crowns of their heads and they felt her whole body shaken as if by a violent wind, but she did not cry. Catherine began to sniffle quietly because everything seemed very serious and very sad. Rufus listened to his mother's shattered breathing and gazed sidelong past her fair shoulder at the sheet, rumpled, and at a rubbed place in the rose-patterned carpet and then at something queer, that he had never seen before, on the bedside table, a tangle of brown beads and a little cross; through her breathing he began once more to hear the quarreling sparrows; he said to himself: *dead, dead*, but all he could do was see and hear; the streetcar raised and quieted its grim, iron cry; he became aware that his cap was pushed crooked against her and he felt that he ought to take it off but that he ought not to move just now to take it off, and he knew why his Aunt Hannah had been so mad at him. He could no longer hear even a rumor of the streetcar, and his mother's breathing had become quiet again. With one hand she held Catherine still more closely against her, and Catherine sniffled a little more comfortably; with the other hand she put Rufus quietly away, so that she could look clearly into his eyes; tenderly she took off his cap and laid it beside her, and pushed the hair back from his forehead. "Neither of you will quite understand for a while," she said. "It's—very hard to understand. But you will," she said (I do, he said to himself; he's dead. That's what) and she repeated rather dreamily, as if to herself, though she continued to look into his eyes, "You will"; then she was silent, and some kind of energy intensified in her eyes and she said: "When you want to know more—*about* it" (and her eyes became still more vibrant) "just, just ask me and I'll tell you because you ought to know." *How did he get hurt,* Rufus wanted to ask, but he knew by her eyes that she did not mean at all what she said, not now anyway, not this minute, he must not ask; and now he did not want to ask because he too was afraid; he nodded to let her know he understood her. "Just ask," she said again, and he nodded again; a strange, cold excitement was rising in him; and in a cold intuition that it would be kind, and gratefully received, he kissed her. "God *bless* you," she groaned, and held them passionately against herself; "*both* of you!" She loosened her arms. "And now you be a good boy," she said in almost her ordinary voice, wiping Catherine's nose. "Get little Catherine dressed, can you do that?" He nodded proudly; "and wash and dress yourself, and by then Aunt Hannah will have breakfast ready."

"Aren't you getting up, Mama?" he asked, much impressed that he had been deputized to dress his sister.

"Not for a while," she said, and by her way of saying it, he knew that she wanted them to go out of the room right away.

"Come on, Catherine," he said, and found, with surprise, that he had taken her hand. Catherine looked up at him, equally surprised, and shook her head.

"Go with Rufus, dear," her mother said, "he's going to help you get dressed, and eat your breakfast. Mother will see you soon."

And Catherine, feeling that for some reason to do with her father, who was not where he ought to be, and her mother too, she must try to be a very good girl, came away with him without further protest. As they turned through the door to go down, Rufus saw that his mother had taken the beads and cross from the bedside table (they were like a regular necklace) and the beads ran among her fingers and twined and drooped from her hands and one wrist while she looked so intently at the upright cross that she did not realize that she had been seen. *She'd be mad if she knew,* he was sure.

Before he did anything about Catherine he put his cap back in the tissue paper. Then he got her clothes. "Take off your nightie," he said. "Sopping wet," he added, as nearly like his mother as possible.

"You're sopping wet too," she retorted.

"No, I didn't either," he said, "not last night."

He found that she could do a certain amount of dressing herself; she got on the panties and she nearly got her under-waist on right too, except that it was backwards. "That's all right," he told her, as much like his mother as he was able, "you do it fine. Just a *little bit* crooked"; and he fixed it right.

He buttoned her panties to her underwaist. It was much less easy, he found, than buttoning his own clothes. "Stand still," he said, because to tell her so seemed only a proper part of carrying out his duty.

"I am," Catherine replied, with such firmness that he said no more.

That was all that either of them said before they went down to breakfast.

Chapter 15

CATHERINE did not like being buttoned up by Rufus or bossed around by him, and breakfast wasn't like breakfast either. Aunt Hannah didn't say anything and neither did Rufus and neither did she, and she felt that even if she wanted to say anything she oughtn't. Everything was queer, it was so still and it seemed dark. Aunt Hannah sliced the banana so thin on the Post Toasties it looked cold and limp and slimy. She gave each of them a little bit of coffee in their milk and she made Rufus' a little bit darker than hers. She didn't say, "Eat"; "Eat your breakfast, Catherine"; "Don't dawdle," like Catherine's mother; she didn't say anything. Catherine did not feel hungry, but she felt mildly curious because things tasted so different, and she ate slowly ahead, tasting each mouthful. Everything was so still that it made Catherine feel uneasy and sad. There were little noises when a fork or spoon touched a dish; the only other noise was the very thin dry toast Aunt Hannah kept slowly crunching and the fluttering sipping of the steamy coffee with which she wet each mouthful of dry crumbs enough to swallow it. When Catherine tried to make a similar noise sipping her milk, her Aunt Hannah glanced at her sharply as if she wondered if Catherine was trying to be a smart aleck but she did not say anything. Catherine was not trying to be a smart aleck but she felt she had better not make that noise again. The fried eggs had hardly any pepper and they were so soft the yellow ran out over the white and the white plate and looked so nasty she didn't want to eat it but she ate it because she didn't want to be told to and because she felt there was some special reason, still, why she ought to be a good girl. She felt very uneasy, but there was nothing to do but eat, so she always took care to get a good hold on her tumbler and did not take too much on her spoon, and hardly spilled at all, and when she became aware of how little she was spilling it made her feel like a big girl and yet she did not feel any less uneasy, because she knew there was something wrong. She was not as much interested in eating as she was in the way things were, and listening carefully, looking mostly at her plate, every sound she heard and the whole quietness which was so much stronger than the sounds, meant that things were not good. What it was was that he wasn't here. Her mother wasn't either, but she was upstairs. He wasn't even upstairs. He was coming home last night but he didn't come home and he wasn't coming home now either, and her mother felt so awful she cried, and Aunt Hannah wasn't saying anything, just making all that noise with the toast and big loud sips with the coffee and swallowing, *grrmmp*, and then the same thing over again and over again, and every time she made the noise with the toast it was almost scary, as if she was talking about some awful thing, and every time she sipped it was like crying or like when Granma sucked in air between her teeth when she hurt herself, and every time she swallowed, *crrmmp*, it meant it was all over and there was nothing to do about it or say or even ask, and then she would take another bite of toast as hard and shivery as gritting your teeth, and start the whole thing all over again. Her mother said he wasn't coming home ever any more. That was what she said, but why wasn't he home eating breakfast right this minute? Because he was not with them eating breakfast it wasn't fun and everything was so queer. Now maybe in just a minute he would walk right in and grin at her and say, "Good morning, merry sunshine," because her lip was sticking out, and even bend down and rub her cheek with his whiskers and then sit down and eat a big breakfast and then it would be all fun again and she would watch from the window when he went to work and just before he went out of sight he would turn around and she would wave but why wasn't he right here now where she wanted him to be and why didn't he come home? Ever any more. He won't come home again ever any more. Won't come home again ever. But he will, though, because it's home. But why's he not here? He's up seeing Grampa Follet. Grampa Follet is very, very sick. But Mama didn't feel awful then, she feels awful now. But why didn't he come back when she said he would? He went to heaven and now Catherine could remember about heaven, that's where God lives, way up in the sky. Why'd he do that? God took him there. But why'd he go there and not come home like Mama said? Last night Mama said he was coming home last night. We could even wait up a while and when he didn't and we had to go to bed she *promised* he would come if we went to sleep and she promised he'd be here at breakfast time and now it's breakfast time and she says he won't come ever any more. Now her Aunt Hannah folded her napkin, and folded it again more narrowly, and again still more narrowly, and pressed the butt end of it against her mouth, and laid it beside her plate, where it slowly and slightly unfolded, and, looking first at Rufus and then at Catherine and then back at Rufus, said quietly, "I think you ought to know about your father. Whatever I can tell you. Because your mother's not feeling well."

Now I'll know when he *is* coming home, Catherine thought.

All through breakfast, Rufus had wanted to ask questions, but now he felt so shy and uneasy that he could hardly speak. "Who hurt him?" he finally asked.

"Why nobody hurt him, Rufus," she said, and she looked shocked. "What on earth made you think so?"

Mama said so, Catherine thought.

"Mama said he got hurt so bad God put him to sleep," Rufus said.

Like the kitties, Catherine thought; she saw a dim, gigantic old man in white take her tiny father by the skin of the neck and put him in a huge slop jar full of water and sit on the lid, and she heard the tiny scratching and the stifled mewing.

"That's true he was hurt, but nobody hurt him," her Aunt Hannah was saying. How could that be, Catherine wondered. "He was driving home by himself. That's all, all by himself, in the auto last night, and he had an accident."

Rufus felt his face get warm and he looked warningly at his sister. He knew it could not be that, not with his father, a grown man, besides, God wouldn't put you to sleep for *that*, and it didn't hurt, anyhow. But Catherine might think so. Sure enough, she was looking at her aunt with astonishment and disbelief that she could say such a thing about her father. Not in his *pants*, you dern fool, Rufus wanted to tell her, but his Aunt Hannah continued: "A *fatal* accident"; and by her voice, as she spoke the strange word, "fatal," they knew she meant something very bad. "That means that, just as your mother told you, that he was hurt so badly that God put him to sleep right away."

Like the rabbits, Rufus remembered, all torn white bloody fur and red insides. He could not imagine his father like that. Poor little things, he remembered his mother's voice comforting his crying, hurt so terribly that God just let them go to sleep.

If it was in the auto, Catherine thought, then he wouldn't be in the slop jar.

They couldn't be happy any more if He hadn't, his mother had said. They could never get well.

Hannah wondered whether they could comprehend it at all and whether she should try to tell them. She doubted it. Deeply uncertain, she tried again.

"He was driving home last night," she said, "about nine, and apparently something was already wrong with the steering mech—with the wheel you guide the machine with. But your father didn't know it. Because there wasn't any way he could know until something went wrong and then it was too late. But one of the wheels struck a loose stone in the road and the wheel turned aside very suddenly, and when . . ." She paused and went on more quietly and slowly: "You see, when your father tried to make the auto go where it should, stay on the road, he found he couldn't, he didn't have any control. Because something was wrong with the steering gear. So, instead of doing as he tried to make it, the auto twisted aside because of the loose stone and ran off the road into a deep ditch." She paused again. "Do you understand?"

They kept looking at her.

"Your father was thrown from the auto," she said. "Then the auto went on without him up the other side of the ditch. It went up an eight-foot embankment and then it fell down backward, turned over and landed just beside him.

"They're pretty sure he was dead even before he was thrown out. Because the only mark on his whole body," and now they began to hear in her voice a troubling intensity and resentment, "was right—here!" She pressed the front of her forefinger to the point of her chin, and looked at them almost as if she were accusing them.

They said nothing.

I suppose I've got to finish, Hannah thought; I've gone this far.

"They're pretty sure how it happened," she said. "The auto gave such a sudden terrible *jerk*"—she jerked so violently that both children jumped, and startled her; she demonstrated what she saw next more gently: "that your father was thrown forward and struck his chin, very hard, against the wheel, the steering wheel, and from that instant he never knew anything more."

She looked at Rufus, at Catherine, and again at Rufus. "Do you understand?" They looked at her.

After a while Catherine said, "He hurt his chin."

"Yes, Catherine. He did," she replied. "They believe he was *instantly killed*, with that one single blow, because it happened to strike just exactly where it did. Because if you're struck very hard in just that place, it jars your whole head, your brain so hard that—sometimes people die in that very instant." She drew a deep breath and let it out long and shaky. "Concussion of the brain, that is called," she said with most careful distinctness, and bowed her head for a moment; they saw her thumb make a small cross on her chest.

She looked up. "Now do you understand, children?" she asked earnestly. "I know it's very hard to understand. You please tell me if there's anything you want to know and I'll do my best to expl—tell you better."

Rufus and Catherine looked at each other and looked away. After a while Rufus said, "Did it hurt him bad?"

"He could never have felt it. That's the one great mercy" (or *is* it, she wondered); "the doctor is sure of that."

Catherine wondered whether she could ask one question. She thought she'd better not.

"What's an eightfoot embackmut?" asked Rufus.

"Em-bank-ment," she replied. "Just a bank. A steep little hill, eight feet high. Bout's high's the ceiling."

He and Catherine saw the auto climb it and fall backward rolling and come to rest beside their father. Umbackmut, Catherine thought; em-*bank*-ment, Rufus said to himself.

"What's instantly?"

"Instantly is—quick's that"; she snapped her fingers, more loudly than she had expected to; Catherine flinched and kept her eyes on the fingers. "Like snapping off an electric light." Rufus nodded. "So you can be very sure, both of you, he never felt a moment's pain. Not one moment."

"When's . . ." Catherine began.

"What's . . ." Rufus began at the same moment; they glared at each other.

"What is it, Catherine?"

"When's Daddy coming home?"

"Why *good golly*, Catherine," Rufus began; "Hold your tongue!" his Aunt Hannah said fiercely, and he listened, scared, and ashamed of himself.

"Catherine, he *can't* come home," she said very kindly. "That's just what all this means, child." She put her hand over Catherine's hand and Rufus could see that her chin was trembling. "He died, Catherine," she said. "That's what your mother means. God put him to sleep and took him, took his soul away with Him. So he can't come home . . ." She stopped, and began again. "We'll see him once more," she said, "tomorrow or day after; that I promise you," she said, wishing she was sure of Mary's views about this. "But he'll be asleep then. And after that we won't see him any more in this world. Not until God takes us away too.

"Do you see, child?" Catherine was looking at her very seriously. "Of course you don't, God bless you"; she squeezed her hand. "Don't ever try too hard to understand, child. Just try to understand it's so. He'd come if he could but he simply can't because God wants him with Him. That's all." She kept her hand over Catherine's a long while more, while Rufus realized much more clearly than before that he really could not and would not come home again: because of God.

"He would if he could but he can't," Catherine finally said, remembering a joking phrase of her mother's.

Hannah, who knew the joking phrase too, was startled, but quickly realized that the child meant it in earnest. "That's it," she said gratefully.

But he'll come once more, anyway, Rufus realized, looking forward to it. Even if he *is* asleep.

"What was it you wanted to ask, Rufus?" he heard his aunt say.

He tried to remember and remembered. "What's kuh, kuhkush, kuh . . . ?"

"Con-*cus*-sion, Rufus. Concus-sion of the brain. That's the doctor's name for what happened. It means, it's as if the brain

were hit very hard and suddenly, and joggled loose. The instant that happens, your father was—he . . ."

"Instantly killed."

She nodded.

"Then it was that, that put him to sleep."

"Hyess."

"*Not* God."

Catherine looked at him, bewildered.

Chapter 16

WHEN breakfast was over he wandered listlessly into the sitting room and looked all around, but he did not see any place where he would like to sit down. He felt deeply idle and empty and at the same time gravely exhilarated, as if this were the morning of his birthday, except that this day seemed even more particularly his own day. There was nothing in the way it looked which was not ordinary, but it was filled with a noiseless and invisible kind of energy. He could see his mother's face while she told them about it and here her voice, over and over, and silently, over and over, while he looked around the sitting room and through the window into the street, words repeated themselves, He's dead. He died last night while I was asleep and now it was already morning. He has already been dead since way last night and I didn't even know until I woke up. He has been dead all night while I was asleep and now it is morning and I am awake but he is still dead and he will stay right on being dead all afternoon and all night and all tomorrow while I am asleep again and wake up again and go to sleep again and he can't come back home again ever any more but I will see him once more before he is taken away. Dead now. He died last night while I was asleep and now it is already morning.

A boy went by with his books in a strap.

Two girls went by with their satchels.

He went to the hat rack and took his satchel and his hat and started back down the hall to the kitchen to get his lunch; then he remembered his new cap. But it was upstairs. It would be in Mama's and Daddy's room, he could remember when she took it off his head. He did not want to go in for it where she was lying down and now he realized, too, that he did not want to wear it. He would like to tell her good-bye before he went to school, but he did not want to go in and see her lying down and looking like that. He kept on towards the kitchen. He would tell Aunt Hannah good-bye instead.

She was at the sink washing dishes and Catherine sat on a kitchen chair watching her. He looked all around but he could not see any lunch. I guess she doesn't know about lunch, he reflected. She did not seem to realize that he was there so, after a moment, he said, "Good-bye."

"What-*is*-it?" she said and turned her lowered head, peering. "Why, Rufus!" she exclaimed, in such a tone that he wondered what he had done. "You're not going to *school*," she said, and now he realized that she was not mad at him.

"I can stay out of school?"

"Of course you can. You must. Today and tomorrow as well and—for a sufficient time. A few days. Now put up your things, and stay right in this house, child."

He looked at her and said to himself: but then they can't see me; but he knew there was no use begging her; already she was busy with the dishes again.

He went back along the hall towards the hat rack. In the first moment he had been only surprised and exhilarated not to have to go to school, and something of this sense of privilege remained, but almost immediately he was also disappointed. He could now see vividly how they would all look up when he came into the schoolroom and how the teacher would say something nice about his father and about him, and he knew that on this day everybody would treat him well, and even look up to him, for something had happened to him today which had not happened to any other boy in school, any other boy in town. They might even give him part of their lunches.

He felt even more profoundly empty and idle than before.

He laid down his satchel on the seat of the hat rack, but he kept his hat on. She'll spank me, he thought. Even worse, he could foresee her particular, crackling kind of anger. I won't let her find out, he told himself. Taking great care to be silent, he let himself out the front door.

The air was cool and gray and here and there along the street, shapeless and watery sunlight strayed and vanished. Now that he was in this outdoor air he felt even more listless and powerful; he was alone, and the silent, invisible energy was everywhere. He stood on the porch and supposed that everyone he saw passing knew of an event so famous. A man was walking quickly up the street and as Rufus watched him, and waited for the man to meet his eyes, he felt a great quiet lifting within him of pride and of shyness, and he felt his face break into a smile, and then an uncontrollable grin, which he knew he must try to make sober again; but the man walked past without looking at him, and so did the next man who walked past in the other direction. Two schoolboys passed whose faces he knew, so he knew that they must know his, but they did not even seem to see him. Arthur and Alvin Tripp came down their front steps and along the far sidewalk and now he was sure, and came down his own front steps and halfway out to the sidewalk, but then he stopped, for now, although both of them looked across into his eyes, and he into theirs, they did not cross the street to him or even say hello, but kept on their way, still looking into his eyes with a kind of shy curiosity, even when their heads were turned almost backwards on their necks, and he turned his own head slowly, watching them go by, but when he saw that they were not going to speak he took care not to speak either.

What's the matter with them, he wondered, and still watched them; and even now, far down the street, Arthur kept turning his head, and for several steps Alvin walked backwards.

What are they mad about?

Now they no longer looked around, and now he watched them vanish under the hill.

Maybe they don't know, he thought. Maybe the others don't know, either.

He came out to the sidewalk.

Maybe everybody knew. Or maybe he knew something of great importance which nobody else knew. The alternatives were not at all distinct in his mind; he was puzzled, but no less proud and expectant than before. My daddy's dead, he said to himself slowly, and then, shyly, he said it aloud: "My daddy's dead." Nobody in sight seemed to have heard; he had said it to nobody in particular. "My daddy's dead," he said again, chiefly for his own benefit. It sounded powerful, solid, and entirely creditable, and he knew that if need be he would tell people. He watched a large, slow man come towards him and waited for the man to look at him and acknowledge the fact first, but when the man was just ahead of him, and still did not appear even to have seen him, he told him, "My daddy's dead," but the man did not seem to hear him, he just swung on by. He took care to tell the next man sooner and the man's face looked almost as if he were dodging a blow but he went on by, looking back a few steps later with a worried face; and after a few steps more he turned and came slowly back.

"What was that you said, sonny?" he asked; he was frowning slightly.

"My daddy's dead," Rufus said, expectantly.

"You mean that sure enough?" the man asked.

"He died last night when I was asleep and now he can't come home ever any more."

The man looked at him as if something hurt him.

"Where do you live, sonny?"

"Right here"; he showed with his eyes.

"Do your folks know you out here wandern round?"

He felt his stomach go empty. He looked frankly into his eyes and nodded quickly.

The man just looked at him and Rufus realized: He doesn't believe me. How do they always know?

"You better just go on back in the house, son," he said. "They won't like you being out here on the street." He kept looking at him, hard.

Rufus looked into his eyes with reproach and apprehension, and turned in at his walk. The man still stood there. Rufus went on slowly up his steps, and looked around. The man was on his way again but at the moment Rufus looked around, he did too, and now he stopped again.

He shook his head and said, in a friendly voice which made Rufus feel ashamed, "How would your daddy like it, you out here telling strangers how he's dead?"

Rufus opened the door, taking care not to make a sound, and stepped in and silently closed it, and hurried into the sitting room. Through the curtains he watched the man. He still stood there, lighting a cigarette, but now he started walking again. He looked back once and Rufus felt, with a quailing of shame and fear, he sees me; but the man immediately looked away again and Rufus watched him until he was out of sight.

How would your daddy like it?

He thought of the way they teased him and did things to him, and how mad his father got when he just came home. He

thought how different it would be today if he only didn't have
to stay home from school.

He let himself out again and stole back between the houses
to the alley, and walked along the alley, listening to the cinders
cracking under each step, until he came near the sidewalk. He
was not in front of his own home now, or even on Highland
Avenue; he was coming into the side street down from his
home, and he felt that here nobody would identify him with
his home and send him back to it. What he could see from the
mouth of the alley was much less familiar to him, and he took
the last few steps which brought him out onto the sidewalk
with deliberation and shyness. He was doing something he
had been told not to do.

He looked up the street and he could see the corner he
knew so well, where he always met the others so unhappily,
and, farther away, the corner around which his father always
disappeared on the way to work, and first appeared on his way
home from work. He felt it would be good luck that he would
not be meeting them at that corner. Slowly, uneasily, he turned
his head, and looked down the side street in the other direction; and there they were: three together, and two along the
far side of the street, and one alone, farther off, and another
alone, farther off, and, without importance to him, some girls
here and there, as well. He knew the faces of all of these boys
well, though he was not sure of any of their names. The moment he saw them all he was sure they saw him, and sure that
they knew. He stood still and waited for them, looking from
one to another of them, into their eyes, and step by step at
their several distances, each of them at all times looking into
his eyes and knowing, they came silently nearer. Waiting, in
silence, during those many seconds before the first of them
came really near him, he felt that it was so long to wait, and be
watched so closely and silently, and to watch back, that he
wanted to go back into the alley and not be seen by them or by
anybody else, and yet at the same time he knew that they were
all approaching him with the realization that something had
happened to him that had not happened to any other boy in
town, and that now at last they were bound to think well of
him; and the nearer they came but were yet at a distance, the
more the gray, sober air was charged with the great energy and

with a sense of glory and of danger, and the deeper and more exciting the silence became, and the more tall, proud, shy and exposed he felt; so that as they came still nearer he once again felt his face break into a wide smile, with which he had nothing to do, and, feeling that there was something deeply wrong in such a smile, tried his best to quieten his face and told them, shyly and proudly, "My daddy's dead."

Of the first three who came up, two merely looked at him with suspicion and the third said, "Huh! Betcha he ain't"; and Rufus, astounded that they did not know and that they should disbelieve him, said, "Why he is so!"

"Where's your satchel at?" said the boy who had spoken. "You're just making up a lie so you can lay out of school."

"I am not laying out," Rufus replied. "I was going to school and my Aunt Hannah told me I didn't have to go to school to-day or tomorrow or not till—not for a few days. She said I mustn't. So I am not laying out. I'm just staying out."

And another of the boys said, "That's right. If his daddy is dead he don't have to go back to school till after the funerl."

While Rufus had been speaking two other boys had crossed over to join them and now one of them said, "He don't have to. He can lay out cause his daddy got killed," and Rufus looked at the boy gratefully and the boy looked back at him, it seemed to Rufus, with deference.

But the first boy who had spoken said, resentfully, "How do *you* know?"

And the second boy, while his companion nodded, said, "Cause my daddy seen it in the paper. Can't your daddy read the paper?"

The paper, Rufus thought; it's even in the paper! And he looked wisely at the first boy. And the first boy, interested enough to ignore the remark against his father, said, "Well how did he get killed, then?" and Rufus, realizing with respect that it was even more creditable to get killed than just to die, took a deep breath and said, "Why, he was . . ."; but the boy whose father had seen it in the paper was already talking, so he listened, instead, feeling as if all this were being spoken for him, and on his behalf, and in his praise, and feeling it all the more as he looked from one silent boy to the next and saw that their eyes were constantly on him. And Rufus listened, too, with as much interest as they did, while the boy said with relish, "In his ole Tin Lizzie, that's how. He was driving along in his ole Tin Lizzie and it hit a rock and throwed him out in the ditch and run up a eight-foot bank and then fell back and turned over and over and landed right on top of him *whomph* and mashed every bone in his body, that's all. And somebody come and found him and he was dead already time they got there, that's how."

"He was instantly killed," Rufus began, and expected to go ahead and correct some of the details of the account, but nobody seemed to hear him, for two other boys had come up and just as he began to speak one of them said, "Your daddy got his name in the paper didn he, and you too," and he saw that now all the boys looked at him with new respect.

"He's dead," he told them. "He got killed."

"That's what my daddy says," one of them said, and the other said, "What you get for driving a auto when you're drunk, that's what my dad says," and the two of them looked gravely at the other boys, nodding, and at Rufus.

"What's drunk?" Rufus asked.

"What's drunk?" one of the boys mocked incredulously: "Drunk is fulla good ole whiskey"; and he began to stagger about in circles with his knees weak and his head lolling. "At's what drunk is."

"Then he wasn't," Rufus said.

"How do *you* know?"

"He wasn't drunk because that wasn't how he died. The wheel hit a rock and the other wheel, the one you steer with, just hit him on the chin, but it hit him so hard it killed him. He was instantly killed."

"What's instantly killed?" one of them asked.

"What do *you* care?" another said.

"Right off like that," an older boy explained, snapping his fingers. Another boy joined the group. Thinking of what instantly meant, and how his father's name was in the paper and his own too, and how he had got killed, not just died, he was not listening to them very clearly for a few moments, and then, all of a sudden, he began to realize that he was the center of everything and that they all knew it and that they waited to hear him tell the true account of it.

"I don't know nothing about no chin," the boy whose father saw it in the paper was saying. "Way I heard it he was a-drivin along in his ole Tin Lizzie and he hit a rock and ole Tin Lizzie run off the road and thowed him out and run up a eight-foot bank and turned over and over and fell back down on top of him *whomp*."

"How do *you* know?" an older boy was saying. "*You* wasn't there. Anybody here knows it's *him*." And he pointed at Rufus and Rufus was startled from his revery.

"Why?" asked the boy who had just come up.

"Cause it's his daddy," one of them explained.

"It's my daddy," Rufus said.

"What happened?" asked still another boy, at the fringe of the group.

"My daddy got killed," Rufus said.

"His daddy got killed," several of the others explained.

"My daddy says he bets he was drunk."

"Good ole whiskey!"

"Shut up, what's *your* daddy know about it."

"Was he drunk?"

"No," Rufus said.

"No," two others said.

"Let *him* tell it."

"Yeah, *you* tell it."

"Anybody here ought to know, it's him."

"Come on and tell us."

"Good ole whiskey."

"Shut your mouth."

"Well come on and tell us, then."

They became silent and all of them looked at him. Rufus looked back into their eyes in the sudden deep stillness. A man walked by, stepping into the gutter to skirt them.

Rufus said, quietly, "He was coming home from Grampa's last night, Grampa Follet. He's very sick and Daddy had to go up way in the middle of the night to see him, and he was hurrying as fast as he could to get back home because he was so late. And there was a cotter pin worked loose."

"What's a cotter pin?"

"Shut up."

"A cotter pin is what holds things together underneath, that you steer with. It worked loose and fell out so that when one of the front wheels hit a loose rock it wrenched the wheel and he couldn't steer and the auto ran down off the road with an awful bump and they saw where the wheel you steer with hit him right on the chin and he was instantly killed. He was thrown all the way out of the auto and it ran up an eight-foot emb—embackment and then it rolled back down and it was upside down beside him when they found him. There was not a mark on his body, my Uncle Andrew says. Only a little tiny blue mark right on the end of the chin and another on his lip."

In the silence he could see the auto upside down with its wheels in the air and his father lying beside it with the little blue marks on his chin and on his lip.

"Heck," one of them said, "how can *that* kill anybody?"

He felt a kind of sullen stirring among the others, and he felt that he was not believed, or that they did not think very well of his father for being killed so easily.

"It was just exactly the way it just happened to hit him, Uncle Andrew says. He says it was just a chance in a million. It gave him a concush, con, concush—it did something to his brain that killed him."

"Just a chance in a million," one of the older boys said gravely, and another gravely nodded.

"A million trillion," another said.

"Knocked him crazy as a loon," another cried, and with a waggling forefinger he made a rapid blubbery noise against his loose lower lip.

"Shut yer Goddamn mouth," an older boy said coldly. "Ain't you got no sense at all?"

"Way I heard it, ole Tin Lizzie just rolled right back on top of him *whomp.*"

This account of it was false, Rufus was sure, but it seemed to him more exciting than his own, and more creditable to his father and to him, and nobody could question, scornfully, whether that could kill, as they could of just a blow on the chin; so he didn't try to contradict. He felt that he was lying, and in some way being disloyal as well, but he said only, "He was instantly killed. He didn't have to feel any pain."

"Never even knowed what hit him," a boy said quietly. "That's what my dad says."

"No," Rufus said. It had not occurred to him that way. "I guess he didn't." Never even knowed what hit him. Knew.

"Reckon that ole Tin Lizzie is done for now. Huh?"

He wondered if there was some meanness behind calling it an old Tin Lizzie. "I guess so," he said.

"Good ole waggin, but she done broke down."

His father sang that.

"No more joy rides in that ole Tin Lizzie, huh Rufus?"

"I guess not," Rufus replied shyly.

He began to realize that for some moments now a bell, the school bell, had been weltering on the dark gray air; he realized it because at this moment the last of its reverberations were fading.

"Last bell," one of the boys said in sudden alarm.

"Come on, we're goana git hell," another said; and within another second Rufus was watching them all run dwindling away up the street, and around the corner into Highland Avenue, as fast as they could go, and all round him the morning was empty and still. He stood still and watched the corner for almost half a minute after the fattest of them, and then the smallest, had disappeared; then he walked slowly back along the alley, hearing once more the sober crumbling of the cinders under each step, and up through the narrow side yard between the houses, and up the steps of the front porch.

In the paper! He looked for it beside the door, but it was not there. He listened carefully, but he could not hear anything. He let himself quietly through the front door, at the moment his Aunt Hannah came from the sitting room into the front hall. She wore a cloth over her hair and in her hands she was carrying the smoking stand and the ash tray with weighted straps, and two pipes. She did not see him at first and he saw how fierce and lonely her face looked. He tried to make himself small but just then she wheeled on him, her lenses flashing, and exclaimed, "Rufus Follet, where on earth have you been!" His stomach quailed, for her voice was so angry it was as if it were crackling with sparks.

"Outdoors."

"Where, outdoors! I've been looking for you all over the place."

"Just out. Back in the alley."

"Didn't you hear me calling you?"

He shook his head.

"I shouted until my voice was hoarse."

He kept shaking his head. "Honest," he said.

"Now listen to me carefully. You mustn't go outdoors to-day. Stay right here inside this house, do you understand?"

He nodded. He felt suddenly that he had done an awful thing.

"I know it's hard to," she said more gently, "but you've got to. Help Catherine with her coloring. Read a book. You promise?"

"Yes'm."

"And don't do anything to disturb your mother."

"No'm."

She went on down the hall and he watched her. What was she doing with the pipes and the ash tray, he wondered. He considered sneaking behind her, for he knew that she could not see at all well, yet he would be sure to get caught, for her hearing was very sharp. All the same, he sneaked along to the back of the hall and watched her empty the ashes into the garbage pail and rap out the pipes against its rim. Then she stood with the pipes in her hand, looking around uncertainly; finally she put the pipes and the ash tray on the cupboard shelf, and set the smoking stand in the corner of the kitchen behind the stove. He went back along the hall on tiptoe and into the sitting room.

Catherine sat in the little chair by the side window with a picture book on her knees. Her crayons were all over the window sill and she was working intently with an orange crayon. She looked up when he came in and looked down again and kept on working.

He did not want to help her, he wanted to be by himself and see if he could find the paper with the names in it, but he felt that he ought to try to be good, for by now he felt a dark uneasiness about something, he was not quite sure what, that he had done. He walked over to her. "I'll help you," he said.

"No," Catherine said, without even looking up. It was the Mother Goose book and with her orange crayon she was scrawling all over the cow which jumped over the moon, inside and outside the lines of the cow.

"Aunt Hannah says to," he said, disgusted to see what she was doing to the cow.

"No," Catherine said, and again she did not look up or stop scrawling for a second.

"That ain't no color for a cow," he said. "Whoever saw an orange cow?" She made no reply, but he could see that her face was getting red. "Besides, you're not even coloring inside the cow," he said. "Just look at that. You're just running that crayon around all over the place and it isn't even the right color." She bore down even harder and harder with the crayon and pushed it in a wider and wider tangle of lines and all of a sudden it snapped and the long part rolled to the floor. "See now, you busted it," Rufus said.

"Leave me lone!" She tried to draw with the stub of the crayon but it was too short, and the paper got in the way. She looked along the window sill and selected a brown crayon.

"What you goana do with that brown one?" Rufus said. "You already got all that orange all over everything, what you goana do with that brown one?" Catherine took the brown crayon and made a brutal tangle of dark lines all over the orange lines. "Now all you did is just spoil it," Rufus said. "You don't know how to draw!"

"*Quit* it!" Catherine yelled, and all of a sudden she was crying. He heard his Aunt Hannah's sharp voice from the kitchen: "Rufus?"

He was furious with Catherine. "Crybaby," he whispered with cold hatred: "Tattletale!"

And there was Aunt Hannah at the door, just as mad as a hornet. "Now, what's the matter? What have you done to her!" She walked straight at him.

It wasn't fair. How did she know he was doing anything? With a feeling of real righteousness he talked back: "I didn't do one single thing to her. She was just messing everything up on her picture and I tried to help her like you told me to and all of a sudden she started to cry."

"What did he do, Catherine?"

"He wouldn't let me alone."

"Why good night, I never even touched you and you're a liar if you say I did!"

All of a sudden he felt himself gripped by the shoulders and shaken and he turned his rattling head from his sister to look into his Aunt Hannah's freezing glare.

"Now you just listen to *me*," she said. "Are you listening?" she sputtered. "*Are you listening?*" she said still more intensely.

"Yes," he managed to get out, though the word was all shaken up.

"I don't want to spank you on this day of all days, but if I hear you say one more rough thing like that to your sister I'll give you a spanking you'll remember to your dying day, do you hear me? *Do you hear me?*"

"Yes."

"And if you tease her or make her cry just one more time I'll—I'll turn the whole matter over to your Uncle Andrew and we'll see what *he'll* do about it. Do you want me to call him? He's upstairs this minute! Shall I call him?" She stopped shaking him and looked at him. "Shall I?" He shook his head; he was terrified. "All right, but this is my last warning. Do you understand?"

"Yes'm."

"Now if you can't play with Catherine in peace like a decent boy just—stay by yourself. Look at some pictures. Read a book. But you be quiet. And good. Do you hear me?"

"Yes'm."

"Very well." She stood up and her joints snapped. "Come with me, Catherine," she said. "Let's bring your crayons." And she helped Catherine gather up the crayons and the stubs from the window sill and from the carpet. Catherine's face was still red but she was not crying any more. As she passed Rufus she gave him a glance filled with satisfaction, and he answered it with a glance of helpless malevolence.

He listened towards upstairs. If his Uncle Andrew had overheard this, there would really be trouble. But there was no evidence that he had. Rufus felt weak in the knees and in the stomach. He went over to the chair beside the fireplace and sat down.

It was mean to pester Catherine like that but he hadn't wanted to do anything for her anyway. And why did she have to holler like that and bring Aunt Hannah running? He remembered the way her face got red and he knew that he had really been mean to her and he was sorry. But what did she

holler for, like a regular crybaby? He would be very careful today, but sooner or later he sure would get back on her. Darn
crybaby. Tattletale.

The others really did pay him some attention, though. Anybody here ought to know, it's him. His daddy got killed. Yeah
you tell it. Come on and tell us. Just a chance in a million. A
million trillion. Never even knowed, knew, what hit him. Shut
yer Goddamn mouth. Ain't you got no sense at all?

Instantly killed.

Concussion, that was it. Concussion of the brain.

Knocked him crazy as a loon, bibblibblebble.

Shut yer Goddam mouth.

But there was something that made him feel wrong.

Ole Tin Lizzie.

What you get for driving a auto when you're drunk, that's
what my dad says.

Good ole whiskey.

Something he did.

Ole Tin Lizzie just rolled back down on top of him *whomp*.

Didn't either.

He didn't say it didn't. Not clear enough.

Heck, how can that kill anybody?

Did, though. Just a chance in a million. Million trillion.

Instantly killed.

Worse than that, he did.

What.

How would your daddy like it?

He would like me to be with them without them teasing;
looking up to me.

How would your daddy like it?

Like what?

Going out in the street like that when he is dead.

Out in the street like what?

Showing off to people because he is dead.

He wants me to get along with them.

So I tell them he is dead and they look up to me, they don't
tease me.

Showing off because he's dead, that's all you can show off
about. Any other thing they'd tease me and I wouldn't fight
back.

How would your daddy like it?

But he likes me to get along with them. That's why I—went out—showed off.

He felt so uneasy, deep inside his stomach, that he could not think about it any more. He wished he hadn't done it. He wished he could go back and not do anything of the kind. He wished his father could know about it and tell him that yes he was bad but it was all right he didn't mean to be bad. He was glad his father didn't know because if his father knew he would think even worse of him than ever. But if his father's soul was around, always, watching over them, like his mother said, then he knew. And that was worst of anything because there was no way to hide from a soul, and no way to talk to it, either. He just knew, and it couldn't say anything to him, and he couldn't say anything to it. It couldn't whip him either, but it could sit and look at him and be ashamed of him.

"I didn't mean it," he said aloud. "I didn't mean to do bad."

I wanted to show you my cap, he added, silently.

He looked at his father's morsechair.

Not a mark on his body.

He still looked at the chair. With a sense of deep stealth and secrecy he finally went over and stood beside it. After a few moments, and after listening most intently, to be sure that nobody was near, he smelled of the chair, its deeply hollowed seat, the arms, the back. There was only a cold smell of tobacco and, high along the back, a faint smell of hair. He thought of the ash tray on its weighted strap on the arm; it was empty. He ran his finger inside it; there was only a dim smudge of ash. There was nothing like enough to keep in his pocket or wrap up in a paper. He looked at his finger for a moment and licked it; his tongue tasted of darkness.

Chapter 17

THEY were told they could eat, that morning, in their
nightgowns and wrappers. Their mother still wasn't there,
and Aunt Hannah talked even less than at any meal before.
They too were very quiet. They felt that this was an even more
special day than day before yesterday. All the noises of their
eating and from the street were especially clear, but seemed to
come from a distance. They looked steadily at their plates and
ate very carefully.

First thing after breakfast Aunt Hannah said, "Now come
with me, children," and they followed her into the bathroom.
There she washed their faces and hands and arms, and behind
the ears, and their necks, and up each nostril, carefully and
gently with soap and warm water; she did not get soap in the
eyes of either of them, or hurt their skins with the washcloth.
Then she took them into the bedroom and opened the bureaus and took out everything bran clean, from the skin out,
and told Rufus to get his clothes on and to ask for help if he
wanted it, and started dressing Catherine. Rufus began to see
the connection between all this and the bath, the night before.
When he had on his underclothes she brought out new black
stockings and his Sunday serge. While she was helping Catherine on with her stockings, which were also new but white, the
phone rang and she said, "Now sit still and be good. I'll be
straight back," and hustled from the room. They heard her say,
rather loudly and distinctly, up the hall, "I'm getting it, Mary,"
then her feet, fast on the stairs. They sat very still, looking at
the open door, and tried to hear. They found they could hear
quite distinctly, for Hannah spoke to the telephone as she did
to her deaf brother and sister-in-law. They heard: "Hello . . .
Hello . . . Yes . . . *Father?*", and when they heard the word
"Father" they looked at each other with curiosity and with an
uneasy premonition. They heard "Yes . . . yes . . . yes . . .
yes . . . yes . . . yes, Father . . . yes . . . yes, as well as could
be expected . . . yes . . . yes . . . Thank you. I'll tell her . . .
yes . . . yes . . . very well . . . yes . . . The *Highland* Avenue
. . . yes . . . yes . . . *any* . . . yes . . . *any* car to the corner

693

of Church and Gay, then transfer to the Highland—yes—very
well . . . yes . . . Thank you . . . we'll be waiting . . . yes . . .
no . . . yes, Father . . . yes F— . . . good b . . . yes, Father
. . . Thank you . . . goo— . . . yes . . . Thank you . . .
good-bye . . . good-bye."

They heard her let out a long, tired, angry breath and they
could hear her joints snapping as she sprinted up the stairs.
They were sitting exactly where she had left them. Rufus
thought, Maybe she will say we were good children, but without a word she finished with Catherine's stockings. She gave
Rufus a new white shirt from which he slowly and with fascination drew the pins, running them between his teeth as he
watched Aunt Hannah help Catherine into her new dress,
which was white, speckled with small dark blue flowers.
Catherine stood holding the hem and looking at the skirt and
at her white-stockinged feet, which she could see through the
skirt. "And now your necktie," Aunt Hannah said. She took
his dark blue tie and made expert motions beneath his chin
while alternately he tried to watch her hands and looked into
her intent eyes behind their heavy lenses. Her eyes looked stern
and sad and exhausted.

Then she cleaned their nails and combed and brushed their
hair, and put a clean handkerchief in Rufus' breast pocket and
blacked their shoes. "Now wait a moment," she said, leaving
the room. They heard her rap softly on their mother's door.

"Mary?" she said.

"Yes," they heard dimly.

"The children are ready. Shall I bring them in?"

"Yes do, Hannah; thank you."

"Come in now and see your mother," she told them from
the door.

They followed her in.

"Oh, they look *very nice*," she exclaimed, in a voice so odd
that it seemed to the children that she must be sorry that
they did. Yet by her face they could see that she was not
sorry. "Hannah, thank you so much, I don't know what I'd
have . . ."

But Hannah had left the room and closed the door.

They stood and looked at her with curiosity. Her eyes
seemed larger and brighter than usual; her hair was done up as

carefully as if she were going to a party. She wore her wrapper and where it opened in front they could see that she had on something dull and black underneath. Her face was like folded gray cloths.

She watched them look at her; they did not move. Her face altered as if a very low light had gone on behind it.

"Come here, my darlings," she said, and smiled, and squatted with her hands out towards them.

Rufus came shyly; Catherine ran. She took one of them in each arm.

"There, my darlings," she said above them, "there, there, my dear ones. Mother's here. Mother's here. Mother has wanted to see you more, these last days; a *lot* more: she just—couldn't, Rufus and Catherine. Just couldn't do it." When she said "couldn't" she held them very tightly and they knew they were loved. "Little Catherine"—and she held Catherine's head still more tightly to her—"bless her soul! and Rufus"—she held him away and looked into his eyes—"you both know how much Mother loves you, with all her heart and soul, all her life—you know, don't you? Don't you?" Rufus, puzzled but moved, nodded politely, and again she caught him to her. "Of course you do," she said, as if she were not speaking to them. "Of course you do.

Now," she said, after a moment. She stood up and drew them by their hands to the bed. They sat down and she sat in a chair and looked at them for a few seconds without speaking.

"Now," she said again. "I want to tell you about Daddy, because this morning, soon now, we're all going down to Grampa's and Grandma's, and see him once more, and tell him good-bye." Catherine's face brightened; her mother shook her head and placed a quieting hand on Catherine's knees, saying, "No, Catherine, it won't be like you think, that's what I must tell you about him. So listen very carefully, you too, Rufus."

She waited until she was sure they were listening carefully.

"You both understand what has happened to Daddy, don't you. That something happened in the auto, and God took him from us, very quickly, without any pain, and took him away to heaven. You understand that, don't you?"

They nodded.

"And you understand, that when God takes you away to heaven you can never come back?"

"*Never* come back?" Catherine asked.

She stroked Catherine's hair away from her face. "No, Catherine, not ever, in any way we can see and talk to. Daddy's soul will always be thinking of us, just as we will always think of him, but we will never see him again after today." Catherine looked at her very intently; her face began to redden. "You must learn to believe that and know it, darling Catherine. It's so."

She seemed to be about to cry; she swallowed; and Catherine seemed to accept it as true.

"We'll always remember him," she told both of them; "*Always*. And he'll be thinking of us. Every day. He's waiting for us in heaven. And someday, if we're good, when God comes for us, He'll take us to heaven too and we'll see Daddy there, and all be together again, forever and ever."

Amen, Rufus almost said; then realized that this was not a prayer.

"But when we see Daddy today, children, his soul won't be there. It'll just be Daddy's body. Very much as you've always seen him. But because his soul has been taken away, he will be lying down, and he will lie very still. It will be just as if he were asleep, so you must both be just as quiet as if he were asleep and you didn't want to wake him. Quieter."

"But I do," said Catherine.

"But Catherine, you can't, dear, you mustn't even think of trying. Because Daddy is dead now, and when you are dead that means you go to sleep and you never wake up—until God wakes you."

"Well when *will* He?"

"We don't know, Rufus, but probably a long, long time from now. Long after we are all dead."

Rufus wondered what was the good of that, then, but he was sure he should not ask.

"So I don't want you to wonder about it, children. Daddy may seeem very queer to you, because he's so still, but that's— just simply the way he's got to look."

Suddenly she pressed her lips tightly together and they trembled violently. She clenched her cheekbone against her left shoulder, squeezing their hands with her trembling hands, and tears slipped from her tightly shut eyes. Rufus watched her with awe, Catherine with forlorn worry. She suddenly hissed out, "Just-a-minute," with her eyes still closed, startling and shocking Catherine, so that she looked as if she were ready to cry. But before Catherine could commit herself to crying, her hands relaxed, pressing them gently, and she raised her head and opened her clear eyes, saying, "Now Mother must get dressed, and I want you to take Catherine downstairs, Rufus, and both of you be very quiet and good till I come down. And don't make any bother for Aunt Hannah, because she's been wonderful to all of us and she's worn out.

"You be good," she said, smiling and looking at them in turn. "I'll be down in a little while."

"Come on, Catherine," Rufus said.

"I'm coming," Catherine replied, looking at him as if he had spoken of her unjustly.

"Mama"; Rufus stopped near the door. Catherine hesitated, bewildered.

"Yes, Rufus?"

"Are we orphans, now?"

"*Orphans?*"

"Like the Belgians," he informed her. "French. When you haven't got any daddy or mama because they're killed in the war you're an orphan and other children send you things and write you letters."

She must have been unfamiliar with the word, for she seemed to have to think very hard before she answered. Then she said, "Of *course* you're not orphans, Rufus, and I don't want you going around saying that you are. Do you hear me? Because it isn't so. Orphans haven't got *either* a father *or* a mother, you see, and nobody to take care of them or love them. You see? That's why other children send things. But you both have your mother. So you aren't orphans. Do you see? Do you?" He nodded; Catherine nodded because he did. "And Rufus." She looked at him very searchingly; without quite knowing why, he felt he had been discovered in a discreditable secret. "Don't be sorry you're not an orphan. *You be thankful.* Orphans sound lucky to you because they're far away and everyone talks about them now. But they're very,

very unhappy little children. Because *nobody* loves them. Do you understand?"

He nodded, ashamed of himself and secretly disappointed.

"Now run along," she said. They left the room. Aunt Hannah met them on the stairs. "Go into the liv—sitting room for a while like good children," she said. "I'll be right down." And as they reached the bottom of the stairs they heard their mother's door open and close. They sat, looking at their father's chair, thinking.

Catherine felt more virtuous and less troubled than she had for some time, for she had watched Rufus being scolded, all to himself, and it more than wiped out her unhappiness at his telling her to come along when of course she was coming and he had no right even if she wasn't. But she couldn't see how anyone could look as if they were asleep and not wake up, and something else her mother had said—she tried hard to remember what it was—troubled her more deeply than that. And what was a norphan?

Rufus felt that his mother was seriously displeased with him. It was the wrong time to ask her. Maybe he ought not to have asked her at all. But he did want to know. He had not been sure whether or not he was an orphan, maybe you had to be French or Belgian to be one, for he never heard people talk about German orphans but there must be some. Then there were orphans in asylums, but they must be like crazy people. Or did your father and mother have to be killed in the war, if you were to be an orphan people would envy you for being, or the right kind of orphans. If he claimed he was an orphan in school and it turned out that he was not, people would all laugh at him. But if he really was an orphan he wanted to know, so he would be able to say he was, and get the benefit. What was the good of being an orphan if nobody else knew it? Well, so he was not an orphan. Yet his father was dead. Not his mother, too, though. Only his father. But one was dead. One and one makes two. One-half of two equals one. He was half an orphan, no matter what his mother said. And he had a sister who was half an orphan too. Half and half equals a whole. Together they made a whole orphan. He felt that it was not worth mentioning, that he was half an orphan, although he privately considered it a good deal better than nothing; and

that also, he would not volunteer the fact that he and his sister
together made a whole orphan. But if anyone teased either of
them about not being an orphan at all, then he would certainly
speak of that. He decided that Catherine should be warned of
this, so that if they were teased, they could back each other up.

"Both of us together is a whole orphan," he said.

"Huh?"

"Don't say 'huh,' say, 'What is it, Rufus?'"

"I will not!"

"You will so. Mama says to."

"She does not."

"She does so. When I say 'huh' she says, 'Don't say "huh,"
say "What is it, Mother?"' When you say 'huh' she tells you
the same thing. So don't say 'huh.' Say, 'What is it, Rufus?'"

"I won't say it to you."

"Yes, you will."

"No, I won't."

"Yes, you will, because Mama said for us to be good. If you
don't I'll tell her on you."

"You tell her and I'll tell on you."

"Tell on me for what?"

"Listening at the door."

"No you won't."

"I will so."

"You will not."

"I will so."

He thought it over.

"All right, *don't* say it, and I *won't* tell on you if you won't
tell on me."

"I will if you tell on me."

"I said I won't, didn't I? Not if you don't tell on me."

"I won't if you don't tell on me."

"All right."

They glared at each other.

They heard loud feet on the porch, and the doorbell rang.
Upstairs they heard their mother cry "Oh, goodness!" They
ran to the door. He blocked Catherine away from the knob
and opened it.

A man stood there, almost as tall as Daddy. He had a black
glaring collar like Dr. Whittaker but wore a purple vest. He

wore a long shallow hat and he had a long, sharp, bluish chin almost like a plow. He carried a small, shining black suitcase. He seemed to be as disconcerted and displeased as they were. He said, "Oh, good morning," in a voice that had echoes in it and, frowning, glanced once again at the number along the side of the door. "Of course," he said, with a smile they did not understand. "You're Rufus and Catherine. May I come in?" And without waiting for their assent or withdrawal (for they were blocking the door) he strode forward, parting them with firm hands and saying "Isn't Miss L . . ."

They heard Aunt Hannah's voice behind them on the stairs, and turned. "Father?" she said, peering against the door's light. "Come right in." And she came up as he quickly removed his oddly shaped hat, and they shook hands. "This is Father Jackson, Rufus and Catherine," she said. "He has come specially from Chattanooga. Father, this is Rufus, and this is Catherine."

"Yes, we've already introduced ourselves," said Father Jackson, as if he thought it was funny. That's a lie, Rufus reflected. Father Jackson left one hand at rest for a moment on Catherine, then removed it as if he had forgotten her. "And where is Mrs. Follet?" he asked, almost whispering "Mrs. Follet."

"If you'll just wait a moment, Father, she isn't quite ready."

"Of course." He leaned towards Aunt Hannah and said, in a grinding, scarcely audible voice, "Is she—chuff-chuff-chuff?"

"Oh yes," Hannah replied.

"But does she Whehf-wheff-whehf-whef-tized?"

"I'm afraid not, Father," said Hannah, gravely. "I wasn't quite sure enough, myself, to tell her. I'm sorry to burden you with it but I felt I should leave that to you."

"You were right, Miss Lynch. Absolutely." He looked around, his head gliding, his hat in his hand. "Now little man," he said, "if you'll kindly relieve me of my hat."

"Rufus," said Hannah. "Take Father's hat to the hat rack."

Bewildered, he did so. The hat rack was in plain sight.

"Now Father, if you won't mind waiting just a moment," Hannah said, showing him in to the sitting room. "Rufus: Catherine: sit here with Father. Excuse me," she added, and she hastened upstairs.

Father Jackson strode efficiently across the room, sat in their father's chair, crossed his knees narrowly, and looked, frowning, at the carefully polished toe of his right shoe. They watched him, and Rufus wondered whether to tell him whose chair it was. Father Jackson held his long, heavily veined right hand palm outward, at arm's length, and, frowning, examined his nails. He certainly wouldn't have sat in it, Rufus felt, if he had known whose chair it was, so it would be mean not to tell him. But if he was told now, it would make him feel bad, Rufus thought. Catherine noticed, with interest, that outside the purple vest he wore a thin gold chain; on the chain was a small gold crucifix. Father Jackson changed knees and, frowning, examined the carefully polished toe of his left shoe. Better not tell him, Rufus thought; it would be mean. How do you get such a blue face, Catherine wondered; I wish my face was blue, not red. Father Jackson, frowning, looked all around the room and smiled, faintly, as his gaze came to rest on some point above and beyond the heads of the children. Both turned to see what he was smiling at, but there was nothing there except the picture of Jesus when Jesus was a little boy, staying up late in his nightgown and talking to all the wise men in the temple. "Oh," Rufus realized; "that's why."

When they turned Father Jackson was frowning again and looking at them just as he had looked at his nails. He quickly smiled, though not as nicely as he had smiled at Jesus, and changed his way of looking so that it did not seem that he was curious whether they were really clean. But he still looked as if he were displeased about something. They both looked back, wondering what he was displeased about. Was Catherine wetting her panties, Rufus wondered; he looked at her but she looked all right to him. What was Rufus doing that the man looked so unpleasant, Catherine wondered. She looked at him, but all he was doing was looking at the man. They both looked at him, wishing that if he was displeased with them he would tell them why instead of looking like that, and wishing that he would sit in some other chair. He looked at both of them, feeling that their rude staring was undermining his gaze and his silence, by which he had intended to impress them into a sufficiently solemn and receptive state for the things he intended to say to them; and wondering whether or no he should reprimand them. Surely, he decided, if they lack manners even at such a time as this, this is the time to speak of it.

"Children must not stare at their elders," he said. "That is ill-bred."

"Huh?" both of them asked. What's "stare," they wondered; "elders"; "ill-bred"?

"Say 'Sir,' or 'I beg your pardon, Father.'"

"Sir?" Rufus said.

"You," Father Jackson said to Catherine.

"Sir?" Catherine said.

"You must not stare at people—look at them, as you are looking at me."

"Oh," Rufus said. Catherine's face turned red.

"Say, 'Excuse me, Father.'"

"Excuse me, Father."

"You," Father Jackson said to Catherine.

Catherine became still redder.

"Excuse me, Father," Rufus whispered.

"No prompting, please," Father Jackson broke in, in a voice pitched for a large class. "Come now, little girl, it is never too soon to learn to be little ladies and little gentlemen, is it?"

Catherine said nothing.

"Is it?" Father Jackson asked Rufus.

"I don't know," Rufus replied.

"I consider that a thoroughly uncivil answer to a civil question," said Father Jackson.

"Yes," Rufus said, beginning to turn cold in the pit of his stomach. What was "uncivil"?

"You agree," Father Jackson said. "Say, 'yes, Father.'"

"Yes, Father," Rufus said.

"Then you are aware of your incivility. It is deliberate and calculated," Father Jackson said.

"No," Rufus said. He could not understand the words but clearly he was being accused.

Father Jackson leaned back in their father's chair and closed his eyes and folded his hands. After a moment he opened his eyes and said, "Little boy, little sister" (he nudged his long blue chin towards Catherine), "this is neither the time nor place for reprimands." His hands unfolded; he leaned forward, tapping his right kneecap with his right forefinger, and frowning fiercely, said in a voice which sounded very gentle but was not, "But I just want to tell . . ." They heard Hannah on the stairs. "Children," he said, rising, "this must wait another time." He pointed his jaw at Hannah, raising his eyebrows.

"Will you come up, Father?" she asked in a shut voice.

Without looking again at the children, he followed her upstairs.

They looked each other in the eyes; their mouths hung open; they listened. It was as they had begun to expect it would be: the steps of two along the upper hallway, the opening of their mother's door, their mother's strangely shrouded voice, the closing of the door: silence.

Taking great care not to creak, they stole up to the middle of the stairs. They could hear no words, only the tilt and shape of voices: their mother's, still so curiously shrouded, so submissive, so gentle; it seemed to ask questions and to accept answers. The man's voice was subdued and gentle but rang very strongly with the knowledge that it was right and that no other voice could be quite as right; it seemed to say unpleasant things as if it felt they were kind things to say, or again, as if it did not care whether or not they were kind because in any case they were right, it seemed to make statements, to give information, to counter questions with replies which were beyond argument or even discussion, and to try to give comfort whether what it was saying could give comfort or not. Now and again their mother's way of questioning sounded to the children as if she wondered whether something could be fair, could possibly be true, could be so cruel, but whenever such tones came into their mother's voice the man's voice became still more ringing and overbearing, or still more desirous to comfort, or both; and their mother's next voice was always very soft. Aunt Hannah's voice was almost as clear and light as always, but there was now in it also a kind of sweetness and of sorrow they had not heard in it before. Mainly she seemed only to agree with Father Jackson, to add her voice to his, though much more kindly, in this overpowering of their mother. But now and again it seemed to explain more fully, and more gently, something which he had just explained, and twice it questioned almost as their mother questioned, but with more spirit, with an edge almost of bitterness or temper. And on these two occasions Father Jackson's voice shifted and lost a bit of its vibrancy, and for a moment he talked as rapidly in a circle, seeming to assure them that of course he did not at all mean what they had thought he meant, but only, that (and then the voice would begin to gather assurance); they must realize (and now it had almost its old drive); in fact, of course— and now he was back again, and seemed to be saying precisely what he had said before, only with still more authority and still less possibility of disagreement. And then their Aunt Hannah murmured agreement in an oddly cool, remote tone, and their mother's voice of acceptance was scarcely audible at all.

Once in a while when these voices came to crises in their subdued turmoil Rufus and Catherine looked into each other's cold, bright eyes which brightened and chilled the more with every intensification of the man's voice, and every softening and defeat of their mother's voice. But most of the time they only stared at the knob on their mother's door, shifting delicately on the stairs whenever they became cramped. They could not conceive of what was being done to their mother, but in his own way each was sure that it was something evil, to which she was submitting almost without a struggle, and by which she was deceived. Rufus repeatedly saw himself flinging open the door and striding in, a big stone in his hand, and saying, "You stop hurting my mother." Catherine knew only that a tall stranger in black, with a frightening jaw and a queer hat, a man whom she hated and feared, had broken into their house, had been welcomed first by Aunt Hannah and then by her mother herself, had sat in her father's chair as if he thought he belonged there, talked meanly to her in words she could not understand, and was now doing secret and cruel things to her mother while Aunt Hannah looked on. If Daddy was here he would kill him. She wished Daddy would hurry up and come and kill him and she wanted to see it. But Rufus realized that his Aunt Hannah and even his mother were on Father Jackson's side and against him, and that they would just put him out of the room and punish him terribly and go right on with whatever awful thing it was they were doing. And Catherine remembered, with a jolt, that Daddy would not come back because he was down at Grandma's and Grandpa's and now they would see him again and then they would never see him any more until heaven.

But suddenly there was a kind of creaking and soft thumping and the voices changed. Father Jackson's voice was even more strongly in charge, now, than before, although it did not seem that he was arguing, or informing, or trying to bring comfort, or even that he was speaking to either of the two women. Most of its theatrical resonance had left it, and all of its dominance. He seemed to be speaking as if to someone at least as much more assured and strong than he was, as he was more assured and strong than their mother was, and his voice had something of their mother's humbleness. Yet it was a very confident voice, as if it were sure that the person who was being addressed would approve what was said and what was asked, and would not rebuff him as he had rebuffed their mother. And in some way the voice was even more authoritative than before, as if Father Jackson were speaking not for himself but for, as well as to, the person he addressed, and were speaking with the power of that person as well as in manly humility before that person. Clearly, also, the voice loved its own sound, inseparably from its love of the sound and contour of the words it spoke, as naturally as a fine singer delights inseparably in his voice and in the melody he is singing. And clearly, although not one word was audible to the children, the voice was not mistaken in this love. Not a word was distinct from where they stood, but the shapes and rhythms and the inflections were as lovely and as bemusing as any songs they had ever heard. In general rhythm, Rufus began to realize, it was not unlike the prayers that Dr. Whittaker said; and he realized, then, that Father Jackson also was praying. But where Dr. Whittaker gave his words and phrases special emphasis and personal coloring, as though they were matters which required argument and persuasion, Father Jackson spoke almost wholly without emphasis and with only the subtlest coloring, as if the personal emotion, the coloring, were cast against the words from a distance, like echoes. He spoke as if all that he said were in every idea and in every syllable final, finished, perfected beyond disquisition long before he was born; and truth and eternity dwelt like clearest water in the rhythms of his language and in the contours of his voice;

his voice accepted and bore this language like the bed of a brook. They looked at each other once more; Rufus could see that Catherine did not understand. "He's saying his prayers," he whispered.

She neither understood him nor believed him but she realized, with puzzlement, that now the man was being nice, though she did not even want him to be nice to her mother, she did not want him to be anything, to anybody, anywhere. But it was clear to both of them that things were better now than they had been before; they could hear it in his voice, which at once enchanted and obscurely disturbed them, and they could hear it in the voices of the two women, which now and again, when he seemed to pause for breath, chimed in with a short word or two, a few times with whole sentences. Both their voices were more tender, more alive, and more inhuman, than they had ever heard them before; and this remoteness from humanity troubled them. They realized that there was something to which their mother and their great-aunt were devoted, something which gave their voices peculiar vitality and charm, which was beyond and outside any love that was felt for them; and they felt that this meant even more to their mother and their great-aunt than they did, or than anyone else in the world did. They realized, fairly clearly, that the object of this devotion was not this man whom they mistrusted, but they felt that he was altogether too deeply involved in it. And they felt that although everything was better for their mother than it had been a few minutes before, it was far worse in one way. For before, she had at least been questioning, however gently. But now she was wholly defeated and entranced, and the transition to prayer was the moment and mark of her surrender. They stared so long and so gloomily at the doorknob, turning over such unhappy and uncertain intuitions in their souls, that the staring, round white knob became all that they saw in the universe except a subtly beating haze pervaded with magnificent quiet sound; so that when the doorbell rang they were so frightened that their hearts contracted.

Then, with almost equal terror, they realized that they would be caught on the stairs. They started down, in haste as desperate as their efforts to be silent. The door burst open above them. She can't see, they realized (for it was Hannah who came out), and in the same instant they realized: but she can hear better than anybody. A stair creaked loudly; terror struck them; against it, they continued. "Yes," Hannah called sharply; she was already on the stairs. The doorbell rang again. On the last stair, they were hideously noisy; they wanted only to disappear in time. They ducked through the sitting-room door and watched her pass; they were as insane with excitement as if they could still dare hope they had not been discovered, and solemnly paralyzed in the inevitability of dreadful reprimand and of physical pain.

Hannah didn't even glance back at them: she went straight to the door.

It was Mr. Starr. Usually he wore suits as brown and hairy as his mustache, but this morning he wore a dark blue suit and a black tie. In his hand he carried a black derby.

"Walter," Aunt Hannah said, "you know what all you're doing means to us."

"Aw now," Walter said.

"Come in," she said. "Mary'll be right down. Children, you know Mr. Starr . . ."

"Course we do," Mr. Starr said, smiling at them with his warm brown eyes through the lenses. He put the hand holding the derby on Rufus' shoulder and the other on Catherine's cheek. "You come on in and sit with me, will you, till your mother's ready."

He walked straight for their father's chair, veered unhappily, and sat on a chair next the wall.

"Well, so you're coming down and visit us," he said.

"Huh?"

"Coming down," Walter said. "Or ma—did your mama say anything about maybe you were coming down sometime, and pay us a visit?"

"Huh-uh."

"Oh, well, there's lots of time. Did you ever hear a gramophone?"

"She can't hardly hear when she does."

"Eigh?" He seemed extremely puzzled.

"Uncle Andrew says she's crazy even to try."

"Who?"

"Why, Granma." Mr. Starr had never before seemed stupid, but now Rufus began to think his memory was as bad as those of the boys at the corner. Could he be teasing? It would be very queer if Mr. Starr would tease. He decided he should trust him. "You know, when she phones, like you said."

Mr. Starr thought that over for a moment and then he seemed to understand. But almost the moment he understood he started to laugh, so he must have been teasing, after all. Rufus was deeply hurt. Then almost immediately he stopped laughing as if he were shocked at himself.

"Well now," he said. "I begin to see how we both got a bit in a muddle. You'd never heard of the thing I was talking about, and it sounds mighty like grandma phone, did you ever hear grandmaphone. Of course. Naturally. But what I was talking about was a nice box that music comes out of. Did you ever hear music come out of a box?"

"Huh-uh."

"Well down home, believe it or not, we got a box that music comes out of. Would you like to hear it sometime?"

"Uh-huh."

"Good. We'll see if that can't be arranged. Soon. Now would you like to know what they call this box?"

"Uh-huh."

"A gram-o-phone. See? It sounds very much like grandma phone, but it's just a little different. Gram-o-phone. Can you say it?"

"Gram-uh-phone."

"That's right. Can Baby Sister say it, I wonder?"

"Catherine? He means you."

"Gran-muh-phone."

"Gra*mm*-uh-phone."

"Gra*mm*-muh-phone."

"That's fine. You're a mighty smart little girl to say a big word like that."

"I can say some ever so big words," Rufus said. "Want to hear? The Dominant Primordrial Beast."

"Well now, that's mighty smart. But of course I don't mean smarter than Sister. You're a lot bigger boy."

"Yes, but I could say that when I was four years old. She's

almost four and I bet she can't say it. Can you, Catherine? Can you?"

"Well, now, some people learn a little quicker than others. It's nice to learn fast but it's nice to take your time, too." He walked over and picked Catherine up and sat down with her in his lap. He smelled almost as good as her father, although he was soft in front, and she looked happy. "Now what does that word 'primordrial' mean?"

"I dunno, but it's nice and scary."

"Is it scary? Yes? Yes, spose it does have a sort of a scary sound. Now you can say it, you ought to find out what it means, sometime."

"What *does* it mean?"

"Not sure myself, but then I don't say it. Don't have occasion." He opened out one arm and Rufus walked across to him without realizing he was doing so. The arm felt strong and kind around him. "You're a fine little boy," Mr. Starr said. "But it isn't nice of you to lord it over your sister."

"What's 'lord it'?"

"Brag about things you can do, that she can't do yet. That isn't nice."

"No, sir."

"So you watch, and don't do it."

"No siree."

"Because Catherine's a fine little girl, too."

"Yes, sir."

"Aren't you, Catherine?" He smiled at her and she blushed with delight. Rufus liked Catherine so well, all of a sudden, that he smiled at her, and when she smiled back they were both happy and suddenly he was very much ashamed to have treated her so.

"I want to tell you two something," they heard Mr. Starr's quieted voice. They looked up at him. "Not because you'll understand it now, but I have to, my heart's full, and it's you I want to tell. Maybe you'll remember it later on. It is about your daddy. Because you never got a real chance to know him. Can I tell you?"

They nodded.

"Some people have a hard, hard time. No money, no good schooling. Scarcely enough food. Nothing that you children have, but good people to love them. Your daddy started like that. He didn't have one thing. He had to work till it practicly killed him, for every little thing he ever got.

"Well, some of the greatest men start with nothing. Like Abraham Lincoln. You know who he was?"

"He was born in a log cabin," Rufus said.

"That's right, and he became the greatest man we've ever had."

He said nothing for a moment and they wondered what he was going to tell them about their father.

"Somehow I never got a chance to know Jay—your father—well as I wish. I don't think he ever knew how much I thought of him. Well I thought the world of him, Rufus and Catherine. My own wife and son couldn't mean more to me I think." He waited again. "I'm a pretty ordinary man myself," he went on. "Not a bad one. Just ordinary. But I always thought your father was a lot like Lincoln. I don't mean getting ahead in the world. I mean a man. Some people get where they hope to in this world. Most of us don't. But there never was a man up against harder odds than your father. And there was never a man who tried harder, or hoped for more. I don't mean getting ahead. I mean the right things. He wanted a good life, and good understanding, for himself, for everybody. There never was a braver man than your father, or a man that was kinder, or more generous. They don't make them. All I wanted to tell you is, your father was one of the finest men that ever lived."

He suddenly closed his eyes tightly behind his glasses, and swallowed; a long sobbing sigh fell from him. Deeply and solemnly touched, they moved closer to him, whether to comfort him or themselves they did not know. "There, there," he said, his eyes still closed. "There, there now. There, there."

Upstairs, they heard the door open.

Chapter 18

WHEN grief and shock surpass endurance there occur phases of exhaustion, of anesthesia in which relatively little is felt and one has the illusion of recognizing, and understanding a good deal. Throughout these days Mary had, during these breathing spells, drawn a kind of solace from the recurrent thought: at least I am enduring it. I am aware of what has happened, I am meeting it face to face, I am living through it. There had been, even, a kind of pride, a desolate kind of pleasure, in the feeling: I am carrying a heavier weight than I could have dreamed it possible for a human being to carry, yet I am living through it. It had of course occurred to her that this happens to many people, that it is very common, and she humbled and comforted herself in this thought. She thought: this is simply what living is; I never realized before what it is. She thought: now I am more nearly a grown member of the human race; bearing children, which had seemed so much, was just so much apprenticeship. She thought that she had never before had a chance to realize the strength that human beings have, to endure; she loved and revered all those who had ever suffered, even those who had failed to endure. She thought that she had never before had a chance to realize the might, grimness and tenderness of God. She thought that now for the first time she began to know herself, and she gained extraordinary hope in this beginning of knowledge. She thought that she had grown up almost overnight. She thought that she had realized all that was in her soul to realize in the event, and when at length the time came to put on her veil, leave the bedroom she had shared with her husband, leave their home, and go down to see him for the first time since his death and to see the long day through, which would cover him out of sight for the duration of this world, she thought that she was firm and ready. She had refused to "try on" her veil; the mere thought of approving or disapproving it before a mirror was obscene; so now when she came to the mirror and drew it down across her face to go, she saw herself for the first time since her husband's death. Without either desiring to see her face, or caring how it looked, she saw that it had changed; through the deep, clear veil her gray eyes watched her gray eyes watch her through the deep, clear veil. I must have fever, she thought, startled by their brightness; and turned away. It was when she came to the door, to walk through it, to leave this room and to leave this shape of existence forever, that realizations poured upon and overwhelmed her through which, in retrospect, she would one day know that all that had gone before, all that she had thought she experienced and knew —true, more or less, though it all was—was nothing to this. The realization came without shape or definability, save as it was focused in the pure physical act of leaving the room, but came with such force, such monstrous piercing weight, in all her heart and soul and mind and body but above all in the womb, where it arrived and dwelt like a cold and prodigious, spreading stone, that she groaned almost inaudibly, almost a mere silent breath, an *Ohhhhhhh*, and doubled deeply over, hands to her belly, and her knee joints melted.

Hannah, smaller than she, caught her, and rapped out, "*Close that door!*" It would be a long time before either of the women realized their resentment of the priest and their contempt for him, and their compassion, for staying in the room. Now they did not even know that he was there. Hannah helped her to the edge of the bed and sat beside her exclaiming, over and over, in a heartbroken voice, "Mary, Mary, Mary, Mary. Oh Mary, Mary, Mary," resting one already translucent, spinster's hand lightly upon the back of her veiled head, and with the other, so clenching one of Mary's wrists that she left a bracelet of bruise.

Mary meanwhile rocked quietly backward and forward, and from side to side, groaning, quietly, from the depths of her body, not like a human creature but a fatally hurt animal; sounds low, almost crooned, not strident, but shapeless and orderless, the sisters, except in their quietude, to those transcendent, idiot, bellowing screams which deliver children. And as she rocked and groaned, the realization gradually lost its fullest, most impaling concentration: there took shape, from its utter darkness, like the slow emergence of the countryside into first daylight, all those separate realizations which could be resolved into images, emotions, thought, words, obligations:

so that after not more than a couple of minutes, during which Hannah never ceased to say to her, "Mary, Mary," and Father Jackson, his eyes closed, prayed, she sat still for a moment, then got quietly onto her knees, was silent for not more than a moment more, made the sign of the Cross, stood up, and said, "I'm ready now."

But she swayed; Hannah said, "Rest, Mary. There's no hurry," and Father Jackson said, "Perhaps you should lie down a little while"; but she said, "No; thank you; I want to go now," and walked unsteadily to the door, and opened it, and walked through.

Father Jackson took her arm, in the top hallway. Although she tried not to, she leaned on him very heavily.

"Come, now," their mother whispered, and, taking them each by the hand, led them through the Green Room and into the living room.

There it was, against the fireplace, and there seemed to be scarcely anything else in the room except the sunny light on the floor.

It was very long and dark; smooth like a boat; with bright handles. Half the top was open. There was a strange, sweet smell, so faint that it could scarcely be realized.

Rufus had never known such stillness. Their little sounds, as they approached his father, vanished upon it like the infinitesimal whisperings of snow, falling on open water.

There was his head, his arms; suit: there he was.

Rufus had never seen him so indifferent; and the instant he saw him, he knew that he would never see him otherwise. He had his look of faint impatience, the chin strained a little upward, as if he were concealing his objection to a collar which was too tight and too formal. And in this slight urgency of the chin; in the small trendings of a frown which stayed in the skin; in the arch of the nose; and in the still, strong mouth, there was a look of pride. But most of all, there was indifference; and through this indifference which held him in every particle of his being—an indifference which would have rejected them; have sent them away, except that it was too indifferent even to care whether they went or stayed—in this self-completeness which nothing could touch, there was something else, some other feeling which he gave, which there was no identifying even by feeling, for Rufus had never experienced this feeling before; there was perfected beauty. The head, the hand, dwelt in completion, immutable, indestructible: motionless. They moved upon existence quietly as stones which withdraw through water for which there is no floor.

The arm was bent. Out of the dark suit, the starched cuff, sprang the hairy wrist.

The wrist was angled; the hand was arched; none of the fingers touched each other.

The hand was so composed that it seemed at once casual and majestic. It stood exactly above the center of his body.

The fingers looked unusually clean and dry, as if they had been scrubbed with great care.

The hand looked very strong, and the veins were strong in it.

The nostrils were very dark, yet he thought he could see, in one of them, something which looked like cotton.

On the lower lip, a trifle to the left of its middle, there was a small blue line which ran also a little below the lip.

At the exact point of the chin, there was another small blue mark, as straight and neat as might be drawn with a pencil, and scarcely wider.

The lines which formed the wings of the nose and the mouth were almost gone.

The hair was most carefully brushed.

The eyes were casually and quietly closed, the eyelids were like silk on the balls, and when Rufus glanced quickly from the eyes to the mouth it seemed as if his father were almost about to smile. Yet the mouth carried no suggestion either of smiling or of gravity; only strength, silence, manhood, and indifferent contentment.

He saw him much more clearly than he had ever seen him before; yet his face looked unreal, as if he had just been shaved by a barber. The whole head was waxen, and the hand, too, was as if perfectly made of wax.

The head was lifted on a small white satin pillow.

There was the subtle, curious odor, like fresh hay, and like a hospital, but not quite like either, and so faint that it was scarcely possible to be sure that it existed.

Rufus saw these things within a few seconds, and became aware that his mother was picking Catherine up in order that she might see more clearly; he drew a little aside. Out of the end of his eye he was faintly aware of his sister's rosy face and he could hear her gentle breathing as he continued to stare at his father, at his stillness, and his power, and his beauty.

He could see the tiny dark point of every shaven hair of the beard.

He watched the way the flesh was chiseled in a widening trough from the root of the nose to the white edge of the lip.

He watched the still more delicate dent beneath the lower lip.

It became strange, and restive, that it was possible for anyone to lie so still for so long; yet he knew that his father would never move again; yet this knowledge made his motionlessness no less strange.

Within him, and outside him, everything except his father was dry, light, unreal, and touched with a kind of warmth and impulse and a kind of sweetness which felt like the beating of a heart. But borne within this strange and unreal sweetness, its center yet alien in nature from all the rest, and as nothing else was actual, his father lay graven, whose noble hand he longed, in shyness, to touch.

"Now, Rufus," his mother whispered; they knelt. He could just see over the edge of the coffin. He gazed at the perfect hand.

His mother's arm came round him; he felt her hand on the crest of his shoulder. He slid his arm around her and felt her hand become alive on his shoulder and felt his sister's arm. He touched her bare arm tenderly, and felt her hand grapple for and take his arm. He put his hand around her arm and felt how little it was. He could feel a vein beating against the bone, just below her armpit.

"Our Father," she said.

They joined her, Catherine waiting for those words of which she was sure, Rufus lowering his voice almost to silence while she hesitated, trying to give her the words distinctly. Their mother spoke very gently.

"Our Father, Who art in Heaven, hallowed be Thy name; Thy kingdom come, Thy—"

"Thy will be d . . ." Rufus went on, alone; then waited, disconcerted.

"Thy will be done," his mother said. "On earth," she continued, with some strange shading of the word which touched him with awe and sadness; "As it is in heaven."

"Give us this d . . ."

Rufus was more careful this time.

"Daily bread," Catherine said confidently.

"Give us this day our daily bread," and in those words still more, he felt that his mother meant something quite otherwise, "And forgive us our trespasses as we forgive those who trespass against us.

"And lead us not into temptation; but deliver us from evil," and here their mother left her hands where they dwelt with her children, but bowed her head:

"For Thine is the kingdom, and the power, and the glory," she said with almost vindictive certitude, "forever and ever. Amen."

She was silent for some moments, and still he stared at the hand.

"God, bless us and help us all," she said. "God, help us to understand Thee. God, help us to know Thy will. God, help us to put all our trust in Thee, whether we can understand or not.

"God, help these little children to remember their father in all his goodness and strength and kindness and dearness, and in all of his tremendous love for them. God, help them ever to be all that was good and fine and brave in him, all that he would most have loved to see them grow up to be, if Thou in Thy great wisdom had thought best to spare him. God, let us be able to feel, to know, he can still see us as we grow, as we live, that he is still with us; that he is not deprived of his children and all he had hoped for them and loved them for; nor they of him. Nor they of him.

"God, make us to know he is still with us, still loves us, cares what comes to us, what we do, what we are; so *much*. O, God . . ."

She spoke these words sharply, and said no more; and Rufus felt that she was looking at his father, but he did not move his eyes, and felt that he should not know what he was sure of. After a few moments he heard the motions of her lips as softly again as that falling silence in which the whole world snowed, and he turned his eyes from the hand and looked towards his father's face and, seeing the blue-dented chin thrust upward, and the way the flesh was sunken behind the bones of the jaw, first recognized in its specific weight the word, *dead*. He looked quickly away, and solemn wonder tolled in him like the shuddering of a prodigious bell, and he heard his mother's snowy lips with wonder and with a desire that she should never suffer sorrow, and gazed once again at the hand, whose casual majesty was unaltered. He wished more sharply even than before that he might touch it, but whereas before he had wondered whether he might, if he could find a way to be alone, with no one to see or ever know, now he was sure that he must not. He therefore watched it all the more studiously, trying to bring all of his touch into all that he could see; but he could not bring much. He realized that his mother's hand was without feeling or meaning on his shoulder. He felt how sweaty his hand, and his sister's arm, had become, and changed his hand, and clasped her gently but without sympathy, and felt her hand tighten, and felt gentle towards her because she was too little to understand. The hand became, for a few moments, a mere object, and he could just hear his mother's breath repeating, "Good-bye, Jay, good-bye. Good-bye. Good-bye. Good-bye, my Jay, my husband. Oh, Good-bye. Good-bye."

Then he heard nothing and was aware of nothing except the hand, which was an object; and felt a strong downward clasping pressure upon his skull, and heard a quiet but rich voice.

His mother was not—yes, he could see her skirts, out behind to the side; and Catherine, and a great hand on her head too, and her silent and astounded face. And between them, a little behind them, black polished shoes and black, sharply pressed trouser legs, without cuffs.

"Hail Mary, full of grace," the voice said; and his mother joined; "The Lord is with thee; blessed art thou among women, and blessed is the fruit of thy womb, Jesus.

"Holy Mary, Mother of God, pray for us sinners, now, and in the hour of *our* death. Amen."

"Our Father, Who art in heaven," the voice said; and the children joined; "Hallowed be Thy name," but in their mother's uncertainty, they stopped, and the voice went on: "Thy kingdom come, Thy will be done," said the voice, with particular warmth, "on earth as it is in heaven. Give us this day our daily bread. And forgive us our trespasses, As we forgive those who trespass against us." Everything had been taken off the mantelpiece. "And lead us not into temptation, But deliver us from evil," and with this his hand left Rufus' head and he crossed himself, immediately restoring the hand, "for Thine is the kingdom, and the power, and the glory, for ever and ever. Amen."

He was silent for a moment. Twisting a little under the hard hand, Rufus glanced upward. The priest's jaw was hard, his face was earnest, his eyes were tightly shut.

"O Lord, cherish and protect these innocent, orphaned children," he said, his eyes shut. *Then we are!* Rufus thought, and knew that he was very bad. "Guard them in all temptations which life may bring. That when they come to understand this thing which in Thy inscrutable wisdom Thou hast brought to pass, they may know and reverence Thy will. God, we beseech Thee that they may ever be the children, the boy and girl, the man and woman, which this good man would have desired them to be. Let them never discredit his memory, O Lord. And Lord, by Thy mercy may they come quickly and soon to know the true and all-loving Father Whom they have in Thee. Let them seek Thee out the more, in their troubles and in their joys, as they would have sought their good earthly father, had he been spared them. Let them ever be, by Thy great mercy, true Christian Catholic children. Amen."

Some of the tiles of the hearth which peeped from beneath the coffin stand, those at the border, were a grayish blue. All the others were streaked and angry, reddish yellow.

The voice altered, and said delicately: "The Peace of God, which passeth all understanding, keep your hearts and minds in the knowledge and love of God, and of his Son Jesus Christ our Lord": His hand again lifted from Rufus' head, and he drew a great cross above each of them as he said, "And the blessing of God Almighty, the Father, the Son, and the Holy Ghost, be upon you, and remain with you always."

"Amen," their mother said.

The priest touched his shoulder, and Rufus stood up.

Catherine stood up. Their father had not, of course not, Rufus thought, he had not moved, but he looked to have changed. Although he lay in such calm and beauty, and grandeur, it looked to Rufus as if he had been flung down and left on the street, and as if he were a very successfully disguised stranger. He felt a pang of distress and of disbelief and was about to lean to look more closely, when he felt a light hand on his head, his mother's, he knew, and heard her say, "Now, children"; and they were conveyed to the hall door.

The piano, he saw, was shut.

"Now Mother wants to stay just a minute or two," she told them. "She'll be with you directly. So you go straight into the East Room, with Aunt Hannah, and wait for me."

She touched their faces, and noiselessly closed the door.

Crossing to the East Room they became aware that they were not alone in the dark hall. Andrew stood by the hat rack, holding to the banister, and his rigid, weeping eyes, shining with fury, struck to the roots of their souls like ice, so that they hastened into the room where their great-aunt sat in an unmoving rocking chair with her hands in her lap, the sunless light glazing her lenses, frostlike upon her hair.

They heard feet on the front stairs, and knew it was their grandfather. They heard him turn to go down the hall and then they heard his subdued, surprised voice: "Andrew? Where's Poll?"

And their uncle's voice, cold, close to his ear: "In—there—with—Father—Jackson."

"Unh!" they heard their grandfather growl. Their Aunt Hannah hurried towards the door.

"Praying."

"Unh!" he growled again.

Their Aunt Hannah quickly closed the door, and hurried back to her chair.

But much as she had hurried, all that she did after she got back to her chair was to sit with her hands in her lap and stare straight ahead of her through her heavy lenses, and all that they could do was to sit quietly too, and look at the clean lace curtains at the window, and at the magnolia tree and the locust tree in the yard, and at the wall of the next house, and at a heavy robin which fed along the lawn, until he flew away, and

at the people who now and then moved past along the sunny
sidewalk, and at the buggies and automobiles which now and
then moved along the sunny street. They felt mysteriously immaculate, strange and careful in their clean clothes, and it
seemed as if the house were in shadow and were walking on
tiptoe in the middle of an easy, sunny world. When they tired
of looking at these things, they looked at their Aunt Hannah,
but she did not appear to realize that they were looking at her;
and when there was no response from their Aunt Hannah they
looked at each other. But it had never given them any pleasure
or interest to look at each other and it gave them none today.
Each could only see that the other was much too clean, and
each realized, through that the more acutely, that he himself
was much too clean, and that something was wrong which required of each of them such careful conduct, and particularly
good manners, that there was really nothing imaginable that
might be proper to do except to sit still. But though sitting so
still, with nothing to fix their attention upon except each
other, they saw each other perhaps more clearly than at any
time before; and each felt uneasiness and shyness over what he
saw. Rufus saw a much littler child than he was, with a puzzled, round, red face which looked angry, and he was somewhat sorry for her in the bewilderment and loneliness he felt
she was lost in, but more, he was annoyed by this look of shut-
in anger and this look of incomprehension and he thought
over and over: "Dead. He's dead. That's what he is; he's
dead"; and the room where his father lay felt like a boundless
hollowness in the house and in his own being, as if he stood in
the dark near the edge of an abyss and could feel that droop of
space in the darkness; and watching his sister's face he could
see his father's almost as clearly, as he had just seen it, and said
to himself, over and over: "Dead. Dead"; and looked with uneasiness and displeasure at his sister's face, which was so different, so flushed and busy, so angry, and so uncomprehending.
And Catherine saw him struck down there in the long box like
a huge mute doll, who would not smile or stir, and smelled
sweet and frightening, and because of whom she sat alone and
stiffly and too clean, and nobody was kind or attentive, and
everything went on tiptoe, and with her mother's willingness a
man she feared and hated put his great hand on her head and

spoke incomprehensibly. Something very wrong was being done, and nobody seemed to care or to tell her what or to help her or love her or protect her from it and there was her too-clean brother, who always thought he was so smart, looking at her with dislike and contempt.

So after gazing coldly at each other for a little while, they once more looked into the side yard and down into the street and tried to interest themselves in what they saw, and to forget the thing which so powerfully pervaded their thoughts, and to subdue their physical restiveness in order that they should not be disapproved; and tiring of these, would look over once more at their aunt, who was as aloof almost as their father; and uneased by that, would look once more into each other's eyes; and so again to the yard and the street, upon which the sunlight moved slowly. And there they saw an automobile draw up and Mr. Starr got quickly out of it and walked slowly up towards the house.

Chapter 19

A s THEY drew near with Mr. Starr, Rufus noticed that a man
who went past along the sidewalk looked back at his
grandfather's house, then quickly away, then back once more,
and again quickly away.

He saw that there were several buggies and automobiles,
idle and empty, along the opposite side of the street, but that
the space in front of the house was empty. The house seemed
at once especially bare, and changed, and silent, and its corners
seemed particularly hard and distinct; and beside the front
door there hung a great knotted bloom and streamer of black
cloth. The front door was opened before it was touched and
there stood their Uncle Andrew and their mother and behind
them the dark hallway, and they were all but overwhelmed by
a dizzying, sickening fragrance, and by a surging outward
upon them likewise of multitudinous vitality. Almost immediately they were drawn within the darkness of the hallway and
the fragrance became recognizable as the fragrance of flowers,
and the vitality which poured upon them was that of the
people with whom the house was crowded. Rufus experienced
an intuition as of great force and possible danger on his right,
and glancing quickly into the East Room, saw that every window shade was drawn except one and that against the cold
light which came through that window the room was filled
with dark figures which crouched disconsolately at the edge of
chairs, heavy and primordial as bears in a pit; and even as he
looked he heard the rising of a great, low groan, which was
joined by a higher groan, which was surmounted by a low
wailing and by a higher wailing, and he could see that a
woman stood up suddenly and with a wailing and bellowing
sob caught the hair at her temples and pulled, then flung her
hands upward and outward: but upon this moment Andrew
rushed and with desperate and brutal speed and silence, pulled
the door shut, and Rufus was aware in the same instant that
their own footsteps and the wailing had caused a commotion
on his left and, glancing as sharply into the sunlit room where
his father lay, saw an incredibly dense crowd of soberly dressed

people on weak, complaining chairs, catching his eye, looking past him, looking quickly away, trying to look as if they had not looked around.

"It's all right, Andrew," his mother whispered. "Open the door. Tell them we'll be in, in just a minute." And she drew the children more deeply into the hallway, where they could not be seen through either door, and whispered to Walter Starr, "Papa is in the Green Room, and Mama. Thank you, Walter."

"Don't you think of it," Walter said, as he passed her; and his hand hovered near her shoulder, and he went quietly through the door into the dining room.

"Now, children," their mother said, lowering her face above them. "We're all going in to see Daddy, just once more. But we won't be able to stay, we can just look for a moment. And then you'll see your Grandma Follet, just for a minute. And then Mr. Starr will take you down again to his house and Mother will see you again later this afternoon."

Andrew came toward her and nodded sharply.

"All right, Andrew," she said. "All right, children." Reaching suddenly behind the crest of her skull she lowered her veil and they saw her face and her eyes through its darkness. She took their hands. "Now come with Mother," she whispered.

There was Uncle Hubert in a dark suit; he was very clean and pink and his face was full of little lines. He looked quickly at them and quickly away. There was old Miss Storrs and there were Miss Amy Field and Miss Nettie Field and Doctor Dekalb and Mrs. Dekalb and Uncle Gordon Dekalb and Aunt Celia Gunn and Mrs. Gunn and Dan Gunn and Aunt Sarah Eldridge and Aunt Ann Taylor, and ever so many others, as well, whom the children were not sure they had ever seen before, and all of them looked as if they were trying not to look and as if they shared a secret they were offended to have been asked to tell; and there was the most enormous heap of flowers of all kinds that the children had ever seen, tall and extravagantly fresh and red and yellow, tall and starchy white, dark roses and white roses, ferns, carnations, great leaves of varnished-looking palm, all wreathed and wired and running with ribbons of black and silver and bright gold and dark gold, and almost suffocating in their fragrance; and there, almost hidden among these flowers, was the coffin, and beside it, two last strangers who, now that they had entered the room, turned away and quickly took chairs; and now a strange man in a long, dark coat stepped towards their mother with silent alacrity, his eyes shining like dark jelly, and with a courtly gesture ushered her forward and stood proudly and humbly to one side; and there was Daddy again.

He had not stirred one inch; yet he had changed. His face looked much more remote than before and much more ordinary and it was as if he were tired, or bored. He did not look as big as he really was, and the fragrance of the flowers was so strong and the vitality of the mourners was so many-souled and so pervasive, and so permeated and compounded by propriety and restraint, and they felt so urgently the force of all the eyes upon them, that they saw their father almost as idly as if he had been a picture, or a substituted image, and felt little realization of his presence and little interest. And while they were still looking, bemused in this empty curiosity, they felt themselves drawn away, and walked with their mother past the closed piano into the Green Room. And there were Grandpa and Grandma and Uncle Andrew and Aunt Amelia and Aunt Hannah; and Grandma got up quickly and took their mother in her arms and patted her several times emphatically across the shoulders, and Grandpa stood up too; and while Grandma stooped and embraced and kissed each of the children, saying, "Darlings, darlings," in a somewhat loud and ill-controlled voice, they could see their grandfather's graceful and cynical head as he embraced their mother, and realized that he was not quite as tall as she was; and their Aunt Amelia stood up shyly with her elbows out. As their mother led them from the room they looked back through the door and saw that the man in the long coat and another strange man had closed the coffin and were silently and quickly screwing it shut.

Walter Starr stood back in the middle of the hall, looking as if he did not know what to do. Their mother went straight up to him.

"Now we're all ready, Walter," she said. He nodded very shyly and stepped a little to one side as she spoke to the children.

"Now it's time to go," she told them. "Back to Mr. Starr's, as he told you this morning. And have a nice time and be very good and quiet and Mr. Starr will bring you back to Mother later this afternoon." She straightened Catherine's little collar, which was wilting. "Now good-bye," she said. "Mother will see you before long." She kissed them lightly.

Before long, now; before long.

They went so quietly past the living-room door and along the hushed porch and down the steps that Rufus felt that they were moving as stealthily as burglars.

When they had driven almost all the way to Mr. Starr's home Mr. Starr surprisingly turned a wrong corner, and then another, and then said to the children, "I think you'll want to see. Maybe not, but I think you'll be glad later on I took you back." And he drove somewhat more rapidly up the silent, empty, back street, then once again turned a corner, moved very slowly and quietly, and came to a stop.

They were in the side street, just across from Dr. Dekalb's house, and across the street corner and the wide lawn. They could see their grandfather's house and everything that went on, and they knew that they were not seen. Six men, their Uncle Andrew, their Uncle Ralph, their Uncle Hubert Kane, their Uncle George Bailey, and Mr. Drake, and a man whom they had never seen before, were carrying a long, gray, shining box by handles very carefully and slowly down the curved brick walk from the house to the street, and they realized that this was the box in which their father lay, and that it must be very heavy. The men were of different heights so that Uncle Andrew, who was tall, and Uncle George Bailey, who was even taller, had to squat slightly at the knees, whereas Uncle Hubert, who was shortest, was leaning outward and lifting upward. Just behind, seeming to walk even more slowly, came their grandfather, and a tall woman all veiled in black whom by her tallness and humbled grace they knew was their mother; and just behind her, with Aunt Jessie on one side and Father Jackson on the other, came a second woman, all veiled in black, who by her shortness and lameness they knew was their Grandmother Follet. And just behind them came Granma and Aunt Hannah, and Aunt Sally and Aunt Amelia, and Aunt Celia Gunn and Mrs. Gunn and Miss Bess Gunn, and old Mr.

Kane, and Miss Amy Field and Miss Nettie Field, and Doctor Dekalb and Mrs. Dekalb and Uncle Gordon Dekalb, and the porch and the porch steps were still full of darkly dressed people whose faces and bearing they could unsurely recognize but whose names they did not know, and of people whom they could not be sure whether they had ever seen before, and more were still shuffling slowly out through the front door onto the porch. And up the hill alongside the house, behind it, stood a shining black automobile, and two, small, quick men dressed in black sped constantly between the house and the wagon, bringing from the house great armsful of bright flowers, and stowing them in the automobile. And down in front of the front steps the man in the long coat who had ushered them to the coffin now made an imperious gesture and, drawn by three shining black horses and one horse of a shining red-brown, a long, tall, narrow box of whorled and glittering black and of black glass was pulled forward a few feet, and then a foot more, so that its black and glittering rear end was just beyond the opening of the steps; and the men who carried their father's coffin now hesitated at the head of the steps, and the man in the long coat nodded courteously as he turned and opened the shining back doors of the tall, blind-looking wagon, so that they carefully and uneasily made their way down the narrow steps, squeezing gingerly together, and he stood aside from the open doors and seemed to speak and to instruct them with his hands; and while their mother and her father hesitated at the head of the steps and behind them, all the dark column of mourners hesitated likewise, the men who carried their heavy father lifted him as if he were hard to lift and they were careful but unwilling, and studiously, with reverent nudgings and hitchings, shoved the coffin so deeply into the dark wagon that only its hard end showed, and they could hear a streetcar coming. And the man in the long coat closed one of the doors, and they could see only a corner of the box, and then he closed the other door and they could not see it at all, and he tightened over the shining silver handle which held the doors locked, and one of the horses twitched his ears, and the streetcar, which had paused, was now louder. And the long, dark wagon was drawn forward a few paces, and paused again, and a closed and shining black buggy moved forward and took its place, and the streetcar moved past and they could see heads turning through its windows and a man took off his hat, and their mother and their grandfather came down the steps and their grandfather helped their mother to climb in, and their Grandmother Follet and their Aunt Jessie and Father Jackson came down the steps and their Grandfather and Father Jackson helped their Grandmother Follet to climb in, and they helped Aunt Jessie in, and the noise of the streetcar was fading, and Uncle Ralph stood aside so that their grandfather might get in, and then they both stood aside so that their Grandmother Lynch might get in, and after some hesitation, their grandmother was helped in and then Uncle Ralph stepped in after her, and the curtains of the windows were drawn and the long, dark wagon and the dark buggy moved forward, and a second buggy took its place, and a long line of buggies and automobiles, after a moment's hesitancy, advanced a few feet, and now a man who had stood in the empty sidewalk across from the house walked westward and crossed the street in front of the children, putting on his hat as he reached the farther curb, and they heard the last of the streetcar, but now they heard the hard chipping of two sparrows, worrying a bit of debris in the street, and Mr. Starr said, "Better go now," and they realized that he had never shut off his engine, for as soon as he said this he began to back the car, as silently as he could and with great care; and he twisted it backward around the corner, and they slowly descended the same quiet back street up which he had brought them.

When he had stopped the car in front of his home, he said, before he moved to get out, "Maybe you'd better not say anything about this." He still did not move to get out, so they too sat still. After a little he said, "No, you do as you think best." He did not look at them; he had not looked at them during all of this time. They watched the shadows work, and the leaves waving.

He got out of the car, and opened the door on their side, and held out his hands to Catherine.

"Up she goes," he said.

Chapter 20

THE HOUSE echoed, and there was still an extraordinary fragrance of carnations.

Their mother was in the East Room.

"My darlings," she said; she looked as if she had traveled a great distance, and now they knew that everything had changed. They put their heads against her, still knowing that nothing would ever be the same again, and she caught them so close they could smell her, and they loved her, but it made no difference.

She could not say anything, and neither could they; they began to realize that she was silently praying, and now instead of love for her they felt sadness, and politely waited for her to finish.

"Now we'll stay here at Granma's," she finally said. "Tonight, anyway." And again there was nothing further that she could say.

Her hands on them began to feel merely heavy. Rufus moved nearer, trying to recover the lost tenderness; at the same moment Catherine pulled away.

He understands, their mother thought; and tried not to feel hurt by Catherine's restiveness. Catherine, aware at this absolute moment that her brother was preferred, was hurt so bitterly that her mother felt it in her body, and lightened her hold, at just the moment when Catherine most desired to be taken close in to her kindness. By the way she held him Rufus realized, she thinks I'm better than I am; he felt as if he had been believed in a lie, but this time it was not a good feeling.

"God bless my children," she whispered. "God bless and keep us all."

"Amen," Rufus whispered courteously; he tried to lose his uneasiness by holding her still more closely, and felt her still more passionate hand; while Catherine, in an enchantment of pain and loneliness, stayed like a stone.

There they stayed quiet, the deceived mother, the false son, the fatally wounded daughter; it was thus that Andrew found them and, with a glimpse of the noble painting it could be, said to himself, crying within himself, "It beats the Holy Family."

"Come for a walk with me," Andrew said; from the front porch Catherine watched them until she could no longer see them. Then she pulled one of the chairs away from the wall and sat in it and rocked. She had a feeling that it would be all right to rock if she could rock without making any noise, and it interested her to try. But no matter how carefully and quietly she moved, the rockers gave out a cobbling noise on the boards of the porch, and the chair squeaked gently. She stopped rocking, less because she felt that the noise was wrong, than because she felt that she did not want to be heard. She sat with her arms and hands high and straight along the arms of the chair and looked through the railing at the lawn and down into the street. A robin hopped heavily along the grass. He gave her a short, hard look, then a second, short and hard as the jab of a needle, then paid her no further attention, but hopped, heavily, and jabbed and jabbed in the short grass with jabs which were much like his short, hard way of looking.

Down across the street she saw Dr. Dekalb come along the sidewalk towards home; he was still in his dark clothes. Remembering how her father always saw her from a distance and waved, she waited for the moment when he would look over and wave, but he did not wave, or even look over; he went straight into his house.

Deep in the side yard among her flowers she saw Mrs. Dekalb in a long, white dress and long, white gloves, wearing a paper bag on her head. She bent deeply above the flowers, rather than squatting, and whenever she moved to another place, she straightened, tall and very thin, and gathered her skirt in one hand and delicately lifted it, as Grandma did when she stepped up or down from a curb. Then she would bend deeply over again, as if she were leaning over a crib to say good night.

There were quite a few people along the sidewalks, and most of them were walking in one direction, away from downtown.

On the sage-orange tree beside the porch the leaves lay along the air as lazily as if they were almost asleep, and ever so quietly moved, and lay still again.

The robin had hold of a worm; he braced his heels, walked backward, and pulled hard. It stretched like a rubber band and snapped in two; Catherine felt the snapping in her stomach. He quickly gobbled what he had, his head in a regular spasm, and, darting his beak even more quickly, took hold of the rest and pulled again. It stretched but did not break, and then all came loose from the ground; she could see it twisting as he flew away with it. He flung himself upward in a great curve among the branches of a tree in the side yard, and Catherine could just hear the thin hissing cries of the little robins.

Now Dr. Dekalb stood beside his wife and they were looking at each other and talking. She was taller than he was, but he was thicker through. He had taken off his coat, and pale blue suspenders crossed on his back. Above his white shirt his neck was dark red.

All the way down the block where the next street crossed she could see that there were still other people along the walks, looking tired yet walking fast, tiny at this distance, and nearly all of these people, too, were walking away from downtown.

Uncle Gordon Dekalb came towards his house. He was still wearing his dark suit and he carried his hat in one hand. His bottom was fat and he walked like a duck. Even from here Catherine could see how choked-up and thick he looked in the face and neck, Uncle Andrew said, as if his mouth was stuffed full of hot mashed potato. He looked up and across at the house and Catherine raised her hand, but he looked quickly away again, and cut across the lawn to join his father and mother. They all three talked.

A small, sudden noise frightened Catherine; then she realized it came from the living room. There was no more sound. She got from the chair in perfect silence and stole to the window in the angle of the porch. Grandma was sitting at the piano and she had opened it; Catherine could see the keys. She sat for a long while without lifting her hands from her lap. Then she stood up and shut the piano and went into the Green Room; she was wearing her apron. But before Catherine could move from the window she came in again (she can't see this far, Catherine quickly reassured herself), looked carefully about with her near-sighted, peering look, pursed her lips, and sat down again at the piano. Now she opened the keyboard once more and curved her hands powerfully above the keys and moved her fingers, but there was no sound. Grandma can't hear very well, Catherine remembered; talk very loud. So she can't hear very well when she plays music, either. She was bent way over, with her good ear close to the keys, the way she always was when she played, and her feet were working the pedals, yet she couldn't hear a sound.

But why can't *I* hear? Catherine suddenly thought. I always do. She watched and listened much more sharply: not one sound.

With sudden pleasure, Catherine thought of listening through a large black ear trumpet, then she realized that she was still hearing the shuffling street and the murmurous city, and knew why she could hear no music. Grandma was just making the notes go down without making any noise.

Then, close beside Catherine, her grandfather came through the door, and stopped abruptly. He was looking at Grandma. He couldn't hear very well either, but he could hear better than Grandma could; he always sat at this far end of the room when there was music. So he knew too. After he had stood a few moments he walked quickly down almost to where she sat with her back to him and both of his hands lifted above her as if he were going to touch her humped-over shoulders or her hair. Then after standing for a moment again, he turned away and walked even more quickly and quietly out by the way he had come in, and his face was so tucked down that Catherine was sure she had not been seen.

Now Grandma finished and left her hands quiet among the keys, moving them only to stroke the black keys and the white ones between. Then she took her hands away and folded them in her lap. Then she stood up, closed the piano, and went into the Green Room.

Dr. Dekalb and Mrs. Dekalb and Uncle Gordon were no longer in the garden.

Where's Daddy?

All of a sudden she felt that she could not bear to be alone. She went into the hall and into the East Room, but her mother was no longer in the East Room. She went down the hall towards the dining room and she could hear her grandmother busy in the pantry, but she knew that she did not want to see her or be found by her. She hurried on tiptoe across the corner of the dining room, hiding behind the table, and into the Green Room, but there was nobody there. She looked out and saw her grandfather standing in the middle of the garden, gazing down into the strong spikes of the century plant. She hurried through the dizzying fragrance of the living room and climbed the front stairs as quickly and quietly as she was able; Aunt Amelia's door was closed.

By now her face felt very hot and she was crying. She hurried along the hallway; shut. Aunt Hannah's door was shut. Behind it there was a coldly tender waning of a voice; Aunt Hannah's voice; her mother's. She set her ear close to the door and listened.

O GOD, the Creator and Preserver of all mankind, we humbly beseech thee for all sorts and conditions of men; that thou wouldest be pleased to make thy ways known unto them, thy saving health unto all nations. More especially we pray for thy holy Church universal; that it may be so guided and governed by thy good Spirit, that all who profess and call themselves Christians may be led into the way of truth, and hold the faith in unity of spirit, in the bond of peace, and in righteousness of life. Finally, we commend to thy fatherly goodness all those who are any ways afflicted, or distressed, in mind, body, or estate; that it may please thee to comfort and relieve them, according to their several necessities; giving them patience under their sufferings, and a happy issue out of all their afflictions. And this we beg for Jesus Christ's sake. Amen.

ALMIGHTY God, Father of all mercies, we, thine unworthy servants, do give thee most humble and hearty thanks for all thy goodness and loving-kindness to us, and to all men. We bless thee for our creation, preservation, and all the blessings of this life; but above all, for thine inestimable love in the redemption of the world by our Lord Jesus Christ; for the means of grace, and for the hope of glory. And, we beseech thee, give us that due sense of all thy mercies, that our hearts may be unfeignedly thankful; and that we show forth thy praise, not only with our lips, but in our lives, by giving up our selves to thy service, and by walking before thee in holiness and righteousness all our days; through Jesus Christ our Lord, to whom, with thee and the Holy Ghost, be all honour and glory, world without end. Amen.

Her mother's voice choked. Aunt Hannah's, with great quietness, spoke what she had been speaking from the beginning, and continued it and brought it to a close. Then, even more quietly, she said, "Mary, my dear, let's stop."

And after a moment Catherine could hear her mother's voice, shaken and almost squeaking, "No, no; no, no; I asked you to, Aunt Hannah. I—I . . ."

And again, Aunt Hannah's voice: "Let's just stop it."

And her mother's: "Without this I don't think I could bear it *at all.*"

And Aunt Hannah's: "There, dear. God bless and keep you. There. There."

And her mother's: "Just a minute and I'll be all right."

And a silence.

And then Aunt Hannah's voice, coldly tender: —————— and her mother's: ——————

In intense quietness, Catherine stole through the open door opposite Aunt Hannah's door, and hid herself beneath her grandparents' bed. She was no longer crying. She only wanted never to be seen by anybody again. She lay on her side and stared down into the grim grain of the carpet. When Aunt Hannah's door opened she felt such terror that she gasped, and drew her knees up tight against her chest. When the voices began calling her, downstairs, she made herself even smaller, and when she heard their feet on the stairs and the rising concern in their voices she began to tremble all over. But by the time she heard them along the hallway she was out from under the bed and sitting on its edge, her back to them as they came in, her heart knocking her breath to pieces.

"Why *there* you *are,*" her mother cried, and turning, Catherine was frightened by the fright and the tears on her face. "Didn't you *hear* us?

She shook her head, no.

"Why how could you *help* but—were you asleep?"

She nodded, yes.

"I thought she was with you, Amelia."

"I thought she was with you or Mama."

"Why, where on earth *were* you, darling? Heavens and earth, have you been all *alone*?"

Catherine nodded yes; her lower lip thrust out farther and farther and she felt her chin trembling and hated everybody.

"Why, bless your little heart, come to Mother"; her mother came toward her stooping with her arms stretched out and Catherine ran to her as fast as she could run, and plunged her head into her, and cried as if she were made only of tears; and it was only when her mother said, just as kindly, "Just look at your panties, why they're *sopping* wet," that she realized that indeed they were.

Andrew had never invited him to take a walk with him before, and he felt honored, and worked hard to keep up with him. He realized that now, maybe, he would hear about it, but he knew it would not be a good thing to ask. When they got well into the next block beyond his grandfather's, and the houses and trees were unfamiliar, he took Andrew's hand and Andrew took his primly, but did not press it or look down at him. Pretty soon maybe he'll tell me, Rufus thought. Or anyway say something. But his uncle did not say anything. Looking up at him, from a half step behind him, Rufus could see that he looked mad about something. He looked ahead so fixedly that Rufus suspected he was not really looking at anything, even when they stepped from the curb, and stepped up for the curb across from it, his eyes did not change. He was frowning, and the corners of his nose were curled as if he smelled something bad. Did I do something? Rufus wondered. No, he wouldn't ask me for a walk if I did. Yes, he would too if he was real mad and wanted to give me a talking-to and not raise a fuss about it there. But he won't say anything, so I guess he doesn't want to give me a talking-to. Maybe he's thinking. Maybe about Daddy. The funeral. (He saw the sunlight on the hearse as it began to move.) What all did they do out there? They put him down in the ground and then they put all the flowers on top. Then they say their prayers and then they all come home again. In Greenwood Cemetery. He saw in his mind a clear image of Greenwood Cemetery; it was on a low hill and among many white stones there were many green trees through which the wind blew in the sunlight, and in the middle there was a heap of flowers and beneath the flowers, in his closed coffin, looking exactly as he had looked this morning, lay his father. Only it was dark, so he could not be seen. It would always be dark there. Dark as the inside of a cow.

The sun's agonna shine, and the wind's agonna blow.

The charcoal scraping of the needle against the record was in his ears and he saw the many sharp, grinning teeth in Buster Brown's dog.

"If anything ever makes me believe in God," his uncle said.

Rufus looked up at him quickly. He was still looking straight ahead, and he still looked angry but his voice was not angry. "Or life after death," his uncle said.

They were working and breathing rather hard, for they were walking westward up the steep hill towards Fort Sanders. The sky ahead of them was bright and they walked among the bright, moving shadows of trees.

"It'll be what happened this afternoon."

Rufus looked up at him carefully.

"There were a lot of clouds," his uncle said, and continued to look straight before him, "but they were blowing fast, so there was a lot of sunshine too. Right when they began to lower your father into the ground, into his grave, a cloud came over and there was a shadow just like iron, and a perfectly magnificent butterfly settled on the—coffin, just rested there, right over the breast, and stayed there, just barely making his wings breathe, like a heart."

Andrew stopped and for the first time looked at Rufus. His eyes were desperate. "He stayed there all the way down, Rufus," he said. "He never stirred, except just to move his wings that way, until it grated against the bottom like a—rowboat. And just when it did the sun came out just dazzling bright and he flew up out of that—hole in the ground, straight up into the sky, so high I couldn't even see him any more." He began to climb the hill again, and Rufus worked hard again to stay abreast of him. "Don't you think that's wonderful, Rufus?" he said, again looking straight and despairingly before him.

"Yes," Rufus said, now that his uncle really was asking him;

"Yes," he was sure was not enough, but it was all he could say.

"If there are any such things as miracles," his uncle said, as if someone were arguing with him, "then *that's* surely miraculous."

Miraculous. Magnificent. He was sure he had better not ask what they were. He saw a giant butterfly clearly, and how he moved his wings so quietly and grandly, and the colors of the wings, and how he sprang straight up into the sky and how the colors all took fire in the sunshine, and he felt that he probably had a fair idea what "magnificent" meant. But "miraculous." He still saw the butterfly, which was resting there again, waving his great wings. Maybe "miraculous" was the way the colors were streaks and spots in patterns on the wings, or the bright flickering way they worked in the light when he flew fast, straight upwards. Miraculous. Magnificent.

He could see it very clearly, because his uncle saw it so clearly when he told about it, and what he saw made him feel that a special and good thing was happening. He felt that it was good for his father and that lying there in the darkness did not matter so much. He did not know what this good thing was, but because his uncle felt that it was good, and felt so strongly about it, it must be even more of a good thing than he himself could comprehend. His uncle even spoke of believing in God, or anyway, if anything could ever make him believe in God, and he had never before heard his uncle speak of God except as if he disliked Him, or anyway, disliked people who believed in Him. So it must be about as good a thing as a thing could be. And suddenly he began to realize that his uncle told it to him, out of everyone he might have told it to, and he breathed in a deep breath of pride and of love. He would not admit it to those who did believe in God, and he would not tell it to those who didn't, because he cared so much about it and they might swear at it, but he had to tell somebody, so he told it to him. And it made it much better than it had been, about his father, and about his not being let to be there at just that time he most needed to be there; it was all right now, almost. It was not all right about his father because his father could never come back again, but it was better than it had been, anyway, and it was all right about his not being let be there, because now it was almost as if he had been there and seen it with his own eyes, and seen the butterfly, which showed that even for his father, it was all right. It was all right and he felt as his uncle did. There was nobody else, not even his mother, not even his father if he could, that he even wanted to tell, or talk about it to. Not even his uncle, now that it was told.

"And *that* son of a bitch!" Andrew said.

He was not quite sure what it meant but he knew it was the worst thing you could call anybody; call anybody that, they had to fight, they had a right to kill you. He felt as if he had been hit in the stomach.

"That Jackson," Andrew said; and now he looked so really angry that Rufus realized that he had not been at all angry before. "'*Father*' Jackson," Andrew said, "as he insists on being called.

"Do you know what he did?"

He glared at him so, that Rufus was frightened. "What?" he asked.

"He said he couldn't read the complete, the complete burial service over your father because your father had never been baptized." He kept glaring at Rufus; he seemed to be waiting for him to answer. Rufus looked up at him, feeling scared and stupid. He was glad his uncle did not like Father Jackson, but that did not seem exactly the point, and he could not think of anything to say.

"He said he was deeply sorry," Andrew savagely caricatured the inflection, "but it was simply a rule of the Church."

"Some church," he snarled. "And they call themselves Christians. Bury a man who's a hundred times the man *he'll* ever be, in his stinking, swishing black petticoats, and a hundred times as good a man too, and 'No, there are certain requests and recommendations I cannot make Almighty God for the repose of this soul, for he never stuck his head under a holy-water tap.' Genuflecting, and ducking and bowing and scraping, and basting themselves with signs of the Cross, and all that disgusting hocus-pocus, and you come to one simple, single act of Christian charity and what happens? The rules of the Church forbid it. He's not a member of our little club.

"I tell you, Rufus, it's enough to make a man puke up his soul.

"That—that butterfly has got more of God in him than Jackson will ever see for the rest of eternity.

"Priggish, mealy-mouthed son of a bitch."

They were standing at the edge of Fort Sanders and looking out across the waste of briers and of embanked clay, and Rufus was trying to hold his feelings intact. Everything had seemed so nearly all right, up to a minute ago, and now it was changed and confused. It was still all right, everything which had been, still was, he did not see how it could stop being, yet it was hard to remember it clearly and to remember how he had felt and why it had seemed all right, for since then his uncle had said so much. He was glad he did not like Father Jackson and he wished his mother did not like him either, but that was not all. His uncle had talked about God, and Christians, and faith, with as much hatred as he had seemed, a minute before, to talk with reverence or even with love. But it was worse than that. It was when he was talking about everybody bowing and scraping and hocus-pocus and things like that, that Rufus began to realize that he was talking not just about Father Jackson but about all of them and that he hated all of them. He hates Mother, he said to himself. He really honestly does hate her. Aunt Hannah, too. He hates them. They don't hate him at all, they love him, but he hates them. But he doesn't hate them, really, he thought. He could remember how many ways he had shown how fond he was of both of them, all kinds of ways, and most of all by how easy he was with them when nothing was wrong and everybody was having a good time, and by how he had been with them in this time too. He doesn't hate them, he thought, he loves them, just as much as they love him. But he hates them, too. He talked about them as if he'd like to spit in their faces. When he's with them he's nice to them, he even likes them, loves them. When he's away from them and thinks about them saying their prayers and things, he hates them. When he's with them he just acts as if he likes them, but this is how he really feels, all the time. He told me about the butterfly and he wouldn't tell them because he hates them, but I don't hate them, I love them, and when he told me he told me a secret he wouldn't tell them as if I hated them too.

But they saw it too. They sure saw it too. So he didn't, he

wouldn't tell them, there wouldn't be anything to tell. That's it. He told me because I wasn't there and he wanted to tell somebody and thought I would want to know and I do. But not if he hates them. And he does. He hates them just like opening a furnace door but he doesn't want them to know it. He doesn't want them to know it because he doesn't want to hurt their feelings. He doesn't want them to know it because he knows they love him and think he loves them. He doesn't want them to know it because he loves them. But how can he love them if he hates them so? How can he hate them if he loves them? Is he mad at them because they can say their prayers and he doesn't? He could if he wanted to, why doesn't he? Because he hates prayers. And them too for saying them.

He wished he could ask his uncle, "Why do you hate Mama?" but he was afraid to. While he thought he looked now across the devastated Fort, and again into his uncle's face, and wished that he could ask. But he did not ask, and his uncle did not speak except to say, after a few minutes, "It's time to go home," and all the way home they walked in silence.

STORIES

Death in the Desert

BETWEEN Springerville and Magdalena lie one hundred and forty miles of desert so deathly that no sane man will undertake them on foot. Accordingly the outskirts of Springerville are scattered with bums, strung out singly along the road and quite frankly waiting for luck.

The night before I had covered nearly two hundred miles, had arrived at about dawn in St. John's and had been five hours getting here. I bought a can of sauerkraut and a loaf of bread at an A.&P., found a quiet spot behind a church, and took my time with my day's meal. I couldn't do much else, as a matter of fact: my jaw was so swollen I could hardly chew. After a cup of coffee in a lunch bar, I fished out a cigarette. I had only four left and a long jump ahead, so I went back to the A.&P. and bought two packs. I was all set, now. I strolled out of town by the eastern highway. The first two cigarettes got some support from breakfast, the third was flat, and the fourth half made me sick: it was getting hotter minute by minute, and my ear was beginning to pound in grand style.

Bums lined the road at intervals of a hundred yards or so. I took up my position at the far end of the line, about half a mile from town. For a while I talked with a peg-legged man of perhaps sixty; he spent his winters with his niece and her husband in St. Louis. In the summers he got out of their way. His luck was always good, he said—too damned good. This summer he'd been through St. Louis twice already. Unless he did something about it, he'd be there again inside of a week. Did I have a cigarette? Thanks. He'd run out that morning. No, he didn't see his niece, either time he was in St. Louis. He'd tried that, three summers ago—just dropped in for supper one night. They'd given him supper and told him to get the hell out, did he think this was cold weather? I was a young fellow, and he wanted to pass on some advice, which was to let well enough alone. All the while, as he talked, he watched the cars come up the road, and flicked his thumb eastward as each one approached. He stood always with his peg leg toward town. Before long a Chandler, after running a half-mile gauntlet of

743

men, slowed down for him. He took another cigarette and was gone.

For the rest of us, rides came more slowly. My ear was too sore, by now, to make talking a pastime. I sat down on my coat and decided that it was rather less than necessary on days like this. After a couple of hours, I considered the manifold advantages of being conspicuously a cripple. After another hour I had the idea of holding up a sign:

SORE EAR

PLEASE

This request seemed a little ambiguous, and a lousy idea at best. As always, I kept watch on the license plates, and as always, had unreasonable hopes of luck from cars of my own state. In the four hours I waited one Maine car passed; it didn't even slow up. So, once more, I enjoyed being pretty sore at Maine. Since I had no right to be, I got a good deal of fun out of it. It was also gratifying to get seven reinforcements to my theory that of all motorists those of Pennsylvania are least hospitable to bums.

Man by man, the line was dwindling. There was no foretelling your luck: half a dozen trucks and ratty Fords might pass; then a new Buick or even, sometimes, a Pierce-Arrow, would stop for one of us. I began to wish I had shaved; sometimes it makes all the difference between a truck and a Pierce-Arrow—and sometimes it doesn't. With my ear in the shape it was, I'd have been willing to travel in a tux or a green gauze chiton for the sake of a good ride. A Transcontinental Bus came piling eastward, just one jump ahead of its blind trail of dust. Two out of three bums stepped into the road and waved frantically. The driver and some of the passengers laughed and waved back. This show of democracy on their part cheered me up, but not for long; my ear was too sore for sustained good humor. A little later a Chrysler with Purdue stickers tore through. Riding in the rumble seat beside a white sweater and an open clean collar and three weeks' fine golden down was a young Polack I had run into in Omaha. He looked back, and waved and grinned from a hundred yards ahead. I persuaded myself that his ride was good for at least a thousand miles, and managed to get thoroughly griped at the world in general. He could damned well have gotten his boy-friends to pick me up. If there wasn't room, well, I'd ridden the running-boards before, and I could do it again. I had a fairly good time elaborating the various phases of this: and about then a car slowed down.

It was a Buick touring car from Oklahoma, five or six years old and in need of paint, but apparently capable of speed. It was funny that even in my present condition, I could be snooty about my cars, but I was; and so is every bum. Few bums, however, are snooty enough ever to refuse a ride.

I climbed into the back seat. There was a boy of ten, asleep in the far corner.

"Thanks," I said, and began to dig a hole in the mass of suitcases, pop bottles and soiled blankets. The man got under way, and drawled into the windshield, "Just move that baggage around any way you like."

"Thanks."

"How far you going?" his wife asked.

"Maine."

"Maine? Gee, you got a long ways to go, ain't you?"

I laughed at that as if it was news to me, and said, "Yeah. But I've come a long ways, too."

He said, "Yeah, I reckon that's right," went into a huddle with himself, and said, "Why? Where'd you come from?"

"The Coast . . . Tia Juana, last."

"Oh, yeah, there. That's a pretty hard place, they tell me. Lots of gambling, lots of liquor, there, huh?"

I was a little too shot to give him his idea of Tia Juana, and said, "Oh, not so bad as it's painted."

"Not, huh?"

His wife heaved around, and said, "Oh. It's not so bad as it's painted, huh?"

"No ma'am," I shot back.

We all thought things over for a few minutes. Then he said: "Been working?"

"Some in the wheat fields, first of the summer." I began to think fast. Was I going to college, or working, or in High School?

"What do you do at home? In school?"

"No, not right now. I been out of High School a couple years. Just doing jobs as they turn up."

"You aim to go on to college?" the man said.

"Well, I don't rightly know. I been thinking some of going to State of Maine, this fall; but I don't know."

His wife leaned round again, got firmly settled, and said: "I want to give you a piece of advice: you go ahead to college. You won't never regret it."

"Well, I know," I said, "education—."

"Education is a great thing," her husband stated. "I sure wisht I'd had the sense to complete mine."

"Well, I know it is if you go at it right. But trouble is with a lot of these college fellows, when they get out in the world they got to unlearn everything they ever learned."

"I do' know. Maybe you're right," he mourned. "But I aim to give my boy the best he can get."

"You must know the Stein Song, don't you?" The woman brightened.

"Oh—no, not very well."

"Can you sing it? Come on, sing it for us." She began to hum it.

"I'd wake up your boy."

"Oh, you can't wake him up. Come on, sing it."

I felt a little foolish. "I'd rather not."

"Aw, let him be. He don't want to sing that song."

"That's a pretty song." She encouraged me by smiling and singing more loudly.

"I'm kind of sick," I despaired; and that was no lie. "It would hurt me to sing."

"What's wrong?"

"I've got a boil in my right ear."

"A what?"

"A boil. It's terrible sore. I can't hardly chew my food."

"A boil in his ear. I never heard of nothing like that, did you, Joe?"

"Sure I have, and so have you. What'd you think was wrong with Dob Foster, last spring?"

"Oh did he have a boil in his ear?"

He turned his head, and said, "You better see a doctor."

"It'll be all right in a day or two."

"Oh, I'd see a doctor if I was you. Dob Foster didn't get no relief till he seen the doctor."

"I've had them before. They don't last long with me."

"Well . . ." —and he disposed of ears and began on doctors. He proposed that they are a blessing to humanity. I admitted the probability of this. He embellished this theme, and by way of "but by jinny a doctor ain't always the thing," modulated to a passage on the efficacy of herbs. His wife said her mother could vouch for the power of certain charms, and her cousins in Arkansas wouldn't have a thing to do with doctors. I tried to get her going on charms and queer cures, but she had nothing new on this. Her husband insisted that doctors are a blessing to humanity and that he never yet seen a charm work. I said well, I didn't know about that, and told of Maine a lie or two I had picked up in Tennessee. His wife cheered up right away, and went over her ground *in re* charm cures. He said she was just ignernt, that was all; and after twenty minutes on this matter they got round to the value of education in general, and from that to the fact that I'd better see a doctor. If I didn't want to see a doctor, why then there were other cures, she didn't care what Joe said. Joe said she could think up cures darn quick for a woman that had never even heard of boils in the ear, five minutes ago. She said she reckoned what was good for ear-*ache* was good for boils in the ear. He said that was an entirely different matter, that any fool could tell her that. She said, could tell her what? He said my God didn't she know what they'd been talking about all this time? She said well! it was too hot to think straight anyhow. He said if her brains were so weak they couldn't stand a little heat she'd a damn sight better stayed home. She said well! she liked that and besides, Centerville, Oklahoma wasn't no icebox. He wanted to know what the hell that had to do with it. She said if he had to cuss at her like that he'd much better quit talking. I felt like telling them both to go to hell, but I found I was half asleep anyway. After a little backing and filling to keep their self-respect, they shut up. Joe allowed her the last tag, and she said nothing when he increased speed ten miles an hour. So they were both fairly happy, but not nearly so pleased as I.

Joe visibly chewed tobacco, but I wanted to smoke; so I

offered him a cigarette. That gave him the satisfaction of calling
my attention to his preference. When that was over, I set fire
to a Lucky and slouched down until I sat on my kidneys. My
face was crawling with fatigue, and now my nose began to itch
unbearably, as it does when I am very hot and tired and unwashed. I mauled it meditatively, and smoked several Luckies,
and was quite contented. I gave my ear all possible comfort in
my cupped hand, and once more felt the film-thin globe of
lead build around my brain. This was the state that passed for
sleep, most of the time, now that I was bumming. In a lazy,
ticklish way, I was acutely conscious, but nothing could worry
or interest me. I was, rather, passively amused at anything. The
dark cage of the Buick and the two backs before me were like
shadows against the great screen of the desert. I could hear the
two backs talking from time to time, but it meant nothing to
me. The man said God, wasn't it hot, and the woman agreed
with him. I thought Oh, Yeah? and felt quite witty. After a
while he said they still had ninety-seven miles to go. She wondered if the water really would last them through. Well, the man
at the filling station said so, didn't he? I thought, ask the
man at the filling station; he knows and knows and knows.
The man at the filling station is trained to help you. He is not
only your servant but your dear friend. He loves you and you
love him. God how you love him. Kindly report any discour-
tesy. That was a howl, too. I performed one of my favorite
tricks, and saw two skeletons in the front seat. One wore a
dirty sleeveless dress and remarked that it sure would be good
to get back to Oklahoma. The other manipulated the steering
wheel, and its skull chewed tobacco mournfully. I allowed this
skull to sprout horns, and they were very funny until I realized
that the lady skeleton couldn't possibly fulfill her requirements. So I dehorned the man.

The car slowed down and the skeletons sprang into flesh.
Nothing I could do prevented it.

"Need any help, brother?"

I looked out. Two men and a good-looking girl were
working on a tire.

"No thanks. Just a flat."

"Got a spare?"

"It's OK. We mend our own tubes," the girl said. She was tall, and darkly blond.

Oh, you mend your own, huh? I thought. Talented girl. Great girl to have around the house. "Please, sir: I majored in domestic science and eugenics. May I be your bride?"

As we started again I leaned out and smiled at her. She grinned and waved and I waved back.

The car was from Massachusetts, and I wished they had picked me up. I also wondered if they were from Boston or Cambridge, and speculated on my chances of seeing the girl again. In spite of all I could do, they seemed pretty thin; so I dropped back into my skeleton routine. But the girl kept breaking in on this train of thought, and I found that a confusion of lovely flesh and Oklahoma bones wasn't as amusing as you might think. So I thought of other swell girls I had seen once and never seen again, and of the very few girls I had not, strictly speaking, lost, and I became rather unhappy; and after a while, with the feeling that all this was pretty sour, I set myself to remembering good walks I had taken.

I could remember a path through Tennessee woods; every turn of it, and every fork; and the place I used to leave it for a trickling ravine that ran down into Shake-Rag Hollow. There was a flat of sand half way down, printed with exciting tracks that I could never identify. Once, a little farther down, I had come suddenly upon a king snake and a rattler, fighting. There had been a silver flash and flex of sinew scattering last year's leaves, and in the end the rattler lay shuddering with a broken back, and slowly, head first, the king had eaten him and crawled into the dark laurels with rattles still purring between his jaws. I had walked home a little sick at my stomach. The fight was very fine, and I ran it through, now, two or three times. There were abandoned coal mines in the hollow; shale and slate and coal were naked and flaky about the tumbled shafts. If you kicked a black stone it fell away in sheets like a broken book. The sheets were one great clear weave of black ferns, every vein and feather of them distinct. They were giants, but they could never have been larger than the ferns in the drop below, that sprang and drooped in the half-light, a sinister ferocious green. It was somehow too terrifying to know that they too would sink into the earth, that this blaring green would be flattened into blackness. Above the ferns the forest leaves lay on the air in wide silver planes; but there was nothing awful in the thought of their death; for I had never seen and could not conceive such foliage stamped on stone. I tried now, knew I would fail, and failed, to feel about it as I had when I was eleven. But the feeling now was so flat, so anaemic, that once had smoked with reality. Waning moons and the wind against trees, obsidian arrow-heads and my Babylonian tablet, the swell of a New Hampshire hill, and water from God knows where forever striking granite forever bound in Maine, the fixed swerve and distance of stars . . . all these things and all things else were categorized and filed away with their proper emotions and their proper metaphors: and in all the world and in all experience there was little enough that was remarkable. I could no longer get excited over these things; I could no longer even think of them without a slight sickened feeling of shame, without ending by laughing at them and at myself.

Something or other is something else again on all fours. Professor Lowes is Professor Babbitt on all fours. Professor Babbitt is Aristotle on all fours. Aristotle on all fours is a sight for sore eyes. How about ears? Your ear, or my ear, or any-body's ear? If you wore your ear around your neck you'd change it oftener. If you ate eggs with your knees you'd look to your garters, if you wore any garters. Personally I think this discussion is getting a little, well. Ah, then, you are a prig. For my part, I think it's just great to see our boys and girls dis-cussing their little problems, heart to heart. Don't you think Sex is interesting, Elvira? I do. It's my hobby. Sex and Stamps. But Sex is lots more fun. Where would we be without it? Prob-ably off shooting pool somewhere, if at all. Or following the ponies. Every healthy American boy follows the ponies. Pick yourself a good, healthy pony with a sense of humor and a knowledge of cooking, and you have the ideal mother of your children. None of these frills, son. Or a brisk set of back-gammon and a cold shower will turn the trick.

The car went over a bump, my elbow slipped, and I struck my ear with the heel of my hand. It felt as if I'd torn half my brain out, and I yelled.

"Hurt?" Joe said.

"Little bit."

His wife said: "It must have hurt you something awful. You drive slower, Joe."

That made Joe pretty sore. He said nothing, and he did not slow down: I knew he was sore at me because his wife had seen fit to register an objection in my behalf. He had as low an opinion of me as if I myself had asked him to slow up. I felt like socking them both; but I had just enough sense to keep quiet.

I couldn't doze now, and I couldn't think; I simply sat there, enclosing the agony of my ear and half-numb fatigue and a simmering gripe at everything on earth. It was terribly hot. The smells of hot oil and hot stale clothing were like a blow in the face, and the wrinkling air on the desert was one great shiver of heat. I decided I might as well get back in Joe's good graces.

I said: "Wouldn't be so good, walking through this, would it?"

"I reckon it wouldn't."

I knew I'd never have been fool enough to try such a walk, but it wasn't my place to bring that up.

Joe said: "I don't reckon many fellers would be fool enough to try walking it, though."

"They'd be crazy if they did. This is one place you've got to wait for a ride, if it's a week coming."

"Well, you were pretty lucky," Joe said complacently.

"Yes. You sure were lucky." So his wife was getting back on his good side, too. For no reason at all, I was fairly disgusted with both of them.

"I sure am glad of the ride," I said; and we all let it go at that. I sat looking at the two backs, recognizing the cheap condescension and the thin antagonism, and not particularly giving a damn.

Far ahead there was a black speck, and as we came nearer it was moving, and was a man, and the man was limping toward us and waving wildly.

"Good God Almighty," Joe said. "How did he ever land out here!"

I was wondering myself. None of us spoke, for there was something about it that shut our mouths. But Joe got all the speed he could out of the Buick, and very soon we were all sure that the man was black.

"Why, it's a nigger," the woman said.

Joe nodded. It was a nigger all right, and every second we saw him more clearly. A nigger, an exhausted nigger, very tall, and with terrible effort limping toward us. He was grinning and crying and laughing, and the noises he made were strange and unintelligible. For some shameful reason, the effect was grotesquely funny, if indeed there was any effect.

There was little on Joe: enough to make him slow down the car; enough to make him hesitate and do a little thinking; enough, in the end, to make him drive past the man, slowly shaking his head and gathering into his original speed. As it became obvious that he did not intend to stop, his wife turned toward him as if jerked by a cord. Her mouth hung open in a silly way. As we passed, it was thus: Joe looking straight ahead, jaw set over his quid, and head wagging definitively. It was thus: His wife staring at him in naked amazement, her mouth open as if she were dead. It was thus: I watching the two of them and the boy asleep in his corner and the nigger in the road; and feeling excited and horrified and ill and quite unable to think. It was thus as we passed: The nigger's laughter and weeping still alive on his face, as a machine still runs when the power is cut off; the laughter and the weeping frozen in a mask and gone; then only an astounded blackness and marbled eyes and a bestial burnt stalk of tongue; and then, as suddenly, he was moving again and letting out wheezing yells, pleading still and still demanding that God bless us; he was running after us, desperately running after us with both arms hooked and waving in the crisping air. His face was gone and his body shrank with the desert, and he progressed eastward and after us with mad and jerky running, like a small black mangled frog. He was still running, he was a speck that seemed not to run, he was gone and I knew he still ran and still waved and still demanded that God bless us.

The woman did not speak, and I could not. After a time Joe said: "I don't aim to pick up no damned nigger."

"Why, Joe you ought not to talk that way. That poor nigger was one of the Lord's creatures, same as you and me." It was wonderful how quickly she had calmed down.

"I don't know about that, but if you think I'm going to allow any damned nigger in the same car with my wife, you got another think coming."

"But Joe. It ain't as if he was all right, near a town or anything. Way out here in the middle of nowheres . . ."

"I don't want to hear another peep about him, see?" As he drove on, he talked in jerks: "What was he doing out here in the middle of nowheres, I'd like to know. Yes sirree, that's what I'd like to know . . . Wasn't out there for no good reason. No doubt about that . . . I reckon someone had took pity on him, picked him up. Then, by glory, he got fresh . . . they had to boot him out. That's the trouble with these damn niggers . . . never will learn to let well enough alone . . . Why it wouldn't even be patriotic to pick up a feller like that . . . How do you know he ain't a dangerous criminal?"

His wife cut in: "You'd a picked him up, if he was a white man."

He started to say a number of things, and finally got out: "Well, what if I had? I didn't, did I? Think I'm going to let some damn sweaty nigger stink up my car? Well I'm not, and the sooner you get that through your head the better.

"I don't know as I'd have picked him up, if he *had* been a white man. This car's crowded, right now.

"I'm no damn nigger-lover.

"Let some of these nigger-loving Yankees pick him up, if they want to. Some of them will do anything, just to favor a nigger."

"You ain't even Christian."

"By God, I'm as good a Christian as the next man, but I ain't no nigger-lover."

"That ain't . . ."

He stopped the car and turned and glared and shouted at her: "Now that's just about enough. I'm pretty damn sick of all this bugling about some filthy nigger that didn't know enough to stay home and let well enough alone. I ain't a Christian, huh? By Jesus Christ, I'll learn you to talk like that to me. Now it's my advice to you to keep your trap shut. My Holy God, I never heard the like of it in my life! I don't want to hear another word about that black bastard. If you care so much about him, maybe you'd like to trot back and look after him. I don't know as I'd put it a-past you."

And he drove on. After a minute she said: "You ought to be ashamed to talk to me like that, Joe Tate."

"Shut up."

There was no more talking.

I have said that during the incident of passing the man, I was "quite unable to think." This is not quite true. The truth is, that my mind was one chaotic wash of nervous emotion, in which thought could at best merely drift aimlessly and shortly sink. But I thought: and my thoughts were chiefly of my own responsibility in this matter, and, more vaguely, of the fact that I was spontaneously jolted by the incident as I was by few things, of late years. These thoughts, disconnected at first, in time took on substance and form; they drew from the conversation I have recorded above; they begot themselves and built upon themselves. The fact that, according to Joe, the car was crowded already, became, for a time, very important to me. I was the extra man in the car. I was the reason why an exhausted Negro remained in the desert near death. I could offer my place; I could refuse to ride any farther, unless something were done to help him. I realized, all the while, that my presence here had nothing to do with Joe's refusal to take him in, and at length this truth reduced that sport of conscience to its logical absurdity. I knew, quite soon, that there was nothing for me to do; yet I felt compulsion to say what his wife had tried to say, and a great deal more. In purely abstract argument I had talked myself red-eyed and ready for murder, on this matter of the Negro and his place; and now, when I was involved in actuality, I could say nothing and do nothing; and my silence made me confederate in a monstrous wrong. His contemptible wife, in her half-minded fashion, had dared to speak what she felt on the matter; and I . . . I did not dare. The thin fact that I was dependent upon this man's charity: that closed my mouth. What business had I to say anything, pro or con? And another thought built upon this: there would be something cheap and mock-heroic in anything I might do, and I despised mock-heroics. And on this built another thought: we had all exaggerated the Negro's plight. With reasonable certainty, someone would pick him up. The little melodrama that had seemed so shatteringly important, was really in no sense melodrama. I had been fool enough to get excited about it in the first place, and by now I was thankful that I had not paraded my idiocy in talk. There was no tragedy here; only after a manner of speaking was there drama. From now on, I would be proof against any such cheap emotional pitfalls. No sort or condition or twist of humanity deserved such weakness. For there was, indeed, no real tragedy in life. Tragedy was the perennial flower of the ego, and the ego is inconsequent manure.

I was rather proud of this quasi-epigram; it occupied my mind, now, for quite a while; it bred other cool and soothing generalizations; and the mass of them did me a great deal of good.

In due time, I admitted these definite facts: I was heartily sorry for my cheap weakness. It was much more to the point to take care of myself; and this I had managed quite creditably to do. I was tired, I needed sleep, my present occupation was bumming. The desert was broad and hot and deadly, and I was extraordinarily weak with the pain of my ear. If I had spoken out of turn, I might conceivably have been dropped in the road without more ado. As it was, I was in reasonable comfort, and I was letting well enough alone.

That was enough for the present as I think it over now, I can see no flaw in my course of reasoning. I feel, at times, that I thought too much. Certainly for a little while, I thought clearly and well; so clearly and so well that thought assumed substance and shape. It was as if my brain had been dipped in lead, that cooled and thickened and moment by moment bound more securely, so that before long I was sleeping soundly for the first time in several days.

"That was the state that passed for sleep, now that I was bumming." But this fool-proof shell outlasted sleep and several mild calamities, and is as serviceable today as it was the day I bought it.

[From *The Harvard Advocate*, October 1930]

They That Sow in Sorrow Shall Reap

THE HOUSE, which was on a main street, near the tracks, and convenient to work, was painted a remote white; barrenly fronted the street, but possessed along one side a comfortable ledge of porch sparsely trellised with morning-glories; appeared to be small, but was rangy and subdivided into many small rooms. The floor of each room was covered by linoleum of one restless pattern; and each lodger's room contained a bed, a bureau, a shallow closet, a straight chair, and, upon request, a table. Throughout the house there was a flat smell of linoleum made warm, this first evening, by the sun. In every bedroom there were clean curtains; a rhomboid of light was projected upon each opposite wall, and across this the sun had stencilled a shifting lace of shadow. As I waited in my bedroom, the sun, descending, cramped the rhomboid of light, and urged the plaque of shadow and light toward the ceiling. The house was extremely clean. I lay across the clean counterpane, very tired, but lying tensely, in the hope that I might not print the counterpane with uncleanliness. I was slippery with rust and clay. I lay on my back and watched the sunlight tilt upward through the pane, and with vague impatience heard a tired man making himself clean in the one bathroom; and knew that other tired people were impatient and were waiting; and breathed the clean odor germinated on the warm linoleum; and saw a sharp gable shoulder cut the sunlight.

This place was so clean; in one corner which the sun never struck I could see traces of a mop; and the linoleum was not ridged through by boards beneath; its checker pattern was everywhere sharp; and shifty, because my eyes were tired; but clean, and pleasant; and altogether the house was far better than the Eagle Hotel. I got up and looked resentfully at the bed, which I had creased with red dirt. It was my turn to wash. I took a bath, shaved with unusual care, and tried to free my hair of rust and clay; and went downstairs feeling very clean and complacently tired, like a patient ready for the operating table.

In the parlor, the boarders sat in a circle, patient but unrelaxed, and silent. The room was ornamented with pampas-plumes, and with nodular vessels of iridescent glass. There was a piano, carefully dusted, and with open music, and with an air of long desuetude. The room was quiet, except for a clock and the irregular ticking of wicker chairs. Between the next room and the next was a hurry of footsteps, and the clash and arrangement of tableware; but here, silence, and people, most of them still unrelaxed, still in poise like birds about to take wing. There were two men; the laborer looked down at his linked hands, which resembled scrubbed roots; the other, younger, a man of forty, furtively ran his nails one beneath another, while he sat self-consciously beneath his thinning hair. The two older women leaned back, now, with knees unflexed; the younger woman maintained an air of anxiety; she sat straight, with knees snapped crosswise like a closed purse. The people were tired, and without emotion they received once more the deliberate edge of evening.

Mrs. Stevens came to the door to say, "Supper is ready," and with abrupt commotion the six of us filed in to the table, where already an old man was standing guard.

The food was abundant and pridefully cooked. Large bowls of it, consumed, were removed, and came again replenished. The woman who carried them said to each boarder, "Good evening," (then calling him by name); "This has been a beautiful day." And she would say no more. The old man her husband, who sat with the meat pie at the head of the table would add, "Yes, a beautiful day. Can't I help you to something, Miss Silk?" She, who had sat primly as a closed purse, would with difficulty reply, "No. Thank you." And in her silence a blush would thicken across her forehead. The old gentleman said, next, "Nor you, Mrs. Bixby?" at the same time nodding inquiry toward the third woman. After this, whatever the result, he would smile with embarrassment, and restore his attention to his own food.

He was a handsome old gentleman. His features were aquiline and finely regular; his cleft lower lip and chin were opulent and weak, and the whole face was drawn into a sort of perfection by a recently combed and waxed moustache. There was in his face a flicker of forgotten arrogance; and in his appearance was a suggestion of continued vanity; for his hair, shining white and fine as a child's, was most carefully set back from his shield-like forehead; and he wore the sort of "sport" shirt that boys wear; a shirt whose collar flared buttonless away from his strong youthful throat. His hands were abnormally small and veinless; as much as possible he kept them folded in his lap. As I have remarked, he spoke very little, but he smiled continually, as if at his own happiness, and he seemed unduly eager to resolve all uncertainties with his own calm.

I found this beauty, this unexpected youthfulness, somehow sinister. As I watched him, however, this repellence vanished, for he showed only gentleness and kindliness, and embarrassing humility, and shortly, I was aware of his remarkable serenity. For, each time his wife was in the room he smiled and watched her as she moved about, and his eyes blazed with peace.

He was especially anxious for Miss Silk's ease, and this, though futile, was praiseworthy. For Mr. Harbison, oblivious of his thinning hair, was brimming over with good fun and pleasant quips. The fun, much of it at Miss Silk's expense, was delivered to the table at large, as were the pleasant quips. A few of the better-turned quips were repeated so that Mother Stevens, in the kitchen, might hear them. They were carelessly deflected by six at the table, but each one struck Miss Silk solidly and with fine effect. A miserably shy woman of twenty-five, she looked straight into her plate and, for fear of her own voice, said nothing. When she was forced to reply to Mr. Stevens, or to a kind question from Mrs. Bixby, she grew red with mortification as she contemplated the rude brusqueness in her voice.

As the boarders, soothed by good food and by a coolness expanding on the air, became more talkative, it was easier to remark their various interrelations. Mr. Harbison, I understood quickly enough, had appropriated the role of star boarder; this he was granted without jealousy and without recognition. He sat opposite Mr. Stevens at the foot of the table, and fought a routine battle of wits best comparable to shadow-boxing. The two older women worked in the office of the canning factory, and were friends of long standing. From time to time Mrs. Bixby, the more gregarious of the two, made casual efforts to engage Miss Silk in conversation; she weathered each failure far more happily than did the young woman. The laborer said very little and paid much attention to his manners, furtively watching Mr. Harbison's use of knife, fork and toothpick. There were, too, certain unchanging group attitudes: mild hostility toward Harbison, tolerance toward the laborer, and a rather disturbing disregard of Mr. Stevens. I felt a faint curiosity concentrated on me, and a gathering apathetic distrust as Mr. Harbison subtly drew me out. Mr. Harbison gathered, from my replies, that I was the scion of a wealthy house, a student in Harvard, working for my health, trying to live down my education, rather a snob, and possibly about town for no good purpose. It was a good thing, he informed me, for a young man to get out and see the world a bit, to mix with all sorts; it would convince me that life wasn't all silver spoons and things. The only way to rise in the world was to start at the bottom and get to know your fellow man. I would find that there were very fine traits even in those poor souls bruised by fortune and left by the side of the road.

(The laborer took his spoon from his cup and looked ashamed.) I made no effort to reinform him or anyone else. Harbison sailed on, inexorably misinterpreting and advising and, I could see, preparing a lecture on his philosophy of life. But even when most drunk with vast ideas, he did not allow himself to forget his duty to his disciples. After every particularly memorable statement he glanced away from me, and asked Miss Silk if that was not so.

Meanwhile, Mr. Stevens, sensing as much guile as sincerity in Harbison's conversation, pitied me in my bewilderment; a number of times he smiled encouragement toward me. As we left the table and moved toward the porch, Mr. Harbison fell into step beside me, asking for my criticism of Mother Stevens' cooking; and Mr. Stevens followed.

There was no safe answer to such a question, and I grew cold in the shadow of Harbison's tall surmise, so I hung back a little and allowed him to overtake Miss Silk. This act, I could see, crystallized various suspicions he had unwillingly entertained. I was glad enough of that; with only a sharp feeling of pity for Miss Silk, I leaned against a porch post and lighted a cigarette.

"This has been a handsome day."

"Yes. Fine."

It was Mr. Stevens who spoke.

"We don't get many days like it."

"No, you're right."

"Most of this summer has been very rainy, very unpleasant."

"It has been pretty lousy."

He smiled brightly. "Yes, it has been very unpleasant, exceedingly unpleasant. But today has been splendid."

"Yes, it's been a lovely day. We don't get many like it."

"I have a feeling we are in for a good spell, now, though. Not a cloud in the sky, all day."

"It has been very clear, today."

He was anxious, for some reason, to talk; but some sixth sense told us that the weather was a delicate subject, and had best be spoken of no more.

"Do you care for a cigarette?"

"No, thank you; I have never touched tobacco in any form." He smiled apologetically and added, "But thank you very much, just the same."

"Surely."

"I don't in the least frown upon smoking, you understand. And I don't take faith in this stuff and nonsense about its doing any physical harm. Only, I don't like to form habits, as one is likely to do with smoking, don't you think?"

"Yes, I think you're right. I know it's a habit with me."

He was very liberal, for several minutes, on the whole matter of smoking and other habitual vices. I liked the old man but, just because I preferred to be alone, I said as little as I politely could in reply. Just when the subject ran encouragingly dry, and I was getting ready to take my leave, he said, "You are satisfied with everything here?"

I assured him that I was. He was very glad: he and his wife tried to make everything as clean and attractive as could be. They were particularly anxious that the young folks should be happy. It was hard, he knew, being young and a long way from home. He had been young himself once, and it had been a great comfort to him when older people were nice, and tried to make everything, although there was no place like home, like home.

"Young people should appreciate it," I said, without men-

tioning any names. Mr. Stevens' eyes showed more understanding than I had bargained for and, genuinely ashamed, I
added that I most certainly did.

Immediately reassured, he said with eagerness that I was to
feel just like one of the family. We exchanged appreciations and
wore through a discourse on loneliness, during which his concentration upon speech gave way before a crescent eagerness.
Across his left cheek, I saw the flutter of some irrelevant sinew,
and the nicely curled moustache was wry and twitching. At the
same time a ticklish, cold weakness rilled through the roots of
my spine.

"It's been a fine day," he said, "but very hot."

"Not so bad."

"It must have been very hot working."

"Not so bad."

"Is your work pretty heavy?"

"Digging a ditch and handling iron, today."

"That must have been hot, on a day like this. Are you used
to such work?"

"Not very. But it wasn't bad."

"Not bad, eh? Ah, my boy, when you're young you can
stand up to any sort of work."

I said nothing.

"A fine, strapping young fellow like you. You can stand up
to anything, can't you?"

His shaky small hand closed upon my arm. "Let me feel
your biceps. Ah, what a fine, strapping young fellow. See, I
can't reach half around it." He slipped one arm across my
shoulders, and his own shoulder, hard and hot, clenched
against my chest. For a moment pretense was lost to him, and
his eyes, narrowed, brilliant with lust, asked me: "Is everything
understood?"

Everything was quite well understood. I smiled back like
one of the family a bit embarrassed at such demonstrativeness,
freed myself without too much obviousness, lighted a cigarette, and said: "I guess it's about time I went in town, I promised to meet some friends."

I went in through the dining-room and upstairs for matches.
I could hear Mrs. Stevens washing the dishes. I hurried out the
front door. As I passed the porch, the old gentleman smiled

and waved; I pretended not to see him. When, in spite of myself, I looked back, he had gone in.

2

The mind is rarely audience to experience in perfection; rarely is it granted the joy of emotions and realities which, first reduced to their essential qualities, are then so juxtaposed in harmony and discord, in sharp accentuation and fluent change, in thematic statement, development, restatement and recapitulation, as to achieve in progress a continuous, and in consummation, an ultimate beauty. As a rule, experience is broken upon innumerable sharp irrelevancies; emotion and reality, obscurely fused and inexplicably tarnished, are irreducible; their rhythms are so subtly involved, so misgoverned by chance, as to be beyond analysis; and the living mind, that must endure and take part, is soon fugitive before, or else, however brave, falls to pieces beneath this broad unbeautiful pour of chaos.

The experience referred to is objective; the same difficulties hold in the case of subjective experience. The true sum of experience is, as a rule, an inconceivably complex interpenetration of subjective and objective experience. And the true sum and whole of experience is doubly chaotic.

It is therefore fortunate that most minds are constructed to float. However rigorous the weave of currents, however huge the plunge of waves, they are forever near the surface. And it is fortunate, God knows, that minds which anatomize experience are given the mercy of a million moods: these complement and relieve one another, and those which are not wholly proof against pain at least shift the weight of experience to a fresh area of the mind. That mood of sustained callousness and irony which I thought one desert afternoon had perpetuated in me, still serves me well. Although it has achieved a few complexities of perception which may perhaps enrich it, it remains my habitual state of mind, it dilutes experience to a fairly palatable beverage of dubious concoction. But, when I attempt to make real use of these instruments of perception, I realize two things: my own weakness and diffuseness of mind, and the fearful unarrangement of life realized with such completeness and sincerity as my mind may be capable of.

But certain moods, if kept as clear as possible of deflecting intellect, reflect a selection and arrangement of experience which approaches beauty: beauty of form, of emotion, of shadowy idea. The experiences during my first meal here, and just after, seemed casual enough as they occurred; Mr. Stevens' revelation struck away that mood, and, after long modulation of moods in my mind, the whole thing, as it occurred, emerged with symmetry and beauty.

But my relation to this progress of experience is broken, is never sure. In the first place, I work nine hours a day, and that violently different life seems severed from this. Then, even when I am here, so much that happens is utterly without direct significance. For instance, I talk with old Stevens every night. All our conversation, because of my avoidance, is oblique to the essential in his mind. In fragments, and by implication, I have been able to recreate his life; and I find the man as a whole pathetic, and appealing, and somehow very important. The mere unfortunate fact of his perversion is, or should be, beside the point. The important things are the complete frustration of a mind that wished to be fine and could have been good, the dwindling, for many years, of his life as an entity, his still persistent eagerness for knowledge, for the company of educated people, and this incredible tranquillity that has come with his old age. As a preacher in Maine, as a fugitive from misunderstanding, as a miserably unsuccessful grocer in this town, he can scarcely have known tranquillity. But now, as he says, he finds time once more for reading, and for music. He reads vastly and without discrimination, and he plays the piano with two fingers. Now permitted, at last, complete nonentity, he is happy. He sits at table quiet and meek, and says little, like a good child. Apparently, he worships his wife, though they have little to say to each other. He seems to have discovered some private formula for complete contentment: yet (discounting his wooer's flattery) he is genuinely grateful for my company, for the chance to talk about books, any books, for the chance to hear music played, however badly, with ten fingers instead of two. I scarcely know whether to be glad for this, or sorry to have wrought as I have upon his ancient illness.

His wife has had a strange life. In the parlor, their wedding picture is hung. In many ways, the old man still resembles the young one there, with curled mouth, and brave moustache, and arrogant Websterian posture. But the girl who stands beside him in full pride of her beauty, intelligence and aggressiveness are frozen in her eyes, and all beauty has departed the body and the grey pebble of a face; and the woman who has time, now, only for swift patience and for thorough housecleaning, for a proper but minimum politeness; and time never for a friend, or for any glint of affection—what bitterness and what unswerving loyalty have wrought this unaccountable change? Can any memory lie behind that unequivocal mask?

What resurgencies may engulf them both, when, each Sunday, they drive away into Maine? Or, is their mutual calm delicately adjusted beyond unbalancing?

I am far from my beginning. I wonder how, or if, I can return to it.

There is no return, and no use returning. I have tried to work out to my own satisfaction, some aspects of the mind's reaction to experience. I have tried to match this reaction with the patterns of music; the idea is incongruous; I should be kicked for trying it. My mind is hopelessly weak and tangential; time and again, as above, I fail to carry one idea through; before I realize it, I am whirled along the rim of another—and so on—ad nauseam.

Yet, from time to time, I am aware of a definite form and rhythm and melody of existence: however fluctuate and intermittent its progress may be, it *is* a progress; out of long, contrapuntal passages of tantalizing and irreconcilable elements there emerges sometimes an enormous clear chord. And at that moment—or, rather, through its reverberations in our brain; the whole commonplaceness of existence is transfigured— becomes monstrously powerful, and beautiful, and significant —assuming these qualities validly but unanswerably—and descends through tangled discords, once more into commonplaceness, with nothing answered, nothing gained, and heaven undisturbed.

I suppose the essentials of which this music is compounded are the facts as they are, tempered by sternness and pity and calm. We are eight people in this house; we are endowed with as many different minds, or souls, and with as many different machines for attacking existence, and defending ourselves against it. The full vision of existence is forever denied us. We live dimly in the center of being, and thence we perform the most ordinary duties, and avoid others; to some extent we guide our lives, to some extent are guided by them; and the whole object of life, whatever it may or should be, is hidden beyond a profound and inescapable confusion of egoism and of altruism and of evil and of good. And so, when these myopic people, concentrated upon their daily tasks, upon their food, or upon their rest, or upon their little loves, their little cruelties, their little aspirations; when, caught in these flimsy inescapable cogs, they are contemplated in their unrealized relation to the timeless severance of the vast radiance of life, and the enormous shadow of death, they become magnificent, and tragic, and beautiful.

I read carefully what I had written; carefully, and slowly, tried to clarify the ideas, to give them some proper connection, to discover any single coherent thought. When I finished I was sick with exhaustion and self-contempt; I wanted to beat my face to bits. I crumpled the sheets into a fistful and looked for a match; and stopped. It was the only attempt I'd ever made to get at the bottom of anything. It was a horrible failure—but in another mood something might come of it, something might be clear in it.

I lay down and read the second act of *The Cherry Orchard*, and realized once more that here, that melody was caught, and that great drama had been made of it. How, I could not tell.

Although it was very late, and I had to get up at six, I felt it necessary to walk. It was a fine night. After two miles of walking, my brain still felt like a shooting gallery. I returned to my room and went to sleep.

3

The morning was very hot and blue, the blue fading as the heat and light increased. Heat rilled above each fragment and long spine of metal, and shimmered like clear smoke over the grass and dusty streets. The gravel showed cool and dark as our shovels turned it; but almost immediately it was white.

The white light grew so wide that it was painful to look into the sky.

To my right, as I turned for each new shovel-load, I saw the half-bushel scoop slicing deep into the gravel, moving in no slower rhythm than my own square-nosed shovel. Before the second truck was loaded, the new man had struck bottom. I turned toward him and together we cleared out solid footing. The truck moved out, and we all rested in the band of shade to one side of the car, drank the already tepid water, and smoked.

Of the many jobs laborers were assigned, this was by all odds the best. Digging a ditch, or screening sand, you took your time, but worked continuously, with one eye on the foreman or his suspected direction of appearance; here, you worked furiously for a few minutes, in the surety of ten minutes of solid loafing. There was much talking during these ten minutes, and ordinarily, I joined in it and enjoyed it. Today, however, I lay flat on my back and said little. It had been nearly two when I returned from my walk; the need for sleep and the extreme heat were like tightening bolts in my temples; they persuaded me to a black and painful concentration upon the problems which had arisen the evening before. I could no longer fix upon any one idea or fragment of idea. A few words burred so constantly in my brain that they spun themselves free of all meaning; and problems, words, phrases, the uncertain nature of my own mind, the lives and the ruling moods of the people in the house, frozen clear of verbal thought, assumed various geometric forms; and these in their turn underwent change, and emerged as long silver arches, thin as rods; none touched, but a current quickened each, and flickered on the intermediary darkness, and they sent forth a low and hideous multitone.

Not one arch was complete.

Despite this resonant pattern I could see and hear a little. I heard voices as one does beneath fathoms of ether; and I saw the man new on the job, prostrate on the cinders, one knee angled to the sky, head resting in a flexile sling of joined hands and bent arms. He was long and heavy and hugely powerful, and his head seemed fashioned of great plates and ridges of iron, strongly joined. When we heard the truck coming he opened his clear unintelligent eyes, smiled by drawing his mouth into a line, and towered into a magnificent repatterning of strength.

He showed some concern over my lack of skill and economy in handling my shovel. During the next rest he offered me a cigarette, and I learned that he came from Lebanon. During the next he asked me, without that leering which is apology, whether I knew any women in town. A little Canuck made the question funny for himself; the new man saw no humor in it; he said: "Do you know any?" "My women are in Manchester," said the Canuck, among other things. "Then you'd better pipe down," said the new man. The Canuck piped down.

"I've got a Chevrolet," the new man said. I told him that women were hard to find in this lousy town. He replied, "I'll find them."

He said very little; he even swore little. He never suspected the existence of humor; he suspected the existence of nothing, I think, except women, work, food and rest.

He was staying, he said, at the Eagle Hotel. He agreed with me that it was a bad place. During the next rest, he asked me whether I knew of a cheaper place that was any good. I replied that I was staying at a cheaper place, that was very good, and that I believed there was room there. It was quite near the tracks; if he liked, we could go over and see.

And as I spoke, I felt my bowels turn to ice; but I continued to speak.

At noon, therefore, after eating lunch, we went over. We stood at the side door, on the porch.

"What's your name?"

"Grafton."

I stepped inside. From the hall I could see the long table. Miss Silk, the keeper of records, and the old gentleman were here at noon. They were broadly separated, at their regular places. As Mrs. Stevens came in from the kitchen I caught her eye and nodded. She smiled faintly, set down the food, and came to the hall.

"Fellow out here wants to board," I said, "if there's room."

As she crossed to the door I could see beyond the fine white hair, swept by sunlight.

"Mr. Grafton," I said.

She looked at him through the opening screen. For an

instant her face lost its quietude, and I was staring at merciless pain and fear. Then, with composure, she slowly said: "How do you do, Mr. Grafton. Yes, I am sure there will be room. I hope you will be comfortable."

"That's good," said Mr. Grafton.

"Shall I show you your room?"

"Don't bother," I said. "We'll get his stuff after work."

"The end of the hall, on the second floor," she said to both of us. And to me, "Thank you."

I watched her as she turned and closed the door and went into the dining-room.

"Sure," I said.

I said to Grafton: "Supper isn't till six. We'll have time to move your stuff then."

"Sure," he said.

By mid-afternoon we had the car cleared, and were back on the big job. I wheeled gravel to the mixer; he was at work digging a ditch in tough clay. Even late in the afternoon it was hot, but the coldness inside me persisted in spasms, and throughout spaces of rest, I was shivering; and watching the town clock, the hands cutting slowly their wheels on the sunlight.

At five I met Grafton, and we drove to the Eagle Hotel in his Chevrolet. As we came downstairs the younger clerk spoke to me:

"How do you like it, up on Water Street?"

"It's OK."

He grinned doggishly. "How do you like the old gent?"

As we drove through the town, among the stores, among the houses, I wondered how spotted those square miles were with knowledge of the old man and his secret.

We lugged Grafton's meager baggage to the room at the far end of the hall. The room was smaller than mine, but like mine, very clean.

"I guess the can is empty," I said. "We'd better hurry up and wash." As I walked to my room, Miss Silk was going downstairs; she looked up and quickly down; and her reddening face disappeared.

My mail was on the bureau; a letter from my mother, and a card from August. My mother wrote that the sea had been lovely all day, and that my sister found life very dull this summer. She was going dancing tonight though. It would be so good to have me home. August wrote that during one week there were five Chaplins and three Garbos in Berlin, and much rain.

I got my razor and soap and towel, and went into the bathroom. Grafton, standing in his work shoes and Sunday pants, was noisily washing. His head and his naked back and shoulders were a great keystone of corded muscle.

It was late, so after washing I shaved also from the bathtub spigot.

"How old are you?" said Grafton, mowing his cheek.

"Twenty."

He snorted. "I'm twenty myself. I'd have to shave twice a day, to keep down my beard."

"Who's the woman went downstairs?"

"Oh, she's no good. Silk's the name."

"Silk, huh?" He was puzzled. After a minute he said, "That's a funny name."

"Yeah."

We got dressed, and walked downstairs and into the parlor. Everyone was clean in the clean parlor, and waiting for supper, sitting patiently but unrelaxed; with labor past, with hands unbusied, with mind unmolested, they sat very tired waiting for their food and for their few hours of quiet and for their few hours of sleep; and for the next morning, and for the next evening, and for a Sunday, and for another week and Sunday; for autumn and for winter, for spring and for summer; for another year, for another ten; for the slow chemistry of change and age; for the loss of fluids and pigments and tissues, of senses and wits, of faculties and of perceptions; for the silencing of all clamor and for the sealing of all sight; for the final levelling of all desire, of all despair, of all joy, of all tribulations; for the final quelling of all fear and pride and love and disaffection; for the final dissolution of the flesh and of all that flesh must suffer, sickness of soul and body, fast-withering delight and clouded love, unkindness and grief and wrong beyond reckoning; for the final resolution of all the good they had wrought, and all the ill; they sat resting after battle, with quiet hands and unperceiving eyes, without emotion to receive once more the deliberate edge of evening.

Mr. Stevens sat with the roast beef at the head of the table; Mrs. Stevens served food, and was busy between two rooms. She greeted each boarder briefly, and the old gentleman added, "A handsome day, but very hot," and asked Miss Silk if he could help her to anything. Miss Silk was sick with mortification, and stared at the center of her plate. Mr. Harbison was pleasant to Miss Silk, and quite the life of the party. Mrs. Bixby and Mrs. Thompson, her friend of long standing, talked quietly and frequently dabbed their mouths with their napkins. Mrs. Stevens came in with more food, and glanced at me and at Grafton, and went out with an empty dish. Mr. Stevens watched her as she moved about the room, and his eyes were bright with serenity. The laborer, Frank Woods, scraped butter from his clean shirt, and was more deliberate in his eating. Mr. Harbison asked Miss Silk for an appointment in some sequestered grove. Miss Silk grew fiery red and said nothing. Grafton ate quickly and with thoroughness, glancing up as he bit, like a dog. I could scarcely eat; a cold weight was in my belly, the fork was cold to my touch, my temples were numb.

I was watching Mr. Stevens. He sat at the head of the table like a good child, meek, happy and silent. As much as possible, he kept his hands in his lap. His silky white hair and white face, and the white sport collar, were bright across the dimming air. From time to time he glanced toward me, and smiled; and he smiled at Grafton.

Supper was over; we all strolled toward the porch.

"Play something," Mr. Stevens said. "Play the pyano."

I was blind with suspicion and fear, and anxious to counter such schemes as he might have. I replied that Grafton and I were going straight into town.

We stood, therefore, at the back of the porch. Nearer the street, the others sat to talk.

"Let's go," I said.

"Let's have a cigarette," said Grafton, and offered one to Mr. Stevens.

The old gentleman refused politely, and added that he had never touched tobacco in any form. To Grafton's silence he replied that it had been a hot day, but a handsome one.

That was true, I said. I was watching the sky; the sunset was unusual; night was rising from east and south and north, like an immense black hood; its edge was apparent against the day. Across the world from us there was an edge of dawn and freshness; there Greece shivered into light; but over a broadness of sea and plain, sharp mountains and the thistled light of cities, enormous shadow prevailed, and over us the shadow hung.

This in an instant I saw, and pitied the nine gathered in the house.

The old gentleman's arm slipped round my shoulder, and as he openly fondled me, he said that we were all one big family, and that Grafton must feel perfectly at home, perfectly at home.

I did nothing and said nothing. There was nothing to do or say. Grafton stood a little away from us, and I saw amazement piercing his stupidity; and scorn, and incredulity. The old man babbled on, and I watched them both, and waited.

His cheek was twitching like a snake killed before sundown; his eyes were glassy and bright with lust; I felt his body trembling, and saw the trembling as, chattering inanely, he swung me toward Grafton, slid an arm about him, and called us his fine boys, his fine boys. And I saw the fine boy stand quietly, his eyes narrowing, the jaw muscles shifting and freezing; while a vein grew full and hard, and sprawled crooked on the old gentleman's forehead. Grafton stood in quiet; then drew away, and with flat palm struck across the mouth the old man, who, mouth flashing blood, for an instant assumed in all amazement the Jeffries sparring stance, with amazement gone raised supplicating tiny hands like a Moslem mole, while, face all blood and streaming tears, he shrank among the sorrowing flowers of morning bitterly crying, and with dependent hands fluttering before head;

while boarders rose from their chairs and looked in amaze and impended to interfere, then drew back and quickly, but staring back, removed from the porch and roomward made kind haste;

and two across the street stopped to stare;

and a second time the boy raised lowered arm through an arc and with flat palm struck through hands the old man's mouth; who, bawling abominable brat, splayed evening with weeping;

while with crashed plate and rushing footsteps

—murderous anger moving me with all strength I struck the

boy, behind the ear: he turned and dealt upon my cheekbone his fist and power, that with split skin and shrouded purpose I sank against wall and floor, Defender of What?

—the old woman his wife ran toward him, nothing saying, seeing none but him, and in her face revealed unfathomable sorrow fear and love, and two lives, broken late in this their day, that otherwise had closed in tranquillity—

—while in tallness and dignity around the corner stalked Grafton—

and five stared from across the street,

and the old woman haled the old gentleman into the kitchen,

and six stared from across the street,

and I recollecting complete consciousness, was frozen in a pratfall, with face bleeding, watched curiously in my sudden aloneness by six people.

I got to my feet and, through the nearest door and the parlor of books, music and strange wedding picture, upstairs to my room, but straightway to the bathroom with towel and handkerchief, to wash the cut across my cheek. It was not deep, and after a short time I stanched the blood. In the mirror I saw one with swollen temple and battered cheek, with dark stupid eyes which shone with no zeal for living. I started for my room. As I opened the bathroom door, another door opened, at the far end of the hall. Grafton, with his baggage, walked slowly toward me, and I toward him. We looked fully at each other, and, as we met in the middle of the hall, paused, as if in delicate balance, still looking at each other, without animosity, without regret, without emotion of any sort; then, after the instant's pause, walked on, I into my room, he down the stairs and out of my future existence.

I changed my shirt and sat down, weak, on a chair in the center of the room. I was within a hollow cube. It seemed to me that from five sides of this cube came excited whispering; and from the sixth, beneath me, came two sounds: the sound of dishes being washed in haste; and the sound of quiet but profound weeping.

It was beyond my endurance, at the time. I left the house and the town, and walked out to a high hill, from which I watched other hills, and fields heavy with crops, and wooded land,

and the distant town, as they lay beneath the night. I was unable to think, and after a little while I did not try to. I stayed on the hilltop for a long while, and returned with mind quiet because unoccupied by thought; and, after packing, went to sleep.

I was early at the table, conspicuous because I was not in my work clothes. Mrs. Stevens said nothing. She did not speak to any of the boarders as, one by one, they came in. Nor did the boarders speak, either to her, or to each other. They carefully avoided looking directly at anyone, and methodically ate what was set before them. Covertly, Mr. Harbison watched me; he said nothing. Mr. Stevens was not at the table; nor was a place set for him. From the kitchen, from time to time, came the sound of a hoarse whisper.

While everyone was still at table, Harbison rose and beckoned to Mrs. Stevens, and they withdraw to the parlor. Their conversation was not audible, but the tone and intention of Harbison's voice, and the tinkle of money withdrawn from a pocket, were quite well understood by all of us.

For the spark of pleasure her liberation would give me, I was watching Miss Silk. I think we all were. Her eyes were quiet and comprehending; her face without expression, as we heard him ascend and descend the stairs. When the front door closed, however, and his footsteps were no longer audible, there was change: in her face, which lost calm and became in some ways a leaf in late autumn; and in her eyes, which grew large and alarming to look upon, and dark with tears. As she lost all control of her emotions, she rose, gnawing at her hand, and hurried from the room. The two women looked at each other, and in silence followed her. The laborer and I continued to eat, he because of a good appetite, I because of his presence. Finally he rose, looked at me with curiosity and kindness, and set out for work.

I stood up and waited for Mrs. Stevens. She came to the door, stopped, and waited for me to speak.

I had nothing to say, and I began to speak words which had no process from my mind:

"I've heard there's very good work near Manchester. They pay fifty an hour there."

Mrs. Stevens looked at me.

"It's road work."

Mrs. Stevens looked at me.

After a few moments I paid her nine dollars, the price for a week's board and lodging. She pulled open a cupboard drawer, opened a cigar-box, and fumbled for change.

"That is right for a week, isn't it," I said.

She counted all the change in the box. "You haven't been here a week," she said. "Your week is up tonight." She gave me a bill. "Have you a quarter?"

I had only a dime in change.

"Don't mind it," I said. "Never mind it, please."

"You shall have the breakfast, then," she said. "Free." In the kitchen I heard an old man, trying to cry quietly. She let her hands fall. I put the dollar and the dime into my pocket. The weeping was suddenly very loud. There was a scuffle across the linoleum, and Mr. Stevens burst through the door. Half the fine moustache had been shaved off, and there were strips of plaster on his lips. He took my right hand in both his, and, with no further attempt to control his sobbing, he spoke rapidly through his tears.

It was a burst of mangled oratory, a sort of ex-sermon, ornamented with quotations from the Bible and with misquotations from Victorian poetry; a much prepared and half-forgotten sermon, upon kindliness, and brotherly love, upon the Christian virtues. This it ceased to be, and became lamentation for his own great sins, and loud praise of me and of all my actions. As he became more florid in his praise of me, the whole was tinged with involuntary salaciousness, and with the sort of flattery supposedly employed by those whose love is hopeless.

Meanwhile, he looked earnestly into my eyes; and his wife watched us both.

I do not think my expression changed, during the several minutes he talked on. He found no encouragement, and no hope of encouragement, and at last he stopped, and, still clutching my hand, merely looked at me, his tears in balance.

Both of them looked at me. They were waiting for me to speak. Anything I might have said would have been better than silence; I knew that then; but there was nothing to say. There was nothing. I merely stood and looked back at them, and as I looked, I saw understanding come to fullness in their minds.

I saw that the old man understood this: although you could not do as I wished, you were kind to me. I was happy in your company, and in talking to you. But you were not truly kind, and you did not truly understand. You deceived me with your kindness. You really despised me in secret, as openly you despise me now. Nobody, nobody on earth has ever understood it, has ever been kind, and nobody ever will.

I saw that the old woman understood this: you despise my husband. The only feeling you have for the whole thing is hatred and disgust. I can't blame you, you are like the whole world in that: but since you hate my husband, I hate you.

The old man, with this understanding to cherish, burst into new wild weeping, and retired to the kitchen. His wife waited, until after a moment, I turned, and walked into the parlor. I heard her go into the kitchen.

I stopped for a minute, and looked at their brave wedding photograph; then took my baggage and walked northward from the town.

On the farms, people had been at work for hours. At about nine I climbed to the hill I had visited the night before, left the road, and came to the crest. The sun was high enough, now, to be free of hills and of the tall clouds along the east. The blue was slowly paling into intense light. On a farm to my right, they were cutting a little patch of wheat. Slowly the machine breasted the standing grain, and left a new band of flatness behind it.

Between sky and countryside the sunlight glanced, like a broad sheet of glass; all that I saw lay stunned beneath its clarity, save only the nearer woodlands and the grain, which swarmed and shifted with devious breezes. The sunlight, elsewhere pure and calm, was shrill upon small twisting streams, and upon far-scattered weathervanes, and upon the town clock and steeples in the town, and upon the track tangential to the town. I saw the town hall, where Miss Silk would be busy with county records; I saw the canning factory, where the two older women were at work. Beyond the town, a road was torn up, for a little space; there, the laborer was at work. In some side street, Harbison was mending shoes. Beyond that grove, the new grade-school was rising by degrees; there, Grafton was finishing his ditch. On Water Street, near the tracks, the old woman would be about her housework, by now.

The header had made a full round, now; it was turning the corner to go around again. A few more rounds, and the entire patch would be cut.

[From *The Harvard Advocate*, May 1931]

A Mother's Tale

THE CALF ran up the hill as fast as he could and stopped sharp. "Mama!" he cried, all out of breath. "What *is* it! What are they *doing*! Where are they *going*!"

Other spring calves came galloping too.

They all were looking up at her and awaiting her explanation, but she looked out over their excited eyes. As she watched the mysterious and majestic thing they had never seen before, her own eyes became even more than ordinarily still, and during the considerable moment before she answered, she scarcely heard their urgent questioning.

Far out along the autumn plain, beneath the sloping light, an immense drove of cattle moved eastward. They went at a walk, not very fast, but faster than they could imaginably enjoy. Those in front were compelled by those behind; those at the rear, with few exceptions, did their best to keep up; those who were locked within the herd could no more help moving than the particles inside a falling rock. Men on horses rode ahead, and alongside, and behind, or spurred their horses intensely back and forth, keeping the pace steady, and the herd in shape; and from man to man a dog sped back and forth incessantly as a shuttle, barking, incessantly, in a hysterical voice. Now and then one of the men shouted fiercely, and this like the shrieking of the dog was tinily audible above a low and awesome sound which seemed to come not from the multitude of hooves but from the center of the world, and above the sporadic bawlings and bellowings of the herd.

From the hillside this tumult was so distant that it only made more delicate the prodigious silence in which the earth and sky were held; and, from the hill, the sight was as modest as its sound. The herd was virtually hidden in the dust it raised, and could be known, in general, only by the horns which pricked this flat sunlit dust like little briars. In one place a twist of the air revealed the trembling fabric of many backs; but it was only along the near edge of the mass that individual animals were discernible, small in a driven frieze, walking fast, stumbling and recovering, tossing their armed heads, or opening their skulls heavenward in one of those cries which reached the hill-side long after the jaws were shut.

From where she watched, the mother could not be sure whether there were any she recognized. She knew that among them there must be a son of hers; she had not seen him since some previous spring, and she would not be seeing him again. Then the cries of the young ones impinged on her bemusement: "Where are they going?"

She looked into their ignorant eyes.

"Away," she said.

"Where?" they cried. "Where? Where?" her own son cried again.

She wondered what to say.

"On a long journey."

"But where *to*?" they shouted. "Yes, where *to*?" her son exclaimed; and she could see that he was losing his patience with her, as he always did when he felt she was evasive.

"I'm not sure," she said.

Their silence was so cold that she was unable to avoid their eyes for long.

"Well, not *really* sure. Because, you see," she said in her most reasonable tone, "I've never seen it with my own eyes, and that's the only way to *be* sure; *isn't* it."

They just kept looking at her. She could see no way out.

"But I've *heard* about it," she said with shallow cheerfulness, "from those who *have* seen it, and I don't suppose there's any good reason to doubt them."

She looked away over them again, and for all their interest in what she was about to tell them, her eyes so changed that they turned and looked, too.

The herd, which had been moving broadside to them, was being turned away, so slowly that like the turning of stars it could not quite be seen from one moment to the next; yet soon it was moving directly away from them, and even during the little while she spoke and they all watched after it, it steadily and very noticeably diminished, and the sounds of it as well.

"It happens always about this time of year," she said quietly while they watched. "Nearly all the men and horses leave, and go into the North and the West."

"Out on the range," her son said, and by his voice she knew what enchantment the idea already held for him.

"Yes," she said, "out on the range." And trying, impossibly, to imagine the range, they were touched by the breath of grandeur.

"And then before long," she continued, "everyone has been found, and brought into one place; and then . . . what you see, happens. All of them.

"Sometimes when the wind is right," she said more quietly, "you can hear them coming long before you can see them. It isn't even like a sound, at first. It's more as if something were moving far under the ground. It makes you uneasy. You wonder, why, what in the world can *that* be! Then you remember what it is and then you can really hear it. And then finally, there they all are."

She could see this did not interest them at all.

"But where are they *going*?" one asked, a little impatiently.

"I'm coming to that," she said; and she let them wait. Then she spoke slowly but casually.

"They are on their way to a railroad."

There, she thought; that's for that look you all gave me when I said I wasn't sure. She waited for them to ask: they waited for her to explain.

"A railroad," she told them, "is great hard bars of metal lying side by side, or so they tell me, and they go on and on over the ground as far as the eye can see. And great wagons run on the metal bars on wheels, like wagon wheels but smaller, and these wheels are made of solid metal too. The wagons are much bigger than any wagon you've ever seen, as big as, big as sheds, they say, and they are pulled along on the iron bars by a terrible huge dark machine, with a loud scream."

"Big as *sheds*?" one of the calves said skeptically.

"Big *enough*, anyway," the mother said. "I told you I've never seen it myself. But those wagons are so big that several of us can get inside at once. And that's exactly what happens."

Suddenly she became very quiet, for she felt that somehow, she could not imagine just how, she had said altogether too much.

"Well, *what* happens?" her son wanted to know. "What do you mean, *happens*?"

She always tried hard to be a reasonably modern mother. It was probably better, she felt, to go on, than to leave them all full of imaginings and mystification. Besides, there was really nothing at all awful about what happened . . . if only one could know *why*.

"Well," she said, "it's nothing much, really. They just—why, when they all finally *get* there, why there are all the great cars waiting in a long line, and the big dark machine is up ahead . . . smoke comes out of it, they say . . . and . . . well, then, they just put us into the wagons, just as many as will fit in each wagon, and when everybody is in, why . . ." She hesitated, for again, though she couldn't be sure why, she was uneasy.

"Why then," her son said, "the train takes them away."

Hearing that word, she felt a flinching of the heart. Where had he picked it up, she wondered, and she gave him a shy and curious glance. Oh dear, she thought. I should never have even *begun* to explain. "Yes," she said, "when everybody is safely in, they slide the doors shut."

They were all silent for a little while. Then one of them asked thoughtfully, "Are they taking them somewhere they don't want to go?"

"Oh, I don't think so," the mother said. "I imagine it's very nice."

"I want to go," she heard her son say with ardor. "I want to go right now," he cried. "Can I, Mama? *Can I? Please?*" And looking into his eyes, she was overwhelmed by sadness.

"Silly thing," she said, "there'll be time enough for that when you're grown up. But what I very much hope," she went on, "is that instead of being chosen to go out on the range and to make the long journey, you will grow up to be very strong and bright so they will decide that you may stay here at home with Mother. And you, too," she added, speaking to the other little males; but she could not honestly wish this for any but her own, least of all for the eldest, strongest and most proud, for she knew how few are chosen.

She could see that what she said was not received with enthusiasm.

"But I want to go," her son said.

"Why?" she asked. "I don't think any of you realize that it's a great *honor* to be chosen to stay. A great privilege. Why, it's just the most ordinary ones are taken out onto the range. But only the very pick are chosen to stay here at home. If you want to go out on the range," she said in hurried and happy inspiration, "all you have to do is be ordinary and careless and silly. If you want to have even a chance to be chosen to stay, you have to try to be stronger and bigger and braver and brighter than anyone else, and that takes *hard work. Every day.* Do you see?" And she looked happily and hopefully from one to another. "Besides," she added, aware that they were not won over, "I'm told it's a very rough life out there, and the men are unkind."

"Don't you see," she said again; and she pretended to speak to all of them, but it was only to her son.

But he only looked at her. "Why do you want me to stay home?" he asked flatly; in their silence she knew the others were asking the same question.

"Because it's safe here," she said before she knew better; and realized she had put it in the most unfortunate way possible. "Not safe, not just that," she fumbled. "I mean . . . because here we *know* what happens, and what's going to happen, and there's never any doubt about it, never any reason to wonder, to worry. Don't you see? It's just *Home,*" and she put a smile on the word, "where we all know each other and are happy and well."

They were so merely quiet, looking back at her, that she felt they were neither won over nor alienated. Then she knew of her son that he, anyhow, was most certainly not persuaded, for he asked the question she most dreaded: "Where do they go on the train?" And hearing him, she knew that she would stop at nothing to bring that curiosity and eagerness, and that tendency toward skepticism, within safe bounds.

"Nobody knows," she said, and she added, in just the tone she knew would most sharply engage them, "Not for sure, anyway."

"What do you mean, *not for sure,*" her son cried. And the oldest, biggest calf repeated the question, his voice cracking.

The mother deliberately kept silence as she gazed out over the plain, and while she was silent they all heard the last they would ever hear of all those who were going away: one last great cry, as faint almost as a breath; the infinitesimal jabbing vituperation of the dog; the solemn muttering of the earth.

"Well," she said, after even this sound was entirely lost, "there was one who came back." Their instant, trustful eyes were too much for her. She added, "Or so they say."

They gathered a little more closely around her, for now she spoke very quietly.

"It was my great-grandmother who told me," she said. "She was told it by *her* great-grandmother, who claimed she saw it with her own eyes, though of course I can't vouch for that. Because of course I wasn't even dreamed of then; and Great-grandmother was so very, very old, you see, that you couldn't always be sure she knew quite *what* she was saying."

Now that she began to remember it more clearly, she was sorry she had committed herself to telling it.

"Yes," she said, "the story is, there was one, *just* one, who ever came back, and he told what happened on the train, and where the train went and what happened after. He told it all in a rush, they say, the last things first and every which way, but as it was finally sorted out and gotten into order by those who heard it and those they told it to, this is more or less what happened:

"He said that after the men had gotten just as many of us as they could into the car he was in, so that their sides pressed tightly together and nobody could lie down, they slid the door shut with a startling rattle and a bang, and then there was a sudden jerk, so strong they might have fallen except that they were packed so closely together, and the car began to move. But after it had moved only a little way, it stopped as suddenly as it had started, so that they all nearly fell down again. You see, they were just moving up the next car that was joined on behind, to put more of us into it. He could see it all between the boards of the car, because the boards were built a little apart from each other, to let in air."

Car, her son said again to himself. Now he would never forget the word.

"He said that then, for the first time in his life, he became very badly frightened, he didn't know why. But he was sure, at that moment, that there was something dreadfully to be afraid of. The others felt this same great fear. They called out loudly to those who were being put into the car behind, and the others called back, but it was no use; those who were getting aboard were between narrow white fences and then were walking up a narrow slope and the men kept jabbing them as they do when they are in an unkind humor, and there was no way to go but on into the car. There was no way to get out of the car, either: he tried, with all his might, and he was the one nearest the door.

"After the next car behind was full, and the door was shut, the train jerked forward again, and stopped again, and they put more of us into still another car, and so on, and on, until all the starting and stopping no longer frightened anybody; it was just something uncomfortable that was never going to stop, and they began instead to realize how hungry and thirsty they were. But there was no food and no water, so they just had to put up with this; and about the time they became resigned to going without their suppers (for now it was almost dark), they heard a sudden and terrible scream which frightened them even more deeply than anything had frightened them before, and the train began to move again, and they braced their legs once more for the jolt when it would stop, but this time, instead of stopping, it began to go fast, and then even faster, so fast that the ground nearby slid past like a flooded creek and the whole country, he claimed, began to move too, turning slowly around a far mountain as if it were all one great wheel. And then there was a strange kind of disturbance inside the car, he said, or even inside his very bones. He felt as if everything in him was *falling*, as if he had been filled full of a heavy liquid that all wanted to flow one way, and all the others were leaning as he was leaning, away from this queer heaviness that was trying to pull them over, and then just as suddenly this leaning heaviness was gone and they nearly fell again before they could stop leaning against it. He could never understand what this was, but it too happened so many times that they all got used to it, just as they got used to seeing the country turn like a slow wheel, and just as they got used to the long cruel screams of the engine, and the steady iron noise beneath them which made the cold darkness so fearsome, and the hunger and the thirst and the continual standing up, and the moving on and on and on as if they would never stop."

"*Didn't* they ever stop?" one asked.

"Once in a great while," she replied. "Each time they did," she said, "he thought, Oh, now *at last*! *At last* we can get out and stretch our tired legs and lie down! *At last* we'll be given food and water! But they never let them out. And they never gave them food or water. They never even cleaned up under them. They had to stand in their manure and in the water they made."

"Why did the train stop?" her son asked; and with sombre gratification she saw that he was taking all this very much to heart.

"He could never understand why," she said. "Sometimes men would walk up and down alongside the cars, and the more nervous and the more trustful of us would call out; but they were only looking around, they never seemed to do anything. Sometimes he could see many houses and bigger buildings together where people lived. Sometimes it was far out in the country and after they had stood still for a long time they would hear a little noise which quickly became louder, and then became suddenly a noise so loud it stopped their breathing, and during this noise something black would go by, very close, and so fast it couldn't be seen. And then it was gone as suddenly as it had appeared, and the noise became small, and then in the silence their train would start up again.

"Once, he tells us, something very strange happened. They were standing still, and cars of a very different kind began to move slowly past. These cars were not red, but black, with many glass windows like those in a house; and he says they were as full of human beings as the car he was in was full of our kind. And one of these people looked into his eyes and smiled, as if he liked him, or as if he knew only too well how hard the journey was.

"So by his account it happens to them, too," she said, with a certain pleased vindictiveness. "Only they were sitting down at their ease, not standing. And the one who smiled was eating."

She was still, trying to think of something; she couldn't quite grasp the thought.

"But didn't they *ever* let them out?" her son asked.

The oldest calf jeered. "Of *course* they did. He came back, didn't he? How would he ever come back if he didn't get out?"

"They didn't let them out," she said, "for a long, long time."

"How long?"

"So long, and he was so tired, he could never quite be sure. But he said that it turned from night to day and from day to night and back again several times over, with the train moving nearly all of this time, and that when it finally stopped, early one morning, they were all so tired and so discouraged that they hardly even noticed any longer, let alone felt any hope that anything would change for them, ever again; and then all of a sudden men came up and put up a wide walk and un-barred the door and slid it open, and it was the most wonder-ful and happy moment of his life when he saw the door open, and walked into the open air with all his joints trembling, and drank the water and ate the delicious food they had ready for him; it was worth the whole terrible journey."

Now that these scenes came clear before her, there was a far-away shining in her eyes, and her voice, too, had something in it of the faraway.

"When they had eaten and drunk all they could hold they lifted up their heads and looked around, and everything they saw made them happy. Even the trains made them cheerful now, for now they were no longer afraid of them. And though these trains were forever breaking to pieces and joining again with other broken pieces, with shufflings and clashings and rude cries, they hardly paid them attention any more, they were so pleased to be in their new home, and so surprised and delighted to find they were among thousands upon thousands of strangers of their own kind, all lifting up their voices in peacefulness and thanksgiving, and they were so wonderstruck by all they could see, it was so beautiful and so grand.

"For he has told us that now they lived among fences as white as bone, so many, and so spiderishly complicated, and shining so pure, that there's no use trying even to hint at the beauty and the splendor of it to anyone who knows only the pitiful little outfittings of a ranch. Beyond these mazy fences, through the dark and bright smoke which continually turned along the sunlight, dark buildings stood shoulder to shoulder in a wall as huge and proud as mountains. All through the air, all the time, there was an iron humming like the humming of the iron bar after it has been struck to tell the men it is time to eat, and in all the air, all the time, there was that same strange kind of iron strength which makes the silence before lightning so different from all other silence.

"Once for a little while the wind shifted and blew over them straight from the great buildings, and it brought a strange and very powerful smell which confused and disturbed them. He could never quite describe this smell, but he has told us it was unlike anything he had ever known before. It smelled like old fire, he said, and old blood and fear and darkness and sorrow and most terrible and brutal force and something else, something in it that made him want to run away. This sudden uneasiness and this wish to run away swept through every one of them, he tells us, so that they were all moved at once as restlessly as so many leaves in a wind, and there was great worry in their voices. But soon the leaders among them concluded that it was simply the way men must smell when there are a great many of them living together. Those dark buildings must be crowded very full of men, they decided, probably as many thousands of them, indoors, as there were of us, outdoors; so it was no wonder their smell was so strong and, to our kind, so unpleasant. Besides, it was so clear now in every other way that men were not as we had always supposed, but were doing everything they knew how to make us comfortable and happy, that we ought to just put up with their smell, which after all they couldn't help, any more than we could help our own. Very likely men didn't like the way we smelled, any more than we liked theirs. They passed along these ideas to the others, and soon everyone felt more calm, and then the wind changed again, and the fierce smell no longer came to them, and the smell of their own kind was back again, very strong of course, in such a crowd, but ever so homey and comforting, and everyone felt easy again.

"They were fed and watered so generously, and treated so well, and the majesty and the loveliness of this place where they had all come to rest was so far beyond anything they had ever known or dreamed of, that many of the simple and ignorant, whose memories were short, began to wonder whether that whole difficult journey, or even their whole lives up to now, had ever really been. Hadn't it all been just shadows, they murmured, just a bad dream?

"Even the sharp ones, who knew very well it had all really happened, began to figure that everything up to now had been made so full of pain only so that all they had come to now might seem all the sweeter and the more glorious. Some of the oldest and deepest were even of a mind that all the puzzle and tribulation of the journey had been sent us as a kind of harsh trying or proving of our worthiness; and that it was entirely fitting and proper that we could earn our way through to such rewards as these, only through suffering, and through being patient under pain which was beyond our understanding; and that now at the last, to those who had borne all things well, all things were made known: for the mystery of suffering stood revealed in joy. And now as they looked back over all that was past, all their sorrows and bewilderments seemed so little and so fleeting that, from the simplest among them even to the most wise, they could feel only the kind of amused pity we feel toward the very young when, with the first thing that hurts them or they are forbidden, they are sure there is nothing kind or fair in all creation, and carry on accordingly, raving and grieving as if their hearts would break."

She glanced among them with an indulgent smile, hoping the little lesson would sink home. They seemed interested but somewhat dazed. I'm talking way over their heads, she realized. But by now she herself was too deeply absorbed in her story to modify it much. *Let* it be, she thought, a little impatient; it's over *my* head, for that matter.

"They had hardly before this even wondered that they were alive," she went on, "and now all of a sudden they felt they understood *why* they were. This made them very happy, but they were still only beginning to enjoy this new wisdom when quite a new and different kind of restiveness ran among them. Before they quite knew it they were all moving once again, and now they realized that they were being moved, once more, by men, toward still some other place and purpose they could not know. But during these last hours they had been so well that now they felt no uneasiness, but all moved forward calm and sure toward better things still to come; he has told us that he no longer felt as if he were being driven, even as it became clear that they were going toward the shade of those great buildings; but guided.

"He was guided between fences which stood ever more and more narrowly near each other, among companions who were pressed ever more and more closely against one another; and now as he felt their warmth against him it was not uncomfortable, and his pleasure in it was not through any need to be close among others through anxiousness, but was a new kind of strong and gentle delight, at being so very close, so deeply of his own kind, that it seemed as if the very breath and heartbeat of each one were being exchanged through all that multitude, and each was another, and others were each, and each was a multitude, and the multitude was one. And quieted and made mild within this melting, they now entered the cold shadow cast by the buildings, and now with every step the smell of the buildings grew stronger, and in the darkening air the glittering of the fences was ever more queer.

"And now as they were pressed ever more intimately together he could see ahead of him a narrow gate, and he was strongly pressed upon from either side and from behind, and went in eagerly, and now he was between two fences so narrowly set that he brushed either fence with either flank, and walked alone, seeing just one other ahead of him, and knowing of just one other behind him, and for a moment the strange thought came to him, that the one ahead was his father, and that the one behind was the son he had never begotten.

"And now the light was so changed that he knew he must have come inside one of the gloomy and enormous buildings, and the smell was so much stronger that it seemed almost to burn his nostrils, and the smell and the sombre new light blended together and became some other thing again, beyond his describing to us except to say that the whole air beat with it like one immense heart and it was as if the beating of this heart were pure violence infinitely manifolded upon violence: so that the uneasy feeling stirred in him again that it would be wise to turn around and run out of this place just as fast and as far as ever he could go. This he heard, as if he were telling it to himself at the top of his voice, but it came from somewhere so deep and so dark inside him that he could only hear the shouting of it as less than a whisper, as just a hot and chilling breath, and he scarcely heeded it, there was so much else to attend to.

"For as he walked along in this sudden and complete loneliness, he tells us, this wonderful knowledge of being one with all his race meant less and less to him, and in its place came something still more wonderful: he knew what it was to be himself alone, a creature separate and different from any other, who had never been before, and would never be again. He could feel this in his whole weight as he walked, and in each foot as he put it down and gave his weight to it and moved above it, and in every muscle as he moved, and it was a pride which lifted him up and made him feel large, and a pleasure which pierced him through. And as he began with such wondering delight to be aware of his own exact singleness in this world, he also began to understand (or so he thought) just why these fences were set so very narrow, and just why he was walking all by himself. It stole over him, he tells us, like the feeling of a slow cool wind, that he was being guided toward some still more wonderful reward or revealing, up ahead, which he could not of course imagine, but he was sure it was being held in store for him alone.

"Just then the one ahead of him fell down with a great sigh, and was so quickly taken out of the way that he did not even have to shift the order of his hooves as he walked on. The sudden fall and the sound of that sigh dismayed him, though, and something within him told him that it would be wise to look up: and there he saw Him.

"A little bridge ran crosswise above the fences. He stood on this bridge with His feet as wide apart as He could set them. He wore spattered trousers but from the belt up He was naked and as wet as rain. Both arms were raised high above His head and in both hands He held an enormous Hammer. With a grunt which was hardly like the voice of a human being, and with all His strength, He brought this Hammer down into the forehead of our friend: who, in a blinding blazing, heard from his own mouth the beginning of a gasping sigh; then there was only darkness."

Oh, this is *enough*! it's *enough*! she cried out within herself, seeing their terrible young eyes. How *could* she have been so foolish as to tell so much!

"What happened then?" she heard, in the voice of the oldest calf, and she was horrified. This shining in their eyes: was it only excitement? no pity? no fear?

"What happened?" two others asked.

Very well, she said to herself. I've gone so far; now I'll go the rest of the way. She decided not to soften it, either. She'd teach them a lesson they wouldn't forget in a hurry.

"Very well," she was surprised to hear herself say aloud.

"How long he lay in this darkness he couldn't know, but when he began to come out of it, all he knew was the most unspeakably dreadful pain. He was upside down and very slowly swinging and turning, for he was hanging by the tendons of his heels from great frightful hooks, and he has told us that the feeling was as if his hide were being torn from him inch by inch, in one piece. And then as he became more clearly aware he found that this was exactly what was happening. Knives would sliver and slice along both flanks, between the hide and the living flesh; then there was a moment of most precious relief; then red hands seized his hide and there was a jerking of the hide and a tearing of tissue which it was almost as terrible to hear as to feel, turning his whole body and the poor head at the bottom of it; and then the knives again.

"It was so far beyond anything he had ever known unnatural and amazing that he hung there through several more such slicings and jerkings and tearings before he was fully able to take it all in: then, with a scream, and a supreme straining of all his strength, he tore himself from the hooks and collapsed sprawling to the floor and, scrambling right to his feet, charged the men with the knives. For just a moment they were so astonished and so terrified they could not move. Then they moved faster than he had ever known men could—and so did all the other men who chanced to be in his way. He ran down a glowing floor of blood and down endless corridors which were hung with the bleeding carcasses of our kind and with bleeding fragments of carcasses, among blood-clothed men who carried bleeding weapons, and out of that vast room into the open, and over and through one fence after another, shoving aside many an astounded stranger and shouting out warnings as he ran, and away up the railroad toward the West.

"How he ever managed to get away, and how he ever found his way home, we can only try to guess. It's told that he scarcely knew, himself, by the time he came to this part of his story. He was impatient with those who interrupted him to ask about that, he had so much more important things to tell them, and by then he was so exhausted and so far gone that he could say nothing very clear about the little he did know. But we can realize that he must have had really tremendous strength, otherwise he couldn't have outlived the Hammer; and that strength such as his—which we simply don't see these days, it's of the olden time—is capable of things our own strongest and bravest would sicken to dream of. But there was something even stronger than his strength. There was his righteous fury, which nothing could stand up against, which brought him out of that fearful place. And there was his high and burning and heroic purpose, to keep him safe along the way, and to guide him home, and to keep the breath of life in him until he could warn us. He did manage to tell us that he just followed the railroad, but how he chose one among the many which branched out from that place, he couldn't say. He told us, too, that from time to time he recognized shapes of mountains and other landmarks, from his journey by train, all reappearing backward and with a changed look and hard to see, too (for he was shrewd enough to travel mostly at night), but still recognizable. But that isn't enough to account for it. For he has told us, too, that he simply *knew* the way; that he didn't hesitate one moment in choosing the right line of railroad, or even think of it as choosing; and that the landmarks didn't really guide him, but just made him the more sure of what he was already sure of; and that whenever he *did* encounter human beings—and during the later stages of his journey, when he began to doubt he would live to tell us, he traveled day and night—they never so much as moved to make him trouble, but stopped dead in their tracks, and their jaws fell open.

"And surely we can't wonder that their jaws fell open. I'm sure yours would, if you had seen him as he arrived, and I'm very glad I wasn't there to see it, either, even though it is said to be the greatest and most momentous day of all the days that ever were or shall be. For we have the testimony of eye-witnesses, how he looked, and it is only too vivid, even to hear of. He came up out of the East as much staggering as galloping (for by now he was so worn out by pain and exertion and loss of blood that he could hardly stay upright), and his heels were so piteously torn by the hooks that his hooves doubled under more often than not, and in his broken forehead the mark of the Hammer was like the socket for a third eye.

"He came to the meadow where the great trees made shade over the water. 'Bring them all together!' he cried out, as soon as he could find breath. 'All!' Then he drank; and then he began to speak to those who were already there: for as soon as he saw himself in the water it was as clear to him as it was to those who watched him that there was no time left to send for the others. His hide was all gone from his head and his neck and his forelegs and his chest and most of one side and a part of the other side. It was flung backward from his naked muscles by the wind of his running and now it lay around him in the dust like a ragged garment. They say there is no imagining how terrible and in some way how grand the eyeball is when the skin has been taken entirely from around it: his eyes, which were bare in this way, also burned with pain, and with the final energies of his life, and with his desperate concern to warn us while he could; and he rolled his eyes wildly while he talked, or looked piercingly from one to another of the listeners, interrupting himself to cry out, '*Believe* me! Oh, *believe* me!' For it had evidently never occurred to him that he might not be believed, and must make this last great effort, in addition to all he had gone through for us, to *make* himself believed; so that he groaned with sorrow and with rage and railed at them without tact or mercy for their slowness to believe. He had scarcely what you could call a voice left, but with this relic of a voice he shouted and bellowed and bullied us and insulted us, in the agony of his concern. While he talked he bled from the mouth, and the mingled blood and saliva hung from his chin like the beard of a goat.

"Some say that with his naked face, and his savage eyes, and that beard and the hide lying off his bare shoulders like shabby clothing, he looked almost human. But others feel this is an irreverence even to think; and others, that it is a poor compliment to pay the one who told us, at such cost to himself, the true ultimate purpose of Man. Some did not believe he had ever come from our ranch in the first place, and of course he was so different from us in appearance and even in his voice, and so changed from what he might ever have looked or sounded like before, that nobody could recognize him for sure, though some were sure they did. Others suspected that he had been sent among us with his story for some mischievous and cruel purpose, and the fact that they could not imagine what this purpose might be, made them, naturally, all the more suspicious. Some believed he was actually a man, trying —and none too successfully, they said—to disguise himself as one of us; and again the fact that they could not imagine why a man would do this, made them all the more uneasy. There were quite a few who doubted that anyone who could get into such bad condition as he was in, was fit even to give reliable information, let alone advice, to those in good health. And some whispered, even while he spoke, that he had turned lunatic; and many came to believe this. It wasn't only that his story was so fantastic; there was good reason to wonder, many felt, whether anybody in his right mind would go to such trouble for others. But even those who did not believe him listened intently, out of curiosity to hear so wild a tale, and out of the respect it is only proper to show any creature who is in the last agony.

"What he told, was what I have just told you. But his purpose was away beyond just the telling. When they asked questions, no matter how curious or suspicious or idle or foolish, he leaned, toward the last, to answer them with all the patience he could and in all the detail he could remember. He even invited them to examine his wounded heels and the pulsing wound in his head as closely as they pleased. He even begged them to, for he knew that before everything else, he must be believed. For unless we could believe him, wherever could we find any reason, or enough courage, to do the hard and dreadful things he told us we must do!

"It was only these things, he cared about. Only for these, he came back."

Now clearly remembering what these things were, she felt her whole being quail. She looked at the young ones quickly and as quickly looked away.

"While he talked," she went on, "and our ancestors listened, men came quietly among us; one of them shot him. Whether he was shot in kindness or to silence him is an endlessly disputed question which will probably never be settled. Whether, even, he died of the shot, or through his own great pain and weariness (for his eyes, they say, were glazing for some time before the men came), we will never be sure. Some suppose even that he may have died of his sorrow and his concern for us. Others feel that he had quite enough to die of, without that. All these things are tangled and lost in the disputes of those who love to theorize and to argue. There is no arguing about his dying words, though; they were very clearly remembered:

"*'Tell them! Believe!'*"

After a while her son asked, "What did he tell them to do?"

She avoided his eyes. "There's a great deal of disagreement about that, too," she said after a moment. "You see, he was so very tired."

They were silent.

"So tired," she said, "some think that toward the end, he really *must* have been out of his mind."

"Why?" asked her son.

"Because he was so tired out and so badly hurt."

They looked at her mistrustfully.

"And because of what he told us to do."

"What did he tell us to do?" her son asked again.

Her throat felt dry. "Just . . . things you can hardly bear even to think of. That's all."

They waited. "Well, *what?*" her son asked in a cold, accusing voice.

"*'Each one is himself,'*" she said shyly. "'*Not of the herd. Himself alone.*' That's one."

"What else?"

"*'Obey nobody. Depend on none.'*"

"What else?"

She found that she was moved. "*'Break down the fences,'*" she said less shyly. "*'Tell everybody, everywhere.'*"

"Where?"

"Everywhere. You see, he thought there must be ever so many more of us than we had ever known."

They were silent. "What else?" her son asked.

"*'For if even a few do not hear me, or disbelieve me, we are all betrayed.'*"

"Betrayed?"

"He meant, doing as men want us to. Not for ourselves, or the good of each other."

They were puzzled.

"Because, you see, he felt there was no other way." Again her voice altered: "*'All who are put on the range are put onto trains. All who are put onto trains meet the Man With The Hammer. All who stay home are kept there to breed others to go onto the range, and so betray themselves and their kind and their children forever.*

"*'We are brought into this life only to be victims; and there is no other way for us unless we save ourselves.'*"

"Do you understand?"

Still they were puzzled, she saw; and no wonder, poor things. But now the ancient lines rang in her memory, terrible and brave. They made her somehow proud. She began actually to want to say them.

"*'Never be taken,'*" she said. "*'Never be driven. Let those who can, kill Man. Let those who cannot, avoid him.'*"

She looked around at them.

"What else?" her son asked, and in his voice there was a rising valor.

She looked straight into his eyes. "*'Kill the yearlings,'*" she said very gently. "*'Kill the calves.'*"

She saw the valor leave his eyes.

"Kill us?"

She nodded, "*'So long as Man holds dominion over us,'*" she said. And in dread and amazement she heard herself add, "*'Bear no young.'*"

With this they all looked at her at once in such a way that she loved her child, and all these others, as never before; and there dilated within her such a sorrowful and marveling grandeur that for a moment she was nothing except her own inward whisper, "Why, *I* am one alone. And of the herd, too. Both at once. All one."

Her son's voice brought her back: "Did they do what he told them to?"

The oldest one scoffed, "Would we be here, if they had?"

"They say some did," the mother replied. "Some tried. Not all."

"What did the men do to them?" another asked.

"I don't know," she said. "It was such a very long time ago."

"Do you believe it?" asked the oldest calf.

"There are some who believe it," she said.

"Do *you?*"

"I'm told that far back in the wildest corners of the range there are some of us, mostly very, very old ones, who have never been taken. It's said that they meet, every so often, to talk and just to think together about the heroism and the terror of two sublime Beings, The One Who Came Back, and The Man With The Hammer. Even here at home, some of the old ones, and some of us who are just old-fashioned, believe it, or parts of it anyway. I know there are some who say that a hollow at the center of the forehead—a sort of shadow of the Hammer's blow—is a sign of very special ability. And I remember how Great-grandmother used to sing an old, pious song, let's see now, yes, 'Be not like dumb-driven cattle, be a hero in the strife.' But there aren't many. Not any more."

"Do *you* believe it?" the oldest calf insisted; and now she was touched to realize that every one of them, from the oldest to the youngest, needed very badly to be sure about that.

"Of course not, silly," she said; and all at once she was overcome by a most curious shyness, for it occurred to her that in the course of time, this young thing might be bred to her. "It's just an old, old legend." With a tender little laugh she added, lightly, "We use it to frighten children with."

By now the light was long on the plain and the herd was only a fume of gold near the horizon. Behind it, dung steamed, and dust sank gently to the shattered ground. She looked far away for a moment, wondering. Something—it was like a forgotten word on the tip of the tongue. She felt the sudden chill of the late afternoon and she wondered what she had been wondering about. "Come, children," she said briskly, "it's high time for supper." And she turned away; they followed.

The trouble was, her son was thinking, you could never trust her. If she said a thing was so, she was probably just trying to get her way with you. If she said a thing wasn't so, it probably was so. But you never could be sure. Not without seeing for yourself. I'm going to go, he told himself; I don't care *what* she wants. And if it isn't so, why then I'll live on the range and make the great journey and find out what *is* so. And if what she told was true, why then I'll know ahead of time and the one *I* will charge is The Man With The Hammer. I'll put Him and His Hammer out of the way forever, and that will make me an even better hero than The One Who Came Back.

So, when his mother glanced at him in concern, not quite daring to ask her question, he gave her his most docile smile, and snuggled his head against her, and she was comforted.

The littlest and youngest of them was doing double skips in his efforts to keep up with her. Now that he wouldn't be interrupting her, and none of the big ones would hear and make fun of him, he shyly whispered his question, so warmly moistly ticklish that she felt as if he were licking her ear.

"What is it, darling?" she asked, bending down.

"What's a train?"

[From *Harper's Bazaar*, 1952]

CHRONOLOGY

NOTE ON THE TEXTS

NOTES

Chronology

1909   Born James Rufus Agee (known to his family as "Rufus") to Laura Tyler Agee and Hugh James Agee (known as "Jay") on November 27, in Knoxville, Tennessee. (Laura, devoutly Anglo-Catholic, comes from a prosperous, cultivated Knoxville home; Jay's roots lie in the mountains north of town. At the time of his son's birth, Jay is working for the Tyler family's construction business, after previous jobs with the U.S. Post Office Department, including an assignment in Panama, and the Louisville and Nashville Railroad.)

1912   Sister Emma born June 22.

1916   On May 16, as Jay Agee is returning to Knoxville after visiting his own ailing father in the hills, his car hits an embankment and flips over; he dies instantly. James, his mother, and his younger sister move out of the family house, but continue to live in Knoxville, near mother's family.

1918–22 Mother spends the summer of 1918 with the children in a cottage near the grounds of the St. Andrew's School, established by Episcopal monks of the Order of the Holy Cross on the Cumberland Plateau near Sewanee, Tennessee. Family moves in 1919 from Knoxville to St. Andrew's. Agee forms close, lifelong relationship with a St. Andrew's teacher, Father James Harold Flye, who serves as his mentor and as a kind of surrogate father. At his mother's direction, Agee lives in the dormitory; unable to visit her freely for the next half decade, he grows closer to Father Flye and his wife, Grace, and becomes deeply involved in the religious rituals of the school. Mother, who serves as a deaconess of the institution, becomes involved with a St. Andrew's staff member, Father Erskine Wright.

1923–24 To be near her sick father, mother takes the family back to Knoxville. Agee enters Knoxville High School mid-term freshman year. Mother marries Father Wright in the spring of 1924. Under medical advice to find a damp yet temperate locale to suit Father Wright's constitution, the newlywed couple explore several southern towns, but eventually settle in Rockland, Maine. Disliking the household's atmosphere of pious gentility, Agee spends little time there.

1925–28   Following a bicycle tour of France and England with Father Flye, Agee enrolls at Phillips Exeter Academy in Exeter, New Hampshire. Writes for *The Phillips Exeter Monthly* and joins the literary society, the Lantern Club (eventually is elected editor of the former and president of the latter). The Lantern Club "is one of the big things to be in here," he writes to Father Flye. "It runs the *Monthly*, and is a literary club. It gets several authors up here each term who give very informal talks in the club room. Booth Tarkington, who graduated here, came several times, and Sinclair Lewis may come this winter. It's a swell idea to have such a thing in a school, don't you think?" Composes stories, criticism, and poetry, including verse narrative "Ann Garner." Develops a crush on a younger male student; begins an affair with a woman several years older than he, Dorothy Carr, an employee of the Exeter Public Library. Begins corresponding with Exeter alumnus and Yale undergraduate Dwight Macdonald. Macdonald and Agee share a love of movies. "To me, the great thing about movies," Agee writes to Macdonald in the summer of 1927, "is that it's a brand new field. I don't see how much more can be done with writing or the stage. In fact, every kind of recognized 'art' has been worked pretty nearly to the limit. Of course great things will undoubtedly be done in all of them, but, possibly excepting music, I don't see how they can avoid being at least in part imitations. As for the movies, however, their possibilities are infinite." Agee barely passes many of his courses, but his teachers, impressed by his literary gifts, provide him with strong recommendations to Harvard, where he is accepted.

1928–29   At Harvard, rooms with future television producer Robert Saudek. Before the end of his first year, contributes a revised version of "Ann Garner" to Lincoln Kirstein's magazine *Hound and Horn*, as well as poetry to *The Harvard Advocate*. Spends a great deal of time at concerts, plays, and movies, and is placed on academic probation. Spends summer as a migrant worker, hiking from one wheatfield to the next in Kansas and Nebraska, then hitchhikes to Tijuana and back to the Northeast; visits Saudek and his family in Pittsburgh. "I had a good summer," he writes Father Flye. "Hard work and little time or provocation to be unhappy." In the same letter he writes, "On the whole, an occasional alcoholic bender satisfies me fairly well. Don't, please, get the idea that this invariably ends in drunkenness. That seldom happens unless I'm down in the dumps at the time."

1930–31   Professor Theodore Spencer, Agee's Harvard tutor (a faculty counselor), takes him on a visit to the Clinton, New York, home of Dr. Arthur Percy Saunders, a chemistry professor at Hamilton College, and his wife, Louisa, a former lecturer in English literature at Cornell. The Saunders, who have social ties to such figures as Robert Frost and Alexander Woollcott, welcome Agee into their circle. Back at Harvard, Agee and poet Robert Fitzgerald take two courses given by the Saunders' friend, the literary critic I. A. Richards. Over Christmas, Agee breaks up with Dorothy Carr. Declares, in a letter to Father Flye, his ambition "to combine what Chekhov did with what Shakespeare did—that is, to move from the dim, rather eventless beauty of C. to huge geometric plots such as Lear." To do so, he says, "I've thought of inventing a sort of amphibious style—prose that would run into poetry when the occasion demanded poetic expression." The Saunders' daughter, Olivia, or "Via," six years older than Agee, moves to Cambridge; Agee begins courting her. Does well enough academically to regain full standing in his class.

1932   As president of *The Harvard Advocate*, Agee scores a popular success and publicity coup with a parody of *Time* that imagines how the news magazine would have covered the world of antiquity. With the help of Macdonald, secures a job at the business magazine *Fortune*, recently founded by Henry Luce. Writes and delivers the class ode at Harvard's commencement exercises. Hitchhikes to New York, where he begins working at Luce's headquarters on floors 50–52 of the Chrysler Building. Takes on various anonymous assignments as part of a staff that includes Macdonald, Archibald MacLeish, and Wilder Hobson (Macdonald's Yale roommate and Thornton Wilder's nephew). Often works alone in the middle of the night, blasting Beethoven on a phonograph. Resides in Brooklyn, first in a barely furnished apartment, then in larger rooms complete with telephone. Via Saunders moves to New York in October, and she and Agee make wedding plans for the new year.

1933   Via and Agee marry at an Episcopal church in Utica, New York, on January 28, and move into a basement apartment in Greenwich Village. Agee continues to write poetry, including "John Carter," a long narrative poem in ottava rima started at Harvard and never completed. At Archibald MacLeish's request, collects his other poems for consideration by the Yale Younger Poets series. Writes first substantial piece for *Fortune*, an evaluation of the Tennessee Valley Authority which attracts considerable attention. Declines offer by Henry Luce to enroll him in Harvard Business School.

1934   Is enthralled by James Joyce's *Ulysses*, which has just been published in America. The Yale Younger Poets series publishes Agee's collection as *Permit Me Voyage*. Contributes articles to *Fortune* including "Cockfighting," "The American Roadside," and "Roman Society." Is impressed by the work of photographer Walker Evans, one of whose pictures illustrated Agee's "American Roadside" article; for Agee, Evans' work "has a kind of Joycean denseness, insight and complexity resolved in its bitter purity."

1935   Agee writes 10,000 words of autobiographical material for a novel. Works hard on a major piece about the Tennessee Valley Authority for *Fortune*, but is frustrated by the magazine's editing of his piece on the orchid industry. In November, struggling to recharge his art and his marriage, travels with Via to Anna Maria, a small coastal town in western Florida. During the first months of an unpaid half-year leave of absence, reads Freud's *The Interpretation of Dreams* and *The Inner World of Childhood* by Francis Wickes, a follower of Jung; records and analyzes his own dreams.

1936   Louis Untermeyer includes four new poems by Agee in his anthology *Modern American Poetry*. Writes "Knoxville: Summer 1915," a lyrical prose recollection of his childhood. On the way back from Florida in April, Agee and Via stop in New Orleans and take in the jazz scene, then observe Easter at St. Andrew's School with Father Flye and Grace. Staying at the Flyes' for most of the month, Agee befriends St. Andrew's student David McDowell (who will be his future publisher). When Agee returns to New York, *Fortune* assigns him a story about the struggle of sharecroppers to survive in the Depression, and teams him with Walker Evans, who has become a close friend. The two travel to Alabama in July to make contact with tenant farmers. Evans makes a first connection with a sharecropping family, but will later credit Agee's seductive "diffidence" for the pair's ability to win the trust of the Tingles and two related families, the Burroughs and the Fields. After three weeks of chronicling the families' lives in intimate detail, Agee and Evans return to New York. *Fortune* editors reject Agee's piece. He hopes to turn the aborted feature into a book, but must persuade *Fortune* to cede ownership of the research and writing on tenant farmers that Agee has done for them while on staff. Writes experimental movie treatment, "Notes for a Motion Picture: The House."

1937   Agee's marriage to Via continues to decline. Begins liaison with Alma Mailman, a young violinist and former protégée of the Saunders. Grows more restless at *Fortune*— his friends Macdonald, Hobson, and MacLeish have already left—and enters into a freelance, rather than staff, arrangement with the magazine. Submits an application for a Guggenheim fellowship listing 47 projects, from "an anti-Communist Manifesto" to "reanalyses of the nature and meaning of love"; the foundation turns him down. *Fortune* permits Agee to use his Alabama work in a book. He accepts a $500 advance from Harper & Brothers, where he will work with editor Edward Aswell, who has recently signed Thomas Wolfe. Agee's last published piece for *Fortune* is a scathing account of a New York to Havana vacation cruise. He visits Wilder and Peggy Hobson on Long Island's North Shore, and the New Jersey retreat of ACLU director Roger Baldwin, Dellbrook Farm. "Notes for a Motion Picture: The House" appears in anthology *New Letters in America*, edited by Horace Gregory.

1938   Via and Agee separate; their divorce becomes final at year's end. Agee goes to live with Alma in a house in the small town of Freetown, New Jersey. Hopes to finish "Three Tenant Families," which he envisions as a short book of "about 200 pages," but is unable to meet an August 1 deadline. "Knoxville: Summer 1915" appears in *Partisan Review*. Samuel Barber composes a musical setting for a poem from *Permit Me Voyage*, "Sure on this Shining Night." Agee and Alma marry in a brief civil ceremony in December.

1939   Agee and Alma move into a Brooklyn home on St. James Place owned by Wilder Hobson's in-laws. Agee accepts a *Fortune* assignment to write about Brooklyn. After *Fortune* rejects the piece, Agee severs his connection with the magazine. Leaves Brooklyn with Alma, who is pregnant, for Monk's Farm in Stockton, New Jersey. Photographer Helen Levitt, a volunteer darkroom assistant to her friend Walker Evans, visits Agee and photographs him and another visitor, Delmore Schwartz. Throughout the summer, Agee reads sections of his still-incomplete book to a succession of guests. Submits an excerpt to the magazine *Common Sense* (edited by Selden Rodman, Macdonald's brother-in-law). Delivers the manuscript to Harper & Brothers before Labor Day; Aswell dislikes the book's profanity and eccentricity, and the publisher rejects it. James and Alma move to 322 West 15th St. in Manhattan. Robert Fitzgerald, now editing the "Books" section at *Time*, gives him a place on his reviewing staff; Agee shares an office with Whittaker Chambers at the new Time-Life Building in Rockefeller Center, and contributes a handful of unsigned reviews each week, starting with the January 1, 1940, issue. Houghton Mifflin accepts "Three Tenant Families," now called *Let Us Now Praise Famous Men*, and schedules it for publication in 1941. For his friend Jay Leyda's journal *Films*, Agee contributes a screen treatment of a section from André Malraux's *Man's Fate* depicting the execution of Chinese Communists in 1927. Becomes romantically involved with Austrian Catholic émigré and *Fortune* researcher Mia Fritsch.

1940   Alma gives birth on March 20 to a son, named Joel for Agee's maternal grandfather.

1941   Alma leaves Agee and takes one-year-old Joel with her to Mexico, where she lives through most of the war years with German Communist writer Bodo Uhse. Agee and

Mia Fritsch live together in a fifth-floor Greenwich Village apartment. Houghton Mifflin publishes *Let Us Now Praise Famous Men*, with Walker Evans' photographs, in August; the book sells only 600 copies before it is remaindered by the publisher. Critical response is marked by hostility or bewilderment; in an essay in *The Kenyon Review*, however, Lionel Trilling, while expressing some reservations, calls it "a great book" and "the most realistic and important moral effort of our generation."

1942   At Time-Life, Agee moves from book to movie reviewing, becoming the regular *Time* film critic in September. Continues to review books for *Time* on special occasions and for isolated two- or three-month periods. The cultural editor of *The Nation*, Margaret Marshall, invites him to become the journal's movie critic while he continues to hold down his position at *Time*. Inaugurates his *Nation* column in December.

1943   Originally classified 3-A, Agee is warned by his draft board of possible reclassification; however, the board passes him over. He and Mia agree to try to have a child.

1944   In the summer, Mia gives birth prematurely to a boy, who dies shortly after birth; soon after, she and Agee marry. For Archibald MacLeish, now Librarian of Congress, Agee compiles an annotated list of films most worthy of preservation. *Time* sends him to Hollywood, where he meets industry figures such as 20th Century–Fox executive Darryl F. Zanuck. His film-related features for the magazine encompass not merely new stars such as Ingrid Bergman and Gregory Peck, but behind-the-scenes forces such as producer Joan Harrison.

1945   Alma returns to New York from Mexico briefly with Joel, now five years old. She lives in Agee's writing studio before getting an apartment of her own. Her New York stay allows Agee to establish a relationship with the son he's barely known. Praises John Huston's battlefield documentary *The Battle of San Pietro* in a review for *The Nation*. Writes unsigned pieces for *Time* about the death of Roosevelt, the atomic bomb, and the American occupation of Europe.

1946   Mia gives birth to Agee's first daughter, Julia Theresa. He contributes the introduction to a collection of photographs by Helen Levitt (the book is not published until 1965).

1947   Begins novel *The Morning Watch*, based on Holy Week observances at St. Andrew's; continues to work on autobiographical novel that will be published as *A Death in the Family*. Samuel Barber sets "Knoxville: Summer 1915" to music for soprano and orchestra. At a New York press conference for Charlie Chaplin's *Monsieur Verdoux*, Agee rises to Chaplin's defense against reporters who charge him with being a fellow traveler and tax evader, asking what "people who care a damn about freedom—who really care for it" can think "when so many of the people of this country pry into what a man's citizenship is, try to tell him his business from hour to hour and from day to day and exert a public moral blackmail against him for not becoming an American citizen . . . in the way that they think he should?" With Chaplin in mind, writes a long film treatment called "Scientists and Tramps," which plunges the comedian's Little Tramp persona into the aftermath of a nuclear holocaust.

1948   Leaves *Time* and *The Nation* and gives up regular movie reviewing. Plans a series of longer pieces for *Life*. Writes his first dramatic screenplay, an adaptation of Stephen Crane's "The Blue Hotel," and continues collaboration with Helen Levitt. After doing some camerawork for her documentary "In the Street," contributes commentary and dialogue for a semi-documentary feature about a young boy in Harlem, *The Quiet One*, which Levitt photographs under the direction of Sidney Meyers. Agee and Mia, who is still on salary at *Fortune*, buy a country retreat in Hillsdale, New York, in the Berkshires. Son Joel is taken to live in East Germany with Alma and Bodo Uhse.

1949   Agee publishes nostalgic essay "Comedy's Greatest Era" in *Life*; the article generates enormous reader response and a revival of interest in comedians of the silent era.

1950   Mia gives birth to their second daughter, Andrea Maria. In a *Life*-sponsored symposium called "What's With the Movies?" Agee says, "Movies are made for respectable people now; were better when made for lowbrows and made with instinct and delight." John Huston agrees to be the subject of an Agee profile, which appears in *Life* as

"Undirectable Director," then hires Agee to help him adapt C. S. Forester's novel *The African Queen*. Before beginning work on the script, Agee spends time with Huston, Chaplin, and producer Frank Taylor and his wife, Nan, as well as her sister, Patricia Scallon, with whom he has an affair.

1951   Houghton Mifflin publishes *The Morning Watch* to respectful reviews. In Santa Barbara, California, Agee drives himself to keep up with Huston both on the tennis court and in their story conferences, while holding to his own insomniac schedule; suffers a heart attack. Peter Viertel, uncredited, helps Huston finish the script. A writer friend from Harvard, Bernard Schoenfeld, finds Agee a house in Malibu. Agee adapts Stephen Crane's story "The Bride Comes to Yellow Sky" and plays a small part in the movie, which is released along with an adaptation of Joseph Conrad's "The Secret Sharer" as a two-part film, *Face to Face*. Has second major heart attack in October; Mia and their children come to the West Coast and remain with him thereafter. Socializes with Bertolt Brecht, Charles Laughton, and Aldous Huxley at the salon of screenwriter Salka Viertel, mother of Peter Viertel.

1952   Agee and family spend the first half of the year in California, the second in New York. For French filmmaker Albert Lamorisse, writes English narration for *White Mane*, a 47-minute film about a wild horse, filmed in the Camargue region. Is commissioned by former Harvard roommate Robert Saudek to write a five-episode, two-and-a-half-hour dramatization of Lincoln's early life for television program *Omnibus*, in which Agee also acts as poet Jack Kelso. The series is a critical success, but historian Allan Nevins charges Agee with historical distortion in a televised discussion of the show. Agee's short story "A Mother's Tale" appears in *Harper's Bazaar*.

1953   Huston offers Agee the chance to adapt *Moby-Dick*, but he turns it down. Writes an original screenplay, "Noa Noa," about the life of Paul Gauguin.

1954   Mia gives birth to John Alexander Agee, the writer's second son. Agee writes screen adaptation of Davis Grubb's novel *The Night of the Hunter* and retains sole credit, although the director, Charles Laughton, drastically prunes his script. Continues to suffer from heart trouble. Contributes ideas and verses, which go unused, for the Lillian Hellman–Leonard Bernstein musical *Candide*. Writes script about young musicians at the Tanglewood Music Festival for director Fred Zinnemann and *New York Times* music critic Howard Taubman.

1955   Agee pushes *A Death in the Family* closer to completion. On May 16, while riding in a New York City taxicab, suffers massive heart attack and dies. Father Flye officiates at the funeral service at St. Luke's Chapel in New York. Is buried in Hillsdale, New York. (*A Death in the Family* is published in 1957 and wins the Pulitzer Prize the following year.)

Note on the Texts

This volume contains James Agee and Walker Evans' book *Let Us Now Praise Famous Men* (1941, revised edition 1960), as well as five works of fiction by James Agee: the novella *The Morning Watch* (1951), the novel *A Death in the Family* (1957), and the short stories "Death in the Desert" (1930), "They That Sow in Sorrow Shall Reap" (1931), and "A Mother's Tale" (1952).

Agee and the photographer Walker Evans spent three weeks in 1936 living in Hale County, Alabama, on assignment for *Fortune* magazine, documenting the lives of three tenant families. The collaboration between writer and photographer was extremely fruitful, and the project became much more ambitious than the magazine had envisioned. *Fortune* rejected the article about the tenant families that Agee submitted in 1936 and later granted him permission to use the material gathered on his assignment for use in a book of his own. In 1937 Harper & Brothers gave him an advance for the proposed book, tentatively entitled "Three Tenant Families," but when he submitted it in summer 1939 it was rejected. The following year the work, now called *Let Us Now Praise Famous Men*, was accepted by Houghton Mifflin. *Let Us Now Praise Famous Men* was published by Houghton Mifflin on August 19, 1941. The book opened with a selection of 31 photographs Evans had taken on their 1936 trip; both Evans' and Agee's names appeared on the title page.

In 1960, five years after Agee's death, Houghton Mifflin published a second edition of *Let Us Now Praise Famous Men*, for which Evans added 37 and removed 6 photographs from the selection that appeared at the beginning of the 1941 edition. He also contributed a brief foreword, "James Agee in 1936." The 1960 Houghton Mifflin edition of *Let Us Now Praise Famous Men* is the source of the text printed here.

The Morning Watch was first published in the journal *Botteghe Oscura* and then published in book form by Houghton Mifflin in 1951. It was not reprinted during Agee's lifetime. The 1951 Houghton Mifflin edition of *The Morning Watch* contains the text printed here.

Agee began writing *A Death in the Family* in the late 1940s. He worked on the novel intermittently until his death in 1955, often putting it aside while working on other projects or because of health problems. The novel was nearly completed when he died. Working from Agee's manuscript and incorporating a fragment written in 1936 entitled "Knoxville: Summer 1915" as a preface, editors at McDowell, Obolensky, the publishing house co-founded by Agee's friend David McDowell, produced an edition of *A Death in the Family* that was published in 1957. Transforming Agee's manuscript into the published edition of *A Death in the Family* required numerous interventions. For example, in several places in the manuscript Agee wrote two variant words or phrases without clearly indicating which variant he preferred. The ordering of the novel also required interpretation by the editors. Agee's handwriting is often difficult to read, and as a result certain errors were introduced into the text of *A Death in the Family* as it was published by McDowell, Obolensky in 1957.

This version of *A Death in the Family* surely differs in some respects from what the novel would have been had Agee lived to see it through the publication process. The Agee scholar Victor Kramer has studied Agee's manuscript and, in his book *Agee and Actuality: Artistic Vision in His Work* (Troy, NY: Whitston Publishing Co., 1991), he has included a list of what he judged to be errors in the published novel. After consulting Kramer's list, the editor of the present volume made an independent comparison between the manuscript, now at the Harry Ransom Humanities Research Center at the University of Texas, and the 1957 McDowell, Obolensky edition. The present volume prints the text of the 1957 McDowell, Obolensky edition of *A Death in the Family* but includes several emendations based on these comparisons with Agee's manuscript. They are listed here, with the present volume's emended reading before the bracket and the 1957 McDowell, Obolensky reading given after it.

476.24–25   streetcar, and "mad]   streetcar, "mad
477.27   picture]   feature
478.32   turned in through]   turned through
478.39   came]   come
480.12   flinched]   flicked
480.34   fall]   face
480.36   rattled]   settled
481.3   privacy]   journey
481.11   for a few]   or a few
483.4   point]   front
483.40   cranking]   creaking
485.19, 21   res dence]   residence
486.9   from thur]   fur this
487.6   exaggerate, and . . ."]   exaggerate . . ."
488.6   broke]   break
488.22   hypocritical]   hypercritical

488.36   said.] said,
493.23   isn't] won't
502.8   blacked] blocked
502.30   coherence] adherence
505.13   the eyes] the the eyes
507.10   alone] down
513.24   we] well
521.34–35   "*Oh, God! God! God! God! God!*" he moaned,] "*Oh, God! God! God! God!*" he moaned,
522.21   comfort in] comforting
534.32   *need never*] *need not ever*
535.26   *ravenousness beyond ravenousness*] *rare monsters beyond rare monsters*
543.17   *ever*] *even*
544.10   *ever*] *even*
546.17   *gentle*] *gently*
556.27   *dis*] *the*
562.29–30   bitter sardonic incredulity] bitter incredulity
568.24   "No, I said: *Have*] "No." I said, "*Have*
570.9   Joel] Jay
572.30   iron] cross
575.12   she] the.
586.12   sipped continuously] sipped
596.35   breath. There wasn't. After] breath. After
597.31   here,"] here;"
599.14   pparalyzed] paralyzed
600.22   contained] continued
609.24   to of.] to.
616.25   room."] room.
621.34   said,] said.
626.17   instant] contact
626.24   during] among
628.36   Papa."] Papa,"
629.12   cracked] crushed
634.39   fist] fists
636.17   or fear.] of fear.
639.7   *knew*] *know*
639.32   *this*] *that*
644.28   *acted*] *asked*
650.16   *pecked*] *pocked*
652.40   *given up*] *giving*
655.10   *chain*] *chains*
656.1   *pile*] *file*
658.10   *towards*] *to*

666.23   shouted,]   shouted

667.8   gray braids]   braids

667.11   *away!*" He shook her.]   *away!*"

667.21   repentance]   repentence

668.23   squeezed]   sneezed

668.26–27   violent wind]   wind [Note: in the manuscript Agee also wrote the variant "strong" with "violent".]

671.8   limp]   wet

676.2   began]   bagan

676.25   long]   little

683.8–9   him with suspicion]   him

686.9   body, my Uncle Andrew says.]   body.

687.30   stand, and the ash tray with weighted straps, and two pipes.]   stand.

688.16   tray]   trays

689.14   lone!]   alone!

690.3   *me*]   me

692.11   them, like his mother said,]   them,

692.14   knew]   know

698.22–27   orphan, maybe you had to be French or Belgian to be one, for he never heard people talk about German orphans but there must be some. Then there were orphans in asylums, but they must be like crazy people. Or did your father and mother have to be killed in the war, if you were to be an orphan people would envy you for being, or]   orphans, or

713.38   self-completeness]   self-completedness

718.38   upon]   amongst

720.35   struck]   stuck

722.2   drew near]   came back

722.35   footsteps]   footstep

724.3   strange]   stranger

724.18   in]   with

726.36   over]   even

730.4–5   had, his head in a regular spasm, and,]   had and

The three stories in this volume are taken from the following sources: "Death in the Desert," *Harvard Advocate*, October 1930; "They That Sow in Sorrow Shall Reap," *Harvard Advocate*, May 1931; and "A Mother's Tale," *Harper's Bazaar*, July 1952.

This volume presents the texts of the original printings chosen for inclusion here, but it does not attempt to reproduce nontextual features of their typographic design. The texts are presented without change, except for the correction of typographical errors. Spelling, punctuation, and capitalization are often expressive features and are not altered, even when inconsistent or irregular. Complementing the list of emendations made to the 1957 McDowell, Obolensky edition of *A Death in the Family* listed above, the following is a list of typographical errors corrected in this volume, cited by page and line number: 102.15, small; 163.6, horse; 175.1, hall, porch; 184.14, Ricketts,'; 246.6, hand; 258.9, tight,; 259.30, Bobsey; 288.35, lightening; 305.26, 'The; 348.35, then; 409.24, dintinguish; 438.17, we'd; 440.19, embarassed; 471.14, grandchild; 757.33, embarassement.

Notes

In the notes below, the reference numbers denote page and line of this volume (the line count includes headings). No note is made for material included in standard desk-reference books. Biblical quotations are keyed to the King James Version. Quotations from Shakespeare are keyed to, *The Riverside Shakespeare*, ed. G. Blakemore Evans (Boston: Houghton Mifflin, 1974). For further biographical background than is contained in the Chronology, see Alfred T. Barson, *A Way of Seeing: A Critical Study of James Agee* (Amherst: University of Massachusetts Press, 1972); Lawrence Bergreen, *James Agee: A Life* (New York: E.P. Dutton, 1984); Victor A. Kramer, *James Agee* (Boston: Twayne, 1975); Erling Larsen, *James Agee* (Minneapolis: University of Minnesota Press, 1971); *Letters of James Agee to Father Flye* (New York: George Braziller, 1962); Michael A. Lofaro, ed., *James Agee: Reconsiderations* (Knoxville: University of Tennessee Press, 1992); James Lowe, *The Creative Process of James Agee* (Baton Rouge: Louisiana State University Press, 1994); David Madden, ed., *Remembering James Agee* (Baton Rouge: Louisiana State University Press, 1974); Genevieve Moreau, *The Restless Journey of James Agee* (New York: Morrow, 1977); Peter H. Ohlin, *Agee* (New York: Obolensky, 1966); Kenneth Seib, *James Agee: Promise and Fulfillment* (Pittsburgh: University of Pittsburgh Press, 1968); Ross Spears and Jude Cassidy, eds., *Agee: His Life Remembered* (New York: Holt, Rinehart and Winston, 1985).

LET US NOW PRAISE FAMOUS MEN

The Walker Evans photographs in this volume were reproduced with advice from Jeff L. Rosenheim, associate curator in the Department of Photography, Metropolitan Museum of Art.

1.2–3 LET US NOW PRAISE FAMOUS MEN] See Ecclesiasticus 44:1: "Let us now praise famous men, and our fathers that begat us."

12.1–9 Poor naked wretches . . . heavens more just.] *King Lear*, III.iv. 28–36.

13.1–2 Workers . . . to win.] Cf. Karl Marx and Friedrich Engels, *The Communist Manifesto* (1848): "The proletarians have nothing to lose but their chains. They have a world to win. Working men of all countries, unite!"

23.32–34 Une chose permise . . . *Critique Indirecte*.] "Anything permitted cannot be pure. The illegal suits me.—*Essay in Indirect Criticism*."

29.2   Dovschenko's *Frontier*]   *Aerograd* (1935) by Alexander Dovzhenko (1894–1956).

40.18–19   Fisk Quartette . . . Mitchell's Christian Singers]   Fisk Quartette, gospel singers from Fisk University; Mitchell's Christian Singers, North Carolina gospel quartet that first recorded in 1934.

83.17–84.5   And seeing the multitudes . . . were before you.]   Matthew 5:1–12.

117.2   I will go unto the altar of God]   Cf. Psalm 43:4.

186.2–3   Rural Electrification]   The Rural Electrification Administration was created as a temporary agency by executive order of Franklin D. Roosevelt in 1935; the following year the Norris-Rayburn Act extended the REA's term from one year to ten years.

208.9   Rube Goldberg]   Cartoonist (1883–1970) known for his depictions of elaborate inventions designed to accomplish mundane tasks by outlandishly circuitous methods.

259.30–31   The Bobbsey Twins . . . The Rover Boys]   The Bobbsey Twins (1904–1979) and the Rover Boys (1899–1926) were children's book series characters created by Edward Stratemeyer, who wrote the early volumes under the respective pseudonyms of Laura Lee Hope and Arthur M. Winfield.

302.12–13   The New Masses or The Saturday Review or Clifton Fadiman]   *The New Masses*, a revived version of the earlier journal *Masses*, began publication in 1926 and in 1948 merged with another left–wing journal to become *Masses and Mainstream*; *The Saturday Review of Literature* (1924–1982), book review journal whose editors included Henry Seidel Canby and Bernard De Voto; Clifton Fadiman (1902–1999), popular book critic and host of the radio show "Information Please" (1938–1952).

303.22–23   race records]   Early music industry term for recordings performed by and primarily marketed to African-Americans.

308.1–17   I will go . . . and my God.]   See Psalm 43.

319.17   the Covered Wagon]   *The Covered Wagon* (1923), epic western directed by James Cruze, based on the novel by Emerson Hough.

333.3   Andersonville]   A Confederate prison camp in southern Georgia where 13,000 Union soldiers died, 1864–65.

335.16   *Introit*]   Introductory part of the Mass sung while the celebrant and ministers enter the church and approach the altar.

388.10–389.11   The tigers of wrath . . . is holy.]   See William Blake, *The Marriage of Heaven and Hell* (1793), for the source of all these quotations, in a different order and with sometimes slightly different wording, with the exception of "Mutual forgiveness of each vice, / Such are the gates of Paradise," whose source is Blake's "For the Sexes: The Gates of Paradise."

THE MORNING WATCH

418.19–20   *he saw more wounds than one*]   See *The Passionate Pilgrim*, IX: "Fair was the morning when the fair queen of love." The poem was published under Shakespeare's name in 1599 but is no longer attributed to him.

A DEATH IN THE FAMILY

475.20   William S. Hart]   Movie actor (1870–1946) known for his roles in westerns such as *The Toll Gate* (1920) and *Tumbleweeds* (1925).

517.10   Barney Oldfield]   Auto racing pioneer (1878–1946) who was the first man to drive one mile in a minute (1903).

529.5–6   *Grammar of Ornament*]   *The Grammar of Ornament: Illustrated by Examples from Various Styles of Ornament* (1856) by Owen Jones, widely influential handbook of design.

565.31   ZuZus]   Snack food manufactured by Nabisco.

581.7   *once more unto the breach*]   From *Henry V*, III.i.1.

661.7–11   *There was a fat man . . . of Bombay.*]   Edward Lear, *A Book of Nonsense* (1845).

STORIES

746.18   Stein Song]   Song (1910) by Lincoln Colcord and E. A. Fenstad, originally published as "Opie—The University of Maine Song." It was successfully revived by Rudy Vallee in 1930.

765.25   *The Cherry Orchard*]   Play (1904) by Anton Chekhov.

Library of Congress Cataloging-in-Publication Data

Agee, James, 1909–1955
    Let us now praise famous men, a death in the
family, & shorter fiction
        p. cm.—(The Library of America ; 159)
    ISBN 1–931082–81–2 (alk. paper)
      1. United States—Social life and customs—Fiction. 2.
Agee, James, 1909–1955—Travel—Alabama. 3. Traffic accident
victims—Fiction. 4. Knoxville (Tenn.)—Fiction. 5. Fathers and
sons—Fiction. 6. Alabama—Rural conditions. 7. Farm tenancy
—Alabama. 8. Boys—Fiction. I. Title: Let us now praise
famous men. II. Title: Death in the family. III. Title: Morning
watch. IV. Series

PS3501.G35A6   2005
818'.5209—dc22   2005045098

THE LIBRARY OF AMERICA SERIES

The Library of America fosters appreciation and pride in America's literary heritage by publishing, and keeping permanently in print, authoritative editions of America's best and most significant writing. An independent nonprofit organization, it was founded in 1979 with seed money from the National Endowment for the Humanities and the Ford Foundation.

This book is set in 10 point Linotron Galliard,
a face designed for photocomposition by Matthew Carter
and based on the sixteenth-century face Granjon. The paper
is acid-free Domtar Literary Opaque and meets the requirements
for permanence of the American National Standards Institute. The
binding material is Brillianta, a woven rayon cloth made by
Van Heek-Scholco Textielfabrieken, Holland. Composition
by Dedicated Business Services. Printing and
binding by Courier Companies, Inc.
Designed by Bruce Campbell.